# Eager Eddy
## The World's Most Active Dude

ATTENTION DEFICIT HYPERACTIVITY DISORDER (ADHD)

Written by Jill Bobula and Katherine Bobula • Illustrated by Rob Hall

Brought to you by Wildberry Productions
as part of the We Are Powerful® children's series.

ISBN 978-0-9784095-0-0


Desktop publishing by Janine Frenken.
Photography by George Karam.
Editing by Nicole Dion.

www.wildberryproductions.ca


Published by Wildberry Productions.
P.O. Box 29028
3500 Fallowfield Road,
Nepean, Ontario
Canada K2J 4A9

Printed by The Lowe-Martin Group
Printed in Canada

First Wildberry Productions printing, September 2007.

We dedicate this book to children and adults touched by Attention Deficit Hyperactivity Disorder (ADHD).

Imagine what the world would be like if we channelled all the high energy of those with ADHD and made the world a better place. Our lives would change so quickly! Let us embrace and celebrate their high energy, creativity and abundant spirit. And above all else, foster the potential that exists in all of us!

**My name is Eddy** and I'm the world's most active dude. I like to move around a whole lot. Some people call me Eager Eddy, others say I have Attention Deficit Hyperactivity Disorder, also called ADHD. ADHD describes my behavior and my high level of energy. I love who I am because I'm such a great kid! My high level of energy is a very precious gift.

Mom tells me I have had ADHD for as long as she can remember. This means I have a lot of extra energy inside of me. There are many things that are special about me. Keep reading and find out what makes me so awesome…

For starters, I'm a pretty busy kid.
I run fast and I'm a very good soccer player.

Dad says I have beans in my pants. My dad says some pretty strange things sometimes. I think he means I'm always moving, eager to do something.

I'm also a great thinker. I think fast, sometimes too fast. Before my teacher is finished asking the class a question, I'm shouting out the answer.

I know I should let others have a chance to answer the questions. I would feel bad too if I didn't have a turn to answer. I suppose it's only fair, but it's not easy being patient.

I work fast at school. I make mistakes because I think and write so fast. I have a hard time focusing on the work because I just want to finish first.

My mom says it doesn't really matter who finishes first. The most important thing is to understand what I'm working on.

I also think and talk fast at home too.
My sister and my brother get angry with me when I don't let them finish talking. I just have so much to say! I'm a smart person and I think everyone should hear what I have to say.

Dad says everyone needs to wait his turn.

Sometimes I get in trouble because of my ADHD. Not everyone understands how I feel and why I behave the way I do.

Because I always want to move, I find it hard to sit still for a long period of time.

When I first started school, I kept my new teacher, Mrs. Dove, busy. I would squirm in my chair and get up many times during the class. There's nothing wrong with leaving my seat, but I would do it when I was supposed to remain seated.

Sometimes I'm so busy thinking, I don't always hear other people talking to me. Mom thinks the walls of the house listen to her more than I do. Should I tell her that walls don't have ears?

When my mom feels the walls are paying more attention to her than I am, she comes and puts her hands on my shoulders. Then, she gently asks me to look straight into her eyes, which helps me focus on what she's saying. I never noticed how beautiful my mom's eyes were until she started doing this little trick.

Every once in a while in class, my mind starts to drift off. I'm busy thinking of what game Jimmy, Omar and I will play after school.

We can't just play any game, these things need to be thought out carefully. When this happens, Mrs. Dove puts her hands on my shoulders and gently asks me to look into her eyes. Mrs. Dove has eyes that sparkle.

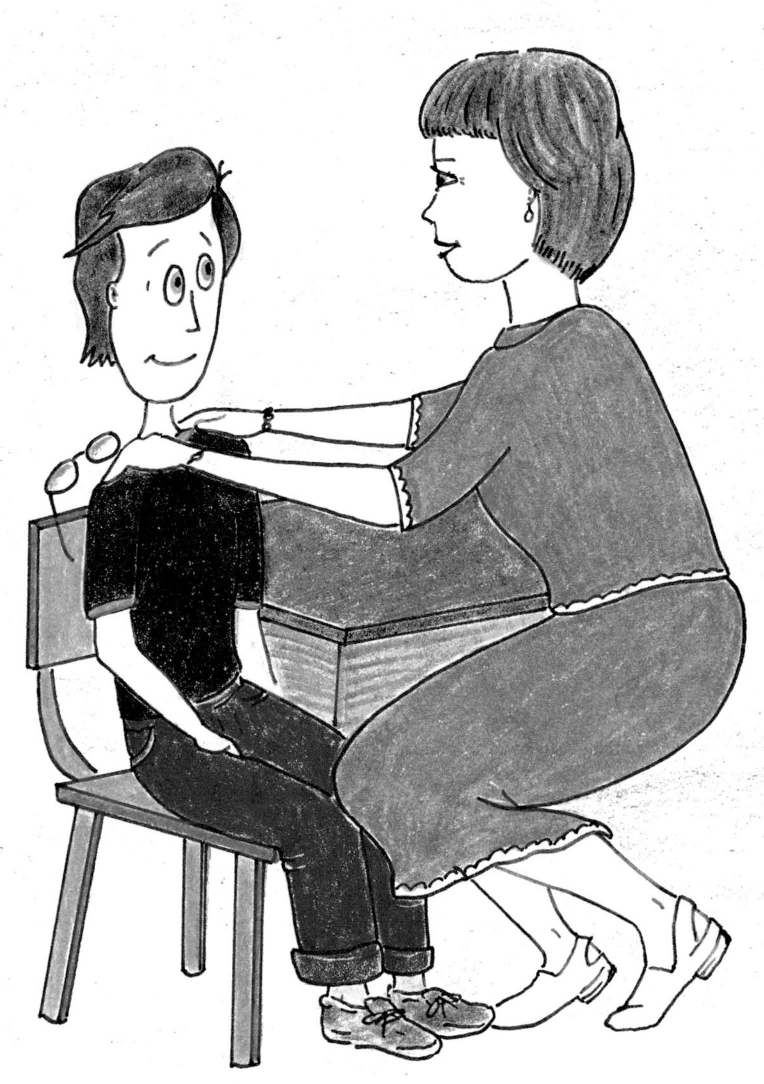

Another special thing to know about me is that I often forget. When dad asks me to pick up my things around the house, I forget.

When I'm supposed to take out
the recycling bin, I forget.

When I have homework to bring home, I forget. After all, I have a bus to catch.

The truth is I have a lot on my mind and I can only remember the important stuff like which card is missing in my baseball collection or which joke book I plan on buying with my allowance.

ADHD includes hyperactivity. I'm learning how to use my extra energy in positive ways. I do a few special things every day to help me release the energy that builds up in my body.

Before I leave home in the morning to go to school, I do exercises. I do 50 jumping jacks and 25 sit-ups. Exercising calms me down.

When I get home from school, I always play outside before I go inside to eat supper and do my homework. I think a few of my neighbours, Jimmy and Omar also have ADHD. They're busy people just like me. I really like playing with them because they can keep up with me.

One day a week, I go to my karate lesson. I learn how to control my need to always move. At first I didn't like going, but now I love it! Dad tells me other kids in my class also have ADHD.

My mom is careful not to give me sugar. When I do eat sugar, watch out!! I become what my mom calls a LITTLE TORNADO!

Having as much energy as I do makes my life very busy and I'm pretty tired by the end of the day.

I enjoy bedtime. The good thing about it is that I have a real cool bed. The bad thing about bedtime is that I have a real hard time falling asleep.

I think a lot at bedtime. I think about my friends or what I want to do in the morning or what games I want to play the next day.

When I have a hard time falling asleep, I read my joke books to my dad. Then, to help further calm me down, mom reads to me. This usually works.

I'm proud of who I am.
I don't mind people describing my behavior as ADHD. After all, my high energy is a gift. Some of the nicest people of all time have ADHD. I think I'm a very special person.

The We Are Powerful® children's book series was conceived and designed to introduce the lives of eight children affected with various disorders, syndromes and learning disabilities. Each book brings to light the experiences of these children affected with Attention Deficit Hyperactivity Disorder (ADHD), Attention Deficit Disorder (ADD), Tourette Syndrome (TS), Obsessive Compulsive Disorder (OCD), Asperger Syndrome (Autism), Fetal Alcohol Spectrum Disorder (FASD), Dyslexia or Dyspraxia.

The books familiarize the reader with the joys and challenges these children experience in their everyday life, at home and in their school settings. Children affected by these disorders, syndromes and learning disabilities are gifted in many ways. The We Are Powerful® children's book series was written to help children, parents, educators, health practitioners and the public in general develop a greater understanding of each child's uniqueness.

Our work at Wildberry Productions is dedicated to the children of the world. We hope we can make everyone's journey a little sweeter, a little easier, one filled with much love.

**Katherine Bobula,**
**Jill Bobula and**
**Rob Hall**

quick and easy

# desserts

Styling SUSIE SMITH, ANNA PHILLIPS
Photography ASHLEY MACKEVICIUS

# Introduction

*Indulge yourself with chocolate, cool off with homemade ice cream, finish the perfect meal with the perfect dessert. Whether it's a family dinner, a special birthday, a festive occasion, a dessert for supper or just because you need a treat, this is the book for you. It is packed with sumptuous desserts to suit any meal.*

*Look for the step-by-step recipes which show how easy it is to make spectacular-looking desserts and check out the hints and tips for variations, do ahead information, storage and variations.*

Published by:
TRIDENT PRESS INTERNATIONAL
801 12th Avenue South
Suite 400
Naples, FL 34102 U.S.A.
(c)Trident Press
Tel: (239) 649 7077
Fax: (239) 649 5832
Email: tridentpress@worldnet.att.net
Website: www.trident-international.com

Quick & Easy Desserts

Production Director: Anna Maguire
Home Economist: Donna Hay
Recipe Development: Lucy Andrews, Sheryle Eastwood
Food Photography: Ashley Mackevicius
Food Styling: Susie Smith, Anna Phillips.



Includes Index
ISBN 1 58279 096 5
EAN 9 781582 790961

Printed September 2002

Printed in the United States of America

## About this Book

### INGREDIENTS

Unless otherwise stated the following ingredients are used in this book:

| | |
|---|---|
| Cream | Double, suitable for whipping |
| Flour | White flour, plain or standard |
| Sugar | White sugar |

### CANNED FOODS

Can sizes vary between countries and manufacturers. You may find the quantities in this book are slightly different to what is available. Purchase and use the can size nearest to the suggested size in the recipe.

### MICROWAVE IT

Where microwave instructions occur in this book, a microwave oven with an output power of 850 watts (IEC705 – 1988) or 750 watts (AS2895 – 1986) was used. The output power of most domestic microwaves ranges between 600 and 900 watts (IEC705 – 1988) or 500 and 800 watts (AS2895 – 1986), so it may be necessary to vary cooking times slightly depending on the output power of your microwave.

### WHAT'S IN A TABLESPOON?

AUSTRALIA
1 tablespoon = 20 mL or 4 teaspoons
NEW ZEALAND
1 tablespoon = 15 mL or 3 teaspoons
UNITED KINGDOM
1 tablespoon = 15 mL or 3 teaspoons

The recipes in this book were tested in Australia where a 20 mL tablespoon is standard. The tablespoon in the New Zealand and the United Kingdom sets of measuring spoons is 15 mL. For recipes using baking powder, gelatine, bicarbonate of soda, small quantities of flour and cornflour, simply add another teaspoon for each tablespoon specified.

# Contents

# Cool Desserts

*Cool, refreshing desserts make the perfect finish on a summer's day. When you want a traditional dessert with a difference, try the Orange and Lime Cheesecake. Or for a more exotic occasion, try the Mango Soup with Sorbet – it's the ideal way to complete an Oriental meal.*

## Orange and Lime Cheesecake

Oven temperature
180°C, 350°F, Gas 4

**155 g/5 oz plain sweet biscuits, crushed**
**90 g/3 oz butter, melted**
**desiccated coconut, toasted**

ORANGE AND LIME FILLING
**185 g/6 oz cream cheese, softened**
**2 tablespoons brown sugar**
**1½ teaspoons finely grated orange rind**
**1½ teaspoons finely grated lime rind**
**3 teaspoons orange juice**
**3 teaspoons lime juice**
**1 egg, lightly beaten**
**½ cup/125 mL/4 fl oz sweetened condensed milk**
**2 tablespoons cream (double), whipped**

1 Place biscuits and butter in a bowl and mix to combine. Press biscuit mixture over base and up sides of a well-greased 23 cm/9 in flan tin with a removable base. Bake for 5-8 minutes, then cool.

2 To make filling, place cream cheese, sugar, orange and lime rinds and orange and lime juices in a bowl and beat until creamy. Beat in egg, then mix in condensed milk and fold in cream.

3 Spoon filling into prepared biscuit case and bake for 25-30 minutes or until just firm. Turn oven off and cool cheesecake in oven with door ajar. Chill before serving. Serve cheesecake decorated with toasted coconut.

*Serves 8*

When limes are unavailable lemon rind and juice can be used instead of the lime rind and juice to make an equally delicious dessert.

*Orange and Lime Cheesecake*

*Layered-fruit Terrine, Nectarine Timbales*

# NECTARINE TIMBALES

$^1/_2$ cup/125 g/4 oz sugar
$^1/_2$ cup/90 mL/3 fl oz water
$^1/_3$ cup/90 mL/3 fl oz orange juice
6 nectarines, halved and stoned
8 teaspoons gelatine
1 cup/250 mL/8 fl oz cream (double), whipped
1 tablespoon orange-flavoured liqueur

ORANGE SAUCE
1 tablespoon sugar
rind $^1/_2$ orange, cut into strips
1 cup/250 mL/8 fl oz orange juice
2 tablespoons orange-flavoured liqueur
2 teaspoons arrowroot blended with 4 teaspoons water

1 Combine sugar, water and orange juice in a saucepan. Add nectarines, bring just to the boil, then reduce heat and simmer for 4-5 minutes or until nectarines are soft. Using a slotted spoon remove nectarines and set aside. Sprinkle gelatine over hot liquid in pan and stir to dissolve.

2 Place nectarines (including skin) and cooking syrup in a food processor or blender and process until smooth. Push mixture through a sieve into a bowl, then fold in cream and liqueur. Spoon mixture into six lightly oiled timbale moulds, cover and chill until set.

3 To make sauce, place sugar, orange rind and juice, liqueur and arrowroot mixture in a saucepan and cook over a medium heat, stirring, until mixture boils and thickens. Cool. To serve, unmould timbales and accompany with sauce.

*Serves 6*

These melt-in-the-mouth desserts are just as delectable made with fresh peaches. If using peaches, peel before puréeing.
If you do not have timbale moulds use small, attractively shaped ramekins or teacups. If using ramekins, choose ones that have a 1 cup/ 250 mL/8 fl oz capacity.

# LAYERED-FRUIT TERRINE

1 star fruit (carambola), sliced
1 peach, peeled, stoned and sliced

MANGO LAYER
2 tablespoons caster sugar
1 cup/250 mL/8 fl oz mango purée
2 tablespoons orange-flavoured liqueur
4 teaspoons gelatine dissolved in $^1/_3$ cup/90 mL/3 fl oz hot water, cooled
$^3/_4$ cup/185 mL/6 fl oz cream (double), whipped

PASSION FRUIT LAYER
2 tablespoons caster sugar
$^1/_2$ cup/125 mL/4 fl oz passion fruit pulp
2 tablespoons orange juice
2 tablespoons melon-flavoured liqueur
4 teaspoons gelatine dissolved in $^1/_3$ cup/90 mL/3 fl oz hot water, cooled
$^3/_4$ cup/185 mL/6 fl oz cream (double), whipped

1 Arrange star fruit (carambola) over base and up sides of a lightly oiled glass 11 x 21 cm/4$^1/_2$ x 8$^1/_2$ in loaf dish.

2 To make Mango Layer, combine sugar, mango purée and liqueur in a bowl. Stir in gelatine mixture, then fold in cream. Pour carefully into loaf dish and chill until firm.

3 To make Passion Fruit Layer, combine sugar, passion fruit pulp, orange juice and liqueur in a bowl. Stir in gelatine mixture, then fold in cream. Place a layer of peach slices over Mango Layer, then carefully pour over passion fruit mixture and chill until set. To serve, unmould terrine and cut into slices.

*Serves 10*

For easy removal, run a spatula around the edge of the terrine to free it from the sides of the dish, before turning out.

*Pink and White Ice Cream, Hazelnut Pinwheels, Double Zabaglione Soufflé*

# Pink and White Ice Cream

Serve scoops of this pretty ice cream with fresh raspberries or other fresh fruit of your choice.

**$1^1/4$ cups/315 g/10 oz sugar**
**$^1/2$ cup/125 mL/4 fl oz water**
**6 egg yolks**
**250 g/8 oz white chocolate, melted**
**1 teaspoon vanilla essence**
**2 cups/500 mL/16 fl oz cream (double), whipped**
**500 g/1 lb raspberries, roughly chopped**

1 Place sugar and water in a saucepan and cook over a low heat, stirring constantly, until sugar dissolves. Bring to the boil, then reduce heat and simmer for 5 minutes or until syrup reduces by half.

2 Place egg yolks in a bowl and beat until thick and creamy. Continue beating, while adding syrup in a thin stream. Add chocolate and vanilla essence and beat until mixture thickens and is cool.

3 Fold cream and raspberries into chocolate mixture, then pour into a freezerproof container, cover and freeze until firm.

***Serves 8***

# Double Zabaglione Souffle

Oven temperature
200°C, 400°F, Gas 6

**$^1/2$ cup/100 g/$3^1/2$ oz caster sugar**
**6 egg yolks**
**1 cup/250 mL/8 fl oz cream (double), whipped**
**4 teaspoons gelatine dissolved in $^1/4$ cup/60 mL/2 fl oz hot water, cooled**
**60 g/2 oz dark chocolate, grated**
**$1^1/2$ tablespoons coffee-flavoured liqueur**
**1 teaspoon instant coffee powder dissolved in 1 teaspoon hot water, cooled**

1 Place sugar and egg yolks in a heatproof bowl over a saucepan of simmering water and cook, beating, for 5-10 minutes or until mixture is thick and fluffy. Place bowl in a pan of ice and beat until mixture is cool.

2 Fold cream and gelatine mixture into egg yolk mixture. Divide mixture into two equal portions and fold chocolate and liqueur into one portion and coffee mixture into the other.

3 Place alternate spoonfuls of each mixture into individual soufflé dishes with 3 cm/$1^1/4$ in high aluminium foil collars attached. Swirl by dragging a skewer through the mixture, then chill until set.

***Serves 4***

Soufflés are delicious served with crisp dessert biscuits such as tuiles.

# Hazelnut Pinwheels

**$^{3}/_{4}$ cup/170 g/5$^{1}/_{2}$ oz caster sugar**
**5 eggs, separated**
**125 g/4 oz hazelnuts, toasted and finely chopped**
**$^{1}/_{4}$ cup/30 g/1 oz self-raising flour, sifted**
**extra caster sugar**

CHOCOLATE HAZELNUT FILLING
**155 g/5 oz chocolate hazelnut spread**
**$^{1}/_{2}$ cup/125 mL/4 fl oz cream (double), whipped**

1 Place sugar and egg yolks in a bowl and beat until thick and creamy. Fold in hazelnuts and flour.

2 Place egg whites in a separate bowl and beat until soft peaks form. Fold egg white mixture into hazelnut mixture. Pour mixture into a greased and lined 26 x 32 cm/10$^{1}/_{2}$ x 12$^{3}/_{4}$ in Swiss roll tin and bake for 20-25 minutes or until cake is cooked. Place a clean damp teatowel over tin and set aside to cool.

3 Turn cold cake onto a piece of greaseproof paper sprinkled with extra caster sugar. Spread with hazelnut spread and cream, then roll up from short end. Chill until required.

***Serves 10***

Oven temperature
180°C, 350°F, Gas 4

Serve roll cut into slices, with extra whipped cream and decorate with hazelnuts. This roll is also delicious filled with just the chocolate hazelnut spread. This variation freezes well and will slice evenly if cut while still frozen. Allow to thaw in serving dishes for 20 minutes.

# TRIPLE-CHOCOLATE TERRINE

Oven temperature
180°C, 350°F, Gas 4

BUTTER CAKE
**125 g/4 oz butter**
**1 teaspoon vanilla essence**
**1/2 cup/100 g/3 1/2 oz caster sugar**
**2 eggs**
**1 cup/125 g/4 oz self-raising flour, sifted**
**1/3 cup/90 mL/3 fl oz milk**

CHOCOLATE FUDGE FILLING
**125 g/4 oz butter**
**2 tablespoons icing sugar**
**90 g/3 oz dark chocolate, melted and cooled**
**1 cup/250 mL/8 fl oz cream (double), chilled**

MILK CHOCOLATE MOUSSE
**200 g/6 1/2 oz milk chocolate, chopped**
**125 g/4 oz unsalted butter**
**2 tablespoons caster sugar**
**2 eggs**
**1 cup/250 mL/8 fl oz cream (double)**
**1 tablespoon dark rum**
**6 teaspoons gelatine dissolved in 2 tablespoons hot water, cooled**

WHITE CHOCOLATE GLAZE
**250 g/8 oz white chocolate**
**100 g/3 1/2 oz unsalted butter**

1 To make cake, place butter and vanilla essence in a bowl and beat until light and fluffy. Gradually beat in sugar and continue beating until mixture is creamy. Beat in eggs one at a time. Fold flour and milk, alternately, into butter mixture. Spoon mixture into a greased and lined 11 x 21 cm/4 1/2 x 8 1/2 in loaf tin and bake for 20-25 minutes or until cooked when tested with a skewer. Stand in tin for 5 minutes, then turn onto a wire rack to cool.

2 To make fudge filling, place butter and icing sugar in a bowl and beat until creamy. Fold in dark chocolate and cream. Chill until required.

3 To make mousse, place milk chocolate and butter in a saucepan and cook over a low heat, stirring constantly, until well blended. Cool. Place sugar and eggs in a bowl and beat until thick and creamy. Fold in chocolate mixture, cream, rum and gelatine mixture.

4 To assemble terrine, cut cake horizontally into three layers. Spread 2 layers with fudge filling and place one of these layers, filling side up, in the base of an 11 x 21 cm/4 1/2 x 8 1/2 in loaf tin lined with plastic food wrap. Top with half the mousse and chill for 10 minutes or until almost set. Place the second layer of filling-topped cake over the mousse with filling facing upwards. Top with remaining mousse and chill until almost set. Place remaining cake layer on top and chill until set.

5 To make glaze, place white chocolate and butter in a saucepan and cook over a low heat, stirring constantly, until well blended. Cool slightly. Turn terrine onto a wire rack, trim edges, pour over glaze to cover. Allow to set.

***Serves 10***

Chocolate should be stored in a dry, airy place at a temperature of about 16°C/60°F. If stored in unsuitable conditions, the cocoa butter in chocolate may rise to the surface, leaving a white film. A similar discoloration occurs when water condenses on the surface. This often happens to refrigerated chocolates that are too loosely wrapped. Chocolate affected in this way is still suitable for melting, however it is unsuitable for grating.

# Mango Soup with Sorbet

LIME SORBET
**1/2 cup/125 g/4 oz sugar**
**1/2 cup/125 mL/4 fl oz water**
**1/2 cup/125 mL/4 fl oz white wine**
**2 teaspoons finely grated lime rind**
**1/2 cup/125 mL/4 fl oz lime juice**
**1 egg white**

MANGO COCONUT SOUP
**1.5 kg/3 lb mangoes, flesh chopped**
**1/3 cup/90 mL/3 fl oz orange juice**
**3/4 cup/185 mL/6 fl oz water**
**1/4 cup/60 mL/ 2 fl oz green ginger wine**
**2 cups/500 mL/16 fl oz coconut milk, chilled**

*Serves 6*

1 To make sorbet, place sugar, water and wine in a saucepan and cook over a low heat, stirring, until sugar dissolves. Bring to the boil, then reduce heat and simmer for 5 minutes. Cool.

2 Add lime rind and juice to sugar syrup and spoon into a freezerproof container, cover and freeze until firm. Remove sorbet from freezer, place in a bowl and beat until smooth. Place egg white in a separate bowl and beat until stiff peaks form, then fold into lime mixture. Return mixture to freezerproof container, cover and freeze until solid.

3 To make soup, purée mangoes. Add orange juice, water and ginger wine and mix to combine. Chill well. To serve, stir coconut milk into soup. Pour soup into serving bowls and top with scoops of sorbet.

If fresh mangoes are unavailable drained, canned mangoes can be used instead. For this recipe you will require two 440 g/14 oz cans.

# Mousse-based Ice Cream

**6 egg yolks**
**3/4 cup/185 g/6 oz sugar**
**1 cup/250 mL/8 fl oz water**
**3 cups/750 mL/1 1/4 pt cream (double), whipped**
**2 teaspoons vanilla essence**

1 Place egg yolks in a bowl and beat until fluffy. Place sugar and water in a saucepan and cook over a low heat, stirring constantly, until sugar dissolves. Bring to the boil and cook until syrup reaches thread stage (107°C/225°F on a sugar thermometer). Beating constantly, gradually pour syrup in a thin stream, into egg yolks and continue beating until mixture leaves a trail and is cool.

2 Fold in cream and vanilla essence. Pour into a freezerproof container and freeze until ice crystals start to form around the edges. Beat mixture until even in texture, then return to freezer. Repeat beating and freezing processes two more times, then freeze until solid.

**Coffee Ice Cream:** Dissolve 2 tablespoons instant coffee powder in 2 tablespoons hot water. Cool. Use in place of vanilla essence.

**Raspberry Ice Cream:** Fold 2 cups/500 mL/16 fl oz raspberry purée into mousse base with cream.

***Makes 1 litre/1 3/4 pt***

For a true vanilla flavour, use vanilla sugar to make the sugar syrup. To make vanilla sugar, fill a large airtight container with sugar, add one or two vanilla beans (pods) and leave for several days. As you use the sugar top up with fresh sugar to keep a ready supply of vanilla sugar on hand. It is great to use for any baked products or custards where a vanilla flavour is required.

*Mango Soup with Sorbet, White Chocolate Mousse*

# White Chocolate Mousse

CHOCOLATE MOUSSE
**185 g/6 oz white chocolate**
**30 g/1 oz butter**
**$^1/_3$ cup/75 g/2$^1/_2$ oz caster sugar**
**4 egg yolks**
**2 teaspoons brandy**
**1$^1/_2$ cups/375 mL/12 fl oz cream (double), whipped**

PEACH COULIS
**440 g/14 oz canned peaches in natural juice, drained**
**1 tablespoon caster sugar**
**1 tablespoon orange-flavoured liqueur (optional)**

1 To make mousse, place chocolate and butter in a saucepan and cook over a low heat, stirring, until melted and well blended. Cool.

2 Place sugar, egg yolks and brandy in a heatproof bowl over a saucepan of simmering water and cook, beating, until mixture is thick and fluffy. Remove bowl from heat and continue beating until mixture is cool. Stir in chocolate mixture, then fold in cream. Spoon into serving glasses and chill until firm.

3 To make coulis, place peaches, sugar and liqueur, if using, in a food processor or blender and process until smooth. Push coulis through a sieve.

***Serves 8***

To serve, spoon coulis over mousse in glasses or serve separately.
This mousse is also delicious served with an apricot or raspberry coulis.

# WATERMELON SORBET

**$^{2}/_{3}$ cup/170 g/5$^{1}/_{2}$ oz sugar**
**1$^{1}/_{4}$ cups/310 mL/10 fl oz water**
**2$^{1}/_{2}$ cups/625 mL/1 pt watermelon purée**
**2 egg whites**

The addition of alcohol to the sorbet mixture prevents it from freezing rock-hard. Sorbets that do not contain alcohol should be softened in the refrigerator for 20-30 minutes before serving to make scooping easier. To prevent the sorbet from melting too quickly, chill the serving dishes.

1 Place sugar and water in a saucepan and cook over a low heat, stirring, until sugar dissolves. Bring to the boil, then reduce heat and simmer for 10 minutes. Cool.

2 Stir watermelon purée into sugar syrup, then pour into a freezerproof container and freeze until almost solid.

3 Place sorbet in a food processor or blender and process until smooth. Place egg whites in a bowl and beat until soft peaks form, then fold into fruit mixture. Return to freezerproof container and freeze until solid.

**Mango and Passion Fruit Sorbet:** Replace watermelon purée with 2 cups/500 mL/16 fl oz of mango purée and the pulp of 4 passion fruit.

**Kiwifruit Sorbet:** Replace watermelon purée with 2 cups/500 mL/16 fl oz kiwifruit purée, $^{1}/_{4}$ cup/60 mL/2 fl oz freshly squeezed grapefruit juice and 2 tablespoons mint-flavoured liqueur.

***Makes 1.2 litres/2 pt***

# CUSTARD-BASED ICE CREAM

**1$^{1}/_{4}$ cups/280 g/9 oz caster sugar**
**8 egg yolks**
**4 cups/1 litre/1$^{3}/_{4}$ pt milk**
**2 cups/500 mL/16 fl oz cream (single)**
**2 teaspoons vanilla essence**

If you don't have an ice-cream maker pour mixture into a freezerproof container and freeze until ice crystals start to form around the edges. Stir with a fork to break up ice crystals. Repeat process 2-3 times, then allow ice cream to freeze solid. The stirring ensures the finished ice cream has a smooth texture with no large ice crystals.

1 Place sugar and egg yolks in a bowl and beat until thick and creamy.

2 Place milk and cream in a saucepan and bring just to the boil. Remove from heat and whisk gradually into egg yolk mixture. Return mixture to saucepan and cook over a low heat, stirring constantly, until mixture coats the back of a wooden spoon. Place pan in a bowl of ice and cool to room temperature.

3 Stir in vanilla essence, then transfer mixture to an ice-cream maker and freeze according to manufacturer's instructions.

**Chocolate Ice Cream:** Reduce caster sugar to $^{3}/_{4}$ cup/170 g/5$^{1}/_{2}$ oz and fold 315 g/10 oz cooled, melted dark or milk chocolate into cooled custard.

**Peach Ice Cream:** Purée 2 x 440 g/14 oz drained, canned peaches and fold into cooled custard.

***Makes 1.5 litres/2$^{1}/_{2}$ pt***

# Summer Wine Jelly

**4 apricots, stoned and halved**
**200 g/6 $^1/_2$ oz green seedless grapes**
**250 g/8 oz strawberries, halved**
**250 g/8 oz fresh or canned cherries, stoned**
**60 g/2 oz gelatine dissolved in $^1/_2$ cup/ 125 mL/4 fl oz hot water, cooled**
**2 cups/500 mL/16 fl oz sweet white wine**
**2 cups/500 mL/16 fl oz apple juice**
**$^1/_3$ cup/90 mL/3 fl oz melon-flavoured liqueur or additional apple juice**

1 Place apricots, grapes, strawberries and cherries in a bowl and toss to combine.

2 Place gelatine mixture, wine, apple juice and liqueur or additional apple juice in a bowl and mix to combine. Pour one-quarter of the wine mixture into a lightly oiled 4 cup/1 litre/1 $^3/_4$ pt capacity mould, add one-quarter of the fruit and chill until set.

3 Repeat three times to use remaining liquid and fruit. When jelly is set unmould and serve with extra fruit, if desired.

**Unmoulding a gelatine dessert:** Moulded gelatine desserts need to be loosened before turning out. This is easily done by placing the mould in warm water for a few seconds. After removing mould from water dry the base and tip it sideways, while at the same time gently pulling the set jelly away from the edge of the mould. This breaks the air lock. Rinse the serving plate with cold water and place upside down on top of the mould. Then, holding firmly, quickly turn over both mould and plate and give a sharp shake. The dessert should fall onto the plate. If it refuses to move, place a hot, wet cloth over the base of the mould for 10-20 seconds. Wetting the plate means that you can easily move the dessert if it does not land in the centre when you unmould it.

***Serves 8***

Almost any fresh fruit can be used to make this dessert, however, avoid fresh pineapple, pawpaw and kiwifruit as they contain an enzyme which prevents the jelly from setting.

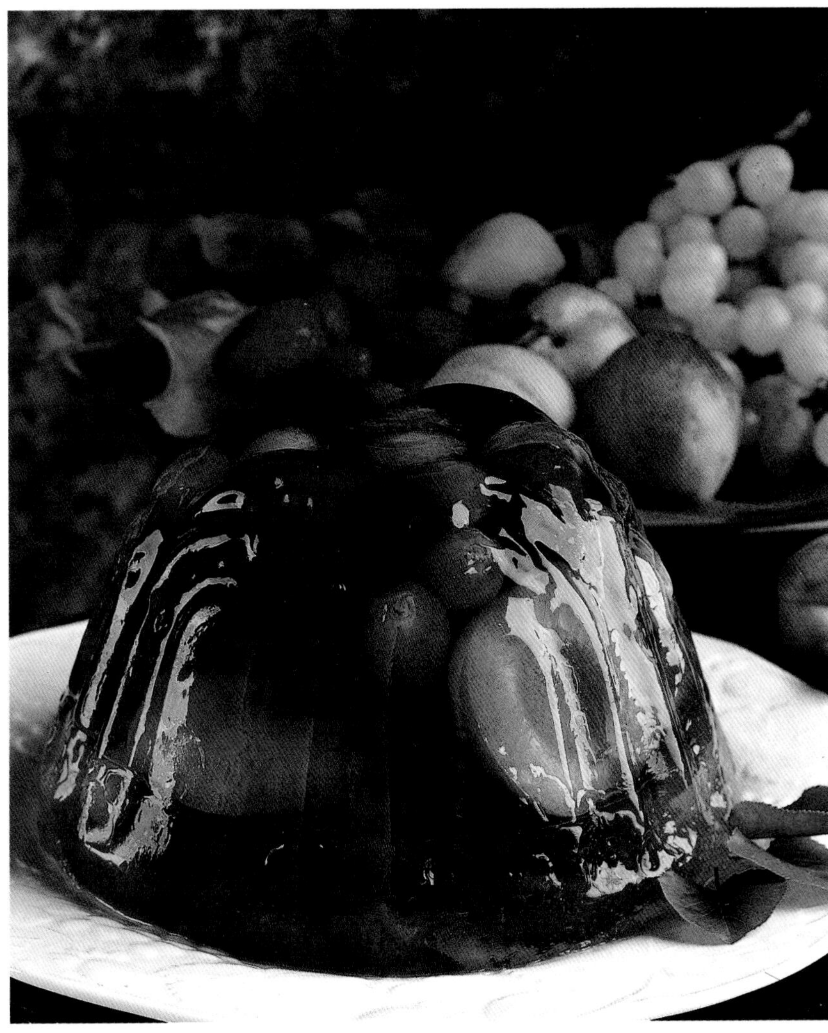

*Summer Wine Jelly*

# *Pies &* Pastries

*Whether it's a picnic in the park, a family dinner or a special occasion, you are sure to find the perfect pie to match the occasion in this chapter.*

## Sour Cream Apple Pie

Oven temperature
200°C, 400°F, Gas 6

Bake blind refers to the technique which is used to bake pastry cases before filling. To bake blind, line the uncooked pastry case with nonstick baking paper then fill with baking weights, uncooked rice or dried beans. Bake as directed in the recipe, then remove weights and paper and bake a little longer as directed in recipe.

*Sour Cream Apple Pie*

**2 quantities Sweet Shortcrust Pastry (page 21)**
**2 tablespoons apricot jam**

APPLE FILLING
**75 g/2 1/2 oz butter**
**3 green apples, cored, peeled and sliced**
**2 tablespoons brown sugar**

CARAMEL SAUCE
**1/4 cup/60 g/2 oz sugar**
**4 teaspoons water**
**1/4 cup/60 mL/2 fl oz cream (double)**
**30 g/1 oz butter, cut into small pieces**

SOUR CREAM TOPPING
**2 cups/500 g/1 lb sour cream**
**4 teaspoons caster sugar**
**1 teaspoon vanilla essence**

1 Roll pastry out to 5 mm/1/4 in thick and use to line a greased, deep 18 cm/7 in fluted flan tin with a removable base. Bake blind for 10 minutes. Remove weights and paper and bake for 8-10 minutes longer or until pastry is golden. Place jam in a saucepan and bring to the boil. Brush hot cooked pastry case with boiling jam and cook for 3-4 minutes longer. Cool.

2 To make filling, melt half the butter in a frying pan over a medium heat, add half the apples, sprinkle with half the sugar and cook, turning slices until they are tender. Remove and repeat with remaining butter, apples and sugar. Layer apples evenly in pastry case.

3 To make sauce, place sugar and water in a heavy-based saucepan and cook over a low heat, stirring until sugar dissolves. Bring to the boil and boil, without stirring, for 8 minutes or until mixture is a caramel colour. Reduce heat, carefully stir in cream and stir until sauce is smooth. Mix in butter and cool slightly. Drizzle caramel over apples in pastry case.

4 To make topping, combine sour cream, sugar and vanilla essence in a bowl. Spoon topping evenly over apples, taking mixture just to rim of pie. Reduce oven temperature to 180°C/350°F/Gas 4 and bake for 5-7 minutes. Cool at room temperature, then chill for several hours or overnight before serving.

***Serves 8***

# Raspberry Mousse Flan

Oven temperature
200°C, 400°F, Gas 6

**500 g/1 lb mixed berries of your choice**

ALMOND PASTRY

**1 1/4 cups/155 g/5 oz flour**
**2 tablespoons caster sugar**
**15 g/1/2 oz ground almonds**
**125 g/4 oz butter, cut into pieces**
**1 egg yolk, lightly beaten**
**2-3 tablespoons water, chilled**

RASPBERRY MOUSSE FILLING

**90 g/3 oz raspberries**
**1/4 cup/60 g/2 oz caster sugar**
**2 eggs, separated**
**1/2 cup/125 mL/4 fl oz cream (double), whipped**
**8 teaspoons gelatine dissolved in 1/2 cup/125 mL/4 fl oz hot water, cooled**

1 To make pastry, place flour, sugar and almonds in a food processor and process to combine. Add butter and process until mixture resembles fine breadcrumbs. With machine running add egg yolk and enough water to form a soft dough. Turn pastry onto a lightly floured surface and knead briefly until smooth. Wrap in plastic food wrap and chill for 30 minutes.

2 Roll out pastry on a lightly floured surface and use to line a lightly greased, deep 20 cm/8 in fluted flan tin with a removable base. Chill for 15 minutes. Line pastry case with nonstick baking paper, weigh down with baking weights, uncooked rice or dried beans and bake for 10 minutes. Remove weights and paper and bake for 10 minutes longer or until pastry case is lightly browned and cooked.

3 To make filling, purée raspberries, then push through a sieve, to remove seeds. Place sugar and egg yolks in a bowl and beat until thick and creamy. Place egg whites in a separate bowl and beat until stiff peaks form.

4 Fold cream and egg whites into egg yolk mixture. Then fold 4 tablespoons of egg mixture into raspberry purée. Fold half the gelatine mixture into the raspberry mixture and the remainder into the egg mixture.

5 Place large spoonfuls of egg mixture into pastry case, then top with smaller spoonfuls of raspberry mixture. Repeat until both mixtures are used. Run a spatula through the mousse to swirl the mixtures. Chill for 2 hours or until mousse is firm. Just prior to serving, top flan with mixed berries.

***Serves 8***

When making pastry have all the utensils and ingredients as cold as possible. In hot weather, chill the utensils before using, wash your hands in cold water and use only your fingertips for kneading. Always preheat the oven before baking pastry. If pastry is put into a cold oven the fat will run and the pastry will be tough and greasy with a poor texture.

*Raspberry Mousse Flan*

# Sweet Shortcrust Pastry

**$1^1/2$ cups/185 g/6 oz flour**
**125 g/4 oz butter, cut into cubes**
**$^1/3$ cup/75 g/$2^1/2$ oz caster sugar**
**$^1/4$ cup/30 g/1 oz cornflour**
**1 egg, lightly beaten**
**1 egg yolk, lightly beaten**
**1 teaspoon vanilla essence**

1 Place flour, butter, sugar and cornflour in a food processor and process until mixture resembles coarse breadcrumbs. Combine egg, egg yolk and vanilla essence and, with machine running, slowly add to flour mixture. Continue processing until a soft dough forms.

2 Turn dough onto a lightly floured surface and knead lightly. Wrap in plastic food wrap and chill for 30 minutes. Use as desired.

Homemade shortcrust pastry is easy to make if you have a food processor. This recipe is suitable to use whenever sweet shortcrust pastry is called for.

# SUGAR-CRUSTED BASKETS

Oven temperature
200°C, 400°F, Gas 6

SUGAR-CRUSTED BASKETS
**6 sheets filo pastry**
**60 g/2 oz butter, melted**
**$^1/_2$ cup/125 g/4 oz sugar**

POACHED FRUIT
**1 cup/250 g/8 oz sugar**
**1 cup/250 mL/8 fl oz water**
**$^1/_2$ cup/125 mL/4 fl oz white wine**
**4 apricots, stoned and quartered**
**4 peaches, stoned and cut into eighths**
**4 plums, stoned and quartered**
**4 nectarines, stoned and cut into eighths**
**16 strawberries**

RASPBERRY CREAM
**125 g/4 oz raspberries, puréed**
**1 tablespoon icing sugar**
**$^3/_4$ cup/185 mL/6 fl oz cream (double), lightly whipped**

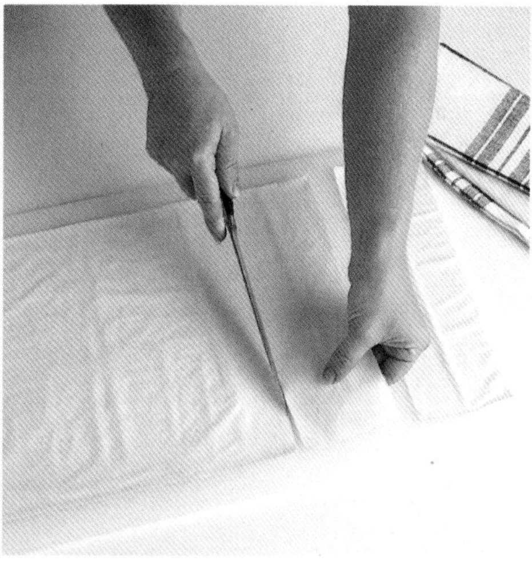

1 To make baskets, cut each pastry sheet crosswise into 8 cm/3$^1/_4$ in wide strips. Grease outsides of four small, round-based ramekins and place upside down on a greased baking tray. Brush pastry strips with butter and lay over ramekins, overlapping each strip, and bringing ends down to lay flat on tray. Brush again with butter and sprinkle generously with sugar. Bake for 10-15 minutes or until pastry is crisp and golden.

2 To poach fruits, place sugar, water and wine in a saucepan and cook over a low heat, stirring, until sugar dissolves. Add apricots, peaches, plums and nectarines and simmer for 3-4 minutes or until fruit is just soft. Remove pan from heat, add strawberries and stand for 5 minutes. Drain.

3 To make Raspberry Cream, push raspberry pureé through a sieve to remove seeds. Fold icing sugar and purée into cream.

4 Just prior to serving, place baskets on individual serving plates, fill with poached fruits and top with Raspberry Cream.

***Serves 6***

These sugar-crusted baskets filled with poached fruit are ideal for entertaining as each part can be made ahead of time. Leave the final assembly until just prior to serving or the fruit will cause the pastry baskets to go soggy and collapse.

*Creamy Caramel Banana Pie, Orange Chocolate Tart (page 26)*

# Creamy Caramel Banana Pie

Oven temperature 190°C, 375°F, Gas 5

There is a way to ensure that a biscuit crust never sticks to the pie plate and that you will always get that perfect slice. It takes a little extra time but is worth the effort. Cut a square of aluminium foil 10 cm/4 in larger than diameter of the pie plate. Turn plate upside down and press foil firmly over it. Remove foil, turn pie plate right way up and press moulded foil firmly into plate. Fold edges of foil over rim of the plate. Next, press crumb mixture firmly into foil-lined plate and bake as directed in recipe. Cool crust to room temperature then freeze for 1 hour or overnight – the crust must be frozen solid. Using edges of foil, carefully lift crust from plate and gently peel away foil a little at a time. Then, supporting base with a spatula, carefully return crust to the pie plate.

**200 g/6½ oz gingernut biscuits, crushed**
**75 g/2½ oz butter, melted**
**4 teaspoons icing sugar**
**½ teaspoon vanilla essence**
**1 cup/250 mL/8 fl oz cream (double), whipped**

BANANA CARAMEL FILLING
**1 cup/250 mL/8 fl oz sweetened condensed milk**
**3 just-ripe bananas, sliced**

1 Combine crushed biscuits and butter in a bowl, then press over base and up sides of a greased 20 cm/8 in pie plate and bake for 10 minutes. Cool.

2 To make filling, pour condensed milk into a shallow 20 cm/8 in pie plate. Cover with aluminium foil, taking the foil over the rim of the pie plate to make it airtight. Place pie plate in a baking dish with enough water to come halfway up the sides of the dish. Increase oven temperature to 220°C/425°F/Gas 7 and cook for 1¼-1½ hours or until condensed milk is a caramel colour. Add water to dish as required during cooking. Cool caramel completely.

3 Place bananas in biscuit crust, then pour over caramel to completely cover.

4 Fold icing sugar and vanilla essence into cream. Place cream mixture in a piping bag fitted with a large star nozzle and pipe rosettes around edge of pie. Chill for at least 4 hours. This pie is best served very cold.

***Serves 8***

# Coffee Nut Pie

This version of the traditional American Mud Pie is sure to be popular as a dessert or as an afternoon tea treat. To make the pie really special, top with chocolate caraques (see page 79) and pipe whipped cream around the edge.

**220 g/7 oz plain chocolate biscuits, crushed**
**125 g/4 oz butter**

COFFEE FILLING
**1 litre/1¾ pt vanilla ice cream, softened**
**2 teaspoons instant coffee powder dissolved in 4 teaspoons hot water, cooled**

CHOC-NUT TOPPING
**200 g/6½ oz dark chocolate**
**½ cup/100 g/3½ oz caster sugar**
**½ cup/125 mL/4 fl oz evaporated milk**
**60 g/2 oz chopped pecans or walnuts**

1 Combine crushed biscuits and butter in a bowl, then press over base of a greased shallow 23 cm/9 in flan dish.

2 To make filling, place ice cream and coffee mixture in a bowl and mix to combine. Spoon over biscuit base and place in freezer.

3 To make topping, place chocolate, sugar and evaporated milk in a saucepan and cook over a low heat, stirring, until chocolate melts and mixture is smooth. Stir in pecans or walnuts and cool. Pour topping over filling and freeze until firm.

***Serves 6***

*Coffee Nut Pie (page 24), Rhubarb and Apple Tart*

# Rhubarb and Apple Tart

Oven temperature 200°C, 400°F, Gas 6

**1 quantity Sweet Shortcrust Pastry (page 21)**

RHUBARB AND APPLE FILLING
**6 stalks rhubarb, chopped**
**2 tablespoons sugar**
**30 g/1 oz butter**
**3 green apples, cored, peeled and sliced**
**1/2 cup/125 g/4 oz cream cheese**
**1/3 cup/90 g/3 oz sugar**
**1 egg**
**1 teaspoon vanilla essence**

For details about blind baking see hint on page 18.

1 Roll out pastry on a lightly floured surface and use to line a greased 23 cm/9 in fluted flan tin with a removable base. Blind bake for 15 minutes, then remove weights and paper and bake for 5 minutes longer. Cool completely.

2 To make filling, poach or microwave rhubarb until tender. Drain well, stir in sugar and cool. Melt butter in a frying pan over a medium heat, add apples and cook, stirring, for 3-4 minutes. Cool.

3 Place cream cheese, sugar, egg and vanilla essence in a bowl and beat until smooth. Spoon rhubarb into pastry case, then top with cream cheese mixture and arrange apple slices on the top. Reduce oven temperature to 180°C/350°F/Gas 4 and cook for 40-45 minutes or until filling is firm.

***Serves 10***

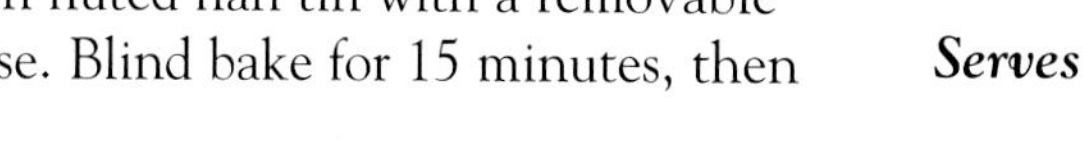

# Orange Chocolate Tarts

Oven temperature 200°C, 400°F, Gas 6

**375 g/12 oz prepared shortcrust pastry**
**125 g/4 oz dark chocolate, melted**

ORANGE FILLING
**2 tablespoons sugar**
**3 egg yolks**
**1 1/4 cups/315 mL/10 fl oz milk, scalded**
**1 tablespoon finely grated orange rind**
**2 tablespoons orange-flavoured liqueur**
**1 1/2 teaspoons gelatine dissolved in 4 teaspoons hot water, cooled**
**1/4 cup/60 mL/2 fl oz cream (double), whipped**

For an attractive presentation, decorate tarts with quartered orange slices and fine strips of orange rind.

1 Roll pastry out and use to line six 10 cm/4 in flan tins. Blind bake for 8 minutes, then remove weights and paper and bake for 10 minutes longer or until pastry is golden. Cool completely. Brush cooled pastry cases with melted chocolate and allow chocolate to set.

2 To make filling, beat sugar and egg yolks in a heatproof bowl over a saucepan of simmering water, until a ribbon trail forms when beater is lifted from mixture. Remove bowl from heat and gradually whisk in milk. Transfer mixture to a heavy-based saucepan and cook over a low heat, stirring, until mixture thickens and coats the back of a wooden spoon. Do not allow the mixture to boil. Place pan in a bowl of ice and stir until cool.

3 Stir in orange rind, liqueur and gelatine mixture, then fold in cream, and spoon filling into pastry cases. Chill.

***Serves 6***

# Quick & Easy

*Easy and irresistible – the desserts in this chapter are ideal for impromptu gatherings or those times when you need a sweet treat.*

## Chocolate Brownie Torte

Oven temperature
180°C, 350°F, Gas 4

**185 g/6 oz dark chocolate, roughly chopped**
**45 g/1 1/2 oz butter, chopped**
**1/4 cup/60 g/2 oz caster sugar**
**1 egg**
**1/2 teaspoon vanilla essence**
**60 g/2 oz slivered almonds**
**1/4 cup/30 g/1 oz flour**
**6 scoops ice cream, flavour of your choice**

1 Place 125 g/4 oz chocolate and butter in a heatproof bowl over a saucepan of simmering water and heat, stirring, for 5 minutes or until chocolate melts and mixture is smooth.

2 Place sugar, egg and vanilla essence in a bowl and beat until mixture is thick and creamy. Beat in chocolate mixture, then fold in almonds, flour and remaining chocolate pieces. Spoon mixture into a lightly greased and lined 20 cm/8 in sandwich tin and bake for 15-20 minutes or until cooked when tested with a skewer. Turn onto a wire rack and cool for 5-10 minutes before serving.

3 To serve, cut warm brownie into wedges and accompany with a scoop of ice cream – coffee-flavoured ice cream is a delicious accompaniment for this dessert.

***Serves 6***

Chocolate melts more rapidly if broken into small pieces. The melting process should occur slowly, as chocolate scorches if overheated.
The container in which chocolate is being melted should be kept uncovered and completely dry. Covering could cause condensation and just one drop of water will ruin the chocolate.

*Chocolate Brownie Torte*

# Dates with Orange Filling

Serve with halved orange slices and thin strips of orange rind.
For a scrumptious after-dinner treat accompany these dates with a cup of rich coffee and an orange-flavoured liqueur.

**315 g/10 oz fresh dates**
**1/4 teaspoon ground cinnamon**
**1/4 teaspoon ground cardamom**
**1/4 cup/60 mL/2 fl oz cognac or brandy**
**1 orange, sliced**
**fine strips orange rind**

ORANGE FILLING
**125 g/4 oz mascarpone**
**4 teaspoons icing sugar**
**2 teaspoons finely grated orange rind**
**4 teaspoons orange juice**

1 Remove seeds from dates, by cutting through centre of dates lengthways then opening out. Place cinnamon, cardamom and cognac or brandy in a glass dish and mix to combine. Add dates and toss to coat. Cover and macerate for 1 hour.

2 To make filling, place mascarpone, icing sugar, orange rind and juice in a bowl and beat until light and fluffy. Spoon mascarpone mixture into a piping bag fitted with a medium-sized star nozzle.

3 Drain dates and pat dry with absorbent kitchen paper. Pipe mascarpone mixture into the centre of each date. Chill until required.

**Variation:** In place of the mascarpone a mixture of cream cheese and cream can be used. Beat 60 g/2 oz softened cream cheese until smooth. Whip 1/4 cup/60 mL/2 fl oz cream (double) until soft peaks form, then fold into cream cheese. Stir in icing sugar, orange rind and juice.

***Serves 4***

# Rocky Road Ice Cream

For a chocolate version of this easy dessert use a rich chocolate ice cream in place of the vanilla.

**1 litre/1 3/4 pt vanilla ice cream, softened**
**2 x 60 g/2 oz chocolate-coated Turkish delight bars, chopped**
**10 pink marshmallows, chopped**
**5 white marshmallows, chopped**
**6 red glacé cherries, chopped**
**6 green glacé cherries, chopped**
**4 tablespoons shredded coconut, toasted**
**2 x 45 g/1 1/2 oz chocolate-coated scorched peanut bars, chopped**
**wafers**

1 Place ice cream in a bowl, then fold in Turkish delight bars, pink and white marshmallows, red and green cherries, coconut and peanut bars. Spoon mixture into a freezerproof container, cover and freeze until firm.

2 To serve, place scoops of ice cream into bowls and serve with wafers.

***Serves 6***

*Pancakes with Orange Sauce (page 32), Dates with Orange Filling, Rocky Road Ice Cream*

# PANCAKES WITH ORANGE SAUCE

**1 cup/125 g/4 oz flour**
**1/2 teaspoon salt**
**1/2 teaspoon bicarbonate of soda**
**1 1/4 cups/250 g/8 oz natural yogurt**
**1/3 cup/90 mL/3 fl oz milk**
**1 egg, lightly beaten**
**extra nautral yogurt (optional)**

ORANGE COINTREAU SAUCE
**2 tablespoons caster sugar**
**1 teaspoon finely grated orange rind**
**1/2 cup/125 mL/4 fl oz orange juice**
**1 teaspoon cornflour blended with 2 teaspoons water**
**2 tablespoons orange-flavoured liqueur**

1 Sift flour, salt and bicarbonate of soda together into a bowl. Make a well in the centre of the flour mixture. Combine yogurt, milk and egg, pour into well in dry ingredients and mix until just combined.

2 Drop spoonfuls of mixture into a heated, lightly greased, heavy-based frying pan and cook until bubbles form on the surface, then turn pancakes and cook on second side until golden.

3 To make sauce, place sugar, orange rind and juice in a saucepan and cook over a medium heat, stirring constantly, until sugar dissolves. Stir in cornflour mixture and cook for 1-2 minutes or until sauce thickens. Stir in liqueur and heat for 1-2 minutes longer. To serve, spoon sauce over pancakes and accompany with extra natural yogurt, if desired.

***Serves 4***

Pancakes, one of the quickest desserts you can make, can be prepared ahead of time then reheated just prior to serving. To reheat, stack pancakes in a microwavable container, cover and heat on MEDIUM (50%) for 1-2 minutes or until pancakes are hot. Take care not to overheat or the pancakes will become tough.

# STUFFED LYCHEES WITH SABAYON

**48 lychees, peeled and seeded**
**200 g/6 1/2 oz blueberries**

BERRY SABAYON
**1/3 cup/75 g/2 1/2 oz caster sugar**
**4 egg yolks**
**100 g/3 1/2 oz mixed berries, puréed and sieved**

1 Stuff each lychee with a blueberry.

2 To make sabayon, place sugar and egg yolks in a heatproof bowl over a saucepan of simmering water and cook, beating, for 5-10 minutes or until mixture is thick and fluffy. Fold in puréed berries. Place lychees in serving bowls, spoon over sabayon and decorate with remaining blueberries.

**Variation:** Redcurrants are a delicious alternative to the blueberries in this recipe.

***Serves 6***

To remove seeds from lychees, cut flesh away from top of seed and gently pull seed away from flesh.

*Stuffed Lychees with Sabayon, Chocolate Millefeuilles*

# Chocolate Millefeuilles

**1 packet chocolate cake mix**
**250 g/8 oz blueberries**
**250 g/8 oz raspberries**
**2 tablespoons icing sugar**

CHOCOLATE CREAM
**155 g/5 oz milk chocolate, melted and cooled**
**2 tablespoons brandy**
**1 cup/250 mL/8 fl oz cream (double), whipped**

1 Prepare chocolate cake following packet directions. Divide batter between two greased and lined 26 x 32 cm/10½ x 12¾ in Swiss roll tins and bake for 8-10 minutes or until cooked when tested with a skewer. Turn cakes onto a wire rack and cool. Using a 7.5 cm/3 in round cutter cut out twelve rounds of cake.

2 To make Chocolate Cream, fold chocolate and brandy into cream.

3 To assemble millefeuilles, spread each cake round with Chocolate Cream. Top six rounds with blueberries and six with raspberries, then sprinkle with icing sugar. Place a blueberry-topped round on a serving plate, then top with a raspberry-topped round. Just prior to serving, sprinkle with remaining icing sugar.

***Serves 6***

Oven temperature as per packet directions

Just raspberries or any berries of your choice can be used in place of the blueberries for these tasty dessert treats.

*Creamy Fruit Parfaits, Ginger Pear Cakes*

# Ginger Pear Cakes

Oven temperature
180°C, 350°F, Gas 4

1/2 cup/125 g/4 oz raw sugar
1/4 cup/60 mL/2 fl oz vegetable oil
1 egg, lightly beaten
1 teaspoon vanilla essence
1 cup/125 g/4 oz flour
1 teaspoon bicarbonate of soda
1/2 teaspoon ground ginger
1/2 teaspoon ground nutmeg
2 pears, cored, peeled and finely diced
155 g/5 oz glacé ginger or stem ginger in syrup, chopped

GINGER CREAM
1 cup/250 mL/8 fl oz cream (double)
1/4 cup/60 g/2 oz sour cream
1 tablespoon honey
1 tablespoon brandy
1/4 teaspoon ground ginger
1 tablespoon finely chopped glacé ginger or stem ginger in syrup

1 Place sugar, oil, egg and vanilla essence in a bowl and beat to combine. Sift together flour, bicarbonate of soda, ginger and nutmeg. Mix flour mixture into egg mixture, then fold in pears and chopped ginger.

2 Spoon batter into six lightly greased large muffin tins and bake for 20 minutes. Reduce oven temperature to 160°C/325°F/Gas 3 and bake for 15-20 minutes longer, or until cakes are cooked when tested with a skewer.

3 To make Ginger Cream, place cream, sour cream and honey in a bowl and beat until soft peaks form. Add brandy and ground ginger and beat to combine. Fold in chopped ginger. Serve cakes hot or warm accompanied by Ginger Cream.

*Serves 6*

Raw sugar is a golden to dark brown colour and is characterised by it larger crystal size and richer flavour. The amount of molasses that a sugar retains will determine its colour. Specific types of raw sugar include demerara and muscovado.

# Creamy Fruit Parfaits

Oven temperature
180°C, 350°F, Gas 4

1/4 cup/60 g/2 oz sugar
1/3 cup/90 mL/3 fl oz white wine
1 tablespoon lime juice
1 1/4 cups/310 mL/10 fl oz cream (double)
1/3 cup/90 mL/3 fl oz mango purée
1 mango, peeled and thinly sliced
2 kiwifruit, peeled and chopped
250 g/8 oz strawberries, sliced

1 Place sugar, wine and lime juice in a saucepan and cook over a medium heat, stirring constantly, until sugar dissolves. Cool at room temperature, then chill.

2 Place cream, mango purée and wine mixture in a bowl and beat until soft peaks form.

3 Arrange a layer of mango slices in the base of four dessert glasses and top with a spoonful of mango cream. Continue layering using kiwifruit, strawberries and mango cream, finishing with a layer of mango cream. Chill.

*Serves 6*

Any fruits of your choice can be used to make this attractive dessert. Puréed, drained mangoes, peaches or apricots are all good alternatives to the fresh mango purée.

# Festive

*Christmas, Easter and Thanksgiving are special times for many people not only because of the religious significance, but also because it's a time when families gather and special meals are prepared.*

## Cassata alla Siciliana

Oven temperature
180°C, 350°F, Gas 4

Decorate this traditional Italian dessert with glacé fruits and serve as a special Easter, Christmas or wedding feast treat.

Cassata alla Siciliana

**4 eggs**
**½ cup/100 g/3½ oz caster sugar**
**¾ cup/90 g/3 oz self-raising flour, sifted**
**⅓ cup/90 mL/3 fl oz brandy**

CASSATA FILLING
**½ cup/125 g/4 oz sugar**
**2 tablespoons water**
**375 g/12 oz ricotta cheese**
**100 g/3½ oz dark chocolate, finely chopped**
**60 g/2 oz glacé cherries, quartered**
**60 g/2 oz mixed peel, chopped**
**45 g/1½ oz unsalted pistachio nuts, chopped**
**½ cup/125 mL/4 fl oz cream (double), whipped**

CHOCOLATE COATING
**315 g/10 oz dark chocolate**
**90 g/3 oz butter**

1 Place eggs in a bowl and beat until light and fluffy. Gradually beat in caster sugar and continue beating until mixture is creamy. Fold in flour. Pour batter into a greased and lined 26 x 32 cm/10½ x 12¾ in Swiss roll tin and bake for 10-12 minutes or until cooked when tested with a skewer. Turn onto a wire rack to cool.

2 To make filling, place sugar and water in a saucepan and cook over a low heat, stirring constantly, until sugar dissolves. Cool. Place ricotta cheese in a food processor or blender and process until smooth. Transfer to a bowl, add chocolate, cherries, mixed peel, nuts and cream and mix to combine.

3 Line an 11 x 21 cm/4½ x 8½ in loaf dish with plastic food wrap. Cut cake into slices and sprinkle with brandy. Line base and sides of prepared dish with cake. Spoon filling into dish and top with a final layer of cake. Cover and freeze until solid.

4 To make coating, place chocolate and butter in a saucepan and cook, stirring, over a low heat until melted and mixture is well blended. Allow to cool slightly.

5 Turn frozen cassata onto a wire rack and cover with coating. Return to freezer until chocolate sets.

***Serves 10***

# French Christmas Log

Oven temperature
180°C, 350°F, Gas 4

**5 eggs**
**$^1/_2$ cup/100 g/3$^1/_2$ oz caster sugar**
**60 g/2 oz dark chocolate, melted and cooled**
**$^1/_2$ cup/60 g/2 oz self-raising flour**
**6 teaspoons cocoa powder**
**icing sugar**

RUM FILLING

**1 tablespoon icing sugar**
**$^3/_4$ cup/185 mL/6 fl oz cream (double)**
**1 tablespoon dark rum**

GANACH ICING

**185 g/6 oz dark chocolate**
**30 g/1 oz unsalted butter**
**$^2/_3$ cup/170 mL/5$^1/_2$ fl oz cream (double)**

CHOCOLATE MUSHROOMS

**1 egg white**
**$^1/_2$ teaspoon vinegar**
**$^1/_3$ cup/75 g/2$^1/_2$ oz caster sugar**
**1 teaspoon cornflour**
**30 g/1 oz dark chocolate, melted**
**1 teaspoon cocoa powder**

1 Place eggs in a bowl and beat until fluffy. Gradually beat in caster sugar and continue beating until mixture is thick and creamy. Beat in chocolate. Sift together flour and cocoa powder, then fold into egg mixture. Pour mixture into a greased and lined 26 x 32 cm/10$^1/_2$ x 12$^3/_4$ in Swiss roll tin and bake for 10-12 minutes or until cake is just firm. Turn cake onto a damp teatowel dusted with cocoa powder, remove baking paper and roll up from short end. Stand for 2-3 minutes, then unroll, cover with a second damp teatowel and cool.

2 To make filling, place icing sugar, cream and rum in a bowl and beat until soft peaks form. Chill until required.

3 To make icing, place chocolate, butter and cream in a saucepan and cook, stirring constantly, over a low heat until mixture melts and is well combined. Chill until mixture thickens and is of a spreadable consistency. Beat mixture until thick.

4 To assemble log, spread cake with filling and roll up. Cover log with icing and mark with a spatula to resemble textured bark. Decorate with mushrooms and dust with icing sugar.

5 To make mushrooms, place egg white and vinegar in a bowl and beat until soft peaks form. Gradually beat in caster sugar and continue beating until mixture is thick and glossy. Fold in cornflour. Spoon mixture into a piping bag fitted with a plain nozzle and pipe seven button shapes for the tops of the mushrooms and small nobs for the stems, onto a greased and lined baking tray. Bake at 120°C/250°F/Gas $^1/_2$ for 30 minutes or until meringue is crisp and dry. Cool meringues on tray, then join tops and stems, using a little melted chocolate, to make mushrooms. Sprinkle with cocoa powder.

***Serves 10***

Decorate serving plate with any remaining mushrooms. Cut log into slices and serve with vanilla ice cream if desired.

*French Christmas Log, Boiled Christmas Pudding (page 40)*

# Boiled Christmas Pudding

**500 g/1 lb sultanas**
**250 g/8 oz raisins**
**125 g/4 oz glacé apricots, chopped**
**125 g/4 oz glacé cherries, halved**
**125 g/4 oz blanched almonds**
**60 g/2 oz mixed peel**
**3/4 cup/185 mL/6 fl oz brandy**
**250 g/8 oz butter, softened**
**1/2 cup/90 g/3 oz brown sugar**
**1 tablespoon finely grated orange rind**
**4 eggs**
**4 teaspoons fresh orange juice**
**1 cup/125 g/4 oz flour**
**1 teaspoon ground cinnamon**
**1/2 teaspoon ground mixed spice**
**1/2 teaspoon ground nutmeg**
**4 cups/250 g/8 oz breadcrumbs made from stale bread**

If the pudding is not to be eaten immediately it may be stored in the refrigerator, wrapped in the oven bag, then reheated by reboiling in the pudding basin for 1 hour.
Check water in saucepan regularly during cooking and add more hot water as required.

1 Combine sultanas, raisins, apricots, cherries, almonds, mixed peel and brandy in a bowl and set aside.

2 Place butter, sugar and orange rind in a bowl and beat until light and creamy. Beat in eggs, one at a time, then mix in orange juice.

3 Sift together flour, cinnamon, mixed spice and nutmeg. Fold flour mixture, fruit mixture and breadcrumbs into butter mixture.

4 Spoon pudding mixture into an 8 cup/2 litre/3 1/2 pt capacity pudding basin lined with an oven bag. Seal oven bag with string, place a piece of aluminium foil over pudding and seal with pudding basin lid. Place basin in a saucepan with enough water to come halfway up the sides of the basin. Boil for 4 1/2-5 1/2 hours or until pudding is cooked through. Serve hot, warm or cold with whipped cream or vanilla ice cream.

***Serves 10-12***

# Spicy Pumpkin Pie

Oven temperature
200°C, 400°F, Gas 6

**1 quantity Sweet Shortcrust Pastry (page 21)**

SPICY PUMPKIN FILLING
**280 g/9 oz pumpkin, cooked and puréed**
**2 eggs, lightly beaten**
**1/2 cup/125 g/4 oz sour cream**
**1/2 cup/125 mL/4 fl oz cream (double)**
**1/4 cup/60 mL/2 fl oz golden syrup**
**1/2 teaspoon ground nutmeg**
**1/2 teaspoon ground mixed spice**
**1/2 teaspoon ground cinnamon**

Serve pie hot, warm or cold with whipped cream.

1 To make filling, place pumpkin, eggs, sour cream, cream, golden syrup, nutmeg, mixed spice and cinnamon in a bowl and beat until smooth.

2 Roll pastry out and use to line a greased 23 cm/9 in flan tin with a removable base. Spoon filling into pastry case. Bake for 20 minutes, then reduce heat to 160°C/325°F/Gas 3 and bake for 25-30 minutes longer or until filling is set and pastry is golden. Stand pie in tin for 5 minutes before removing.

***Serves 8***

# *Fabulous* Favourites

*This chapter is filled with desserts that are loved around the world. Delight your family with a pavlova – the all-time favourite in Australia and New Zealand. Try your hand at an American angel food cake or the rich, smooth, creamy toffee-topped French crème brûlée. And who can resist the ever-popular English bread and butter pudding?*

## The Perfect Pavlova

Oven temperature 120°C, 250°F, Gas 1/2

For extra crunch sprinkle the top of the pavlova with nuts. Both Australia and New Zealand claim to have created this truly marvellous dessert. However, both agree that it is named after the famous Russian ballerina.

**6 egg whites**
**1 1/2 cups/315 g/10 oz caster sugar**
**6 teaspoons cornflour, sifted**
**1 1/2 teaspoons white vinegar**
**1 1/4 cups/315 mL/10 fl oz cream (double), whipped**
**selection of fresh fruits, such as orange segments, sliced bananas, sliced peaches, passion fruit pulp, berries or sliced kiwifruit**

1 Place egg whites in a bowl and beat until soft peaks form. Gradually beat in sugar and continue beating until mixture is thick and glossy.

2 Fold cornflour and vinegar into egg white mixture. Grease a baking tray and line with nonstick baking paper. Mark a 23 cm/9 in diameter circle on paper, then grease and dust with flour.

3 Place one-quarter of the egg white mixture in the centre of the circle and spread out to within 3 cm/1 1/4 in of the edge. Pile remaining mixture around edge of circle and neaten using a metal spatula or knife. Bake for 1 1/2-2 hours or until firm to touch. Turn off oven and cool pavlova in oven with door ajar. Decorate cold pavlova with cream and top with fruit.

***Serves 8***

*The Perfect Pavlova*

# Blackberry Creme Brulee

Any fruit or a mixture of berries can be used instead of the blackberries. If using fruits such as apricots, plums or peaches they will need to be lightly poached first.

**200 g/6 1/2 oz blackberries**
**2 cups/500 mL/16 fl oz cream (double)**
**1 vanilla bean (pod)**
**1 cup/220 g/7 oz caster sugar**
**5 egg yolks**

TOFFEE TOPPING
**1/2 cup/125 g/4 oz sugar**
**1/4 cup/60 mL/ 2 fl oz water**

1 Divide berries between six 1/2 cup/125 mL/4 fl oz capacity ramekins. Place cream and vanilla bean (pod) in a saucepan and bring to the boil. Place caster sugar and egg yolks in a bowl and beat until thick and creamy. Continue beating while slowly pouring in hot cream. Return mixture to pan and cook over a low heat, stirring, until mixture thickens. Remove vanilla bean (pod). Pour cream mixture into ramekins and refrigerate until custards are set.

2 To make topping, place sugar and water in a saucepan and cook over a medium heat, stirring, until sugar dissolves. Bring mixture to the boil and boil, without stirring, until sugar syrup is golden. Swirl pan once or twice during cooking. Carefully spoon toffee over cold brûlées and set aside to harden.

***Serves 6***

# Berry Chocolate Mud Cake

Oven temperature
120°C, 250°F, Gas 1/2

**315 g/10 oz dark chocolate**
**250 g/8 oz butter, chopped**
**5 eggs, separated**
**2 tablespoons caster sugar**
**1/4 cup/30 g/1 oz self-raising flour, sifted**
**250 g/8 oz raspberries**
**whipped cream, for serving**

RASPBERRY COULIS
**250 g/8 oz raspberries**
**sugar to taste**

1 Place chocolate and butter in a heatproof bowl over a saucepan of simmering water and heat, stirring, until chocolate melts and mixture is smooth. Cool slightly.

2 Beat egg yolks and caster sugar into chocolate mixture, then fold in flour.

3 Place egg whites in a separate bowl and beat until stiff peaks form. Fold egg whites and raspberries into chocolate mixture. Pour into a greased and lined 20 cm/8 in round cake tin and bake for 1 1/4 hours or until cooked when tested with a skewer. Turn off oven and cool cake in oven with door ajar.

4 To make coulis, place raspberries in a food processor or blender and process until puréed. Push purée through a sieve to remove seeds. Add sugar to taste. Serve cake with coulis and cream.

***Serves 10***

*Berry Chocolate Mud Cake, Blackberry Crème Brûlée*

# Jaffa Self-saucing Pudding

125 g/4 oz butter
2 teaspoons finely grated orange rind
3/4 cup/170 g/5 1/2 oz caster sugar
2 eggs
100 g/3 1/2 oz chocolate chips
1 1/2 cups/185 g/6 oz self-raising flour, sifted
1/2 cup/125 mL/4 fl oz orange juice
1/4 cup/30 g/1 oz cocoa powder
1/2 cup/100 g/3 1/2 oz caster sugar
1 1/2 cups/375 mL/12 fl oz boiling water

1 Place butter and orange rind in a bowl and beat until light and fluffy. Gradually beat in sugar and continue beating until mixture is creamy.

2 Beat in eggs one at a time. Toss chocolate chips in flour, then fold flour mixture and orange juice, alternately, into batter. Spoon batter into a greased ovenproof dish.

3 Sift cocoa powder and sugar together over batter in dish, then carefully pour over boiling water. Bake for 40 minutes or until pudding is firm.

*Serves 8*

Oven temperature
180°C, 350°F, Gas 4

Serve this simple family dessert with vanilla or chocolate ice cream or lightly whipped cream.

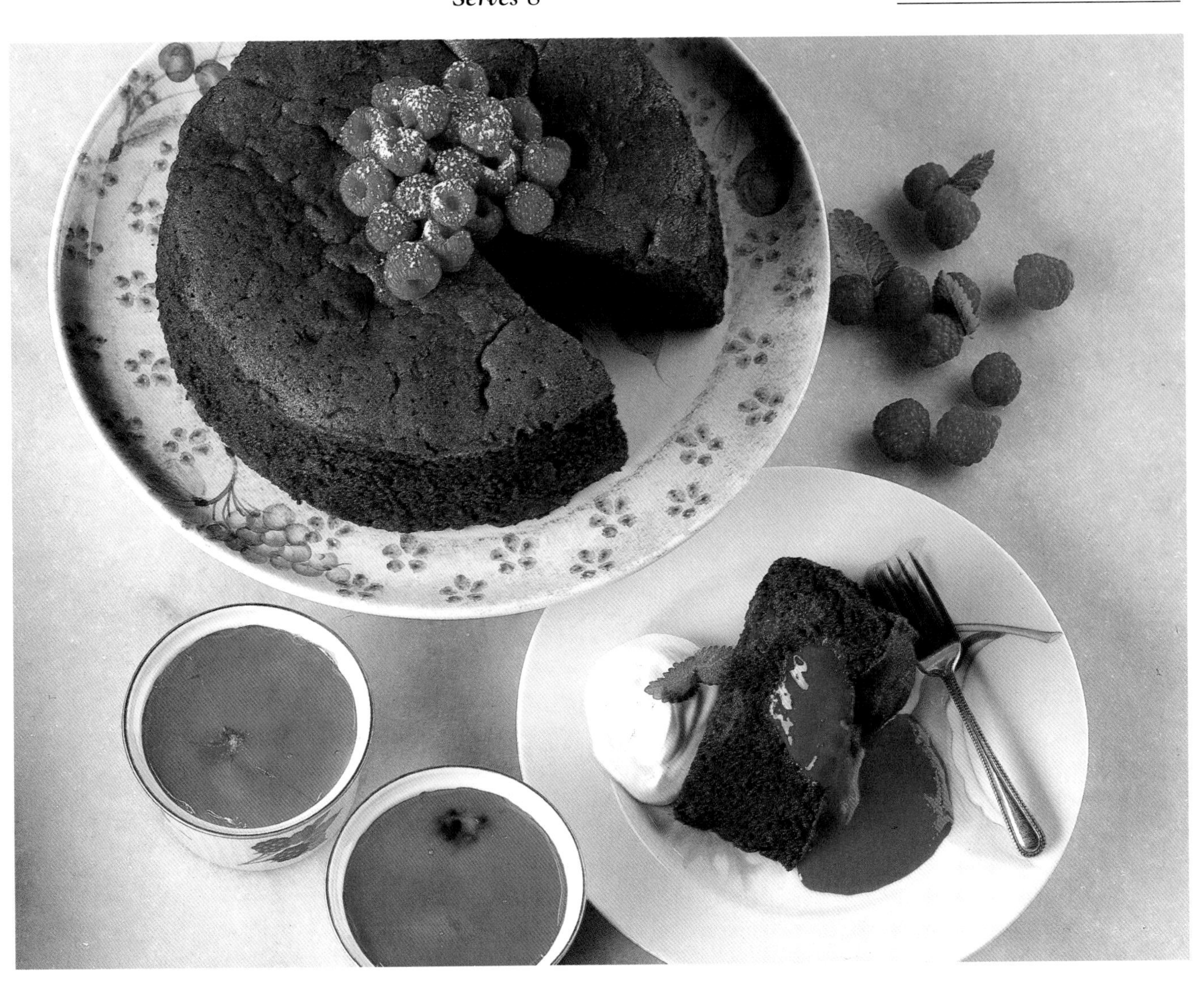

# Coconut Angel Food Cake

Oven temperature
180°C, 350°F, Gas 4

**3/4 cup/90 g/3 oz flour**
**1/4 cup/30 g/1 oz cornflour**
**1 cup/220 g/7 oz caster sugar**
**10 egg whites**
**1/2 teaspoon salt**
**1 teaspoon cream of tartar**
**8 teaspoons water**
**1 teaspoon vanilla essence**
**45 g/1 1/2 oz shredded coconut**

FLUFFY FROSTING
**1 1/4 cups/315 g/10 oz sugar**
**1/2 cup/125 mL/4 fl oz water**
**3 egg whites**
**90 g/3 oz shredded coconut, lightly toasted**

1 Sift flour and cornflour together three times, then sift once more with 1/4 cup/60 g/2 oz of the caster sugar.

2 Place egg whites, salt, cream of tartar and water in a bowl and beat until stiff peaks form. Beat in vanilla essence, then fold in remaining sugar, 1 tablespoon at a time.

3 Sift flour mixture over egg white mixture then gently fold in. Lastly sprinkle coconut over top of batter and fold in. Spoon batter into an ungreased angel cake tin, then draw a spatula gently through the mixture to break up any large air pockets. Bake for 45 minutes. When cake is cooked invert tin and allow the cake to hang while it is cooling.

4 To make frosting, place sugar and water in a saucepan and cook over a medium heat, without boiling and stirring constantly, until sugar dissolves. Brush any sugar from sides of pan using a pastry brush dipped in water. Bring the syrup to the boil and boil rapidly for 3-5 minutes, without stirring, or until syrup reaches the soft-ball stage (115°C/239°F on a sugar thermometer). Place egg whites in a bowl and beat until soft peaks form, then continue beating while pouring in syrup in a thin stream. Continue beating until all syrup is used and frosting stands in stiff peaks. Spread frosting over top and sides of cold cake, then press toasted coconut onto sides of cake.

***Serves 12***

An angel cake tin is a deep-sided ring tin with a removable base that has a centre tube higher than the outside edges. If you do not have an angel cake tin use an ordinary deep-sided ring tin with a removable base. However, when you invert the tin for the cake to cool, place the tube over a funnel or bottle. Never grease an angel cake tin as this stops the cake rising.

# Lemon Sultana Cheesecake

Oven temperature
220°C, 425°F, Gas 7

PASTRY
**½ cup/60 g/2 oz flour**
**¼ cup/30 g/1 oz cornflour**
**¼ cup/30 g/1 oz custard powder**
**4 teaspoons icing sugar**
**60 g/2 oz butter**
**1 egg yolk**
**iced water**

CHEESECAKE FILLING
**½ cup/100 g/3½ oz caster sugar**
**2 teaspoons finely grated lemon rind**
**375 g/12 oz cream cheese, softened**
**¼ cup/45 g/1½ oz natural yogurt**
**2 eggs**
**1 teaspoon vanilla essence**
**170 g/5½ oz sultanas**

LEMON TOPPING
**½ cup/125 mL/4 fl oz cream (double)**
**2 teaspoons lemon juice**
**½ teaspoon finely grated lemon rind**

1 To make pastry, sift flour, cornflour, custard powder and icing sugar together into a bowl. Using fingertips, rub in butter until mixture resembles coarse breadcrumbs. Make a well in the centre of the flour mixture, then stir in egg yolk and enough water to make a firm dough. Wrap in plastic food wrap and chill for 30 minutes.

2 Roll out pastry to fit the base of a greased 20 cm/8 in springform tin. Using a fork, prick pastry base and bake for 10 minutes. Cool.

3 To make filling, place caster sugar, lemon rind, cream cheese, yogurt, eggs and vanilla essence in a bowl and beat until smooth. Fold in sultanas. Spoon mixture into prepared cake tin. Reduce oven temperature to 180°C/350°F/Gas 4 and bake for 20-25 minutes or until filling is firm. Turn off oven and cool cheesecake in oven with door ajar.

4 To make topping, place cream, lemon juice and rind in a saucepan and bring to simmering, then simmer, stirring, for 5 minutes or until mixture thickens. Pour topping over cooled cheesecake and chill until required.

***Serves 8***

Orange rind and juice are tasty alternatives to the lemon in this recipe.

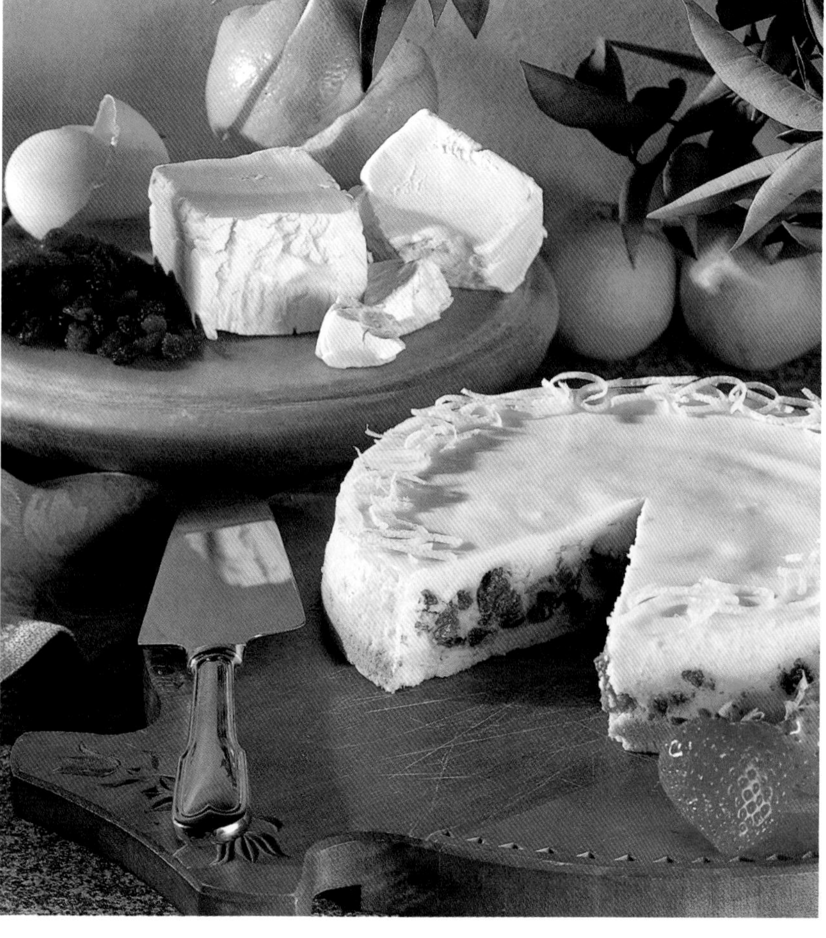

*Left: Lemon Sultana Cheesecake*
*Right: Devil's Food Cake*

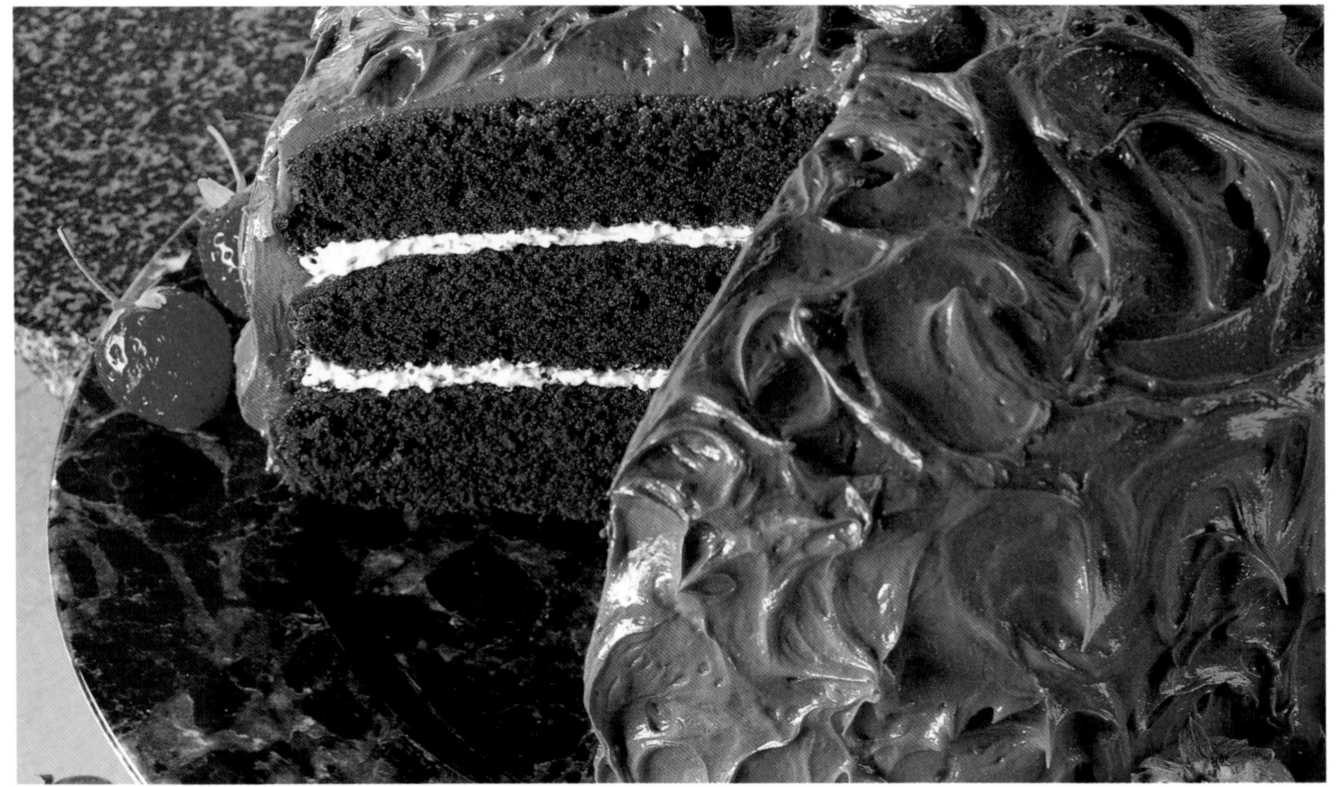

# Devil's Food Cake

1 cup/100 g/3½ oz cocoa powder
1½ cups/375 mL/12 fl oz boiling water
375 g/12 oz unsalted butter, softened
1 teaspoon vanilla essence
1½ cups/315 g/10 oz caster sugar
4 eggs
2½ cups/315 g/10 oz flour
½ cup/60 g/2 oz cornflour
1 teaspoon bicarbonate of soda
1 teaspoon salt
½ cup/125 mL/4 fl oz cream (double), whipped

CHOCOLATE BUTTER ICING
250 g/8 oz butter, softened
1 cup/155 g/5 oz icing sugar, sifted
2 egg yolks
1 egg
185 g/6 oz dark chocolate, melted and cooled

1 Combine cocoa powder and water in a bowl and mix until blended. Cool. Place butter and vanilla essence in a bowl and beat until light and fluffy. Gradually beat in caster sugar and continue beating until mixture is creamy. Beat in eggs, one at a time.

2 Sift together flour, cornflour, bicarbonate of soda and salt. Fold flour mixture and cocoa mixture, alternately, into egg mixture.

3 Divide batter between three greased and lined 23 cm/9 in sandwich tins and bake for 20-25 minutes or until cakes are cooked when tested with a skewer. Stand cakes in tins for 5 minutes before turning onto wire racks to cool.

4 To make icing, place butter in a bowl and beat until light and fluffy. Beat in icing sugar, egg yolks and egg. Beat in chocolate and continue beating until icing is thick. Sandwich cakes together using whipped cream then cover top and sides with icing.

*Serves 12*

Oven temperature
180°C, 350°F, Gas 4

The uniced, undecorated layers of this cake can be frozen in an airtight container for up to 3 months.

*Fruity Bread Pudding, Banana Fritters, Jaffa Self-saucing Pudding (page 45)*

# Fruity Bread Pudding

Oven temperature
180°C, 350°F, Gas 4

**60 g/2 oz butter**
**1/2 cup/90 g/3 oz brown sugar**
**440 g/14 oz canned sliced apples**
**90 g/3 oz sultanas**
**1/2 teaspoon ground cinnamon**
**12 thick slices fruit loaf, buttered and crusts removed**
**1 1/4 cups/310 mL/10 fl oz milk**
**3/4 cup/185 mL/6 fl oz cream (double)**
**3 eggs**
**1/2 teaspoon vanilla essence**

1 Melt butter in a frying pan over a medium heat, add sugar and cook, stirring constantly, until sugar dissolves. Stir in apples, sultanas and cinnamon and cook for 1-2 minutes longer. Cool.

2 Cut bread into triangles and arrange one-third, buttered side up, in the base of a greased ovenproof dish. Top with half the apple mixture and another layer of bread. Spoon over remaining apple mixture, then top with another layer of bread and finally arrange remaining triangles around the edges.

3 Place milk, cream, eggs and vanilla essence in a bowl and whisk to combine. Carefully pour into dish, then place dish in a baking dish with enough water to come halfway up the sides. Bake for 45-50 minutes or until pudding is firm and top is golden.

***Serves 8***

Allowing the pudding to stand for an hour before baking allows the bread to absorb the cream mixture, resulting in the cooked pudding having a softer and moister texture.

# Banana Fritters

**4 large firm bananas, cut in half then split lengthways**
**2 tablespoons lime juice**
**vegetable oil for deep-frying**

BATTER
**1 cup/125 g/4 oz self-raising flour**
**2 tablespoons caster sugar**
**1/2 cup/125 mL/4 fl oz milk**
**1 egg, lightly beaten**
**1 egg white**

CARAMEL SAUCE
**1/2 cup/125 g/4 oz sugar**
**1/2 cup/125 mL/4 fl oz water**
**1/2 cup/125 mL/4 fl oz cream (double)**
**2 teaspoons whisky (optional)**

1 To make batter, sift flour in a bowl and make a well in the centre. Combine caster sugar, milk and egg, then mix into flour mixture to make a batter of a smooth consistency. Stand for 10 minutes.

2 To make sauce, place sugar and water in a saucepan and cook over a low heat, stirring constantly, until sugar dissolves. Bring to the boil, then reduce heat and simmer, without stirring, for 5 minutes or until mixture is golden.

3 Remove pan from heat and carefully stir in cream and whisky, if using. Return pan to a low heat and cook, stirring, until combined. Cool.

4 Beat egg white until soft peaks form, then fold into batter. Heat oil in a saucepan until a cube of bread dropped in browns in 50 seconds. Brush bananas with lime juice, dip in batter to coat then drain off excess. Cook bananas in hot oil for 2-3 minutes or until golden. Serve immediately with sauce.

***Serves 4***

Fruit fritters are always popular, especially with children. You might like to make these using other fruits, such as apples, peaches or canned pineapple rings.

# Light & Low Delights

*Low in calories and light in texture, these sinfully delicious desserts are hardly wicked at all. Even if you are not on a diet, these desserts make the perfect finish.*

## Coeur a la Creme

**185 g/6 oz cottage cheese**
**60 g/2 oz reduced-fat cream cheese**
**1 tablespoon icing sugar**
**1/4 cup/60 mL/2 fl oz cream (double)**
**1/2 teaspoon vanilla essence**
**1 tablespoon orange-flavoured liqueur**
**250 g/8 oz mixed fruits, such as berries of your choice, plums, peaches or melons**

Start preparing this dessert the day before serving as it has to sit in the refrigerator overnight.

1 Place cottage cheese in a food processor or blender and process until smooth. Add cream cheese, icing sugar, cream and vanilla essence and process to combine.

2 Line four coeur à la crème moulds with a double thickness of damp muslin or gauze and pack cheese mixture into moulds. Place moulds on a wire rack, on a tray. Cover and refrigerate for 24 hours. Turn crèmes onto serving plates, sprinkle each with a little liqueur and garnish with fruit.

**Coeur à la crème moulds:** These are china, heart-shaped moulds with draining holes in the base. Before lining with the muslin you should rinse them in cold water, but do not dry. You can make your own moulds, using small empty plastic containers. Cut the containers down to make sides of about 2.5 cm/1 in, then, using a skewer, punch holes in the base. These moulds will not be heart-shaped like the traditional ones but the dessert will still look and taste wonderful.

***Serves 4***

*Coeur à la Crème*

# Peach Compote

Other fruits such as nectarines, plums, apples and pears are also good prepared in this way. Remember the cooking time will be a little longer for harder fruits.

**6 firm ripe peaches, halved and stoned**
**1 cup/250 mL/8 fl oz red wine**
**2-3 tablespoons honey**
**1 cinnamon stick**

Cut peaches into thick slices. Place wine, honey and cinnamon stick in a saucepan and bring to the boil, reduce heat and simmer for 5 minutes. Add peaches and cook for 5-10 minutes or until slightly softened. Cool, then chill.

*Serves 4*

# Rhubarb Fool

Oven temperature 190°C, 375°F, Gas 5

**750 g/1 1/2 lb rhubarb, trimmed and cut into 1 cm/1/2 in pieces**
**1 cup/170 g/5 1/2 oz brown sugar**
**1/4 teaspoon ground cloves**
**2 tablespoons lemon juice**
**2 tablespoons orange juice**
**1/2 teaspoon vanilla essence**
**3/4 cup/185 mL/6 fl oz cream (double)**
**1/2 cup/100 g/3 1/2 oz natural yogurt**

ORANGE BISCUITS
**75 g unsalted butter**
**1/4 cup/60 g/2 oz caster sugar**
**1 egg**
**1 1/2 teaspoons grated orange rind**
**3/4 cup/90 g/3 oz flour**

1 Place rhubarb, brown sugar, cloves, lemon and orange juices and vanilla essence in a saucepan. Bring to the boil, then reduce heat and simmer, stirring occasionally, for 15 minutes or until rhubarb is soft and mixture thick. Chill.

2 Place cream in a bowl and beat until soft peaks form. Fold yogurt into cream, then fold in chilled rhubarb mixture to give a marbled effect. Spoon into individual serving glasses and chill.

3 To make biscuits, place butter and caster sugar in a bowl and beat until light and creamy. Add egg and orange rind and beat to combine. Stir in flour. Place teaspoons of mixture, 5 cm/2 in apart, on lightly greased baking trays and bake for 10 minutes or until golden. Stand biscuits on trays for 1 minute before transferring to wire racks to cool. Accompany each fool with two or three biscuits.

*Serves 8*

Rhubarb is the edible stalk of the rhubarb plant and as such is in fact a vegetable. However, because of the way it is used we tend to think of it as a fruit. The leaves of the rhubarb plant are very toxic and should never to cooked or eaten.

# Raspberry Tarts

HAZELNUT PASTRY
**1 cup/125 g/4 oz flour, sifted**
**60 g/2 oz unsalted butter, chopped**
**30 g/1 oz hazelnuts, ground**
**1 tablespoon icing sugar**
**1 egg, lightly beaten**
**1 egg yolk, lightly beaten**

CREAM FILLING
**375 g/12 oz reduced-fat cream cheese**
**2 tablespoons caster sugar**
**$^1/_4$ cup/60 mL/2 fl oz cream (double)**

RASPBERRY TOPPING
**350 g/11 oz raspberries**
**$^1/_3$ cup/100 g/3$^1/_2$ oz raspberry jam, warmed and sieved**

1 To make pastry, place flour, butter, hazelnuts and icing sugar in a food processor and process until mixture resembles fine breadcrumbs. Add egg and egg yolk, and process to form a soft dough. Wrap dough in plastic food wrap and chill for 1 hour.

2 Knead pastry lightly, then roll out to 3 mm/$^1/_8$ in thick and use to line six lightly greased 7$^1/_2$ cm/3 in flan tins. Bake pastry cases blind for 10 minutes. Remove weights and paper and bake for 15 minutes or until golden. Cool.

3 To make filling, place cream cheese, and caster sugar in a bowl and beat until smooth. Beat cream until soft peaks form, then fold into cream cheese mixture. Cover and chill for 20 minutes.

4 To assemble, spoon filling into pastry cases, then arrange raspberries attractively on top. Brush warm jam over raspberries and chill for a few minutes to set glaze.

***Serves 6***

Oven temperature
200°C, 400°F, Gas 6

Any berries such as strawberries, blueberries or blackberries can be used to make these divine individual tarts. For more information about baking blind see hint on page 18.

*Peach Compote, Raspberry Tarts*

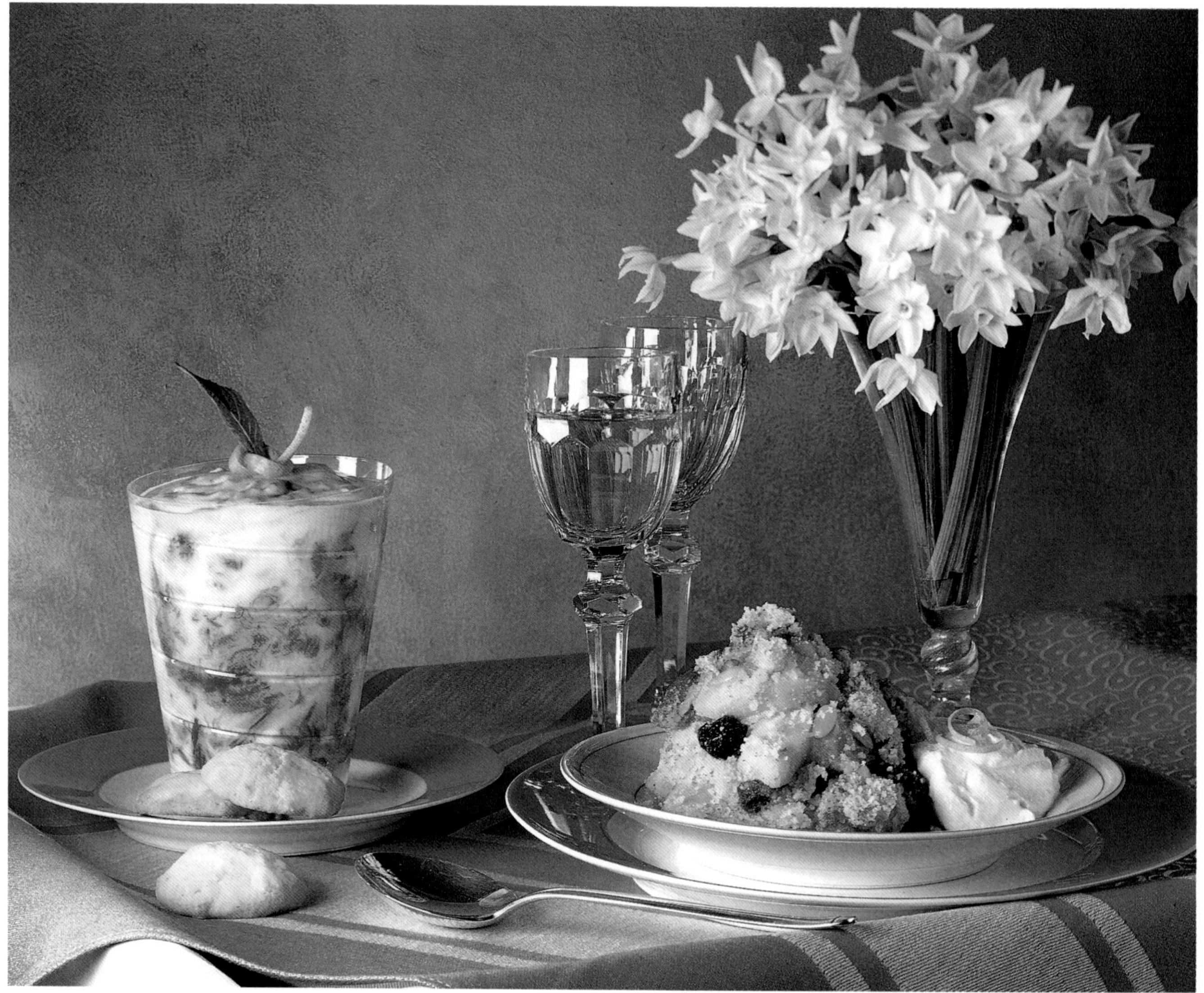

*Apple Pudding, Rhubarb Fool served with Orange Biscuits (page 54)*

# Apple Pudding

Oven temperature
200°C, 400°F, Gas 6

6 green apples, cored, peeled and cut into 1 cm/$^1/_2$ in slices
100 g/3$^1/_2$ oz raisins
60 g/2 oz pine nuts, toasted
1 cup/250 mL/8 fl oz orange juice
$^1/_4$ cup/90 g/3 oz honey
60 g/2 oz ground almonds
1 tablespoon finely grated orange rind
6 whole cloves
$^1/_2$ teaspoon ground cinnamon

RICOTTA CREAM

100 g/3$^1/_2$ oz fresh ricotta cheese
100 g/3$^1/_2$ oz cottage cheese
1-2 tablespoons milk
1-2 tablespoons caster sugar

1 Layer apples, raisins and pine nuts in a shallow ovenproof dish. Pour over orange juice, then drizzle with honey, and scatter with almonds, orange rind, cloves and cinnamon. Cover dish with aluminium foil and bake for 35-40 minutes or until apples are tender.

2 To make cream, place ricotta and cottage cheeses in a food processor or blender and process until smooth. Add a little milk if the mixture is too thick and sweeten with sugar to taste. Serve with apple pudding.

*Serves 4*

The Ricotta Cream served with this pudding is a delicious alternative to cream. You might like to try it as an accompaniment to other desserts.

# Individual Summer Puddings

**$^1/_2$ cup/100 g/3$^1/_2$ oz caster sugar**
**2 cups/500 mL/16 fl oz water**
**875 g/1$^3/_4$ lb mixed berries, such as raspberries, strawberries, blueberries or blackberries**
**14 slices white bread, crusts removed**

BERRY SAUCE
**2 tablespoons icing sugar**
**155 g/5 oz mixed berries, such as raspberries, strawberries, blueberries or blackberries**
**2 tablespoons water**
**1 tablespoon fresh lemon juice**

1 Place caster sugar and water in a saucepan and cook over a low heat, stirring constantly, until sugar dissolves. Bring to the boil, then reduce heat, add berries and simmer for 4-5 minutes or until fruit is soft, but still retains its shape. Remove from heat. Drain, reserving liquid, and set aside to cool.

2 Cut 8 rounds of bread to fit the base of $^1/_2$ cup/125 mL/4 fl oz capacity ramekins. Line four ramekins with 4 rounds of the bread, reserve the remaining rounds for tops of puddings. Cut remaining bread slices into fingers and line the sides of the ramekins, trimming bread to fit if necessary. Spoon fruit into ramekins then pour over enough reserved liquid to moisten bread well. Cover with remaining bread rounds. Reserve any remaining liquid. Cover tops of ramekins with aluminium foil, top with a weight, and refrigerate overnight.

3 To make sauce, place icing sugar, berries, water and lemon juice in a food processor or blender and process to make a purée. Push mixture through a sieve to remove seeds and chill.

4 Turn puddings onto serving plates, spoon sauce over or pass separately.

***Serves 4***

Use either fresh or frozen berries to make this dessert. For an attractive serving presentation garnish with additional berries and accompany with natural yogurt or Ricotta Cream (see recipe on page 56).

*Individual Summer Puddings*

# *Something* Spectacular

*For a special occasion, a fabulous home-cooked dinner followed by a spectacular dessert is the perfect way to celebrate.*

## Austrian Coffee Cake

Oven temperature
180°C, 350°F, Gas 4

Chocolate-coated coffee beans are available from specialty food shops and some supermarkets.

**4 eggs, separated**
**1/4 cup/60 g/2 oz caster sugar**
**45 g/1 1/2 oz ground almonds**
**3 teaspoons instant coffee powder dissolved in 4 teaspoons boiling water, cooled**
**1/2 teaspoon vanilla essence**
**1/4 cup/30 g/1 oz flour**
**chocolate-coated coffee beans or chocolate dots**
**finely grated chocolate**

COFFEE CREAM

**1 tablespoon caster sugar**
**1 teaspoon instant coffee powder dissolved in 2 teaspoons boiling water, cooled**
**2 tablespoons coffee-flavoured liqueur**
**1 cup/250 mL/8 fl oz cream (double), whipped**

1 Place egg yolks and sugar in a bowl and beat until thick and creamy. Beat in almonds, coffee mixture and vanilla essence.

2 Place egg whites in a bowl and beat until stiff peaks form. Sift flour over egg yolk mixture and fold in with egg white mixture. Spoon batter into a greased and lined 20 cm/8 in springform tin and bake for 20-25 minutes or until cooked when tested with a skewer. Stand in tin for 10 minutes, before turning onto a wire rack to cool.

3 To make Coffee Cream, mix sugar, coffee mixture and liqueur into cream. Split cold cake horizontally and use a little of the Coffee Cream to sandwich halves together. Spread remaining Coffee Cream over top and sides of cake. Decorate top of cake with coffee beans or chocolate dots and grated chocolate. Chill and serve cut into slices.

***Serves 10***

*Austrian Coffee Cake*

# Orange and Almond Gateau

Oven temperature
180°C, 350°F, Gas 4

The secret to this spectacular cake is to pour the hot sugar syrup over the cooked cakes while they are still hot. Do not pour cold syrup over hot cakes or hot syrup over cold cakes or the cakes will become soggy.

**75 g/2½ oz flaked almonds, toasted**

SOUR CREAM ORANGE CAKE

**1 cup/220 g/7 oz caster sugar**
**3 eggs**
**4 teaspoons orange juice**
**1 tablespoon finely grated orange rind**
**1¾ cups/220 g/7 oz flour**
**¼ cup/30 g/1 oz cornflour**
**1½ teaspoons baking powder**
**1 teaspoon bicarbonate of soda**
**1 cup/250 g/8 oz sour cream, lightly beaten**
**250 g/8 oz butter, melted and cooled**

ORANGE SYRUP

**½ cup/125 g/4 oz sugar**
**¼ cup/60 mL/2 fl oz orange juice**
**¼ cup/60 mL/2 fl oz orange-flavoured liqueur**

ORANGE BUTTER CREAM

**½ cup/125 g/4 oz sugar**
**½ cup/125 mL/4 fl oz water**
**4 egg yolks**
**250 g/8 oz unsalted butter, softened**
**2 teaspoons finely grated orange rind**
**¼ cup/60 mL/2 fl oz orange juice**
**2 tablespoons orange-flavoured liqueur**

1 To make cake, place caster sugar, eggs, orange juice and rind in a bowl and beat until thick and creamy. Sift together flour, cornflour, baking powder and bicarbonate of soda. Place sour cream and butter in a bowl and whisk lightly to combine. Fold flour and sour cream mixtures, alternately, into egg mixture.

2 Spoon batter into three lightly greased and lined 23 cm/9 in sandwich tins and bake for 15-20 minutes or until cooked when tested with a skewer.

3 To make syrup: Five minutes before cakes complete cooking, place sugar, orange juice and liqueur in a saucepan and cook over a medium heat, stirring constantly, until sugar dissolves.

4 Turn cakes onto wire racks and, using a skewer, pierce surface of cakes to make holes that reach about halfway through the cakes. Spoon hot syrup over hot cakes and cool.

5 To make butter cream, place sugar and water in a saucepan and cook over a medium heat, stirring constantly, until sugar dissolves. Bring syrup to the boil and cook until mixture reaches the soft-ball stage (115°C/239°F on a sugar thermometer). Place egg yolks in a bowl, then beat to combine and continue beating while slowly pouring in sugar syrup. Beat for 5 minutes longer or until mixture cools and is of a thick mousse-like consistency. In a separate bowl beat butter until light and creamy, then gradually beat into egg yolk mixture. Beat in orange rind and juice and liqueur.

6 To assemble, sandwich cakes together with a little butter cream, then spread remaining butter cream over top and sides of cake. Press almonds around sides of cake.

***Serves 10***

*Orange and Almond Gâteau*

# Fresh Berry Tart

Oven temperature
200°C, 400°F, Gas 6

**1 quantity Sweet Shortcrust Pastry (page 21)**
**500 g/1 lb mixed berries**

MASCARPONE ORANGE FILLING
**500 g/1 lb mascarpone**
**2 tablespoons icing sugar**
**1 teaspoon finely grated orange rind**
**3/4 cup/185 mL/6 fl oz orange juice**
**1/4 cup/60 mL/2 fl oz orange-flavoured liqueur**

STRAWBERRY GLAZE
**1/4 cup/75 g/2 1/2 oz strawberry jam**
**1/2 cup/125 mL/4 fl oz orange juice**
**2 teaspoons gelatine**

1 Roll out pastry to fit a 23 cm/9 in square flan tin with a removable base. Bake blind for 10-15 minutes, then remove weights and paper and cook for 5-10 minutes longer or until pastry is golden. Cool.

2 To make filling, place mascarpone, icing sugar, orange rind and juice and liqueur in a bowl and beat to combine. Spoon filling into cold pastry case, then top with berries.

3 To make glaze, place jam and orange juice in a saucepan, sprinkle over gelatine and heat over a low heat until gelatine dissolves. Cool slightly, then brush over tart.

***Serves 8***

A combination of cream cheese and cream can be used in place of the mascarpone in this recipe if you wish. Place 250 g/8 oz softened cream cheese in a food processor and process until smooth. Add 250 mL/8 fl oz cream (double) and beat until mixture is creamy. The tart can also be made in a 25 cm/10 in round flan tin.

# Filled Chocolate Cups

**440 g/14 oz milk chocolate, melted**

PEACH CREAM
**1 1/4 cups/315 mL/10 fl oz cream (double)**
**2 tablespoons icing sugar, sifted**
**2 peaches, peeled, stoned and flesh puréed**
**1/4 cup/60 mL/2 fl oz passion fruit pulp**

PEACH COULIS
**3 peaches, peeled, stoned and flesh puréed**
**1/3 cup/90 mL/3 fl oz passion fruit pulp**
**sugar**

1 To make chocolate cups, cut six 15 cm/6 in squares of nonstick baking paper. Place small moulds or ramekins upside down on a tray and cover with paper squares. Spoon chocolate over base of mould and allow to run down sides of paper. Spread chocolate with a small spatula if it does not run freely. Allow chocolate to set, then carefully peel off paper.

2 To make Peach Cream, place cream in a bowl and beat until soft peaks form. Fold in icing sugar, peach purée and passion fruit pulp.

3 To make coulis, push peach purée and passion fruit pulp through a sieve to make a smooth purée. Add sugar to taste. To assemble, flood serving plates with coulis, place chocolate cups on plates and fill with Peach Cream.

***Serves 6***

This dessert is delicious garnished with crushed praline. To make praline, place 1 cup/250 g/8 oz sugar and 1 cup/250 mL/8 fl oz water in a saucepan and cook over a low heat, stirring, until sugar dissolves. Increase heat and simmer until syrup is golden. Scatter 3 tablespoons slivered, toasted almonds on a greased baking tray, then pour over toffee. Allow to harden then break into pieces. Place in a food processor and process until toffee resembles coarse breadcrumbs.

# Raspberry Truffle Cakes

Oven temperature
180°C, 350°F, Gas 4

**1/2 cup/45 g/1 1/2 oz cocoa powder, sifted**
**1 cup/250 mL/8 fl oz boiling water**
**1 3/4 cups/400 g/12 1/2 oz caster sugar**
**125 g/4 oz butter**
**1 1/2 tablespoons raspberry jam**
**2 eggs**
**1 2/3 cups/200 g/6 1/2 oz self-raising flour, sifted**
**410 g/13 oz dark chocolate, melted**
**raspberries for garnishing**

RASPBERRY CREAM
**125 g/4 oz raspberries, puréed and sieved**
**1/2 cup/125 mL/4 fl oz cream (double), whipped**

CHOCOLATE SAUCE
**125 g/4 oz dark chocolate**
**1/2 cup/125 mL/4 fl oz water**
**1/4 cup/60 g/2 oz caster sugar**
**1 teaspoon brandy (optional)**

These rich little chocolate cakes filled with a raspberry cream and served with a bittersweet chocolate sauce are a perfect finale to any dinner party. Follow the step-by-step instructions and you will see just how easy this spectacular dessert is.

1 Dissolve cocoa powder in boiling water, then cool.

2 Place sugar, butter and jam in a bowl and beat until light and fluffy. Beat in eggs one at a time, adding a little flour with each egg. Fold remaining flour and cocoa mixture, alternately, into butter mixture.

3 Spoon mixture into eight lightly greased 1/2 cup/125 mL/4 fl oz capacity ramekins or large muffin tins. Bake for 20-25 minutes or until cakes are cooked when tested with a skewer. Stand cakes in tins for 5 minutes then turn onto wire racks to cool. Turn cakes upside down and scoop out centre leaving a 1 cm/1/2 in shell. Spread each cake with chocolate to cover top and sides, then place right way up on a wire rack.

4 To make cream, fold raspberry purée into cream. Spoon cream into a piping bag fitted with a large nozzle. Carefully turn cakes upside down and pipe in cream to fill cavity. Place right way up on individual serving plates.

5 To make sauce, place chocolate and water in a saucepan and cook over a low heat, stirring, for 4-5 minutes or until chocolate melts. Add sugar and continue cooking, stirring constantly, until sugar dissolves. Bring just to the boil, then reduce heat and simmer, stirring, for 2 minutes. Cool for 5 minutes, then stir in brandy, if using. Cool sauce to room temperature and serve with cakes.

***Serves 8***

# Hot Puddings

*You will find the puddings of childhood memories in this chapter. Pancakes, crumbles and self-saucing puddings along with soufflés and cobblers will remind you of the puddings that mother used to make. Served on their own or with custard and ice cream these desserts are a wonderful way to end a winter meal.*

## Rhubarb Souffle

Oven temperature
220°C, 425°F, Gas 7

**500 g/1 lb rhubarb, trimmed and cut into 2.5 cm/1 in pieces**
**$^1/_4$ cup/60 g/2 oz sugar**
**$^1/_2$ cup/125 mL/4 fl oz water**
**4 teaspoons cornflour blended with $^1/_4$ cup/60 mL/2 fl oz water**
**$^1/_2$ cup/100 g/3$^1/_2$ oz caster sugar**
**5 egg whites**
**icing sugar, sifted**

1 Place rhubarb, sugar and water in a saucepan and cook over a medium heat for 10 minutes or until rhubarb is soft.

2 Stir in cornflour mixture and cook for 2-3 minutes longer or until mixture thickens. Stir in half the caster sugar and cool slightly.

3 Place egg whites in a bowl and beat until soft peaks form. Gradually beat in remaining caster sugar and continue beating until mixture is thick and glossy. Fold in rhubarb mixture and spoon into a greased 20 cm/8 in soufflé dish. Bake for 15-20 minutes or until soufflé is well risen and golden. Dust with icing sugar and serve immediately.

***Serves 8***

Step 1 of this recipe can be cooked in the microwave. Place rhubarb, sugar and water in a microwavable dish and cook on HIGH (100%) for 5-8 minutes or until rhubarb is tender.

*Rhubarb Soufflé*

# Brandied Plum Clafouti

Oven temperature
180°C, 350°F, Gas 4

500 g/1 lb plums, quartered and stoned
1/3 cup/90 mL/3 fl oz brandy
2 tablespoons sugar
1/4 cup/30 g/1 oz flour, sifted
1/4 cup/60 g/2 oz caster sugar
1 cup/250 mL/8 fl oz milk
3 eggs, lightly beaten

BRANDY ORANGE SAUCE
2 tablespoons sugar
1/2 teaspoon ground cinnamon
3/4 cup/185 mL/6 fl oz orange juice
2 teaspoons arrowroot blended with 4 teaspoons water

1 Place plums and brandy in a bowl, sprinkle with sugar, cover and stand for 30 minutes. Drain plums and reserve liquid. Arrange plums in a lightly greased shallow ovenproof dish.

2 Place flour and caster sugar in a bowl, make a well in the centre, then stir in milk and eggs and mix to make a smooth batter. Pour batter evenly over plums and bake for 45-50 minutes or until firm.

3 To make sauce, place sugar, cinnamon, orange juice, arrowroot mixture and reserved liquid from fruit in a saucepan and cook over a medium heat, stirring constantly, until mixture boils and thickens. Serve with clafouti.

*Serves 4*

Clafouti is a wonderful classic French pudding, traditionally made with fresh cherries. This recipe uses plums, but you might like to try apricots, peaches, nectarines or, of course, cherries.

# Toffee Figs with Sabayon

1 cup/250 g/8 oz sugar
1/2 cup/125 mL/4 fl oz water
2 tablespoons brandy
6 fresh figs, halved

MARSALA SABAYON
1/3 cup/90 g/3 oz sugar
4 egg yolks
1/4 cup/60 mL/2 fl oz Marsala or dry sherry

1 Place sugar and water in a saucepan and cook over a low heat, stirring constantly, until sugar dissolves. Stir in brandy, bring to the boil and cook until golden. Remove pan from heat, dip figs in toffee, then plunge into iced water for a few seconds to harden.

2 To make sabayon, place sugar and egg yolks in a heatproof bowl over a saucepan of simmering water and cook, beating, for 5-10 minutes or until mixture forms a ribbon. Beat in Marsala or sherry. To serve, spoon sabayon over figs.

*Serves 4*

This dessert is also delicious made using other fresh fruit such as apples, pears, apricots and strawberries.

*Brandied Plum Clafouti, Toffee Figs with Sabayon, Berry Pancakes with Sauce (page 74)*

# Apple and Berry Crumble

Oven temperature
180°C, 350°F, Gas 4

Blueberries have been used to make this delicious crumble, but blackberries, raspberries or strawberries are equally delicious. Serve with natural or fruit-flavoured yogurt.

**1/4 cup/60 g/2 oz caster sugar**
**1/2 cup/125 mL/4 fl oz water**
**4 green apples, peeled, cored and sliced**
**440 g/14 oz canned blueberries, drained**

CRUMBLE TOPPING
**1 3/4 cups/250 g/8 oz crushed shortbread biscuits**
**45 g/1 1/2 oz unsalted butter, softened**
**4 tablespoons ground almonds**
**2 tablespoons demerara sugar**
**1/2 teaspoon ground cinnamon**
**1 egg yolk**
**1 1/2 tablespoons cream (double)**

1 Place caster sugar and water in a saucepan and cook over a medium heat, stirring constantly, until sugar dissolves. Bring to the boil, then add apples and cook, over a low heat, for 8-10 minutes or until apples are tender. Cool.

2 Drain apples and place in a shallow ovenproof dish. Add blueberries and mix to combine.

3 To make topping, place crushed biscuits, butter, almonds, demerara sugar, cinnamon, egg yolk and cream in a bowl and mix until just combined. Scatter topping over fruit mixture and bake for 20-25 minutes or until golden.

***Serves* 6**

# Peach and Berry Cobbler

Oven temperature
180°C, 350°F, Gas 4

As with most fruit desserts other fruits can be used for this one. You might like to try the following combinations: apricots and apples; pears and blueberries; or apples and blackberries.

**2 x 440 g/14 oz canned sliced peaches, drained**
**440 g/14 oz canned blackberries, drained**
**4 teaspoons cornflour blended with 1/4 cup/60 mL/2 fl oz water**
**1 tablespoon brown sugar**

COBBLER DOUGH
**1/2 cup/60 g/2 oz self-raising flour**
**1/4 cup/30 g/1 oz flour**
**2 tablespoons caster sugar**
**60 g/2 oz butter**
**1 egg, lightly beaten**
**2 teaspoons milk**

1 To make dough, sift flours together into a bowl. Stir in caster sugar, then using fingertips, rub in butter, until mixture resembles fine breadcrumbs. Make a well in the centre of the dry ingredients, then add egg and milk and mix to form a soft dough.

2 Arrange peaches and blackberries in a greased, shallow ovenproof dish, then pour over cornflour mixture. Drop heaped spoonfuls of dough around edge of dish, then sprinkle with brown sugar and bake for 30-35 minutes or until topping is golden.

***Serves* 6**

*Apple and Berry Crumble, Peach and Berry Cobbler*

# Hazelnut Crepes

**$^3/_4$ cup/90 g/3 oz flour**
**90 g/3 oz hazelnuts, ground**
**$1^1/_4$ cups/315 mL/10 fl oz milk**
**1 egg, lightly beaten**
**2 teaspoons hazelnut or vegetable oil**

ORANGE AND LIME TOPPING
**1 lime**
**$^1/_2$ cup/100 g/$3^1/_2$ oz caster sugar**
**$^1/_4$ cup/60 mL/2 fl oz ginger wine**
**2 oranges, peeled, white pith removed and segmented**

1 Sift flour into a bowl, then stir in hazelnuts. Make a well in the centre of the flour mixture, then stir in milk, egg and oil. Mix to make a smooth batter, cover and stand for 30 minutes.

2 To make topping, remove rind from lime using a vegetable peeler and cut into thin strips. Set aside. Squeeze juice from lime and place in a saucepan with sugar and ginger wine. Cook over a medium heat, stirring constantly, until sugar dissolves. Bring to the boil, then reduce heat and simmer for 4 minutes. Remove pan from heat and stir in lime rind and orange segments. Cool slightly.

3 Pour 2-3 tablespoons batter into a heated, greased crêpe pan and cook over a medium heat until lightly browned on both sides. Remove from pan and repeat with remaining mixture to make eight crêpes.

4 To serve, fold crêpes into triangles, place two on each serving plate, spoon over topping and serve immediately.

***Serves 4***

For the topping on these delicious crêpes lemon can be used in place of the lime.

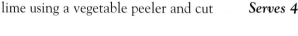

# Nutty Plum Crumble

Oven temperature
180°C, 350°F, Gas 4

**4 x 440 g/14 oz canned dark plums, drained and $^3/_4$ cup/185 mL/6 fl oz liquid reserved**
**1 teaspoon finely grated orange rind**

CRUMBLE TOPPING
**$^1/_2$ cup/60 g/2 oz flour**
**1 teaspoon ground mixed spice**
**60 g/2 oz butter, chopped**
**$^1/_3$ cup/60 g/2 oz brown sugar**
**90 g/3 oz hazelnuts, chopped**

1 To make topping, place flour and mixed spice in a bowl, then using fingertips, rub in butter until mixture resembles fine breadcrumbs. Stir in sugar and hazelnuts.

2 Place plums, reserved liquid and orange rind in a greased, shallow ovenproof dish. Toss to combine, then scatter with topping and bake for 30-35 minutes or until topping is golden.

***Serves 6***

Accompany with whipped cream or yogurt for a really wonderful family dessert.

*Nutty Plum Crumble, Hazelnut Crêpes*

# Berry Pancakes with Sauce

**$1^{1}/_{2}$ cups/185 g/6 oz self-raising flour**
**$^{1}/_{3}$ cup/75 g/$2^{1}/_{2}$ oz caster sugar**
**2 teaspoons finely grated lemon rind**
**2 eggs, separated**
**$1^{1}/_{2}$ cups/375 mL/12 fl oz milk**
**30 g/1 oz butter, melted**
**155 g/5 oz blueberries**

BERRY SAUCE

**90 g/3 oz raspberries**
**$^{3}/_{4}$ cup/185 mL/6 fl oz water**
**$^{1}/_{4}$ cup/90 mL/3 fl oz light corn syrup**
**4 teaspoons arrowroot blended with $^{1}/_{3}$ cup/90 mL/3 fl oz water**
**1 tablespoon lemon juice**
**90 g/3 oz strawberries, quartered**

1 Place flour, sugar and lemon rind in a bowl. Add egg yolks, milk and butter and mix to combine. Place egg whites in a separate bowl and beat until soft peaks form, then fold into batter with blueberries. Cook spoonfuls of mixture in a lightly greased preheated frying pan for 2-3 minutes each side or until golden. Keep warm.

2 To make sauce, place raspberries, water, corn syrup, arrowroot mixture and lemon juice in a saucepan and cook over a medium heat, stirring, for 4-5 minutes or until sauce boils and thickens. Add strawberries and mix gently to combine. To serve, spoon sauce over pancakes and serve.

*Serves 4*

Pancakes can be made in advance, stacked between sheets of freezer wrap and frozen in an airtight container for 2-3 months. Reheat before using. For details on reheating see hint on page 32.

# Apricot Pie

Oven temperature 200°C, 400°F, Gas 6

**$^{1}/_{2}$ quantity Sweet Shortcrust Pastry (page 21)**

APRICOT FILLING

**3 x 440 g/14 oz canned apricot halves, drained and sliced**
**$^{1}/_{4}$ cup/45 g/$1^{1}/_{2}$ oz brown sugar**
**$^{1}/_{2}$ teaspoon ground nutmeg**
**$^{1}/_{2}$ teaspoon ground cinnamon**

1 To make filling, place apricots, sugar, nutmeg and cinnamon in a bowl and mix to combine.

2 Spoon filling into a greased 23 cm/9 in pie plate. Roll out pastry to 3 mm/$^{1}/_{8}$ in thick. Mark centre of pastry and cut four 10 cm/4 in slits, crossing at the centre. Place pastry over filling and trim edges 5 mm/$^{1}/_{4}$ in wider than rim of plate. Fold back flaps of pastry from centre of pie. Make a large scalloped edge by placing your thumb against the inside pastry edge and moulding the pastry around it with fingers of other hand.

3 Bake pie for 20-30 minutes or until pastry is golden and cooked through.

*Serves 6*

Reroll leftover scraps of pastry, then cut out decorative shapes and use to decorate tops of pies.

# Cherry Pie

**1 quantity Sweet Shortcrust Pastry (page 21)**

CHERRY FILLING

**3 x 440 g/14 oz canned, pitted black cherries, drained**
**2 tablespoons brown sugar**
**4 teaspoons flour**
**1 teaspoon ground mixed spice**

1 To make filling, place cherries on sheets of absorbent kitchen paper to absorb excess moisture. Place cherries, sugar, flour and mixed spice in a bowl and mix to combine.

2 Roll out two-thirds of the pastry to 3 mm/1/8 in thick and use to line a greased 23 cm/9 in pie dish. Spoon filling into pastry case. Roll out remaining pastry and cut into 2 cm/3/4 in wide strips. Twist each strip and arrange in a lattice pattern over filling. Brush edge of pie with a little water and seal each strip to edge.

3 Bake pie for 20 minutes, then reduce temperature to 160°C/325°F/Gas 3 and bake for 30-40 minutes longer or until pastry is golden and cooked through.

***Serves 6***

Oven temperature
220°C, 425°F, Gas 7

Instead of making a lattice topping on this pie you might like to cut out leaf shapes and arrange them in an overlapping pattern on top of the pie. The whole top need not be covered, just make sure that the pattern is symmetrical.

# Apple Pie

**1 1/2 quantities Sweet Shortcrust Pastry (page 21)**

APPLE FILLING

**2 x 440 g/14 oz canned sliced apples**
**1/4 cup/60 g/2 oz sugar**
**1/2 teaspoon ground cloves**
**1/2 teaspoon ground cardamom**

1 To make filling, place apples, sugar, cloves and cardamom in a bowl and mix to combine.

2 Roll out two-thirds of the pastry to 3 mm/1/8 in thick and use to line a greased 23 cm/9 in pie dish. Spoon filling into pastry shell.

3 Roll out remaining pastry to fit over top of pie. Cut out two apple shapes on opposite sides of pastry. Brush pastry with a little water and place apple shapes on pastry between cut-outs. Place pastry over filling, trim edge and fold under bottom pastry layer. To form a rope edging, pinch edge at a slant using your thumb and index finger and at the same time pulling back with your thumb.

4 Bake pie for 20 minutes, then reduce temperature to 160°C/325°F/Gas 3 and bake for 30-40 minutes longer or until pastry is golden and cooked through.

***Serves 6***

Oven temperature
220°C, 425°F, Gas 7

# Sweet Finishes

## Chocolate Chestnut Truffles

**100 g/3½ oz dark chocolate, melted**

CHESTNUT FILLING
**¼ cup/60 mL/2 fl oz cream (double)**
**315 g/10 oz finely chopped dark chocolate**
**30 g/1 oz butter**
**2 tablespoons brandy**
**½ cup/220 g/7 oz canned chestnut purée**

1 Spread the inside of 36 small aluminium foil cases with the melted chocolate. Allow to set.

2 To make filling, place cream in a saucepan and bring to the boil. Remove pan from the heat, add chopped chocolate and butter and whisk, using a balloon whisk, until chocolate melts and mixture is smooth. Whisk in brandy, then stir in chestnut purée.

3 Transfer mixture to a bowl, cover with plastic food wrap and chill for 2-3 hours.

4 Spoon filling into a piping bag fitted with a small fluted nozzle and pipe swirls into chocolate cases. Chill for 1 hour or until firm. Store in an airtight container in the refrigerator for up to 2 weeks.

***Makes 36***

*Florentines (page 78), Sweet Cinnamon Bows, Chocolate Chestnut Truffles, Miniature Profiteroles (page 78)*

# Sweet Cinnamon Bows

**250 g/8 oz cream cheese**
**250 g/8 oz unsalted butter**
**1 cup/125 g/4 oz flour**
**$^1/_4$ cup/60 g/2 oz caster sugar**
**2 teaspoons ground cinnamon**
**icing sugar, sifted**

1 Roughly chop cream cheese and butter and stand at room temperature for 10 minutes. Place flour, caster sugar and cinnamon in a food processor and process briefly to sift. Add cream cheese and butter and process, using the pulse button, until mixture is combined. Turn dough onto a lightly floured surface, gather into a ball and knead briefly. Wrap in plastic food wrap and chill for at least 1 hour.

2 Roll out dough to 3 mm/$^1/_8$ in thick, then cut into strips 1 cm/$^1/_2$ in wide and 20 cm/8 in long. Shape each strip into a bow and place on baking trays lined with nonstick baking paper. Cover and chill for 15 minutes. Bake for 5 minutes, then reduce temperature to 150°C/300°F/Gas 2 and bake for 10-15 minutes or until bows are puffed and golden. Cool on wire racks, then store in airtight containers. Just prior to serving sprinkle with icing sugar.

***Makes 50***

Oven temperature
190°C, 375°F, Gas 5

# Miniature Profiteroles

Oven temperataure
250°C, 500°F, Gas 9

**45 g/1 1/2 oz butter, cut into pieces**
**2/3 cup/170 mL/5 1/2 fl oz water**
**1/2 cup/60 g/2 oz flour, sifted**
**2 eggs**

CREME PATISSIERE FILLING
**2 cups/500 mL/16 fl oz milk**
**1/2 cup/100 g/3 1/2 oz caster sugar**
**5 egg yolks**
**2 tablespoons flour, sifted**
**4 teaspoons cornflour, sifted**
**2 tablespoons coffee-flavoured liqueur**
**2 teaspoons instant coffee powder dissolved in 2 teaspoons boiling water, cooled**

Other liqueurs and flavourings can be used to flavour the filling if you wish. For an orange filling use 2 tablespoons orange-flavoured liqueur and 1 teaspoon finely grated orange rind in place of the coffee mixture and coffee-flavoured liqueur.
For an attractive finish decorate profiteroles with melted chocolate as shown in picture on previous page.

1 Place butter and water in a saucepan and bring to the boil. Using a wooden spoon, quickly stir in flour, then cook over a low heat, beating constantly, for 2 minutes or until mixture leaves sides of pan. Cool slightly. Beat in eggs, one at a time, then continue beating until mixture is glossy. Spoon batter into a piping bag fitted with a large fluted nozzle and pipe swirls onto wet baking trays lined with nonstick baking paper. Bake for 8 minutes, then bake pastries with oven door ajar for 10 minutes or until golden and crisp. Make a slit in the base of each pastry, reduce oven temperature to 120°C/250°F/Gas 1/2 and bake for 5 minutes or until centres dry out. Cool on wire racks.

2 To make filling, place milk in a saucepan and bring just to the boil. Cool for 10 minutes. Place sugar and egg yolks in a bowl and beat until thick and creamy. Whisk in flour and cornflour, then slowly whisk in warm milk. Pour into a clean saucepan and bring to the boil over a medium heat, beating constantly with a wooden spoon, until mixture thickens. Beat liqueur and coffee mixture into filling, then cover surface of filling with plastic food wrap. Cool.

3 Spoon cold filling into a piping bag fitted with a plain nozzle and pipe filling into profiteroles.

*Makes 30*

# Florentines

Oven temperature
180°C, 350°F, Gas 4

**45 g/1 1/2 oz butter**
**1/4 cup/45 g/1 1/2 oz brown sugar**
**2 tablespoons honey**
**1/4 cup/30 g/1 oz flour sifted with 1/4 teaspoon ground ginger**
**45 g/1 1/2 oz slivered almonds**
**30 g/1 oz glacé cherries, chopped**
**1 tablespoon mixed peel, chopped**
**100 g/3 1/2 oz dark chocolate, melted**

For a professional finish to the florentines, when the chocolate on the base is almost set, mark wavy lines in it using a fork.

1 Place butter, sugar and honey in a saucepan and bring to the boil. Cool for 5 minutes. Stir flour mixture, almonds and cherries into butter mixture. Drop teaspoons of mixture 8 cm/3 1/4 in apart onto baking trays lined with nonstick baking paper. Bake for 12-15 minutes or until brown and crisp. Stand on trays for 1 minute then transfer to wire racks to cool.

2 Spread underside of each florentine with melted chocolate.

*Makes 50*

# Decorative *Touches*

## CHOCOLATE

**Chocolate curls and shavings:** Can be made by running a vegetable peeler down the side of a block of chocolate. If the chocolate is cold you will get shavings, if at room temperature, curls.

**Chocolate caraques:** Are made by spreading a layer of melted chocolate over a marble, granite or ceramic work surface. Allow the chocolate to set at room temperature. Then, holding a metal pastry scraper or large knife at a 45° angle slowly push it along the work surface away from you to form chocolate into cylinders. If chocolate shavings form, then it is too cold and it is best to start again.

**Chocolate leaves:** Choose non-poisonous, fresh, stiff leaves with raised veins. Retain as much stem as possible. Wash leaves, then dry well on absorbent kitchen paper. Brush the underside of leaves with melted chocolate and allow to set at room temperature. When set, carefully peel away leaf. Use one leaf to decorate an individual dessert, or make a bunch and use to decorate a larger dessert or cake.

**Piped chocolate decorations:** Are quick and easy to make. Trace a simple design onto a sheet of paper. Tape a sheet of baking or greaseproof paper to your work surface and slide the drawings under the paper. Place melted chocolate into a paper or material piping bag and, following the tracings, pipe thin lines. Allow to set at room temperature and then carefully remove, using a metal spatula. If you are not going to use these decorations immediately, store them in an airtight container in a cool place.

## FROSTED FRUITS

Frosted, strawberries, cherries, small bunches of grapes or redcurrants make wonderful decorations for cold desserts and cakes.

**To frost fruit:** Rinse fruit and drain well on absorbent kitchen paper. Break into small bunches or single pieces and

remove any leaves or unwanted stems. Place an egg white in a small bowl and whisk lightly. Dip fruit in egg white. Remove, set aside to drain slightly, then coat with caster sugar. Stand on a wire rack to dry for 2 hours or until set. Frosted fruit is best used on the day you do it, but will keep for 12 hours in an airtight container.

You can also crystallise miniature roses, rose petals and mint leaves using this method.

## FEATHERED ICING

This technique is most effective if you use Glacé Icing. To make Glacé Icing, place 200 g/6 1/2 oz sifted pure icing sugar in a bowl and beat in 1/3-1/2 cup/ 90-125 mL/3-4 fl oz warm water to make an icing of spreadable consistency. Mix in 1/4 teaspoon vanilla essence. Glacé Icing should be used immediately. Before covering cake place 2 tablespoons of icing in a separate bowl and colour with a few drops of food colouring. Stand cake on a wire rack and pour over plain Glacé Icing. Place coloured icing in a piping bag and pipe thin straight lines across cake surface. Draw a skewer across the lines at 2 cm/3/4 in intervals and then back in the opposite direction between the original lines. This technique works well for all shapes of cakes.

For a spider web effect on a round cake, start at the centre and pipe the icing in a spiral. Then, starting at the centre, divide the cake into eight portions by dragging a skewer out towards the edge. Finally divide the cake eight more times by dragging the skewer in the opposite direction between the original lines.

QUICK DECORATING IDEAS

Flaked almonds, chopped nuts (such as pistachios, pecans and macadamias), and chopped or grated chocolate are all good for decorating the sides of cakes. Spread the sides with butter icing then roll them in your chosen decoration. Try the following decorating suggestions:

- chocolate sprinkles
- hundreds and thousands
- chocolate thins
- warmed sieved jam
- glacé and dried fruits
- sifted icing sugar
- cinnamon sugar
- sugared violets
- crushed meringue
- sifted cocoa powder
- wafer biscuit rolls
- strawberry halves dipped in chocolate

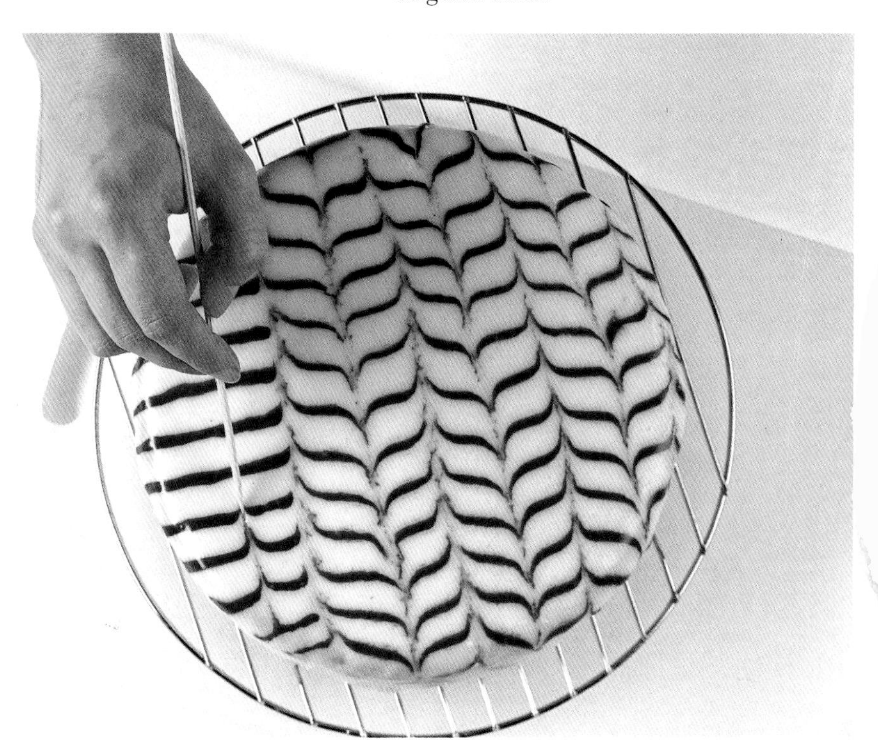

# INDEX

# Historical Atlas of the Outlaw West

Richard Patterson

Johnson Books
BOULDER

Sixth printing 1997

Cover design: Trish Wilkinson
Grateful acknowledgement is made for permission to use the maps on pages viii, 166, 167, and 188 from *Rand McNally's Pioneer Atlas of the American West* published by Rand McNally and Company. Copyright © 1956.

ISBN 0-933472-89-7
LCCN 84-082543

Printed in the United States of America by
Johnson Publishing Company
1880 South 57th Court
Boulder, Colorado 80301

# CONTENTS

# PREFACE

The idea for this book came from an article by Jim Dullenty in the March 1983 issue of *True West*. The article, "Outlaw Hangouts You Can Visit," started me thinking that no attempt has ever been made to provide a gazetteer's look at western outlaw history. Tour books on the Old West do exist, but they are concerned more with dining and accommodations than with highlighting the West's renegade years.

Although the heyday of Hollywood westerns may be over, interest in the history of the American West has slackened little. Every summer the highways are crowded with western buffs and vacationers flocking to the land where the sky has no corners. Unfortunately, much of yesterday's frontier is now buried under asphalt and cement, but many sites remain or have been restored and can be visited and relished. I hope this book will lead the reader to some.

Many people deserve thanks for helping with this book. In addition to providing me with the idea, Jim Dullenty, formerly with Western Publications as editor of *True West*, *Old West*, and *Frontier Times*, deserves much credit for keeping interest in the frontier alive. Many Western history magazines have come and gone, but those of Western Publications, first produced by the tireless Texan Joe Austell Small and now in the stable of a determined Bob Evans of Perkins, Oklahoma, have always stood above the others. The best writers of popular western nonfiction have appeared in the pages of these magazines, and I have found their accounts valuable in preparing this book.

Personal thanks also are due dedicated outlaw researcher Roy O'Dell of Cambridge, England, stalwart member of the English Westerners' Society. And I am particularly indebted to western historians C. L. Sonnichsen, Glenn Shirley, Leon Metz, William A. Settle, Joseph Rosa, Robert K. DeArment, and Bill O'Neal, upon whose works I have greatly depended and which I especially admire. Thanks also to the prolific Carl Breihan and to my fellow members of the Western Writers of America whom I have pestered for information. The same goes for my friends in The National Association for Outlaw and Lawman History.

I am also grateful to research librarian Michelle Unrue of the Franklin–Johnson County Public Library, Franklin, Indiana, whose online searches delivered nearly every source I requested.

Many local historical societies and museums have assisted me over the past year. Foremost are the Friends of the James Farm, Kearney, Missouri; the Clay County Department of Parks, Recreation and Historical Sites, Kearney, Missouri; The Dalton Museum of Coffeyville, Kansas; the Dodge City Museum, Dodge City, Kansas; the Sharlot Hall Museum, Prescott, Arizona; and the St. Joseph Museum, St. Joseph, Missouri.

Also a special thanks to Marian C. Parker of Goodland, Kansas; Robert Rybolt of Sidney, Nebraska; Mrs. Ellen D. Stull of the Oliver Historical Museum, Canyon City, Oregon; Ken Longe, Research Specialist for the Union Pacific System, and the staff at the Union Pacific Railroad Museum at Omaha; Mrs. Paul J. McDougal of the University of Wyoming Archives–American Heritage Center, Laramie; Arizona Historical Society; the Bancroft Library, University of California; Colorado Historical Society; El Paso Public Library, El Paso, Texas; Idaho State Historical Society; Kansas State Historical Society; Montana Historical Society; Nebraska State Historical Society; Nevada Historical Society; Museum of New Mexico, Santa Fe; Oklahoma Historical Society; the University of Oklahoma; Oregon Historical Society; South Dakota State Historical Society; Utah State Historical Society; the Wells Fargo Bank and History Room, San Francisco; and the Wyoming State Archives and Historical Department. Special thanks also go to Denver book and map specialist Paul Mahoney and to Rand McNally and Company for permission to reprint portions of its nineteenth century atlas.

Again, as with earlier efforts, I had much help from

Johnson Books, and I am extremely grateful to Publisher Barbara Johnson Mussil, Editorial Director Michael McNierney, and all the staff at Boulder.

Closer to home: thanks to my wife, Wynonia, who saw me through another book with love and patience, and a helping hand when needed.

One final word to the reader. Since the West is vast, only so many trails could be followed on this trip. I apologize to those of you whose favorite story did not make these pages. Let me hear from you—there is always more to be said.

November, 1984 Richard Patterson

**Note:** An asterisk following a name in the text indicates that the place has a separate entry of its own.

*To Wynonia, with love.*

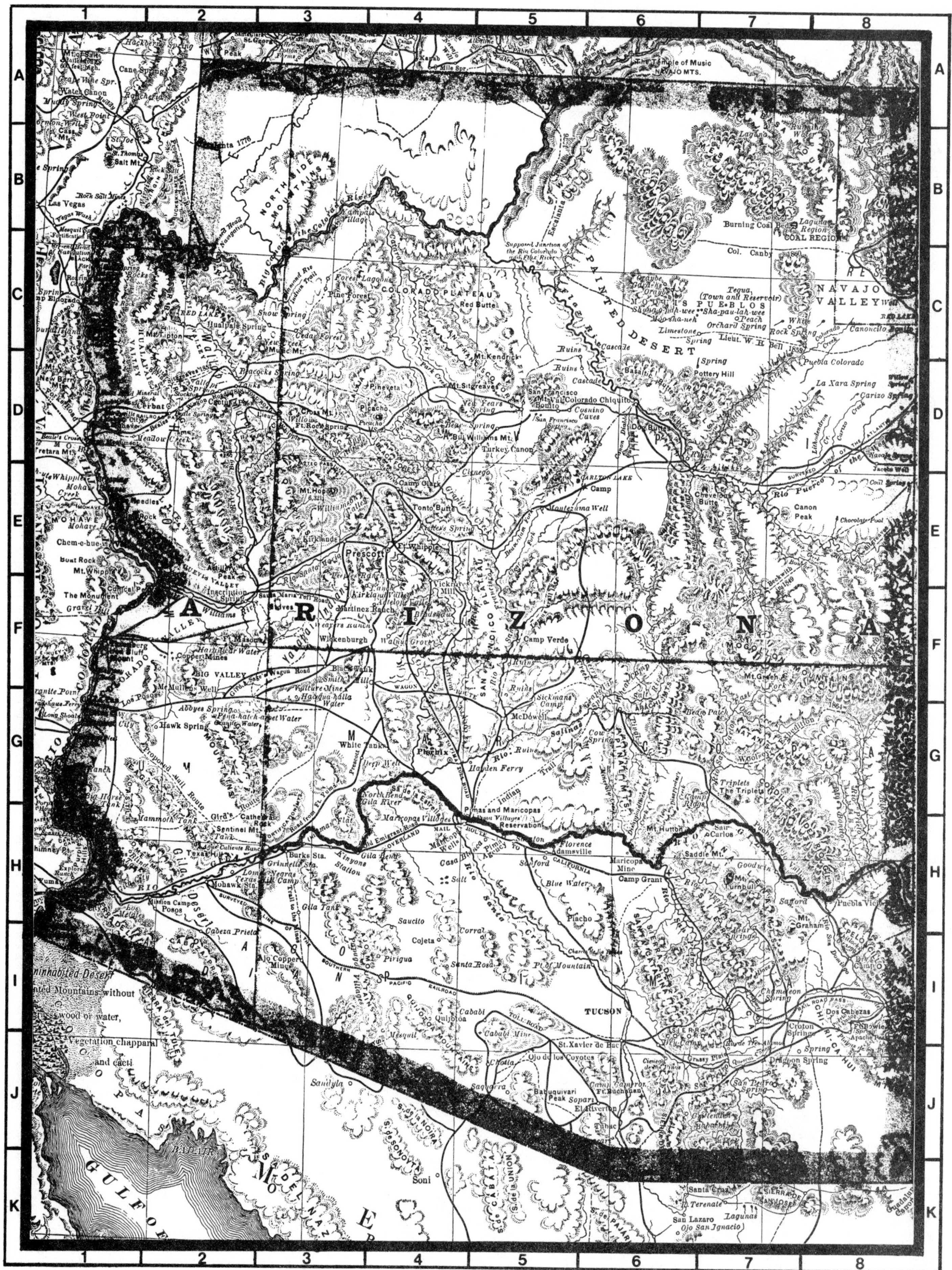


Arizona 1876

# ARIZONA

## Colossal Cave
### Pima County

The crystal-walled chambers of Colossal Cave reach far back into the Rincon Mountains. Formed years ago by seeping water that eventually hollowed out an underground river and tributaries, the cavern today is bone dry and maintains a constant temperature of 72°. Of the miles of twisting passageways, only a little over a mile is made easy for visitors by steps and walkways. A guided tour takes about an hour.

If you visit the cave, located just northeast of Vail on Interstate 10 between Tucson and Benson, think twice if someone offers you a treasure map showing where train robbers hid $62,000 in loot in 1884. The money was probably hidden there, possibly for nearly twenty years, but apparently it was eventually reclaimed by one of the bandits, a shrewd and patient fellow who put one over on the authorities, even though they were sure he would someday return for the treasure.

The loot came from a robbery on the Southern Pacific Railroad near Pantano Siding, about ten miles from the cave, known locally as "The-Hole-in-the-Wall." The bandits had planned well in advance to use the cave as a hideout: plenty of food and water had been stored away at the 120-foot level, enough to withstand weeks of seige. Also, unknown to the posse that trailed the outlaws to the cavern, the gang had a secret exit, a tight "chimney" that went forty yards straight up and out on the far side of a cactus-covered ridge, nearly a mile from the entrance. At the end of the third week of the seige, when it appeared that the posse was as stubborn as the bandits, the gang used their exit to escape. Delighted with their victory, the outlaws descended on nearby Wilicox to celebrate. Word reached the hot and dusty possemen waiting at the cave entrance, and they rode to Wilicox and shot three of the four robbers dead on the spot. The fourth, a young fellow named Phil Carver, survived to face the law.

Carver was only twenty-two years old. Although questioned thoroughly, he maintained that he had no idea where the cache was hidden. He claimed that his job with the gang was to guard the cave entrance, and he was there when the rest of the gang buried the loot. He stuck to his story and was sentenced to twenty-eight years at the Territorial Prison at Yuma.

While in prison Carver's health failed, and he was released after eighteen years. The authorities had not forgotten the robbery, however, and they put a tail on him immediately. But at the end of a week, Carver disappeared. A rumor circulated that he had been seen in Mexico; another placed him in England. But apparently both were false, because shortly thereafter he was spotted north of Tucson, and later, near the Rincon Mountains. A posse was quickly dispatched to search the cave. At the 120 foot level they found three empty canvas mail bags—the kind used at the time of the robbery. The original consignment tickets were still tied to them. But the gold was gone. And there was no trace of Carver.

The cave today is much the same as it was in 1884, except that the narrow chimney through which the outlaws escaped has been partially blocked, the result of a series of minor earthquakes in the 1920s. Although the gold may be gone, a trip to the cave is worthwhile. Pima County Park, which surrounds the cavern, offers excellent camping and picnic grounds and an excellent view of Tucson and the desert.

## Contention City
### Cochise County

What is left of Contention City lies about twelve miles northwest of Tombstone on the San Pedro River, midway between Fairbank and St. David. Today, crumbling adobe marks the site of its best saloons, the Dew Drop and the Headlight, which sprung up with the construction of a nearby stamping mill in 1879. It is said that the town got its name from a disputed mining claim. In outlaw history, Contention City is remembered for the holdup of the Tombstone stage on March 15, 1881. The stage was a night coach to Tucson and carried $26,000 in bullion and eight passengers. Just north of town on a steep grade, three masked men stepped out of the darkness and brought the driver to a halt. Then, for no apparent reason, they shot the man riding shotgun, Budd Philpot. He fell forward, frightening the team, and the coach lunged ahead nearly out of control. The driver, a Wells Fargo special agent named Bob Paul, squeezed off a desperate shot at his attackers and hit one, Bill Leonard, in the groin. The other two bandits, believed to be Harry "The Kid" Head and Jim Crane, opened fire, killing a passenger, Pete Roerig, who had been riding on top. Bob Paul finally got the team under control by leaping on the tongue Hollywood style and retrieving the reins. It was later rumored that the would-be robbers were not robbers at all but were out to kill Paul, who had been sent to the area by Wells Fargo to investigate stagecoach robberies. At Contention City he had changed seats with the driver to give him a rest. It was also rumored that the notorious Doc Holliday, then residing in Tombstone, was in on the plot.

Doc Holliday was not too well-liked in Tombstone at the time. Also, there was evidence that he was known to occasionally visit a hacienda near where the suspects appeared to have camped the week before the attack. Doc laughed off the charges, claiming that he had a good alibi. But the following July a warrant was sworn out for his arrest, issued on an affidavit signed by Kate Elder, his girlfriend. Doc was taken into custody but was soon released on bond, the money being put up by his friend, Wyatt Earp, and several others. Four days later the case was dismissed for insufficient evidence. Whether Doc was actually involved in the affair has never been determined. Some say he knew it was to take place but was in no way connected.

In the history books the shooting is sometimes referred to as the attempted robbery at "Drew's Station."

## Diablo Canyon Station
### Coconino County

Train robberies in Arizona Territory and in most parts of the West were often successful because local law officers refused to cross county lines. Few county coffers were full enough to reimburse posses for lengthy chases. Unless local officials knew that the railroad or express company would pay off with a healthy reward, the chase was usually abandoned after a day, sometimes after only a few hours. Thus the story of Yavapai County Sheriff William Owen "Buckey" O'Neill's pursuit of the Diablo Canyon Station train robbers in March 1889 is an unusual one, at least to those who did not know Buckey well.

Buckey O'Neill was an ambitious man. For persistence, few peace officers in the West could match him, although he was apparently cursed with a "weak stomach" (see *Prescott, Arizona*). A "saloon-wise" gambler who could quote Lord Byron while spitting Bull Durham, Buckey had his eye on a political career. Catching and convicting the Diablo Canyon robbers would be a stepping stone, and an important one.

Diablo Canyon Station was the third stop east of Flagstaff on the old Atlantic and Pacific Railroad (now the Sante Fe), about twenty-six miles west of Winslow. You can seldom find it on the roadmaps today; the site can best be located by following Interstate 40 west out of Winslow to the point where the highway appears to intersect with the southern border of the Navajo Indian Reservation. Some of the old maps are confusing: the station was not located where the tracks cross the canyon named "Diablo;" that was Dennison, fourteen miles to the east.

In March 1889 four bandits attacked the A. & P.'s eastbound No. 2 while it was picking up wood at Diablo Canyon Station. Holding the crew at gunpoint, they broke into the express car and rode off with $7,000 in cash, several pocket watches, and a set of diamond earrings. In those days Diablo Canyon Station was part of Yavapai County and therefore within Sheriff O'Neill's jurisdiction. With deputies Jim Black and Ed St. Clair and two railroad detectives, Carl Holton and Fred Fornoff, O'Neill picked up the robbers' trail north of the tracks on what is now the Navajo reservation. Riding

Diablo Canyon Posse. Bucky O'Neill is second from right. *J. B. Rice Collection.*

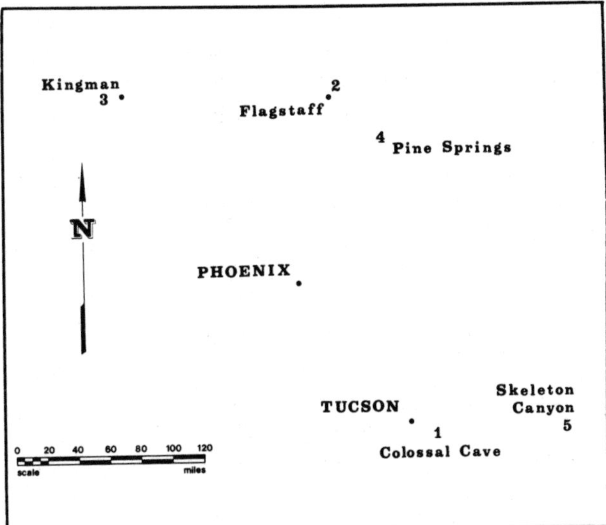


**Lost outlaw loot in Arizona.** **1.** Over $60,000 from a train robbery at nearby Pantano Siding was reportedly stashed in Colossal Cave in 1884; however, one of the outlaws may have returned for it 18 years later. (See *Colossal Cave.*) **2.** In the mountains above Flagstaff a cache of $125,000 may be hidden near a spot called Veit Springs. (See *Flagstaff.*) **3.** Southwest of Kingman near an old stage stop called Beale Spring, a stagecoach and $200,000 in gold ingots may lie buried in the desert. (See *Kingman.*) **4.** Deep in the Coconino National Forest, $225,000 in uncirculated gold coins is believed to be hidden near the site of an 1879 holdup on the Old Star Stage Line. (See *Pine Springs.* ) **5.** Skeleton Canyon may still hold the loot from a robbery of a Mexican pack train carrying gold bullion in 1881. (See *Smuggler's Trail.*)

at a furious pace, the posse gained a little on the outlaws each day. By the time they crossed into Utah two weeks later, they were finding warm campfires. The lawmen caught up with the bandits near Wah Weep Canyon, a Mormon settlement near Cannonville. In the gunfight O'Neill's horse was killed and pinned him to the ground, but Holton pried the sheriff loose, and after another five minutes of fighting, the outlaws surrendered. Most of the cash from the express car was recovered, as were the watches. The diamond earrings had been lost.

Not wanting to try a return trip on horseback, the posse and their captives headed further north. At Salt Lake City, O'Neill bought nine tickets for Denver on the Denver & Rio Grande Railroad. At Denver, he bought nine more for Prescott, Arizona, on the Santa Fe. By the time he, the posse, and their three prisoners (one had escaped by slipping off his shackles near Raton, New Mexico), O'Neill had spent $8,000 for his three-week, four-state trek. Despite a hero's welcome, including a hearty congratulations from Territorial Governor Louis Wolfley, the sheriff's request for full reimbursement from the county was turned down. O'Neill's roundabout train ride was, concluded the Board of Supervisors, a piece of bad judgment and extravagant. Buckey sued for his money, lost on appeal, and was personally stuck with part of the bill, about $2,200.

# Douglas
## Cochise County

Douglas is at the bottom of US 80's sweep through outlaw-rich Cochise County. Douglas got a late start (1901) and never could match its neighbors to the north as a hell-raising town. But Cochise County had no shortage of badmen, and hard cases did ride in and out of this border town, some at a fast enough clip to make things interesting.

The Arizona Rangers discovered this the year the town was born. Ranger Dayton Graham was sent to Douglas to bring in an outlaw named Bill Smith. He and a Douglas peace officer, Tom Vaughn, met Smith head-on in front of the town's general store. Smith was the quickest: Graham fell with wounds in the chest and arm, and Vaughn took a bullet in the neck. Smith made a hasty exit. Ranger Graham was so badly injured that his superiors summoned his family for the death watch, but the spunky lawman recovered and devoted the next year to tracking down his assailant. According to frontier researcher Carl Breihan he eventually found him in a southern Arizona saloon and left him dying on the floor.

Later the same year Douglas erupted in gunfire again; this time in the popular Cowboy Saloon. Three Arizona Rangers stepped into a fight between the saloon owner and a gambler, and ended up killing the former and crippling the latter.

Considering the total number of Arizona Rangers on duty in 1901, it seems unusual that so many were stationed at Douglas. The town may have been tougher than we think.

If you are ever in Douglas, stop by the Calvary Cemetery. There is a "Pearl Reed" buried there, said to be the daughter of outlaw Belle Starr.

# Fairbank
## Cochise County

Fairbank is not much to look at today, but at the turn of the century it was an important stop on the railroad to Mexico and a stage terminal for mail and express. Some say the name came from a corruption of "faro bank," but more likely the town took its name from a Chicago merchant, K.N. Fairbank, who had many mining interests in the area.

The most exciting day Fairbank ever experienced was February 15, 1900, the day of the attempt to rob a Wells Fargo express car. Most western train robberies occurred on a lonely stretch of track, usually far enough outside the nearest town to give the robbers plenty of time to raid the express car or the passenger coaches and disappear over the nearest ridge. The robbery attempt at Fairbank was unique in that it took place at the depot in the midst of a crowd.

The holdup was planned by the notorious Burt Alvord and his gunhappy henchman, Bill Stiles. At the time both were peace officers at Wilcox, Arizona. To carry out the affair, Alvord called on local hard cases "Three-Fingered Jack" Dunlap, George and Louis Owens, Bravo Juan Yoas, and a man named Bob Brown. The plan was to hit the Wells Fargo car just as it was unloading at the station, using innocent bystanders as shields. In arranging the details, Alvord and Stiles took great pains to select a night on which Wells Fargo express messenger Jeff Milton, a former lawman and Texas Ranger, was not on the run. Milton was an experienced gunfighter, and the outlaws did not want to have to contend with him. But as luck would have it, Milton substituted for another messenger that night, and when the train pulled in around dark, there he was at the door of the car, ready to hand out packages.

When a voice from the station platform shouted "Hands up!" Milton thought it was a joke and continued with his work. But the next command was "Throw up your hands and come out of there," and a shot knocked off Milton's hat. Jeff had left his pistol on his desk inside the car. His sawed-off shotgun was within reach beside the door, but he could not use it for fear of hitting bystanders. The bandits' next shots struck Jeff in the left arm, knocking him to the floor of the car. His attackers, thinking he was finished, rushed the door. But Milton now had his shotgun, and he put eleven pellets into the belly of the first robber, Jack Dunlap. A twelfth pellet hit Bravo Juan Yoas, taking the fight out of him and sending him on his way to find his horse.

The three remaining attackers riddled the interior of the car with their Winchesters. Inside, Milton, although weak from loss of blood, pulled the keys to the safe from his pocket and threw them into a corner behind some packages. Then he passed out. The bandits, unable to find the keys and not prepared to force the safe, put their wounded comrade on his horse and galloped off.

Little remains of the holdup site today. Fairbank's main link with the early days is its adobe general store and post office, in later years serving the town's handful of survivors in much the way it did three-quarters of a century ago. To find the town, take Interstate 10 east out of Tucson to US 80, then go south to State Road 82. Turn west and go eight miles to San Pedro River.

## Flagstaff

### Coconino County

It is called the "Dead Outlaws' Loot" and may consist of a fortune in gold and silver. Some of it may have been found; maybe all of it, but then again maybe it is still there. For years treasure hunters have searched the area, a secluded mountain spot called Veit Spring 8,500 feet above Flagstaff.

Arizona abounds with tales of lost treasure. This cache stems from a stagecoach robbery in 1881. On May 10 of that year two mail bags were removed from the boot of a stage traveling between Canyon Diablo and Flagstaff, the route now followed by Interstate 40. In the bags were small gold and silver bars and some coins, a total value at the time of about $125,000. Because of recent robberies in northern Arizona, Wells Fargo officials thought it smart to hide the treasure in the mail, in two whiskey kegs wrapped tightly in paper. But word of the plan leaked out and five bandits were waiting on the trail. Since the robbery involved the United States mail, a cavalry troop joined in on the chase. Scouts picked up the robbers' trail and tracked them into the mountains to the spot now known as Veit Spring. There the soldiers found five men camped in a one-room cabin built against a giant boulder. One of the men matched the description of one of the robbers. The gang opened fire and the soldiers killed all five. The dead men were buried in a common grave. According to the report of the officer in charge, Captain E.C. Hentig, no gold or silver was found. Hentig was later killed in a skirmish with Indians.

In the summer of 1913 a local character named "Short Jimmy" McGuire reportedly turned up with what may have been some of the stolen coins. While buying drinks for the house at Black's Saloon in Flagstaff, he claimed he located the loot by using a water witch's willow fork. A crowd soon gathered. After his fourth drink, McGuire became ill and collapsed. A doctor rushed to his side and pronounced him dead, apparently from a heart attack. His pants pockets were stuffed with coins, more money than he had ever been seen to carry. Treasure seekers raced from the saloon and converged on Veit Spring. They found McGuire's tracks and his campsite, but no trace of any diggings. People are still looking.

## Globe

### Gila County

Globe, named for a globe-shaped piece of almost pure silver reputedly found nearby, lies east of Phoenix on scenic US 60. Although seldom mentioned in outlaw chronicles, Globe may have been the home of Butch Cassidy from 1908 to around 1910. Cassidy biographer Larry Pointer offers strong evidence that Butch did not die in South America but returned to the United States, assumed the name William T. Phillips, married a Michigan woman (Gertrude Livesay), and moved to Globe in 1908, presumably for his wife's health. There is no evidence that Butch returned to his outlaw ways while in Globe, although he may have earned some money as a sharpshooter during the unrest in Mexico. Pointer believes Cassidy, as Phillips, left Globe in 1910.

While in Globe, Butch may have helped lay the copper roof on the county courthouse. The building still stands and can be visited today. Some who doubt the story point to an inscription above the steps which says the building was built in 1906, two years before Cassidy was supposed to have arrived in Globe. It is possible, however, that the building was completed in 1906 but the roof was not coppered until later.

Phillips' connection with Globe was uncovered by Jim Dullenty, editor of *True West*, who has done much research on Cassidy. His sources include old-time Globe residents and Phillips' adopted son.

Globe was also the stomping ground of Pearl Hart, sometimes called the "last of the lady road agents." As with many lady outlaws, the stories surrounding Pearl have been exaggerated. Some say she began her wayward path by luring unsuspecting lovers into her diggings where a confederate bashed in their heads and took their money. She later turned to stage robbery. On the Globe–Casa Grande run on July 14, 1899, Pearl and a companion, Joe Boot, emptied the pockets of the passengers for $431.20 and two pistols. They then returned one dollar to each victim "so they wouldn't be busted." A posse caught up with the two outside Benson. While confined to jail in Tucson, Pearl agreed to an interview with a writer for *Cosmopolitan Magazine* and posed for pictures, one of which showed her brandishing sixshooters (unloaded) to show how she held up the stage. Boot was sentenced to thirty years at the Territorial Prison at Yuma, and Pearl got five. He escaped the following year, and Pearl was released in 1902, some say because she convinced the prison authorities that she was made pregnant under circumstances that would have been embarrassing to them. Out of prison, she turned to picking pockets, then for a while appeared with Buffalo Bill's Wild West Show. Nearing middle age, Pearl changed her name, quieted down, and little more was heard from her. Some say she lived to be near ninety, which would have placed her death in the 1960s. Others say she died in 1955, probably in or near Globe.

## Holbrook
### Navajo County

Holbrook lies on the old Atlantic & Pacific Railroad route about midway between Flagstaff and the New Mexico line. It began in the 1880s mainly as a cowtown. Its Saturday nights were sometimes wild, but it never became an outlaw town, thanks largely to a sheriff named Commodore Perry Owens.

Owens had the reputation of being a dead shot, but so did many other frontier peace officers. In Owens' case he proved it and then some. The date was September 4, 1887, a warm Sunday afternoon. Owens had a warrant for a murderer named Andy Blevins whose widowed mother, Eva, lived on the edge of Holbrook. Although he did not expect to get much information from Eva, he felt it was his duty to ride out and question her. If Owens had been expecting trouble on the trip, he probably would have taken along some help. But as he neared the house, he must have gotten an uneasy feeling, because he slipped his Winchester out of its scabbard and cradled it in his arm as he walked up to the porch. It was well he did. Standing just inside one of the two front doors was the man he was after, sixgun in hand and ready to shoot. The two men fired almost simultaneously; Blevins' shot missed, and the sheriff's bullet knocked the outlaw back into the house. A gun appeared at the other door—John Blevins, Andy's brother. But his shot missed too, and the Winchester barked again, shattering John's right shoulder.

The widow Blevins had three sons, and Owens figured his troubles were just starting. In need of cover, he raced to the side of the house, just as Mose Roberts, a Blevins brother-in-law, came around from the rear. The sheriff dropped him with one shot. Back he darted to the front, just in time to catch the third brother, Sam Blevins, coming out the door. Again, one shot was all it took, and Sam went down. In less than a minute, Sheriff Commodore Perry Owens had killed three men and wounded a fourth.

Few hard cases rode into Holbrook looking for trouble after the story of that Sunday afternoon made the rounds.

## Kingman
### Mohave County

Kingman lies due west of Flagstaff, at the junction of Interstate 40 and US 66, almost in the dead center of Mohave County. About two miles west of Kingman, somewhere south of an old stagecoach stop called Beale Spring, may lie the buried remains of a stage, its team and driver, and three passengers. Also, nearby, may be a heavy wood and iron box filled with gold ingots valued in 1880 at $200,000.

The fact that the stage disappeared is in the records. It left Beale Spring for Needles, California, on a June night in 1880. Four men saw it leave the station. It is believed it was later stopped by three bandits, one of whom was "Hualapai Joe" Desredo. Shortly after the disappearance Desredo and his comrades were killed in a gunfight with lawmen. Before he died, Desredo admitted holding up the stage and burying the box of gold. He denied harming the driver, a man named John "Johnny Jumpup" Upshaw, or the passengers. Desredo said that after unloading the box he and his men allowed the stage to proceed on toward Needles. He added, however, that a strange thing happened as the stage was leaving. "I could hear wheels cracking against rocks and Johnny Jumpup yelling at his team," said Desredo. "Then all at once I couldn't hear the stage wheels and Johnny Jumpup yelling no more." It just "vanished into nowhere."

The area was searched, including the spot where Desredo said he and his men buried the box (the bandits intended to return later with a wagon and haul it away). Nothing was found: no horses, men, stage, or gold.

As the years went by, nearly everyone forgot about the incident. Then in 1940 an Arizona historian who wrote under the name Maurice Kildare was approached by a Mohave County character named Max Bordon. Bordon, a hermit who lived most of his life in and around the Black Mountain range of western Mohave County, claimed he had found the stage. It had been swallowed up by a wide fissure at the edge of a deep wash. Apparently in the darknass, Upshaw had wandered off the trail and into the crack. Much of the remains had been washed away, but part of the coach was still there, and some of the bones of the passengers were still inside. Bordon took Kildare to the spot but made him promise that he would tell no one else. Max evidently did not want to be disturbed by treasure seekers. Kildare kept his word. Then World War II came along. During the war years, Bordon apparently died. After the war, Kildare informed the Mohave County sheriff of the incident, but the sheriff did not seem interested.

More years went by. Maurice Kildare is now gone. The stage is probably still out there, and maybe the gold. Kildare did not say if he tried to return to the spot, only that he "couldn't begin to find that place" again. Probably so: when Kildare went with Bordon to the site, they approached it from the south, from Bordon's camp in the Sacramento Valley west of Yucca. Did Kildare try reaching it from Beale Springs, following the most likely route that would be used by a stage line in 1880?

## Nogales
### Pima County

Nogales is the nearest border town to Tucson, easily reached by heading south on Interstate 19. Although rich in Spanish history, the town was not a hangout for Arizona outlaws. When they were that far south, they crossed the border for the pleasures of Old Mexico.

One interesting item does appear in the old newspaper records: an attempted bank robbery on a hot summer day in 1896. The account was notable in that much of the story was undoubtedly dictated by the hero of the tale, a newspaperman named Frank King. On August 6 swarthy Will "Black Jack" Christian and his outlaw gang, the "High Fives," rode into town and held up the International Bank of Nogales. Believed to be with Christian were sidekicks "Three-Fingered" Jack Dunlap, George Muskgrave, Jess Williams, and Bob Hays. As the robbers were leaving the bank, King spotted them from across the street and opened fire. Although veterans at bank robbery and similar crimes, the gang, for some reason, panicked. Williams and Hays, who were carrying the loot, dropped it and ran for their lives. Christian, Dunlap and Muskgrave, who were supposed to be covering them, spurred their horses and raced out of town. The courageous King (at least by his account), climbed on an unhitched buggy horse and went after the outlaws, in the process wounding two of their horses. Somewhere just outside of town, it likely occurred to King that one newspaperman should not pursue five armed outlaws too strenuously, and he returned to write up his hair-raising story.

## Pantano Station
### Pima County

Pantano Station, near the Cienaga Wash between Benson and Tucson (a route now followed by Interstate 10), was one of several desolate stops on the lonely Southern Pacific tracks stretching west from the New Mexico line. In the late 1880s that stretch of track accounted for more train robberies per mile than any other on the frontier. Typical of these holdups was the robbery of the S.P.'s westbound No. 20 on April 27, 1887. When the train failed to show up at Tucson by midnight, a crew went looking for it. They found it disabled near Esmond Station, on what is now the southeast corner of David-Monthan Air Force Base. Robbers had obstructed the track and stopped the locomotive with a hail of lead at 9:55 p.m. Engineer Bill Harper was marched back to the Wells Fargo express car and forced to persuade messenger Charles F. Smith to open up or be blown to pieces by black powder. Smith complied and the robbers emptied the safe of about $3,000. He saved $5,000 by stuffing it into the car's pot-bellied stove.

On August 10 the same train was hit again, about a mile east of the site of the earlier holdup. This time the engineer did not stop in time, the locomotive hit the obstruction, and it and the tender overturned. Several persons were injured but none were killed. The express car was robbed of an undetermined amount. Charles F. Smith was again the messenger on duty, and one of the bandits informed him that his "stove racket" would not work this time. After loading up their horses, the robbers rode off toward the Rincon Mountains. Posses searched the area for weeks with no luck.

## Phoenix
### Maricopa County

In striving to become cosmopolitan, Phoenix has nearly lost the vestiges of its frontier period. A visitor can no longer capture the feel of the dusty territorial capital. Replicas, such as the 1880 bank on the lower level of the Interstate Bank Plaza (100 W. Washington Street), the 1890 Bayless Cracker Barrel Store and Museum (118 W. Indian School Road), and Pioneer Arizona (north of Bell Road off Interstate 17), offer some flavor, but will hardly interest a true Old West buff.

In the beginning, frontier Phoenix was little different from its neighbors. Growing from a cavalry hay camp in 1864 to a thriving adobe trade center of 1,500 people in the 1870s, it suffered some from its rough element, especially along "Whiskey Row," the north side of Washington Street between Central and First, but it never developed a reputation for lawlessness as did the Cochise County towns to the southeast. One reason was probably a gutsy little law officer named Henry Garfias.

Garfias began as a Phoenix constable around 1874. From the start, he refused to back down from trouble, regardless of the odds. Shortly after pinning on his badge he was called upon to quiet a disturbance at Washington Street's frisky Capitol Saloon. When he arrived, a husky troublemaker ordered the little lawman to "start dancing." The man started to draw, but Garfias' gun was already out. The man was dead when he hit the floor. A second man whipped out his sixshooter and Garfias dropped him, too.

On a Sunday in May 1879, a hard case named Juan Gallegos, apparently out of pure meanness, rode through a crowd of spectators at a horse race on Washington Street and slashed eight with a saber. Garfias trailed him all the way to Mexico, knocked him in the head, and brought him back to Phoenix for trial. But a few days later, while being escorted to meet his lawyer, Gallegos tried to smack Garfias in the head with a stick, and the constable shot him dead.

In 1881 Garfias was appointed a deputy sheriff of Maricopa County. He celebrated the promotion by riding north to Gillett and solving a series of mysterious stagecoach robberies committed by a robber who left no tracks and disappeared without a trace after each holdup. In 1888 he rounded up the Valenzuela gang, a band of thieves and killers that operated on the outskirts of the county.

Garfias helped keep Phoenix tame into the 1890s, when old gunshot wounds and a case of tuberculosis finally forced him to retire. He died in 1896, following a fall from his horse.

## Pine Springs
### Coconino County

Deep in Coconino National Forest, about eight miles north of Happy Jack on the county road between Flagstaff and State Road 87, National Forest Road No. 22 forks southeast from the county road. Five miles down No. 22 lies Mahan Mountain. Where the road bends close to the mountain a rough trail leads you past the remains of several old buildings, the Mahan homestead. About a half-mile farther lies Pine Springs, once a station on the old Star Stage Line that operated between Prescott and Santa Fe, New Mexico. Somewhere near that station may lie buried a fortune in uncirculated gold coins—three boxes of them, estimated in 1879 to be worth $225,000.

The boxes were shipped in secret from Santa Fe on a six-horse stage, hidden beneath bags of mail. But somehow word leaked out, and four robbers attacked the driver and one passenger at Pine Springs. The passenger was killed, but the driver, Mose Stacey, escaped in the brush and rode off to find a posse just a few miles away. The lawmen closed in and trapped the outlaws at the station. After an overnight seige, the station was set on fire and all four bandits were killed trying to flee. The gold, however, was never found, despite years of searching. The robbers had less than an hour to hide the loot before the posse arrived, and from then until their deaths they were trapped in or near the station. The gold, if still there, has to be somewhere nearby.

Be careful if you go looking for the loot, however. Over the years there have been reports of treasure hunters being shot at from the dense pines on Mahan Mountain.

## Prescott
### Yavapai County

Prescott had its beginnings in 1863 when gold was discovered on Granite Creek. A year later the town became Arizona'a first territorial capital. Mindful of its

Prescott, Arizona. *Sharlot Hall Museum.*

past, Prescott honors its early period with its Frontier Days Celebration and Rodeo each July 4th, an event dating back to 1888.

On February 5, 1886, Prescott was the scene of Arizona's last classic "legal public hanging," the kind treated as a holiday with elaborate press coverage, the closing of stores and offices, and in some cases, a generous sale of tickets. The victim on that day was a cattle rustler named Dilda who had killed a Yavapai County deputy sheriff named Murphy. The grim affair was capped off by an embarrassing incident involving a stalwart Prescott peace officer and later mayor, William Owen "Buckey" O'Neill. O'Neill, then captain of the Prescott Greys, a local uniformed militia outfit, marched his men in precise military formation to the scene of the hanging. As the condemned man's end neared, Captain O'Neill and his troops drew their sabers and presented arms. All went well until Dilda dropped through the door. As the body jerked to a halt at the end of the rope, Captain O'Neill fainted.

Whatever the reason Buckey O'Neill faltered that day, it was not from an aversion to violence. He later became an agressive and dedicated lawman (see *Diablo Canyon Station, Arizona*) and was the first volunteer in the Spanish-American War from the Territory of Arizona. After helping organize the First United States Volunteer Cavalry (Teddy Roosevelt's Roughriders), O'Neill was killed by a sniper's bullet on July 1, 1898, near San Juan Hill. Today O'Neill is honored by a statue on Prescott's courthouse plaza, the work of Solon Borglum, brother of Gutzon Borglum of Mt. Rushmore fame.

## St. Johns
### Apache County

At the turn of the century St. Johns, a Mormon-settled town of tall poplars lying fifty-three miles south of Interstate 40 at the junction of US 180 and US 666, was the center of operations of one of the last major outlaw gangs in Arizona. The gang, led by Jack Smith, specialized in rustling and roamed without much difficulty in and around the mountains of Apache County and along the Little Colorado River between St. Johns and Holbrook. But by early 1900 the ranchers began complaining, and Apache County Sheriff Ed Bealer took a few men and rode north, in the general direction of what was thought to be Smith's hideout area. Probably to the sheriff's surprise, he stumbled directly onto the outlaws' camp. In a brief gunfight, one of the outlaws was wounded and the rest fled. Before following the gang farther into the mountains, Bealer sent a man into St. Johns for reinforcements. But when the help arrived, the sheriff and his posse were gone. Rather than look for the sheriff, the second group forged ahead. They were seven townsmen, armed but not professional lawmen, and the Smith gang quickly disposed of two of them, Frank Lesueur and Gus Gibbons. Several days later two federal officers, U.S. Marshal George Scarborough and deputy W. Birchfield, met a similar fate at the hands of the gang, and the following month the outlaws added still another two peace officers to their list of victories.

Moving their operations to the mountains south of St. Johns near northern Graham County, the Smith bunch roamed unmolested for nearly a year. Then in the summer of 1901 the territorial legislature created the Arizona Rangers, a fighting force to be patterned after the successful Texas organization. The Smith gang was high on the Rangers' priority list, and before long they had an arrest: Tod Carver, an admitted member of the gang. Carver confessed his part in the killings, but before he could be tried the gang broke him out of jail. A posse chased the outlaws into what is now the Gila National Forest where two more possemen were killed in a gunfight: Ranger Carlos Tofolla and a volunteer, Bill Maxwell. Two outlaws were also killed, but the rest escaped. After adding more men from St. Johns, the posse followed the outlaws' trail deep into the forest. Apparently Smith and his bunch did not expect this, and they were finally captured at their hideout cabin near the San Francisco River.

On being returned to St. Johns, the outlaws were housed in the Apache County jail, but once more they could not be held. They overpowered a guard and escaped, never to be seen again in Arizona.

## Smugglers' Trail
### Cochise County

The trail is nearly gone in some parts now, having slowly disappeared under parched grass and sagebrush. Even local ranchers would have difficulty following it to its end. At its busiest in the 1880s and 1890s it probably did not even have a name, other than perhaps "The Trail," or maybe the "Sonora Trail." It offered a secluded path through almost uninhabited country. Many of southern Arizona's thieves and killers used it to slip from Tombstone down to Old Mexico and back again. It eventually became the "Smugglers' Trail" from a steady stream of contraband, everything from cattle to pesos, that flowed northward into Tombstone and Tucson.

Starting from the westernmost terminus, Tombstone, the trail generally followed what is now the county road joining that town and McNeal. Then it curved northward a little through the Coronado National Forest and ducked south into Skeleton Canyon and slightly east toward the isolated Peloncillo Mountains of New Mexico. From the Peloncillos it continued southeastward into the Animas Valley, then cut due south and finally southwest past Cloverdale, re-entering Arizona just above the Mexican Border. It then made a final turn south into Sonora.

Highwaymen used the trail to raid unsuspecting pack trains. In 1881 a large Mexican train carrying bullion was attacked in Skeleton Canyon. From human bones recovered over the years at the site, it appears that from six to nineteen men were killed. According to old timers, the treasure is still likely buried somewhere in the canyon, since none of it ever showed up in the area. Tombstone outlaw Curly Bill Brocius is occasionally mentioned as the leader of the raiders.

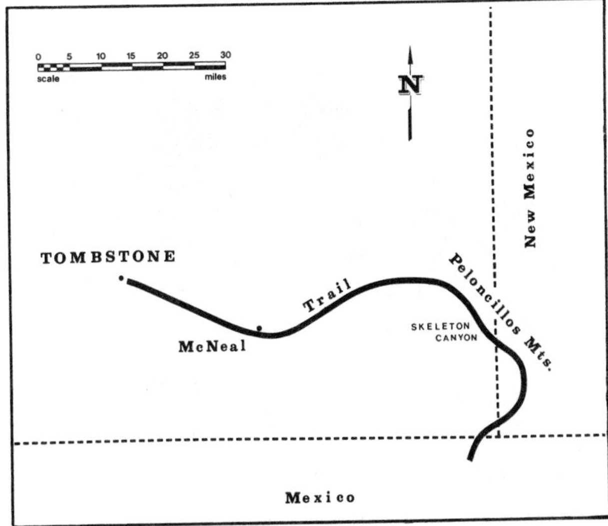

Smugglers' Trail. Trail used by southeastern Arizona outlaws to travel between Tombstone and Old Mexico. In the 1880s and 1890s, a steady stream of contraband flowed northward along the route to Tombstone and Tucson. Loot from a raid in 1881 on a pack train carrying bullion may still lie buried in Skeleton Canyon.

## Tombstone
### Cochise County

It was called "The Town Too Tough to Die," and it is probably the town most often associated with outlawry on the frontier. Born in 1877 as a result of a rich silver deposit, it was named, so the legend goes, by its prospector-founder, Ed Schieffelin, who was told by doubters that all he would find in the area (still inhabited by Apaches) was his "tombstone." The area prospered, however, and by 1881 the town boasted of 10,000 people. But the mines were plagued with water, production fell, and by 1886 its heyday was over.

Tombstone reeks with history and myth, and western researchers are still sorting through the legends for the truth. In January 1881 Wyatt Earp was supposed to have single-handedly held off a gigantic mob bent on lynching a gambler named Johnny "Behind-the-Deuce" O'Rourke in front of Vogan's Saloon. The tale is typical of Tombstone embellishment. Newspaper accounts of the day suggest that O'Rourke did arrive in town just ahead of a throng of angry pursuers (miners who accused him of killing one of their men), but his neck was saved

Tombstone ladies, a diversion for Cochise County hard cases. *Arizona Historical Society.*

through a cooperative effort of local officials. Maybe Earp was there, but he seems to have gone unnoticed by witnesses.

Probably no shootout is more steeped in myth and controversy than the "Gunfight at the O.K. Corral" on October 26, 1881. The argument over who were the good guys and who were the bad guys will never be settled. Wyatt Earp fans will never believe the fight was not a fair one, yet there are those who would call the deaths out and out murder. It is agreed that the Earp brothers—Wyatt, Morgan, and Virgil—had been feuding for some time with four alleged rustlers, Ike and Billy Clanton and Frank and Tom McLaury. The reason is not clear. Some say the Earps, being peace officers of sorts, wanted to rid the town of such characters. Others suggest that the Earps, together with Doc Holliday, wanted in on the action.

The ruckus that led to the famous showdown actually began the previous day, but at that point did not go beyond threats and shouting. Then the following morning Virgil Earp, at the time town marshal, encountered Ike Clanton on the street and clubbed him over the head with his pistol barrel. A short time later Wyatt did a similar number on Tom McLaury. And around noon Ike got it again from all three Earp brothers. Thus the stage was set.

The big shootout occurred around two o'clock in the afternoon; not in the O.K. Corral, as many tourist books still say, but on Fremont Street several doors away. There were numerous witnesses, but their accounts vary. The Clantons and the McLaurys had gathered near Fly's Photograph Gallery, some say with the intention of riding out of town, others say with the idea of meeting the Earps. The Earps, accompanied by Doc Holliday, approached from Fourth Street, some say to arrest the Clantons and McLaurys, others say to gun them down. By now the Clanton-McLaury group had been joined by a fifth man, Billy Claibourne. Billy Clanton, Frank McLaury, and Claibourne were armed with six-shooters, and Frank's horse standing close by carried a rifle in a scabbard. Tom McLaury and Ike Clanton were unarmed. The Earps all carried pistols, and Holliday had a shotgun.

The two groups squared off at the front edge of a narrow lot between Fly's gallery and a house owned by a man named Harwood. What was said is not clear. It is generally agreed that the Earp faction got off the first shots, although Wyatt later said he did not know for sure. A bullet ripped into Billy Clanton's right hand while he was trying to draw, and he slumped against the side of the Harwood home. Frank McLaury was struck in the stomach, and Holliday's shotgun blew a hole the size of a hand in Tom McLaury's chest. Ike Clanton lunged at Wyatt Earp, and Wyatt, seeing he was unarmed, shouted something like "Go to fighting or get away!" With that, Ike ran south between the two buildings toward the O.K. Corral. By now Billy Clanton had drawn his sixshooter with his left hand and put a slug into Virgil Earp's leg. Meanwhile, Frank McLaury had managed to get out his pistol. Holliday, having discarded his shotgun, was also drawing his. They fired simultaneously, as did Morgan Earp, standing to Doc's right. McLaury's bullet struck Holliday in the hip, and either Doc's or Morgan's bullet hit McLaury just below the ear. Meanwhile, Billy Clanton, although by now bleeding from two or three holes, put a slug into Morgan's shoulder. As Morgan went down he fired, as did Wyatt, and one of their bullets finished Billy.

It was all over. Out of eight participants, six had spilled blood. Tom and Frank McLaury were dead, Billy Clanton would soon be, and Virgil Earp, Morgan Earp, and Doc Holliday were wounded. Wyatt Earp emerged unscathed, as did Ike Clanton. Billy Claibourne, although armed, had slipped into the rear door of the gallery and avoided the action.

Although presumably representing the law (Morgan Earp was Virgil's assistant, and Virgil had allegedly deputized Holliday), the Earp bunch was accused of murder. Wyatt and Holliday were in fact jailed, but eventually the killings were deemed "justified" by the local magistrate.

But the issue was not settled. On the evening of March 18, 1882, Morgan Earp was playing a game of pool at Campbell and Hatch's Billiard Parlor on Allen Street. As he was about to chalk his cue, shots rang out from the rear of the room. He fell to the floor with a bullet lodged near his spine. Wyatt Earp was also present but was not hit. As Morgan lay on a sofa in the nearby card room, he whispered to his brother, "This is the last game of pool I'll ever play." He died within the hour. His death was attributed to revenge for the "O.K. Corral" shooting. The prime suspects were Clanton supporters Frank Stilwell and Pete Spence.

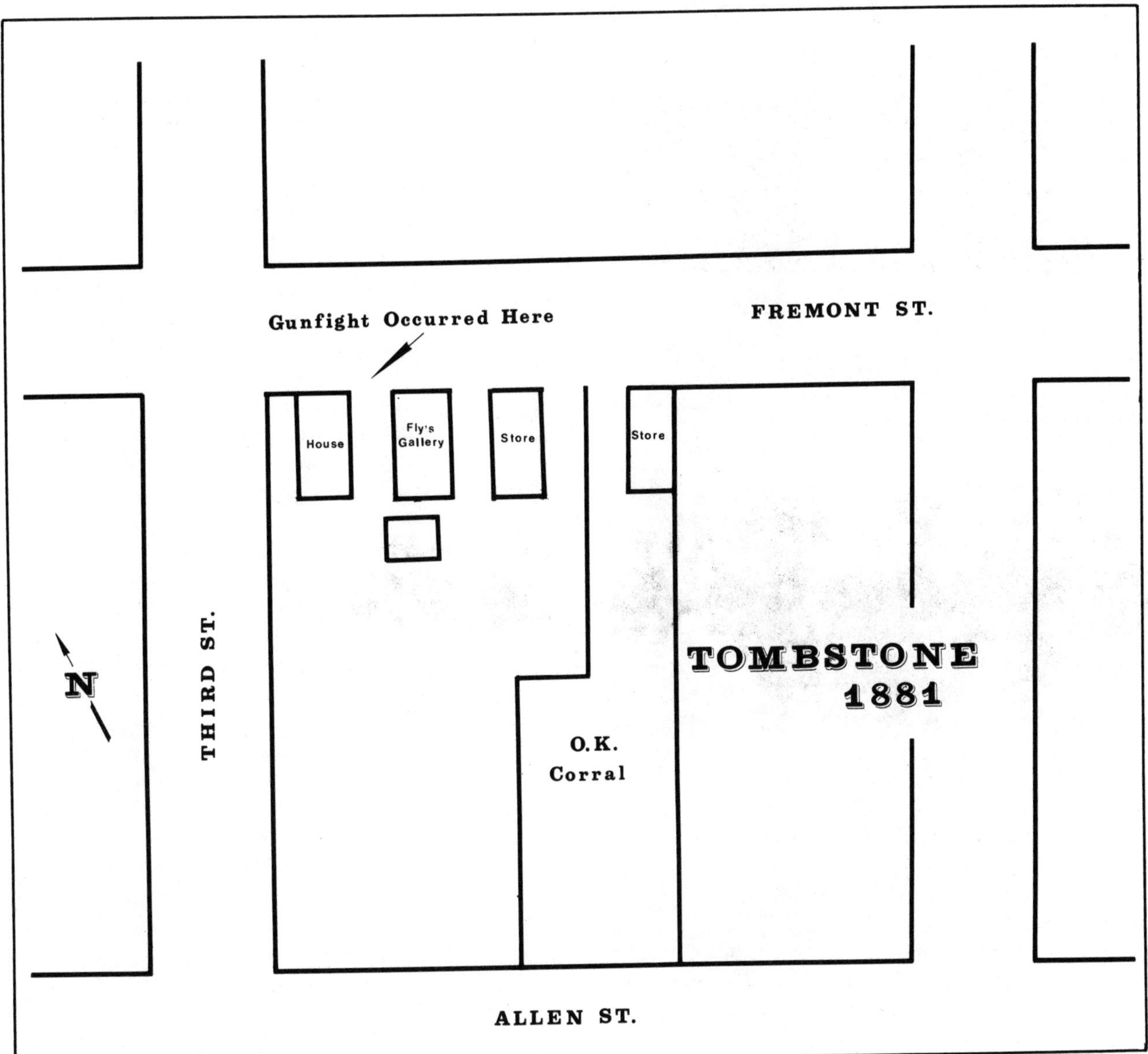


**The Earp-Clanton gunfight at Tombstone.** The October 26, 1881, shootout between the Earp and Clanton factions at Tombstone is popularly known as the "Gunfight at the O.K. Corral." Actually, the battle was fought on Fremont Street, a block away from the main entrance to the corral, which was on Allen Street.

Visitors to Tombstone today can get a pretty good picture of the town when the Earp and Clanton factions met on Fremont Street. Thanks to a retired Detroit attorney, Harold Love, much restoration has taken place. In addition to the gunfight site, tourists can visit the restored Bird Cage Theater, Schieffelin Hall, Boot Hill, the old City Hall, the old Courthouse, and the Crystal Palace Saloon.

The Clanton ranch outside Tombstone still exists. Some of the buildings are gone and the remainder are in need of repair. There is some effort being made to restore it, but the site is too far from town to attract tourists, and nature will likely take its course.

## Tucson
### Pima County

Tucson is one of the oldest Spanish settlements in the West, having at one time been the only walled town in Arizona. The city is proud of its frontier heritage, and has attempted to preserve it. A large section of downtown Tucson has been renovated, but much territorial architecture has been retained, and it blends well with the modern.

While the streets never flowed with blood as was the case in some southwestern towns, a "general climate of

End of the line for Tuscon stage robber Bill Brazelton. *Wells Fargo Bank History Room.*

lawlessness was reflected in the daily life of the community," reports Tucson chronicler C.L. Sonnischsen. As an example, Sonnichsen lists the following entries in a Tucson citizens' diary for the years 1882 and 1883:

> Oct 9. Fine morning. Two men dead. One natural death, the other named Hewitt, supposed to have been beat till he died.
> Nov. 2. Chinaman got a bad beating this morning.
> Nov. 2. Day passed off quiet until night—a row occurred at the Park Theater. Alex Levin in trying to stop it got 2 bad cuts on his head. John Dobbs got knocked under a table. Several others beaten by the railroaders. No one killed.
> Jan. 1. White, jailor, opened cell door. Two prisoners jumped out and gave him a terrible beating and escaped. Paul (Bob Paul, the sheriff) is red hot.
> Jan. 17. Paul took a prisoner to the hospital today. He was shot in the act of robbing a man 5 days ago. Both bones and elbow broken and shattered badly. He will not steal with that hand in a long time.
> March 3. Some son of a gun came in my room and appropriated a pound of fine cuty tobacco, leaving me without a chew. That was very unkind.

On March 20, 1882, Tucson was the scene of what probably was a spill-over of violence from the famous Earp-Clanton shootout at Tombstone the previous fall. Two days earlier Morgan Earp had been killed while playing pool in Tombstone. A primary suspect was Frank Stilwell, a Clanton associate and a well-known Earp-hater. On the night of the 20th, Wyatt and Warren Earp, Doc Holliday, and several other friends of the Earps escorted Virgil Earp and his wife to the railroad depot at Tucson. Stilwell and Ike Clanton, who survived the "O.K. Corral" shootout, were in town. When spotted by the Earps, Stilwell and Clanton disappeared into the darkness. The Earp bunch followed Stilwell, and a few minutes later shots were heard. Stilwell's body was found with over twenty holes in it. The palm of one hand was burned, as if he had tried to fight off his attackers by grabbing the barrel of a shotgun.

Another hard case to meet his end in Tucson was Jim Levy. Levy, who some say was one of the most underrated gunslingers of his day, had left a trail of dead foes from Nevada (see *Pioche*) to Wyoming (see *Cheyenne*). He was a gambler by trade and quarrelsome by nature. On June 4, 1882, he got into an argument with John Murphy, faro dealer at the Fashion, one of Tucson's more popular saloons. Words led to threats, and by evening the two had agreed to meet the next morning and settle the matter for good. But dawn never came for Levy. Shortly after midnight Murphy, with two friends, Bill Moyer and Dave Gibson, spotted Levy at the front door of the Palace Hotel. Jim was unarmed, but the three did not know it. As the door casing splintered around him, Levy dashed into the street, apparently thinking the shots were coming from inside. He ran directly in front of the blazing guns. When it was discovered that he was not armed, Murphy, Moyer, and Gibson were jailed. Four months later they escaped, and there is no record of their ever being recaptured.

Tucson was the home of an interesting bandit named Bill (sometimes called "Jim") Brazelton. Those who knew Brazelton did not seem to agree on just what kind of character he was. Some said he was "big and tough, boasted he was not afraid to die, carried a Spencer carbine and a pistol twenty-four hours a day, and was a hard man to say no to." Others said he was a "gentleman bandit," who seldom ever bothered a stagecoach passenger, was considerate of his victims, and even made it a point to place a stolen Wells Fargo express box beside the trail so the next stage could return it to the company office.

Brazelton worked at Leatherwood's stable in Tucson when he was not robbing stages. His favorite holdup site was northwest of Tucson on the road to Phoenix near a stage stop called Picacho. The area was called the "Cactus Forest" because of the tall saguaro cactus that grew there. These picturesque sentinels of the desert provided Brazelton with a perfect hiding place to await the arrival of a night coach. Moreover, in the eerie desert moonlight, it was easy to mistake a saguaro for a man. A single bandit could command a driver to throw off the box, because the victim was never sure the robber was not accompanied by confederates just off the trail.

Brazelton's end came in August 1888 when a passenger tracked him back to Tucson by noticing his horse had a crooked hoof. It was rumored that an associate of Brazelton's, one Dave Nimitz, agreed to tell what he knew about the robber on the condition that Brazelton be killed so he could not seek revenge.

When visiting Tucson, remember that "Old Tucson," twelve miles west on Speedway Boulevard in Tucson Mountain Park, is not the original town. It is a movie set erected in 1940 by Columbia Pictures for the film, *Arizona*. It has been used for several other films over the years and for the television series, *High Chapparral*.

## Willcox
### Cochise County

Although the ranches in the hills and valleys around Willcox were said to be notorious as refuges for fugitive gunslingers, the town itself is seldom mentioned in outlaw history. Willcox was, however, the end of the line for an Earp brother, Warren, in 1900. Warren Earp missed out on the famous "O.K. Corral" gunfight at Tombstone,* but he was involved in much of the trouble before and after. He was probably in on the killing of Frank Stilwell at Tucson.* By 1900 Warren had dissipated some from intemperate drinking, and one night in a Willcox saloon he challenged an old enemy, Johnny Boyet, to a fight, forgetting that he had left his gun in his hotel room. Boyet whipped out his pistol and shot Warren dead, later pleading that he certainly did not expect a famous Earp brother to go out at night unarmed. He was acquitted.

## Yuma
### Yuma County

A visit to Yuma, on Interstate 8 near the California line, must include a tour of Yuma Territorial Prison State Historical Park. The park is on a bluff on the south side of the Colorado River and can be reached by taking the 4th Street exit off the interstate. The baked adobe walls of the prison stand as a tribute to the lusty territorial period, described by one observer as the "West's last frenzied attempt to escape being civilized." Built in 1876, the prison boasted of walls eight feet thick at the base and four feet at the top. A Gatling gun, capable of firing 350 rounds per minute, commanded the main watchtower. Legend has it that it was once manned by the warden's wife during an attempted break. The prison served the territory until 1907, when a new facility was built at Florence. It is now a museum.

Escapes were few from the Yuma prison. An exciting attempt occurred in October 1887. While warden Thomas Gates was walking near the gate he was jumped by two knife-wielding inmates. The scuffle sparked a general riot as guards rushed to the scene. A prisoner named Puebla was about to finish off the warden, who was already bleeding badly from a bullet in the neck, when another inmate, Barney Riggs, who later became a noted Texas gunslinger, picked up a fallen revolver and shot Puebla. In return for saving his life, Gates arranged a pardon for Riggs, who was serving time for murder.

All the news out of Yuma did not concern the prison. In November 1875 the notorious Cleovaro Chavez, successor to Tiburcio Vasquez as California's most dreaded badman, was brought into Yuma feet first by two ranch hands. Chavez had been hiding out in Mexico and drifted north to near Stanwix Station, where he hired on with a rancher named Baker. Luis Raggio, a hand on a neighboring ranch, recognized Chavez, and with the help of two companions got the drop on the outlaw while he was digging a ditch. Chavez tried to reach his rifle but was killed by one of Raggio's companions. On arriving at Yuma with the body, Raggio and his friends were told by the authorities that they could not collect the reward on Chavez unless they delivered the corpse to California for positive identification. Traveling with corpses was not easy in those days, so they persuaded a local doctor to sever the outlaw's head and place it in a five gallon can of alcohol. This seemed to satisfy the state of California, and the three cowhands eventually collected their reward.

California 1886

# CALIFORNIA

## Badger
### Tulare County

Badger is east of Fresno, at the northern edge of Tulare County on mountainous State Highway 245. On a narrow grade a mile and a half above the town, then called Camp Badger, the notorious California train robbers and renegades Chris Evans and John Sontag held up the Visalia stage in an unsuccessful attempt to dispose of their old nemisis, Southern Pacific Railroad detective Will Smith. The date was April 29, 1893. Evans and Sontag had learned that Smith, a dogged manhunter who had dedicated his remaining years to their capture, would be on board. But he was not; urgent business had taken him to San Francisco at the last minute, a trip that saved his life.

Disappointed at missing their prey, the two ragged fugitives, whiskered and gamey after a winter of hiding in what is now Sequoia National Forest, settled for ordering all the passengers off the stage for a quick search to see if any Southern Pacific officials, lawmen, or bounty hunters were among them. Finding none, the outlaws bade all a farewell, and returned to their mountain lair, where the authorities would finally catch up with them the following June.

## Bakersfield
### Kern County

Bakersfield was the stomping ground of Jim McKinney, for a while in 1903 California's most wanted outlaw. McKinney's early career as a badman was unspectacular. He was in and out of jail a few times, and he may, for several months, have ridden with Wyoming's Wild Bunch. Bakersfield first heard his gun roar in 1899, when he killed a former gambling partner, Long Tom Sears, for mistreating Jim's mistress. McKinney confronted Sears behind Cohen's General Store. Long Tom, knowing he was no match for the gunman, tossed his pistol on the ground and tried to talk his way out of his fix. According to witnesses, Sears said "All right Jim. If we can't be friends you just might as well shoot me." Jim needed no further urging, and pulled the trigger. A deputy sheriff, John Crawford, was answering the call of nature in a nearby privy. He rushed out with one hand holding up his unsuspendered trousers but quickly departed when Jim creased his backside with two bullets.

Somehow McKinney managed to get acquitted for Sears' death, but the town made it clear to Jim that he was to move on. He did; first to Porterville* in Tulare County, where he killed another man, and then south to Arizona, where he may have killed two more.

In 1903 Jim slipped back into Bakersfield, seeking refuge with an old friend, Al Hulse, who had a room on the first floor of a Chinese joss house. He was spotted, and the next morning, April 19, a posse closed in. Two lawmen burst through the front door and Jim shot them dead, but when he tried to escape he got only a few steps. A shotgun blast caught him in the neck and a rifle bullet tore into his chest. He was still trying to rise when a final blast put an end to his violent life.

## Bodie
### Mono County

Bodie is a ghost town today, but enough remains to make it an interesting trip. It can be reached by taking US 395 south out of Carson City, Nevada, to Bridgeport, California. Just south of Bridgeport is State Highway 270 heading east. The only town on that road is Bodie.

Bodie was never visited by the famous outlaws, yet it was an unruly town. Legend has it that the undertakers in neighboring towns complained that "as soon as the local talent get to thinking they're tough, they go to try it out in Bodie and Bodie undertakers get the job of burying them." One visitor to Bodie in 1879 noted that during the first week he was there, there were six fatal shootings. Another legend is that a little girl whose family was moving from the town of Aurora, across the line in Nevada, was heard to end her nightly prayer with "Goodbye, God: we're going to Bodie."

The town's heyday was between 1878 and 1881, when prosperous mines in the area kept it bustling twenty-four hours a day. At its height, Bodie boasted of two banks, three breweries, a half dozen hotels, a sizable red light district, several newspapers, and a well-populated Boot Hill. The town was its toughest in 1879 when local citizens finally got enough and lynched one of the offenders. Apparently things quieted a bit in town, but the badmen went on the road. Some say that during 1880 the stage running between Bodie and Aurora, Nevada, was robbed no less than six times.

The town began to fade in 1881, when a rumor spread that its mines were faltering, and Bridgeport, a few miles to the west, was selected as the permanent county seat.

The townsite is now operated as a state historical park.

## Campo
### San Diego County

Campo lies on scenic State Highway 94 southeast of San Diego, between the Baja California town of Tecate and Interstate 8. In 1875 Campo was one dusty street and a handful of dried-out shacks. In fact, much of the time the town consisted of only five people: a telegraph operator at the lonely railroad station; two brothers, Silas and Luman Gaskill, who ran the general store, blacksmith shop, and post office; and Luman's wife and small son.

Gaskill Brothers' store, Campo. *Union Title Insurance Company, San Diego.*

Because of its isolated location, in December of 1875 a gang of ruthless bandits led by a Mexican named Cruz Lopez picked Campo for their last raid in California before heading south to Sonora for a campaign against Mexican villages. Cruz's gang numbered fifteen. Some say it was made up of remnants of the legendary "Murietta gang" that once plagued much of California; others believe the outlaws were part of Cleovaro Chavez's cutthroats, inherited by Lopez on Chavez's death the previous month in Arizona (see *Yuma*). Whoever the outlaws were, they were ruthless thieves and killers, and the seemingly helpless town of Campo was a tempting target.

Lopez chose five of his toughest followers to ride with him into town. The remaining nine were to wait in the hills, then on his signal bring in two four-team wagons to carry away the loot. The outlaws had gotten careless, however, and somehow a local Mexican learned of the intended raid and rode into town to warn the Gaskills. Ordinary men would have packed up and left until the danger was over, but Silas and Luman Gaskill were not ordinary. Although neither had ever fired a gun in anger, they calmly cleaned and oiled what weapons they had, stashed them about the town at strategic spots, and went about their daily routine, confident that when trouble came they could handle it.

Trouble came the following day. Luman Gaskill was in the store when the outlaws arrived. He had a shotgun hidden at the far end of the counter, but he could not reach it in time. A bullet from Lopez's gun pierced his lung and he dropped to the floor, apparently dead. Silas Gaskill had been working near the blacksmith shop. He reached his shotgun but was hit in the shoulder and side. As he went down, however, he blew a hole in the chest of one of his attackers and shot a second one as he was fleeing.

Just then a local sheepherder came riding into town for supplies, and quickly joined the fight. One of his first shots struck the startled Lopez as he rushed out of the store. In the next instant, however, the outlaws riddled the herder with bullets. In the meantime, Luman Gaskill had regained consciousness. He picked up his shotgun, which the outlaws had overlooked, and blasted one of the gang members that had shot the sheepherder. Just then another bandit came around the corner of the blacksmith shop and Luman dropped him. This ended the battle.

The two Gaskill brothers would survive, as would three of the bandits. The nine outlaws waiting with the wagons never joined the fight. The town of Campo was seldom bothered by troublemakers after that day.

## Camptonville
### Yuba County

Although early express company records probably deserve more probing, most historians agree that one of the first attempts at a stagecoach robbery in the mining regions of north central California occurred on the morning of August 11, 1856, on the route from Camptonville to Marysville, just southwest of where the country road to Dobbins now joins State Highway 49. The stage driver was John Gear, a veteran at the reins. Beside him rode Bill Dobson, a swarthy messenger for the Langton Express Company. Beneath their seat was a strongbox containing almost $100,000, property of a Camptonville dealer in raw gold named Rideout, who that morning was riding alongside the stage on horseback.

The road southwest of Camptonsville ran part way along the winding course of a creek that sometimes flooded. For a short stretch a new road had been built higher up on the side of the ravine. When the stage reached the fork, Gear took the team along the lower path, while Rideout chose the higher road because it was cooler. Near where the two courses again joined, three masked men stepped out of the brush by the side of the higher road and ordered Rideout off his horse. Three more bandits waited hidden in the undergrowth, ready to spring out as the stage drew near. Too late, they realized they had chosen the wrong path. Below them, the stage was about to pass. Forgetting Rideout, the six bandits raced toward the lower road, firing as they ran. From his perch up front, Dobson returned their fire, as did two of the passengers. Later accounts say over thirty shots were fired. One bandit was killed and another wounded. Three passengers were hit; one, the wife of a Marysville banker, later died. The bandits, rattled over the resistance they encountered, finally fled.

## Cedar Ridge
### Nevada County

In 1873, just southeast of Cedar Ridge on what is now State Highway 174 between Grass Valley and Interstate 80, the Colfax-to-Grass Valley stage was held up by four men wearing blue muslin masks. The holdup came to be known as "the robbery that built a railroad."

Although Grass Valley and nearby Nevada City were two of the richest mining towns in northern California, and gold shipments were common, robberies were practically unheard of in 1873. Wells Fargo considered their treasure shipments secure, mainly because the gold was snugly tucked away in stout strongboxes firmly bolted under the rear seat. Often the drivers did not even carry weapons. But at a secluded spot on the road that day the express company's confidence suddenly gave way in a shattering blast of black powder. After empyting the stage of its passengers, the bandits boldly blew open the treasure box—one of the few times explosives were used in stage robberies. (Probably as a result, Wells Fargo wisely decided it might be better to give up a few boxes than to have their stages blown apart and the company did not require that all lines bolt down their safes.)

The robbers' haul that day was $7,000, but they had little time to enjoy it. In two weeks they were rounded up and jailed. But the robbery so unnerved the mining interests in the area that they soon financed the construction of a shortline narrow gauge railroad to carry shipments to and from the Central Pacific Railroad at Colfax.

Desperate for arrests, the authorities picked up two of the Dalton brothers, who were already known as troublemakers back in Oklahoma. Grat Dalton was charged with the crime, and brother Bill, who at the time was living in Paso Robles,* was charged with being an accessory. Grat was eventually convicted, but most historians doubt his guilt. Many believe Dalton was set up and that his own attorney, a prominent California trial lawyer, only went through the motions in putting up a defense. But on September 18, 1891, three days before he was to be sentenced, Grat escaped jail. Later, the Supreme Court of California overturned the conviction.

## Ceres
### Stanislaus County

About four miles south of Modesto, just off State Highway 99, is the site of the famous "Ceres Holdup," an attempted robbery of a Wells Fargo express car on Southern Pacific Train No. 19. The date was September 3, 1891, and the attack was the fourth in a series of train holdups first attributed to the Dalton gang and then to California renegades Chris Evans and John Sontag. The methods used in all the holdups were virtually the same. At Ceres two masked men apparently slipped aboard behind the tender as the train pulled away from the Ceres water tank. A mile south of town the engineer was ordered to stop, and he and the fireman were forced to walk back to the express car. The Wells Fargo messenger, U.W. Reed, was told to open up, but he refused. He and his helper, a man named Charles, doused their lights and prepared for an assault.

The attackers came ready with dynamite and blew a sizable hole in the side door. They then forced the fireman to climb through with a lighted lamp. Messenger Reed, however, sternly told the fireman to crawl back outside or he would shoot him. The fireman, apparently fearing Reed more than the bandits, retreated. A second bomb was tossed through the hole, but it failed to go off. By now, two Southern Pacific Railroad detectives who had been riding in a passenger car opened fire on the bandits from along the side of the train. The robbers dodged beneath the car and returned the fire, striking one of the detectives, Len Harris, in the neck. Calling it a night, the bandits released their captives, ran to their horses waiting nearby, and rode away south toward what is now the town of Newman.

## Earlimart
### Tulare County

Earlimart lies about forty miles north of Bakersfield on State Highway 99. In 1891 the town was called Alila, and on February 6 of that year it was the scene of the third in a series of express car holdups. They began in 1899 at Pixley,* five miles farther north, and were apparently perpetrated by the same men. The bandits—some say the Dalton brothers and others say the California renegades Chris Evans and John Sontag—presumably slipped aboard as the train pulled out of Alila. About a mile south of town they drew their guns and ordered the engineer to halt. The Wells Fargo messenger, C. C. Haswell, refused to cooperate and put up a good fight. Although nearly blinded by blood streaming down his face from a scalp wound, he fired repeatedly through the slats of the express car door at the voices outside. He later said he heard one of the robbers drop his gun and groan, but this may have been the fireman, a man named Radcliff, who had been marched back to the car with the engineer. During the battle Radcliff was shot in the stomach.

The messenger's stout defense of his car discouraged the bandits, and when they failed to dislodge him with a barrage of gunfire, they fled without taking a cent. But law enforcement officers, possibly from frustration over another clean getaway by the attackers, sought vengeance against Haswell by charging him with shooting the fireman. At his trial, Haswell testified that there were three bandits in on this affair, the third having remained on the opposite side of the train from the other two, and it was he, Haswell claimed, who fired the shot that struck Radcliff. Other witnesses supported his testimony as to the third man, and Haswell was finally acquitted when his lawyer proved that the bullet that hit Radcliff had "ranged slightly upward" and thus could not have come from the messenger's gun, since he was firing down through the grating in the lower part of the car door.

## Farmersville
### Tulare County

Farmersville, on State Highway 216 a mile south of Visalia, was the hometown in the early 1880s of the notorious Jim McKinney, a hard-drinking, hard-riding gunslinger who became one of the San Joaquin Valley's most wanted renegades shortly after the turn of the century. Although legend has it that McKinney killed his first man in Leadville, Colorado at the age of eighteen, the best available evidence suggests that his first serious brush with the law was in Farmersville, when he cracked the skull of a local schoolmaster for paddling his younger brother. Not satisfied with clubbing his victim senseless, McKinney notched the man's ear with his Bowie knife while he lay unconscious. And when a deputy sheriff tried to arrest him, Jim turned the knife on him, slicing his arm.

Somehow McKinney avoided conviction for both assaults and soon drifted off to launch a life as a killer and fugitive, finally meeting his end in the famous "joss house shootout" at Bakersfield.*

## Firebaugh
### Fresno County

Firebaugh is west of Fresno, about twenty miles east of Interstate 5, off the second exit south of the Los Banos exit. Six miles north of the town, not far from the long slough that once connected the Tulare Lakes with the San Joaquin River, a sturdy sycamore was used to end the career of Tom Bell, one of California's earliest stage robbers.

"Tom Bell" was actually an alias. Just minutes before his hanging, Bell revealed his true name, Thomas Hodges, in a hastily written letter to his mother back in Tennessee. Tracing the letter, authorities discovered that Bell, as Hodges, had once been a doctor and had practiced medicine in Nashville, although there was no record of his ever having attended medical school. In 1853 he had come west to seek his fortune in the California gold fields. When this proved unsuccessful, and a short-lived "medical practice" was equally unrewarding, Hodges, as Bell, donned a flour sack with slits for eye holes and became a road agent.

A stretch at Angel Island Prison in 1855 only slowed the Tennessee bandit briefly. Feigning illness to obtain a transfer to the San Francisco County Jail, Bell and a handful of prisoners escaped. Soon after, they formed a gang and began terrorizing travelers in the San Joaquin Valley.

Tom's farewell letter to his mother has been preserved.

In it he advised others who might follow his path: "Tell them to beware of bad associations, and never to enter any gambling saloons, for that has been my ruin."

After the outlaw's death, it was discovered that there were actually two "Tom Bells." The other one, whose name really was Bell, was also a bandit. Doctor Hodges apparently adopted the same name to create confusion.

The town of Firebaugh also fell victim to the famous California bandit Tiburcio Vasquez and his gang of thieves. Few towns in Fresno County were ever safe from these outlaws, and Firebaugh's turn came on the evening of February 25, 1873. Vasquez, his sidekick Cleovaro Chavez, and three others rode up to Hoffman's store near the ferry (the town was then closer to the San Joaquin River). They stormed through the front door with guns drawn, tied up and robbed several customers, and pillaged the shelves for food and supplies. As they were finishing up, the stage arrived, and they helped themselves to the Wells Fargo strongbox, after which they turned to the passengers and driver. All were robbed except one traveler, a Mexican, who, needless to say, was highly unpopular with his fellow passengers during the rest of the trip.

Tiburcio Vasquez. *J. B. Rice Collection.*

# Fresno
## Fresno County

Although the facts are sketchy, two of the Dalton brothers, Bob and Grat, may have used Fresno as a base of operations around 1890-91. The extent of their outlawry is not known, but it is believed that Grat may have worked as a professional gambler at the Grand Central Hotel, hustling strangers into one-sided games.

Fresno was the scene of the trial of train robber Chris Evans for the murders at Young's Cabin (see *Sequoia National Forest*). In December 1893, following his conviction, Evans engineered a break from the Fresno County jail with the help of his daughter, Eva, and a local waiter, Ed Morell, who was hired by the county to deliver meals to the jail. Morell slipped a gun into Evan's cell, and the two men forced the jailer, Ben Scott, to lead them out the front door. Morell had a team of horses waiting a few blocks away, but on the way they ran into Fresno's chief of police, John D. Morgan. There was a scuffle, and Morell shot Morgan, causing the horses to bolt and run. The two fugitives then raced down an alley where, about a block away, they commandeered a newspaper boy's one-horse cart. They rode east out of town, through the outskirts of Sanger, up the Hume-Sanger flume along the north bank of King's River and into the mountains.

Evans remained free until February 1894, when he was captured visiting his family at Visalia.*

# Goshen
## Tulare County

Goshen's contribution to the history of outlawry in California occurred on the night of January 20, 1890, with the robbery of a Wells Fargo express on the Southern Pacific line, almost a duplicate of a holdup eleven months earlier twenty-five miles down the track at Pixley.* As passenger train No. 19 pulled away from the station at Goshen, which is on State Highway 99 about forty miles south of Fresno, two robbers apparently swung aboard behind the tender. A little over two miles south of the town they climbed forward to the locomotive and ordered the engineer, S. R. DePue, to halt the train. DePue and his fireman, W. G. Lovejoy, were marched back to the express car where the Wells Fargo messenger was told to throw out the strongbox. He did, and as the robbers were preparing to leave, a tramp who had been riding under the car chose that moment to drop to the ground and run. A bullet from one of the robbers caught him between the shoulder blades.

View from the cab of one of the earliest Central Pacific locomotives on the main line east of Sacramento. The railroad and its successor, the Southern Pacific, were robbed 59 times before the train robbery era ended. *Southern Pacific.*

Although the exact figure was never revealed, the bandits reportedly got $20,000 for their night's work. Irate Southern Pacific officials issued orders that they were to be caught regardless of the cost. Railroad police converged on the scene and a dozen suspects were picked up and questioned, but all were eventually released for lack of evidence.

In time the robbery was blamed on two Southern Pacific haters, Chris Evans and John Sontag, who in the next three years were the subject of one of the largest manhunts ever conducted in California (see *Sequoia National Forest*; *Visalia*).

## Kerman
### Fresno County

On August 3, 1892, the fifth in a series of express car holdups on the Southern Pacific line occurred thirteen miles west of Fresno near the station of Kerman (then called Collis). Two bandits stopped the train near midnight just east of town by sticking guns in the ribs of the engineer, Al Phipps, and the fireman, Will Lewis. Apparently the bandits had slipped aboard as the train was pulling away from the station. Once on the ground, the engineer was handed a "dynamite bomb" and told to place it against the left cylinder of the locomotive. The blast crippled, but did not totally disable, the engine (a point which later raised speculation that at least one of the bandits knew something about locomotives and thus may have been a railroader).

The Wells Fargo express car on this train was new and soundly built, and the robbers wasted no time in going to work with more dynamite. Six charges were set off, one at a time, until the stubborn express messenger, George D. Roberts, lay dazed and unable to defend his car.

All appeared to be going the robbers' way until shots came from a nearby field. A team of threshers were camped overnight no more than 100 years away. Two of them, J. W. Kennedy and John Arnold, began taking pot shots at the shadowy figures beside the express car. But thanks to an especially dark night, the robbers were able to load up and leave safely, making their escape down the track to a waiting wagon.

The exact amount of the haul was never revealed. Some reports ran as high as $30,000 to $50,000, but serious researchers doubt these figures, pointing out that three time-locked safes on board were never opened. Also, most of the stolen money was in silver, some of it Peruvian coins. Estimates given by the messenger and the fireman, both of whom were forced to carry the money sacks down to the wagon, were that the total weight was probably no more than 125 pounds.

At first the Dalton gang was blamed, especially after it was discovered that more than two men may have been involved. (Some witnesses said that there were additional robbers stationed on either side of the tracks to guard against passengers wandering up from the coaches.) But later attention was directed toward Chris Evans and John Sontag, who eventually led hundreds of law enforcement officers on a lengthy chase through the rugged Sierras (see *Sequoia National Forest*).

## Los Angeles

Early Los Angeles was as wild as the cattle and gold rush towns that later gained fame in the Old West. In the 1850s it could probably match any of them; a review of Los Angeles papers during that period suggests gunfights were frequent. This Los Angeles *Star* item is typical: "Last Sunday night was a brisk night for killings. Four men were shot and killed and several wounded in shooting affrays." The fact that so little space was devoted to an item describing four violent deaths suggests such news might have been commonplace.

In 1874 Los Angeles County was the scene of the capture of one of California's most notorious outlaws, Tiburcio Vasquez. Vasquez was wanted for a number of crimes but particularly for the murders of two innocent bystanders during the robbery of a general store at Tres Pinos.* The bandit had come to the Los Angeles area to sell stolen loot. Word reached the authorities that he was negotiating with an unsavory character

Los Angeles, 1889. Broadway at Second Street. *Security Pacific National Bank Collection: Los Angeles Public Library.*

named George Allen, better known as "Greek George," a local fence. "Greek George" lived in Alison Canyon in the Cahuenga Hills. The Los Angeles County Sheriff's Department quickly organized a raid. Among the special deputies sworn in was one George Beers, a local correspondent for the San Francisco *Chronicle*. According to Beers' later account, he and an undersheriff named Johnson rode up to the house in the bed of a wagon, hidden by a piece of canvas. Vasquez saw them and leaped through a rear window. Johnson fired and missed, and Beers, carrying a shotgun, delivered a load of buckshot into the outlaw's legs (some accounts credit others with the disabling shot). An hour later Vasquez was behind bars in the Los Angeles County Jail. A year later he was swinging from the gallows.

The present Los Angeles suburb of El Monte, southeast of Pasadena near the junction of Interstates 605 and 10, was an early hell-hole town for outlaws and toughs. Founded in 1850, the community was soon overrun with unsavory characters driven out of the mountains by miners' courts and by outlaws who drifted up from Mexico. Saloons and gambling houses did a thriving business, and horse races were held regularly on Main Street. Legend has it that at one time the town's honest citizens chipped in and offered up to $10,000 a year in salary and perks for the job of head peace officer in "The Monte," as it was then called, and no one could be found who could handle the office. In 1855 a group of townsmen took matters into their own hands. Without benefit of trial, justice was dispensed swiftly. Concentrating on the crimes of murder and horse stealing (lessor offenses were largely ignored), the vigilantes, calling themselves the "Monte Boys," would race to the scene of a crime and hang the best suspect. Frequently, after a lynching, the boys would return to the El Monte stage depot, known as "Willow Grove," and enjoy a grand feast accompanied by "plenty of whiskey and fast fiddle music." Although crime decreased markedly under the system, federal authorities began policing the area in the late 1850s and demanded that defendants be given fair trials. The Monte Boys did not halt their practice entirely, but gradually the leaders died off or got too old to ride. Sometime in the 1860s the group disbanded. Visiters to the region today can still probably find descendants of these vigilantes willing to pass on an exciting tale or two.

The Oklahoma outlaw Belle Starr and her first husband, Jim Reed, are believed to have lived in Los Angeles from 1869 to 1871. Belle, then known as Myra Maybelle Reed, had yet to become the notorious "Bandit Queen." Reed, however, was at odds with the law and was wanted by the California authorities for passing counterfeit money. Reed fled the city in March 1871, and Belle followed shortly after.

Butch Cassidy may have spent some time in Los Angeles during the summer of 1899. According to the "Bandit Invincible," an unpublished manuscript which may have been written by Cassidy himself, Butch headed north following the robbery of a Union Pacific express in June of that year at Wilcox, Wyoming.* From Montana he boarded a Northern Pacific train for Seattle, Washington. There he signed on a ship (the *Elinor*), steamed down the coast to San Pedro, and eventually found quarters in an out-of-the-way sailors' hotel in Los Angeles, where he spent most of the time in his room, amusing himself by reading about holdups back in Montana and Colorado still being credited to his gang.

Elzy Lay, who rode with Cassidy and the Wild Bunch in the 1890s, died in Los Angeles on November 10, 1934, and was buried in Forest Lawn Cemetery (Lot 3338) under the name William Ellsworth Lay.

Wyatt Earp lived in Los Angeles during the early 1900s and reportedly had an apartment near 17th and Washington. Because of his reputation as a peace officer, he could still get occasional special duty police and security work. In 1909 he was hired by the I.W. Hellman Bank to quell a riot at its doors brought about by a newspaper item suggesting that the bank was in trouble. Earp and a side-kick from his law officer days, A. M. King, took the job for "a couple hundred dollars," apparently payable on accomplishing the task. According to a later account by King, Earp's job was to convince the bank's depositers that the bank was sound. Earp pulled it off by bringing in a wagonload of fake money ($10,000 coin sacks stuffed with washers). When the depositers saw the "money" being placed in the bank's vault, their fears were calmed. When later asked how he came up with the idea, Earp said he had once helped several banks in Wichita, Kansas, do the same thing, using sand and poker chips.

An interesting story crops up now and then about a near-shootout in the streets of Los Angeles between the notorious Emmett Dalton and an old enemy from his Oklahoma outlaw days. The incident, possibly fictitious, supposedly occurred sometime in the 1920s. The story has been attributed to a Western magazine writer named Chuck Martin who is said to have been a witness. Martin claimed Emmett actually drew an ancient six-shooter and was about to fire away when Martin saved the day by calming the old outlaw down. The tale is suspect because it was unlike Dalton, who had mellowed considerably in his middle years, to cause trouble. It could also have been a movie stunt, possibly to hype a film. Dalton had come to Los Angeles with his family in 1916 or 1917 to try to captitalize on his outlaw reputation in the motion picture industry. He set up his own production company, Southern Feature Film Corporation. The company's first and only film was *Beyond the Law*, which retold the story of the Dalton gang. Emmett wrote the script and played the lead. The film was amateurish, even for its day, and Dalton was no actor. He toured with the picture, giving a "law and order" sermon following each showing. The profits were meager and the company disbanded. Emmett then turned to the construction business and was moderately successful. Occasionally he returned to the studios where he would pick up a writing assignment or a small part. His last days were spent in Hollywood, where he lived at 1224 Meyer Avenue. He died peacefully on July 13, 1937.

The film industry also attracted Oklahoma train robber Al Jennings. After serving a stretch in prison, Jennings, with the help of a professional writer, Will Irwin, wrote his life story, *Beating Back*, which was turned into a motion picture. Al starred in the film, and it made some money, prompting Vitagraph Studios to offer the ex-outlaw a job in Hollywood. Jenning's first film after that was *Dead Shot Baker* (1917), in which he appeared as a supporting actor and served as a technical advisor. The picture was a success, and Al, who was once a practicing lawyer (see *Woodward, Oklahoma*), decided to set up his own production firm, which he called Capitol Film Company. The new company's first effort was *Lady of the Dugout*, released in 1918. Al hyped the film by announcing that it was based on actual incidents and would reveal how "it really was" during his outlaw days. The company made a profit for a few years, but with so many western films being produced, Capitol Films fell behind in the race. The company folded in 1921, forcing Jennings to seek small roles with other producers. He eventually faded from the scene, returning briefly in 1936 as technical advisor on James Cagney's *The Oklahoma Kid*. Al's remaining years were spent in Los Angeles, where he died in 1962.

## Murphy's
### Calaveras County

Most researchers today agree that the famous bandit Joaquin Murietta never existed—that there were probably a handful of renegades who committed the robberies attributed to the phantom Murietta. Then again, there are a few who say there indeed was such a man. According to legend Murietta, his gang, or some other gang operating in the early 1850s, hid much of their loot in the vast Calaveras Forest near the town of Murphy's, on the county road that runs from State Highway 49 just north of Angel's Camp northeast to Pioneer on State Highway 88. Some have tried to estimate the loot taken by these bandits, whoever they were, and have come up with the figure of $150,000.

The town of Murphy's is one of the better preserved gold camps. Named for the founding brothers, Daniel and John Murphy, it first served as a placer mining center and later as gateway to the Calaveras Grove of the giant sequoia trees. The old hotel, built as the Sperry Hotel in 1855, is said to have preserved its early register books which contain the names of famous visitors during the nineteenth century, among them Mark Twain and Ulysses S. Grant.

Another visitor may have been the notorious Black Bart, at least the hotel register contains "Charles Bolton, Silver, Montana," said to be a name and address Bart sometimes used.

## Nevada City
### Nevada County

Nevada City has been called a "story-book town" because of its successful modernization of gold rush buildings without the loss of their historic flavor. Situated in eastern California, at the junction of State Highways 49 and 20 just west of Interstate 80, it is easily reached and a joy to visit.

The town was a staging center for the early Yuba River gold camps and by the early 1850s boasted some 250 buildings and tents. A bit more refined than most of the gold rush towns in the area—it even had a theater and hosted the likes of Edwin Booth—Nevada City was never an outlaw hangout. But stage robbery was common on the outskirts of town in the late 1850s and early 1860s, the most frequent culprit being a local bandit by the name of Jack Williams.

The most famous outlaw to spend time in Nevada City was the notorious Henry Plummer, later of Montana fame, who began his violent career there as a teenager around 1852. Plummer's first job was in a bakery; later he took on the duties of town marshal, but he was too ready with fists and gun, and he was convicted of killing the husband of a woman with whom he was having an affair. After less than a year in prison, he was paroled and returned to town to once more enter the bakery business. His temper got him in trouble again, and after seriously wounding a man in a bawdy house brawl, he fled to the mountains and became a full-time outlaw. On another return visit to Nevada City he got in yet another fight in a brothel and chalked up his second murder. Back to prison he went. This time he bribed his way out and left California for good.

## Paso Robles
### San Luis Obispo County

Frank and Jesse James are believed to have spent some time in Paso Robles in the summer of 1869, at a spa called Hot Sulphur Springs, owned by an uncle, Drury Woodson James. Although the James brothers have been mentioned in connection with a stagecoach robbery near San Diego, little is known about any criminal activity on the part of the two Missouri outlaws during their stay in California.

Paso Robles was the home of Bill Dalton of the famous Dalton brothers. Bill moved to California from Kansas in the 1880s, about the time his brothers were stealing horses back in Indian Territory in preparation for becoming big-time outlaws. Bill, probably the brightest of his clan, dabbled in California politics and dreamed of becoming a state legislator.

Dalton and his family rented a ranch outside town from a San Francisco judge named Cotton. The neighbors generally liked Bill but became nervous when his brothers visited him in the early 1890s. They spent much time "drinking and brawling" in Paso Robles and nearby towns. On Bill's ranch one of their favorite pastimes was target-shooting. They would hang a small piece of hide on a tree and ride in circles, shooting from horseback. According to a neighbor, at one time there were more than a hundred slugs in the tree. The tree still stands, on the bank of the Estrella River.

According to this same source, the brothers were all in hiding in Bill's attic when the sheriff and Southern Pacific detectives came looking for them following the express car robbery near Earlimart* in February 1891. The Daltons' possible involvement in the robbery doused Bill's hopes for a political career, and he later returned to Oklahoma and followed the outlaw trail himself.

## Pixley
### Tulare County

It was February 22, 1889, a cold, cloudy night in the San Joaquin Valley. As Southern Pacific's southbound No. 17 pulled slowly away from the Pixley station, two masked men slipped out of the shadows and swung aboard behind the tender. Two miles south of town, the engineer, Pete Boelenger, felt a gun barrel in his back. Once the train was halted the masked men marched Boelinger and his fireman back to the Wells Fargo express car. When a single shout to the messenger, J. R. Kelly, brought no response, the robbers stuffed a dynamite charge under the car.

Meanwhile the conductor, James Symington, had spotted the trouble and was seeking out Ed Bently, a deputy sheriff from Modesto, who was a passenger in the smoking car. Symington also summoned the brakeman, named Anscon, and another man, believed to be a Southern Pacific employee named Gabert. The four men dropped to the ground beside the tracks and cautiously began working their way forward.

Just as the dynamite went off beneath the express car, one of the robbers saw Anscon's lantern and fired off a blast from a shotgun, seriously wounding Gabert. On the opposite side of the train a second blast riddled deputy sheriff Bently. Symington, seeing the situation was hopeless, ran down the track toward Pixley.

Although dazed from the explosion, the express messenger still refused to open up until the robbers convinced him they would kill the engineer and fireman unless he cooperated. Reluctantly, he threw out the strongbox, and the robbers disappeared in the darkness.

The robbery was the first of a series along the Southern Pacific line in the San Joaquin Valley. In the beginning the Dalton gang was suspected, but later blame was placed on two California renegades, Chris Evans and John Sontag, who eventually led authorities on the biggest manhunt in California history (see *Sequoia National Forest*; *Visalia*).

## Placerville
### Eldorado County

Placerville is about halfway between Sacramento and the Nevada state line on US Highway 50. It is a charming town, nestled in the Sierra foothills just west of the Eldorado National Forest.

In June 1857 the town was the departure point for the first stage over the Sierras to what eventually would become Nevada Territory. Four years later it was the site of the first Wells Fargo robbery. Although stagecoach holdups occurred in California in the early 1850s, according to sketchy Wells Fargo files (most of the company's records were destroyed by the 1906 San Francisco earthquake and fire), the first robbery of a Wells Fargo shipment occurred in September 1861 just out of Placerville at a relay point then known as Strawberry Station. The bandits, three in number, struck just as the team was being changed. They ordered the passengers out of the coach, lined them up, and relieved them of their money and valuables. Turning to the strongbox, they smashed it and scooped out approximately $3,000 in gold coins. A fourth member of the gang was waiting with their horses down the trail. He appeared at a signal, and the outlaws galloped away.

Placerville, California. *Western History Collections, University of Oklahoma.*

## Porterville
### Tulare County

Porterville, about forty-five miles north of Bakersfield on State Highway 65, is the last resting place of California gunslinger Jim McKinney. McKinney briefly rode the outlaw trail in Arizona and possibly Wyoming but was never included among the Old West's leading desperadoes. In the San Joaquin Valley, however, his reputation as a turn-of-the-century renegade probably was exceeded only by the notorious train robbers, Chris Evans and John Sontag.

McKinney's path of violence began in Farmersville, led to Visalia and Porterville, and finally ended in Bakersfield (see these towns), where he was killed by lawmen in 1903. In Porterville he is remembered mainly for one wild July night in 1902 when he "went a little crazy" at Zalaud's saloon. He began by shooting up Zalaud's ceiling fan. Next he sent customers scurrying by shattering light bulbs and whiskey bottles. When the town marshal rushed in and hit Jim over the head with a stick, Jim responded by putting a bullet through both sides of his mouth. Figuring he was in for a rough night, McKinney went looking for a shotgun. On returning to the scene, he spotted a man in the street whom he thought was the marshal, and with one blast nearly tore him in two. When he got closer, he found that he had shot a good friend, Will Linn. Before he finally rode out of town, he shot two more men, one a printer who had prepared some handbills denouncing Jim as an "undesirable citizen" and calling for his banishment from the town.

Five miles south of Porterville at Terra Bella is an organization devoted to compiling information on McKinney's spectacular career. Anyone wanting more facts on this outlaw, or having information to share, is invited to get in touch with R. P. "Sundown" Dutschmann, The Jim McKinney Research Team, Box 201, Terra Bella, CA 93270.

## Raymond
### Madera County

There were many stage robberies during California's frontier years, but only one has ever been photographed in progress. The date was August 15, 1905. The site was on the road to Yosemite, a few miles northeast of Raymond, which is northwest of Fresno on the northern edge of Madera County between State Highways 99 and 41. The stage had left Fresno that morning. On

Stage robbery in progress near Raymond, California. *Yosemite National Park.*

board were ten passengers, six women and four men. One of the men, Anton Veith, was the Austrian Consul at Milwaukee. Veith, on an extended tour of the West, had with him a fine camera, the kind used by professional photographers.

As the stage rounded a slight bend past a patch of short brushy trees, a man dressed in a battered felt hat and a dirty linen duster stepped into view and ordered the driver to halt. In minutes he had the passengers lined up and was emptying their pockets. Unlike some chivalrous highwaymen of the day, this bandit did not hesitate to rob the ladies in the group. They, like the men, were forced to hand over their cash. Only the driver was spared. "I don't want a workingman's money" was the robber's answer when the driver asked if he was to be searched, too.

When the robber had taken all the passengers' money, Anton Veith, on an impulse, made a startling request. "How about letting me take a picture of you by the stage? It'll only take a minute."

To Veith's surprise, the robber answered "Go ahead and get your camera. No one can recognize me in the get-up anyway. Hurry it up, though."

The result was a remarkable photograph, which was published several days later in the Fresno *Morning Republican*. Credit for bringing the photo to light goes to veteran Western history researcher and writer William B. Secrest of Fresno who found the original in the possession of Anton Veith's son, George. Hats off to Secrest; an exceptional find!

## Redding
### Shasta County

The northern California town of Redding lies at the junction of Interstate 5 and State Highway 299. In the Trinity foothills southwest of town may be buried a fortune in outlaw gold. Naturally, nobody knows the exact location. The loot was reportedly hidden by a gang of bandits led by Dick Barter, alias "Rattlesnake Dick". The treasure was part of a shipment of $100,000 which left Yreka in Siskiyou County by wagon in the summer of 1856. The gang struck just south of Redding on what is now State Highway 273. They overpowered a team of Mexican mule drivers, then quickly transported the shipment to a prearranged hiding place—presumably due west or slightly southwest, toward Igo or Cloverdale.

The reason some think the gold may still be there is because it is likely that none of the bandits were able to return for it. The entire gang was killed or captured in the weeks that followed. Barter himself returned to outlawry after a stint in jail, but he operated much further south in Placer County, where he was killed in July 1859.

Redding was also more or less the center of operations of the notorious stage robber, Black Bart, during his ventures into the northern mining country in 1879 through 1882 (see *San Andreas*).

## San Andreas
### Calaveras County

From the standpoint of geography, probably the most difficult California outlaw to pin down is the prince of stage robbers, Black Bart. This dapper little bandit robbed stages as far north as the Oregon border and as far west as the Coast Ranges in Mendocino County. The town

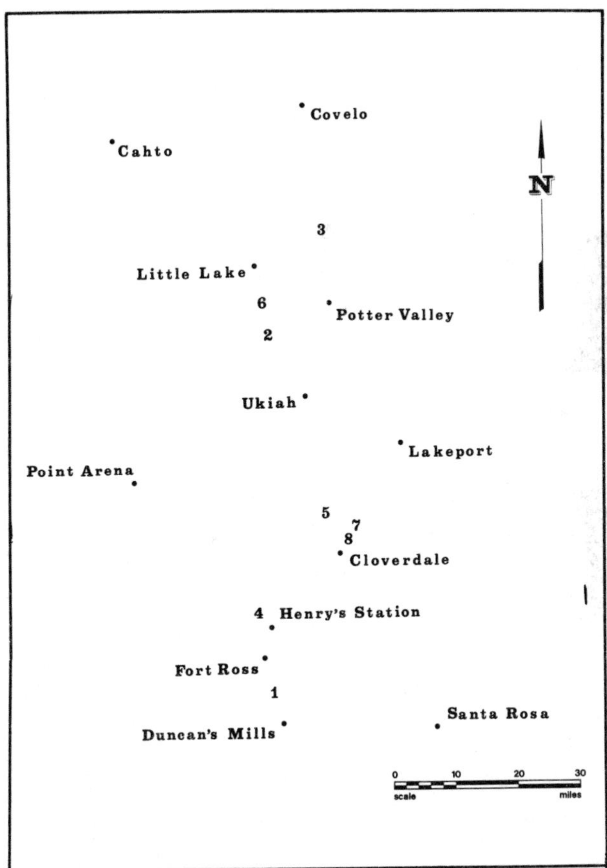


**Wells Fargo stagecoach robberies attributed to Black Bart—Northwestern California, 1877-1883. 1.** Stage from Point Arena to Duncan's Mills, August 3, 1877, between Fort Ross and Duncan's Mills. **2.** Stage from Cahto to Ukiah, October 2, 1878, twelve miles from Ukiah. **3.** Stage from Covelo to Ukiah, October 3, 1878, ten miles from Potter Valley. **4.** Stage from Point Arena to Duncan's Mills, July 22, 1880, two and one half miles from Henry's Station. **5.** Stage from Ukiah to Cloverdale, January 26, 1882, six miles from Cloverdale. **6.** Stage from Little Lake to Ukiah, June 14, 1882, three miles from Little Lake. **7.** Stage from Lakeport to Cloverdale, November 24, 1882, six miles from Cloverdale. **8.** Stage from Lakeport to Cloverdale, April 12, 1883, five miles from Cloverdale.

of San Andreas, however, takes a special proprietary interest in Bart because it was the end of the line for him as an outlaw.

Nobody knows exactly how many stages Bart held up during his career. Wells Fargo records list him as responsible for twenty-eight robberies or attempted robberies of their shipments, but he probably robbed many independent lines, too. He seemed to have had three centers of operations: in the far north he roamed around Redding in Shasta County; to the west he worked out of Ukiah near the Coast Ranges; and in the eastern part of the state, Oroville in Butte County seemed to be his base.

Bart's first victim was probably the stage from Sonora to Milton on July 26, 1875. The site was four miles northeast of Copperopolis on what is now State Highway 4. His last robbery, at least according to Wells Fargo records, was on November 3, 1883, only a mile away from the scene of the first. In between, Wells Fargo credited the dapper bandit with twenty-six other holdups on its lines, for a total haul of possibly $40,000 (this may not seem like much, but it must be remembered that the days of the big gold shipments in California were over).

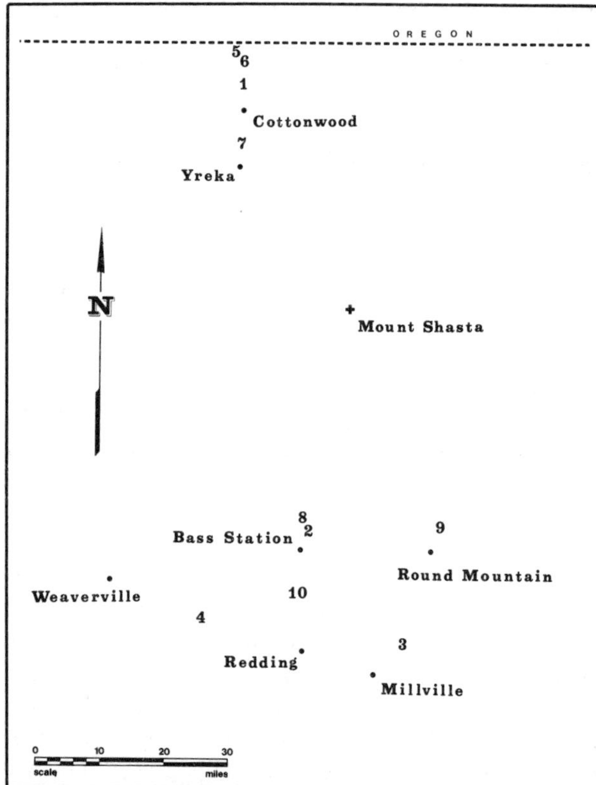


Wells Fargo stagecoach robberies attributed to Black Bart—North-central California, 1876-1882. **1.** Stage from Roseburg, Oregon, to Yreka, June 2, 1876, five miles from Cottonwood. **2.** Stage from Roseburg, Oregon, to Redding, October 25, 1879, two miles from Bass Station. **3.** Stage from Alturas to Redding, October 27, 1879, twelve miles above Millville. **4.** Stage from Weaverville to Redding, September 1, 1880. **5.** Stage from Roseburg, Oregon, to Yreka, September 16, 1880, one mile from Oregon line. **6.** Stage from Redding to Roseburg, Oregon, November 20, 1880, one mile from Oregon line. **7.** Stage from Roseburg, Oregon, to Yreka, August 31, 1881, nine miles from Yreka. **8.** Stage from Yreka to Redding, October 8, 1881, three miles from Bass Station. **9.** Stage from Lakeview to Redding, October 11, 1881, two miles from Round Mountain. **10.** Stage from Yreka to Redding, September 17, 1882, fourteen miles from Redding.

The outlaw's routine seldom varied. He always chose a spot near the top of a steep grade where a tired team had nearly slowed to a walk. He would step out of his hiding place brandishing a doubled-barreled shotgun. Almost always he was dressed in a long linen duster and wore a flour sack with narrow slits for eyeholes. His command was usually a terse "Throw down the box!"

Bart acquired his name from a note he left on August 3, 1877, after removing a Wells Fargo strongbox from a stage on the Point Arena to Duncan's Mills route. On the back of the waybill he wrote these lines:

> I've labored long and hard for bread,
> For honor and for riches,
> But on my corns too long you've tread
> You fine haired sons of bitches.

It was signed "Black Bart, the PO8."

Bart left only one other poem, the following year near Berry Creek on the Quincy to Oroville route. He was, however, firmly established as California's "bandit poet," and newspaper feature writers spread his fame throughout the West, often with embellishment. From a common road agent, Bart grew to become a daring Robin Hood seeking equity for the little man against corporate giants.

The bold bandit was finally caught in 1883. During the November 3 robbery three miles northeast of Copperopolis he was winged by a nineteen-year-old lad who had hitched a ride on the stage to go deer hunting in the mountains. Bart escaped, but Wells Fargo detectives found an expensive silk handkerchief at the scene; it had blood on it, and a laundry mark. The mark was traced to a San Francisco laundry and a customer named C. E. Bolton. Bolton, whose real name was believed to be Charles E. Boles, originally from Decatur, Illinois, was quietly picked up and taken to Calaveras County. What transpired there is a mystery. Rumor had it that the bandit made a deal with Wells Fargo to confess to the last robbery and turn over the loot in return for a light sentence and the company dropping all previous charges. On November 17, 1883, officials at San Andreas accepted Bart's guilty plea to the November 3 holdup, and he was sentenced to six years in prison. In just over five years he was once again seen on the streets of San Francisco, expensively dressed and dapper as

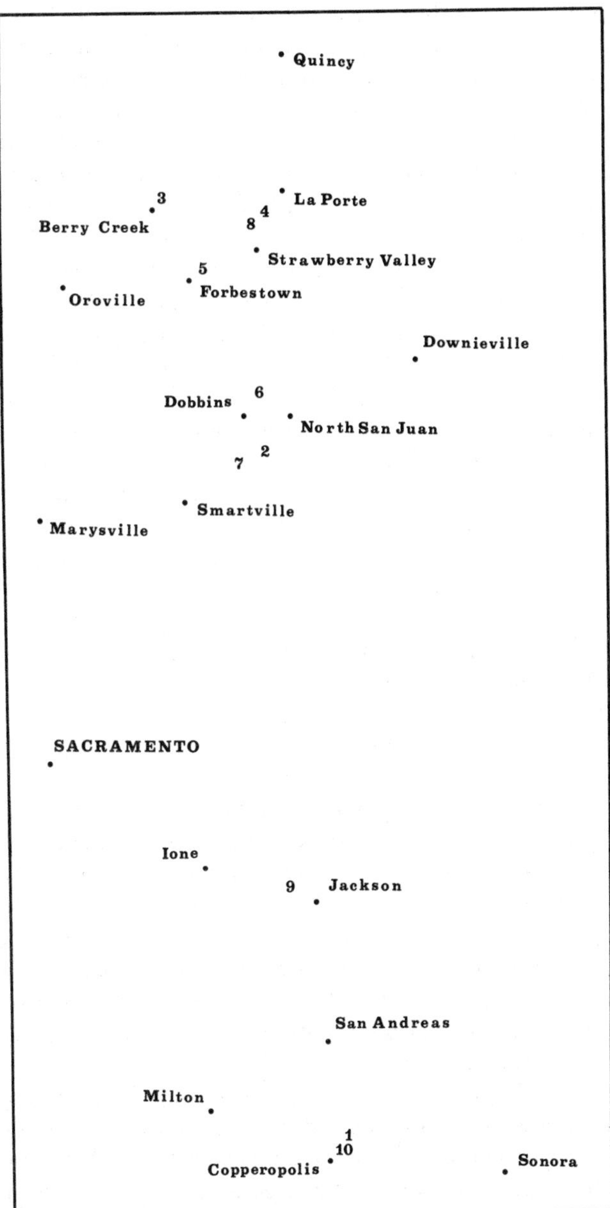


**Wells Fargo stagecoach robberies attributed to Black Bart—Northeastern California, 1875-1883. 1.** Stage from Sonora to Milton, July 26, 1875, four miles from Copperopolis. **2.** Stage from North San Juan to Marysville, December 28, 1875, ten miles from North San Juan. **3.** Stage from Quincy to Oroville, July 25, 1878, one mile from Berry Creek. **4.** Stage from LaPorte to Oroville, July 30, 1878, five miles from LaPorte. **5.** Stage from LaPorte to Oroville, June 21, 1879, three miles from Forbestown. **6.** Stage from Downieville to Marysville, December 15, 1881, four miles from Dobbins. **7.** Stage from North San Juan to Smartville, December 27, 1881. **8.** Stage from LaPorte to Oroville, July 13, 1882, nine miles from Strawberry Valley (attempted robbery). **9.** Stage from Jackson to Ione, June 23, 1883, four miles from Jackson. **10.** Stage from Sonora to Milton, November 3, 1883, three miles from Copperopolis.

ever. There were those who said they saw him occasionally calling at the general offices of Wells Fargo on Montgomery Street, which led to rumors that as part of the deal he was put on the company's payroll. This seems unlikely; a more reasonable explanation is that if there were a deal, Bart may have had to keep the company informed as to his whereabouts.

Some time in 1888 Bart left the state. Now and then a report would come in that he had been seen in one of the large cities—St. Louis, New Orleans, Mexico City—but eventually these stories dwindled, and nothing more was heard about him.

San Andreas was also the town where the legendary bandit and murderer Joaquin Murietta (also spelled Murrieta) supposedly launched his crime wave in the early 1950s. Devoted researchers have proved that the Joaquin story was mostly if not all fiction, but the San Andreas area did have a Mexican trouble-maker who terrorized Calaveras County for several months in 1853, which probably was the basis for the dime novel exploits attributed to the notorious Joaquin.

## San Francisco

San Francisco's troubles began soon after gold was discovered in California. As miners flocked to the state, the town became a center for their entertainment. Word spread that men carried gold dust in the streets, and soon a steady stream of criminals flowed into the city to relieve them of it.

A particularly troublesome bunch was a group of New York toughs calling themselves the "Hounds." Many of its members had served in or deserted from the Mexican War, later tried their hand at mining but found it too much work, and finally drifted to the Bay City to prey on its citizens. Loosely organized, the Hounds slept by day and ravaged by night, sometimes in small groups and other times in a large, warlike gang, which usually concentrated on the foreign quarters. After an especially violent night-long raid in mid-July 1849, a local newspaper editor, Samuel Brannan, called upon local residents to organize and fight these terrorists. Volunteers came from everywhere, and immediately four companies of a hundred men each were formed. Almost overnight nineteen of the worst of the gang members were rounded up. A "people's court" was created, defense counsels were appointed, and witnesses were called to testify. Nine of the accused were found guilty and banished from the city.

Flushed with success, the new crime fighters decided that they needed a jail. Rather than wait to have one built, they chipped in and bought a brig moored in the harbor, the *Euphemia*, and converted it to a floating hoosegow.

But no sooner had the Hounds been tamed, than another gang rose out of the hovels of Sydney Town, a scruffy settlement at Clark's Point. The miners were their special victims in the streets and the crowded gambling dens. From robbery and assault they quickly graduated to murder; dusty records suggest that as many as a hundred occurred in the bay area over a period of only a few months. The city was now bursting with a population of nearly 50,000, and law and order was falling behind. When a suspect was caught, trial was often delayed until witnesses were killed or frightened off. Editor Sam Brannan took charge again. In the summer of 1851 he and his followers formed a new citizens' group, this time calling themselves the "Vigilance Committee." Their first victim was an Australian named John Jenkins, whose worst crime was burglarizing an office. In quick succession he was tried, convicted, and sentenced. No banishment this time—that had not kept the lid on—this time the penalty was death. Following a token resistance from the police department, Jenkins was hanged in the Plaza in front of the Customs House. A month later the rope was used again: this time on an Englishman named James Stuart who, it was rumored, had a reputation for thievery and murder up in the mining districts.

The Stuart execution was quickly condemned by city and state officials, but the city's newspapers supported the committee's efforts, claiming the vigilantes were merely inflicting the penalties the elected officials should have been carrying out. In July 1851 the San Francisco *Herald* asked its readers, "Whenever the law becomes an empty name, has not the citizen the right to supply its deficiency?"

Two more criminals felt the rope later in the year. The committee proved so successful that the idea spread to surrounding towns, and in San Francisco order was restored to the extent that the vigilantes were deactivated, retaining only a "watchdog committee."

The city was relatively quiet for several years, but by 1856 corrupt officials had once again let crime get out of hand. When the fiery editor of the San Francisco *Bulletin*, a former vigilante named James King, was killed by a city supervisor, James Casey, following an editorial exposing Casey's criminal record, the committee reorganized and hanged Casey and another politician, Charles Cora, who had bought off a jury trying him for murder. Two months later, on July 29, 1856, two more murderers were strung up: another Englishman named Joseph Hetherington and an outlaw from upper New York state, Philander Brace.

Once again the vigilantes' actions had an impact on the city's criminals. Murders dropped to less than one a month, compared to fifteen prior to the committee's revival. By mid-August the vigilantes felt they could again disband. A formal parade was held to announce deactivation. Over six thousand men marched in military order, as a warning to San Francisco's underworld that the strength was still there and could be called upon at a moment's notice.

Victims of San Francisco's Vigilance Committee. *New York Historical Society.*

## Sequoia National Forest
### Fresno & Tulare Counties

Ten miles northeast of Squaw Valley near the western edge of Sequoia National Forest, fugitive train robbers Chris Evans and John Sontag engaged a ten-man Tulare County posse near an abandoned mining area called Sampson's Flat in what has become known as "The Battle of Young's Cabin." It was the fall of 1892. The two renegades, wanted for a series of robberies on the Southern Pacific (see *Earlimart*, *Goshen*, *Kerman*, and *Pixley*), had already killed a deputy sheriff and wounded two other pursuers at Visalia.* At Young's cabin the posse walked into a death trap. Thrown off guard by the sight of a local hermit named Mainwaring, whom the outlaws had sent out of the cabin for a bucket of water, the lawmen carelessly walked to within fifteen feet of the door. Evans and Sontag calmly stepped out and killed Vernon Wilson, a hired manhunter from Texas, and severely wounded a Modesto deputy sheriff, Andy McGinnis. The rest of the posse scattered for safety, and the outlaws escaped into a nearby woods.

About a mile from the scene the authorities found a miniature fortress built by the fugitives. Dug by hand into the slope of an overhanging precipice, the bastion looked down upon a valley and the only trail that led up to it. The outlaws had carefully placed large boulders around the front edge, leaving narrow openings through which they could fire with almost perfect safety. Well-stocked with provisions and hundreds of rounds of rifle and shotgun ammunition, the dugout could have been defended for months against anything less than field artillery. Although the site can still be visited today (it is marked on geological survey maps as Sontag Point),

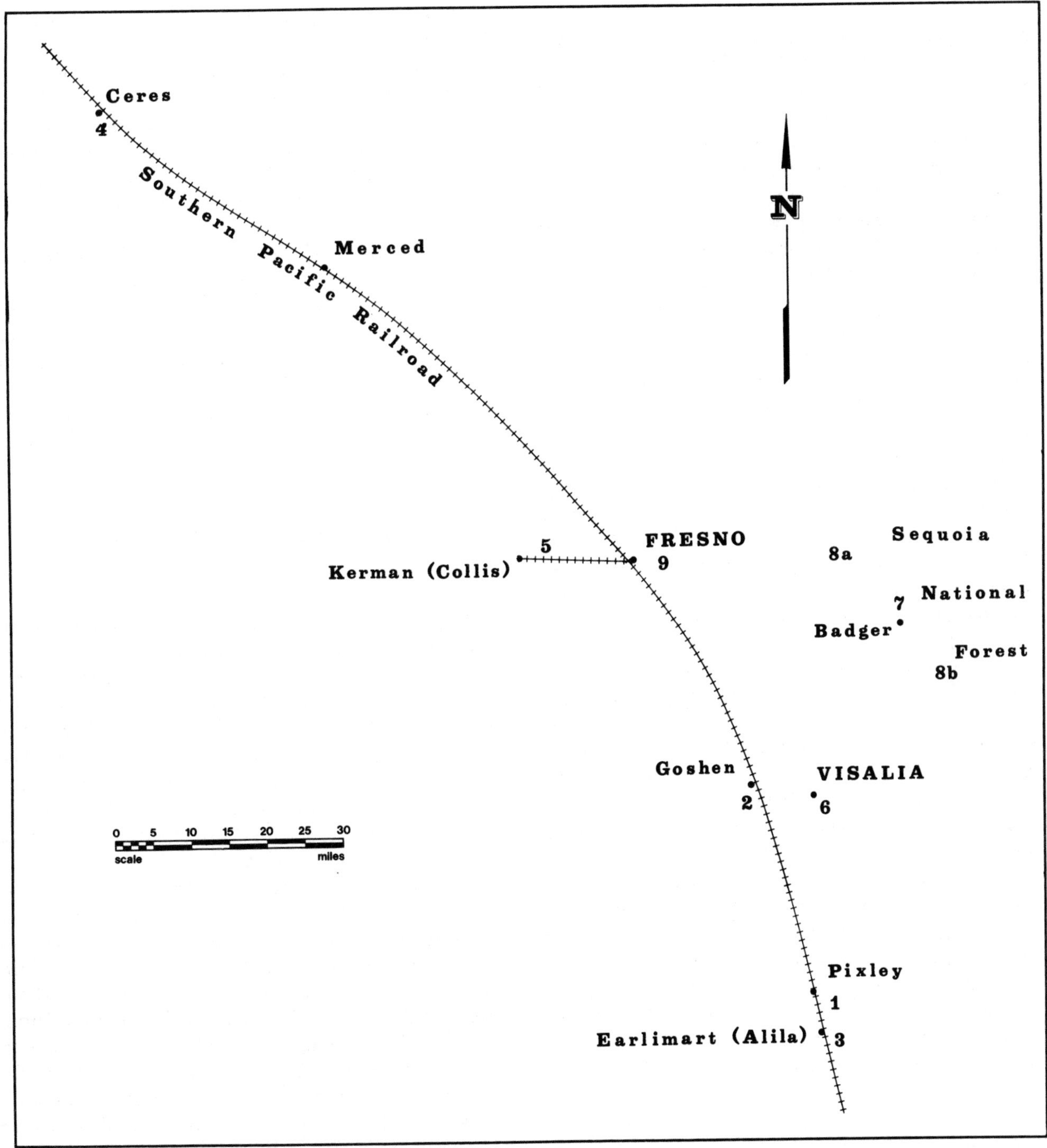


**The saga of Chris Evans and John Sontag.** 1. Robbery of a Wells Fargo express car two miles south of Pixley on February 22, 1889; the first in a series of train robberies in the San Joaquin Valley thought to be the work of the Dalton brothers, but later attributed to Evans and Sontag. **2.** Robbery of a Wells Fargo express car two miles south of Goshen on January 20, 1890. **3.** Attempted robbery of a Wells Fargo express car one mile south of Earlimart (then called Alila) on February 6, 1891. Grat Dalton was tried for the crime, but escaped following trial; the conviction was later overturned. **4.** Attempted robbery of a Wells Fargo express car one mile south of Ceres on November 3, 1891. **5.** Robbery of a Wells Fargo express car east of Kerman (then called Collis) on August 3, 1892. **6.** Visalia; home of Chris Evans. The hunt for Evans and Sontag began here in August 1892, when the two outlaws shot and wounded Southern Pacific Railroad detective Will Smith and a deputy sheriff who called at Evans' home to question him about the Collis robbery. Later that night the outlaws killed another deputy before escaping into the mountains. **7.** Stage holdup by Evans and Sontag on August 29, 1893, one and one-half miles north of Badger in an unsuccessful attempt to dispose of their nemesis Will Smith. He was not on the stage. **8a-8b.** General area of one of the biggest manhunts in California history. From August 1892 to June 1893 Evans and Sontag led lawmen in a chase through the mountainous region that now forms the western edge of the Sequoia National Forest. Sontag was fatally wounded during the outlaws' capture. **9.** Fresno; scene of Chris Evans' trial for the murder of two possemen during the chase through the mountains. Evans later escaped and was recaptured the following February at Visalia.

Chris Evans, following his capture in June, 1893. *Wells Fargo Bank History Room.*

the possemen loosened and rolled the boulders down the slope before they left, just in case the outlaws returned.

Having to abandon their stronghold, the fugitives spent the winter under a cliff above the bed of Dry Creek, a small stream that winds through Dark Canyon, a few miles southeast of Badger near Eshom Valley. They continued to elude the authorities through spring. Evans even made a half dozen trips back to his home in Visalia to visit his family, several times under the very nose of guards hired to watch his home. On April 29 the two outlaws stopped a stagecoach near Badger* because they heard that one of their most hated pursuers, Southern Pacific detective Will Smith, would be on board. He was not, having changed his plans at the last minute.

The end finally came for the two fugitives during the second week of June 1893 at a site on local maps known as Stone Corral. At the time there was a vacant cabin there (the "Widow Baker's Place"), which made an ideal hideout. It lay in a remote valley, cleared of trees and underbrush, so that anyone in the cabin had a commanding view for hundreds of yards in every direction. It would have been a safe retreat for the outlaws, had they arrived a little sooner, but they were one day too late: a posse made up of federal marshals and local deputy sheriffs were waiting for them.

Evans and Sontag came walking up to the cabin around sunset. It was the reverse of the Young's cabin affair. Had trigger fingers been less itchy, the matter would have ended in minutes, but Fred Jackson, a federal officer called in from Nevada, squeezed off a rifle shot while the outlaws were still at least seventy-five yards away. The bullet caught Evans in the left arm, and he and Sontag dived for cover behind a pile of straw and manure. While the manure pile kept the officers from having a clear shot, it offered little protection. More bullets reached their mark. Sontag took a hit in his right arm, rendering it useless. Minutes later another slug ripped into his side. Evans raised to look at his wounded partner, and a bullet creased his back. Sontag, bleeding badly, pleaded with his comrade to put him out of his misery. Evans declined, then took another hit himself, this time the right arm. Seconds later three buckshot caught him in the right eye, tearing it from its socket. The outlaws were no longer a threat, but the officers had no way of knowing this. As night fell, they ceased fire, content to wait out the darkness.

At daybreak the lawmen cautiously approached the manure pile. They found Sontag, unconscious but still alive. In the night he had received two more scalp wounds in the head; this time by his own hand, in a futile attempt to end his life. Evans was gone. Somehow he had managed to crawl six miles from the scene to a cabin in Wilcox Canyon, where a family took him in and bandaged his wounds. When he fell asleep they sent for the sheriff. Although he still had a pistol, Evans offered no resistance. The manhunt was over.

With proper maps, it is possible to visit much of the area over which Evans and Sontag led authorities during their year-long chase. Check with the Public Information Officer, Sequoia National Forest, 900 W. Grand Avenue, Porterville, CA 93257.

Bullet-riddled body of John Sontag, June 1893. *Wells Fargo Bank History Room.*

# Stockton
## San Joaquin County

California towns tended to blossom early as outlaw hangouts, much earlier than the rest of the frontier. Stockton, forty miles south of Sacramento on Interstate 5, was no exception. In the spring of 1850 a local resident described the town's hard cases this way:

> They always carried a large-sized Colt's revolver and a knife in their belts, and woe to the man who dared to cross them! . . . On Sundays they filled up with whiskey, mounted their horses and rode around town looking for a row, and "raising hell" generally. They would ride into a saloon, up to the bar, and drink without dismounting.

Stockton is not without its hidden outlaw loot. Some local historians say that just east of town, buried in a cave or hidden by dense underbrush, may lie part of some $250,000 in cash and jewels stolen by the outlaw Tom Bell who preyed on the Mother Lode area in the mid-1850s. It is doubtful that Bell was that successful, but maybe there is something there.

# Tehachapi
## Kern County

Tehachapi is on State Highway 58 about thirty miles east of Bakersfield. Deep in Tejon Canyon in the rugged mountains nine miles southwest of town, lie the remains of the hideout of the Mason-Henry gang, a band of killers and robbers who plagued the San Joaquin Valley during the final years of the Civil War. At first the outlaws terrorized the valley under the guise of Southern sympathizers sent to harass Northerners for the "cause" of the Confederacy. But soon it was clear that the bandits were merely out for what they could steal from the citizenry.

According to Virginia Bartholomew, who researched the gang's activity during those years, the outlaws' hideout in Tejon Canyon was at the end of a trail that "ran down a long, sharp ridge with a bluff many hundreds of feet high on the west side." The east side of the trail was "so steep and full of brush it was impossible to get a horse down to the canyon floor." The path was only about five feet wide, and at one spot where it passed around a giant boulder, it was just three feet. What makes the hideout interesting, according to Bartholomew, is that quite possibly near the bottom of the trail there still lies buried gang leader Mason's saddlebag and money belt, stuffed with cash taken from a robbery in Tehachapi.

Tehachapi Loop. *Southern Pacific.*

The gang apparently operated for several years until shortly after the end of the war when the leaders began to die off. Mason's partner, Henry, is believed to have died in a shootout in San Bernadino County, the exact date of which is unknown. The details on Mason's demise are also cloudy: there is some evidence he was killed by a jealous lover of one of his mistresses the very day he hid his saddlebag and money belt in Tejon Canyon.

In January 1883 a Southern Pacific express was resting on the steep grade near Tehachapi Summit, just east of the town of Tehachapi. Suddenly the seven cars behind the tender broke loose and began to roll backward down the mountain. The summit is nearly 3,800 feet above sea level, and within minutes the runaway cars reached a speed of over seventy miles per hour. Four miles down the grade at the center of a long curve, the cars left the track. When the last of the bodies was removed from the wreckage, it was considered a miracle that only fifteen persons were killed. Within a week Southern Pacific officials announced that two of the victims, neither of whom could be identified, resembled two men who had been seen at the station just before the train broke loose. It was speculated that these two had intended to rob the train, their plan being to release the brakes gradually and control the speed of the cars so they could bring them to a stop somewhere down the track.

# Tres Pinos
## San Benito County

This tiny town, on State Highway 25 eight miles south of Hollister, was the scene of the "Tres Pinos Massacre" on August 26, 1873, which led to the conviction and execution of California's notorious bandit chief Tiburcio Vasquez. Vasquez's gang descended on the town to rob Andrew Snyder's general store. While three of the outlaws were filling grain sacks with money and supplies inside the store, Vasquez stood out front watching the horses. A sheepherder came walking up, knowing nothing of the robbery in progress, and Vasquez shot him dead. This frightened two teamsters who were hitching their horses nearby, and they began to run. Vasquez shot one of them. A local boardinghouse owner, A. M. Davidson, saw what was happening, and ran to warn his wife. Vasquez put a bullet in him. Inside, a young boy tried to escape out the back door, and an outlaw clubbed him in the head.

Vasquez was captured the following year (see *Los Angeles*) and charged with the murders. At his trial he argued that his gang members did the killing, not he, but the jury did not believe him. He was convicted and sentenced to hang. According to witnesses his last request before going to the gallows was to see his coffin. It was brought to his cell, and as he admired the satin lining, he remarked, "I can sleep here forever very well." He began his sleep on March 19, 1875.

# Ventura
## Ventura County

Some have called it the silliest bank robbery in California frontier history. Ventura, located on US Highway 101 midway between Los Angeles and Santa Barbara, was not a town bothered much by outlaws. In fact, by the 1880s it was so peaceful that the sheriff, A. J. Snodgrass, did not always carry his gun. Often in midday he would leave it at the jail when he ate lunch at his favorite cafe, a few doors away. So it was that on April 25, 1889, an unarmed Sheriff Snodgrass emerged from his mealtime break to find the Collins and Sons Bank on Main Street in the process of being robbed.

The robber was a penniless drifter named Jim McCarthy. He had scouted the bank and found that the owner, J. E. Collins, always went to lunch promptly at noon, leaving only one teller, Jack Morrison, on duty. On seeing McCarthy with a gun, teller Morrison made a hasty retreat out the back door. McCarthy gathered up a tray full of money and hurried back to his horse, which he had tied to a wagon wheel. While McCarthy was in the bank, the horse had taken a few steps forward, and

Peaceful Ventura in 1885. *Security Pacific National Bank Collection: Los Angeles Public Library.*

McCarthy's reins were now on the bottom of the wheel, partly buried in the dirt. Teller Morrison in the meantime had emerged from an alley and was shouting that the bank was being robbed! And as McCarthy fumbled with the knot in his reins, his horse shied and backed away, pulling the knot even tighter.

Morrison's shouts finally brought a shopkeeper out of his store. He had picked up an old revolver that had been lying around for years, but he could not get it cocked. By now McCarthy had dropped the teller's tray and was on his hands and knees trying to gather up the spilled money. Morrison was jumping up and down screaming for help, and the shopkeeper stood at the door of his store fumbling with his gun.

Such was the scene when Sheriff Snodgrass stepped from the door of the cafe. He quickly ran over to the shopkeeper, grabbed the gun out of his trembling hand and ordered McCarthy to surrender. The hapless robber, by now convinced that it was just not his day, tossed the money back on the gound, and then his gun. "I give up," he sighed, and he raised his hands.

## Visalia
### Tulare County

Visalia was the home of train robber Chris Evans, who with partner John Sontag led peace officers and Southern Pacific detectives on a not-so-merry chase through the Sierra Nevadas in the early 1890s.

Evans owned a small farm on the south edge of town. In August 1892 Southern Pacific detective Will Smith and a local deputy sheriff, a man named Witty, called at the farm, looking for Sontag. Although at the time there was no evidence linking either Evans or Sontag to any of the robberies, the most recent of which had occurred August 3 at Kerman,* the two apparently panicked at seeing Smith and Witty and began shooting. (Evan's 16-year-old daughter, however, told a different story, claiming that Smith and Witty fired first. There are local residents today who will tell you that Evans and Sontag were innocent and ran only from fear of rough treatment by the authorities.) After wounding Smith and Witty, Evans and Sontag fled, presumably for the mountains. Later that night, however, they returned for provisions. Two deputy sheriffs and a constable were posted near the barn, and a gunfight erupted. One of the deputies, Oscar Beaver, was killed.

Over the next year the two fugitives led the authorities on one of the biggest manhunts in California history. They were finally captured in June 1893, following a gunfight at Stone Corral, near the western edge of what is now the Sequoia National Forest.* Both were wounded severely in the fight. Sontag died, and Evans was tried for murder. But in December 1893 Evans escaped from jail at Fresno and once again disappeared into the mountains. He remained loose until February 1894, when he was surrounded by peace officers while visiting his family at Visalia. He was sent to prison where he remained until 1911, when he was pardoned by California governor Hiram Johnson. He died in 1917.

Visalia had another hard case to endure during its frontier years: the bad-tempered and hard-drinking Jim McKinney. Although not well-known outside California, McKinney enjoyed the reputation as the San Joaquin Valley's most feared killer shortly after the turn of the century. Visalia was introduced to Jim's special brand of violence when he put a bullet in a saloon girl's bottom because her dancing did not please him. According to one account, on sobering up, McKinney saw that the poor woman received medical treatment; later, the two became lovers.

McKinney may have ridden with the Wild Bunch and reportedly was wanted for killings in Arizona. Most of his violence, however, was inflicted in Tulare and Kern Counties (see *Farmersville*; *Porterville*; *Bakersfield*). He finally fell before lawmen's guns at Bakersfield in 1903.

Colorado 1886

# COLORADO

## Brown's Park
### Moffat County

This rugged canyon area (also called Brown's Hole) on the Green River, about ten miles as the crow flies south of the Wyoming line and just east of Utah, was a notorious outlaw hideout. The following item which appeared in the March 11, 1898, issue of the Denver *News* aptly describes the area's attraction for fugitives:

> Hunting men in a thickly settled country or on the plains or open country is one thing, but to hunt them in these mountains snowcapped in sections the year around, cut by impassable canyons, unfordable rivers, gulches, gullies and where nearly every section of land affords a hiding place, is another proposition.

The area was also ideal because of its proximity to the state lines. Pursuing posses tended to tie up when they reached the end of their jurisdiction. Outlaws could merely shuttle back and forth across the borders, depending on who was chasing them.

Butch Cassidy, Harry Longabaugh (the Sundance Kid), and their fellow Wild Bunch members found Brown's Park a safe harbor between robberies. Cassidy likely used it for the first time following the San Miguel Valley Bank robbery at Telluride.*

The hideout was also used by outlaw Harry Tracy in the winter of 1898, following his escape from a Utah jail. Tracy and a companion, Dave Lent, were pursued into the area by a posse led by lawman Valentine Hoy. The two outlaws, joined by a third, Swede Johnson, were cornered on March 1, and Hoy was killed during the fight.

## Colorado Springs
### El Paso County

In October 1881 the biggest train robbery in Colorado history occurred a few miles north of Colorado Springs. The northbound express of the Colorado and Southern Railroad had barely gained speed for the long haul to Denver when it was jolted to a stop by a stack of ties on the tracks. Three masked men sprang out of the darkness and ordered the engineer and fireman to raise their hands. With near military precision the bandits marched the two trainmen back to the express car. The engineer pleaded with the express messenger to open his door, claiming that refusal could mean death for them all. Just then the conductor and several curious passengers stepped down from the first coach. A volley of shots from the robbers sent them scurrying back to safety and at the same time convinced the messenger that he had better open up. In minutes the bandits blew open the safe and cleaned out its contents—$105,000 in cash and about $40,000 worth of jewelry. After securing the loot to their horses, the robbers rode north into the darkness.

The train backed into Colorado Springs, and the crew sounded the alarm. A posse was quickly formed and tracked the three riders for ten miles above the site of the robbery. There they found the outlaws' horses, where a fresh relay team had been standing by. The tracks then led northwest, toward the mountains, where the pursuers soon lost them on the rocky slopes.

Later the authorities would learn that the robbers crossed the mountains into Utah, where they buried the loot near Corinne.*

## Creede
### Mineral County

Creede lies just west of Rio Grande National Forest on State Highway 149, a little over twenty miles northwest of US 160. As a bonanza town it was a late arrival, the first silver lode being discovered in 1889. It thrived for about three years, then dwindled.

At first Creede's boomtown days were not accom-

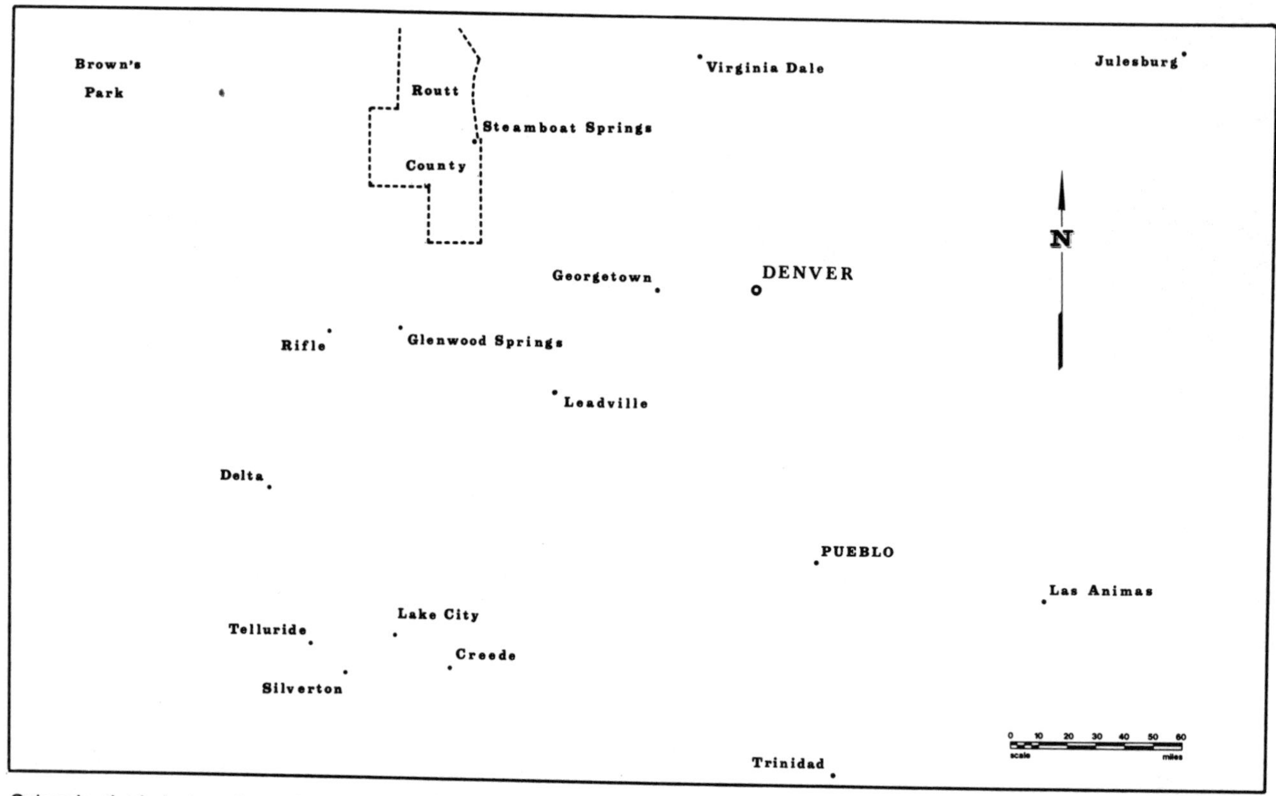


**Colorado, the lodestone for outlaws and gunfighters.** Although Colorado produced few hard cases of its own, the state attracted many of the West's outlaws and gunfighters. **Brown's Park**: Hideout for Butch Cassidy, Harry Longabaugh (The Sundance Kid), and the Wyoming Wild Bunch. **Creede**: Bat Masterson helped keep the lid on in the early nineties; Bob Ford was killed here in 1892. **Delta**: Scene of the McCarty gang's disastrous bank robbery in 1893. **Denver**: Base of Dave Cook's Rocky Mountain Detective Association; also playground for Doc Holliday and Bat Masterson. **Georgetown**: Wild Bill Hickok found the town too quiet in the early 1870s. **Glenwood Springs**: Doc Holliday spent his last days there. **Julesburg**: Jack Slade killed Jules Beni here. **Lake City**: Wyatt Earp was wounded in a saloon fight in 1884. **Las Animas**: Scene of a Clay Allison shootout in 1876. **Leadville**: A reckless town during the boom years; Luke Short and Doc Holliday were among the undesirables; the town also spawned Jim McKinney, later one of California's worst badmen. **Pueblo**: Drew Dodge City's top gunfighters in 1879 for the showdown of the "Royal Gorge War." **Rifle**: May have been the scene of Harvey (Kid Curry) Logan's demise in 1904. **Routt County**: Hired killer Tom Horn made two business trips to the area in 1900. **Silverton**: Bat Masterson called in to quiet the town in the 1880s. **Steamboat Springs**: Meeting place of the legendary "Train Robbers' Syndicate" in 1898. **Telluride**: Early home of Butch Cassidy; he may have returned in 1889 to rob the San Miguel Valley Bank. **Trinidad**: Plagued by outlaws migrating from Dodge City; the Masterson brothers tried to calm things down in the early eighties. **Virginia Dale**: Jack Slade founded the town as a stage stop in 1860s and probably used it as a base for rustling operations in southern Wyoming.

panied by the violence often found in the riotous mining camps of Colorado. Some say this was due in part to the presence of ex-Dodge City peace officer Bat Masterson, whose reputation as a gunfighter kept the lid on an otherwise spirited citizenry. Masterson did not wear a badge in Creede but managed the best gambling house in town, Mart Watrous's Denver Exchange. While Bat's fame as a gunman may have been grossly exaggerated, it was effective, and apparently few rowdies felt like taking on the steely eyed former marshal.

Bat himself was not sure that the town's early calm was a good sign. In an interesting interview reported in the *Colorado Sun* on February 25, 1892, Masterson said: "I don't like this quiet; it augurs ill. I have been in several places that started out this way and there were generally wild scenes of carnage before many weeks passed. . . . It only needs a break to raise Cain here. The same thing happened in other notorious camps. It seems as though there must be a little blood-letting to get affairs into proper working order."

Bat's prediction came true. The town eventually burst at the seams. On July 8, 1892, in a tent saloon operated by Bob Ford (the man who killed Jesse James ten years earlier in St. Joseph, Missouri) a seedy character named Ed Kelly (also called O'Kelly) walked in the front door with a shotgun and emptied both barrels into the former Missouri bandit. The motive was never clear. There was some talk abut Ford having "done him dirt" one time or another; another version has it that Ford had earlier accused Kelly of stealing his diamond ring, and when he stormed in Ford's tent to argue the matter, Ford had him thrown out. And of course it is possible that Kelly merely wanted to be the man who killed the man who killed Jesse James.

Creede, Colorado, around 1890. *Denver Public Library, Western History Department.*

# Delta
## Delta County

Delta has a place in the history of Colorado's outlaw years because of one incident—the robbery of the Farmers and Merchants Bank on September 7, 1893. There are several versions of the affair. According to a Delta resident, Ben Laycock, who was there when it happened, three men, later determined to be Tom and Bill McCarty (who some say rode with Wyoming's Wild Bunch) and their nephew, Fred McCarty, had been casing the bank for several days. About 3:30 in the afternoon two of the McCartys (some say Bill and Fred, others say Bill and Tom) entered the bank and ordered all hands up. The third McCarty stayed with the horses at the rear of the building. As the robbers in the bank were issuing their orders, the cashier, Andrew Blachly, "let out a yell," and one of the McCartys, apparently thinking he was going to run for help, shot him. Quickly stuffing as many greenbacks into their shirts as they could carry, the two bandits ran to the back door, which led to the office of a lawyer, W. R. Robertson. Robertson had seen what was happening and had locked the door, but the robbers easily kicked it open and dashed through the office into the alley.

According to Laycock, the McCarty who had been left holding the horses panicked and fled. The horses, however, were still there, and the other two robbers jumped in the saddles and raced north up the alley toward Third Street. Meanwhile, a local hardware merchant, W. Ray Simpson, had heard the shot, and was standing ready with a loaded rifle as the fleeing bandits arrived at Third. According to Laycock, Simpson calmly drew a bead on Fred and put a bullet into his left temple. The outlaw's horse, however, never missed a stride, and Fred, still upright in the saddle, rode straight ahead toward Second Street. Simpson, probably believing he had missed, quickly jacked another shell into the chamber and fired at Bill. His aim was true again, and the outlaw's body tumbled into the alley, behind a cowbarn owned by a man named Bailey. In the meantime, the life had finally drained from Fred, and as his horse turned west on Second Street, he toppled from the saddle and rolled up against the fence that surrounded a barn owned by a family named Hammond. Tom, the last McCarty, continued on, heading north to the Delta bridge and then west toward Wells Gulch. Riding south through the gulch to the Dominguez Switch, he worked his way to an island in the Gunnison River where he and his companions had stashed fresh mounts. After changing horses, Tom forded the river to the south bank, rode up Dominguez Creek, and disappeared over a ridge into the Sinbad area.

# Denver

Outlaw activity in Denver seemed to have come in waves. One of the first bad years was 1860, when the town was suddenly overrun with thieves and toughs. Local law enforcement was ineffective, and soon a "People's Court" was formed. In traditional vigilante style, judgment was hastily rendered on the spot. Often there was a "trial," but there were no delays, stays, appeals, or imprisonment. Before the year was out, five troublemakers saw the end of a rope.

A typical case was that of one Jim Gordon. Gordon, who tended to get crazy when drunk, shot a man in a saloon brawl. He skipped town but foolishly wrote back to a friend. The letter fell into the hands of a member of the People's Court. Vigilante groups seldom strayed far from home, but the Denver bunch wanted no blots on its record. Gordon was found and returned. A "trial" was held, and on October 6, 1869, Gordon was marched to the gallows. As the rope was readied, the doomed man was heard to cry "Oh, if some good friend would only shoot me." When no such friend came forward, Gordon pleaded, "Please remember to fix the knot so it will break my neck instantly." This request was granted.

Another bad year was 1864, thanks mainly to a hard winter which drove miners into town, some of whom turned to crime. The years following the Civil War saw another upsurge in outlawry, as veterans came west to seek their fortune and found none. Like the miners, some turned to crime. In 1866 a crusading young crimefighter, Dave Cook, was made Denver city marshal. Cook, a tireless man who thrived on tracking down outlaws, was not content with protecting just Denver. He established an organization called the Rocky Mountain Detective Association, a network of cooperating law officers throughout Colorado. The group became a real problem for outlaws from Wyoming to New Mexico, particularly rustlers. In one instance Cook invaded the prominent Colorado Stock Growers Association and found that some of its leading members were operating rustling rings under the very noses of the association's honest stockmen. Soon thereafter he helped break up another band of horse thieves, the Musgrove gang, which operated out of a saloon on Denver's Holladay Street. In 1869 Cook was elected sheriff of Arapahoe County, the first of several terms. In 1874 he was appointed a major general in the Colorado state militia. The following year he launched a successful investigation of the famous "Italian Murders," a grisly case of four deaths stemming from a Denver extortion ring. For nearly forty years Cook and his association rode hard on the Denver area's criminal element, logging 3,000 arrests and solving over thirty murders.

Frontier Denver, at least to the roving outlaw, was Holladay Street. They called it "The Street of a Thousand Sinners." One observer described it as "four blocks [that] held more prostitute flesh, saw more wickedness [and] more sin than any four other blocks in the Old West."

In the 1860s the city's rough element was encased in a cluster of log cabins on the south bank of Cherry Creek, west of Larimer Street. But then as gold began to flow in from the mountains, the residents on Holladay Street moved to more fashionable quarters, leaving their roomy brick houses to be taken over by the red-light district crowd.

Holladay Street, named after the Overland Stage Line's Ben Holladay, plus adjacent areas on Blake and Larimer, became "the gayest, gaudiest, most brazen tenderloin west of the Mississippi." By the 1880s it was said that these three Denver streets provided at least a thousand "brides of the multitude" for the lonely pleasure-seeker. Foremost among the bawdy houses were Mattie Silks's and Lizzie Preston's, Jennie Rogers's House of Mirrors, Belle London's The Fashion, Verona Baldwin's Paradise Alley, Gouldie Gould's Club Annex, and Rose Lee's elegant House of Rose.

Gambling houses were also abundant: Ed and John Chase's Cricket Club, the Progressive Club, and the Palace Variety Theatre and Gambling Parlor, to name a few.

Denver buzzed with excitement over another "Holliday" in May 1882, when the famous Doc Holliday was arrested by a peace officer named Perry M. Mallan. Mallan claimed Doc was wanted for various crimes back in Arizona. Doc argued that the charges were a hoax and that certain Arizona parties, including John Behan, sheriff of Cochise County, wanted him dead for personal reasons. Behan, indeed, had petitioned for extradition papers to get Doc back, and it appeared that he would succeed until Doc's good friend, Bat Masterson, at the time town marshal at Trinidad, Colorado, interceded by falsifying charges of his own against Doc and requesting that he be released in Bat's custody for return to Trinidad. Bat's plan worked, and it likely saved Doc's life. Later a Denver newspaper editor checked up on peace officer Mallan and found that he was no peace officer at all, but a small-time swindler, possibly hired by Doc's enemies to bring him back to Arizona.

In 1888 Bat Masterson, who had accumulated a sizeable bankroll from proficient gambling, purchased the Palace Variety Theatre and Gambling Parlor, a two-story brick landmark at Blake and 15th Streets. The 750-seat theatre was a grand place, with curtains of heavy velvet

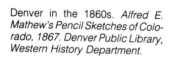

Denver in the 1860s. *Alfred E. Mathew's Pencil Sketches of Colorado, 1867. Denver Public Library, Western History Department.*

and luxurious private boxes where beer sold for a dollar a bottle but a free midnight snack of roast pork, venison, and breast of prairie hen was available. The gambling room sported a huge gas chandelier which radiated light from 500 glass prisms over twenty-five spiffy dealers. Vaudeville acts were booked from the East, headed by the popular Eddie Foy and Lottie Rogers, the "Leadville Nightingale." Masterson operated the Palace for over two years, until a vigorous reform movement swept the city in the early nineties. When the Palace was proclaimed an evil "death-trap to young men [and] a foul den of vice and corruption" by local crusaders, Bat chose to avoid trouble and sold out. He left Denver for the new silver camp of Creede, Colorado, where he took a job as manager of another gambling operation.

Masterson returned to Denver in 1897 and provided the city with some excitement during the municipal elections that spring. Bat had been hired as a special deputy to keep order at the polls. At a polling booth at 18th and Larimer Streets, it was reported that several challengers had been kicked out by supporters of one of the candidates for alderman, James Doyle. Bat arrived on the scene and announced that no ballots would be counted until the challenges were resolved. The election judges ignored Bat and kept counting. Bat drew his gun, as did a local city detective, Tim Conners, a Doyle backer. Bat was the quicker, and suddenly Conners had a change of heart (some say Bat's bullet knocked Conners's pistol from his hand). A bystander was hit by the ricocheting slug but was not seriously injured. It was the last time Bat would fire a gun in anger.

During this period Bat and his wife, Emma, lived at 1825 Curtis Street.

A rather far-fetched story has been handed down regarding Masterson's departure from Denver for good in 1902. According to the tale, taken from an unpublished manuscript written by a Denver district attorney, Harry Lindsley, Bat had become boozy and troublesome after another election day incident in which he was challenged as a voter. Denver police wanted him out of town but wanted it done peacefully. They called on an old friend of Bat's, Jim Marshall, then a law officer in Cripple Creek. Bat learned that Marshall was on his way and sent word that he would meet him at a certain barber shop. Bat was there but Marshall did not show up. Later, while Bat was having a drink at his favorite morning saloon, Marshall walked in and drew his gun on his old friend. What followed resembles a classic Hollywood western script.

"Does this mean a killing, Jim?" said Bat.

"Depends on whether you are reasonable, Bat," Marshall replied.

"Meaning just what?"

"Meaning that it is for you to say. Denver is too big a town for you to hurrah, Bat. Time for you to move on." Marshall then proposed that Bat be on a train that afternoon.

"Reckon so," Bat replied.

The incident might have been true, but if so, it suffers from a lack of supporting witnesses.

An 1890 bawdy house. One of the attractions that drew lonely outlaws to Denver. *Denver Public Library, Western History Department.*

## Georgetown
### Clear Creek County

Georgetown was noted for its renowned Hotel de Paris, built in 1875 by a moody Frenchman, Louis Dupuy, who strived to bring elegance to a spartan mining town. Dupuy's guests slept in solid walnut beds, washed in marble-topped basins fitted with hot and cold faucets, and dined on sparkling white linen and Haviland china. Down the street was Charlie Utter's rooming house, hardly elegant, but that is where Wild Bill Hickok stayed in 1872.

Wild Bill gravitated toward the action, and in the early seventies it appeared that Georgetown would be an action town. The gold rush of the 1860s had faded, but then silver took hold. The town flourished but never turned wild. Whiskey flowed, but blood did not. Hickock spent most of his time at the poker tables and was in no gunfights. Either the stakes were not high enough, or he was just plain bored. For whatever reason he left after six weeks. Georgetown's first and last gunfighter had come and gone and did not leave a mark.

Obsessed with protecting their town from fire, Georgetown residents established some of the best hook and ladder companies in Colorado. As a result the buildings today are much the same as they were in the gold and silver rush days—a delight to visit. Take Interstate 70 west out of Denver. Georgetown is about half way to Vail, at the second exit after Idaho Springs.

## Glenwood Springs
### Garfield County

Glenwood Springs, just off Interstate 70 between Denver and Grand Junction, was the home of the notorious Doc Holliday during his last illness. Doc had been plagued with what was probably tuberculosis, or "galloping consumption" as they called it then. After a miserable spring in Leadville and Denver, during which his health failed rapidly, Doc sought the hot springs of Colorado's newest and most popular health resort. He checked into the luxurious Glenwood Hotel in May 1887 to take the steamy cure. But Doc's condition was too advanced to be helped by mineral waters. As summer approached he spent more and more time in his room. He lingered until fall, the end coming on November 8.

According to his obituary, Doc was only thirty-six years of age, but "he looked like a man well advanced in years, for his hair was silvered and his form emaciated and bent." Cursed by liquor and an ornery disposition during most of his life, Doc was well-liked by few people who crossed his path. But apparently approaching death mellowed him. He was described as "quiet and gentlemanly," and showed "fortitude and patience" that "made him many friends" during his final days.

He was buried in Linwood, the local cemetery. His tombstone is inscribed, "He died in bed."

## The Higgins Ranch
### Park County

The "Higgins Ranch" lies about eighteen miles southwest of Lake George, which is on US 24 west of Colorado Springs, just across the line in Park County. The ranch is not much different from hundreds of others in the mountains of central Colorado, with one exception: every now and then the land turns up a cache of outlaw booty.

It began near the turn of the century. One day one of the owners stumbled across an old shack in the rugged northern section of the valley near the base of a large cliff. Inside he found a chest, the kind used by stage and express companies for hauling gold and silver. There was no treasure inside; instead, it contained food. Several months later the Higgins family noticed riders coming in and out of the area. One day shortly thereafter a stranger appeared at the Higgins's door. He had been shot and was near death. He told the Higginses that he was part of a gang of outlaws who had used the shack for a hideout. He added that he was now the only survivor of the bunch and that he had received his wounds during a recent holdup. Before he died he told the Higginses that there was much loot hidden near the shack and in the surrounding bluffs. On searching the area the Higginses did find a cache, a shirt stuffed in a crevice in the cliff. Inside were coins and jewelry. A month later a bucket of coins was found buried in the ground near where the Higginses were digging post holes. Later two more caches were discovered.

Apparently nothing more was found. In 1957 the last of the Higgins clan sold the property and moved to California. In the 1970s a well-known treasure hunter heard the story and searched the area. It is believed that he found still another cache, suspended in the limbs of a thick pine tree.

By now the area has probably been picked clean—or has it?

## Julesburg
### Sedgwick County

Julesburg, in the northeastern corner of the state, was the home of Jack Slade, possibly Colorado's most notorious outlaw. Slade may have been overrated as a desperado. As with so many colorful characters, fact gave way to legend early. Although described by some as a hard-nosed killer, scant evidence has been turned up that he was more than a part-time robber and a troublesome drunk. Mark Twain even once described him as "friendly" and "gentle-spoken." He did, however, leave his mark on Julesburg.

The Jack Slade–Jules Beni (sometimes called Reni, or René) story has been told and retold. It is generally agreed that Jules Beni, who is credited with establishing Julesburg as a trading post in the 1850s, was in charge of the local stage line. Sometime in the early 1860s, when word spread to company officials that Beni was involved in thefts and robberies on his own line, Jack Slade (whose real name was Joseph Alfred Slade), an allegedly tough character from Illinois, was sent to replace him. On a trip out to Beni's ranch to gather up horses and mules belonging to the company, Slade made the mistake of turning his back on Beni and Jules put a bullet in him. Here the accounts vary, but apparently Beni pumped several more slugs into Slade, and then topped it off with a blast from a shotgun. How badly Slade was injured is not known, but Beni assumed he was dead. Another employee of the stage line, who had accompanied Slade out to the ranch, threw his bleeding body over his saddle and took him back to Julesburg.

Somehow Slade survived, and after recuperating back in Illinois, he returned to Julesburg and to his job with the stage line. Beni was still around and apparently still stealing from the company. Slade made another call on him and this time did not turn his back. Details of this fight are also sketchy, but most agree that Beni's lifeless body was found tied to a corral post with the ears cut off. It is said that Slade carried one of them for years, occasionally pulling it out and slapping it on a bar to show fellow customers, sometimes in return for free drinks.

Eventually Slade's taste for liquor got the best of him, and he lost his job with the stage line. He drifted around, finally settling in Montana where his troublesome nature got him lynched during the vigilante craze in 1865.

## Lake City
### Hinsdale County

Lake City's population has declined considerably since 1876-77, when it enjoyed a population of 2,500 and nearly 500 buildings and tents. Major outlaws avoided the town, which had little patience with them. For example, when Sheriff E. N. Campbell was killed by robbers in April 1882, the residents, after a day of mourning, marched the killers down Silver Street and hanged them from a crossbeam of the bridge over Hanson Creek. The next morning the schoolchildren in town were taken down to see the bodies as an object lesson. As an afterthought, a hastily summoned "grand jury" found that the culprits "came to their deaths at the hands of unknown parties."

Wyatt Earp found Lake City saloons a bad place to cheat at cards in September 1884. Wyatt was accused of bending a few rules of the game during a poker marathon. A fight started, and Wyatt picked up a bullet in the arm.

Lake City is most remembered for a chap named Alfred Packer. Hired to guide a party of goldseekers, Packer was convicted in 1874 of killing and eating his companions after they became lost in a winter storm.

The town can be visited today and is popular with vacationers because of nearby Lake San Cristobal, from which the community got its name. If you are out that way, take US 50 six miles west of Gunnison, then head south on State Highway 149 and be prepared for a spectacular sixty-mile drive.

## Las Animas
### Bent County

Las Animas is in southeastern Colorado on US 50, midway between Pueblo and the Kansas state line. On December 21, 1876, the Olympic Dance Hall at Las Animas was the scene of a shootout between Texas gunslinger Clay Allison and Charles Faber, a deputy sheriff and local constable. Allison and his brother, John, were causing a disturbance at the dance hall. Both probably drunk, they were accused of being belligerent and stepping on the toes of other dancers. Seeing trouble coming, Faber had asked the two Texans to check their guns while in town, but they refused. Faber left, got a shotgun, and appointed two special deputies to back him up. When he returned to the Olympic, Clay Allison was standing at the bar with his back to the door, and John was on the dance floor. As Faber entered, someone shouted "Look out!" Thinking John was going for his gun, and possibly mistaking him for Clay who had a widespread reputation as a killer, Faber fired, striking John in the chest and shoulder. As his brother went down, Clay whipped out his gun and went after Faber. Witnesses say he got off four shots. One tore into Faber's chest near the heart, and he died instantly. As Faber fell, the other barrel of the shotgun discharged, sending another load of buckshot into the helpless John Allison.

Faber's special deputies, who had been watching from the door, had seen enough and turned and ran. Clay rushed to the door and emptied his gun into the darkness. Then, thinking his brother was dying, he dragged Faber's lifeless body over to where John lay to show him that he had evened the score. But John recovered, and no witnesses could be found that would testify that Clay had not shot in self defense. Charges against him were dropped, and he was released.

## Leadville
### Lake County

Leadville lies thirty miles south of Vail on US 24. During its boom period from the late 1870s to the early

Leadville street in the late 1870s. *Denver Public Library, Western History Department.*

1890s, many of the well-known outlaws passed through town, and like many Colorado mining camps, it suffered at the hands of scores of nameless criminals. The following is a description of one visitor's evening in Leadville, probably in the spring or summer of 1879.

> . . . Footpads were to be found lurking in every corner, lying in wait for belated business men or wealthy debauchers on their way home. The ominous command, "Hold up your hands," accompanied by the click of a pistol, was heard almost nightly, and the newspaper reporter who failed to secure one or more hold-ups during his daily rounds, felt that he had failed in one of the duties of his position. Men were robbed within the shadows of their own doors; stripped of their valuables in their own bed-chambers, whither they had been followed by daring criminals; and no part of the city was so well guarded as to be safe from the attempts of the rogues whom success had emboldened. Men whose duties compelled them to be out late at night, walked with naked pistols in their hands, and not infrequently with a second in reserve, taking the middle of the street to avoid being ambushed from dark corners. Every object, the exact nature of which was unknown, was critically scrutinized, and when two men chanced to meet, a wide berth was given by each. No man who could help it went out after dark alone. When men connected with the mines were caught in town at night, they either stopped at a hotel or went to their quarters in squads for mutual protection. One young man, a confidential employee of a prominent company, in a fit of drunken bravado, exhibited a large roll of bills in one of the variety theaters. A few minutes afterward he started for his room; on turning the first corner, a crowded thoroughfare with the lights from saloons making the locality as light as day, he received a blow from a bludgeon, and two hours later awoke to consciousness, lying in the gutter in which he had fallen, and discovered that his gold watch and a thousand dollars of his own and company's money had been taken from him. The next day he was sent to his Eastern home in disgrace. A gentleman who had been visiting a sick friend in a locality within a short distance of Harrison Avenue, left the house only to return in a few minutes with the astounding intelligence that he had been held up and robbed within ten yards of his door. Another gentleman left a well known saloon to go to his room but a short distance away, and was robbed before half the distance had been accomplished, though he was armed at the time. It seemed as if the city was given up to the criminal classes, and the authorities were powerless to prevent it. The charge was frequently made that the police were in league with the robbers, and many circumstances seemed to give the charge color.

The bloodiest night in Leadville's history occurred on May 8, 1879, and was known as the "Night Hell Let Loose." The evening's events were reported the next day in the *Carbonate Chronicle* under these separate headlines: "Murderous Attack upon Kokomo Freighter," "Assault and Robbery on Harrison Avenue," "A Tenderfoot Garroted on Capitol Hill," "Daring Robbery of a Man at the Comique," and "Arrest of a Notorious Confidence Man."

The town continued to be harassed by toughs through the fall. The climax came in November through a means becoming alarmingly common in the West: masks and ropes. The victims' names were Frodsham and Stewart. The former was a Wyoming desperado who specialized

Leadville saloon during the town's heyday. *Denver Public Library, Western History Department.*

in "lot jumping," and the latter was a thief and mugger. Pinned to Frodsham's body was this warning: "Notice to all thieves, bunko steerers, footpads, thieves [sic] and chronic bondsmen for the same, and sympathizers for the above class of criminals: This is our commencement, and this shall be your fates. We mean business, and let this be your last warning . . . Vigilantes' Committee. We are 700 strong."

They say nearly 400 "undesirables" left Leadville within twenty-four hours after the lynchings.

Leadville was a haven for the knights of the green cloth. As it prospered the town became a leading gambling center of the West, where it was not uncommon for $1,000 to change hands on one turn of a faro card. Of the three top gambling towns of the period, Dodge City, Leadville, and Deadwood, most agree that Leadville took the prize for the number of games running and the stakes involved.

The dapper gambler-gunman Luke Short is believed to have got his start in both professions in Leadville. Luke drifted into town in 1879. Up to then he had made his living peddling whiskey to Indians and scouting for the army. In Leadville he developed a proficiency at the tables and at whipping out his gun—much to the dismay of another gambler named Brown whose draw one night on Harrison Avenue was slightly slower than Short's and who, as a result, lost part of his cheek.

Bat Masterson almost settled in Leadville in 1880 after his defeat for re-election as Ford County sheriff in Kansas. Several of Leadville's gambling houses wanted Bat as a combined dealer-bouncer and reportedly offered him a handsome salary, but Bat's interests lay elsewhere.

In 1883 Doc Holliday drifted to Leadville. It was a bad choice for Doc, whose lung problem had worsened. He needed a much healthier climate than an altitude of 10,000 feet and long winters, but Doc was a gambler, and Leadville offered what he excelled at. Almost from the day he arrived, Doc faced trouble from old enemies. First he renewed a feud with Johnny Tyler, a tinhorn he had embarrased in a showdown back in Tombstone; later, he tangled with a friend of Tyler's, Billy Allen, who tried to sucker him into a fist fight. The frail dentist was too smart to go at it hand-to-hand with the brawny Allen, but one evening in August 1884 at Hyman's saloon on Harrison Avenue, Billy pushed Doc too far, and he put a bullet through Allen's right arm. Doc was not a particularly good shot, and he probably was trying to kill Billy, but a bystander grabbed him and prevented him from finishing the job. Doc had to stand trial, but was acquitted on a plea of self-defense. It was the ailing dentist's last gunfight (see *Glenwood Springs, Colorado*).

Leadville also spawned the dangerous Jim McKinney, called by some California's last great outlaw. McKinney moved to Leadville in 1878 with his family. His father, Andrew, was a teamster, and the family lived at 506 Eighth Street. According to local legend, Jim engaged in his first gunfight while in Leadville, but the details have been lost to history. Jim left town around 1880, possibly because of the shootout, and settled near Visalia, California.*

# Meeker
## Rio Blanco County

As the crow flies, Meeker lies only seventy-five miles from Colorado's notorious outlaw hideout, Brown's Park. But the big-name desperados did not frequent the town. In outlaw annals, Meeker's claim to fame stems from a bungled bank robbery—probably the most bungled in Colorado frontier history.

The date was October 13, 1896. The 13th was on a Tuesday that month, but for the trio of would-be robbers who tried to hold up the Bank of Meeker, it was the unluckiest day they would ever spend. Their plan was fairly sound: in traditional "Wild Bunch" fashion they even posted a relay of fresh horses outside of town. But they would never get a chance to use them.

The three men walked into the Hugus & Company store, adjacent to the bank, about midafternoon. One of the three, Jim Shirley, walked with a slight limp. A second, an older man named George Law, was powerfully built and had reddish hair and mustache. The third man was young, clean shaven, and in his early twenties. He was known only as "The Kid."

These three men may have been experienced bank robbers, but that day they seemed to do everything wrong. George Law reached through the teller's cage with his pistol to frighten the assistant cashier, David Smith, and the gun went off. Not once, but twice! Merchants along Main Street heard the shots and ran for their own guns. With half the town alerted, the trio should have turned and ran, but Shirley, apparently the leader, insisted they stay and collect the money.

When a sack of money was finally produced from the vault, the robbers grabbed three hostages and backed out the door. When they reached the street they found it deserted—a sure sign of trouble. Suddenly Shirley spotted a man with a rifle peering from behind the grain warehouse next door, and he dropped him with a bullet in the chest. This panicked the hostages and they broke and ran. Once their fellow townsmen were safely out of the field of fire, the citizens of Meeker opened up on the hapless bandits. Shirley went down first with a slug in the lung. "The Kid" took five hits and tumbled off the sidewalk into a patch of weeds. George Law made a run for it, but after only a few steps he fell with a bullet in the back and another in the leg. When the smoke cleared, Shirley and "The Kid" were dead. Law lived long enough to suffer even further humiliation. In the excitement, the robbers forgot to pick up the money sack. It still lay on the floor of the Hugus & Company store, just outside the door to the bank office.

## Park County

Park County lies between Leadville and Denver. In 1863 and 1864 it was the scene of operations of the Jim Reynolds gang, a notorious band of robbers who preyed on gold-carrying stages. Most of the robberies took place along what is now US 295.

One of the first holdups occurred near Bailey. The bandits reportedly got $45,000 in gold and cash, none of which was ever recovered. The gang's two main hideouts were near Kenosha Pass and on Elk Creek, about four miles from Shaffer's Crossing. According to local legend, somewhere in these mountainous areas may be hidden the bulk of the stolen loot, estimated at as much as $100,000 in cash and an undetermined amount of gold (by today's standards, perhaps as much as $500,000).

About eleven miles northwest of Bailey, near the present town of Grant, lies the buried remains of one of the gang members, believed to be a man named Showalter. He was killed by a posse in the fall of 1864. The posse was on the gang's trail following a robbery near Kenosha Pass. From the site of the grave the gang was trailed up Geneva Creek, then east over the divide between Mount Logan and Mount Rosalie to the head of Deer Creek. After riding down Deer Creek for about seven miles, the outlaws crossed to South Elk Creek, which they followed for three or four miles to the north branch. About half a mile up North Elk they made camp in a large cave. Here the posse caught up with them again. Some of the outlaws were killed, and some may have escaped. Four, including Reynolds, were captured. No loot was found.

The outlaws were taken to Denver where the same posse was deputized to take them on to Fort Lyons, east of Pueblo, for trial. But the captives never made it. South of Denver, near Castle Rock, all four were apparently lined up and shot, possibly in an attempt to force them to tell where the loot was hidden.

Stories persist to this day about the Reynold gang's treasure. In 1939 a local man, Vernon Crow, may have found one of the gang's camps; he was certain that he found the bones of one of the outlaws. He also found what may have been a marker designed to locate the loot—a dagger stuck in a tree. Crow looked for the gold for a while but finally gave up. It is rumored that another man, a Texas lawman, was told the location of the treasure by a surviving gang member. According to the rumor this Texan visited the area for a while, then left, telling several persons that he found nothing. But someone reportedly checked on him back in Texas and learned that he had retired from the law enforcement business a wealthy man. This story has not discouraged treasure hunters, however. The land is now part of Pike National Forest.

## Pueblo
### Pueblo County

In June 1879 Pueblo was the scene of a major battle between the Santa Fe and the Denver & Rio Grande railroads in what has become known as the "Royal Gorge War." Both railroads wanted the lucrative route through the Royal Gorge to ore-rich Leadville. The battles were fought both in the courts and in the gorge, where the right to lay rails was claimed by both railroads.

By 1879 the situation had become unbelievably complicated. Weakened financially from the struggle, the Denver & Rio Grande had been pressured into an attempted compromise by its stockholders and had been forced to lease its line to the larger railroad. But in March the fiery D&RG president, General William Palmer, declared the lease broken and demanded his railroad back. Both companies put out a call for gunfighters, and on June 11 the forces met at Pueblo. The Santa Fe contingent barricaded themselves in the telegraph office and roundhouse. Bolstered by hired guns from Dodge City, including Bat Masterson, Ben Thompson, and probably Doc Holliday, the defenders braced for a seige. The Denver & Rio Grande group, armed with a state court order calling for the return of all track and equipment and supported by the local sheriff and 100 special deputies (drawn mainly from D&RG workers), marched first on the telegraph office. Shots were fired and a Dodge City volunteer, Harry Jenkins, fell dead. The deputies stormed the building, a free-for-all erupted, and the outnumbered Santa Fe forces surrendered.

At the roundhouse, however, the numbers were closer to even. According to most accounts, the Santa Fe group, led either by Masterson or Thompson, had stolen a cannon from the state armory and trained it on the attackers. It looked like a standoff, and by afternoon the two sides agreed to talk. After a brief meeting between Masterson and D&RG officials, Bat ordered his forces to turn over the roundhouse.

Masterson later received much criticism for surrendering. There were rumors that he and his men were paid to call its quits. One version has the payoff sum as high as $25,000. More likely, Bat, who was then sheriff of Ford County, Kansas, accepted the court order as proof the D&RG was entitled to have its railroad back.

Pueblo, Colorado. *Charles C. Goodhall Collection.*

# Rifle
## Garfield County

Following an assault on a Denver & Rio Grande express car near Parachute, Colorado, on June 7, 1904, the outlaws were trailed east to near Rifle where they were cornered in a gully. During the ensuing gunbattle, one of the robbers was heard to cry out "I'm hard hit and going to cash in quick . . . you go on." At dawn the posse rushed the gully and found a lone dead outlaw; he had a revolver in his hand and two bullet wounds, one apparently self-inflicted. He was tentatively identified as Tap Duncan, a local cowboy.

But as more lawmen arrived on the scene, word spread that the body might very well be that of the notorious Harvey Logan, alias "Kid Curry" of the Wyoming Wild Bunch. The dead man had a scar on his right arm said to be identical to one Logan carried. The Pinkerton office in Denver requested a photograph of the body. On examining it, Pinkerton superintendent James McParland declared the body was indeed that of Logan. But several other lawmen, some of who claimed they once knew Logan, would not accept this finding. Agency head William Pinkerton sent one of his special agents, Lowell Spence, to have the body exhumed and examined again. Spence had become quite familiar with Logan while the outlaw was confined to a jail in Tennessee two years earlier. He stated positively that the man was Logan. This appeared to settle it, but then William T. Canada, Chief of Special Agents of the Union Pacific Railroad, released a statement that he also knew Logan and he was just as positive that it was not Logan's body.

The Pinkerton agency then sent the photographs to Knoxville, Tennessee, for viewing by law officers who had known Logan while he was confined to jail there. Several of these officers confirmed that the pictures were of Logan. But the matter was still not settled. Three years later, in an address before a convention of police chiefs at Jamestown, Virginia, William Pinkerton let it slip that Logan was still at large.

What happened to Logan is still in question. Some say he later joined Butch Cassidy and Harry Longabaugh (the Sundance Kid) in South America. The Logan issue is still a fertile area for outlaw researchers.

Rifle lies just off Interstate 70 about sixty-five miles east of Grand Junction.

## Routt County

It is believed that killer-for-hire Tom Horn made at least two business trips to Routt County in 1900. In July of that year they say he drifted into the Cold Springs Mountain area under the alias "James Hicks" looking for a rustler named Matt Rash. He found Rash's cabin and waited outside with his rifle. When Rash stepped out the door for an after-supper smoke, Horn put three bullets in him. Rash crawled back inside and made it to his cot, where he dipped his finger in his own blood and tried to write a message on the back of an envelope. He died before he could make any legible marks.

Three months later, on October 3, Horn returned. This time his target was Isom Dart, another suspected rustler. Again Horn posed as James Hicks, and again he hid outside his victim's cabin. Dart died with a 30-30 slug in his head.

## Silverton
### San Juan County

Dodge City lawman Bat Masterson served as a special city marshal in Silverton during the mid-1880s. Silver was king and the town was raw and rough. Following the killing of town marshal Clayton Ogsbury by a pair of Durango toughs and the subsequent hanging of an innocent citizen by an enraged mob, the town council called on Masterson for help. Bat issued a warning that Silverton was no longer a welcome place for troublemakers. Thanks to his reputation, the warning was sufficient.

Silverton, on US 550 between Montrose and Durango, is a delight for Old West buffs. The false-front stores of Blair Street, which during the bonanza days sported twenty-four-hour pleasure palaces, have been restored with frontier flavor and cater to the tourist well.

## The Spanish Peaks
### Huerfano County

Over the years a story has persisted that south of Walsenburg, somewhere in the vicinity of the twin Spanish Peaks, lies buried some more of the "lost gold of the Reynolds gang" (see *Park County*). Jim Reynolds and his brother, John, were Texans who migrated to Colorado around 1862, where they formed a gang and robbed stages. During the Civil War the brothers got caught up in the cause of the South and recruited frontier toughs to ride thinly disguised as Confederate guerrillas. One of their early raids was on a gold shipment bound from Mexico to Santa Fe. They made off with $60,000 in newly minted gold coins and headed for the mountains of Huerfano County. On the way, however, an argument arose over disposition of the loot. According to one version, the Reynolds brothers wanted to bury the gold temporarily until it could be turned over to the Confederates. Other members of the gang were not so enthusiastic about the cause and wanted the loot divided up on the spot. The gang split into two groups. The dissenters apparently took their shares, and those who sided with the Reynolds brothers rode on to somewhere in the vicinity of the Spanish Peaks, where they buried their portion.

## Steamboat Springs
### Routt County

Steamboat Springs is the center of a popular winter resort area in northwestern Colorado. The town lies on US 40 about forty miles east of Craig. Legend has it that in 1898, shortly after the onset of the Spanish-American War, the town was the scene of a huge gathering of outlaws, called possibly by Butch Cassidy, to discuss an en masse enlistment in the United States Army, perhaps with the intention of working out some form of amnesty with the authorities. One source suggests that there were at least fifty desperados in attendance and that when word of the convention leaked out, it "was a situation to worry the most lymphatic peace officers." And as for the edgy express companies, "there was not one of their cars went through that did not carry two or more heavily armed guards in addition to the messenger." If such a meeting took place, it probably was responsible for the turn-of-the-century rumor that western outlaws were planning to unite and form a "train robbers' syndicate" for wholesale ravishment of railroads and express companies.

# Telluride
## San Miguel County

Telluride lies in the San Miguel Valley on State Highway 145 southwest of Ouray. One of the older towns in Colorado, it was originally called Columbia. The name Telluride is said to be a corruption of the word "tellurium," a mineral used for years in ceramics and later to alloy stainless steel and lead. But some old timers around the area will tell you that the name stems from the phrase, "To hell you ride."

Butch Cassidy called Telluride home in 1884, when he was about eighteen. Charged with rustling steers back home in Utah (see *Circleville*), Butch fled eastward, stopping for a while in Telluride to work at the mines driving a mule train. While there, Butch ran afoul of the law over a dispute with a rancher concerning the ownership of a certain horse. The boy spent a few days in jail in Montrose until his father came to clear things up. On his release, Butch left the mines for work on the range.

It is believed Cassidy returned to Telluride in June 1889 with two or three fellow outlaws (the reports differ) to relieve the San Miguel Valley Bank of about $20,000. The robbers apparently hung around the saloons near the bank until they saw the cashier step out to do some collecting. This left only a clerk on duty. According to a June 27 report in the *Rocky Mountain News*, as the clerk "was bending over the desk examining the check [given to him by one of the robbers] this party grabbed him around the neck, pulling his face down on the desk, at the same time admonishing the surprised official to keep quiet on pain of instant death." Scooping up the money, the robbers raced out the door. "When they had ridden a couple of blocks they spurred their horses into a gallop, gave a yell, discharged their revolvers and dashed away."

The bandits rode down the San Miguel Valley, then over to Keystone Hill where they had stashed a fresh relay of horses. A hastily formed posse nearly caught up with them a few miles on, but several warning shots from the outlaws slowed them down. When the lawmen drew near again, the robbers tied a branch to the tail of an extra horse, spooked it, and sent it racing down the narrow trail toward the pursuers. By the time the possemen gained control of their own frightened mounts, the bandits had escaped.

There was some talk later about the Telluride town constable, Jim Clark, being in on the affair and taking a share of the loot to be out of town on the day of the robbery. According to the story, the gang left Clark's share under a log along the trail they had used for their getaway.

# Trinidad
## Las Animas County

As early as 1867 the southeastern Colorado town of Trinidad was plagued by outlaws. The troublesome bunch was a gang from the Oklahoma Panhandle led by "Captain" Bill Coe. The captain and his crew operated out of a stronghold near the New Mexico line just south of Black Mesa,* and Trinidad was their choice for hell-raising, much to the dismay of its peaceful citizens. What little law enforcement there was in Trinidad in those days was no match for the Coe gang, which at its peak numbered nearly fifty. When things got particularly bad, the town sought the help of ranch hands from a spread northeast of town owned by cattleman Charles Goodnight. Goodnight knew Coe and was one of the few men alive whom the outlaw respected. Also, many of Goodnight's wranglers were as tough as Coe's renegades. Rather than have it out with the Goodnight outfit, Coe's bunch would saddle up and ride back to Black Mesa.

Later on, Trinidad seemed to draw a parade of hard cases from Dodge City. By 1882 the town had a sizeable collection of former Dodge saloonkeepers, dealers, and gamblers. To help maintain order, the town council hired Jim Masterson, Bat's brother, to serve on the police force. Jim knew most of the crowd from his days as city marshal in Dodge.

As in Dodge City, gunfights frequently erupted over cards. A good example was the shootout between Cock-eyed Frank Loving and John Allen on April 16, 1882. Loving had a reputation as a cool customer in a show-down and already had at least one killing to his credit during a similar fracas three years earlier back in Kansas.

This fight, however, which began in the Imperial Saloon and ended in Hammond's Hardware Store, went to Allen. Following the killing a Denver newspaper labeled the town "Turbulent Trinidad." Gunfights soon became so frequent that the Trinidad *Daily News* announced that it was going to play them down to keep the town from developing an even worse reputation.

In 1882 Bat Masterson himself was called in to try to calm things down, but it did not help. In August there was even a fatal battle between two peace officers. The feud arose over a jail break. The jail was managed by the county, and following the escape the sheriff's office received a scathing attack by Olney Newell, editor of the Trinidad *Daily News*. Fiery M. B. McGraw, Las Animas County undersheriff, retaliated with an attack published in the rival Trinidad *Democrat*. After another blast by Newell, McGraw realized that somebody was feeding the editor with inside information—it turned out to be a Trinidad police officer, George Goodell, whom McGraw had once fired from the county force. McGraw then went to work on Goodell, charging in print that the officer was a pimp and his wife a prostitute. As expected, the next encounter between the two was in the street. On August 19 in front of Jaffa's Opera House, McGraw slapped Goodell's face and both men went for their guns. Goodell was quicker and his shot tore into McGraw's right arm. Although McGraw dropped his gun, Goodell continued firing, putting three more slugs in him, until another deputy sheriff grabbed his gun. But Goodell, mad with rage, broke loose, picked up McGraw's pistol, and pumped two more bullets into his helpless victim. Somehow McGraw lived two days with six holes in him. At the coroner's inquest, Goodell was exonerated, following a finding that he had not killed McGraw "with felonious intent."

That same month the lobby of Trinidad's Armijo Hotel was almost the scene of what might have become Colorado's most famous shootout. Pat Garrett, who a year earlier had gunned down the notorious Billy the Kid (see *Fort Sumner, New Mexico*), came face to face with Joe Antrim, Billy's grim and seemingly revengeful brother. Antrim, while clearly no match for Garrett in a fair gunfight, was not necessarily the kind to invite a fair fight. Humorless and tight-lipped, Joe Antrim lacked the color of his famous outlaw brother, but there was no reason to believe he could not be as deadly. Yet, if he ever notched his gun there was no record of it. Most of his life was spent as a faro dealer in the shadowy districts of Denver. He had never tasted fame as Billy had, but on that day in Trinidad he had his chance. However, the two men merely talked quietly for several hours and at the end arose and shook hands. Later

Trinidad, Colorado. *Colorado Historical Society.*

Antrim told a reporter that he now understood why Garrett did what he did. A confrontation that might have been talked about for years passed virtually unnoticed.

During Bat Masterson's tour as city marshal, the office was changed from appointive to elective. In 1883 he had to run for the job and was defeated in a landslide by an assistant, Lou Kreeger, a home town candidate—no doubt a message to Bat that he had not accomplished what had been expected of him.

## Virginia Dale
### Larimer County

Legend has it that this tiny roadstop on US 287 just south of the Wyoming line was founded by the notorious Jack Slade shortly after he left Julesburg, Colorado,* where he had killed the founder of that town, Jules Beni. According to the story, Slade had married a comely woman named Virginia Maria and opened a stage division at this site, naming it after his wife. In addition to the stage business, Slade reportedly launched a long-range horse stealing and stage robbing operation throughout northern Colorado and southern Wyoming. According to one source, Slade and his men accidentally killed a Frenchman named Savoie and his wife while chasing a fellow horse thief near Fort Bridger, Wyoming. The thief, said to be Mexican or Spanish, was thought to be hiding in the Savoie home, and Slade had it burned down. The Savoies' two small children escaped the fire, but one, a girl, died from exposure. Slade and his wife took in the other child, a boy named Jimmy, and raised him as their own.

## Wray
### Yuma County

Wray, at the junction of US 34 and US 385 in eastern Colorado, has been mentioned as the boyhood home of William Ellsworth (Elzy) Lay, member of the Wyoming Wild Bunch. Lay, who often rode under the name William McGinnis, may have been the gang member closest to Butch Cassidy. Butch's sister, Lulu Parker Betenson, claimed that most of the episodes in the popular 1969 motion picture *Butch Cassidy and the Sundance Kid* actually involved Elzy Lay rather than Sundance (Harry Longabaugh), but, said Mrs. Betenson, "who would go to a movie entitled *Butch Cassidy and Elzy Lay*?"

Serious Western buffs interested in the career of this outlaw might do well to spend some time probing around the town of Wray.

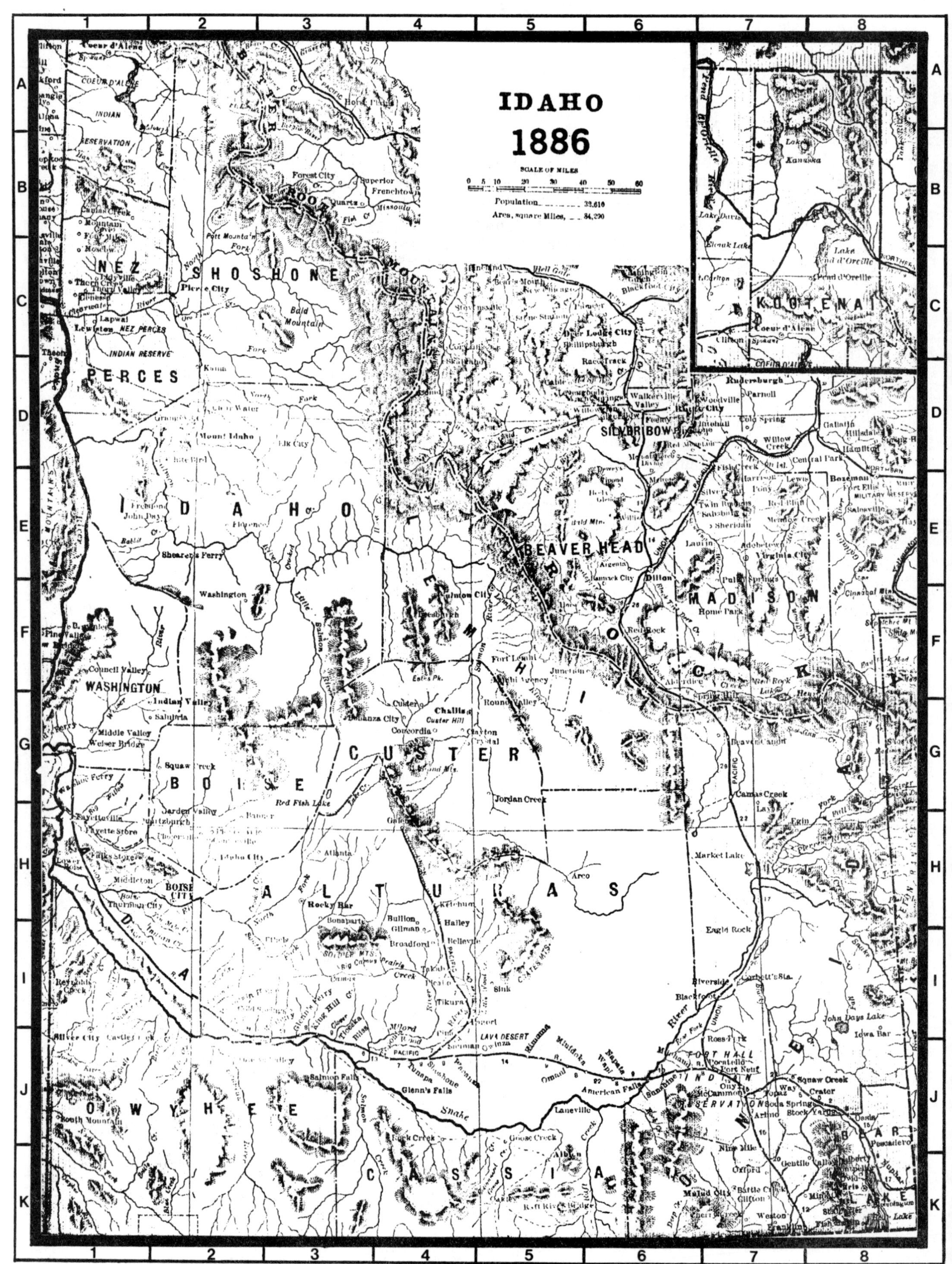
IDAHO
1886
SCALE OF MILES
Population 32,610
Area, square Miles, 84,290
NEZ PERCES
SHOSHONE
IDAHO
WASHINGTON
BOISE
CUSTER
LEMHI
ALTURAS
ADA
OWYHEE
CASSIA
ONEIDA
BEAR LAKE
KOOTENAI
BEAVER HEAD
MADISON
SILVER BOW
ROCKY
BITTER ROOT MOUNTAINS
LAVA DESERT
FORT HALL INDIAN RESERVATION
Lewiston
Boise City
Hailey
Challis
Blackfoot
Eagle Rock
Market Lake
Dillon
Deer Lodge City
Mount Idaho
Washington
Rocky Bar
Silver City
Salmon Falls
Glenn's Ferry
American Falls
Arco
Camas Creek
Bozeman
Snake

Idaho 1886

# IDAHO

## Boise
### Boise County

In the early 1860s Boise fell victim to the same riff-raff who plagued most of the mining country of the northwest. Describing the situation in 1864, a local pioneer wrote, "Boise contained at that time a spendid assortment of murderers, robbers and tinhorn gamblers . . . offscourings of all the abandoned and worn-out mining camps of the territory." The worst of the bunch were the Updyke and Dixon gangs, both of which terrorized the area from 1863 to 1866. In 1866 a vigilante group was formed. A short time later gang leader Dave Updyke was found hanging in a Boise shed. A note pinned to his body read "Dave Updyke, the aider of murderers and horse thieves." The note was signed "XXX", the mark of the vigilantes. James Dixon was next. On his body was pinned a list of his most vicious crimes.

But the lawlessness did not stop; new outlaws merely stepped in to take up the slack. Typical, and perhaps most often remembered by Idaho chroniclers, is the 1880 robbery of the Salisbury, Gilmore and Company stage down river from Boise at Glenn's Snake River Ferry. Prior to the stage's arrival two bandits jumped the station hostler as he hung out his lantern. They bound and gagged him and threw him into the stable. When the stage pulled up they ordered the driver and single passenger down and proceeded to empty the Wells Fargo express box and mail bags. Their mistake, however, was to operate too closely to the lighted station. The driver and passengers gave excellent descriptions of the road agents to Wells Fargo officials, and a week later they were dragged before the federal judge at Boise. Justice was swift and harsh: life in the penitentiary.

## Florence
### Idaho County

Florence is a ghost town today, though it was once a thriving gold camp. In the 1860s a pan of Florence gravel brought $500. In the spring of 1862 it is said gold dust taken from this "superficially rich" camp was weighed by the pound. A single placer miner supposedly "rocked out" $4,600 in one day.

Early cabin in Boise City. *J. B. Rice Collection.*

Florence, Idaho. *Idaho Historical Society.*

Like most gold camps, Florence drew its share of undesirables. The notorious Montana outlaw-sheriff Henry Plummer once operated in the area, as did a renegade known as Cherokee Bob, who was killed in the town and lies beneath a deteriorating wooden marker in the Florence cemetery. The details on this outlaw are sketchy. Some say he was once part of a Montana gang of thieves and was wanted for murdering two soldiers in Walla Walla, Washington.

The bones of Florence lie on the eastern edge of the Gospel Hump Wilderness Area. The old road north to Lewiston, which winds today through Mount Idaho as State Road 14, was where robbers most often did their plundering. Today Florence has dropped off the maps. One should check locally before trying to reach the town.

## Fort Hall
### Bingham County

Near Fort Hall, which lies today just off Interstate 15 between Idaho Falls and Pocatello, is the site of the most tragic stage robbery in Idaho history. In July 1865 six or seven armed bandits rushed out of the sagebrush to halt a southbound stage driven by a veteran driver named Frank Williams. In and on the coach were eight passengers, nearly all of whom foolishly opened fire on the would-be robbers. The bandits, some of whom carried shotguns, returned the fire, and the passengers fell like clay targets. Four were killed outright and Williams was wounded. Two managed to escape into the underbrush. One passenger, a man named William Carpenter, lay on the floor of the coach in the midst of his dead comrades. He was uninjured, but he was so covered with the blood of his fellow passengers, the bandits assumed he was finished and honored his pleas to let him die in peace. Another passenger, William Brown, lay beneath him, wounded, but also still alive. Carpenter begged the bandits to spare Brown's life, so he could help him (Carpenter) in his dying moments. The bandits obliged, and busied themselves with opening the treasure box, from which they took $60,000 and rode off.

## Idaho City
### Boise County

Located in the Boise National Forest about forty miles northeast of Boise on State Road 21, Idaho City was once the largest city in the territory and for a while was

Old Fort Hall. *Idaho Historical Society.*

a contender for the territorial capital. The town sprang to life in the early 1860s following the discovery of gold to the north. It was soon the center of a mining area that produced more gold than Alaska.

Desperados moved into the area to prey on newcomers. By 1865 records showed sixty violent deaths without a conviction. Despite the violence, Idaho City grew to become the commercial center of the territory. With a population of nearly 12,000 the town boasted of 250 mercantile establishments by 1867, including four breweries, four theaters, and a "reliable express service to all parts of Boise Basin and the Southern Owyhee District." But reliable as this express service was, it soon fell victim to bandits, especially a gang led by one Yank Kinney. Had this bunch limited their attacks to stages and freight wagons, they might have persisted, but in July 1867 Kinney and his outlaws waylaid four miners who had friends in town. A vigilante committee was formed and warnings posted. Some undesirables left the area, but Kinney and his gang remained. Shortly thereafter, the committee stormed the Idaho City saloons, grabbed Kinney and nine of his comrades, and marched them to a grove of cottonwoods at the edge of town. Yank's last words were "to hell with you," as the noose was slipped over his head. The lynchings did not stop crime in Idaho City, but the trails were no longer dominated by road agents.

Idaho City was the site of the first Idaho Territorial Prison. Built of logs in 1870, the old structures had badly deteriorated until the Sons and Daughters of the Idaho Pioneers stepped in and began a program of restoration. There are now guided walking tours of the prison and grounds. Also of interest is Idaho City's Boot Hill Cemetery, with its intricate iron fencework and intriguing headboards telling of murders and lynchings during the town's reckless years.

Also worth visiting are the nearby ghost towns of Centerville, Placerville, and Pioneerville.

## Lewiston
### Lewis County

Lewiston, in northern Idaho on the Washington line, was a campsite for explorers Lewis and Clark in 1805 and again in 1806. In the early 1860s, when gold was discovered in the nearby mountains, the town served as a supply point for mining camps. It later became the territorial capital.

As Lewiston blossomed, it drew the attention of the notorious Henry Plummer, later to become Montana's most famous outlaw. The story is told that Plummer was in town only a few days when he had his first gunfight. A local miner laughed at Plummer's eastern accent (he was born in Connecticut). Plummer responded with an insult and both men drew their guns. Plummer was the faster and he added another victim to his list, which began in Nevada City, California, in 1857 and ended in Bannack, Montana, in 1863 (see these towns).

Plummer's demise at Bannack was at the end of a vigilance committee's rope. He may have barely avoided the same fate by leaving Lewiston. By 1862 the town began to supplement legal justice with extra-legal means. The following item in a local newspaper in November of that year was typical for the period:

> David English, Nelson Scott and Wm. Peoples who were arrested here a week or two [ago] on charges of highway robbery were hung by the citizens of Lewiston, on Saturday night last. If guilty the retribution was just—that they were guilty there was not the remotest doubt.

In response to the continuing harsh treatment handed out by the vigilantes of the area, a reader of the same newspaper later wrote in complaining about such "dangerous innovations creeping into our system of jurisprudence." Calling himself "a retired road agent," the writer argued that the dashing road agents of the region should be treasured since they add flavor to society and provide the "ladies with their most elegant beaux." Vigilante action, he maintained, should be discouraged. The editor replied to the writer that "You may be a 'retired road agent,' but your retiracy from the valley would make the thing (vigilance committees) appear plausible."

## Montpelier
### Bear Lake County

The town of Montpelier, said to be named after Brigham Young's birthplace in Vermont, was never a hotbed of outlaw activity. In fact, when the bank was robbed there in the summer of 1896, presumably by Butch Cassidy and the Wild Bunch, the town's part-time deputy sheriff, a clerk at nearby Brenan and Davis Mercantile, had no gun and no horse and had to give chase on a high-wheeled bicycle. The deputy, Frederick Cruikshank, had to endure years of jibes from his friends about his unorthodox pursuit of the outlaws. He was forever explaining that he had never intended to catch up with the gang, only to track them far enough to determine their route, so he could send the information to the proper authorities.

Until the summer of the big robbery, Montpelier's greatest contribution to crime was polygamy practiced by local Mormons, which occasionally brought bounty hunters into the area for the $50 they could collect by turning in violaters.

The bank robbery occurred around noon. There were probably five robbers in all. As with most Wild Bunch holdups, it is not certain just which members of the gang participated. Cassidy and Elzy Lay are usually mentioned. The outlaws rode east out of town, zig-zagged some, then headed for Montpelier Canyon. Two of the outlaws may have followed the trail that is now US 89 northeast to Afton, Wyoming, where they holed up in an isolated log cabin.

Several figures have been given for the amount taken: $30,000, $28,000, and $7,165, the last amount being that reported by bank teller A. N. MacIntosh. Legend has it that Cassidy buried some of the loot along the trail in the Wind River Mountains in a hole dug in the sand at the base of a large lightning-shattered stump.

## Salmon
### Lemhi County

Salmon lies in eastern Idaho at the junction of US 93 and State Road 28, just west of the Montana line and the Continental Divide. During Idaho's frontier days the town was the center of an active mining and prospecting region, although the area produced little wealth in comparison to some of the other regions in the state.

The town was never seriously troubled by outlaws, thanks partly to a deputy sheriff named John W. Snook, Sr. who had a reputation of "never losing a man." There is a story that Snook once followed four horse thieves into Nevada. After several weeks he returned with the stolen animals. When asked about the thieves, he replied that all four "had died in quicksand."

In 1884 Snook may have captured John Bender, the patriarch of a notorious Kansas family of murderers who killed and robbed patrons of their roadhouse. Positive identification was never made because the suspect died while trying to escape. The town of Salmon had no official jail, so when somebody had to be locked up, Snook used the basement under a store building on the corner of St. Charles and Main streets. The man who may have been Bender bled to death one night after partially amputating his foot in an attempt to slip out of his shackles. There were no means of preserving a body in Salmon in those days, and it deteriorated before anyone familiar with Bender could be summoned to identify it.

## Twin Falls
### Twin Falls County

Two and one-half miles east of Twin Falls on US 30, near a stagecoach stop called Desert Station, possibly the most unusual stage robbery in Idaho history occurred in a dark evening night in 1869. The story may have been embellished over the years, but apparently a local character named "Stove Pipe Sam" had "done poorly at cards" and found "little or nothing at the diggings," and in desperation decided to become a road agent. Having no helpers, and realizing that a lone bandit might not present enough of a threat to a stage driver to cause him to rein up, Sam ingeniously rigged up two lifelike dummies out of sagebrush and driftwood, and propped them up near the side of the trail. As the stage slowly rounded a curve, Sam, who reportedly was not even armed, stepped up beside the dummies and shouted for the driver to halt and throw out the treasure box. The driver complied immediately, and as soon as the box hit the ground, he gave his horses the whip and sped away. At Sam's feet lay $1,500 in bagged gold dust.

But Sam's next move was a bad one. For some reason he felt he needed help in cashing in the dust and sought the assistance of a card-playing friend, one Frederickson, to whom he offered a share of the loot. Frederickson at first agreed, but when a $750 reward was posted for the man who held up the Twin Falls stage that night, Frederickson weakened and turned old Sam in.

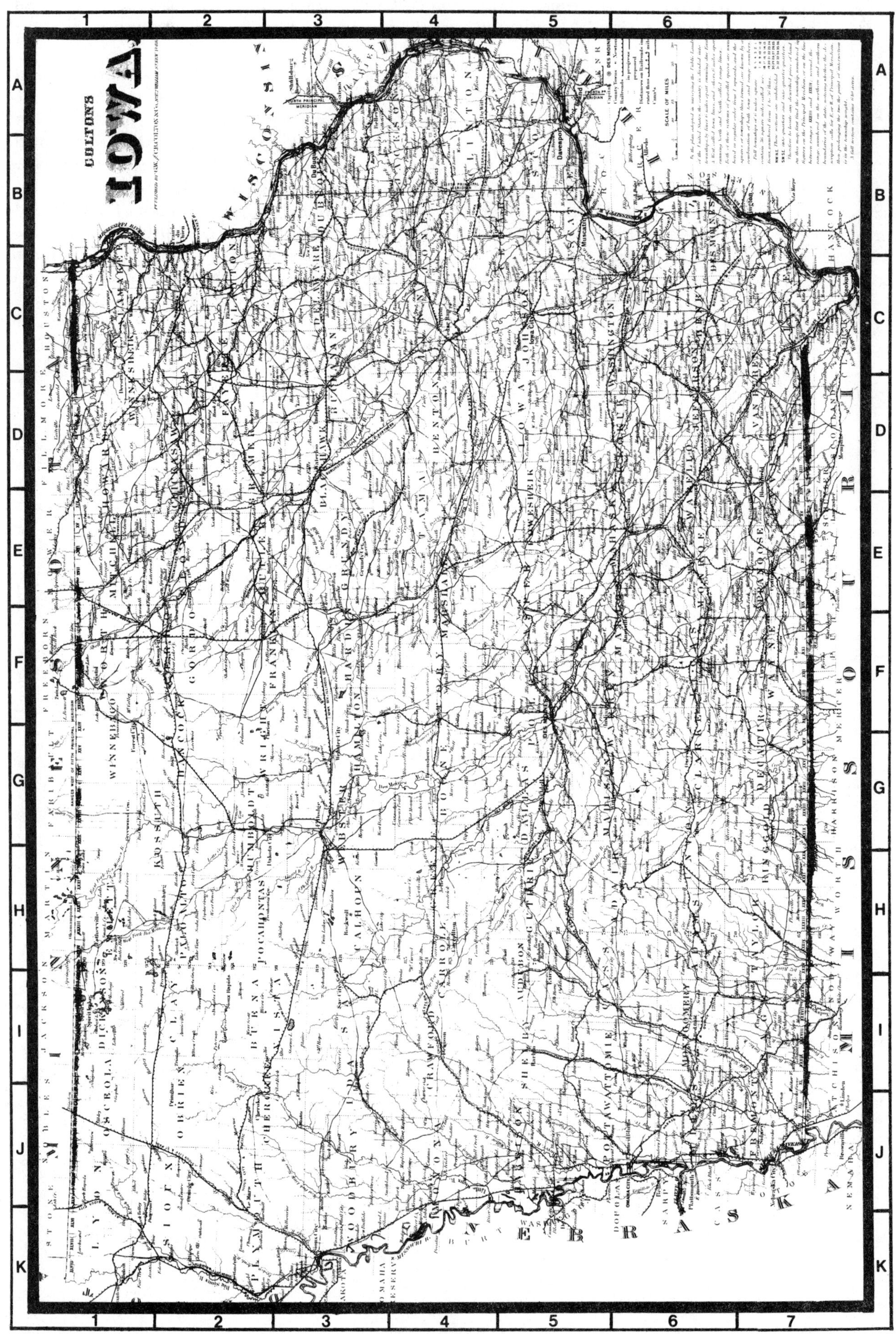


Iowa 1886

# IOWA

## Adair
### Adair County

Adair is in western Iowa, just off Interstate 80 about midway between Des Moines and the Nebraska line. The wreck and robbery of a Chicago, Rock Island and Pacific Railroad passenger train near the town on the night of July 21, 1873, occasionally has been labeled the first train robbery in the United States. It was not (notwithstanding a marker placed near the site in 1954, the 81st anniversary of the holdup, which made such a claim). The robbery was, however, believed to be the first holdup of a train by Jesse James and his gang.

The wreck was accomplished by yanking a loosened rail just as the locomotive was about to reach it. The engine toppled, killing the engineer, John Rafferty, in the boiling wreckage. The fireman, Dennis Foley, survived by clawing his way out and rolling in dew-ladened grass to extinguish his flaming overalls.

The amount taken in the robbery is not known. Some reports say the gang recovered $2,000 from the express car and then turned to the passenger coaches, collecting money and valuables worth as much as $24,000. This is probably an exaggeration. The robbers fled southward toward Missouri. Those who claim they saw them gave vague descriptions of two of the gang which roughly matched those of Jesse and Frank James.

## Albert City
### Buena Vista County

It was the biggest gun battle ever fought in frontier Iowa. The date was November 16, 1901; the place was Albert City, a quiet town of around 800 a few miles north of State Road 3 on the eastern edge of Buena Vista County, about eighty miles east of Sioux City. Earlier in the day, town marshal Carlos Lodine had received a wire that three men suspected of burglarizing a Greenville, Iowa, bank were heading in his direction. Almost before he could spread the word that he might need a posse, Lodine was informed that there were three strangers hanging around the train depot. They had come in from the north, apparently along the tracks of the Wabash and St. Louis Railroad. Lodine quickly rounded up five men, mostly merchants, and armed them with rifles and pistols.

Marshal Lodine was not a man to waste words. As he approached the strangers at the depot, he shouted, "You are our prisoners!" In an instant they went for their guns. At least 64 shots were fired in the next several minutes. Marshal Lodine was the first man hit and went down with a bad wound, apparently in the abdomen. A townsman, John Sundblad, was also hit in the side and chest. The depot offered the gunmen good protection, but obviously they knew that soon more help would come from town. Therefore, when the next train pulled in, they used it for cover and dashed across the tracks, where they took shelter behind a large corncrib.

Not too far from the corncrib was a shed to which the local grain elevator operator, named Bush, had hitched his horse that morning. One of the gunmen made an attempt to reach it. Posseman Mike Collins got off one quick shot and hit him in the leg. As he slowed, a second bullet struck him in the stomach. Just then a farmer named Peterson pulled up with his wagon. The remaining two gunmen ran for it, firing over their shoulders. On reaching the wagon, they shouted for Peterson to lash his horses and head out of town.

A silence then fell over Albert City. Marshal Lodine, bleeding badly, had crawled into a root cellar. He would soon die as would his friend, John Sundblad. The wounded gunman was also dying. The two who had escaped made it only as far as a cornfield south of the town of Laurens, about six miles away. There they surrendered following another exchange of shots. They were returned to Albert City where there was brief talk of lynching, but a lawman called in from Sioux Rapids quickly discouraged it. What rage the town had left was spent the next day at the dead gunman's "funeral." A rough box was hurriedly nailed together from scrap lumber and the body was tossed into a round hole in the public graveyard. A townsman named Geyer picked up a handful of dirt and threw it on the coffin. In mock bereavement he muttered, "Ashes to ashes, dust to dust. If God won't have you the devil must."

Should you visit Albert City today, and the old Wabash & St. Louis depot is still standing, check about head high on the north wall. You should be able to see at least five bullet holes, a testament to "Iowa's big gun battle."

## Bellevue
### Jackson County

This tiny Mississippi River town, twenty-five miles south of Dubuque on US 52, set an early precedent for its neighbors further west on how to deal with outlaws. In 1837 Bellevue was overrun by a gang of horse thieves and counterfeiters led by a local hotel owner named W. W. Brown. The bunch was tolerated until January 1840 when several members of the band stepped over the line by mistreating a young woman during a robbery of a residence. The owner of the residence fought the outlaws, killing one. This infuriated the gang, and they tried to blow up the man's house with gunpowder.

The citizens of Bellevue had had enough. They formed a posse and stormed Brown's hotel. Brown and two of his men were killed in the battle, thirteen were captured, and six escaped. The townspeople had four men killed and seven wounded. When the shooting was over, the town was divided on what to do with the captured outlaws. Some were for hanging and others preferred whipping. They voted, using a ballot box, and chose whipping. After the culprits were soundly beaten, they were placed on flatbottom boats with three days' rations and set adrift on the river.

## Corydon
### Wayne County

Corydon lies at the junction of State Roads 2 and 14, just thirteen miles north of the Missouri line, almost in the center of the state. On June 3, 1871, seven strangers walked into the county treasurer's office and ordered the clerk on duty to open the safe. Petrified with fear, the clerk pleaded with the outlaws saying the safe had a time lock on it and could not be opened. He suggested instead that they go down the street to the bank. Perhaps one of the outlaws examined the lock; in any event, they apparently decided the clerk was telling the truth. Holstering their guns, they bid the clerk good day and departed for the Obocock Brothers Bank. There they found the money accessible.

At neither the treasurer's office nor the bank did the gang encounter any customers. Nearly everybody in Corydon was at the public square for a town meeting. This fact seemed to inspire the robbers. Perhaps the robbery had been too easy, or maybe the outlaws were just in a devilish mood. For whatever reason, they pulled their masks back over their faces, saddled up, and headed for the square.

The speaker was dumbfounded when the leader of the masked riders interrupted him and asked if he could address the group. Still astride his horse, he turned and faced the crowd. His exact words have been forgotten, but he said something to the effect that while the townspeople were having their fun at the meeting, he and his companions were also having fun—down at the bank—which they had just robbed of every dollar it held. He thanked the group for their attention, nudged his horse, and with his comrades at his side, rode off.

At first the townspeople thought the whole thing was a joke. When they finally discovered what happened, they quickly formed a posse and picked up the gang's trail. It led south into Missouri. At one point the pursuers got close enough to exchange a few shots, but they lost the tracks somewhere in Jackson County.

Before the trail was lost, it led deep into the home territory of the James-Younger gang. Thus, it has been assumed that they were responsible for the robbery. Actually, there has been little evidence turned up over the years to prove or disprove this. A sometimes James-Younger gang member, Clell Miller, was later arrested in Kansas City and charged with participating in the crime. He was returned to Corydon for trial, but none of the witnesses could identify him as one of the culprits.

## Tama
### Tama County

Tama is in eastern Iowa, about fifty miles west of Cedar Rapids, at the junction of US 30 and US 63. There is some evidence that the town was the birthplace of the notorious Harvey Logan, alias "Kid Curry" of Wild Bunch fame, and his brothers Lonnie (Lonie), Henry, and Johnny.

Writers occasionally give Kentucky as the origin of

the Logans (all of whom except Henry at times called themselves "Curry"), but according to Wild Bunch researcher Larry Pointer, the brothers, while living in Montana, gave Tama as their birthplace on voting records. Actually, the Logans spent much of their boyhood with an aunt in Dodson, Missouri,* where Henry, the oldest, remained most of his life, refusing to join his brothers on the outlaw trail.

No evidence has ever been found suggesting that the Logans frequented Tama during their renegade years, but according to Pointer, Butch Cassidy may have paid a visit to the area in the late 1890s.

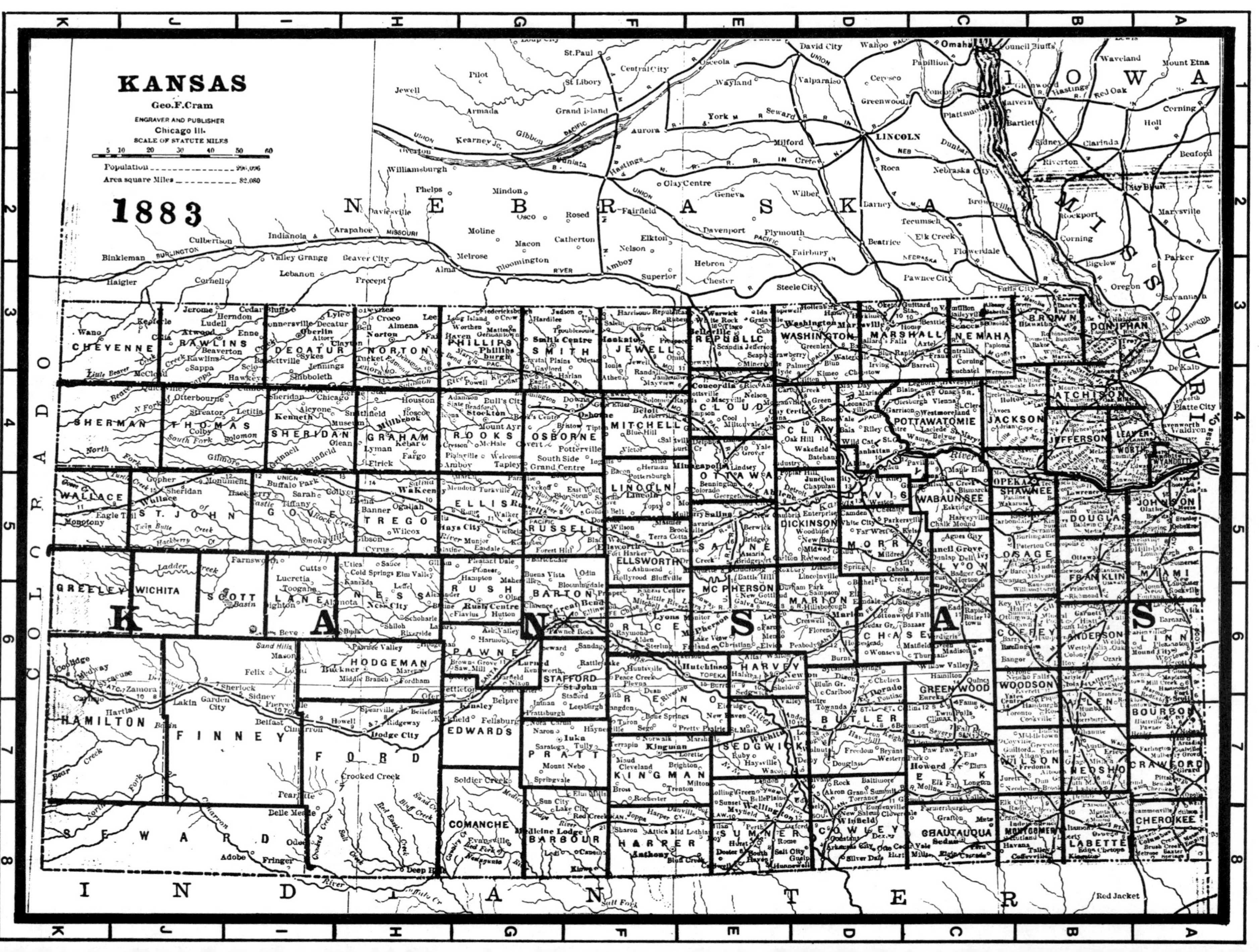
KANSAS
Geo.F.Cram
ENGRAVER AND PUBLISHER
Chicago Ill.
SCALE OF STATUTE MILES
Population 996,096
Area square Miles 82,080
1883
NEBRASKA
IOWA
MISSOURI
KANSAS
COLORADO
INDIAN TER.

Kansas 1883

# KANSAS

## Abilene
### Dickinson County

Abilene's reputation as a rip-roaring town probably was the result of the nature of its birth. In most Kansas boomtowns there was an early core of sound citizens who pushed for law and order. But in Abilene when the Texans hit the town with their herds in the late 1860s they outnumbered permanent residents as much as six to one. One observer described young Abilene as "a wide-open settlement, with no civic organization, no jail, no court, practically no attempt at police control," where everybody was "free to be drunk anywhere, to gamble in public, to shoot to kill." Texas gunslinger John Wesley Hardin supposedly said, "I have seen many fast towns, but I think Abilene beats them all." And a correspondent for the New York *Tribune* wrote, "Gathered together in Abilene and its environs is the greatest collection of Texas cowboys, rascals, desperados, and adventuresses the United States has ever known. There is no law, no restraint in this seething cauldron of vice and depravity."

The town calmed down some in 1870 during the reign of Marshal Bear River Tom Smith. According to witnesses, Smith, reportedly an ex-policeman from New York, often subdued Abilene's riff-raff by bashing in their heads. Apparently, visiting cowboys generally complied with Smith's edict that all weapons be checked with bartenders while in town. But Smith lasted only four months. In November he was killed by a pair of ranchers out on Chapman's Creek while serving a warrant. Some versions of Smith's short career in Abiline have him patrolling the streets unarmed. This is doubtful. Although he seldom used a gun, it is believed he wore two pistols on his belt. Also, he rode up and down the saloon district astride a silver-gray horse called Silverheels, which obviously gave him a decided advantage in bashing heads. Furthermore, most of the time he was assisted by two deputies, J. H. McDonald and a man named Robbins.

Wild Bill Hickok succeeded Smith as marshal of Abilene. He was hired April 15, 1871, and served until the end of the year. He inherited a relatively tame town and for the most part kept it that way, despite the presence of such gunslingers as Ben and Billy Thompson and John Wesley Hardin. Hickok and Ben Thompson tangled early over a sign Ben was using for his Bull's Head Tavern. The sign displayed a grossly exaggerated part of a bull's anatomy which many persons considered obscene. Hickok ordered Thompson to take the sign down or paint over the offending part. Thompson complied, apparently without complaint.

Shortly thereafter Hickok allegedly had a run-in with John Wesley Hardin, but the only report of the incident is found in Hardin's autobiography and must be viewed in this light. According to Hardin, when Hickok ordered him to hand over his guns (in compliance with the rule of no weapons in town) Hardin gave his pistols the old "reverse twirl" (also called the "road agent's roll") and backed Hickok down. Other than this questionable, if not fictional, account by Hardin, he and Hickok never tested one another. Hardin left Abiline in August 1871.

Many thought Hickok and Ben Thompson also might square off, but Ben left Abilene that summer to visit his family in Texas.

On October 5, 1871, Abilene witnessed a tragic affair involving Hickok and the death of a special agent, Mike Williams. Hickok, in attempting to quiet a rowdy troublemaker named Phil Coe who was shooting up the street in front of the Alamo Saloon, accidentally killed Williams when he rushed around the corner of the building into Wild Bill's line of fire. Infuriated, Hickok then put two slugs into Coe's belly. There are other versions of these killings, none of which place Wild Bill in a good light. In one account Hickok was supposed to have used Derringers and shot Coe in the back. There was also some speculation that Hickok and Coe might have been interested in the same woman, Jessie Hazell.

There is another interesting story, possibly true, about some kind of "deal" made between Hickok and the James gang of Missouri. The source of the tale was Charles Gross, a room clerk at the Drover's Cottage in Abilene where Hickok lived when he first came to town. Gross revealed the "deal" years later in a letter to a friend, J. B. Edwards, which is on file at the Kansas State Historical Society at Topeka. According to Gross, the James boys had done Hickok a favor back in Missouri during the Civil War, and he repaid the debt by allowing the brothers to hide out in Abilene with no questions asked. The Jameses, in return, agreed not to cause any trouble.

Hickok's term as marshal ended on December 13, 1871, when Abilene chose not to invite the Texans and their cattle back. Without the unruly cowboys, the town fathers felt they could get along with a less expensive peace officer.

To some extent, visitors to Abilene today can relive the frontier days through "Old Abilene Town," a tourist replica of a handful of the false fronts of the original settlement.

# Ashland
## Clark County

Ashland is in southern Kansas, forty miles south of Dodge City. A story has circulated for years that in May, 1885, a shooting occurred in Ashland involving the famous "Mysterious Dave" Mather. It goes like this: Dave's brother Josiah had a job tending bar in Ashland's popular Junction Saloon. On May 10 Dave spent the evening there playing cards, mostly with a local grocer, Dave Barnes. Mather, who at times earned his living as a gambler, experienced a streak of bad luck. Embarrassed over losing several games of Seven-Up to a rank amateur, he threw his cards at Barnes and reached to scoop up the pot which his opponent had just won. Possibly unaware of Mather's reputation as a gunslinger, or perhaps feeling that he had enough local support to back him up, Barne's brother John, who was standing nearby, went for his gun. But Clark County Sheriff Pat Sughrue was on hand and grabbed the young man's arm, preventing him from shooting. As they were struggling, Dave Barnes whipped out his pistol as did Dave Mather. Barne's shot creased Mather's head. This brought Josiah Mather into the fray, and either his shots or his brother's downed Dave Barnes as well as bystanders C. C. Camp and John Wall. When it was all over Sughrue arrested the Mathers. Bond was set at $3,000 for each. They paid it, saddled up, and rode out of town. The incident did occur, but in the Junction Saloon in Dodge City, not Ashland.

# Bluff City
## Harper County

Harper County, Kansas, on the south edge of the state about thirty miles west of the Kansas Turnpike, would have gone virtually unmentioned in the annals of outlaw history had it not been for the brief but noisy visit by Texas gunman John Wesley Hardin in July 1871. For most of his life Hardin would be pursued by the law, but on this day he was the pursuer. A week earlier a friend of Wes's, Bill Cohron, had been killed by a Mexican cowboy named Bideno at a trail camp outside Newton, Kansas. The killer had fled south, with Hardin and two fellow Texans in hot pursuit. On July 7 the Mexican, figuring he had swapped enough horses along the way to cover his tracks, stopped for a noonday meal at a saloon in Bluff City, a tiny community about five miles north of the Oklahoma line. While Bideno was still eating, Hardin walked in, his right hand at his side close to his sixgun. If one were to believe Hardin's later account, he gave his victim a chance to surrender. This is doubtful. Hardin's blast sent the Mexican backward over his chair. When they rolled him over, he had a bullet hole squarely in the center of his forehead.

Kansas towns never took kindly to Texans storming into saloons and killing people, even if the victim himself was a stranger. A crowd gathered fast, but fortunately for Hardin, his companions had thought to obtain a copy of a warrant naming Bideno as a fugitive. The crowd wandered off, and Hardin and his friends, after leaving a $20 bill to bury the hapless cowboy, bid Bluff City farewell.

# Burden
## Cowley County

This peaceful southern Kansas community, located on US 160 about twenty miles northeast of Winfield, once served as a temporary hideout for the notorius Oklahoma train robber and gunslinger Bill Doolin. The gang split up in the summer of 1895, and the following September Bill sneaked his wife and small child out of her parents' home in Lawson, Oklahoma, and the three of them toured the sparsely populated Osage country in a covered wagon. But during the trip Mrs. Doolin became ill, and Bill drove north to Burden where his wife had relatives. While there the family lived in a tent pitched near spring about a mile and a half west of town on a farm owned by a man named Johnnie Wilson. In and around Burden, Doolin used the name Thomas Wilson and posed as an impoverished would-be-homesteader who had not yet found his piece of land. Every couple of weeks he drove into town for supplies "in a dilapidated old wagon hitched to a team managed with rope lines, dressed in ragged clothes and looking the typical played-out Oklahoma boomer he pretended to be." Although Bill probably had enough stolen loot stashed away to buy and sell half the people in town, word got around about "that poor suffering family out there in the tent," and Burden citizens pitched in with food and clothing.

Meanwhile, Oklahoma lawman Bill Tilghman, who had been on Doolin's trail for many months, received a tip as to the outlaw's whereabouts and headed for Kansas. But about the same time, Doolin began to get uneasy over all the attention that was being paid to him and his family, and two days before Tilghman rode into town, Bill packed up and left, leaving no trail to follow.

## Caldwell
### Sumner County

The West was never short of tales of gunfighters who spent years tracking down a lawman to avenge a grievance. Caldwell's story occurred in December 1881, and

Caldwell marshal Henry Brown and deputy Ben Wheeler captured following bank robbery at Medicine Lodge. *Charles C. Goodhall Collection.*

Caldwell, Kansas, hotel in the 1880s. *Kansas State Historical Society.*

involved the town's mayor, Mike Meagher. As with most stories of this kind, the facts have become blurred over the years; as with many gun battles, the witnesses often spent more time ducking than witnessing. This is one version of what happened.

Mayor Mike Meagher had been marshal of Wichita when that town was a flourishing terminus for Texas steers. One day in the line of duty he killed a small-time outlaw named Powell. The incident would have been forgotten except that Powell had a cousin, Jim Talbott (also known as Jim Sherman) who fancied himself as quite a badman. Talbott, said to be a former Missouri bushwhacker, vowed he would avenge his cousin's death.

Five years had passed since Powell's killing when Talbott and a gang of eight toughs rode into Caldwell. The years, however, had not mellowed Talbott. His plan was to start enough trouble to call out the Caldwell town marshal who, being outnumbered nine to one, would probably seek assistance from former lawman Meagher. Talbott would than have his man. A local saloon-keeper, George Speer, owner of the Red Light, got wind of the scheme and asked to join up, claiming he also had a score to settle with the mayor (Meagher had arrested his brother for murder).

Talbott and his bunch started their riot, and as expected the town marshall called on Meagher for assistance. Meagher, however, possibly sensed trouble and brought extra help of his own. This evened the odds some. The ensuing battle was something to behold. Caldwell's storefronts would carry bullet holes for years. In the end Talbott accomplished his mission. Meagher, usually a cautious sort, let his foe slip around a building and get behind him. He fell with a bullet in a lung. Seeing the mayor dying, Talbott and his band raced for their horses. Speer failed to make it; as he started to mount he was shot through the heart.

Years later Talbott was apprehended and returned for trial. But too many witnesses to the fight had disappeared, and he was never convicted.

The killing of Meagher convinced the people of Caldwell they needed strong law enforcement. In July 1882 they found what they were looking for in a deputy marshal named Henry Newton Brown. While his background was sketchy, he was obviously fearless, and he knew how to handle a gun. In a few months he was promoted to marshal, and with the help of a another hard case from Texas, Ben Wheeler (real name, Ben Robertson), he soon tamed Caldwell's criminal element. In appreciation the town presented Brown with a shiny new Winchester with an inscription extolling his "valuable services to the citizens of Caldwell." All seemed to be going well until the following fall, when the town was shocked to learn that Brown and his sidekick Wheeler were caught robbing a bank in nearby Medicine Lodge.* Brown was killed trying to escape and Wheeler was hanged.

Caldwell is located forty miles south of Wichita and about fifteen miles west of the Kansas Turnpike. The town is proud of its frontier heritage and is well worth a visit. At the Border Queen Museum in the city park is a carefully constructed replica of the town in the mid-1880s. This scale model contains nearly 100 structures, exact as possible in every detail. This fascinating display was built by Western researcher Bill O'Neal in connection with his biography of Marshal Brown. A handful of these old buildings still stand in downtown Caldwell. In the words of O'Neal, "in just the right light it is not difficult to imagine the sounds of a frontier saloon, of cattle hoofs, and gunfire."

## Caney
### Montgomery County

Some students of outlaw history believe the express car robbery on the night of October 13, 1892, at Caney was part of a hoax perpetrated by Dalton gang member Bill Doolin on the neighboring town of Coffeyville (eighteen miles to the east) in retribution for the slaying of the Dalton bunch eight days earlier (see *Coffeyville*). Doolin's plan, they think, was to make everybody believe the gang would descend on Coffeyville when in fact they had their eye on one of the nearby towns. The day before the Caney holdup, John J. Kloehr, one of the principals in the Coffeyville affair, received a letter from the "Dalton Gang" promising revenge on the town for the "killing of Bob, Grat and the rest." Coffeyville town fathers, expecting an invasion, called for help from the surrounding towns. This left Caney and other railroad stops in the vicinity, vulnerable to a raid.

The robbers at Caney, presumably led by Doolin, nearly struck out from the standpoint of a haul; they probably garnered less than $100. The holdup went off without a hitch, however, and launched Doolin as an outlaw in his own right. Over the next several years he and his companions would ravage many an Oklahoma town and be a constant threat to the railroads and express companies.

## Cimarron
### Gray County

Cimarron, sixteen miles west of Dodge City, was the scene of the famous "battle for the county seat." Cimarron and its neighbor six miles to the west, Ingalls, were vying for the right to be the seat of Gray County. Cimarron already held the title but was challenged by Ingalls in a new election. The results were protested and ended up in court. In the meantime, an Ingalls man was elected county clerk and demanded the county records from the Cimarron courthouse. When Cimarron officials refused, the Ingalls faction organized a raiding party.

The raid was scheduled for January 2, 1889. To beef up their forces, the Ingalls group employed a handful of hired guns from Dodge City. Leading this contingent was Bill Tilghman and Jim Masterson, brother of the famous Bat. Also along were Dodge City stalwarts Neal Brown, Fred Singer, Ben Daniels (all former Dodge City peace officers), and younger but no less spirited cowtown mercenaries George Bolds, Ed Brooks, and Billy Allensworth.

The Dodge City group was cloaked with semi-official status, being specially deputized for the job by Tilghman, who had in turn been appointed temporary Gray County sheriff by the new Ingalls county clerk, Newt Watson. (The current sheriff, Joe Reynolds, was laid up with a gunshot wound.)

The raiders drove up with a wagon and began loading up records. Watson, Masterson, Singer, and Allensworth were inside the courthouse, and the rest were near the wagon when Cimarron residents opened fire. Tilghman was hit in the leg, Brooks doubled over with a gut shot, and Bolds was struck three times—once in the leg and twice in the abdomen. The wagon driver, Charlie Reicheldeffer, was also hit. Miraculously they all managed to climb aboard and race out of town. Meanwhile, the four raiders trapped in the courthouse returned the attackers' fire from the second-story windows. These men were deadly shots and three Cimarron citizens soon fell.

The attackers tried to rush the stairway but failed. Next they raised a ladder to a rear window but Masterson kicked it away. The attackers then tried firing through the wooden floor from below, but the defenders climbed on top of filing cabinets, desks, and a steel safe. The seige lasted six hours, ending when the Cimarron forces received a telegram from Bat Masterson informing them that if his brother and his comrades were not allowed to leave town safely, Bat would "hire a train and come in with enough men to blow Cimarron off the face of Kansas."

When it was all over, the casualty count was one dead and three wounded for the Cimarron group and four wounded for Ingalls. The raiders were later tried for the death of the Cimarron man J. W. English but were acquitted.

The town of Cimarron also made the headlines four years later. On June 11, 1893, at 1:20 A.M. the Bill Doolin gang held up the Sante Fe's Southern California and New Mexico Express No. 3 a half mile west of town. The gang stopped the train by displaying a danger signal on the track. The engineer was forced to march back to the Wells Fargo car and batter in the door with a sledge hammer. The express carried $10,000 in the through safe, but the messenger did not have the combination, and the robbers had to be content with about $1,000 in money and valuables from the local safe. The gang fled southeast, crossing Clark County near Ashland. In northern Oklahoma they encountered a posse, and Doolin was shot in the foot.

## Coffeyville
### Montgomery County

Coffeyville was established shortly after the Civil War on the banks of the Verdigris River. Being practically on the Kansas-Oklahoma line, the town soon became a hangout for bootleggers peddling illegal whiskey in Indian Territory. Although wild in the beginning, the town mellowed over the years while neighbors like Dodge City and Wichita grew tougher.

Billy-the-Kid supposedly lived in Coffeyville for a while as a youngster, as did the notorious Dalton brothers. In 1888 Bob Dalton, who with brothers Grat and Emmett would later make the town famous, laid one of his first victims to rest on the south side of the Santa Fe tracks at the home of a cattle dealer named Ted Seymour. The victim was a whiskey peddler, Charlie Montgomery, who some say made the mistake of running off with a young lady named Minnie Johnson, a distant cousin of the Daltons whom Bob considered his personal property. Officially the records shows that Montgomery was shot resisting arrest (at the time Bob was with the Indian Police in Oklahoma), but most Coffeyville residents suspected otherwise.

The year of the famous "Dalton Raid" was 1892. Coffeyville had prospered in the four years since the Dalton clan had moved on to become the most dreaded outlaw gang in Indian Territory. The town could boast of two flourishing banks, a generous number of wholesale and retail establishments, and the shiny tracks of three railroads. The town was successful, and that meant the bank vaults held a goodly supply of cash.

Sometime during the last week of September the authorities received a tip that the Daltons might be paying a visit to Coffeyville. According to the source, the gang's targets would be both the town's banks, the First National, located on the east side of Union Street, and the C. M. Condon Company, just across the street on the north side of the plaza. A meeting of town officials was quickly called, and a plan was drawn up whereby the two banks could be defended by volunteers at a few minutes' notice. Arrangements were made to store weapons at the Isham Brothers & Mansour Hardware

Bullet-riddled entrance to Coffeyville's Condon & Company Bank. Photo was taken shortly after the "Dalton Raid." *Dalton Museum, Coffeyville.*

Dalton gang casualties following the Coffeyville raid. *Dalton Museum, Coffeyville.*

next door and immediately south of the First National. From the front of this store, one also could command a good view of the Condon & Company Bank. Guns were also made available at Coffeyville's other hardware store, A. P. Boswell & Company, across the plaza.

The Daltons rode into town on the morning of October 5. Despite an assortment of fake whiskers and mustaches, they were recognized by several townspeople as they reined up. Word quickly spread, and no sooner than Bob and Emmett Dalton entered the lobby of the First National, a dozen townsmen headed for the hardware stores. The First National cashier, Tom Ayres, saw that the outlaws had been spotted and began stalling for time.

Over at the Condon bank the scene was much the same. Grat Dalton, accompanied by Bill Powers and Dick Broadwell, ordered the bank's co-owner, C. T. Carpenter, and cashier Charles M. Ball to fill their grain sacks with cash. Ball, like his counterpart at the First National, stalled for time, telling the robbers that the time-lock on the vault would not open for another ten minutes.

Bob and Emmett were the first to draw fire. When they stepped out of the First National's front door, two shots range out from Rammel Brothers' Drug Store, immediately north of the bank. As they ducked back in, the townsmen turned their rifles toward the Condon bank across the street. Bob and Emmett headed for the bank's back door which opened onto an alley between Union and Depot streets. Apparently only one townsman was guarding that spot. His name was Lucious Baldwin, a clerk at Read Brothers General Store. The outlaws left him lying in the alley, a bullet in his left breast. They then raced north to Eighth Street and turned west. As they crossed Union they spotted George B. Cubine standing in the doorway of Rammel Brothers. Although nearly forty yards away, the outlaws hit him with three shots. Townsman Charles Brown ran to Cubine's body, picked up his Winchester, and turned toward the robbers, now almost across Union Street. Four more shots rang out and Brown sank to the sidewalk. An instant later Tom Ayres, the cashier at the First National, leaned out the doorway of Isham's Hardware for a better view and took a slug just below the left eye.

Meanwhile, across Union Street at Condon's bank, Grat Dalton, Bill Powers, and Dick Broadwell were fighting for their lives. At least a dozen guns were blasting away at the plate glass windows and two sets of double doors. Most of the firing was coming from Isham's where owner Henry H. Isham, a town carpenter named Anderson, and a third man, Charles Smith, all manned shiny new Winchesters. A fourth townsman, hardware clerk Lewis Dietz, was keeping a sixgun hot. All four men had an unobstructed view of the route these outlaws would have to take to reach their horses, tied up over a block west, in what is now known as "Death Alley." And probably a half-dozen other townsmen were positioned in various doorways on the south and west sides of the plaza, all with guns trained on the bank's front doors.

Coffeyville's "Death Alley." *Kansas State Historical Society.*

For the Coffeyville defenders it was a shooting gallery. With guns blazing, the outlaws kicked open the door on the southwest corner of the building and dashed onto Walnut Street. Grat Dalton and Bill Powers were hit before they made twenty yards. Witnesses said they could see dust flying from their clothes as the bullets struck. But they kept running. Grat found cover under a wagon about a third of a block down the alley. Powers tried to duck into a doorway but found the door locked. He then raced back into the alley, took another bullet in the back, and fell dead. Grat ran from his hiding place under the wagon to the rear of a barn that jutted out into the alley, which for the moment provided him cover from the deadly fire coming from the east. Broadwell had been hit but was still moving, running zig-zag toward the horses. He reached his animal, climbed on, and kept going west, toward Maple Street. Before he reached Maple and turned north he took two more hits.

Coffeyville city marshal Charles Connelly had worked his way north from Ninth Street through a vacant lot.

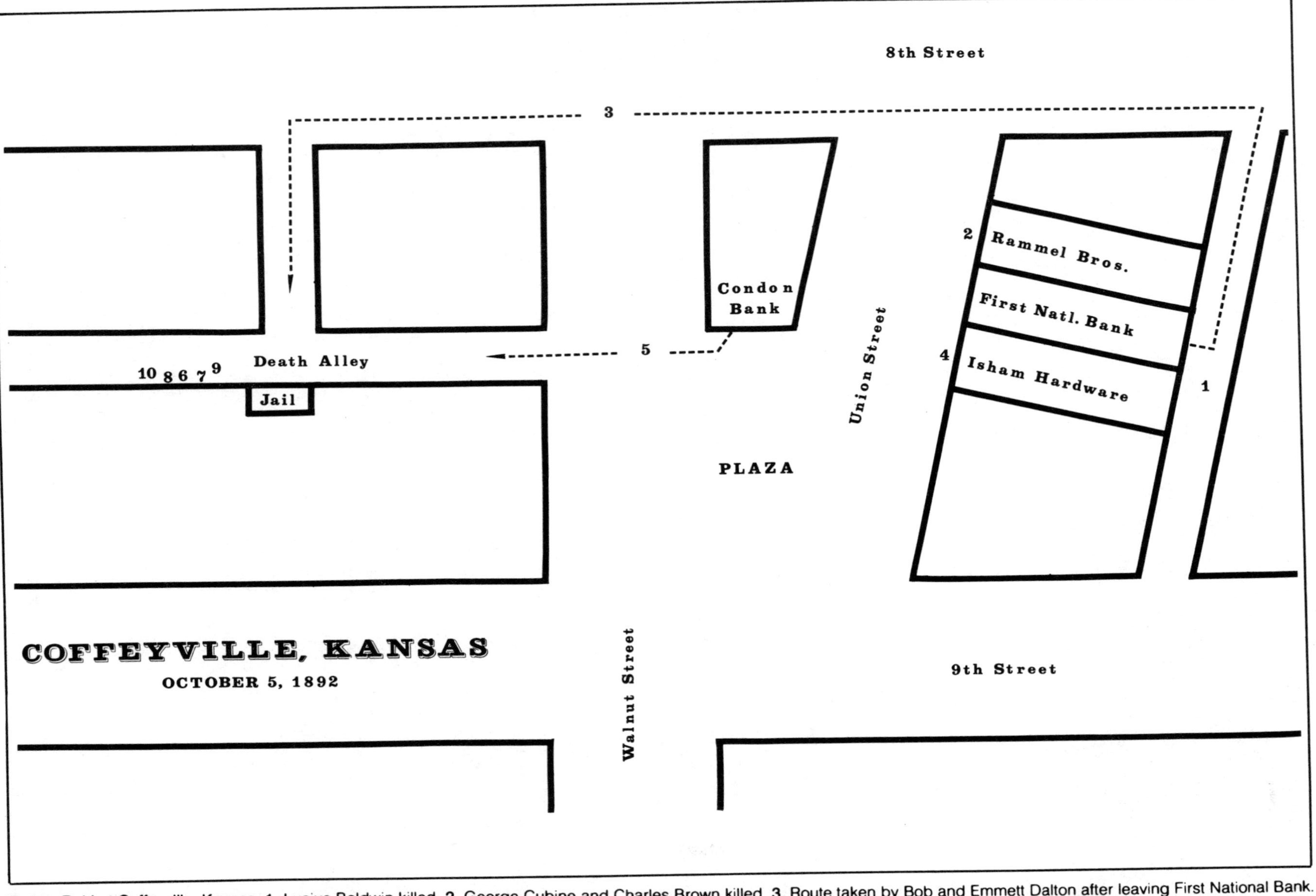


**Dalton Raid at Coffeyville, Kansas.** 1. Lucius Baldwin killed. **2.** George Cubine and Charles Brown killed. **3.** Route taken by Bob and Emmett Dalton after leaving First National Bank. **4.** Tom Ayres wounded. **5.** Route taken by Grat Dalton, Bill Powers, and Dick Broadwell after leaving Condon Bank. **6.** Marshal Charles Connelly killed. **7.** Bob Dalton killed **8.** Grat Dalton killed. **9.** Emmett Dalton wounded. **10.** Bill Powers killed.

When he reached the alley he apparently thought Grat Dalton was to the west of him. He stepped into the alley and turned to look in that direction. Grat, just a few yards away, had only to raise his rifle hip-high to put a bullet in the lawman's back.

By this time Bob and Emmett had reached the alley from the north and emerged from a driveway near the middle of the block, across from the rear of Slosson's Drug Store. Bob spotted F. D. Benson at the window of the store. As he fired off a quick shot, he stepped too far out in the alley. A rifle slug sent him staggering across the alley into a pile of curbstones near a tiny stone building that served as the town jail. As he lay there he saw John Kloehr, owner of the local livery, inside the fence near Slosson's store. He fired at Kloehr and missed. Dazed, he got to his feet and hugged the rear of a barn to the west of the jail. Kloehr followed, and when Bob turned toward him again, he put a bullet in the outlaw's chest.

Meanwhile, Grat had almost reached his horse, but Kloehr spotted him and put a bullet through his throat, breaking his neck.

Emmett Dalton, still unscathed, had worked his way along the north edge of the alley, almost across from where the horses were tied. But as he tried to make it across, he was hit in the left hip and the right arm. Still, he was able to mount up, and for an instant it appeared that he might escape, but he hesitated (some say he rode over to where Bob lay dying), and a townsman named Carey Seamen emptied both barrels of his shotgun into his back. The last Dalton had fallen.

Emmett survived thanks to the skilled hands of three Coffeyville physicians. Dick Broadwell's body was found near the edge of town. It was brought back and deposited in the town jail with those of his dead comrades for a grisly group picture that has now become famous.

Tourists today can visit "Death Alley" and the graves of three of the gang in Elmwood Cemetery. Plaques mark the sites in the streets and alleys where the four Coffeyville residents fell. The Condon & Company bank can be visited, as well as the old stone jail. A "Dalton Musuem" has been established at 113 E. Eighth Street, adjacent to the alley from which Bob and Emmett emerged on their dash out the rear of the First National. The museum's collection includes memorabilia of the battle and other items of interest to Old West buffs.

## Dodge City
### Ford County

Dodge City was born in the early 1870s to serve the soldiers at nearby Fort Dodge and soon developed as a trading center for buffalo hunters. Later, its success was assured when it became a shipping point for Texas longhorns. Established for commerce, the town immediately drew gamblers and prostitutes and soon acquired a reputation for wickedness. Yet, probably because it operated at a faster pace then most of its sister towns, Dodge quickly sported a strong vigilance committee followed by a series of law enforcement officers sturdy enough to challenge the rough element that often terrorized lesser communities. Dodge paid a price for these hearty "peacemakers," however, because many straddled the line between right and wrong themselves.

But the respectable citizens knew where the danger lay. If one wanted to avoid trouble he stayed out of the brothels and gambling parlors during the day and off Front Street at night. Travelers were warned to skirt Dodge during its wildest days, but these warnings often came from neighboring towns who competed with Dodge for the cattle trade.

There is some disagreement as to just how dangerous it was in Dodge. According to an article in the Dodge City *Democrat* on June 19, 1903, the town saw fifteen killings the year it was born (1872), which necessitated the establishment of Boot Hill Cemetery on a barren mound just west of the center of town and a half-mile north of the Arkansas River. Official records, however, suggest things quieted down considerably. Some researchers have documented only a *total* of fifteen homicides in Dodge during what was supposed to be its wildest years, 1876-1885, for an average of only 1.5 killings a year.

As in most towns of the Old West, Dodge City killings usually resulted from feuds and arguments, frequently enhanced by whiskey. Cowboys often got out of hand on Saturday night, or on whatever night they were paid, and sixguns began popping. Town marshal Ed Masterson, brother of Bat, fell victim to a drunken trail herder in April 1878. The following July a similar fate befell U.S. Deputy Marshal Harry T. McCarty. Later that month Bat's other brother, Jim Masterson, and Wyatt Earp, both on the city payroll at the time, shot it out with three soused troublemakers, one of whom died. And things did not let up: in September there were six shootings in one week, making the year 1878 the high-point for bloodshed in the streets of Dodge.

A myth arose surrounding Ed Masterson's death. He was killed scuffling with two cowboys outside the Lady Gay Saloon on Front Street. One of the cowboys was killed and the other severely wounded. Some accounts have Bat Masterson, then Ford County sheriff, charging down the street with guns blazing, settling the score on the spot. One version has Bat dropping his victims from sixty feet away; another has him picking off an additional five Texans who happened to be standing nearby. No evidence supports these tales. The cowboys apparently

Bat Masterson. *Charles C. Goodhall Collection.*

were hit in the exchange with Ed. They did have four companions in the saloon, and Bat later arrested them on warrants but they were released. This incident is typical of the exaggerated claims about Bat Masterson as a gun-wielding peace officer. Careful research has turned up only one instance in which he shot a man while making an arrest, and that involved shooting a fleeing suspect with a rifle. It occurred in 1878 also; the victim was Jim Kennedy, wanted for the killing of dance hall singer Dora Hand.

There is also disagreement among history buffs as to Wyatt Earp's role in taming Dodge during the seventies. Some say he was city marshal for awhile, but others point to records disputing it, claiming he was only an assistant. Wyatt himself tended to exaggerate about those years, and his recollections can not be relied upon. The Masterson brothers Jim and Ed did both serve as city marshal, and Bat served a two-year stint as Ford County sheriff (1878-1880).

The enigmatic Doc Holliday called Dodge home in 1877 and 1878, during an off-and-on-again relationship with crib-girl Katherine "Big Nosed Kate" Elder. Doc's role in the town's history was minor: when not drinking and frolicking with Kate, he gambled and nourished a friendship with Wyatt Earp, all the while fighting a worsening case of tuberculosis which would bring on an early death.

The Long Branch Saloon's most spectacular shooting fray occurred on April 5, 1879. "Cockeyed Frank" Loving, a gambler who was handy with a revolver, got into an argument with Levi Richardson, a freighter. Tempers flared and both men went for their guns. Loving's misfired and Richardson missed. Diving for cover behind a stove, Richardson got off two shots but only nicked Loving in the hand. Loving carefully took aim and put bullets in his foe's chest, arm, and side. Richardson, staggering backward, fired several more wild shots before he dropped. Loving, still enraged, had to be restrained from emptying his gun into his dying victim.

With regard to Dodge City gunfighters, some say Jim Masterson may have been tops. At least one contemporary, George Bolds, thought he may have been the best in the West:

> I can still shut my eyes and see him walking down the street, six-shooter under his coat, hat tilted to one side, a cigar in the corner of his mouth and his face as impassive as an Indian's. I maintain he was the most deadly man with a gun outside Harvey Logan, the executioner of the Wild Bunch in Wyoming. If Jim Masterson had ever met Logan or that buck-toothed little Billy the Kid, my chips would have been on Jim.

Since its inception, Dodge more or less had been run by a political faction that encouraged the vice on Front Street. More than one public official had his fingers in the pie, but by 1881 some citizens were beginning to complain. In March of that year a local Adams Express Company Agent, M. C. Ruby, felt obligated to expose some of the wrongs he saw. Among his gripes to reach print was this item:

> The mayor is a flannel mouthed Irishman and keeps a saloon and gambling house which he attends to in person. The city marshal and assistant are gamblers and each keep a "woman" as does the mayor also. The marshal and assistant for their services (as city officials) receive one hundred dollars per month each. The sheriff owns a saloon and the deputy sheriff is a bartender in a saloon... The ex-chairman of the Board of County Commissioners runs a saloon and dance hall, where the unwary are enticed, made drunk and robbed.... There are many good people here, but the bad ones are so numerous we almost lose sight of the good.

The following month the mayor and city council defeated in their bid for re-election, but the new mayor merely set up his own system of vice. Two years later another attempt was made at reform, bolstered by a vigilante force that challenged the gambling and saloon group. The situation became tense enough for the governor to put two companies of national guardsmen on alert, but before things boiled over, a compromise was reached wherein gambling and saloonkeeping were permitted on a regulated basis.

April 1881 is remembered for the famous "Battle of the Plaza." Bat Masterson had left Dodge the year before after failing to be re-elected as Ford County sheriff. His brother Jim, after serving his term as city marshal, became partners in the Lady Gay Saloon. In April Jim got into an argument with his partner, A. J. Peacock, and Peacock's brother-in-law, Al Updegraff, who tended bar at the Lady Gay. Friends of the Mastersons wired Bat, who was then in Tombstone, that his brother would probably end up being killed. Bat took the next train for Dodge, arriving at noon on the 16th. When he got off at the depot, Peacock and Updegraff were waiting for him. It is not clear who fired first, but a battle suddenly erupted all over Front Street, then called "The Plaza." Friends of both sides joined in and managed to put holes in most of the surrounding store fronts. Only one man was hit, Updegraff, and he survived. Bat was fined for "discharging a pistol upon the streets." The tale of the battle was told and retold across the West, each time growing larger. By the time it reached the newspapers, it had Bat killing both Peacock and Updegraff because they had killed Jim. Some reporter also added that this made twenty-six victims for Bat during his career as a peace officer and gunman. The truth was that Bat had killed only one man in a gunfight, a drunken soldier in a brawl in Mobeetie (then Sweetwater), Texas, in 1876.

Another famous Dodge City shootout occurred in 1884, when "Mysterious Dave" Mather killed Tom Nixon. The two had been feuding since Nixon was given Mather's job as an assistant city marshal. The details are sketchy, but it seems on July 18 Nixon took a shot at Mather, claiming that he saw Dave about to draw on him. Nobody was hurt and apparently nobody believed Nixon. Mather was a noted gunslinger, and it was presumed that had Mather started to draw, Nixon would have been dead. Nixon was arrested and then released on bond. Three days later, Nixon was on duty at the corner of Front Street and First Avenue. Mather walked up to him, called his name, and then shot him dead. Despite the testimony of several witnesses who said Nixon had not drawn his gun, Mysterious Dave was acquitted by a jury after only twenty-seven minutes of deliberation.

Long Branch Saloon, Dodge City, in the 1880s. *Kansas State Historical Society.*

Things began to quiet down some in Dodge following the Nixon killing. By 1885 the town's wildest days were over. For visitors today, Front Street has been restored, if not faithfully at least colorfully, in the style of the 1870s. Names from the past include the Long Branch Saloon, Zimmerman Hardware Store, Rice Brothers Saddle Shop, City Drug Store, Saratoga Saloon, the Beatty and Kelly Restaurant, and a few others. All are part of the Boot Hill Museum which also features a large collection of firearms, the old Fort Dodge jail (circa 1865), a restored Santa Fe depot, and special daily events.

## Douglass
### Butler County

Douglass lies southwest of Wichita on US 77, about twenty miles north of Winfield. In 1870 a large gang of outlaws began operating along the Arkansas River between Wichita and Winfield. On learning that the thieves had driven over 250 stolen mules from Kansas to Texas, Winfield citizens formed a vigilance committee. When they were fairly sure the gang had returned to Kansas, the committee organized a scouting party and went looking for them. They found four hiding out in a house near Douglass at the Walnut River crossing. When the committee ordered all to come out with their hands up, only one came. The house was riddled with bullets, the three remaining outlaws were killed, and the one who had surrendered was promptly hanged. One of the bodies was left on the river bank as a warning to the rest of the gang. A placard read: "Killed for stealing horses."

Apparently before he died, the outlaw who was hanged named most of the members of the gang. Some lived right in Douglass. A few weeks later, four of these were picked up and taken a mile and a half south of town to near Olmstead's Mill, where they, too, were put to the rope. The remainder of the names were then published in a local newspaper. No further warning was necessary. It was the end of the gang's operations in Butler County.

# Ellsworth
## Ellsworth County

Ellsworth, just below Interstate 70 about 55 miles west of Salina, almost enjoyed the privilege of being the first Kansas town tamed by Wild Bill Hickok. Wild Bill ran for sheriff of Ellsworth County in November 1867 but along with three other candidates was defeated by incumbent E. W. Kingsbury. Two years later Hickok began his career as a town-tamer at Hays, Kansas.

Actually, in 1867 Ellsworth did not need much taming. It was not until the Kansas Pacific Railroad came to town that Ellsworth sprouted horns. As the rails moved west across Kansas, the newest railhead each summer became the preferred shipping point for Texas beef, and if a town was receptive to the rowdy Texans, it could generally count on a succeeding year of prosperity. Cowboys measured a town by what it offered a thirsty wrangler and how well he was treated by the peace officers.

Ellsworth's turn came in 1872. Things had been going fairly well, and the town merchants looked forward to 1873. But as the Texans began to pour in the following summer, a group of Ellsworth citizens decided they wanted law and order more than Texas cash. The town council divided. At first, the pro-Texans won, and the town's police force was reduced in size and told to "take it easy." But within two weeks the council reversed its decision. The climax came on August 15 when a quick-tempered gunfighter from Abilene named Billy Thompson (brother of the notorious Ben Thompson) unloaded a shotgun on Ellsworth's respected sheriff, Chauncy Whitney, who was unarmed at the time. Thompson's fellow Texans claimed the killing was an accident (they argued Billy had tripped and dropped his gun), and they armed themselves with full intention of taking on the town. Ellsworth's three-man police force took too much time pondering the Texans' challenge, and the town's fiery mayor, Jim Miller, canned them. Cooler heads prevailed and they were reinstated. Perhaps embarrassed by their reprimand, the lawmen returned to the streets with blood in their eyes and killed a wrangler named Cad Pierce. The Texans retaliated by wiping out two-thirds of the department (Jack Merko and Ed Crawford).

The shootings marked the end of Ellsworth's tumultuous years. In 1874 the Texans moved on to other towns. Ellsworth had had its wild and wooly times.

# Fort Riley
## Riley County

During 1866 James Butler "Wild Bill" Hickok served as a deputy U.S. marshal at Fort Riley, which is located near Manhattan in northeastern Kansas. Little has been recorded of Hickok's activities during this period which probably deserves more attention from Western researchers and writers. Wild Bill served as a lawman at Riley for less than a year, which was just prior to his career as an army scout. As a deputy U.S. marshal, Hickok's primary duties involved chasing down military deserters and, occasionally, horse thieves and other outlaws. He was also expected to help maintain order and settle disputes among military personnel and civilians.

Although Western adventure writers had not yet made Wild Bill a living legend in 1866, he had acquired a reputation by that time as an effective lawman, and he left a favorable impression on the citizens of the surrounding Kansas towns. He so impressed a twelve-year-old Kansas lad named Billy Tilghman, who met him on the road to Atchison one day that summer, that Billy vowed that he, too, would someday become a daring federal marshal and carry lightning-fast sixguns. He did.

# Galena
## Cherokee County

For several months in late 1879, the town of Galena, a few miles west of Joplin on the Kansas-Missouri line, was the focal point of a bizarre story that the notorious Jesse James had been shot and killed by one of his own gang. On November 4 Kansas City newspapers reported that Jesse had been killed by gang member George Shephard, a one-eyed former Civil War guerrilla leader who had once ridden with James and who later returned to the gang as a spy for a Kansas City marshal, James Ligget. According to the tale, Ligget found Shephard working in Kansas City as a teamster and hired him to rejoin the James outfit to help engineer Jesse's capture. The reports said Ligget was interviewed and confirmed this much of the story.

According to Shephard, he and Ligget had set the James gang up to be ambushed during a bank robbery at Short Creek, Missouri, a small town near Joplin, but Jesse had called the raid off when he spotted an extra guard at the bank. Shephard said he and Ligget then decided that Shephard would kill Jesse at a designated spot and then flee, leading the rest of the gang into an ambush.

The spot chosen by Shephard was just outside Galena. Shephard said that while riding along, he suddenly turned on Jesse and drew his gun. Jesse also went for his weapon, but Shephard fired first, striking Jesse in the head and killing him. In escaping Shephard said he was shot in the leg by gang member Jim Cummings. After rescuing Shephard, Marshal Ligget and his men rode to the scene but failed to find Jesse's body. At first the story was labeled a hoax, but then several newspaper reports began changing people's minds. Former James gang member Cole Younger, interviewed in prison, said he believed the story. A week later a Jefferson City, Missouri, newspaper ran an unverified story that word was received from gang member Jim Cummings that Shephard had told the truth. Then rumors began circulating that a body claimed to be Jesse's had actually arrived at Kearney, Missouri, by train from Kansas City and had been buried somewhere in Clay County.

When it was eventually discovered that Jesse had not been killed, it was decided that Jesse and Shephard had concocted the story to split the reward money and to take whatever advantage could be gained out of the outlaw's being thought dead.

It is believed the notorious "Bandit Queen" Belle Starr, then known as Myra Maybelle Reed, lived in Galena in 1878 or 1879. Although some early writers produced exaggerated accounts of her outlaw activities before and during this period, there is no proof that she engaged in any lawlessness while in Galena, except perhaps illegal cohabitation with Bruce Younger, a half-brother of the father of the Younger clan of outlaws. Even here there is some evidence that they may have been married.

Younger and Belle lived at the Evans Hotel in Galena where, according to one old timer who remembered her, "Belle was always well behaved" and was "no worse than the rest" of the rough characters who roamed the frontier in those days.

## Goodland
### Sherman County

At the turn of the century it was known as the Bartholomew Place—a typical Kansas farm except perhaps for the house, which had once been a soddy but to which a neatly built frame two-story addition had been added. It was a good house by Sherman County standards. On August 10, 1900, it was burned to the ground by local lawmen to rid the West of two train robbers, Jim and John Jones. (You can still visit the site, about three miles northeast of town; Goodland is on Interstate 70 about seventeen miles east of the Colorado line.)

The Jones brothers had robbed the Union Pacific eastbound out of Limon, Colorado, on August 5, killing a passenger in the process. They fled with a modest amount of loot into Kansas via the Rock Island line. Why they got off the train at Goodland nobody knows; possibly it was as far as their money would take them. At Goodland they posed as travelers from Iowa heading for California. The Bartholomew family, kindly by nature, took them in.

Sherman County sheriff William Walker knew of the train robbery, and when word about the Bartholomews' guests reached town, he became suspicious. On August 10 he and two special deputies, John Riggs and George Cullins, rode out to the farm pretending to be cowboys with a herd of horses. Their plan was to stop and ask for water while the rest of their posse, armed with shotguns and rifles, waited a safe distance away. The plan did not work. The two outlaws raced for the house as soon as they saw the three riders, and a gun battle erupted in seconds. Deputy Riggs was hit in the belly. A few minutes later, John Jones tried to escape, and a Winchester slug split his skull. The Bartholomews took advantage of the confusion to flee to safety, and Jim Jones retreated to the second story window where he could command a good view of his attackers.

It appeared to be a standoff. Word spread throughout the area, and several hundred people came out to watch. Those with rifles crawled in close enough to take potshots at the house. Late in the afternoon it was decided to set the dwelling on fire; apparently the Bartholomews were consulted, and county officials agreed to reimburse them for the loss. Three men crawled close enough to lob railroad torpedos onto the roof, and soon the house was in flames.

Jim Jones never came out. At 10:00 that night deputies found his body. It appeared that he killed himself before the flames reached him. On John Jones's body they found the two masks the men had used in the robbery and a watch belonging to the passenger they had killed.

Burning of the Bartholomew farm home. *M. C. Parker, Goodland, Kansas.*

# Hays
## Ellis County

Hays is in west central Kansas at the junction of Interstate 70 and US 183. The town was born with the arrival of the railroad in 1867 and spent its first two years searching for a sheriff who could keep the lid on the saloons and gambling parlors that were kept roaring twenty-four hours a day by drunken buffalo hunters and soldiers from nearby Fort Hays. In August 1869 the town found him: James Butler "Wild Bill" Hickok, former deputy U.S. marshal and scout for the army at Fort Riley.

It was Wild Bill's first elected office and he went to work immediately. Although never the terror-spreading gunslinger Western writers of the day portrayed him to be, Hickok did manage to bury a local hard case within days after he took office. The victim's name was Bill Mulvey (or Mulrey), and the generally accepted version of the story is that Mulvey got the drop on the new sheriff, but Wild Bill distracted him (possibly with a variation of the old "look out behind you" trick) and whipped out his own weapon. Mulvey died a day or two later.

Hickok soon drew blood again. This time it was Sam Strawhim, another troublemaker whom the local vigilance committee had been trying to chase out of town for months. The facts surrounding Strawhim's demise are also clouded. According to an article in the September 30 edition of the Lawrence, Kansas, *Daily Tribune*, the incident occurred in a house owned by a man named John Bittles, but another source places it at Oderfeld's Saloon on Fort Street. Apparently Hickok and his deputy, Pete Lanihan, were called to the scene because Strawhim was creating a disturbance. Strawhim reportedly made some statements against Wild Bill, and as one reporter told it, "in his [Hickok's] efforts to preserve order, Samuel Stringham (sic) was shot through the head by him, and instantly killed." The incident was investigated and a coroner's jury returned a verdict of justifiable homocide.

But Hickok soon became a marked man in Hays. He began watching his step when he walked past lighted doorways on his nightly rounds. Apparently more than once a bullet whizzed past his head and buried itself into a storefront. When he entered a saloon at night, he did so with haste, quickly stepping to the side to avoid becoming a tempting silhouette from the opposite side of the darkened street.

Hickok served as sheriff of Ellis County through the end of 1869, when he was defeated for election by Pete Lanihan. The voters were probably not unhappy with Wild Bill's performance, but the county was heavily Democrat, as was Lanihan, and Hickok ran as an independent.

Hays has preserved the flavor of its early days with "Old Hays City," between Fort and Main streets near the Union Pacific tracks. The Chamber of Commerce furnishes maps for self-guided tours of some twenty-seven markers and monuments placed to show the "stomping grounds" of Wild Bill and other frontier characters.

# Kinsley
## Edwards County

The train robbery era in the West lasted over sixty years, and while many gangs became highly efficient at plundering express cars and passenger coaches, some bandits were just not cut out for the task. And apart from bungled jobs by amateurs, some robbery attempts failed out of just plain bad luck. If records were kept of such things, probably the prize winner was a fiasco that occurred in January 1878 during an attempt to rob a Santa Fe express at Kinsley, a small town northeast of Dodge City at the junction of US 183 and US 56.

The would-be robbers were not amateurs; in fact they were led by Mike Rourke, a seasoned outlaw. It was just a matter of things not going their way. To begin with, the plan was to hold up the train at the water tank two miles west of Kinsley. But the train did not stop. Having run low on water early, the engineer had taken some on at Dodge City. Disappointed but undaunted, the outlaws leaped into their saddles and raced for Kinsley, hoping to catch the train there.

When they arrived at the depot, they found only the night operator, a young lad named Andrew Kinkade, on duty. Rourke drew his guns and ordered the boy to hand over all the money in the station. Kinkade, a courageous lad, jerked open an empty money drawer and announced, "I have no money here." Rourke pointed to the company safe standing in the corner and demanded that the boy open it. Kinkade answered that he did not have the key, that the day operator had it, and he was at the hotel. While the outlaws pondered this, they heard a train whistle in the distance—but it came from the east, not the west, which meant they had missed the train they were after.

In the meantime, two men came walking up to the depot, apparently intending to board the approaching westbound. Kinkade saw them and shouted that he was being robbed! Afraid the two strangers would spread the alarm, the outlaws ran out to the platform to grab them. In the confusion, Kinkade slipped out of Rourke's grasp and also ran out on the platform. The westbound

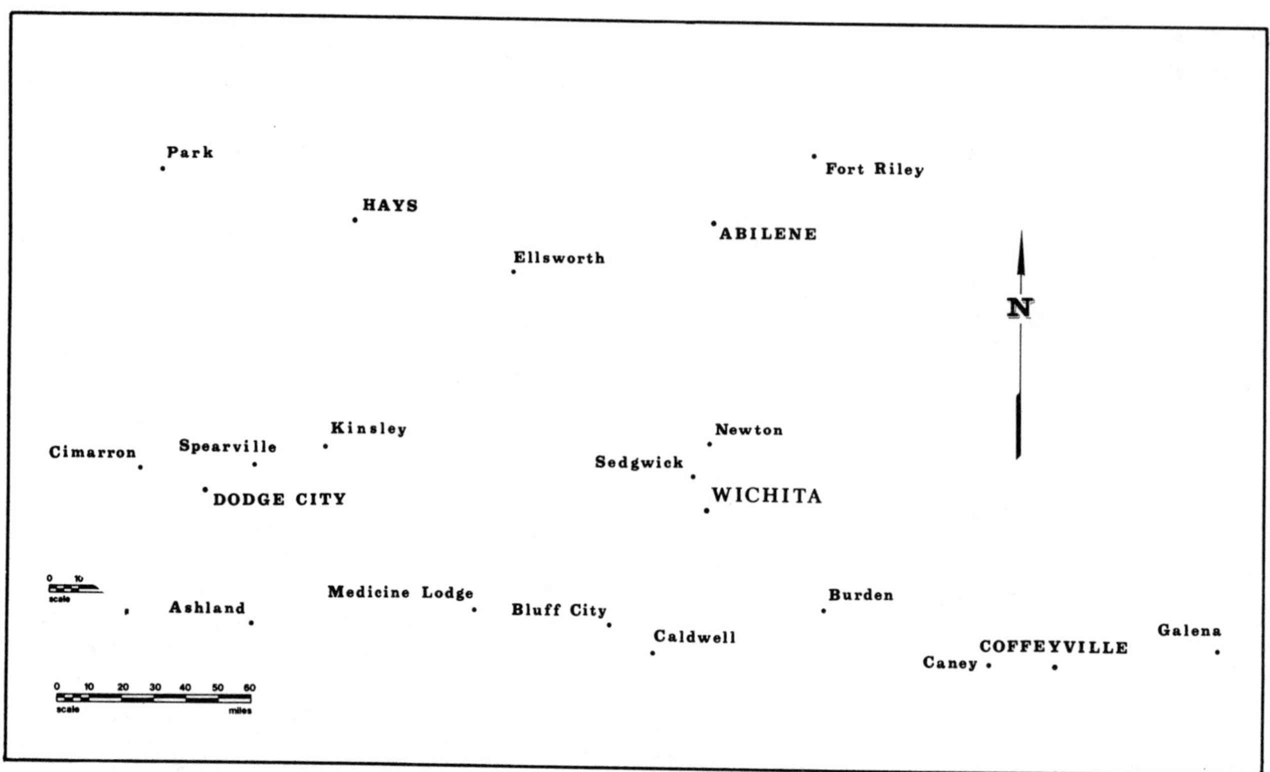


**Frontier Kansas: 1871-1895. Abilene:** Once called the "fastest town in the West" by gunman John Wesley Hardin; Marshal Wild Bill Hickok helped tame the town in 1871. **Ashland:** "Mysterious Dave" Mather paid a visit in May 1885 and left bodies on the floor of the Junction saloon. **Bluff City:** Scene of the John Wesley Hardin's killing of Juan Bideno in July 1871. **Burden:** A Bill Doolin hideout in 1895. **Caldwell:** Scene of the Talbott-Meagher shootout in 1881. **Caney:** Express car robbery here in October 1892 was Bill Doolin's first after inheriting the remnants of the Dalton gang. **Cimarron:** Scene of the 1889 "Battle for the County Seat" involving Dodge City gunslingers. **Coffeyville:** End of the trail for the Daltons in October 1892. **Dodge City:** Wildest of the Kansas cowtowns—Wyatt Earp, Doc Holliday, Dave Mather, the Mastersons—they were all here. **Douglass:** Rustlers were taught an early lesson at Walnut River Crossing and Olmstead's Mill. **Ellsworth:** The lid blew off with the arrival of Texas beef in 1873. **Fort Riley:** An early Hickok stomping ground. **Galena:** Scene of the Jesse James "assassination" in 1879; also a stopping-off place for Belle Starr. **Hays:** Marshal Hickok's first assignment. **Kinsley:** Site of Mike Rourke's hard-luck assault on the Santa Fe in 1878. **Medicine Lodge:** Scene of the McCluskie-Anderson duel; also the end of the line for Henry Newton Brown. **Newton:** The shootout at the Tuttle Dance Hall is still talked about, as is Wes Hardin's battle with the Mexicans. **Park:** Last stop for two Sam Bass gang members. **Sedgwick:** Once the home of the Masterson clan. **Spearville:** Scene of a Doolin gang bank robbery in 1892. **Wichita:** Remembered for the New Years' Day gunfight of 1877.

was now almost to the depot. Kinkade jumped off the platform and raced across the tracks, just ahead of the slowing locomotive. Racing alongside the train, he shouted that there were six armed men on the station platform! To Kinkade's delight, the train kept on rolling, right on past the station. At first, Kinkade thought the engineer had heard him; later he found out that the brakes were faulty, and the engineer was having difficulty stopping.

The train finally pulled to a halt a hundred yards or so down the tracks. The outlaws had run after it, and Rourke and another robber climbed up onto the locomotive. Pointing his gun at the engineer, Rourke ordered him to start up again and "take her out of town." But the engineer, probably faking, claimed that the steam was too low. Back in the express car, the Adams Express Company messenger had seen what was happening and was ready when two of the outlaws approached his door. He caught the first one full in the face with a shotgun blast. Hearing the shot, Rourke and his comrade left the cab and came running back to the express car. As soon as they had passed the tender, the engineer slammed the throttle forward and the train lunged ahead. The outlaws gave up and rode off.

As if the gang's luck had not been bad enough, the Adams Express Company engaged the services of Bat Masterson to go after them. Bat had recently been elected sheriff of Ford County and wanted to make a good showing. Also, he had hunted buffalo over the very route the outlaws had taken and he knew it well. Four days after Bat began his search, he and his posse captured two of the gang at a cattle camp on Crooked Creek, fifty miles southeast of Dodge. Two more were captured in March by Bat's brother Ed Masterson, then Dodge City marshal. The following October Mike Rourke, the leader, was turned in by one of his own gang members. He confessed to the holdup attempt at Kinsley and was sentenced to ten years at hard labor.

# Medicine Lodge
## Barber County

One of the most spectacular duels ever seen was fought in front of Harding's Trading Post on Medicine Lodge's main street. In August 1871 a Texan named Hugh Anderson and several companions killed a part-time law officer, Mike McCluskie, in Newton, Kansas.* Mike's brother Art vowed that he would avenge Mike's death. In June 1873 Art found Anderson working as a bartender at Harding's. If the details of the encounter are true, it reads like a Hollywood script.

McCluskie sent word to Anderson that there was to be a fight to the death, and Anderson could choose the weapons—either guns or knives. Anderson, the smaller of the two, chose guns. The contest was refereed by Harding, Anderson's employer. He stationed the foes twenty paces apart with their backs to each other. When he gave the signal, the contestants whirled and let go. McCluskie's second shot ripped into Anderson's arm, knocking him to the ground. But Anderson, from his knees, put a bullet through the big man's jaw. Blind with rage, McCluskie lunged forward, cocking his gun for another shot. Anderson let him draw near, then calmly put slugs into his shoulder and belly. When McCluskie went down, the crowd closed in, thinking the battle was over. But McCluskie was not through. Slowly he raised his gun and squeezed off another shot, this time hitting Anderson in the belly.

No doubt knowing that he himself was finished, McCluskie wanted to make sure his foe was too. His face contorted with pain, he drew his knife from his belt and slowly began dragging himself toward Anderson. Several bystanders had seen enough and pleaded with Harding to end the fight. But Harding said no, insisting that it was to go to the finish.

As McCluskie drew near his fallen enemy, Anderson rolled over on his side, drawing his own knife. When McCluskie was within reach, Anderson lunged, driving the blade into McCluskie's neck. The big man gurgled and, with a final effort, drove his knife into Anderson's side. In one giant pool of blood, the two enemies died.

Medicine Lodge also hit the headlines in 1884. It was in April on a rainy, dreary morning. Most of the men were at the livery watching a handful of local ranchers and their wranglers getting their gear together for a roundup over on Antelope Flat. As a result, few people noticed the four men who ride into town and stopped in front of the Medicine Valley Bank. The bank's president, Wylie Payne, had just opened up. With him was his cashier, George Geppert.

Wylie Payne was not your typical banker. He had earned his wealth the hard way by punching cattle and then building a herd from scratch. He was tough and seldom side-stepped a fight. So, when one of the strangers commanded, "Hands up!" Wylie Payne's first reaction was to reach for the pistol in his desk drawer. It was a fatal mistake.

A second gun barked, and cashier Geppert pitched backward with bullets in his chest and head.

At the sound of the gunfire the town marshal, Sam Denn, raced up the street toward the bank. He spotted the outlaw who had been left outside with the horses. Denn squeezed off a quick shot but missed. The outlaw returned the fire and also missed. Just then the three robbers burst out the front door of the bank with guns blazing. Denn dived for cover, and the outlaws saddled up and galloped out of town.

The four outlaws headed southwest into a driving rain toward a range of low-lying hills called the "Gypsums." By mistake they wandered into a boxed-in draw, and within a hundred yards they were up to their horses' knees in mud and water. The posse had only to wait at the entrance for the outlaws to decide to give up or fight. They chose to give up.

To their astonishment, the posse found the leader of the gang to be none other than Henry Brown, city marshal of nearby Caldwell, Kansas. With Brown was his assistant marshal, Ben Wheeler. Brown was no stranger to the situation in which he found himself. He had spent enough time on both sides of the law to know that he and his comrades might never see a courtroom. His first impulse was to make a deal. "We'll give you $1,000 if you'll save our lives till daylight," he told the county attorney that night in Medicine Lodge's tiny jail. The answer he got was not encouraging. Brown's next move was to try to lie his way out of his predicament. The robbery was a "set-up" he claimed. Payne and Geppert had engineered it themselves to hide a shortage in the bank funds. The shooting, Brown said, was a mistake. When Payne went for his gun, Brown thought he was being double-crossed. Nobody bought the tale.

As Brown feared, about ten o'clock that night a crowd gathered at the jail. There was a brief flurry of gunshots, and the mob entered the building. As Brown was being wrestled out the front door, he made a break for it. A load of buckshot nearly cut him in two. Wheeler was the next to run. A barrage of bullets brought him down at a hundred yards—wounded but still alive.

Wheeler and the remaining two outlaws were dragged down to the bottoms east of town between Spring and Elm creeks, where three ropes were thrown over a low limb on a huge elm. Wheeler cried and begged for his life. The second outlaw, John Wesley, requested for his last wish that his mother never be told how he died. The third man, Billie Smith, merely muttered, "What's the use," and asked that they get it over with.

Henry Brown researcher Bill O'Neal has dug up an interesting sidelight to this story. It seems that the gang had arranged to disappear through a gap in the Gypsum Hills where they had hidden a team of fresh horses. They had marked the entrance to the gap by the end of a partially completed barbed wire fence. The day of the robbery, however, the farmer stringing the fence had added several hundred feet of posts and wire. As a result, Brown and his companions rode too far and turned into the wrong draw.

Today a modern bank building stands at the site of the old Medicine Valley Bank, but a few blocks to the east local residents can show you the remains of the "hanging tree" and also direct you to the graves of the outlaws.

# Mill Creek
## Johnson County

Mill Creek, a tiny settlement southwest of Kansas City in Johnson County, was once the home of James Butler "Wild Bill" Hickok. He moved there in 1855, living first at the residence of a John Owen; later he bought farmland of his own in Monticello Township. Because Hickok was very friendly with Owen's daughter Mary and because Owen's wife was a Shawnee, some historians have mistakenly reported that Hickok married an Indian girl while in Mill Creek. There is no proof of this.

In 1858 Hickok was elected constable of Monticello Township. It is believed that while he was away one day on official business, his homestead was burned to the ground by Missouri marauders. He left the area soon after to take a job driving a stage for the Russell, Majors and Waddell line.

# Muncie
## Wyandotte County

Muncie, just west of Kansas City on the old Kansas Pacific line (now the Union Pacific), was the site of a train robbery attributed to the James-Younger gang. On December 8, 1874, five men forced section hands to pile railroad ties across the track. The train was then halted by waving a red scarf. The crew was required to uncouple the express and baggage cars from the rest of the train, and the engineer was ordered to pull ahead. The robbers removed about $30,000 from the express car safe.

The James-Younger gang was implicated when it was reported that Jesse James and one of the Younger brothers had been seen in Kansas City a few days before the holdup. Then, not long after the robbery, Kansas City police picked up a drifter named Bud McDaniel who was known to be an associate of the James brothers. He was carrying $1,000 in cash and several pieces of jewelry taken during the robbery, but before he could be tried, he escaped jail and was shot to death by a farmer near Lawrence, Kansas.

# Newton
## Harvey County

Newton can still boast of a gun battle that Hollywood writers find difficult to match: the shootout at the Tuttle Dance Hall. The years have colored the facts some, but the story remains an exciting one.

Newton's big year was 1871, when the advancing rails of the Santa Fe Railroad made the town more convenient for shipping Texas beef east than Abilene, a good fifty miles further north. Saloons and dance halls sprang up overnight, and by August the town was swollen with rowdy cowboys and operating twenty-four hours a day. One such cowboy, a gunslinger named Bill Bailey (also called Baylor), got into an argument with a local man, Mike McCluskie, a railroader and part-time peace officer. The two shot it out in the street and only McCluskie walked away. Several friends of Bailey vowed to avenge his death, notably another Texas hard case, Hugh Anderson. A few nights after the killing, Anderson and four companions encountered McCluskie in Tuttle's Dance Hall.

McCluskie had an acquaintance named Riley (first name possibly Jim) who accompanied big Mike everywhere he went. Riley was a contrast to the two-fisted McCluskie. Small, weakened by consumption and subject to coughing fits, the frail Riley did not look long for this world. Perhaps McCluskie felt sorry for him. In any event, Riley, as usual, was with McCluskie the night Hugh Anderson and his pals challenged Mike at Tuttle's.

What was said between Anderson and McCluskie was not recorded, but suddenly Anderson went for his gun and shot Mike through the neck. The dying man tried to retaliate, but Anderson's comrades finished him off as he lay on the floor. Riley, not far away, went into a rage. He ran to the door of the hall, shut it, and turned to face the Texans. Despite his frailness, Riley evidently carried a gun. He whipped it out and made it talk. One, two, three shots, and three Texans dropped, possibly not even knowing where the shots were coming from. Four, five, six. Six shots from Riley's gun and six bodies lay on the floor. At this point the story clouds. Some say the bartender doused the lights and more shots were fired—maybe by the dying Texans or others in the crowd. In some versions the total body count was nine (including McCluskie). Of Anderson's friends, it is believed that one died instantly and three more died later (two were said to be shot through the lungs). Anderson recovered. No one knows what happened to Riley. He survived the battle but disappeared that night.

Anderson would later be challenged by McCluskie's brother, Art, in a battle to the death in the streets of Medicine Lodge, Kansas.*

Another Hollywood-style shooting match occurred on the prairie outside Newton the same year. Again, the accounts vary, and it is the kind of tale that invites embellishment, but the popular version goes this way. The notorious Texas gunslinger John Wesley Hardin was bringing a herd of longhorns up the Chisholm Trail. Hardin was only eighteen years old at the time, but already he had a reputation of being one of the "quickest trigger fingers" in Texas. Apparently a group of Mexican cowboys were pushing another herd just behind Hardin's. They insisted on crowding his cattle, at times mixing the herds, and no doubt picking up a few stragglers along the way. Hardin rode back and issued a warning, but the Mexican trail boss only laughed at him. When Hardin persisted, the Mexican threatened to shoot him. Few men made such threats to Hardin and lived to tell about it.

When Hardin rode back the next time, he was joined by his pal Jim Clements. It was two against six. (Hardin reportedly told the rest of the trail hands to stay out of it.) Witnesses said the two Texans charged the Mexicans head-on with guns blazing. Soon the foes joined and circled, their horses kicking up so much trail dust nobody could see anybody. When it was all over, six Mexicans lay on the ground, and Hardin and Clements did not have a scratch.

Witnesses swore it happened just that way.

## Park
### Gove County

Few Western buffs can recall Park, Kansas, playing a role in outlaw history. It did, but under a different name. In 1877 this tiny dot on the wind-swept prairie was a lonely Kansas Pacific whistle-stop called Buffalo Station, just about an even 100 miles east of the Colorado line. In 1877 it was not even a town, just a bare bones depot, water tank, and section house—all maintained by a man named Jim Thompson.

In September of that year a Union Pacific eastbound was robbed of over $60,000 at Big Springs, Nebraska.* The robbers, Sam Bass, Joel Collins and four others, split up and headed for Texas. Collins and another, Bill Heffridge, rode south into Kansas. The outlaws had been spotted at the Republican River near the Nebraska-Kansas line, and the authorities were fairly certain of their course. When word reached Hays, Kansas, the Ellis County sheriff and ten soldiers from Fort Hays climbed aboard a train heading west. They estimated the route of the outlaws, guessed it would come somewhere close to Buffalo Station, and chose it as their base of operations. They did not have long to wait.

The two outlaws rode in early on the morning of September 25. There was a heavy fog, and they did not see the soldiers camped on a small ridge near Thompson's section house. Nor did the soldiers see the outlaws. The two men rode up to the station and asked the telegraph operator, Bill Sternberg, about purchasing supplies. They told him they were Texans who had come north with a herd and were on their way home. Sternberg took them up to Thompson's house.

While the men were paying for their grub, Sternberg noticed an envelope sticking out of Collins' pocket with his name on it. He recognized it as being mentioned in connection with the train robbery, and he quietly slipped out to tell the sheriff.

The sheriff and the troopers caught up with the two outlaws a short distance south of the station. Seemingly unperturbed, the two men agreed to ride back so the sheriff could check out their story. But after going only a few hundred feet, the outlaws went for their guns. The soldiers, however, were ready with theirs. The crack of gunfire echoed across the silent prairie, and the two outlaws were pitched from their saddles, dying as they hit the ground.

## Sedgwick
### Sedgwick County

A farm near Sedgwick was the first western home of Bat Masterson and his brothers, Ed and Jim. Their father, Thomas Masterson, moved his family there from near St. Louis in June 1871. His land was in Grant Township, about fourteen miles northeast of Wichita.

Bat and Ed did not stay on the farm long—probably less than a year. Bat was eighteen and Ed, nineteen, and both were eager to strike out on their own. After helping their father build a sod house and harvest his first crop, they headed west to hunt buffalo. Brother Jim joined them a year or so later.

The father lived on the land until 1921. The sons returned for visits now and then, especially Bat, during his years as Ford County sheriff at Dodge City.

Early Wichita. *Kansas State Historical Society.*

# Spearville
## Ford County

Bill Doolin, erstwhile Dalton gang member, led his newly formed band in a raid on the Ford County Bank at Spearville on November 1, 1892. Accompanied by Bitter Creek Newcomb and Ol Yantis, Doolin hit the bank about three o'clock in the afternoon. Leaving Yantis to watch the horses, Doolin and Newcomb placed Winchesters under the nose of cashier J. R. Baird and ordered him to hand over all cash on hand. In three minutes the robbers left with a tote bag filled with over $1,600 in bank notes and currency. In classic James gang fashion, the three outlaws sent passersby scurrying by firing wildly in the air, then sped out of town to the southeast, toward the Arkansas River. A few townsmen saddled up and tried to follow but were easily outdistanced. Ol Yantis was eventually traced to his sister's ranch near Orlando, Oklahoma,* where he was killed in a gun battle with law officers. Doolin and Newcomb would plague Kansas and Oklahoma another three years before the law would catch up with them.

# Wichita
## Sedgwick County

Old timers like to tell the story of the famous New Year's Day gunfight between Wichita city marshal Mike Meagher and a rowdy stage driver, Sylvester Powell. The date was January 1, 1877. Early in the day, Powell allegedly stole a horse from the town hitching rail. The owner complained and Powell threatened him. The owner then went to Meagher who threw Powell in jail. Later that evening, Powell's boss bailed him out, and Powell, probably braced with a few whiskeys, went looking for the marshal.

Powell found Meagher sitting in the outhouse behind Hope's saloon. Without even waiting for his victim to finish what he was doing, Powell opened fire with his sixgun. One bullet hit Meagher in the leg, and a second ripped a hole in his coat. Thinking the marshal might be dead, Powell cautiously approached. Just as he reached the door, Meagher burst out and lunged at his attacker. Powell got off another shot and hit the marshal in the hand. But Meagher still kept coming and Powell lost his nerve. As he turned and ran, Meagher fired but missed. Once out of Meagher's range of fire, Powell slowed to a walk. Possibly he thought the marshal was too badly injured to follow. He was wrong. When Meagher reached the street, he saw Powell standing in front of Hill's Drug Store. The marshal carefully took aim and put a bullet into Powell's heart.

Wichita relives its yesterdays with its Cow Town Museum, 1871 Sim Park Drive, consisting of over thirty-five relocated and restored buildings, including the town's first permanent house, church, and jail. Also worth visiting is the Wichita-Sedgwick County Historical Museum, 204 S. Main Street, which includes the renovated former city hall building (1892) and a recreation of a turn-of-the-century drug store.

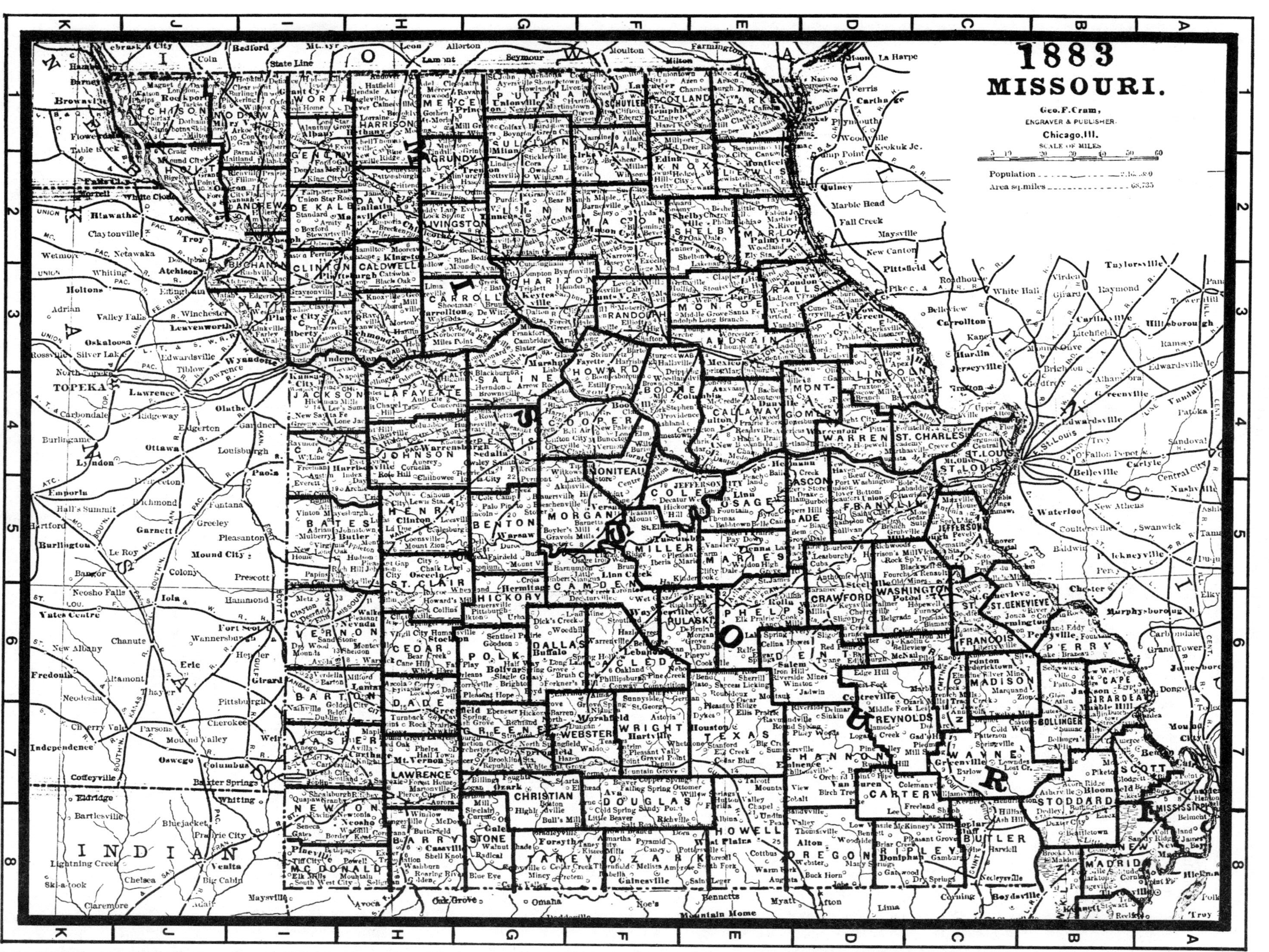


Missouri 1883

# MISSOURI

## Blue Cut
### Jackson County

The "Blue Cut," also occasionally called the "Rocky Cut," was nothing more than a slice carved out of a thirty-foot hillside for the tracks of the Chicago and Alton Railroad about two miles west of the Glendale Station in Jackson County. In the annals of Missouri outlaw history, the train robbery that occurred there on the night of September 7, 1881, is frequently confused with two other train robberies: at Rocky Cut near Otterville* in Cooper County in 1876 and at nearby Glendale Station* in 1879. All three holdups have been credited by most writers to Jesse James and his gang.

All the robbers at Blue Cut were masked except the leader, who was bearded, and who kept telling his victims that he was indeed the notorious Jesse James. He claimed that he and his men were there to avenge the Chicago and Alton Railroad's participation in the generous reward put up after the Winston, Missouri* robbery to induce a member of the gang to turn Jesse and Frank in.

The Blue Cut robbery was carried out in traditional James gang fashion: warning flags were placed on the track to stop the train. Further down, rocks and logs were piled on the rails in case the engineer failed to stop. The robbers broke open the door of the express car while the passengers were kept in line by occasional rifle shots. Once in the express car, however, the outlaws appeared upset by the small amount of cash in the safe, and they took out their anger by beating the express messenger on the head with their pistol butts. (It was later rumored that had they waited for the next train they would have found $100,000.)

The holdup almost resulted in a tragic train wreck. A freight was following the express, and a brakeman, Frank Burton, made a heroic dash down the tracks to flag it.

In a final act of bravado, the outlaw leader saluted the engineer of the robbed train, and gave him two silver dollars from the loot, with which he was told to "drink to the health of Jesse James."

Doubt was cast on the James' boys role in the robbery when in the following weeks several local characters were rounded up and charged with the crime. At least one reportedly confessed and named three companions, none of whom were Jameses. But later, two members of the James gang were caught, and both placed Jesse and Frank at the Blue Cut affair.

## Carthage
### Jasper County

Carthage, about twenty miles northeast of Joplin, was the birthplace of the notorious "Bandit Queen" Belle Starr. Born Myra Maybelle Shirley in 1848, Belle received an excellent early education at a local private school run by William Cravens in a second floor room over the Masonic Hall on the northwest corner of Carthage's public square. Belle's father, John Shirley, operated the Carthage Hotel, located several doors to the east.

The Shirley family lived in Carthage until the summer of 1864, when they moved to Scyene, Texas, a few miles southeast of Dallas.

There is a story that while the family was living in Carthage, Belle's father and the outlaw Jim Reed, whom Belle later married, got into a shooting match, apparently over Reed's attentions to the girl. The fight supposedly occurred in 1861, which meant that Belle would have been only thirteen years old. According to the account, neither Shirley nor Reed were injured in the affair.

# Forsyth
## Taney County

Forsyth is on US 160 about thirty-five miles south of Springfield. Just southwest of Forsyth, on the old Harrison-Springfield Road, are the "murder rocks," a narrow and tortuous spot on the trail bordered by a deep gorge on one side and a sharp ledge of a jagged cliff on the other. The spot was a perfect place to ambush travelers and a favorite hangout of a maniacal bushwhacker named Alf Bolin.

By the age of sixteen Bolin was said to be leading a gang of guerrillas in war-torn southern Missouri. In 1862 he reportedly killed his own foster father who had chosen to side with the Union. Living off the country, more animal than human, Bolin specialized in rape and torture, especially torture. It seems he enjoyed ripping open his victim's bellies, plucking out their tongues and cutting off their ears. It made little difference to Alf who came down the trail. If a traveler carried money, Alf took it, and only if the rider was very lucky did he live to tell about it.

The deranged Alf had no social life, and some say most of what he stole he stashed away in a cave somewhere in Taney County, probably near the Arkansas border. It may still be there today.

Bolin's career came to an end near the end of the war, allegedly at the hands of a Union solder who posed as a friendly Rebel and caught the outlaw off guard. The details are sketchy, but apparently Alf met his match in ruthlessness. It is said that one day Alf's severed head showed up at the Federal headquarters at Ozark. It is believed the soldier who brought it in was paid an unspecified sum out of a special fund set up for such purposes.

# Gads Hill
## Wayne County

The holdup at Gads Hill, a flag station on the Iron Mountain Railroad about 100 miles south of St. Louis, was Missouri's first train robbery. It is also believed to be the first in the nation in which the robbers took complete control of a station and awaited the arrival of the train. The gang, numbering five men, placed a signal on the track calling for the engineer to stop. When he did, the robbers boarded the passenger coaches and the express car, garnering from $2,000 to $22,000, depending upon whose account is accepted.

The holdup occurred on January 31, 1874, and is generally believed to represent the return of the James-Younger gang to Missouri after successful robberies in Iowa and Arkansas. The Gads Hill affair perpetrated the myth that the James-Younger bunch were Robin Hood types who pillaged only the rich. Stories circulated that the outlaws asked to see the hands of their male victims to see if they were "working men" or "plug-hat gentlemen." And, of course, it is said the outlaws refused, in true chivalrous fashion, to rob the ladies.

# Gallatin
## Daviess County

In November 1867 the Daviess County Treasurer's Office at Gallatin, which is just east of Interstate 35 about half-way between Kansas City and the Iowa line, fell victim to John Reno, a member of the famous Reno brothers gang of Indiana. Reno and another gang member, Volney Elliott, broke into the office after hours and rummaged two safes for around $22,000 in bills and coins. The outlaws fled on foot to the southeast along the Grand River, hiding by day and traveling by night, until they reached Chillicothe. There they boarded a stock train which eventually would take them to Chicago.

Through a tip from a Gallatin resident named Clay Abel (whom Reno later would claim suggested the burglary), the authorities picked up Reno in Indiana several weeks later and returned him to Missouri. (According to Pinkerton records he was snatched by their operatives at the train station in Seymour, Indiana, but Reno for some reason denied this and claimed he was captured by Indianapolis police.) Back in Gallatin, Reno at first argued his innocence, but fearing a lynching by an angry crowd that gathered around the jail, he finally admitted his guilt and was sentenced to the state prison at Jefferson City.

Gallatin made the news again in 1869. On December 7, two men entered the Daviess County Savings Bank and asked for change for a $100 bill. As the cashier, John W. Sheets, sat at his desk counting out the money, one of the robbers for apparently no reason, shot him. A clerk, William A. McDowell, dashed out the door and spread the alarm. The robbers ran for their horses, one of which bolted and dragged its rider for a dozen yards. The other outlaw halted, pulled his companion up on his horse, and the two raced out of town. After stealing another horse from a farmer named Daniel Smoot, the outlaws headed south toward Clay County. Near Kidder, on the Caldwell County line, they forced a local resident named Helm to guide them over back trails around the town.

The outlaws' abandoned horse, a spirited black mare, was eventually traced to Jesse James. This was the first evidence directly connecting the James brothers to bank robberies in the area. (Jesse later issued "alibi cards" saying that he had sold the horse to a man from Topeka, Kansas, two days before the Gallatin holdup.) The authorities converged on the James's brothers home in Clay County, Missouri, but Jesse and Frank escaped following a brief gun battle.

## Glendale Station
### Jackson County

The town of Glendale, now absorbed by sprawling St. Louis, is occasionally mentioned as the site of a James-Younger gang train robbery on October 8, 1879. There was a robbery on that date, but at a different Glendale. This Glendale was located just southeast of Independence, Missouri, on the old Chicago and Alton Railroad.

The gang rode in at sunset, probably expecting the town to be deserted. It was not. Several farmers, having arrived late for afternoon shopping and small talk, were gathered on the board sidewalk in front of the general store. The group eyed the strangers as they rode up, and this must have made them nervous. They drew their guns and ordered the entire bunch to march down the street to the depot. At the depot the outlaws wrecked the telegraph key and forced the station agent to change the signal from green to red, which would halt the 8:00 P.M. express.

As the train rolled to a stop, the express car messenger smelled trouble and began stuffing the money from his safe into a valise. When the robbers banged on the station-side door of his car, the messenger tried to climb out the window on the opposite side, but he was spotted. Angered by his attempt to flee, the outlaws knocked him in the head with a pistol butt. After searching the car for any additional loot, the gang saddled up and rode off.

Early reports of the holdup estimated the loss at upwards of $40,000. The figure was later reduced to about $6,000 in cash and an undetermined amount of non-negotiable paper. A story soon circulated that the robbers left a note with the station agent which read: "We are the boys who are hard to handle, and we will make it hot for the boys who try to take us." At the bottom were the names of Jesse and Frank James plus six companions.

Whether the note was genuine is not known. There were rumors that Jesse James was spotted in Kansas City in the weeks preceding the robbery, and there were witnesses who claimed they recognized him as the leader of the gang. In 1880 a man named Tucker Bassham was arrested and charged with participating in the Glendale affair. He implicated others and testified that the group was led by Jesse. A second man, Dick Liddil, the gang member who testified against Frank James following his surrender to the authorities in 1882, told substantially the same story.

## Hughesville
### Pettis County

By 1898 train robbery had become a fashionable crime in the American West. Thanks to the exploits of the James and Youngers, Missouri had picked up the sobriquets "Outlaw Paradise" and "The Train Robber's State." Although by 1898 the James and Youngers were long gone, the memory of their escapades were still fresh in the minds of many a Missourian, so it was not surprising that three out-of-work employees of the Missouri Pacific Railroad spent the summer of that year plotting how they would rob an express car on the Lexington Branch of the road for which they had once toiled.

The ex-railroaders were Jim West, E. H. Adams, and Eli Stubblefield. West and Adams had been engineers; Stubblefield's occupation is not known. They picked November 29 to stage their affair. Their plan was to ride out in Adam's surrey to a spot along the tracks near Hughesville, which is on County Road H about twelve miles northwest of Sedalia. West and Stubblefield would stop the train and rob the express car, and Adams would pick them up later at Sedalia. The plan was good, with one exception: Adams got cold feet and told the Missouri Pacific officials at Sedalia all about it.

On the night of the robbery, extra guards were riding the locomotive cab. Stubblefield swung a lantern to stop the train and was met with a roar of gunfire. West, waiting from the top of a nearby embankment, ran for his life. Both men were captured and sent to prison.

## Kansas City

As an attraction for outlaws, Kansas City probably was at its peak in 1880, when there were from thirty to forty gambling houses in town. Bat Masterson spent six months there that year following his defeat for reelection as sheriff of Ford County, Kansas. Masterson was never the deadly gunfighter many writers made him out to be nor was he a troublemaker, and his days in Kansas City were quiet ones. He spent most of his time playing faro at one of three popular Main Street parlors—Doc Frame's, Major James S. Showers's, or Joe Bassett's—or over on Missouri Avenue at Bob Potee's place.

Bob Potee's "Number 3 Missouri Avenue" was one of the top gambling houses in the West. Covering the entire second floor above one of the finest restaurants in the city, it boasted of luxurious appointments such as a lengthy entrance hall lined with perfumed lovelies, each claiming to be "Lady Luck." Well-heeled guests were encouraged to "touch" their favorite beauty before playing the tables— a sure-fire guarantee that they would not lose, especially if they tipped their lady a $20 gold piece.

Rivaling Potee's palace was Joe Bassett's "Marble Hall," a favorite of the Texas cattlemen, located on Main between Fifth and Missouri. Wild Bill Hickok was a frequent visitor to Bassett's, as were Jesse and Frank James and Cole Younger.

Many believe the James brothers paid a special visit to Kansas City on September 26, 1872, to rob the annual Kansas City Fair of its gate receipts. At four o'clock that afternoon, two horsemen rode up to the main gate with guns drawn. A fair official named Ford was ordered to hand over the cash box containing about $10,000. The money had just been counted and was awaiting deposit with the First National Bank of Kansas City which had arranged to pick it up by special messenger. After taking the box, the robbers fired their revolvers in the air to clear a path through the crowd. Ford later said that one of the robbers looked like Frank James. Several reports of the incident mentioned three gunmen instead of two, and at times, Cole Younger's name was brought up. According to dedicated James-Younger gang researcher Carl Breihan, years later Frank James admitted that it was he and Jesse who went to the fair that day.

In October 1898 Missourians could not believe what they were reading in the Kansas City newspapers: "Jesse James arrested for train robbery!" The notorious Jesse had been dead since 1892, the victim of fellow outlaw Bob Ford's treachery (see *St. Joseph, Missouri*). But there it was: Jesse James once again accused of robbing an express car, this time on the Missouri Pacific Railroad at Leeds, just southeast of Kansas City. Closer reading of the account, however, revealed that the suspect was Jesse James, Jr., son of the famous bandit.

After Jesse, Sr.'s death his widow, Zee, had moved to Kansas City with her children, Jesse, Jr., and Mary. Jesse, Jr., a likeable lad, had gone to work at age fifteen as an office boy for a Kansas City law firm. Former Missouri governor Thomas Crittenden, impressed by the youth's willingness to work hard, later took him under his wing and arranged for him to receive the lucrative cigar and confection concession at the Jackson County courthouse. But while working at the courthouse, Jesse became acquainted with an unsavory character known as "Quail Hunter" Jack Kennedy. Kennedy, a man with a shady past, had grown up in the "Cracker Neck" area of Jackson County where many local youths regarded the James-Younger gang as heroes. It was not surprising, therefore, that he sought the acquaintance of the young son of outlaw Jesse.

It is believed that Kennedy already had at least two train robberies to his credit when he and young Jesse met. Jesse, Jr., apparently was taken in by the flamboyant bandit and did not hesitate to admit on one occasion that he considered Kennedy a "friend." As a result, several weeks after the holdup at Leeds, presumably the work of Kennedy, Kansas City police arrested young Jesse. It seems a member of the Kennedy gang had a note in his pocket bearing Jesse, Jr.'s signature. Under questioning, the outlaw named the boy as a member of the gang.

Ex-governor Crittenden and other political officials promptly came to the boy's aid. The best lawyers were hired, and he was quickly acquitted. It is said the lad was so impressed by the eloquence of the defense put up on his behalf, he announced that he wanted to become a lawyer himself. Once again his influential friends helped out, and he achieved his goal. He was admitted to the bar and later practiced in Kansas City and in California, where he lived until his death in March 1951.

## Kearney
### Clay County

The boyhood home of Jesse and Frank James is two miles east of Kearney, which itself is twenty miles north of Kansas City on Interstate 35. The outlaws' father, Robert James, settled in Clay County in 1842, where he became pastor of the New Hope Baptist Church. He also farmed and eventually accumulated 275 acres of good crop land. An educated man, James help found William Jewell College in nearby Liberty and served as one of the school's first trustees. But in 1850 Robert James caught gold fever and set out alone for California. Several weeks after arriving there, he took ill and died.

Zerelda James, Jesse's and Frank's mother, remarried twice. Her third husband was Dr. Reuben Samuel, a country physician who devoted most of his time to farming. Samuel moved into the James home, and it eventually became known as the "Samuels' place."

During Jesse's and Frank's early outlaw years the farm was a semi-safe haven. The brothers came and went as they pleased, although probably in disguise. As they became more well-known, they had to be more careful, but even then they probably made many midnight visits to see their mother, Dr. Samuel, and step-brothers and sisters. There are several accounts of the boys using nearby wooded areas to rendezvous their gang.

The farmhouse was the scene of a tragic incident on January 26, 1875. Doctor Samuel and his wife awakened in the night to discover an object, described later as

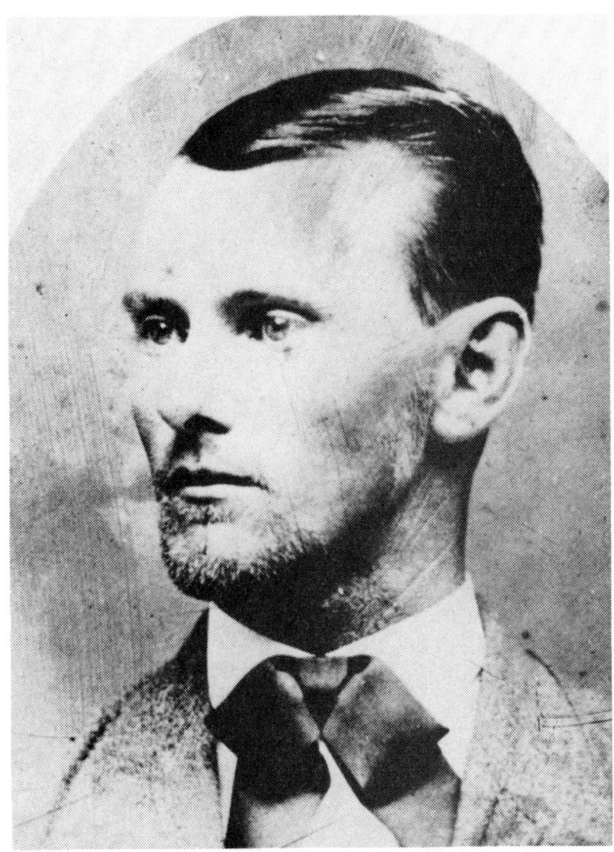

Jesse James. *Kansas State Historical Society.*

some kind of cloth ball saturated with a flammable liquid, aflame on their kitchen floor. They shoved it into the fireplace before it could do any major damage. Seconds later another ball came crashing through a window. When Dr. Samuel pushed this one into the fireplace it exploded. A piece of the object struck young Archie Samuel, nine-year-old half-brother of Jesse and Frank, tearing a gaping hole in his side. Another fragment hit Mrs. Samuel, severely injuring her hand and arm. The boy died an hour later, and Mrs. Samuel's arm eventually had to be amputated.

Later it was discovered that a group of men, thought to be Pinkerton agents, had arrived in the area that night by train. They converged on the house, thinking that Jesse and Frank were hiding inside. The flaming objects were incendiary devices made of oil-soaked cotton wrapped around pieces of metal. Apparently they were intended to smoke the outlaws out. The one probably exploded when the oil-soaked material was touched off by hot coals.

The attackers were never identified. It was believed that a neighbor's hired hand, Jack Ladd, was involved and that he may even have been a Pinkerton agent. It was also said a gun was found at the scene bearing the initials "P.G.G." which was supposed to stand for "Pinkerton Government Guard." Sympathy for the family resulted in an outcry for an investigation. One was held and some of the results were published in local newspapers, but the full report has never been found. The following March a Clay County grand jury indicted Allan Pinkerton, Jack Ladd (who disappeared immediately after the attack), and a third man, Robert J. King, for the murder of the Samuel boy. Another suspect, a Liberty attorney named Samuel Hardwicke, was mentioned but apparently cleared when the only evidence that could be found against him was that he had been retained by the Pinkerton agency around the time of the attack. Allan Pinkerton stayed out of Missouri, and no attempt was made to extradite him from Illinois. No arrests were made, and the matter was eventually dropped.

Some light has recently been shed on the possible identity of the raiders. A man named Howard Meck, whose grandfather, Edward Davis, lived in Liberty at the time, revealed in January 1983 that his grandfather had admitted to being part of the raiding party that night. According to Meck, his grandfather was a Clay County deputy sheriff who, along with five fellow deputies, was temporarily assigned to assist the Pinkertons in an attempt to capture the James brothers. Following the raid, deputy Davis left Missouri, apparently out of fear of retaliation. Meck, who now lives in Annapolis, Maryland, has the deputy sheriff's badge his grandfather said he wore that night.

Not long after Jesse James's death (see *St. Joseph, Missouri*), Mrs. Samuel turned the homestead into a tourist attraction. Until 1902 Jesse's grave remained in the yard, decorated by flowers, many of which came from seeds sent by well-wishers from across the nation. Mrs. Samuel entertained paying visitors with tales of her outlaw sons, accompanied by tears of grief and oaths of vengeance against the Pinkertons and others. For an extra 25¢, a visitor could purchase pebbles from Jesse's grave. In

James Farm, Kearney, Missouri, now under restoration. *Clay County Department of Parks, Recreation and Historical Sites.*

An aged Frank James playing host to James Farm visitors. *Clay County Department of Parks, Recreation and Historical Sites.*

1902 Jesse's remains were transferred to the Mount Olivet Cemetery at Kearney. A prominent marker was placed on the grave, but over the years souvenir hunters chipped away pieces until little was left.

The old farmhouse deteriorated over the years. By the 1970s the outbuildings were gone, and the oldest wing of the house, where Jesse was born, was in ruins. The newer front area, containing the room where Frank died in 1915, was in only a little better shape. To save the site, the county purchased it in 1978. Historic preservation specialists were called in and restoration was begun. An organization called "Friends of the James Farm" was formed to finance restoration and to sponsor writing and research on the James family.

Across the road from the farm is Claybrook, a pre-Civil War plantation house that was the home of Jesse's daughter, Mary James Barr, from 1899 to 1921. It too is being restored, and both the James farm and Claybrook are open to the public under the supervision of the Clay County Department of Parks, Recreation and Historic Sites.

The "Friends of the James Farm" invite interested persons to become members. It is a private, non-profit organization. Members receive newsletters, free admission to the site, and discounts on purchases. The group sponsors an annual James Family Reunion the third weekend in September in conjunction with the town of Kearney's "James Festival" celebration which features rodeos, parades, dances, craft shows, and other events. Interested persons can write to James Farm, Route 2, Box 236, Kearney, Missouri 64060.

## Lexington
### Lafayette County

Lexington is east of Kansas City on US 24. The town, which was founded on a bluff overlooking the Missouri River, boasts of one, possibly two encounters with Jesse and Frank James. On October 30, 1866, cashier J. L. Thomas of the banking house of Alexander Mitchell and Company was robbed by two men who removed $2011.50 from his cash drawer. Waving menacing pistols at Thomas, they demanded an additional $100,000 they said they heard was deposited in the safe. Thomas swore there was no such sum, and, after a search failed to produce a key to the safe, the outlaws stormed out. A posse was quickly formed, but it was soon outdistanced.

Later, when Jesse and Frank James became famous,

local storytellers attributed the robbery to them. Little proof of this has ever been turned up.

Lexington's second alleged run-in with the James brothers is supported by more evidence but not much. It occurred nearly eight years later on August 30, 1874, north of town, on the far side of the Missouri River. The victims were passengers on a local stagecoach used to shuttle travelers between Lexington and the railroad that paralleled the north bank of the river. Three armed men held up the nine passengers. The amount taken was not reported. There were witnesses to the robbery, all Sunday afternoon strollers on the south side of the river. Helpless, they watched the outlaws stop the driver at gunpoint and order the passengers out of the coach. One witness, Miss Mattie Hamlet, claimed she recognized the robbers as the James brothers and one of the Younger brothers. Later, however, she refused to sign an affidavit to this effect. The editor of the Lexington *Caucasian* praised the bandits as "brilliant, bold and indefatigable roughriders," perpetuating the myth that they were Robin Hood types. One of the victims, a school teacher from Kentucky, was quoted as saying "he was exceedingly glad, if he had to be robbed, that it was done by first class artists, by men of national reputation."

# Liberty
## Clay County

Liberty, just off Interstate 35 north of Kansas City, is the seat of Jesse and Frank James's home county and possibly was the site of their first (and some say the nation's first) bank robbery. On February 13, 1866, ten to twelve men robbed the Clay County Savings Association of from $60,000 to $70,000 in cash, government bonds, and gold and silver. According to the files of the Liberty *Tribune*, the men, dressed in blue army overcoats, forced the cashier, Greenup Bird, to transfer the contents of the bank's vault into a large wheat sack.

The robbery was accomplished swiftly and quietly, but on making their escape, the outlaws shot at two passersby, S. H. Holmes and George Wymore. Wymore, a student at nearby William Jewell College, was killed. In what would become a classic outlaw fashion, the band wildly fired their guns in the air to frighten off any additional onlookers and rode south out of town toward the Missouri River.

While the robbery is credited by some as being the first peacetime daylight bank holdup in America, there is no solid proof that the James brothers were in fact involved. Some James gang researchers who claim the brothers were not on the scene point to evidence that Frank was in Kentucky at the time and Jesse was home sick in bed.

Tourists can visit the site of the robbery today at 104 E. Franklin Street, on the town square. The building, originally built in 1858, has been restored and houses the Jesse James Museum, which displays James memorabilia, original and period furnishings, and a pre-Civil War banking exhibit. The town's 1833 jail has also been restored and contains a museum. It is located one block north of the square.

# Mexico
## Audrain County

Mexico, located on US 64 seventeen miles north of Interstate 70 between Columbia and St. Louis, is too far east to have been frequented by the James-Younger gang during Missouri's outlaw years. But the town is mentioned in the annals of outlaw history because of one Jim Berry, a hometown boy who rode with the Sam Bass gang during its stage-robbing days in the Black Hills. Also, Berry was along at Big Springs, Nebraska,* for the holdup on the Union Pacific Railroad which netted the gang over $60,000 in twenty-dollar gold pieces.

Big Springs was Jim Berry's last robbery. Following the holdup he returned to Mexico to spend some of his share of the loot. He arrived in town on October 5, 1877, a Friday, carrying his gold pieces in a pair of worn saddlebags. The next morning he did a very stupid thing. As soon as the town's three banks opened, he traded in $9,000 of the coins for currency. As was their practice, the banks immediately shipped part of the coins to a St. Louis depository. The following Monday they were informed that the coins were probably from the Big Springs robbery. By Tuesday detectives were in town conferring with Audrain County sheriff Henry Glasscock.

A search of Berry's family home failed to turn up the outlaw. However, the following Saturday a man from nearby Callaway County called at Blum's Department Store in Mexico and presented a claim check for a suit of clothes Berry had ordered the first day he was in town. The man, R. T. Kasey, said Berry had told him he could have the suit if he paid the balance due on it. Having no better lead, Sheriff Glasscock staked out Kasey's home, near Shamrock. Sunday morning a posse found Berry hiding in a woods about a mile away. When Berry saw the lawmen he ran, but Glasscock brought him down with a load of shotgun pellets in the legs. Berry, resigned to his fate, pleaded with Glasscock to shoot him rather than make him stand trial. The sheriff declined and loaded the outlaw into a wagon for the trip back to town.

Infection set into Berry's wounds and he had lost much blood. After lingering for two days, he died. He was buried on October 17 next to his aged mother who had preceded him in death by only a few hours—some say from a broken heart over learning that her beloved son was an outlaw.

## Monegaw Springs
### St. Clair County

Monegaw Springs is on County Road 3 near the southwestern end of the Harry S. Truman Reservoir in St. Clair County. In March 1874 it was the scene of a shootout between John and Jim Younger, members of the James-Younger gang of outlaws, and two Pinkerton agents accompanied by a former deputy sheriff. Details of the incident are sketchy, but it seems that the Pinkertons, Louis J. Lull and John Boyle, had joined up with former deputy Edwin B. Daniel to look for the Youngers. All three were strangers to the region, and they stopped to ask directions at a farmhouse owned by a Theodrick Snuffer. As luck would have it, Snuffer was a friend of the Youngers, and the two outlaws were at the house at the time. They became suspicious of the strangers and decided to follow them.

According to a newspaper account based on a story Jim Younger later gave Snuffer, when he and his brother caught up to the three men, John Boyle suspected trouble and rode off in a hurry. The Youngers then ordered Lull and Daniel to unbuckle their gun belts and drop them on the ground. As the outlaws were picking them up, Lull drew out a concealed Derringer and shot John Younger through the neck. Lull spurred his horse and started for a nearby woods, but Younger, as he was falling, got off one shot and knocked the Pinkerton from his saddle. Daniel then made his break and Jim Younger shot him. John Younger and Daniel both died at the scene. Lull lived about six weeks.

John Younger was buried in the old family lot on the Chalk Level Road about three miles from Osceola. His remains were later transferred to a cemetery at Lee's Summit, Missouri.

## Norwood
### Wright County

Norwood is about fifty miles east of Springfield on US 60. On September 23, 1898, a robbery of a Southern Express car on the old Kansas City, Ft. Scott & Memphis Railroad five miles west of Norwood brought to an end the brief career of "Quail Hunter" Jack Kennedy, a small-time Kansas City outlaw who fancied himself another Jesse James.

The holdup, which was actually at a tiny flag station called Macomb, was unremarkable among the hundreds of train robberies that occurred during the last decade of the nineteenth century, except for how the train was stopped. Kennedy and his comrades hit upon the idea of hiring an innocent farmer. When the train stopped to let him off, Quail Hunter and his bunch were waiting. Unfortunately for the outlaws, they left a trail that was easy to follow, and Kennedy became a guest of the Missouri State Penitentiary for seventeen years.

Kennedy, a colorful character who once tried to recruit the son of Jesse James to ride in his gang (see *Kansas City*), supposedly acquired his nickname from an incident that occurred a few years prior to the robbery that landed him in prison. It seems he was picked up by lawmen late one night carrying a shotgun and a pistol and wearing a black mask and a set of false whiskers. When asked what he was doing with such paraphernalia in the middle of the night, he answered that he was "quail hunting."

## Otterville
### Cooper County

Otterville is just north of US 50 about ten miles east of Sedalia. About a mile east of Otterville the Missouri Pacific tracks cross the Lamine River. On approaching the bridge from the west, the rails pass through a rugged slice in the cliffs called Rocky Cut. On the night of July 7, 1876, eight men hid in a nearby woods until well past sunset, then sneaked out and overpowered the watchman at the bridge. Using the watchman's red lantern, they gave the westbound express the signal to stop. As the engineer pulled to a halt, the leader of the gang shouted from the darkness that they were holding up the train.

The express company safes contained over $15,000, which two of the robbers quickly stuffed into sacks. Back in the coaches, the stunned passengers sat quietly under the steady gaze of the robbers' confederates. In one of the coaches a preacher was softly praying that the lives of all aboard would be spared.

After dividing their loot, the outlaws saddled up and disappeared in the night. Some say there were only half-hearted attempts to pursue them, probably because no posseman wanted to face a bullet from the blackness of the dense Missouri woods.

Not long after the holdup, law officers picked up a young drifter named Hobbs Kerry in the town of Granby, south of Joplin. Although the town was over

150 miles from the scene of the robbery, Kerry was flashing a wad of money which looked like it might have been part of the shipment. Kerry's description was sent to witnesses in and around Cooper County, and a farmer from Sedalia identified him as one of a group of strangers who stopped at his house just a week before the holdup. Kerry soon broke down and confessed his part in the crime. Moreover, he named his confederates: Jesse and Frank James, Cole and Bob Younger, and three others, marking the first time the James-Younger gang had been directly linked to one of the many robberies in central and western Missouri.

## Princeton
### Mercer County

This tiny northern Missouri community, at the junction of US 36 and US 65, is believed to be the birthplace of Calamity Jane (Martha Jane Cannary or Conarray). Various dates have been given for her birth, including 1850, 1852, and possibly as early as 1844. There is evidence that her family left Princton in 1865, moving further west to Virginia City, Montana. Many tales have been told about Calamity's exploits in later years, particularly her years in Deadwood, Dakota Territory. Details on her early life, however, are scarce.

## Richmond
### Ray County

By late spring 1867 bank employees in small towns surrounding Kansas City were cautiously eyeing nearly every stranger who walked through the door. In the preceding year banks at Liberty, Lexington, and Savannah had been raided. Everybody was wondering who was next. On May 22 it was the Hughes and Wasson Bank at Richmond.

Richmond lies just east of Clay County on State Road 10 about eight miles north of the Missouri River. According to witnesses four or five masked men entered the bank and helped themselves to about $4,000. While they were inside a crowd gathered, and several shots were fired. The outlaws returned the fire, hitting the town's mayor, John B. Shaw, and two others—B. G. Griffin, the local jailer, and his son Frank.

A posse chased the robbers until sundown, once coming close enough to exchange more shots, but they eventually lost them in the dense woods. The identity of the robbers was never established. Some time later three suspects were rounded up, accused of the crime, and lynched by angry citizens. Still later a witness was supposedly uncovered who claimed he was on the scene and could positively identify Jesse and Frank James as the culprits, aided by two of the Younger brothers.

## Ste. Genevieve
### Ste. Genevieve County

This little Mississippi River town, about fifty miles south of St. Louis, was the first permanent settlement in Missouri. On May 27, 1873, four riders tied their horses outside the Ste. Genevieve Association's Banking House. Two went inside with guns drawn and came out with from $3,500 to $4,000. Using the cashier as a shield against any trouble from bystanders, they joined their comrades who had been left holding the horses. As the four rode out of town, they shouted "Hurrah for Hildebrand!"

The reference was apparently to Sam Hildebrand, a desperado from nearby St. Francis County, who had specialized in bushwhacking Union troops in southeastern Missouri and northern Arkansas during the Civil War. Rumors quickly spread that the robbers were former members of his gang. Others, however, blamed the holdup on Cullon Baker, an Arkansas outlaw, while still others attributed it to Jesse James and his followers. The identity of the bandits was never established. The James gang became the most popular suspects mainly because the robbery was carried off in a manner almost identical to those in western Missouri in the late 1860s which most authorities attribute to Jesse, Frank, and the Younger brothers.

The safe from which the robbers took their loot has been preserved and is on display. Also of interest are the collections at the Historical Museum, located at Merchant Street and DuBourg Place.

## St. Joseph
### Buchanan County

In the 1880s busy St. Joseph was an ideal hideout town for outlaws. The city had grown rapidly in the last half of the century, being the last port in northwestern Missouri having direct river communication with the East. The town also was one of the most popular points of departure for immigrants heading west. The community bustled, and with travelers coming and going by the hundreds daily, it was easy for a person to get lost in the crowd. It is not surprising, therefore, that when Jesse James temporarily put aside his guns to spend some time with his wife and family, he chose a quiet St. Joseph neighborhood for a safe haven. Jesse's address was 1318 Lafayette Street; it would be his last.

Bob Ford, killer of Jesse James. *St. Joseph Museum.*

Early reports that the notorious Jesse James had been killed were taken lightly. There had been similar stories over the years, and this time some of the newspapers cautioned their readers to await confirmation. But this time the details began to check out. On April 3, 1882, a man named Thomas Howard, said to be the name used by Jesse, was shot to death at his home on Lafayette Street. The killer was named Robert Ford, a recently recruited member of Jesse's gang. Ford and his brother Charles had turned themselves over to the St. Joseph authorities immediately.

According to the story given by the Fords, they had been living with Jesse and his wife, Zee, while plans were being made for a robbery of a bank at Platte City, Missouri. Shortly after breakfast on April 3, while the Ford brothers and Jesse were in the bedroom, Jesse took off his guns and laid them on the bed, apparently intending to step up on a chair and dust a picture. As he did, Bob Ford drew his revolver and put a bullet in Jesse's brain.

There were those who continued to doubt that the dead man was indeed Jesse, until reports were released that the outlaw's mother, Zerelda Samuel, had arrived at the house the following morning and was seen suffering from what appeared to be genuine grief. Later the body was positively identified as Jesse's by the Clay County sheriff and several former neighbors.

Ford apparently killed James for the reward offered by Missouri governor, Thomas T. Crittenden. How much he actually collected is not known.

Shortly after Jesse's death the house in which he was killed was open to the public as a tourist attraction. Interest eventually waned and the structure fell into disrepair. At one time in the 1930s it was nearly sold for taxes. In 1938 it was saved and moved from its original site to its present location at 12th and Penn streets. The house has now been restored and furnished with original and period pieces, including personal items of Jesse's. It is open to the public for a fee.

## Savannah
### Andrew County

This county seat town on US 71 just north of St. Joseph was the scene of the third assault on a western Missoui bank later attributed to the James gang. On March 2, 1867, five men rode into town and headed for a private banking house owned by a man named by John McLain. One of the riders waited outside with the horses while the others entered the building. McLain was inside, as was his son. When he saw the strangers he slammed the door of his safe shut and reached for a revolver he always kept under the counter. The intruders scattered and the bankers' shots went wild. The outlaws' aim was better, and McLain dropped to the floor with a bullet in his chest. The banker's son raced out the door and spread the alarm. The outlaws ran to their horses and galloped out of town.

Two suspects were later arrested, Bud McDaniel and Sam Pope, but both had alibis and were eventually released. Although the James gang has been credited by many with the attempted robbery, there has never been any solid proof that they were involved.

## South West City
### McDonald County

Missouri banks were relatively safe following the demise of the James-Younger gang in the early 1880s, but occasionally Oklahoma outlaws would venture across the line to cause trouble. On May 10, 1894, the Bill Doolin gang rode north into the corner of Missouri to raid the bank at South West City. The gang, then numbering seven (Doolin, "Dynamite Dick" Clifton, Charley Pierce, William "Tulsa Jack" Blake, Little Dick West, Bill Raidler and Red Buck), probably expected little trouble. Two of the outlaws were left to guard the horses, two were stationed outside the bank, and three entered with a sack to scoop up the money. The affair seemed to go well at first: in ten minutes the robbers collected between $3,000 and $4,000 and were ready to leave. However, someone had spread the alarm; the gang had no sooner hit the saddle when townsmen converged on the scene with guns blazing. But in their excitement their aim was bad; the outlaws, on the other hand, were seasoned gunslingers, and they left a trail of bleeding citizens in their wake.

Deputy U.S. Marshal Simpson F. Melton was felled with a bullet in the thigh. J. S. Seaborn, a leading businessman and former Missouri state auditor, was hit in the groin and later bled to death. His brother Oscar Seaborn was also wounded, as was the town shoemaker, Mart Pembree, who suffered a shattered leg. Only one outlaw was hit, and his identity and the seriousness of his wound were never determined. A posse followed the gang west into the Cherokee Nation but lost them near the Grand River.

## Springfield
### Greene County

On Friday, June 21, 1865, Springfield citizens on the public square witnessed what perhaps was a near-classic Western shootout: the killing of Dave Tutt by James Butler "Wild Bill" Hickok. As usual the details are blurred. Hickok especially has been the subject of outrageous tales of skill and daring, and there are several versions of this story.

The showdown stemmed from some kind of argument that occurred the night before. Hickok and Tutt had been playing cards at the Old Southern Hotel (also called the Lyon House) on the east side of South Street. The two may have been feuding for some time; some say over a woman, others say gambling debts. In one version of the story Tutt reportedly picked up Hickok's expensive Waltham watch from the table, telling him that he was keeping it as settlement of a debt. Talk turned to meeting the next day on the public square; some say that Hickok said Tutt better not show up wearing the watch. The versions agree that the two men left on bad terms.

The following day Tutt was on the square and so was Wild Bill. Possibly it was the classic showdown: face-to-face, ready to draw. Apparently Hickok got his shot off first, and the bullet struck Tutt in the heart. Hickok was tried and acquitted, much to the displeasure of the editor of the Missouri *Weekly Patriot* who, on August 10, wrote:

> The citizens of this city were shocked and terrified at the idea that a man could arm himself and take a position at a corner of the public square, in the centre of the city, and await the approach of his victim for an hour or two, and then willingly engage in a conflict with him which resulted in his instant death; and this, too, with the knowledge of several persons who seem to have posted themselves in safe places where they could see the tragedy enacted.

Wild Bill came across even worse in 1883 in the *History of Greene County Missouri*. After describing Hickok as "by nature a ruffian . . . a drunken, swaggering fellow who delighted, when on a spree, in frightening nervous men and timid women . . ." the author claimed Wild Bill had gunned down Tutt before he had a chance to defend himself. (And in this version of the story, the night before the shooting, Hickok, after losing at cards, had thrown them out the window in a fit of anger, and Tutt had forced him to go out and pick them up.)

In general it seems Wild Bill Hickok was more fond of Springfield than the town was of him. The following fall he ran for town marshal but was defeated 107 votes to 63.

## Winston
### Daviess County

In November 1879 Jesse James was reportedly killed by a member of his own gang on the outskirts of Galena, Kansas. Rumors also circulated that Frank James was dead. In January 1881 the Sedalia *Daily Democrat* raised doubts about these reports when it ran an article telling of a meeting between a member of the newspaper's staff and Jesse in Denver, Colorado, that winter. Jesse, the reported claimed, wanted to know if he could return to Missouri and live a "peaceful" life under some form of amnesty.

Was Jesse dead or alive? On July 15, 1881, the question was answered for many Missourians when an express on the Chicago, Rock Island and Pacific Railroad was robbed at Winston, and the conductor, William Westfall, was brutally killed as he stood with his hands raised. Conductor Westfall, it was revealed, had been in charge of the train that had allegedly carried detectives into Clay County, Missouri, on the night of January 26, 1875, which culminated in the "bombing" of the James family home, the killing of Jesse's and Frank's half-brother, Archie, and the mutilation of their mother, Zerelda Samuel (see *Kearney*).

The senseless killing of Westfall and a passenger in the smoking car did not follow the usual James gang pattern in train robberies, but most James historians agree the affair marked the outlaws' return to mischief in their home state following nearly a two-year layoff.

After his surrender in 1882 Frank James was tried for the Winston murder and acquitted. The only direct evidence against him was the testimony of gang member Dick Liddil, whom the jury apparently believed was merely trying to save his own neck.

Montana 1886

# MONTANA

## Bannack
### Beaverhead County

Bannack was born in the early 1860s and soon beame headquarters for placer mining on the eastern slope of the Rockies. As with most towns near strikes, an unwanted element converged on the settlement and quickly rivaled the honest folk. Some communities in this situation elected or appointed sturdy law enforcement officers to give the lawbreakers a run for their money. Bannack tried this but came up with a bad choice. In May 1863 the town pinned a star on a young California gunslinger named Henry Plummer. A bigger mistake could not have been made. Plummer already had served time for one murder and had been involved in at least three others. He had broken out of jail in California and was currently the ringleader of a loosely-organized band of outlaws operating in the area.

Plummer immediately hired three of his outlaw confederates as deputies. A third deputy, an honest citizen named D. H. Dillingham, was forced on him by townspeople. Dillingham lasted but a month. On June 29, 1863, he was gunned down by Plummer's bandits in nearby Virginia City.

But an organization the size of Plummer's could not go undetected forever, and eventually rumors circulated that the sheriff was working on both sides of the law. Little was done about it, however, until late in 1863, when several cold-blooded murders in the surrounding region spurred residents of nearby Nevada City to form a vigilance committee. After a couple of necktie parties involving Plummer associates, one of the gang members made a detailed confession of how the sheriff's operation worked. Braced with this information, Bannack citizens established their own vigilante group and put sheriff Plummer's name at the top of the list.

On a cold and windy Sunday afternoon, January 10, 1864, several committee members noticed horses belonging to Plummer and his deputies being brought to the sheriff's rooming house from the livery stable. It suggested to them that the sheriff and his pals might be planning to leave town. That evening a delegation called on Plummer, and a similar group paid a visit to his deputies. Within minutes all three were standing with hands tied under a makeshift gallows. Plummer was the last to swing. Fearing his death would be prolonged, he pleaded with his captors to give him a "good drop." He got his wish.

Today Bannack, which is twenty miles west of Dillon on State Road 278, is an enchanting semi-ghost town and state park. A replica of the gallows that finished off Plummer and his followers stands in what has now been labeled "Hangman's Gulch." Although weather-worn and decayed Skinner's Saloon is still visible—headquarters for Plummer and his confederates between raids.

## Bearmouth
### Granite County

Bearmouth is in western Montana on Interstate 90 about fifty miles east of Missoula. The town is situated on the old Great Northern Railroad and on October 4, 1902, was the scene of an assault by the colorful train robber George F. Hammond.

On that night, while the Great Northern's No. 2 was taking on water, Hammond slipped aboard behind the tender and pointed two revolvers at the engineer and fireman. The fireman was ordered to climb down and put out the kerosene light on the front of the locomotive. As he was doing so, the engineer, Dan O'Neal, tried to jump the robber and in the scuffle took a bullet in the belly. Hearing the shot, the fireman ran to a clump of bushes near the track and hid.

Leaving the dying engineer in the cab, Hammond hurried back to the express car and demanded that the messenger open the safes. When the messenger claimed he did not have the combinations, Hammond leaned dynamite sticks against the doors and ordered the messenger to light the fuses. The blast wrecked the car, but blew open both doors. Hammond, after threatening several crew members who came forward from the passenger coaches, calmly sorted through the debris and filled his gunny sack with several thousands of dollars.

Two years later, on June 16, 1904, Hammond struck again at the same site. This time both the engineer and the fireman were on the ground when Hammond and a second masked man approached from the darkness. The two trainmen were marched back to the express car, and the messenger was ordered to open up. He refused, and Hammond once more reached into his sack for dynamite. This blast blew the door off his hinges, and the robbers entered. After rifling one safe, Hammond blew apart a second, emptied the contents into his sack, and he and his companion rode off into the night.

Bloodhounds led a posse to the banks of Hell Gate River where the robbers stashed a rowboat. After searching the shoreline for several hours, they abandoned the chase. Hammond and his partner, later identified as John Christie, were eventually captured and sent to prison. On being questioned about the second robbery, Christie said he and Hammond buried most of the loot at several locations west of Bearmouth. He gave descriptions of the hiding places but nothing was found. On their release from prison (Hammond was sentenced to fifteen years and Christie, seven), both robbers were undoubtedly placed under surveillance on the chance that they would lead the authorities to the caches, but there are no details on this. In the 1930s an old prospector thought he had discovered part of the loot in an abandoned cabin near Maxville, south of Bearmouth, but what appeared to be a stack of rotting bank notes (as reported by a Butte, Montana, newspaper) turned out to be a bundle of worthless stock certificates.

## Cook Stove Basin
### Bighorn County

Cook Stove Basin, in the northeastern leg of the Bighorn Mountains overlooking Bighorn Canyon, was a little known but often used outlaw hideout for many years. According to local ranchers, horse thieves used the basin as a stopping point in the mid-1870s when transporting stolen mounts from Idaho and Utah to the lucrative markets in the gold-rush towns of the Black Hills. A cabin in the basin, thought to be built by a rustler named Sam Garvin in the early 1890s, may also have been used by Butch Cassidy and the Wyoming Wild Bunch. Well supplied with water, grass, and game, the locale was an ideal bandit hideaway. Across the canyon to the west, in the Pryor range, another cabin was found with the name "Kid Curry" carved on one of the logs. Wild Bunch member Harvey Logan often rode under this alias.

Although the area is still worth exploring, much of it is now under the waters of the Yellowtail Reservoir.

## Deer Lodge
### Powell County

Deer Lodge, the second oldest town in Montana, is on Interstate 90 midway between Yellowstone and Glacier National Parks.

Jesse James may have spent the winter of 1873-4 in Deer Lodge. In December 1873 a letter signed "Jesse

Deer Lodge in the 1870s. *Montana Historical Society.*

W. James" was received by the editor of the St. Louis *Dispatch* in which the writer proposed that he and his brother, Frank, return to Missouri and give themselves up in return for the governor's guarantee of a "fair trial" plus protection from mobs and from Iowa authorities who wanted them for the Adair train robbery.* The letter was dated December 20 and presumably mailed from Deer Lodge. If genuine, it was the first of several letters that are believed to have been written by James to newspapers for publication during his outlaw career. If the letter was from Jesse he must have felt safe in Deer Lodge since he used his real name. He closed by saying, "Any communication addressed to me at Deer Lodge, Montana Territory, will be attended to."

Actually, at the time, Deer Lodge was an unlikely choice for a wanted outlaw as a hideout. The territorial prison was located there, having been established as a private venture in 1869 by two Montana men, Frank Conley and Archie McTague, who contracted with the territory to house its convicts at a specified charge per head. The venture was profitable for the entrepreneurs since they used prison labor to work their farm. The state finally took over the operation in 1889.

The prison, which was used continuously until 1979, can be visited today (1100 Main Street). Guided tours are conducted daily during the summer months.

## Harlem
### Blaine County

Harlem is thirty-four miles east of Havre on US 2. In the 1890s Lonny Logan, then using the name Lonny Curry, who was brother of the notorious Wild Bunch outlaw Harvey Logan (Kid Curry), operated the Curry Brothers Club Saloon in Harlem. Lonny's "brother" in the operation was actually his cousin Bob Lee who also adopted the name Curry. When not tending bar Lonny and Bob occasionally joined Harvey on his raids. All three probably were in on the robbery of the Union Pacific's Overland Flyer at Wilcox, Wyoming,* in June 1899. Five bank notes stolen from that robbery led the Pinkertons to Harlem later that year. By then, however, Lonny and Bob had sold the saloon and had left town. Both were tracked down the following year. Lonny was killed in a shootout at his aunt's house in Dodson, Missouri,* and Bob was arrested dealing three-card Monte at Cripple Creek, Colorado.

Helena in 1865. *Montana Historical Society.*

## Helena
### Clark County

By 1865 the vigilantes' ropes had left little doubt in southwestern Montana that organized outlawry would not be tolerated (see *Bannack* and *Virginia City*). But a new opportunity opened up for desperados 125 miles to the north. Recent strikes had produced another treasure gulch, and a brand new town, Helena, was ripe for plucking.

Helena probably would have gone wild in a hurry but for an early "citizens' trial" and hanging of one John Keene. Keene had shot an old enemy, Harry Slater, when he found him snoozing in the doorway of Sam Greer's saloon. Slater was a professional gambler and not much of a loss to the town, but Helena citizens had a precedent to establish. The killer was whisked away from the sheriff, who with his deputies conveniently took leave, and a two-day kangeroo court sealed his fate. In the words of an observer, the "execution was electrical." The hard cases who had converged on the town "saw that the citizens of Montana had determined that outrage should be visited with condign punishment, and that prudence dictated an immediate stampede from Helena." In simpler words the roughest of the criminal element saw that Helena was not a safe place to be and moved on.

Old West buffs will be interested in Frontier Town, which is thirteen miles west of Helena on US 12. Atop the Continental Divide at McDonald Pass, the town offers a seventy-five-mile view of Montana scenery. The town itself is a replica of frontier days with period furnishings and pioneer collectibles. Also of interest is the frontier theme museum at the Montana Historical Society headquarters at 225 N. Roberts Street in Helena.

Vigilantes' hanging tree near Helena, 1870. Victims were Joseph Wilson and J. L. Compton. *Montana Historical Society.*

## Landusky
### Phillips County

Landusky lies north of US 191, just below the Blaine County line. The town was named after Pike Landusky, an early Montana pioneer who was also the first victim of the notorious Harvey Logan (Kid Curry), later of the Wild Bunch. Harvey and his brothers owned a ranch near town. After Landusky's death in Jew Jake's Saloon on December 27, 1894, Logan left town to launch his life of outlawry. His brother Johnny (then also going by the name Curry) was killed on a neighboring ranch in 1896 by one Jim Winters in a dispute over irrigation rights. Harvey, at the time rustling cattle in Wyoming, sent word back that he would someday avenge his brother's death. It took him until 1901. According to a witness, Abram Gill, Harvey returned one morning and shot Winters while the rancher stood on his back porch brushing his teeth.

If you are ever in Landusky, ask an old timer to give you directions to the Logan and Winters ranches.

## Laurin
### Madison County

Little is left of the original Laurin, which is eleven miles northwest of Virginia City on State Road 287, but in its heyday as a mining camp it rivaled its more popular neighbor as a gathering place for the rich and greedy. Two of the famous Henry Plummer gang, Red Yager and G. W. Brown, met their end there in July 1864, courtesy of vigilante ropes.

About three miles north of town is "Robbers Roost," a roadhouse preserved from frontier days which was used by Plummer's outlaws as a headquarters from which they raided stagecoaches and unwary travelers.

## Lavina
### Golden Valley County

During the fourth week of September 1897, the tiny Musselshell River town of Lavina, which is about forty-five miles northwest of Billings, became the center of attention in a three-state area following news of the capture of the notorious Harvey (Kid Curry) Logan and Walt Punteney, members of Wyoming's Wild Bunch. On September 19 Logan, Punteney, and a third man—possibly Harry Longabaugh (the Sundance Kid)—were spotted in the town of Red Lodge, down in Carbon County. A story later circulated that they had gone there to bribe the town marshal, Byron St. Clair, to leave town while they held up the Red Lodge bank.

St. Clair refused to go along with the scheme and reported the incident to Carbon County sheriff John Dunn. The three outlaws, at the time suspects in the June 28 robbery of the Butte County Bank at Belle Fourche, South Dakota,* were trailed north, by way of Absarokee and Columbus (along what is now State Road 78), and then into Stillwater County toward the Musselshell River. They were finally caught making camp at a spring just outside of Lavina. A newspaper article which appeared the following month in the Fremont County (Wyoming) *Clipper* reported:

> On being summoned to surrender, the two men at the spring jumped over the bank and attempted to defend themselves, but whenever they showed their heads the officers fired. . . . The one with the horse parlied [sic], and getting behind the horse he drew his revolver, when a shot went through the horse's neck and the man's wrist, causing him to drop the revolver. He mounted the horse and ran a mile before it fell, shot dead. The man surrendered.

The injured man was Logan. All three outlaws were returned to Dakota to await trail for the Belle Fourche robbery, but on October 31 they broke out of jail at Deadwood.*

## Malta
### Phillips County

A train robbery near the northern Montana town of Malta (located between Havre and Glascow on US 2) on November 27, 1892, is believed to have been Harry Longabaugh's (the Sundance Kid) first venture into big-time outlawry. At Malta Longabaugh and two fellow robbers, Bill Madden and Harry Bass, slipped aboard the blind baggage of the Great Northern's westbound No. 23 as the train was pulling away from the station. The caboose had hardly cleared town when the engineer and fireman heard the three intruders climbing over the tender. Facing three sixshooters, the engineer quickly braked to a stop. The bandits marched their prisoners back to the express car, where express agent Jerry Hauert was ordered to open up. The robbers ransacked a small local safe for about $20 in cash and a few items of value, but the larger "through" safe was locked with a combination which, explained Hauert, was known only by Great Northern station agents at principal stops along the line. Disgusted, the bandits ordered the engineer to return to his cab, and they rode off into the night.

Longabaugh was familiar with the Malta area, having worked on a ranch thirty-five miles southeast of town in 1889, and he headed southwest toward Great Falls. Madden and Bass, however, unwisely returned to Malta and the nearest saloon, Alex Black's place, where they had spent some time before the robbery, probably gathering information on train arrivals and express shipments. It did not take long for local officials to guess that these two strangers had a hand in the holdup. They confessed under questioning and implicated Longabaugh, but he was long gone, well on his way to Wyoming, where he would soon cross paths with a cowboy calling himself Butch Cassidy.

## Miles City
### Custer County

Frontier Miles City, in eastern Montana near the junction of Interstate 94 and US 12, was a classic cowboy's town. Main Street prospered in two shifts: on the north side of the street were the banks, retail businesses, and pawnshops which operated by day, and on the south side were the saloons, gambling parlors, and brothels which thrived by night.

Malta, Montana. *Montana Historical Society.*

There is some evidence that Butch Cassidy called the Miles City area home in 1886. According to an old cowpuncher, John F. Kelly, who claimed he knew him well, Butch worked for a rancher west of town on the south side of Yellowstone River, across from Forsythe. Apparently this was just before Butch decided to choose full-time outlawry as his way of life.

Harry Longabaugh (the Sundance Kid) also frequented Miles City about the same time; possibly this is where the two outlaws first met. Longabaugh also worked on a ranch outside town, probably for about six months, and then drifted over to Wyoming. While there he stole a horse, saddle, and gun from the employees of a Crook County ranch called the Three V. He was traced back to Miles City where he was arrested in April 1887 by Crook County sheriff James Ryan. On the return trip by train Longabaugh escaped by picking the locks on his shackles while Ryan was using the commode. Foolishly, Longabaugh returned to Miles City where he may have committed several robberies and was once more arrested. Ryan came calling again and this time returned Harry to Wyoming where he was convicted and sentenced to eighteen months in the Crook County jail.

## Missoula
### Missoula County

In December 1972 a man was killed in a Missoula Hotel fire. On checking his identity, authorities learned that he had once claimed to be the illegitimate son of Harry Longabaugh, alias the Sundance Kid. Following the release of the successful 1969 motion picture *Butch Cassidy and the Sundance Kid*, the man traveled around the country posing as first Robert, then Harold, Longabaugh, supposedly the son of the outlaw and a woman whom he insisted was the sister of Sundance's longtime girlfriend, Etta Place. The man claimed that Etta's real name was Thayne and that she died in Oregon in 1940, living under the name Hazel Tryon. Sundance, he said, lived in Wyoming until August 28, 1957, under the name Harry Long.

Serious researchers doubt the truth of the man's story.

## Virginia City
### Madison County

Virginia City is in southwestern Montana, about fifteen miles west of US 287, midway between Interstate 90 and the Idaho state line. From a prospectors' strike on Alder Creek in 1863 the area blossomed into a lawless gold camp. To combat thieves and killers that plagued the region the citizens turned to vigilance committees early. The leader of the road agents, Henry Plummer, who also happened to be sheriff of nearby Bannack,* was strung up in that town on January 10, 1864. The Virginia City committee concentrated on rounding up Plummer's confederates, and five were put to the rope on January 14 (Frank Parrish, George Lane, Boone Helm, Jack Gallagher, and Hayes Lyons). The regulators then spread out to neighboring ranches and gathered up a handful more. By the end of February, twenty-two outlaws had felt the hemp, and probably twice that many fled across the line into Idaho. For Virginia City citizens, only one troublemaker was left to deal with—the enigmatic Jack Slade.

Jack Slade had drifted to Montana in 1863 after a

A legal Montana hanging. Many were not. *Montana Historical Society.*

violent career as division superintendent for stage lines in Julesburg* and Virginia Dale,* Colorado. Slade was no Henry Plummer, but he was a quarrelsome alcoholic with a murderous temper, and the residents of Virginia City apparently feared him. While still flush from their success with the Plummer outfit, the committee members invited Slade to leave town. Instead of going, Jack headed for the saloon and tied one on, probably spending the evening informing all who would listen just what the town of Virginia City could do with its vigil-

Robbers Roost, on the old stage road at Laurin, between Virginia City and Bannack. *Montana Historical Society.*

ance committee. Shortly thereafter Jack was found hanging by the neck from the crossbeam of a town corral gate.

Slade's widow vowed that her husband would not be buried in Montana soil and had his body stuffed into a zinc and tin-lined coffin which she filled with whiskey. Thus pickled, Jack was stored in a rented Virginia City house until the roads were open in the spring. In June the widow Slade lashed the coffin to the top of a stagecoach bound for Salt Lake City, where Jack was buried in the town cemetery. Due to a clerical error, however, the location of the body was lost, and it was not until the 1970s that Jack's gravesite was found (see *Salt Lake City*).

Today Virginia City is a popular tourist attraction, thanks mainly to two local frontier enthusiasts, the late Charles Bovey and his wife, Sue. More than twenty early buildings have been restored or reconstructed, including the Wells Fargo office and the Bale of Hay Saloon. Visitors can also enjoy a narrow-gauge train ride from Virginia City to nearby Nevada City, also a restored ghost town. The train, the Alder Gulch Short Line, features nineteenth century railroad cars fashioned into a walk-through railroad museum.

## Wagner
### Phillips County

The tiny town of Wagner can be found in northeastern Montana on US 2 about midway between Havre and Glascow. The midday robbery on July 3, 1901, of the Great Northern Coast Flyer near Wagner is believed to be the last strike by the Wyoming Wild Bunch before the gang split up to go their separate ways. Just which members of the gang were involved in the holdup is not known for certain—probably Butch Cassidy and Harvey (Kid Curry) Logan, and possibly Ben Kilpatrick, Bill Carver, and a newcomer, O. C. Hanks.

Some say the Wagner area was chosen for the holdup because of Logan's familiarity with the region; also, some say the Great Northern Railroad was picked because the Union Pacific was by then using crack teams of manhunters in "horse cars" which were rushed to the scene of a robbery on a special train.

The robbery was actually committed at Exeter Switch, some two miles east of Wagner. Although accounts differ, it is believed that one of the outlaws (possibly Kilpatrick) boarded the train at Malta, while another (some say Logan) slipped aboard behind the tender. A few miles out Logan worked his way forward and put a gun in the back of the engineer, Tom Jones. The train was stopped at Exeter, where the rest of the gang were waiting. In traditional Wild Bunch fashion, random shots were fired along the sides of the coaches to keep the passengers in order (several were struck by ricochetes), while other members of the gang separated the train behind the express car. The front section was pulled ahead, and the express company safe was blown open with dynamite, making available from $40,000 to $65,000 in cash and bank notes. After loading the loot onto their horses, the outlaws forded the nearby Milk River and rode south, across the trail that is now State Road 363 and then east, into what is today the Charles M. Russell National Wildlife Refuge. Some of the robbers were later spotted near Miles City, where they spent part of the stolen bank notes on four fresh horses.

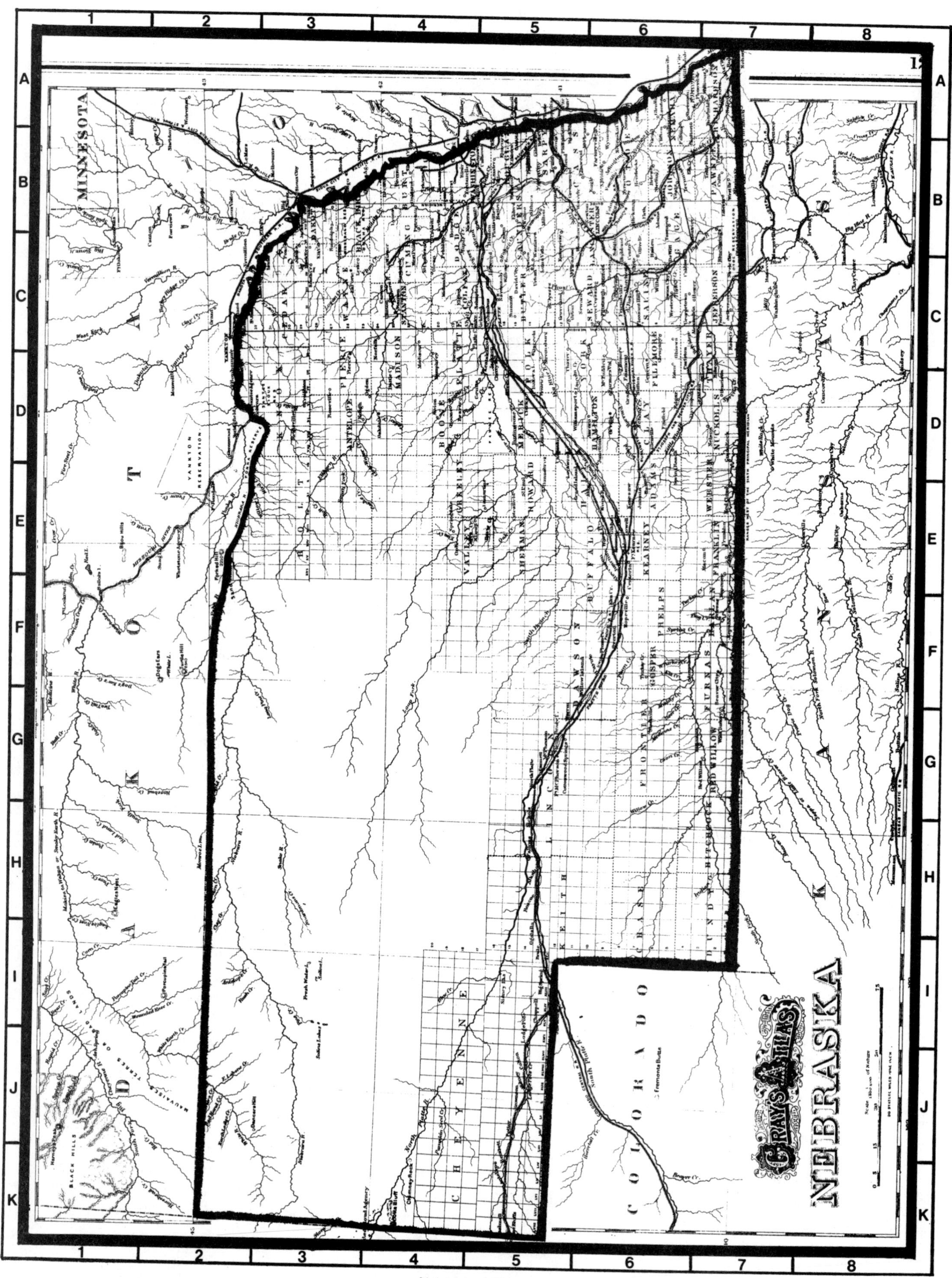


Nebraska 1874

# NEBRASKA

## Big Springs
### Deuel County

The train robbery at Big Springs on September 18, 1877, was one of the most profitable in the history of the Old West. According to most accounts the haul was over $60,000. The Sam Bass gang is generally credited with the holdup, but it is believed that Joel Collins, Bass's partner in crime, was in charge of this affair.

Big Springs is located on US 30 in the western part of the state, just north of Julesburg, Colorado. The Union Pacific eastbound No. 4 was due that day at 10:48 P.M. The outlaws, six in all, arrived shortly after ten. The station agent, George Barnhart, was alone. Seeing pistols pointing at him from all directions, he quickly complied with the order to put his telegraph key out of commission. Next, he was forced to hang out a red signal light to stop the train.

Obeying the signal, engineer George Vroman brought the locomotive to a halt. But when he saw the six gunmen, he became enraged and began throwing coal at them. This was soon discouraged by a few shots. Once inside the express car, the robbers knocked the agent to the floor and took his keys. The "through" safe had a combination lock on it which the agent claimed he could not open; however, rummaging through the express packages, the outlaws found three wooden boxes, each containing $20,000 in freshly minted gold pieces. These they dragged out onto the station platform. Still not satisfied with their haul, the robbers proceeded to go through the coaches, ordering passengers to hand over their money and valuables. They even tried to enter the sleeping cars but found them locked. On hearing the whistle of a freight train approaching from the west, the outlaws sent the conductor down the track to stop it. While he was gone, they saddled up and disappeared in the night.

Following the robbery, Big Springs is no longer mentioned in the annals of western outlaw history. But in 1889 it may have come close to making the headlines again. That year three of the notorious Dalton brothers came to town; at least their names appear on the register of Big Springs's Phelps Hotel. On the register today can be seen the names "Grat Dalton," "Emit Dalton," and "Robert Dalton," all from "I.T." which then stood for Indian Territory. Doubters might ask why would Emmett Dalton mispell his first name. Maybe the desk clerk merely asked Emmett his name and wrote it in himself.

In 1889 the Daltons were yet to become hunted outlaws. Grat, Emmett, and Bob were all working as Indian police in what is now Oklahoma. Perhaps they had come north trailing a fugitive. But already they were getting involved in petty crimes and probably rustling; it is possible that somewhere in Nebraska a big deal was in the offing. Additional research around Big Springs might turn up an interesting story.

## Chadron
### Dawes County

The town of Chadron, in the northwestern corner of the state near the junction of US 20 and US 385, was as tough as any frontier community of the 1880s. Unlike many Nebraska towns, however, it was born ahead of the railroad, being situated on the banks of the White River, several miles northwest of where the present Chadron now stands. The original Chadron came to life in 1883, a hastily built collection of shanties "thrown together with canvas, logs, rough lumber or whatever material was cheapest and nearest," as one observer wrote.

Outlaws no doubt frequented Chadron's early saloons (and probably its primitive jail), but the hard case most often mentioned was a woman. Her name is believed to have been Jane Woodard (at least she referred to herself by that name at times), but she soon became known as "Red Jacket," because of a flaming red coat she seemed to favor. Although Red Jacket owned a piece of land at the edge of the river, she was considered "riff-raff" and something of a mental case by "respectable" townspersons. But she did seem to have business sense, operating an apparently successful roadhouse on her property where she offered travelers food, drink, and a place to bed down.

One day the town announced plans to build a bridge across the river. Part of it would be on Red Jacket's land and she objected. When her protests were ignored, she warned that if any of her property was taken, she would shoot the first person to cross the bridge. The bridge was built, and there is no record that she carried through with her threat, but in late 1885 a stranger was found shot to death not far from Red Jacket's roadhouse. Red Jacket was the mostly likely suspect and she was arrested. As she sat in jail awaiting trial, her mind seemed to deteriorate. Complaining that her cell was infested with rats, she somehow talked her jailer into lending her a pistol to kill them. When the jailer was not looking, she stuck the gunbarrel through a crack in the logs of her cell wall and took a shot at the town judge as he walked down the street. He saved himself by diving behind a rainbarrel. This incident, plus a few others, led her lawyer to plead that she was mentally deranged and she was acquitted.

Red Jacket's story could have ended there but there is more. As soon as her trial was over, she marched to the judge's house and informed his wife that she had just played quite a trick on the town. Knowing that the law would not let her be tried again for the same crime, she admitted that she had killed the stranger and robbed him of a large amount of cash. Furthermore, she said that he was not her first victim; he was in fact the sixth—all well-heeled travelers who had stopped at her roadhouse. The town did not wait to find out if her gruesome tale was true; Red Jacket was promptly adjudged insane and whisked away to an institution where she could do no more harm.

Chadron is also the resting place of "Flat Nose" George Currie, member of the Wild Bunch of Wyoming. His gravesite in the town cemetery is marked by a headstone. Currie was Canadian by birth; his connection with Chadron is not clear, other than the fact his body was claimed by a relative living there at the time. It is believed he rode in the 1880s with rustlers who made use of the "Hole-in-the-Wall"* in Wyoming. Sometime thereafter he joined the Wild Bunch, participating in several robberies including the bank at Bell Fourche, South Dakota,* in 1897 and the Union Pacific express at Wilcox, Wyoming,* in 1899. He was killed in April 1900 on the bank of the Green River in Utah, where a posse out of Vernal mistook him for a local rustler.

Chadron celebrates its frontier days in mid-July with its annual Buckskin Rendezvous, featuring shooting contests with nineteenth century firearms and tomahawk throwing.

## Long Pine
### Brown County

Long Pine, which is in north central Nebraska near the junction of US 20 and US 183, was the last known stomping ground of "Mysterious Dave" Mather, a one-time Dodge City gunslinger who worked both sides of the law and left a trail of victims over much of the West. Mather's last killing of record is believed to occurred in 1885 at Ashland, Kansas,* for which he probably was still wanted when he rode into Long Pine in 1887. While in Long Pine, Dave worked at the railroad hotel. He was in town about a year, and then, true to his name, he mysteriously disappeared. Researchers interested in this outlaw might benefit from more digging into Long Pine's dusty past. Dave Mather was not the kind to die with his boots off.

"Mysterious Dave" Mather, last seen in Long Pine, Nebraska. *Charles C. Goodhall Collection.*

# Ogallala
## Keith County

Ogallala is on US 30 about fifty miles west of North Platte. For years after the train robbery at nearby Big Springs,* an Ogallala store owner, M. F. Leech, entertained listeners with a tale of how he single-handedly trailed the robbers and almost recovered part of the stolen gold. A day or two before the robbery, one of the outlaws, Jim Berry, had stopped at Leech's store to buy a pair of boots and a half-dozen red bandanas. Leech was acquainted with Berry, having known him several years earlier when they both lived at North Platte. At the time Berry was not a known outlaw, but he did have a reputation as sort of a scoundrel. Leech gave the incident no further thought until, as part of the posse, he visited the Big Springs robbery site. There he found a piece of red bandana, the same kind he had sold Berry. Later, while searching the countryside for the robbers, he found another piece at a campsite on the outskirts of Ogallala.

Leech had sold red bandanas to many cowboys that summer, but he could not get Jim Berry out of his mind. Apparently he said nothing to the sheriff about what he had found, thinking that he could follow up the clue himself and claim a reward. He arranged to have someone watch his store, packed his saddlebags for a long trip, and set out along the trail that led away from the campsite. He rode hard, southward, into the rough country east of Julesburg, Colorado. At the end of two days, somewhere near the Arikaree River, he came upon the robbers' camp. It was night, and while the outlaws sat around the fire, Leech crawled up close enough to hear them discussing their plans. And if Leech is to be believed, on either that night or the next, he even tried to sneak into their camp while they were sleeping and steal back some of the gold, but he made too much noise and had to give up the idea.

Leech continued to follow the outlaws, and at one point managed to reach a telegraph office and report their whereabouts to the Wells Fargo office in Omaha. Later, when the outlaws split up, Leech followed two of them, Berry and Tom Nixon, who appeared to be heading for Kansas City. Leech was still on Berry's trail when the outlaw met his end at Mexico, Missouri.*

Old timers around Ogallala still talk about the time the notorious Bat Masterson put one over on the town's law officers. Around 1880 Texas troublemaker Bill Thompson, brother of the noted gunslinger Ben Thompson, was spending some time in Ogallala when he got into an argument with Bill Tucker, owner of the Cowboy's Rest Saloon. A gunflight erupted in the saloon, resulting in Thompson shooting off Tucker's thumb and parts of three fingers. Thompson thought he had killed Tucker and left. As Thompson was crossing the street, Tucker put five shotgun pellets into his back and legs. Tucker then swore out a complaint against the Texan, and Thompson was patched up and put under guard in his hotel room.

According to Bat Masterson, who told this part of the story years later, Thompson's brother Ben asked Bat to go to Ogallala and rescue Bill. Ben claimed he could not go because he had once caused some trouble in Ogallala himself and would be arrested. Bat went and did succeed in sneaking Thompson out of his hotel (with the help of a friendly bartender who drugged the guard) and down to the depot where they caught an eastbound train. Again, according to Masterson (who was known to tell a good story), Bat took the still ailing Texan to North Platte, where he hid him out at the ranch owned by Buffalo Bill Cody. Several days later Cody lent Bat a carriage, and the two men returned to Dodge City.

Gunslingers did not always get off so easy in Ogallala. In 1883 Texas rustler and shootist Charlie Reed found this so. While drinking in an Ogallala saloon, probably the Cowboy's Rest, Reed became involved in a quarrel with a man named Dumas. Reed became enraged, whipped out his sixshooter, and shot Dumas to death on the spot. Apparently local citizens considered the Keith County judicial process would be too slow in handling the matter; before dawn Reed's neck was stretched by a rope.

Ogallala has attempted to restore some of its "end of the trail" flavor with Front Street tourist attractions, including a saloon, dance hall, and a cowboy museum.

# Omaha

No western history buff should pass up an opportunity to visit the Union Pacific Railroad Museum in Omaha. Although most of the collection is devoted to railroad history, there are several outlaw displays, including personal items belonging to the outlaw Tom Horn (knife and sheath, Colt revolver, cat's eye ring, braided horsehair lead rope, and a piece of the rope used to hang him in 1902). The museum also has the leg irons used on "Big Nose" George Parrott the day he was hanged, plus his skull cap which was removed by a Rawlins, Wyoming, physician before he was buried. Jesse James is also represented: on display is a revolver said to have been used by Jesse during the Northfield, Minnesota, robbery. This item, however, has not yet been authenticated. Train robbery enthusiasts will be especially interested in the U.P.'s collection of photographs and file histories.

Tom Horn display at the Union Pacific Railroad Museum, Omaha. Tom's hand-made knife and sheath, cat's eye ring, a piece of the rope used to hang him, his own horsehair lead rope, and his Colt revolver.

"Big Nose" George Parrott display at Union Pacific Museum, Omaha. At left and right are George's death masks. In the center is a piece of his skin. In the foreground are the shackles used in his capture.

## Rock Creek Station
### Jefferson County

Wild Bill Hickok called the Rock Creek area home during the spring and summer of 1861. In July of that year Hickok, who was employed by the Overland Stage Company, established himself as a gunslinger and killer as a result of the famous "McCanles Affair."

The station itself was owned by Dave McCanles. According to one version of the incident, McCanles got into an argument with the local superintendent of the stage line, Horace Wellman, over a contract calling for the company to purchase the station property. Apparently the company, at the time in financial trouble, was behind on its payments to McCanles. Hickok, who served as acting superintendent when Wellman was away, had not actually chosen sides in the dispute, but it was rumored that he and McCanles were at odds, possibly over a woman.

The dispute came to a climax on July 12 at Wellman's house near the station. McCanles, his son Monroe, and two other men, James Woods and James Gordon, rode into the yard and ordered Wellman to come out, apparently to inform him that McCanles was either to get his money or he was terminating the contract with the company. Hickok was in the house with Wellman. The men began to argue and a shot was heard. Woods and Gordon raced toward the house. Woods was the first to reach the door, and was shot (according to McCanles's son) by Hickok. Gordon tried to run and was also hit. At this point apparently two other men joined Hickok and Wellman, one a stage driver, George Hulbert, and a man named Doc Brink. These four then went after Gordon, who was trying to escape along the creek bank. They found him, and although he was already wounded and probably no longer a threat, one of the four finished him off with a shotgun. When the authorities arrived, they also found Dave McCanles in the house with a bullet in his heart.

The following day warrants were issued for the arrest of Hickok, Wellman, and Brink, but they eventually were acquitted after pleading self defense. As the story was told and retold it took on outrageous proportions. In an 1867 article in *Harper's New Monthly Magazine*, Colonel George Ward Nichols had Hickok single-handedly killing McCanles plus nine of his "gang"; Nichols had changed McCanles from the owner of Rock Creek Station to the "captain of a gang of desperadoes, horse-thieves, murderers, and cut-throats . . ." Thanks to author Nichols, Hickok became an instant legend. The article was picked up by other writers and even further distorted, creating a reputation which Hickok probably never wanted and certainly did not deserve.

The site of the old Rock Creek Station, just off State Road 8 southeast of Fairbury, is now a state historical park.

## Sidney
### Cheyenne County

Sidney is in western Nebraska, near the junction of Interstate 80 and US 385. An unverified story has been told that sometime in 1874 or 1875 Wild Bill Hickok killed three men during a visit to Sidney. According to the tale, Wild Bill was quietly drinking in Tim Dyer's

Dance Hall and Hotel when three buffalo hunters began baiting him, probably about his appearance. Hickok had pinned up his famous long hair and was wearing a hat and a long black overcoat, giving the impression of "an offensive preacher" as one observer described it. One of the men knocked Wild Bill's hat off, and his hair fell down around his shoulders. If the men then recognized him, it was too late. Hickok drew his guns and killed all three. If true, the story has an interesting footnote: one of the three men, known as "Big Jack," was supposedly a friend of Jack McCall, who later killed Hickok at Deadwood, South Dakota.* The tale must be questioned. Although it originated with a contemporary of Wild Bill's, W. F. (Doc) Carver, who allegedly arrived on the scene shortly after the shooting, no other evidence has been turned up that the incident ever occurred.

Sidney's most popular outlaw story involves the "Big Gold Robbery" of 1880. On March 9 of that year approximately $120,000 in gold bars arrived in Sidney on the Deadwood stage. It was scheduled to be put aboard a Union Pacific car for shipment east. The stage was one of the "armored" variety occasionally used in the Black Hills to discourage road agents. On this trip the trail was muddy, and the heavy vehicle kept getting stuck. When it finally arrived in Sidney, there was less than a half-hour before the next eastbound train was to pull out. The Union Pacific freight agent, Chester K. Allen, claimed there was not enough time to load the shipment, and he refused to sign for it. Stage officials thought there was enough time to load, but Allen would not budge. As a result, the gold was stored overnight under guard in the stage line's vault.

The next morning the gold was returned to the depot, signed over to the railroad, and placed on a baggage cart in the freight room to await the afternoon train. Scott Davis, in charge of security for the stage company, complained, arguing that the gold would be safer back in his company's vault. Freight agent Allen disagreed, insisting that since the shipment had been signed over to the U.P., it was his responsibility, and he wanted it in the U.P. freight room. Davis gave in and went to lunch. While he was eating he heard a commotion back at the depot. When he got there the gold was gone! According to Allen, when he returned from lunch he found a hole sawed in the wooden floor of the freight room. Apparently the gold had been taken down the hole, out through a crawl space, and loaded on a wagon.

It did not take long for Union Pacific officials, led by their ace detective James L. "Whispering" Smith, to figure out that freight agent Allen had a hand in the heist. Also put under arrest was a friend of Allen's, a former Cheyenne County sheriff C. M. "Con" McCarty, then owner of Sidney's popular Capitol Saloon. But when it came time to make a case, the evidence against the two men was weak: Allen was acquitted, and McCarty was not even brought to trial.

Commercial Hotel, Sidney, formerly the Lockwood House, where James L. "Whispering" Smith shot it out with Dennis Flanigan. *Robert Rybolt Collection.*

Detective Smith was furious. He was convinced Allen and McCarty were guilty, but he could do nothing about it. On May 24 he started an argument in McCarty's saloon and ended up shooting the bartender, Patrick Walters. He was thrown in jail, but was bailed out by a local businessman, Charles A. Moore, and a group of merchants who hated McCarty. But Smith's temper had not cooled. He tangled with another McCarty henchman, a gunman named Dennis Flanigan, on the stairs of Sidney's Lockwood House. When the smoke cleared, Flanigan lay dead with three bullets in him, and Smith went back to jail. Once again Charles Moore and his group bailed him out. At this point Moore and his friends took over. Appointing themselves "regulators" of a town gone corrupt, they posted notices that lawlessness would no longer "run riot" in Sidney. That night they stormed the Capitol Saloon and dragged McCarty and a handful of his confederates off to jail. One McCarty gunman, John "Red" McDonald, put up a fight and was lynched.

In January 1908 the Capitol Saloon burned to the ground. In the ashes were found what appeared to be two gold bars. At first they were thought to be part of the stolen shipment, but on examination they turned out to be brass covered with gold paint. Further investigation suggested that after he was released from jail, Con McCarty concocted a scheme to produce fake gold bars and sell them to out-of-town customers, telling them that they were from the "Big Robbery." There is some evidence that for a while McCarty may have been assisted in his scheme by Doc Holliday, at the time using the name Tom McKay.

NEVADA
1886
SCALE OF MILES
Population 62,266
Area, square Miles 109,740
Longitude West from Washington
HUMBOLDT
ELKO
LANDER
EUREKA
CHURCHILL
STOREY
LYON
DOUGLAS
ESMERALDA
NYE
WHITE PINE
LINCOLN
CALIFORNIA
ARIZONA
Pyramid Lake
Walker Lake
BLACK ROCK DESERT
RALSTON DESERT
Winnemucca
Elko
Carson City
Virginia City
Austin
Eureka
Hamilton
Belmont
Pioche
Reno
Wells
Carlin
Battle Mountain
Tuscarora
Mountain City
WESTERN SHOSHONE INDIAN RES.
MOAPA RIVER INDIAN RESERVE
Dayton
Genoa
Hawthorne
Aurora
Candelaria
Columbus
Tybo
Ely
Cherry Creek
Ruby Valley
Bunkerville
St. Thomas
St. Joseph
Mesquite
Panaca
Hiko
Bodie
Bridgeport
Benton
Ivanpah
Mineral Park
El Dorado City
Vegas Wash
Colorado
Dry Lake
ASH MEADOWS
Humboldt River
Franklin Lake
Ruby Lake


Nevada 1886

# NEVADA

## Aurora
### Mineral County

Today Aurora is a ghost town, a few structures remaining of what was a booming mining center. During its peak years, the 1860s and 1870s, the town also was the center of operations for Milton Sharp, considered by some western historians to have been Nevada's premier highwayman. Sharp was Nevada's Black Bart. Lean and handsome, with a neatly trimmed mustache and goatee, Sharp made a science out of holding up stages. According to one observer he "robbed stages whenever he wanted to and with great thoroughness, never making a mistake and never finding an empty treasure box."

Milton Sharp arrived in Aurora sometime around 1869 and soon took up a dual career as miner and road agent. His favorite hunting ground was the Bodie to Carson City stage route, which ran through Aurora and then northward, across the east fork of the Walker River. The reason for Sharp's unusually lengthy career as a holdup artist probably was his appearance of frugality. Unlike his California counterpart, Black Bart, Sharp lived modestly. Taking only a few dollars from each of his hauls, he buried the rest, apparently against the day he would accumulate enough to retire in luxury.

Although the details are sketchy, it seems near the end of the 1870s Sharp's name did begin to appear on Wells Fargo's list of possible suspects. Perhaps for this reason the nervy bandit began to speed up his operations, probably hoping to top off his earnings quickly and call it quits. According to Wells Fargo records, Sharp robbed six of its shipments in a four month period in 1880, four of the holdups taking place at the same spot—the bridge over the east fork of the Walker River, about ten miles northwest of Aurora. On the fourth try Sharp's luck ran out. An accomplice, W. C. (Bill) Jones (alias Frank Dow), was shot and killed by a Wells Fargo messenger. Sharp escaped but was later captured in San Francisco. He was returned to Aurora and convicted of one of the robberies, the first at the Walker River bridge. But while awaiting sentencing, he broke jail by removing bricks from his cell wall. He was eventually recaptured and sentenced to twenty years in the state prison. The prison, however, could not hold him either. On August 15, 1889, he slipped out, probably by bribing one or more guards (he still had a small fortune buried somewhere back in Mineral County). Whether he ever returned to claim his hidden loot is not known.

Wells Fargo guards, heavily armed to discourage stagecoach robberies. *Wells Fargo Bank History Museum.*

Should you want to visit Aurora, take US 395 south out of Carson City to Bridgeport, California. Just south of Bridgeport take County Road 270 west through Bodie. The remains of Aurora lie just to the east, across the Nevada line. Not much of the town is left: just some vague outlines of foundations and shapeless piles of brick. A few of the streets can still be seen among the sagebrush. Vandals and gold hunters have nearly demolished the rest.

Wells Fargo stage, target for Nevada robbers. *Wells Fargo Bank History Room.*

# Carson City
## Ormsby County

The old United States Mint at Carson City (now housing the Nevada State Museum) drew many a stage robber to western Nevada. One of the most successful was a local lad, saloonkeeper-bandit Jack Harris, who proved an exception to the adage that crime does not pay. Harris, a transplanted New Englander, opened his saloon around 1861. For the next four years he nightly filled the glasses of his customers, always keeping alert to their whiskey-loosened tongues, especially when talk turned to valuable shipments coming and going by Wells Fargo express. Often Jack would be on the road waiting with mask and rifle.

Business was good for Harris well into 1865, but in June of that year he broke one of his cardinal rules: he took in two accomplices. One of their first targets was a $14,000 payroll shipment destined for Comstock district. Near Silver City they stopped the stage and made off with the money without a hitch. Somewhere not far away they buried most of it, keeping only a few hundred dollars each. But for the first time in his career, Jack's name came up as a suspect. In fact, all three men were called in and questioned. Evidence against them was slight, and if they had held fast, the charges against them probably would have been dropped. But one of Jack's confederates, a drifter calling himself Red Smith, weakened under pressure.

Harris was now in a bind, but he was good at making deals. He had important information about other crimes and other outlaws, and for a light sentence and a promise to leave Nevada, he offered to tell many things the express officials wanted to know. Wells Fargo got their information, and Harris walked out of prison two months later.

There is a legend that a Carson City grave was once marked by a board which read:

He had sand in his craw,
But he was slow on the draw,
So we planted him under the daisies.

Carson City had its share of badmen who were planted under the daisies, but the famous outlaws seemed to avoid the town. An exception was the notorious Henry Plummer of Montana fame (see *Bannack, Montana*). Plummer supposedly used Carson City as a hideout for a while in the early 1860s. According to the story, he was taken in by a friend, a local gambler named Billy Mayfield. Mayfield himself was no pushover. When the sheriff, Jack Blackburn, heard that Plummer had been hiding out at Mayfield's place, he paid a call on Billy. By then Plummer was gone, but Blackburn tore into Mayfield, ready to thrash him thoroughly for harboring the famous outlaw under the sheriff's nose. Mayfield promptly drew his Bowie knife, and carved a hole in Blackburn's belly.

# Elko
## Elko County

Elko is in northeastern Nevada about fifty miles west of US 93 on Interstate 80. The town is the center for the state's "Cattle Country," and during the western migration served as a waystation for wagon trains.

It is believed that Elko was visited by three members of Wyoming's famous Wild Bunch in the spring of 1899. Sometime in March of that year, Harry Longabaugh (the Sundance Kid), Harvey (Kid Curry) Logan, and "Flat Nose" George Currie rode into town and rented rooms at a local boardinghouse. Using the names Joe Stewart, John Hunter, and Frank Bozeman, they spent most of their evenings at the gambling tables along Elko's saloon row. Their luck was bad, however, and they were soon tapped out. Perhaps they felt they were cheated, or maybe they just needed traveling money, but around midnight on April 6, three masked men entered the Club Saloon and demanded all the money in the safe. It is not certain how much they got: some accounts say $550, others, $3,000. The next day travelers Stewart, Hunter, and Bozeman were gone.

## Eureka
### Eureka County

The county graveyard at Eureka, which is on US 50 just east of the center of the state, holds the remains of the legendary Jack Davis, leader of the gang that committed the first train robbery west of the Rockies (see *Verdi, Nevada*). Davis served a stretch in the penitentiary for that affair, then some say when he got out he joined up with the Sam Bass gang, but according to careful researchers, this was another Jack Davis. Nevada Jack Davis's career ended forty miles south of Eureka, at tiny Willows Station on the Eureka-to-Tybo stage line.

Davis and two companions overpowered the hostler and lay in wait for the stage. But when it arrived the two express messengers, Jimmy Blair and Eugene Brown, had no intention of parting with the strongbox. Both sides began firing, and Brown was hit in the leg, but before he gave up the fight, he unloaded his shotgun into Davis. The old outlaw died on the trail back to Eureka.

## Genoa
### Douglas County

In the mid-1850s Genoa was the headquarters of a ruthless gang of robbers, horse thieves, gamblers, and killers. It was rumored that the leader was a local rancher and businessman, Lucky Bill Thorrington. Thorrington was called "Lucky Bill" because he seemed to be a success at everything he tried. What he had not acquired through hard work, investment, and speculation, he won at the gambling tables. He bought and sold ranches, held mortgages throughout the valley, and even owned the Carson Canyon Toll Road. Yet, apparently this still was not enough, and he added to his already healthy assets through a share in the proceeds of nearly every robbery in the area.

Thorrington had his way until early spring 1858 when word spread that he and two pals, Bill Edwards and John Mullen, had been in on the killing of an honest and respected rancher named Henry Gordier. Citizens of Carson Valley formed a vigilance committee and began gathering evidence. Thorrington and his confederates were rounded up, and in June 1858 a week-long trial resulted in convictions all around. Lucky Bill's luck had run out. He was sentenced to swing from a rope. His body still lies in Genoa in an unmarked grave.

Genoa was also the site of a stage robbery (date unknown) in which the loot, a wooden keg filled with gold coins, was allegedly buried "at the foot of a certain pine tree" and never recovered. Unfortunately, further details have been lost to history, thanks mainly to the tendency of the small, independent stage companies in those days not to preserve records of such things. The tale periodically surfaces, and treasure hunters converge on the town, which in the early days was called Mormon Station, and which lies due south of Carson City just northwest of Minden.

## Humboldt
### Pershing County

While the Wild Bunch of Wyoming were blamed for many robberies in the late 1890s, it was usually difficult to pin down the actual participants. The gang had many members, frequently riding in groups of three or four, often interchanging, and sometimes covering hundreds of miles between holdups. Today, as more and more researchers dig into the gang's history, they are beginning to connect names with crimes.

A holdup on the Southern Pacific Railroad outside Humboldt on July 14, 1898, which at the time was reportedly committed by "two white men and a negro" (according to the engineer), is now thought to have been the work of Wild Bunchers Harry Longabaugh (the Sundance Kid), Harvey Logan (Kid Curry), and "Flat Nose" George Currie. In 1898 dusty railway passengers called Humboldt the "oasis in the desert" because of its lush irrigated landscape. Today the Southern Pacific's tracks still run through the town, which is just off Interstate 80 about 140 miles east of the California line. The site of the 1898 robbery is about a mile northeast of the town. Shortly after 1:00 A.M., three masked men ordered the engineer to put on the brakes at that spot. Apparently the intruders had climbed aboard behind the tender as the train pulled away from the station. The engineer and fireman were marched back to the express car where the Wells Fargo messenger, named Hughes, opened the door on the threat of black powder. In traditional fashion, one bandit periodically fired his gun alongside the coaches to keep the passengers in line while the other two blew the safe and gathered up between $20,000 and $26,000.

## Huntington Valley
### White Pine County

Huntington Valley, just east of the Diamond Mountains on State Road 228, about midway between Interstate 80 and US 50, may have been Butch Cassidy's and the Wyoming Wild Bunch's hideout following the robbery of the Union Pacific express on August 29,

1900, at Tipton, Wyoming.* According to the manuscript "Bandit Invincible," purportedly written by Cassidy himself long after his outlaw days, Butch and his confederates headed west out of Tipton to stay with some "very close friends" who had a small ranch in the foothills ten miles from "a place called Huntington." In the manuscript the writer mentioned a ranch owned by a man named "Hammit." Cassidy biographer Larry Pointer researched the area and found that there was a town called Huntington in the valley which had a post office from 1873 to 1904, and that there is a place called "Hammet Canyon" at the headwaters of Huntington Creek. Also in the manuscript, the writer mentions that the loot taken at Tipton, allegedly $45,000, was buried by the outlaws "as it was too dangerous to try to dispose of it at that time." Was it buried somewhere in Huntington Valley? Did the outlaws ever return for it?

Adding credence to the story that the outlaws used the valley as a hideout in early September 1900 is the fact that the next robbery for which the gang is credited was the bank at nearby Winnemucca* on September 19.

## Montello
### Elko County

Montello lies on State Road 233 about twenty-five miles northeast of Interstate 80. On January 23, 1883, it was the site of "Aaron Ross's stand," a courageous fight put up by a stubborn Wells Fargo messenger against robbers trying to raid his express car.

The outlaws had taken over the town, a tiny dot on the Central Pacific (now Southern Pacific) route map, consisting of a rickety depot, tank house, wood shed, and a few dilapidated shacks. Ross had been napping in his car when the train was flagged down by the robbers. He was greeted by a voice from the station platform demanding that he open up. Before becoming a Wells Fargo messenger on the Central Pacific, Aaron Ross had driven a Concord in Montana. Bandits had tried to rob his stage twice, and twice they had ridden away empty-handed, on one occasion leaving behind dead comrades. True to form, Ross answered his attackers with his pistol. Guns now roared from outside the car. Ross was six feet four inches tall and weighed nearly 250 pounds. All he had for protection were his green Wells Fargo safe, a package chest, and his bedroll. A bullet struck him in the hand, a second sliced his hip, and a third gouged out flesh just below a rib. Although bleeding badly, the stubborn messenger continued to return the outlaws' fire.

When the attackers realized they could not drive him out with their Winchesters, they backed up the locomotive and smashed the express car, hoping it would telescope in and split its sides. But the car was too heavy and the frame too stout. Next they tried to burn the car. Ross could hear the flames crackling and smell the smoke, but the robbers could not get a large enough blaze going and gave up. After a final barrage of gunfire, the disgusted outlaws rode off.

Ross recovered and was proclaimed a hero by Wells Fargo. He was whisked off to the home office in San Francisco where company officials proudly touted him as an example of the sturdy stock of which Wells Fargo messengers were made: stalwart and brave, eager to take the measure of anyone threatening the company's cargo.

## Pioche
### Lincoln County

Pioche is on the eastern edge of Nevada, far removed from the rich Comstock area which attracted so many hard cases during the bonanza days. But Pioche had its tough characters too, most notably Jim Levy, who some contemporaries claim was one of the best and possibly the most underrated gunfighter of the Old West. Levy drew his first blood in Pioche, and according to an acquaintance, "was himself no longer."

It began in 1871 with a fight between two other men, miners Mike Casey and Thomas Gossan. These two shot it out in the street and Casey won. Before he died, Gossan bequeathed $5,000 to whomever would kill Casey. Whether Jim Levy went after the money, or just did not like Casey, is not known. The details of their

Pioche, Nevada. *Nevada Historical Society.*

fight are sketchy. Apparently it took place in the street, in front of Freudenthal's General Store. Levy put a bullet into Casey and then finished him off by beating him over the head with his pistol. Levy, in turn, took a slug in the jaw from one of Casey's friends. They carted Casey off to the undertakers, and Levy collected Gossan's $5,000.

Levy hung around Pioche several more years and was involved in at least one more killing: Thomas Ryan in January 1873. There was not enough evidence for a conviction and Jim was turned loose. He finally left Pioche sometime between 1873 and 1875.

## Verdi
### Washoe County

On a cool crisp night on November 1870, train robbery was introduced in the Far West on the Central Pacific (now Southern Pacific) Railroad just east of Verdi. The holdup was engineered by a former Sunday school superintendent, John T. Chapman, of Reno. Chapman, however, played it safe: he was in San Francisco on the night of the robbery, having telegraphed the information on the Wells Fargo shipment to his confederates in Nevada.

Verdi was an ideal spot for a holdup—a quiet, isolated tank town just east of the California line. It was easy for the five-man band of robbers to slip on the train and take command along the deserted stretch of track that parallels the Truckee River between Verdi and Reno. The gang was led by Jack Davis, not to be confused with the Jack Davis who rode with Sam Bass (see *Big Springs, Nebraska*). His helpers were John Squires, James Gilchrist, Tilton Cockerill, and R. A. Jones, all hard cases but relative amateurs at big time crime. The robbery had been well rehearsed. While the train was still moving, the robbers slipped the pin behind the express car, and the passenger coaches fell back (a nifty trick seldom used by subsequent train robbers). The Wells Fargo messenger gave the intruders no trouble when they demanded that he open up. Ahead, in the locomotive cab, the outlaws ordered the engineer to pull to a stop at an abandoned stone quarry a few miles east of Verdi. Ten minutes later the robbers rode off with nearly $40,000 in gold and silver coins.

But the outlaws did not keep their loot long. Wells Fargo officials converged on Reno and surrounding

A scene often mistakenly identified as the site of the first train robbery in the West, in Truckee Canyon near Verdi, Nevada. According to the records of the Southern Pacific Railroad, the photograph is actually of a rail-bending crew curing iron rail in Ten-Mile Canyon along the Humboldt River in the Nevada Palisades about 432 miles east of Sacramento. The photograph was taken by official Central Pacific photographer Alfred A. Hart in 1868. *Southern Pacific.*

towns and began asking questions. While the gang had stolen the money with a professional touch, they spent it foolishly. Word got around. Jones was the first picked up, and he could not explain his newly found wealth. Soon he confessed and named the others. In the end the company got back $37,000 of the stolen shipment.

"The Great Verdi Robbery" is occasionally referred to as the first train robbery in America. It was not, of course, having occurred over four years after the holdup which is generally accepted as the first—a raid on an Adams Express Company car by the Reno gang on the Ohio & Mississippi Railroad near Seymour, Indiana, in October 1866. The mistake is mainly due to the efforts of one man, Sam Davis (no relation to Jack Davis), a journalist who prowled the Comstock Lode in the 1880s and 1890s and who later became a respected Nevada historian. Sam Davis was either a careless researcher or just plain stubborn. Years later a colleague, newspaperman Wells Drury, suggested that Davis never fully gave up on the idea that the crime of train robbery was born that night at Verdi. Perhaps because the crime eventually became nearly an exclusively western enterprise, Davis felt that it was only fitting that it should have its roots in a western state.

## Virginia City
### Storey County

While Milton Sharp may have been Nevada's premier highwayman (see *Aurora*), a dashing Spanish-born renegade named Nicanor Rodrigues was probably the territory's most outrageous outlaw. Rodrigues, known in the Comstock area as "Nickanora" or "Nick," had cut his teeth robbing stages in California. After a short stretch in prison he was pardoned because of his tender years, and he drifted to Nevada sometime in the 1870s. While Nick continued ordering down strongboxes on the roads in and out of Virginia City, he also began "visiting the fountainhead," as one observer called it: he and his band began ravaging quartz mills. On one raid, Nick hauled off a load of unretorted bullion (from the Pacific Mill in lower Gold Hill), which he buried in a graveyard and later turned into neat bars well suited for sale. A story is told that he once even stole three gold bricks off a stage without anyone being the wiser. One day he saw the bricks being loaded in the front boot of the stage to Reno. He bought a ticket and asked to sit beside the driver. While the driver's eyes scoured the trail for bandits, Nick removed the bricks one by one and dropped them off the side. Later, he rented a buggy and retrieved them.

Stories about Nick's daring abound. It was said he eventually tired of outwitting express officials and talked the Wells Fargo company into hiring him to *prevent* its stages from being robbed. Thanks to the 1906 San Francisco earthquake and fire, there is no record in the Wells Fargo files of any such agreement, but if anybody could have cut such a deal, it was Nick.

Virginia City, Nevada, in the 1880s. *The Bancroft Library, University of California..*

The dashing robber's luck finally ran out in the late 1870s, and one day he found himself in jail. Before he could be shipped off to prison, however, he engineered an escape. Years later a miner said he thought he saw him in Mexico, living under the name Don Felipe Castro. According to the miner, he had a thriving ranch and "possessed more horses than any other man within fifty miles." That would be Nick.

Nevada newspaperman Wells Drury, who saw more than one hanging during his days in Virginia City, often told the story of one hapless victim who tried to prolong his last hours by oratory. The execution was a legal one, the law had taken its course and the accused was duly convicted and sentenced. During his final days, this particular prisoner somehow got the idea that it was not legal in Nevada to hold an execution after sunset. So when he was told that his hanging was scheduled late in the day, he laid plans to delay it. Using every device he could muster, he managed to prolong the fatal moment until the shadows began to fall long over the town. Pleading for a few more "last words," he took a deep breath and began his final speech. As Drury described it, "he launched into a ghastly kind of filibuster, talking against time—till the sun went down. The sheriff tried to break in and stop the flow of halfwit oratory, but to no avail; and finally the trip was sprung in the midst of a long periodic sentence, as the late sun was gilding the heights."

Virginia City experienced an interesting jailbreak in the late 1870s. Five prisoners escaped, lead by a local hard case named "Red Mike" Langan. The interesting part is that Red Mike, who was charged with doing away with an old enemy in a street fight, had helped build the very jail in which he was being held. He knew that while the outside walls were over two feet thick, the mortar holding the bricks was worthless and would crumble to sand with the slightest probing. In a half hour, Langan and his fellow inmates punched out a hole with a brace taken from a bedstead—probably the easiest jailbreak in Nevada history.

Virginia City is just north of Carson City off US 50. The town has done much to restore the spirit of its bonanza days. There are many small museums, especially on C Street, including The Wild West Museum, The Way It Was Museum, the Delta Saloon, and the Ponderosa Saloon, the last offering daily underground mine tours. And Western buffs interested in collectibles and frontier items should visit Virginia City on Memorial Day weekend during the annual May Antique Show. It is one of the largest shows in the region, drawing major dealers from most of the western states.

## Winnemucca
### Humboldt County

As with most robberies attributed to the Wyoming Wild Bunch, there is disagreement among researchers as to which members of the gang were in Nevada on September 19, 1900, to hold up the Bank of Winnemucca. It is unlikely the same Wild Bunchers who robbed the Union Pacific express on August 29 at Tipton, Wyoming,* would have had enough time to ride all the way to Winnemucca (located in northern Nevada at the junction of Interstate 80 and US 95), camp out a week near town to case the target, and then pull off the robbery by September 19. Since an eyewitness swore that Butch Cassidy was at Winnemucca, some writers doubt that he was at Tipton.

The eyewitness was young Vic Button, a boy of ten, whose father owned a ranch east of Winnemucca. Button claimed that Cassidy and two others, believed to be Harry Longabaugh (the Sundance Kid) and Bill Carver, camped near a haystack about four miles from the Button Ranch the week before the holdup. Young Button would ride down each day and visit with the three men, and they would ask him questions about the town and surrounding area, especially routes and shortcuts.

Writers have speculated as to why the Wild Bunch traveled so many miles from their usual area of operation to rob a bank in Nevada. Several reasons have been suggested. One is that this part of the gang was already in Nevada, hiding out with friends of Cassidy's (see *Huntington Valley*). Another is that they were invited to rob the bank. Some researchers claim that a bank employee had embezzled funds and, in the hope of covering up the crime, got word to the Wild Bunch that a

Winnemucca, Nevada. *Charles C. Goodhall Collection.*

robbery would not be "too vigorously resisted." The robbery was, in fact, carried off with ease. The outlaws walked in, ordered all hands up, and forced everyone to lie down on the floor. In minutes they scooped up all the money from the open vault (the amount varies: some say around $30,000, others, over $40,000) and rode off.

You can roughly trace the bandits' escape route today over Winnemucca's streets. After leaving the bank the robbers ran down the alley behind the building for a block to the rear of the F. C. Robbins store where they had left their horses. From there they rode to Second Street and turned east, crossed Bridge Street, then raced to the narrow wooden bridge over White's Creek, a small stream that wandered down to the Humboldt River. At the bridge one of the gang dropped a sack of money. He jumped off his horse, quickly retrieved the sack, and galloped after his comrades who by then were heading east on the road to Golconda.

A posse nearly caught up with the robbers in nearby Clover Valley, but a change of horses from a carefully prepared relay team sped them on their way.

Today a photograph of the Wild Bunch (the one said to have been taken in Fort Worth, Texas, in 1900) hangs in the bank, now the First National Bank of Nevada. It is said to be an enlargement of an original sent by Cassidy to Vic Button in 1900.

Despite the photograph, some researchers question whether the Wild Bunch was involved at all. George Nixon, part owner of the Bank of Winnemucca, and the person who probably got the best look at the robbers, did not believe they were Cassidy and his bunch. Nixon felt the holdup was organized by a group of local men; several names were mentioned, among them a Willie Wier and two brothers, March and Melville Fuller. Nixon himself was suspected by some of planning the robbery, but no evidence of this was ever turned up. He later became a United States senator.

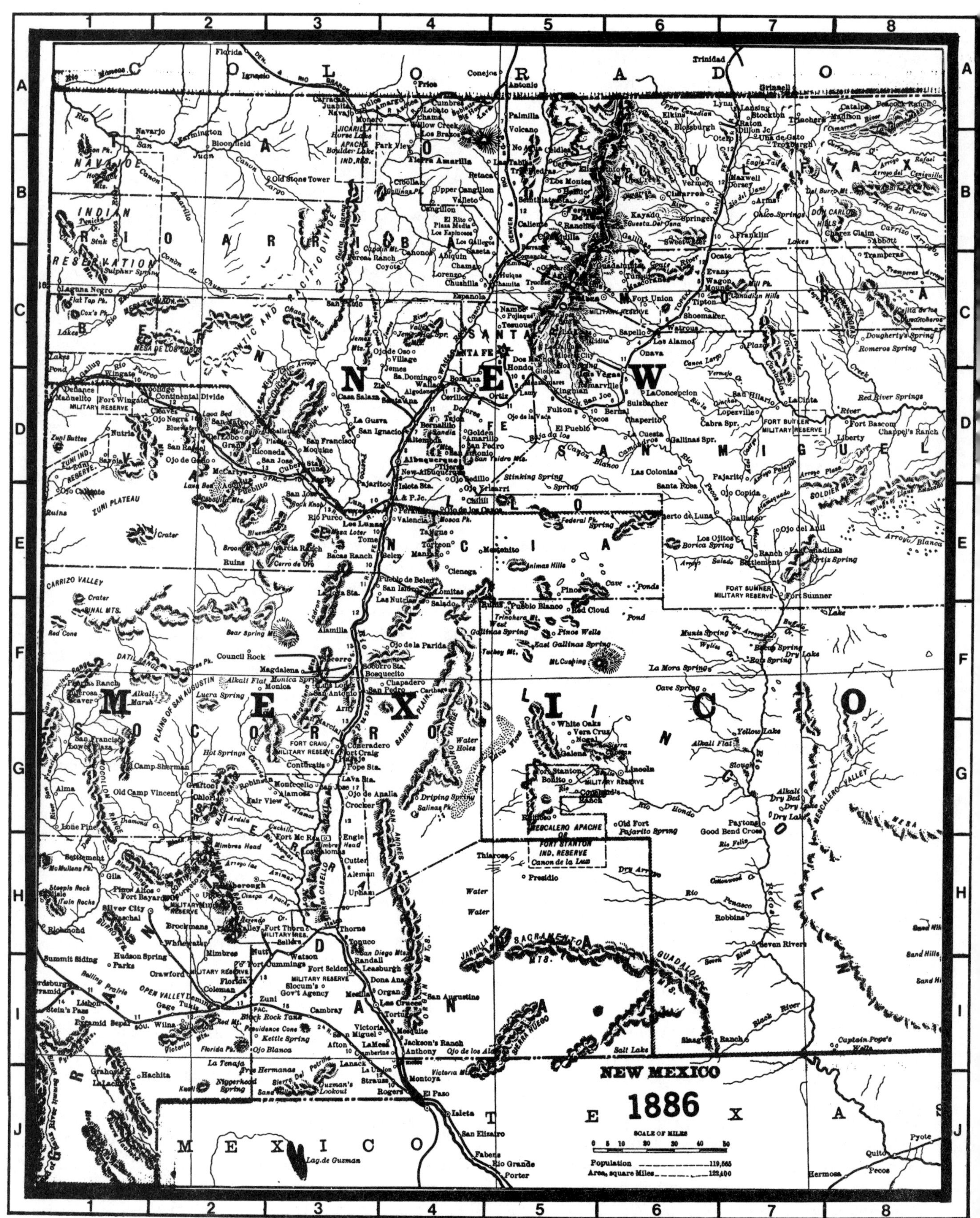


New Mexico 1886

# NEW MEXICO

## Alma
### Catron County

Alma is located on US 180 in southwestern New Mexico, just north of the Grant County line. In the late 1890s the town and the surrounding area was a favorite hideout spot for Butch Cassidy and members of the Wyoming Wild Bunch, including Harry Longabaugh (the Sundance Kid) who is believed to have spent some time there in the summer of 1898. Cassidy, using the name Jim Lowe, supposedly worked on the nearby W. S. Ranch, owned by William French who later wrote of those days. According to French, Butch at times tended bar in town and once in 1899 had the pleasure of serving a Pinkerton agent who had come to Alma, tracing bank notes stolen from the Union Pacific holdup at Wilcox, Wyoming,* the previous June. Feeling their hideaway may have been discovered, the outlaws moved on to Texas later that year.

The old W. S. Ranch lies just north of Alma on US 180, along the San Francisco River. A tiny graveyard on the ranch survives to this day, although none of the markers carry names of any of the famous outlaws who may have gathered there. It is interesting, though, that those who are buried there were all struck down by bullets in their prime—fitting indeed for the ranch's reputation.

Some say Billy the Kid also lived in Alma for a while in 1873 or 1874. His stepfather, William H. Antrim, reportedly was a part-owner of a blacksmith shop on the outskirts of town. The remains of the old adobe building, later converted to a garage, can still be seen.

## Cimarron
### Colfax County

Cimarron is in northern New Mexico, on US 64 about thirty miles west of Interstate 25. The town was home ground for the famous Clay Allison, a successful rancher by profession and a feared killer by reputation. Allison's mean streak apparently stemmed from his fondness for the bottle. He was first labeled a man to avoid in the fall of 1870. While drinking in a saloon in nearby Elizabethtown, now a ghost town just north of Baldy Peak, Clay and his friends were interrupted by an hysterical woman with a tearful story that she had just discovered that her husband was a murderer. Clay and his companions rushed to the women's cabin where they found her husband, Charles Kennedy, even drunker than they. After putting Kennedy in jail the men searched the cabin. They found a cache of bones, which may or may not have been human, but they did not wait to find out. They dragged Kennedy from the jail and hanged him. Then, so the story goes, Allison decapitated the victim, jammed his head on a stick, and took it to Cimarron where he put it on display at Henri Lambert's saloon.

On January 7, 1874, Allison provided more entertainment for the residents of Cimarron. While having dinner at Tom Stockton's Clifton House, just south of town near the river, Clay got into an argument with a local hard case named Chunk Colbert. Details vary, but apparently instead of reaching for his coffee, Colbert went for his gun. He missed, and Allison drilled him in the forehead, killing him instantly. It is said Colbert's remains still lie buried behind the old roadhouse.

Cimarron's St. James Hotel saloon was the site of Allison's next gunbattle. On November 1, 1875, Clay palmed a revolver and pumped three bullets into the belly of Pancho Griego, a Colfax County pistoleer, who had been feuding with Allison over the mysterious death of one of Griego's employees. Clay may have had help in this one for as the shots rang out the lights in the room were suddenly extinguished, and Allison escaped in the darkness, thus avoiding settling the matter with two of Griego's companions.

One of the bloodiest gunfights in northern New Mexico occurred in Turkey Creek Canyon near Cimarron on July 16, 1899. Five days earlier a train was held up near Folsom. Three of the robbers were trailed to isolated Turkey Creek Canyon by a posse. The outlaws, later identified as Elzy Lay (alias William McGinnis), Sam Ketchum (brother of the notorious "Black Jack" Ketchum), and a man known only as G. W. Franks, had made camp for the night. According to one version of the shootout, during the early morning hours the possemen spotted Lay heading for the creek with his canteen to get water, and they put two bullets in him. Ketchum came out of his bedroll firing but was disabled by a shot that shattered his left arm. Franks, however, had good cover and put up a terrific fight, killing one of the possemen, Ed Farr, and wounding another, Henry Love. All three outlaws escaped, but Ketchum, who had lost much blood, was found at a cabin a few miles away. Lay was captured a month later at a ranch in Eddy County. Franks was never apprehended, at least under that name. There was some speculation that he was really Wild Bunch desperado Harvey (Kid Curry) Logan.

There are still some remains of old Cimarron. The St. James Hotel, although altered, still stands, as does one of the old saloons, the Don Diego Tavern, and the original jail.

A New Mexico lynching, 1886. *Denver Public Library, Western History Department.*

## Clayton
### Union County

On April 25, 1901, Clayton (in northeastern New Mexico at the junction of US 56 and US 87) was the site of the hanging of "Black Jack" Ketchum. As he was being marched up the steps of the gallows, this cocky outlaw taunted his executioners with "I'll be in hell before you start breakfast, boys." Once the rope and hood were in place, Ketchum gave the order "Let her rip!" They did, and the trap door was released. Most hangmen in those days prided themselves on not letting a victim suffer because of a "short fall" on the rope. In Kethum's case there was no problem. When Black Jack's body reached the end of the rope, the noose severed his head from his torso and the head went skittering across the ground. A witness to the gruesome scene, Trancito Romero, brother-in-law of the sheriff, was not certain just what caused the decapitation. He later said "perhaps the scaffold was too high, the noose too tight, or perhaps the rope was too slender to hold so heavy a man."

A rumor spread that just before Ketchum was hanged, a stranger appeared at the front of the crowd, presumably a member of Black Jack's gang, and Ketchum "nodded" to him. Romero discounted the story. Contrary to the popular notion that the town of Clayton turned the execution into a grand spectacle, with hundreds in attendance, "the crowd was not large," said Romero. "The people of Clayton did not like to see men killed. . . . Its inhabitants lived a sane, quiet life—their calm shattered only by occasional outlawry and such gun display as we associate with mass movement westward."

## Columbus
### Luna County

Columbus, near the Mexican border south of Deming, is known mainly for the famous raid by Pancho Villa in March 1916. There is even a Pancho Villa State Park on State Highway 11 west of town. Not so well-known is a tale involving a site east of Columbus where there still may be buried a cache of stolen outlaw loot.

According to an old cowboy, Bert Judia, "thousands" of dollars were buried on a ranch at that location, loot from a robbery down in Cananea, Mexico. The year was 1908. Judia had met up with a Texan named Jim Strickland who had vaguely outlined a "project" south of the border at Cananea in which he wanted Judia's help. Bert at first thought it had something to do with mining, since Cananea was near several large mines. As it turned out, Strickland used Judia to transport the proceeds of a robbery which Strickland and several others had committed. The plans were for Strickland to meet Judia afterward at the ranch near Columbus, but the Texan never showed up. Judia later learned that he had been killed shortly after the holdup.

Bert Judia was not an outlaw, and he was afraid to keep the money. He buried it near the windmill on the ranch which he later described as "a few miles out of Columbus at the edge of the sand dunes." In an interview made public in 1974, Judia said he hid the loot in cans and fruit jars on the east side of a sand dune "on a direct line from the windmill, toward the peak of a mountain." He said he went back once to see if it was still there, but did not dig it up. At times he said he thought of retrieving it and putting it in a bank, but he was afraid somebody might become suspicious and connect him with the robbery.

## Corona
### Lincoln County

On the old White Oaks–Las Vagas Road near Corona, which is at the junction of US 54 and State Highway 42, is the site of a ranch house and trading post once operated by "Whiskey Jim" Greathouse. During the fall of 1880, it became a frequent hangout for Billy the Kid and his followers. On November 30 of that year a posse out of White Oaks, led by a deputized blacksmith named Jim Carlyle, cornered Billy's bunch at the Greathouse place. When it appeared the posse might decide to burn the outlaws out, Whiskey Jim suggested that he offer himself as a hostage to the posse in return for Carlyle coming inside to negotiate with Billy. The exchange was made, but Billy and Carlyle could not come to terms. When Carlyle did not return to his posse as expected, word was sent in that Billy had five minutes to release him, or Greathouse would be shot. Shortly thereafter a gunshot was heard from where the posse was hidden. Thinking Greathouse was dead and he would be next, Carlyle made a break for it by diving through a window. As he struggled to his feet he was cut down by bullets, either from inside the house or from the posse which may have mistaken him for one of the outlaws. Shaken by the death of their leader, the posse gave up and returned to town. Two days later someone burned the Greathouse place to the ground.

## Engle
### Sierra County

A ranch in the rugged San Andres Mountains east of Engle, on what now is the western edge of the White Sands Missile Range, may have been the granddaddy of all outlaw hideouts in the Old West. No one knows for sure because the source of the information was Western novelist Eugene Manlove Rhodes who at times blended fact with fiction.

Rhodes owned the ranch and during the 1890s was, as he once put it, "the only settler in a country larger than the state of Delaware." The area was indeed ideal for a hideout. From several lookout points one could spot a posse miles away, and to the south lay an easy ride to Texas or Mexico, both of which offered even better sanctuary to the man on the run.

Rumor had it that Rhodes maintained an open invitation to all desperadoes: if they worked for their keep, he would keep his mouth shut and guarantee a safe haven. If the stories Rhodes told are true, his guest book for the 1890s included the names of such luminaries as the Dalton brothers, Tom (Black Jack) Ketchum, Bob and Will Christian, Bill Doolin, and the Apache Kid.

## Folsom
### Union County

In the early days Folsom (located in northeastern New Mexico on State Highway 72 due east of Raton) was called Madison after its first settler, Madison Emery. The town was then the nearest settlement to Oklahoma's Black Mesa which was the hangout of a ruthless gang of outlaws led by "Captain" Bill Coe (see *Black Mesa*). When the gang needed to replenish their supply of whiskey or a night's entertainment, they headed for Madison (Folsom). After tanking up at the saloons, they repaired to Emery's hotel where they slept off the last few hours before dawn. This continued until July 1868 when Mrs. Emery apparently got fed up with Coe's impudence and tipped off a troop of cavalry that was camped outside town. Coe was arrested and taken to Pueblo, Colorado, where a group of vigilantes stormed his jail cell and lynched him.

Folsom is better remembered for the capture of the notorious stage and train robber Thomas "Black Jack" Ketchum. On August 16, 1899, Ketchum tried to rob a train singlehandedly just outside of town. He shot the express messenger in the jaw and wounded the conductor, Frank Harrington, in the neck. But just as Harrington was hit he unloaded a barrel of buckshot which shattered Ketchum's right arm. The night was dark, and the outlaw ducked under the express car, crawled across the tracks, and disappeared in the sagebrush. By morning, however, he was convinced that he would bleed to death if he did not get help, and he flagged down a freight train and surrendered to the crew.

The town is interesting to visit today because many of its original buildings were built of stone and remain intact.

## Fort Sumner
### De Baca County

Old Fort Sumner, about fifty-five miles west of Clovis just off US 60, is where Pat Garrett killed Billy the Kid. The site of the old fort, on State Highway 212 just southwest of the present town of Fort Sumner, is now a state monument.

Billy's career came to an end on the night of July 14, 1881, in an old adobe dwelling that had once served as the post's officers' quarters. Billy had escaped jail the previous April (see *Lincoln, New Mexico*) and was hiding out around Fort Sumner, sometimes practically under sheriff Garrett's nose. On a tip from Pete Maxwell, who lived in the dwelling on the fort and whose sister Billy was regularly visiting, Garrett and two assistants, John Poe and Tip McKinney, were waiting at the house when Billy arrived. Garrett was sitting in Maxwell's darkened bedroom talking to Pete when the outlaw entered. Billy had seen the sheriff's fellow lawmen outside but did not recognize them; nor did they recognize him. But Billy became suspicious and drew his gun as he entered the room. He saw Garrett sitting on the bed but in the dim light could not identify him. In Spanish, Billy asked Maxwell, "Quien es?" (Who is it?). Garrett's holster had slipped around his belt to the back, and as he struggled to reach it, the movement startled the outlaw. Jumping back, he again cried "Quien es? Quien es?" Garrett now had his gun out. He fired twice and saw Billy drop to the floor. Not sure his bullets had reached their mark, he dashed out of the room, as did Maxwell. Cautiously they huddled outside on the porch for several minutes until they thought they heard "a rattle" from Billy's throat. They lighted a candle and held it to the window. Billy was on his back, his dead eyes staring at the ceiling.

Billy was quickly buried in the cemetery that served the fort, reportedly between two of his gang who had predeceased him, Tom O'Folliard and Charles Bowdre. Although the grave can be visited today, whether Billy's body actually still lies there is open to question. The original wooden marker disappeared many years ago, probably in one of the Pecos River floods that wash over the low parts of the site on occasion. It is also possible that the body, together with those of O'Folliard and Bowdre, were disinterred by the military years later when most of the Fort Sumner corpses were moved to the Santa Fe National Cemetery. Notwithstanding, an appropriate stone marker decorates the site today which is visited by thousands of tourists annually.

As often happens with the death of a famous outlaw, there have been those who say that Billy did not die at all that night. Years later a close friend of Billy's, Ygenio Salazaar, claimed he received a letter from the outlaw telling him that the Fort Sumner affair was fabricated. Also, there is the story of a California priest who came to New Mexico in the 1930s, supposedly on a mission to get in touch with Billy's former friends in the Mexican community. The priest told of an old man who died in an isolated area of California who, on his death, confessed that he was Billy, and as a last request asked the priest to let his Mexican friends know the truth.

## Hillsboro
### Sierra County

Hillsboro, which is in southwestern New Mexico between Silver City and Interstate 25, was the scene of the famous Lee-Gilliland trial in the summer of 1899. Oliver Lee and James Gilliland were charged with the February 1896 killing of Messila lawyer Albert Jennings Fountain and his young son, Henry, near the desert area that is now White Sands National Monument.* The case was transferred from Otera County, Lee's home, because he was too popular there. (Lee, a former deputy U.S. marshal and successful rancher, later became a prominent businessman and state legislator; today, a state park, just south of Alamogordo, is named after him.)

The trial was a culmination of years of feuding between Dona Ana County (and later Otero County) political factions, one led by friends of Fountain and the other by his one-time arch enemy, fellow Messila lawyer Albert Fall, who defended Lee and Gilliland against the murder charges. On the side of the prosecution was Pat Garrett (also a bitter enemy of Lee) who unsuccessfully tried to arrest him and Gilliland at the "Battle of Wildy Well" (see *Orogrande*). The trial lasted eighteen days. The disappearance of key prosecution witnesses coupled with defense attorney Fall's brillant cross-examinations resulted in an acquittal of both defendants.

It was the greatest event Hillsboro ever witnessed. The town overflowed. People came from miles around, filling the Union Hotel and all available rooming houses. Many camped in the surrounding hills. But the affair was the town's swan song. Soon after, the mines in the area played out, and the county seat was taken away. Today Hillsboro is a ghost town with only crumbling remains of the once sturdy brick courthouse to remind visitors of the famous trial.

# Las Cruces
## Dona Ana County

About four miles northeast of downtown Las Cruces, near Alameda Arroyo on the old Mail-Scott Road to Organ, is the spot where the famous New Mexico lawman Pat Garrett was mysteriously gunned down on March 1, 1908. Who killed Garrett and why is still a mystery. The old lawman had retired from chasing fugitives and was struggling to make a go of a not-too-successful cattle ranch near Organ. On the day of his death he was riding to Las Cruces with a man named Carl Adamson, at the time a partner in a cattle operation with gunslinger "Deacon Jim" Miller. (Adamson was negotiating with Garrett over a deal to fatten up Mexican cattle on Garrett's grassland.) Present also was Jesse Wayne Brazel, a local cowboy who was trying to make a living raising goats on land rented from Garrett.

The men had stopped by the side of the road, apparently to relieve themselves, when, according to Adamson, Brazel suddenly drew his gun and shot Garrett. Brazel, who later confessed to the crime, claimed he shot in self defense: that he and Garrett had been arguing and the old lawman was threatening to shoot him. The case went to trial and Brazel was acquitted—some say under highly suspicious circumstances. For one thing, Adamson, the only witness, was never called to testify. For another, the evidence suggested that Garrett was shot in the back of the head, and that at the time he was shot he was in the act of urinating.

There has been much speculation over the years that others were involved: a local rancher and long-time enemy of Garrett's named W. W. Cox; a partner of Brazel's, a hard case named Print Rhode; and "Deacon Jim" Miller himself who had a long history of hired killings to his credit. Also, some believe Adamson was the murderer. Most votes seem to be for Miller, as part of a grand collusion of all parties involved. The best evidence, however, still points to Brazel who likely did get into an argument with Garrett over Pat's insistence that he sell his goats so Garrett could lease the land to Miller and Adamson.

The old lawman was buried in a weed-covered corner of the Las Cruces Odd Fellows Cemetery. He lay there until 1957 when he was transferred to a family plot in the town's Masonic Cemetery.

# Las Vegas
## San Miguel County

Many towns claimed to be the wildest in the West, but perhaps Las Vegas deserves special recognition, at least if we are to believe Miguel Otero, one-time governor of New Mexico who wrote about his days there in the late 1870s and early 1880s. According to Otero, in one month (he does not say which one), twenty-nine men died violently.

Regardless of the accuracy of Otero's figures, Las Vegas was indeed a hangout for outlaws. A spectacular shootout occurred in January 1880 when city marshal

Las Vegas, New Mexico in the 1880s. *Denver Public Library, Western History Department.*

Joe Carson and deputy "Mysterious Dave" Mather challenged the Tom Henry gang at the Close and Patterson Saloon. Carson was killed, but Mather shot Henry and two of his companions, William "Big" Randall and James West. Randall died on the spot. Henry and another gang member, John Dorsey, fled but were captured several weeks later. They, along with West, were promptly dragged from their jail cells and gunned to death in the town plaza. The coroner's report listed the culprits as "parties unknown"; some say they were led by Dave Mather.

Like many western towns, Las Vegas seemed cursed with peace officers who operated on both sides of the law. John Joshua Webb and and Dave Rudabaugh were good examples. Both were transplants from Dodge City. Rudabaugh had ridden briefly with Kansas outlaw Mike Rourke, but after turning state's evidence against Rourke following an attempted train robbery at Kinsley, Kansas, Rudabaugh became friends with Webb, at the time one of Bat Masterson's special deputies. Rudabaugh and Webb drifted to Las Vegas where they became law officers, working under a crooked justice of the peace named H. G. Neill. In March 1880 Webb was charged with taking part in the robbing and killing of a local cattleman and was jailed. Rudabaugh, well-fortified with cantina juice and determined to rescue his friend, single-handedly stormed the jail, shot the jailer, and took his keys and threw them into Webb's cell. Rudabaugh then raced for his horse and rode out of town, but Webb, possibly stunned by his pal's antics, was slow to gather his wits and was still in his cell when the marshal arrived.

In June of the same year Las Vegas may have been the scene of a shootout between the notorious Doc Holliday and a bartender named Charley White. Some say it happened, some say it did not. Governor Otero said it did. According to the story, Holliday and White had got into a fuss back in Dodge City, and Doc ran the bartender out of town, claiming that if he ever saw him again he would kill him. Otero said they met again that June in a saloon on Las Vegas's plaza and both started shooting. Holliday's biographer, Pat Jahns, claims Doc was a terrible shot, and this gunfight confirmed it. Apparently many bullets were fired with the only wound being a crease along White's back. Doc, however, thought he killed White and raced to his hotel to tell his girlfriend, Kate Bender, all about the big gun battle.

Christmas week 1880 saw Dave Rudabaugh back in town, this time a member of Billy the Kid's gang of troublemakers. The week before Billy and four of his bunch had been captured by lawman Pat Garrett (see *Stinking Spring, New Mexico*). One was killed and the rest, including Billy and Rudabaugh, were delivered in irons to the Las Vegas jail, pending transfer to Santa Fe. As Garrett loaded his prisoners onto the train, angry townsmen stormed the coach demanding that Rudabaugh be turned over to them so they could settle the score for his killing of the town jailer the previous March. Things looked bleak, especially when Garrett could not find a crew to operate the train. Finally, after Garrett temporarily backed the crowd down with his sixshooters, a deputy U.S. marshal, J. F. Morley, volunteered his help and managed to start the locomotive and pull the train out of the station.

Dave Rudabaugh was eventually convicted of killing the jailer and sentenced to hang. In the fall of 1881 he was returned to Las Vegas to await execution. But on December 3 he tunneled through his cell wall and escaped. It was later reported that he fled to Parral, Mexico, where he resumed his outlaw ways and for a while terrorized the town until the villagers shot him, cut off his head, and mounted it on a broomstick to warn other gringos to stay away from their pueblo.

## Lincoln
### Lincoln County

The town of Lincoln was the center of the famous "Lincoln County War," a deadly struggle for political power and control of the beef industry during the 1870s. The trouble came to a head in February 1878 with the hired killing of wealthy English rancher and businessman John Henry Tunstall in a wooded canyon near Ruidoso. Skirmish lines were immediately formed and Lincoln became the battlefield. On April 1 a gunfight erupted on Lincoln's main street. Sheriff William Brady, reportedly controlled by the faction that had eliminated Tunstall, died instantly. Beside him lay his deputy, George Hindman. Ranch hands turned gunmen held sway. Three days later guns roared again west of town near Sierra Blanca: the "Fight at Blazer's Mill" where Andrew "Buckshot" Roberts, a scrawny gunslinger who had been in on Tunstall's killing, stood off the gang that had downed Sheriff Brady, killed one attacker, Dick Brewer, and wounded another. Although Roberts fought off the attack, he later bled to death from a gut shot.

The gang, bent on avenging Tunstall's death, called themselves the "Regulators." Among them was Billy the Kid who had worked for Tunstall. They now rallied behind a Lincoln lawyer-merchant, Alexander McSween, and continued to defy the authorities. The climax came in a five-day seige that began July 14, 1878. McSween and the Regulators barricaded themselves in an adobe compound in Lincoln and fired sporadic pot shots at local lawmen now led by Brady's successor, former deputy George "Dad" Peppin. On July 19 the army was called in. When they saw the troopers' Gatling gun the majority of McSween's men called it quits, but fifteen or so remained, including Billy the Kid. The end came on the 19th when the buildings were set on fire. McSween and three of his supporters were killed. Billy was among those who escaped.

Things calmed down with the appointment of Civil War general Lew Wallace as Territorial Governor. Wallace could not determine who should be punished, so he granted amnesty to all participants, provided they were bona fide residents of New Mexico. In February 1879 Billy the Kid returned to Lincoln to meet with Jesse Evans, leader of the gang that killed Tunstall, to work out a truce. While in town they ran into a Las Vegas lawyer named Huston A. Chapman who had been hired by the widow of Alexander McSween to prosecute her husband's killers. Apparently Chapman and Evans got into an argument, and Evans, with the help of a fellow outlaw, James Dolan, shot Chapman and set his body on fire.

Billy the Kid was eventually tried and convicted for the killling of Sheriff William Brady (see *Mesilla*). In April 1881 he was returned to Lincoln to await execution. He was housed in the then vacant two-story Murphy-Dolan store which had been hastily converted into a combined courthouse, jail, and sheriff's office. However, Billy's stay there was short. On April 28, using a pistol a confederate had left hidden for him in the privy, he shot and killed one of his two guards, deputy sheriff J. W. Bell, at the top of the stairs leading to the second floor. Dragging his leg irons, Billy then rushed to the window at the side of the building and unloaded a shotgun into the other guard, deputy Bob Olinger, as he came running from a restaurant across the street. Using a miner's pick, Billy struggled with his chains for almost an hour (during which time no townsman dared to approach him) but managed to free only one leg. Tying the loose shackle to his belt, he saddled up and rode out of town.

Lincoln is located on US 380 about sixty miles west of Roswell. The makeshift courthouse where Billy escaped has been turned into a museum. Among the items that can be seen there is a photostatic copy of the coroner's report of Billy's death in 1881 at Fort Sumner.* A steel marker also designates the spot outside of town where John Tunstall was killed. In celebration of the town's frontier days, Lincoln holds an annual festival the first weekend in August. Events include a re-enactment of Billy's escape from the courthouse.

## Mesilla
### Dona Ana County

Mesilla, just south of Las Cruces on State Highway 28, was the scene of the murder trial of Billy the Kid in April 1881. Billy was charged with the killing of Lincoln County sheriff William Brady in a shootout three years earlier at Lincoln.* Most observers agree

McSween Store, Lincoln. *Museum of New Mexico.*

Lincoln County Court House where Billy the Kid escaped in 1881. *Museum of New Mexico.*

Billy the Kid. *Museum of New Mexico.*

that the trial was pretty much rigged against Billy, although there was little doubt that he had a hand in the killing. His defense was handled by the noted Mesilla lawyer, Albert Jennings Fountain, who undoubtedly knew it was a futile effort from the start. Billy was found guilty and sentenced to hang, but such would not be his fate (see *Lincoln*).

The adobe building in which the trial was held still stands at the southeast corner of the plaza.

## Orogrande
### Otero County

A few miles southeast of Orogrande, on what is now the Fort Bliss Military Reservation, lay Wildy Well, an adobe line shack on land owned by a tough character named Oliver Lee. Lee had served as a deputy U.S. marshal, and would one day become a successful rancher, businessman, and state legislator. However in July 1898 Dona Ana County sheriff Pat Garrett considered him and a sidekick, James Gilliland, prime suspects in the killing of Mesilla lawyer Albert Jennings Fountain and his son on a desert trail which is now part of White Sands National Monument.* Garrett, killer of outlaw Billy the Kid, had one of the finest records of any New Mexico peace officer, but on the night of July 12, 1898, he and his small posse came out second best in what has become known as the Battle of Wildy Well.

Garrett and his men sneaked up on the dwelling, but the crafty Lee and friend Gilliland were sleeping on the roof. In a quick exchange of gunfire, Lee put two bullets into posseman Kent Kearney. From their commanding position Lee and Gilliland easily pinned down the lawmen, forcing them to call it quits. It was a humiliating experience for the proud Garrett, who seldom was bested in a fight.

## Outlaw Rock
### Dona Ana County

Just off Interstate 25, about four miles west of Fort Selden State Monument and a half-mile or so north of Radium Springs, can be seen a craggy peak local residents call "Outlaw Rock." The name stems from scratches on the rock purported to be placed there by Billy the Kid and several members of the gang he ran with in the late 1870s and early 1880s. If one climbed to the base of the peak and carefully inspected a spot a short way up a narrow arroyo, one would find the names "Bonney" and "Bowdre," the letters "Off" and the initials "D. R." Legend has it that "Bonney" was scratched there by Billy himself (who at times used the alias William Bonney), and "Bowdre" was written by his outlaw pal Charles Bowdre. The "Off" is presumed to be the nickname of another gang member, Tom O'Folliard, and the initials "D. R." are said to be those of the notorious killer Dave Rudabaugh.

According to the owners of the land on which the peak is located, the site, an ideal hideout spot with a commanding view of the surrounding area (especially Fort Selden), was once said to include the remains of an adobe hut which was dismantled a few years ago by a Hollywood movie crew for use on a set.

## Raton
### Colfax County

A dispute over the legality of land grants and fraudulent surveys brought trouble to this northeastern New Mexico area in 1884. Word spread that there might be violence, and gunfighters began drifting in looking for work. One was Dick Rogers, a nasty Texan who reportedly had laid at least four men to rest within the past year. By December the situation became so tense the governor authorized the creation of a militia company at Raton to keep order. Jim Masterson, Bat's younger brother, was brought down from Trinidad, Colorado, and given the authority to recruit thirty-five volunteers. Shortly thereafter, Rogers and Masterson squared off one night at a Raton dance hall. The outlaw got the better of the hard-nosed lawman and made him dance to the tune of his sixgun. Later, Masterson's militia, backed by the local Maxwell Land Grant Company, was forced to disband under accusations that it became too abusive in attempting to persuade settlers to abandon their claims. The anti-grant faction, led by Rogers and his collection of gunslingers, formed a quasi-militia group of their own and escorted Masterson and his bunch to the Colorado line.

## San Patricio
### Lincoln County

This little village, on US 70 between Roswell and Alamogordo, was a favorite hangout of Billy the Kid in the late 1870s and early 1880s. Rumor has it that he has descendents living there today. Walter Noble Burns, one of Billy's biographers, supposedly talked with some of the outlaw's kin. Billy never married, and Burns agreed to preserve the privacy of his offspring. It is said that two of Billy's children, both girls, died in infancy, but a son lived until the 1950s.

## Silver City
### Grant County

Consistent with the popular notion that most of the badmen of the West got that way because the law had "done them wrong" sometime during their early years, is the tale that Billy the Kid, as a child in Silver City, was wrongfully thrown in jail for stealing a bundle of clothes from "two Chinamen." According to the story, the bundle was actually stolen by a companion of Billy's. Billy was lodged in the Silver City jail but escaped by climbing up the chimney. Disgusted with "how the law operated," Billy headed for Arizona and eventually the outlaw trail.

Also, sometimes Silver City is mentioned as the site of Billy's first murder: reportedly a stabbing in Ed Moulton's Saloon when Billy was only twelve. This tale has been pretty well disproved.

According to Dalton chronicler Harold Preece, Silver City was the site of the first official robbery by the Dalton gang. Actually, the holdup was just outside of town at a mining camp on the road to what was then called Santa Rosa (not to be confused with the Santa Rosa in Guadalupe County). The year was 1890, and the victims were the owners and customers of a Mexican cantina. The gang at that time apparently consisted of Bob and Emmett Dalton, Charley Bryant, Bitter Creek

Silver City, New Mexico. *Museum of New Mexico.*

Newcomb, and Bill McElhanie. The outlaws simply walked in, played a few hands of faro, and drew their guns. It is not known how much was taken, but evidently it was enough to cause the victims to form a posse and quickly ride in pursuit. They caught up with the gang in a wooded canyon northeast of Silver City the following morning, and in the shootout that resulted, Emmett Dalton was wounded in the arm. Although the outlaws appeared to be trapped, Bob Dalton ordered a "cavalry-like charge," and the pursuers were taken by surprise and scattered.

## Stinking Springs
### Curry County

Stinking Springs, an overnight way station for cattle drivers and sheepherders, was the scene of Pat Garrett's capture of Billy the Kid and four of his gang on December 23, 1880. After a shootout on December 19 at Fort Sumner, Garrett and his posse trailed Billy and his men to the Springs, about twenty-five miles east of the fort. They arrived at night and lay in wait until morning, hoping to pick off Billy which Garrett felt would cause the rest to surrender.

The outlaws were holed up in a dilapidated rock house. Around dawn one of the gang emerged. Although the light was dim, Garrett was pretty sure he had Billy himself in his sights, and he squeezed off a round. The rest of the possemen followed suit. The outlaw screamed, staggered, and fell backward into the doorway of the building. Seconds later a voice was heard from the inside, telling Garrett that he had wounded gang member Charlie Bowdre and that Bowdre wanted to surrender. Garrett shouted back to send the man out. The outlaws did, but as Bowdre stepped through the door, Billy shoved a gun into his hand and told him something to the effect that he was as good as dead anyway, so why didn't he get revenge and "kill some of the sonsofbitches" before he died. Bowdre took the gun but did not use it. With blood gushing from his mouth, he staggered into the waiting arms of Sheriff Garrett, moaning that he was finished. The rest of the gang held out the day but finally surrendered when hunger weakened their resolve.

# White Sands National Monument
## Otero County

During New Mexico's outlaw years, the area around White Sands National Monument was a favorite hiding place for bushwhackers who preyed upon travelers between Tularosa and Mesilla. Today, if one spent enough time digging in the mesquite-covered dunes along US 70, a few bleached bones of long dead victims would likely turn up. At the time local residents blamed many of the mysterious disappearances on "Texas riff-raff" who had been run out of that state by the Rangers.

This lonely stretch of sand was still accumulating victims as late as 1896. On February 1 of that year a prominent Mesilla lawyer, Albert Jennings Fountain, and his nine-year-old son, Henry, disappeared on a trip back from Lincoln. Fountain had been Billy the Kid's lawyer in 1881 when Billy was convicted of killing Sheriff William Brady (see *Lincoln*). Two of Fountain's political enemies, Oliver Lee and James Gilliland, were eventually tried for the murders, but both were acquitted (see *Hillsboro*).

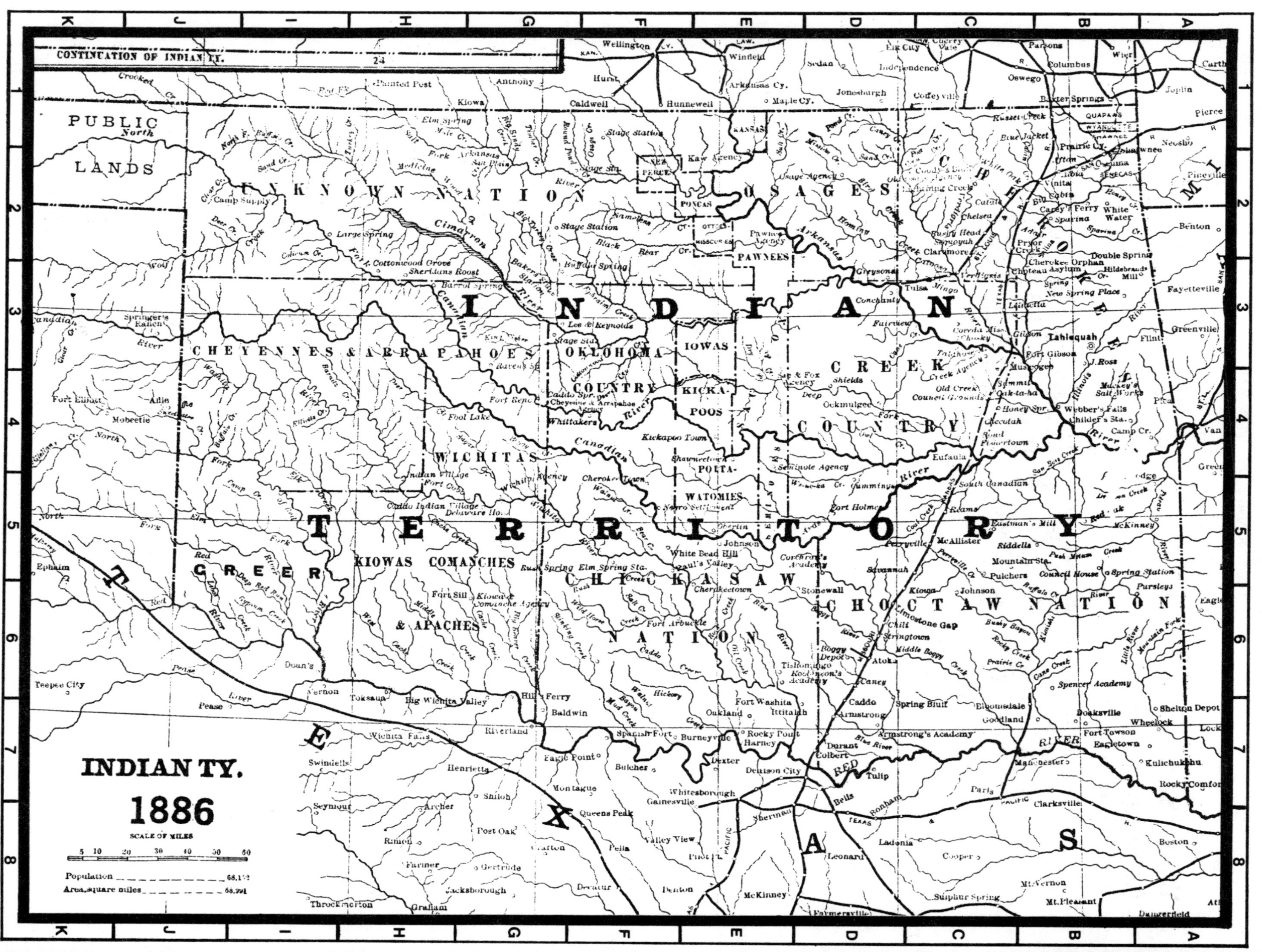


Oklahoma 1886

# OKLAHOMA

## Ada
### Pontotoc County

Ada, twenty-three miles east of Interstate 35 on State Highway 19, was a town that carried its frontier toughness well into the twentieth century. As late as 1908 there were thirty-six murders committed in the immediate vicinity during one year, and this was a community that could boast of but a few more than 5,000 residents. Part of the reason for the high crime rate was a dismal conviction record. Killers with money and the right connections often went free. Those who were tried frequently gained acquittal through the efforts of one lawyer, Moman Pruiett. Attorney Pruiett's record was astounding: during his career he defended 342 accused murderers throughout Oklahoma. He got 304 off without any punishment at all, and of the 38 that were found guilty, not one was executed. Only one was sentenced to death, and he was granted presidential clemency.

During the years 1900 to 1908 Ada and the surrounding area was virtually controlled by three powerful cattlemen—Angus A. (Gus) Bobbitt, Jesse West, and Joe Allen. A bitter feud developed between Bobbitt and the other two. Fierce competition led to questionable dealings and finally to ruthless acts. Both sides put out a call for hired gunslingers. The town of Ada put up with the bloodshed until 1908. That year the citizens rebelled and forced the West-Allen faction to leave the area. But the following year the two cattlemen got even. On February 27, 1909, while taking a wagon home from Ada to his ranch southwest of town (just off the road that is now State Highway 1), Gus Bobbitt was killed by a shotgun blast from a dense grove of elm trees. A neighbor riding behind Bobbitt saw the killer and described him as wearing a black frock coat, white collar, and striped tie and riding a brown mare. A posse trailed the suspect to a farm just south of Francis, Oklahoma, where they found the brown mare. The farm was owned by a young man named John Williamson. Faced with arrest and possibly much worse, he broke down and admitted that he had lent the horse to his uncle "Deacon Jim" Miller, a Texan known to be a notorious "killer-for-hire."

Miller vehemently denied any part in the murder and readily agreed to waive extradition and come to Ada to "clear things up." (At the time he did not know about his nephew's damaging statements.) Soon another witness was found who could link Miller with the cattlemen Jesse West and Joe Allen. And then a fourth suspect was picked up: one Berry B. Burrell who allegedly had "spotted" Bobbitt for Miller. All four suspects were charged with murder and confined to the county jail at Ada.

West, Allen, and Burrell seemed resigned to their fate, but Miller stubbornly refused to accept defeat. Brash and impudent, he joked about the "stupidity" of the town officials and bragged that the famous Moman Pruiett would win them all acquittals. This turned out to be their undoing. Knowing full well of Pruiett's won-and-lost record in criminal cases, Ada citizens decided to take no chances. Shortly after 2:00 A.M. on April 19, forty masked men seized the jail. In minutes the four prisoners were dragged from their cells, down an alley, and into an abandoned livery stable where ropes were quickly thrown over ceiling beams. Jesse West was first; then Allen and Burrell. When the haughty Miller's turn came, and he was asked if he wanted to confess to Bobbitt's murder, he replied, "Just let the record show that I've killed fifty-one men."

## Adair
### Mayes County

Adair was the site of the last train robbery committed by the Dalton gang, and it was nearly a disaster. The date was July 15, 1892. According to a story later told by Emmett Dalton, the gang had planned to rob the train ten miles to the south, at Pryor, but the outlaws' camp was discovered that morning by a farmer, and they were afraid he might have notified the authorities.

At Adair, which is on US 69 eight miles south of Interstate 44, the gang was successful in taking the station agent by surprise, but just as they were about to make their move on the train, gunfire broke out from a shed near the tracks. Three lawmen and a railroad guard had spotted the attackers and had opened fire. Working on the opposite side of the train, three of the outlaws forced their way into the express car while the rest turned their rifles on the shed. The structure was thin-walled and offered little protection. In minutes all four men inside were hit, one seriously. Also, several shots went wild and shattered the window of the town drugstore where two doctors were sitting at a table. Both were injured, and one, W. L. Goff, later died.

Once the fight was taken out of the four defenders in the shed, the Daltons completed their work, ransacking the express company safe for an undetermined amount. When they were done, they mounted up and fled toward the rugged Dog Creek Hills.

## Ames
### Major County

A few miles southwest of Ames, in a sandy basin of the Cimarron River, one can probably still find cartridges buried at the scene of what the editor of the Hennessey *Clipper* called a fight "without parallel in the annals of Oklahoma." The battle was fought on April 4, 1895, between six deputy U.S. marshals and six members of the Bill Doolin gang (Doolin, Bitter Creek Newcomb, Charlie Pierce, William "Tulsa Jack" Blake, Bill Raidler, and Red Buck Waightman). The previous night the gang had held up the Rock Island's passenger train No. 1 at Dover.* After the robbery, the outlaws headed west four miles, then turned northwest to Hoil Creek near Ames, then west again into the sand hills leading to Cimarron. The posse, led by Marshal Chris Madsen, split into two groups, one circling south and west up the Cimarron, and the other staying with the outlaws' tracks, which apparently they made no attempt to hide.

The lawmen came upon the bandits east of the river. The gang was resting and had left one man on guard. He saw the six officers the same time they saw him and sounded the alarm. The battle raged for three-quarters of an hour, with neither side gaining an edge. The posse, having slightly less fire power, could not close in. Finally, the outlaws escaped by working their way down a ravine the officers could not cover. When the lawmen later converged on the campsite, they found the body of Tulsa Jack. Also, several miles from the battle scene,

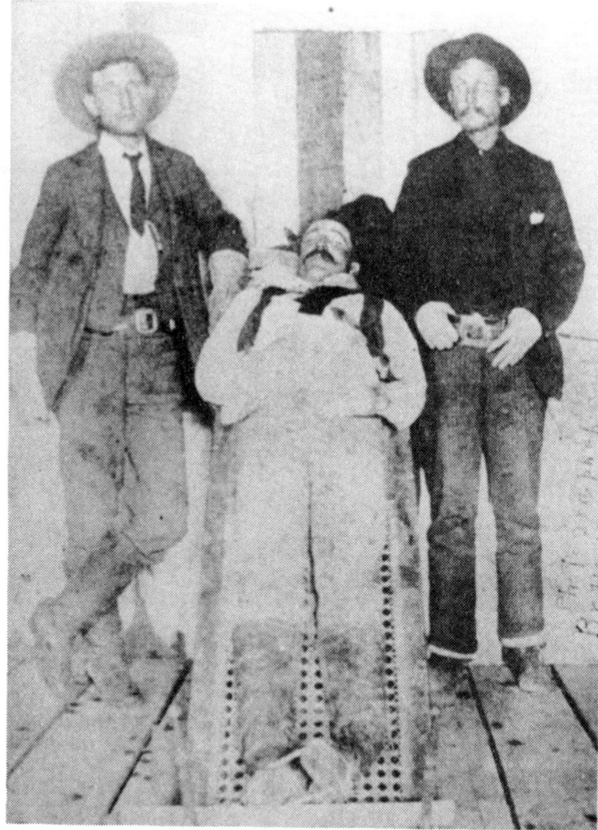

Tulsa Jack Blake, killed near Ames in 1895. *Glenn Shirley Collection.*

they came upon a dead horse. The saddle was splattered with blood, suggesting that the rider had been hit. It was later discovered that the horse belonged to Bill Raidler, who had been shot in the hand. (According to a story appearing a year later in a Guthrie newspaper, one of Raidler's fingers had been shattered by a bullet and was dangling by skin and muscle. The spunky little outlaw promptly took out his pocket knife, cut the finger off, and threw it away.)

For some reason the posse did not pursue the outlaws further. That evening the gang picked up fresh horses to the south, at a farm belonging to an elderly preacher named Godfrey whom they killed. Later, they crossed the Cimarron about seven miles northeast of Okeene, then headed northwest once more. Another posse eventually picked up their trail again but lost it in the foothills of the Glass Mountains near Fairview.

## Arapaho
### Custer County

Arapaho, which is on US 183 five miles north of Interstate 40, was the hometown of Alice Noyes, a spirited storekeeper's wife whose stubborn courage matched that of any Oklahoma frontiersman. Alice's husband operated the prosperous general store on Arapaho's main street. In October 1895 the notorious Red Buck Waightman, formerly of the Bill Doolin gang, and two companions entered the store with guns drawn. Storekeeper Noyes told the intruders that all the cash had been sent to the bank at El Reno that morning. Rather than leave empty-handed, the three outlaws relieved Noyes of his gold watch and then helped themselves to clothes, food, and supplies. As they started to leave, Buck spotted Alice Noyes's diamond ring and ordered her to hand it over. "The only way you'll get that ring is by cutting it off my finger," she answered.

Buck laid his sixshooter on the counter and began pulling on the ring. Alice grabbed the gun, and the two began to struggle. Finally, the outlaw wrenched the pistol away and jammed it against the fiery woman's breast. With his other hand around her throat, he shouted, "I'll kill you, Alice!"

Undaunted, Alice looked him straight in the eye and replied, "You wouldn't have the nerve to kill a woman."

Buck turned and stalked out.

Alice Noyes and Red Buck were to meet again, but only Alice would tell of this second encounter. In March 1896 she was called to the Arapaho jail to view the outlaw's bullet-riddled body, to identify him as the man who robbed her husband's store. Buck and his band finally came to a finish at a lonely dugout hideaway west of Arapaho at the head of Oak Creek. Lawmen from three counties closed in on March 4, killing the fiesty renegade as he charged out the door with guns blazing. At Arapaho Buck's body was roped to an undertaker's board, propped up, and photographed, as was the custom with outlaws for whom rewards were offered (Buck brought $4,800). When no one appeared to claim the remains, Buck was buried in the Arapaho cemetery at the county's expense. A common brick was placed in the ground at the foot of his grave. On it was scratched simply "Red Buck". The brick remained there for years, possibly as late as the 1930s. Today it probably adorns some collector's den.

## Ardmore
### Carter County

A farmhouse outside Ardmore marked the end of the trail for outlaw Bill Dalton, last of the clan to turn renegade. After Bill's brothers were wiped out at Coffeyville, Kansas,* he joined up with Bill Doolin and his gang for a while, then formed his own outfit composed of George Bennett, Bill Jones, and Jim Wallace. But these four long riders made only one raid, on a bank in Longview, Texas,* where Bennett was killed in a near repeat of the Coffeyville disaster.

While Bill Dalton was on his trip to Longview, he sent his wife, Jennie, and his six children to near Ardmore to stay with Jim Wallace's brother's family, the Houston Wallaces. Following his narrow escape at Longview, Bill joined them there, planning to lie low for a while. But Bill left a trail: at Duncan, Oklahoma, he and Jim Wallace bought a wagon with money stolen from the Longview robbery, and federal officers were soon roaming the area.

Once Dalton and Jim Wallace made it back to the Ardmore farmhouse, they probably would have been safe, but Bill became very careless. Running low on provisions, Bill sent Houston Wallace and his wife, accompanied by Dalton's wife, Jennie, into town to buy supplies. To pay for them, Bill gave Houston $200 from the robbery. Apparently unknown to Bill, Houston Wallace's reputation as a farmer was not too good in Ardmore, and when he plunked down $200 cash at the general store, it aroused the interest of Ardmore deputy marshal T. S. Lindsay. He and fellow officers followed Houston and the two women over to the express office where they picked up a shipment of whiskey Dalton had ordered earlier under an assumed name. This all led to further checking by the authorities, and soon a match was made between the wagon Houston Wallace was driving and the one Dalton purchased at Duncan with the stolen money. The next morning, June 8, 1894, a posse of nine men surrounded the Wallace farmhouse and ordered the outlaws to come out. Dalton tried to escape by leaping out a rear window and dashing for a nearby ravine, but one of the posseman put an end to the outlaw's career with a single bullet in his abdomen.

## Bartlesville
### Washington County

Three miles west and slightly south of Bartlesville near US 60, where the old road ran between two hills along Liza Creek, is the site of the most spectacular highway robbery in the history of Oklahoma. The amount taken was not all that much: three horses, three saddles, a gold watch, and an undetermined amount of cash (probably less than $500); what made the holdup sensational was that there were over seventy-five victims (some say closer to 100). The perpetrators were the Martin gang—brothers Sam and Will Martin and Clarence Simmons—all Oklahoma hard cases wanted for numerous robberies of stores and banks from Kansas to New Mexico.

The date was June 14, 1903, a warm Sunday afternoon. The victims were mostly farm families heading home after Sunday visits with friends. At first, as the victims rode into the shady hollow, one of the robbers would step out of the brush and stop them at gunpoint. In each instance they were carefully guided off the road into a nearby secluded clearing. About mid-afternoon a farmer came along with a big hay wagon which was too large to maneuver into the woods so the outlaws left it where it stood to serve as a roadblock. The farmer was forced to join the rest of the prisoners, all sitting or standing in a tight group under the watchful eyes of the robbers. The bandits seemed especially interested in finding three good horses, and it took them nearly all afternoon to do so. When they finally found what they wanted, they told their captives they could go.

On June 20 the Bartlesville *Weekly Examiner* gave an account of the affair, calling it "one of the most remarkable acts of lawlessness in the history of Indian Territory." Nobody was harmed, and one victim reported that the outlaws were "courteous and well-mannered." The writer of the newspaper article went on to say that the holdup "partook more strongly of a whimsical caper of drunken cowboys than it did of a raid by frontier bandits."

As whimsical as the caper may have seemed, when the law finally caught up with the bandits the following August, there was no whimsy to be found in the outcome. Discovered at a campsite at a place called Wooster's Mound* about seven miles southeast of Pawhuska, the Martin brothers were killed in a raging gunbattle, and the leader of the posse, deputy U.S. marshal Wiley G. Haines, nearly died from his wounds.

Bartlesville was also the home of Bill Dalton in the early 1890s. Although presumably in the real estate business at the time, Billy's primary occupation probably was operations manager for his outlaw brothers who hid out in the nearby hill country between raids. Bill later rode the outlaw trail himself, until killed by a posseman's bullet in 1894 near Ardmore, Oklahoma.*

## Black Mesa
### Cimarron County

Black Mesa, the highest point in the state, rises to just under 5,000 feet on the western edge of the Oklahoma Panhandle. To the south, across twisting Carrizo Creek near a smaller jut of rocks called Lookout Peak, lay the remains of an outlaw fortress dating from the 1860s: the hideout of the notorious Coe gang.

"Captain" Bill Coe came to the area sometime during the Civil War and put together a renegade band of ruffians who terrorized wagon trains, ranchers, and isolated settlements for nearly three years. Some local historians say part of the gang's stolen loot may still lie buried somewhere among the rocky crags near the fortress site.

The fortress itself was an impressive sight. Although given the popular title, "Robbers' Roost," the bastion was anything but a typical outlaw lair. A sturdy rock structure that spanned sixteen by thirty-five feet, it had walls thirty inches thick and no windows, just "loopholes" from which rifles could stand off the largest of posses. Built for year-round living, the bulwark had grand fireplaces at each end, and, according to one report, was equipped with a full-sized bar and even a piano. Rumor had it that on occasion Coe would import young women from Old Mexico for the entertainment of his men.

Coe's raiders became troublesome enough the very first year, 1865, that troops from newly-built Fort Nichols, twelve miles to the south, were required to escort wagon trains through the area. However, budget cuts closed the new fort after only a few months, and the outlaws resumed their plundering.

At its peak, the Coe gang numbered some forty or fifty members, sometimes splitting into smaller groups for simultaneous raids. Coe eventually became so confident that he even led attacks against the military at Fort Union in New Mexico where he stole government mules and horses. Flushed with success, he followed up with a similar raid on Fort Lyon in Colorado. This time the army retaliated, and on an excursion down the Carrizo, troopers surprised eleven of Coe's men sleeping in an abandoned shack. According to rumor, they were all promptly hanged. Coe himself was later captured but escaped. Another expedition was sent to the Black Mesa, this time armed with a cannon. This excursion was not well documented, but from local accounts it seems the six-inch gun was dragged up the mesa to a point overlooking the outlaws' fortress. Although over a mile from the target, the gunner's aim was true, and at least one direct hit blasted a hole in the bastion. Coe's men scattered in all directions; later, many were rounded up, and again, according to rumor, all except Coe were hanged. Coe, it is believed, was taken back to Fort Lyon, but once more he escaped.

The bandit leader was recaptured by a detail of soldiers in July 1868 at Folsom, New Mexico.* This time he was taken to Pueblo, Colorado. On July 21, while in jail waiting trial, he was dragged from his cell and hanged from a cottonwood tree on nearby Fountain Creek.

## Bond
### McIntosh County

Bond is located in eastern Oklahoma just south of the junction of Interstate 40 and US 69. In 1897 Al

Jennings and his brother Frank, lawyers-turned-outlaws from Woodward, Oklahoma,* were captured by federal lawmen just east of Bond on Carr Creek, near a ranch owned by a man named Sam Baker. The Jennings brothers, together with a fellow gang member Pat O'Malley, had been offered refuge by Baker who told them he could also arrange for them to leave the territory by a special escape route, or at least so the outlaws thought. Actually, Baker had been in touch with the authorities and had informed federal marshals of the fugitives' whereabouts.

During the early morning hours on December 6, 1897, federal officers, under the leadership of James F. (Bud) Ledbetter, rode to the Baker Ranch. Once satisfied the outlaws were there, they quietly felled a large tree across the only road leading out. A few hours before daylight, the Jennings and O'Malley came down the trail in a wagon Baker had provided, which had been filled with straw and provisions. Frank Jennings was driving, and Al and O'Malley, both of whom were nursing wounds from a recent shootout, were hidden under the straw. When the lawmen closed in, all three renegades surrendered without a fight—a rare occurrence in the annals of Oklahoma outlaw history.

## Caddo
### Bryan County

Caddo, in southeastern Oklahoma at the junction of US 69 and State Highway 22, was the stomping ground of Henri Stewart, said to have been the only Harvard Medical School graduate known to have robbed trains and stagecoaches. Outlaw researcher Wayne Walker has identified Dr. Stewart as the mysterious Henry Underwood, who rode with Sam Bass and his gang during their reckless romp around Denton, Texas,* in the late 1870s. Stewart, as Underwood, barely escaped several encounters with Texas posses in the spring of 1878 and then made his way back across the Red River where he hid out with friends in the Choctaw Nation.

At Caddo, Stewart got into an argument with a fellow physician Dr. J. B. Jones. (One source suggests Jones may have delivered the baby of Stewart's girl friend and while doing so, learned of his outlaw connections.) On August 7, 1878, Dr. Jones was gunned down on the platform of the railroad station at Caddo, presumably by Stewart and his cousin Wiley Stewart. Indian police were soon on their trail, and in a running gun battle, several lawmen were wounded. Stewart escaped, but later, through a letter to his girlfriend back at Caddo, he was traced to Monett, Missouri, where he was arrested. In May 1879 he was convicted of killing Dr. Jones, and on August 29 he died on the scaffold in Fort Smith, Arkansas. His tragic life was summed up by a brief note in the Fort Smith *Elevator*: "A sad sight to see a man of fine personal appearance, good address, possessing a good education, and just in the prime of manhood—placed in such a horrible position through his own reckless folly."

## Canton
### Blaine County

The town of Canton is in northwestern Oklahoma on State Highway 51, thirteen miles east of US 281. Four miles east of Canton, in the yard of a farmhouse owned by a widow named Jones, the elusive outlaw Isaac (Ike) Black was shot to death by a posse of sheriff's deputies. Black and his sidekick, Nathaniel (Zip) Wyatt, who also rode under the names "Wild Charlie" and "Dick Yeager," had led law officers a tortuous chase for several months. Working mainly out of the nearby Glass Mountains, the two desperados had terrorized settlers in Major and Blaine Counties throughout the summer of 1895. In several encounters with posses, the outlaws had picked up wounds, and by the end of July they were running pretty ragged.

Late in the afternoon on August 1, they stopped at the Jones house looking for fresh horses. A high cornfield bordered the house on two sides, offering reasonable seclusion, so they decided to rest a while and maybe eat supper. But the law was much closer than they suspected. Spotting the outlaws' horses, a posse closed in and surrounded the house. When the two renegades finally emerged, the officers shouted for them to throw up their hands. Both men reached for their guns, as the lawmen expected them to, and Black went down immediately. As one observer later said, he died "with a chew of tobacco in his mouth big enough to choke a horse." Zip Wyatt was quicker. Diving for cover in the adjacent cornfield, Zip took only one bullet—a wound in the breastbone that failed to strike a vital organ. Not knowing how seriously the outlaw was injured, nor how much fight was left in him, the lawmen hesitated to follow him into the tall corn. When they did enter, they found his tracks leading out of the field and into a nearby row of sand hills. From there they followed his footprints about a mile to the house of a doctor. There he had told the doctor that he was a federal officer and had just been wounded in a fight with outlaws. The doctor bandaged his wound and lent him a horse.

From the doctor's house Wyatt rode northeast about seven miles to near the town of Homestead where he came across a young boy driving a cart. Figuring the authorities would be looking for a lone man on horseback, he abandoned the doctor's horse, leaped in the cart beside the boy and ordered him to drive north. After a zig-zag route of about twenty-five miles, the outlaw let the boy go and took the cart on alone, eventually disappearing somewhere along the Cimarron River.

## Checotah
### McIntosh County

Oklahoma train and bank robber "Dynamite Dick" Clifton came to his end on November 7, 1897, in a hideout cabin in a woods not far from present-day US 266 about ten miles west of Checotah (which is on US 69 about twenty miles south of Muskogee). Clifton had ridden with the Bill Doolin gang from 1893 to 1895 and later with the Jennings gang. In October 1897 he split with the Jennings brothers and formed an outfit of his own near Tulsa. Later that month local peace officers heard that he was hiding near Checotah, and they staked out an area west of town. On Sunday morning, November 7, Clifton was spotted at the edge of a woods near a farm owned by a man named Sid Williams. As the lawmen approached, the outlaw tried to make a fight of it. A bullet from a posseman's gun broke his arm and knocked him from the saddle. Scampering for underbrush, the spunky outlaw managed to elude the officers in the dense timber.

Although bleeding and on foot, Clifton stayed ahead of his pursuers throughout the day. Near sundown the posse was just about ready to give it up when they discovered a tiny cabin in one of the thickest areas of the woods. On the chance that he might be inside, the lawmen fired their Winchesters in the air and shouted that they were going to burn the cabin down. In a few minutes an Indian woman and a child emerged. Shortly thereafter, the door was suddenly kicked open and Clifton rushed out, guns blazing. He made only a few yards before bullets cut him down. Two days later he was buried at the government's expense in the town cemetery at Muskogee.

## The Corner
### Pottawatomie County

"The Corner" was a piece of river bottom land east of present-day US 177 and south of what is now State Highway 39 in the extreme southeastern edge of Pottawatomie County. About 300 yards north of the Canadian River, in the center of a thicketed cluster of jack oak, cottonwood, and briar brush, was a rough-hewn log saloon, also called "The Corner." Many saloons and trading posts dotted the river bank shortly after the turn-of-the-century. Most catered to thirsty homesteaders and Indians, and some became dangerous outlaw hangouts. None, however, was worse than the Corner. Ownership changed hands several times over the years, but the class of clientele never improved. By 1905 it was described as the "worst den of iniquity" in the territory, a place "where men of evil name, fame and reputation congregated for the purpose of cursing, drinking, shooting and performing unlawful acts." During one period of ten months, from October 1904 to July 1905, the Shawnee *Daily Herald* listed sixteen cases of assault to kill, nine cases of murder, and 81 liquor violations "directly traceable to the Corner." The Oklahoma *State Capital*, which claimed to keep even closer tabs on such things, warned its readers the same year that the Corner had been the "scene of at least fifty murders" and that "the river waters are like an abultion [sic] of blood."

The Corner did not simmer down until around 1908 when its owners, then a pair of lawless cattlemen named Joe Allen and Jesse West, were forced to leave the area by irate citizens. Later, these same two were lynched by an angry mob because of their involvement in the death of another cattleman, Gus Bobbitt (see *Ada, Oklahoma*).

## Cromwell
### Seminole County

Cromwell, just south of Interstate 40 on State Highway 56, was the end of the line for veteran Oklahoma lawman Bill Tilghman. The old marshal was nearing seventy when Cromwell boomed into existence in 1923. Oil flowed and lawlessness reigned, and Seminole County officials could not keep the lid on the town. A citizens commitee sought out Tilghman from retirement, and with added persuasion from the governor, Bill took the job of police chief.

One of Tilghman's first problems came from a local federal prohibition officer named Wiley Lynn. Bill was convinced Lynn was on the take and immediately included him in his personal list of troublemakers to weed out. But Bill never got the chance. On the night of October 30, 1926, Lynn got drunk and began shooting up the town. Tilghman confronted him on Main Street and disarmed him, but Lynn whipped out a second gun and put three bullets into the aging lawman.

It was the end for Bill Tilghman, but in death Bill helped achieve what he had set out to do. Wiley Lynn fled Cromwell as did many of the local riff-raff, mainly out of fear of wholesale arrests in response to the killing of Tilghman. A few days later, however, he was killed in a brawl in another town.

Cromwell is nearly a ghost town today. Other oil

fields drew the people away. From 10,000 inhabitants at the time of Bill Tilghman's death, the town dwindled to 250 by 1930. Today only a handful of stores and houses remain.

## Curtis
### Woodward County

The tiny tank town of Curtis lay on the old Santa Fe tracks in eastern Woodward County between Mooreland and Quinlan. On September 12, 1895, a westbound express was ransacked by four robbers in a deep cut two and a half miles out of Curtis. It was believed the gang was led by "Red Buck" Waightman who had ridden the previous two years with the notorious Bill Doolin gang. Waightman's companions on the raid were thought to be two Texas fugitives, Joe Beckham and Elmer (Kid) Lewis, and possibly a man named Charlie Smith.

The attack took place in broad daylight, about 3:15 in the afternoon, and was accomplished by stacking railroad ties across the track to stop the train. The engineer drew the locomotive to a halt, but the quick-thinking Wells Fargo messenger, a man named Kleaver, ran from his car and hid in the baggage car. When the robbers could not find him nor the key to the express company safe, they took a revolver and some shells from the messenger's shotgun case and departed, riding northeast toward the Glass Mountains.

## Cushing
### Payne County

It probably was an ego-deflating experience for a proud bunch of Oklahoma long riders: a night time burglary just to get food and supplies. The site was Cushing, about thirty miles southeast of Stillwater, at the junction of State Highways 33 and 18. Shortly after midnight on October 29, 1897, the town's main general merchandise store, then operating under the name Crozier & Nutter, received a visit from the notorious "Dynamite Dick" Clifton, "Little Dick" West, and the famous lawyers-turned-bandits, Al and Frank Jennings. Clifton and West, both alumni of the once highly regarded Bill Doolin gang who had joined up with the Jennings brothers to rob trains. After a couple of unsuccessful attempts (see *Edmond, Oklahoma* and *Pocasset, Oklahoma*), the boys swallowed their pride and settled, at least temporarily, for warm clothes, some grub, and a big jug of storekeeper Lee Nutter's whiskey.

This quartet of outlaws, sometimes called the "Dynamite Dick gang" and other times, the "Jennings gang," has received much ridicule by Old West historians for their inauspicious first year as train robbers. The criticism is probably unjustified. Although the Jennings brothers were fairly new at the game, Clifton and West were not, and their rocky beginning was likely more the result of bad luck than ineptness.

## Dover
### Kingfisher County

Dover is about midway between Enid and El Reno on the old Rock Island tracks, which roughly parallel present-day US 81 on its north-south route through the state. In 1895 the famous Bill Doolin gang was responsible for Dover's niche in Oklahoma outlaw history.

It was April 3, and five men—probably "Bitter Creek" Newcomb, Charlie Pierce, William "Tulsa Jack" Blake, Bill Raidler, and "Red Buck" Waightman—held up the Rock Island's southbound passenger train No. 1 a few hundred yards south of Dover. The locomotive was halted in classic fashion: two outlaws slipped aboard behind the tender at the station, and as the locomotive neared the water tank at the edge of town, the engineer was ordered to ease her to a stop. A bit nervous, however, he pulled the brakes suddenly, causing one of the outlaws to lose his balance and discharge his gun. This alerted the conductor who came forward and was quickly taken prisoner.

The train crew was marched back to the express car where the robbers encountered their first problem—stubborn express messenger J. W. Jones—who refused to open up, even after taking nasty wounds in the wrist and leg from the outlaws' guns. Finally, when the robbers threatened to kill the entire crew, he gave in. But the bandits ran into more bad luck: the mail sacks held nothing of value, nor did the way safe. The through safe probably contained cash (reportedly a $50,000 payroll destined for federal troops in Texas), but Jones, still defiant, convinced the gang that the safe had been locked in Kansas City and could be opened only by the express agent at Fort Worth.

The outlaws had brought along a brace and bit, but they had not anticipated the hardness of the steel, and they abandoned the idea of drilling the safe after an hour. Next, they turned to the passenger coaches, but because of the time wasted in the express car, many of the passengers had managed to hide away their money and valuables in nooks and crannies. One man slid his expensive gold watch under the stove; another stuffed a $500 roll of bills into a crack in a seat cushion. All told, the bandits' earnings that night consisted of about $435 in cash, seven or eight watches, and some jewelry valued at about $1,000.

# Edmond
## Oklahoma County

An unsuccessful attempt to rob a southbound Santa Fe express on August 16, 1897, near Edmond (which is just north of Oklahoma City on US 77) was believed to be the work of the "Jennings gang." Al and Frank Jennings, both of whom gave up the practice of law to turn outlaw (see *Woodward, Oklahoma*), were relatively new at holding up trains. "Dynamite Dick" Clifton and "Little Dick" West, however, had ridden with the Bill Doolin gang in 1894 and 1895 and knew about such things. The fifth and sixth members of the gang that night were probably Pat and Morris O'Malley, mainly known as "two wild Irish boys" always looking for fight.

Although several versions of the holdup have been given, according to the conductor (a man named Beers), three men got on board as passengers at Ponca City and rode as far as Edmond. There, as the train was pulling away from the station, these three apparently slipped back on board between the front of the baggage car and the rear of the tender. Working their way forward, they put guns into the backs of the engineer and fireman and forced them to halt about three miles south of town, where three more men were waiting in the tall brush beside the tracks. After firing several shots down the sides of the passenger coaches, the men commanded the Wells Fargo messenger, W. H. May, to open up the express car. Once inside, however, the would-be robbers could not open the safe, despite two attempts to blow it with dynamite. Disgusted, the outlaws climbed down and ordered the engineer to return to his cab and get under way.

# Guthrie
## Logan County

Guthrie is on Interstate 35 about thirty miles north of Oklahoma City. In July 1896 the town was the scene of a scandalous jailbreak involving the notorious outlaw Bill Doolin. The Guthrie jail was a relatively new structure and considered as escape-proof as any around. But as with most jails on the frontier, it proved to be only as sound as the guards that manned it. The break was apparently engineered by Doolin who had been captured the previous January in Arkansas. For several weeks Doolin had complained of illness, and when he began to suffer "a number of fits," he was allowed to leave his stifling hot cell during the day and roam around in the cooler bull pen to which several of the cells were connected.

On Sunday evening, July 5, while Doolin and several other prisoners were still in the bull pen, a prisoner in one of the cells reached through the bars and grabbed one of the two night guards, pinning him against the cell door. The second guard had just let himself into the bull pen, apparently to check some of the cells. Before he could close the bull pen door, Doolin dashed out and locked it behind him, leaving the guard unarmed and helpless among the prisoners. Shoving the first guard's gun into his face, Doolin soon convinced him to open the main cell block door leading to the jail office. There Doolin disposed of the last guard (a trustee who manned the office desk), and Doolin and thirteen prisoners, including his train robbing sidekick, "Dynamite Dick" Clifton, escaped into the darkness of the Guthrie streets.

The citizens of the territory were stunned by news of the escape. Doolin and his gang had terrorized Oklahoma for years, and the taxpayers had spent thousands of dollars to bring about their capture. Newspapers called the escape "a public crime against law and order and society," and decried the "terrible condition of official incompetency" that surrounded the jail of which the city had once been so proud.

Being the seat of the territorial government, Guthrie became the burial site for outlaws laid away at government expense. The town's Summit View Cemetery was the site of the burial of outlaw Charlie Pierce in May 1895. He was laid to rest in the Boot Hill section, Pauper's Grave No. 65. Death came to Pierce, one of the members of Bill Doolin's gang, during an ambush on May 2 a few miles southeast of Ingalls, Oklahoma.* Not far away in the same cemetery, Bill Doolin himself

Harrison Avenue, Guthrie. *Oklahoma Historical Society.*

was put to rest in August 1896, following his death at the hands of deputy U.S. marshal Heck Thomas at the home of the outlaw's wife's parents in Lawson (now Quay), Oklahoma (see *Quay*). Doolin's grave was marked by a twisted, rusty buggy axle.

Southwest of Guthrie, about a half-hour's ride by horse toward Cottonwood Creek, lay a farm once owned by a man named Harmon Arnett. It was there, on April 8, 1898, that "Little Dick" West, another Doolin gang member, fought his last gunfight. West had hired on as a hand on a neighboring farm owned by Ed Fitzgerald. While shopping in Guthrie one day, Harmon Arnett's wife told a friend that Fitzgerald's hired man was trying to get her husband to "join him in a robbery." Word reached Logan County sheriff Frank Rinehart who passed it on to deputy U.S. marshal Heck Thomas. When it was discovered the hired man's description fit that of "Little Dick" West's, a posse was soon on its way to the Fitzgerald place.

The hired man was not there, but the officers found a horse that matched the description of the one ridden by West the previous October during a daylight holdup of a Rock Island express at Pocasset, Oklahoma.* Suspecting that West might be at Arnett's, the posse headed across the adjoining fields in that direction. They had gone but a short distance when they spotted a man at the edge of a woods. On seeing the lawmen, he appeared to change his course. When the posse arrived at the Arnett house, they saw him again, this time near the barn where he apparently was about to saddle a horse. It was West.

Early Guthrie. *Western History Collections, University of Oklahoma.*

When the officers shouted for the outlaw to halt, he drew his pistol, fired three quick shots, and began to run. The two officers nearest to him took careful aim, and as he dived under a wire fence, they hit him in the left side. He rolled under the fence, got to his feet, and started to run again, reloading his pistol as he ran. Then, as he turned to fire, he fell dead.

## Hennessy
### Kingfisher County

Hennessy is in north central Oklahoma at the junction of US 81 and State Highway 51. In 1891 the town was the scene of the capture of Dalton gang member "Blackface" Charley Bryant. In July of that year Bryant, who suffered from an advanced case of veneral disease (probably syphilis), became seriously ill while hiding out somewhere west of Hennessy, probably in Major County. He had recently heard of a physician in Mullhall, which is about thirty miles east of Hennessy, who was successful in treating such diseases. He started out but became worse and made it only as far as Hennessy, where he was taken in by Ben and Jean Thorne who owned the Rock Island Hotel.

Bryant was there only a few days when deputy U.S. marshal Ed Short learned of his whereabouts. Bryant, too ill to resist, gave up with only a token struggle. There was no jail in Hennessy, and Short dragged Bryant down to the train depot and loaded him into an express car for a trip north to the federal district courthouse at Wichita. Near Waukomis, about twelve miles out of Hennessy, Bryant gathered enough strength to grab the express messenger's pistol and empty it into Short. As he was falling, the officer got off a few shots himself. Two minutes later, when the train pulled into the station at Waukomis, both men were dead.

## Herd
### Osage County

In September 1895 about five miles northwest of the tiny town of Herd, the outlaw career of Bill Raidler came to an end. The site was the old Sam Moore ranch on Mission Creek, which is west of Stage Highway 99 and about fifteen miles due south of Elgin, Kansas. Raidler had ridden with the Bill Doolin gang during the previous two years. When that outfit split up in the summer of 1895, Raidler wandered around the Lower Caney River country, then headed north to Little Caney Creek above Bartlesville. Toward the end of August, deputy U.S. marshal Bill Tilghman received a tip that Raidler was hiding in Osage County near the Moore ranch and on September 6 Tilghman and two fellow officers went after him.

At the ranch Moore told the lawmen that Raidler was not there, but under questioning he admitted that the outlaw might show up that evening. Apparently Raidler's practice was to hide out in the timbered area near Mission Creek during the day and come down to the ranch for supper after sundown. Concealing themselves along the path Moore said Raidler usually took, the deputies settled in to wait.

The outlaw arrived about dusk. Tilghman let him get abreast and then shouted for him to surrender. Raidler broke into a run, firing at the sound of the voice as he ran. Tilghman was carrying a double-barreled shotgun. He fired one blast and knocked the outlaw to the ground. Despite six buckshot wounds, including one in the neck and two in the head, Raidler later told a local doctor who gave him only twenty-four hours to live, "I will live to attend your funeral." Raidler survived and the following year was convicted of his part in the train robbery the previous April at Dover, Oklahoma.*

## Ingalls
### Payne County

Ingalls, on State Highway 51 about ten miles east of Stillwater, developed the reputation of an "outlaws' town" in the early 1890s, mainly because of the coming and going of the Bill Doolin gang. Stories have been handed down that the Doolin bunch frequently shot up the town yet were still adored by the local citizens. This was hardly true. The gang did hang out at Ingalls occasionally, primarily because Doolin courted and secretly married a local girl, Edith Ellsworth. More accurate accounts suggest that the outlaws behaved themselves while in Ingalls and that the town tolerated them partly out of fear and partly because the merchants appreciated their business.

The Doolin gang actually had two hideouts outside of Ingalls: the Bill Dunn homestead two and one-half miles southeast on Council Creek and an open cave under a large overhang on Deer Creek, where it flows into the Cimarron River.

On September 1, 1893, the town was the scene of the famous "Ingalls Raid," a shootout between the Doolin bunch and federal officers. The outlaws were playing poker at Ransom's Saloon when the officers arrived hidden in two covered wagons. A gang member noticed the wagons, and "Bitter Creek" Newcomb was sent to investigate. As Newcomb rode up, one of the lawmen, federal officer Dick Speed, was standing in the doorway of the Pierce and Hostetter feed barn, questioning a young boy. When the officer saw Newcomb and asked the boy who he was, the youth said, "Why that's Bitter Creek." Seeing the boy pointing at him, Newcomb reached for his Winchester. Officer Speed was quicker, and his shot knocked the magazine off Newcomb's rifle, the bullet richocheting downward into the outlaws's right leg. Newcomb managed one shot, then wheeled his horse to escape. Speed stepped from the doorway for another shot, just as gang member "Arkansas Tom" Jones leaned out of an upper window of the O.K. Hotel. Jones saw Speed and put a bullet into the lawman's shoulder. Dazed, Speed ran for the wagon instead of taking shelter in the barn, and a second shot from Jones's rifle killed him. In the meantime Newcomb was racing for the road south of town. Doolin and the rest of the gang (Bill Dalton, "Dynamite Dick" Clifton, William "Tulsa Jack" Blake, and "Red Buck" Waightman) were firing from the saloon, trying to cover Newcomb's escape.

The officers now converged on the saloon, firing as they advanced. Inside, the saloon owner, Ransom, was hit twice—in the rib and in the arm. The outlaws, however, seemed blessed with good luck: the lawmen overlooked a side door, and all five desperados slipped out and dashed for the livery stable where they had left their horses. As Doolin and Clifton threw on the saddles, Dalton, Tulsa Jack, and Red Buck held off their attackers. Meanwhile, Arkansas Tom Jones had chopped a hole in the roof of the hotel and put two bullets into another deputy, Tom Hueston (sometimes spelled Huston), who was firing from behind a pile of lumber.

Back at the stable, when all the horses were saddled, the outlaws broke in two directions: Doolin and Clifton raced out the rear door toward the southwest in the direction of the deep ravine a few hundred yards away and Dalton, Tulsa Jack, and Red Buck burst through the front door, then turned and also headed for the ravine. All made it to safety except Dalton. A bullet hit his horse in the jaw and another broke its leg. He leaped from his saddle, scrambled over an embankment, and ran on foot until spotted by Tulsa Jack, who returned and took him aboard his horse.

These five outlaws all escaped. The only casualty was Clifton, having taken a bullet in the fleshy part of his neck. Newcomb also escaped. Back in town, Arkansas Tom Jones was still firing from the O.K. Hotel. While his comrades were racing away from the livery stable, he picked off another officer, Lafe Shadley. But Jones was trapped and he knew it. On learning that all his comrades had left him, he threw out his weapon.

Ransom Saloon in Ingalls. *Glenn Shirley Collection.*

The Doolin gang operated for another year and a half or so, then began to split up. Bitter Creek Newcomb and another gang member, Charlie Pierce (who missed the Ingalls battle), met their end at the Dunn ranch the first week of May 1895. The details of their deaths are shrouded in mystery. Three or four versions of the story exist. Some say the two outlaws were ambushed by federal marshals, others say they were killed by the Dunn family (probably brothers John and Bill Dunn). One version has Pierce dying from a blast of Winchesters as he peered out the door of the Dunn farmhouse during an early morning raid led by a mysterious "special deputy" brought in from Texas. This account has Newcomb being shot as he tried to escape through a window. Another version has the two outlaws slain as they rode into the Dunn barnyard, and still another has them killed in their sleep—a story which stemmed from a report that the soles of Pierce's feet indicated that he had been shot with his boots off. Some later writers have even misreported the date, placing the deaths in July. The only sure fact seems to be that the outlaws Newcomb and Pierce were killed and killed on the Dunn ranch.

After the Doolin gang period, Ingalls declined. In 1938 hopes were raised that the town could be revived as a tourist attraction, and a monument was erected to honor the officers slain in the big battle. Today, however, there is no major highway to take visitors to the site, and the town of Ingalls, scene of the famous shootout, is bypassed by most travelers.

# Inola
## Rogers County

A mile south of Inola is a treeless hump rising several hundred feet above the flat prairie and brushy ravines. Known as "Belle's Mound," it was the legendary lookout point used by "Bandit Queen" Belle Starr and her "outlaw gang" who supposedly preyed on travelers in the 1880s.

Tales involving the site have circulated in Rogers County for years, and the mound has become a landmark. When used by bandits, the mound was supposed to have had a rock tower on top which has since eroded away.

The hill is certainly worth seeing (take State Highway 33 east out of Tulsa for thirty-three miles), but the stories about its popularity as a robbers' lookout may very well be as exaggerated as the stories about Belle Starr, the "Bandit Queen."

# Kingfisher
## Kingfisher County

Kingfisher, on US 81 between Enid and El Reno, was the home of the Dalton brothers' family during the boys' escapades in the early 1890s. Aleline Dalton, the outlaws' mother, lived on a piece of bottom land six miles northeast of Kingfisher. The Dalton home was a comfortable one and one-half-story house on a bend in picturesque Kingfisher Creek. The place was well secluded, off the main road and largely hidden by thick trees and giant lilac bushes. At night, between raids, the outlaws would frequently sneak home and visit the family.

A story is told that Texas rustler-turned-rancher King Fisher took his name from this town. According to the tale, he was up from Texas on his way to Kansas when he was stopped by a lawman and asked to identify himself. Having ridden on the wrong side of the law for several years, the young Texan did not want to give his true name and quickly tried to think of another one. He remembered passing a sign some miles back on the trail and replied "King Fisher." The story is pure fiction. King Fisher was born John King Fisher in Collin County, Texas, in 1854.

# Lenapah
## Nowata County

Lenapah is in northeastern Oklahoma on US 169 just ten miles below the Kansas line. This town's quiet streets carry the memory of a shootout between train robber Henry "Bearcat" Starr and lawman Floyd Wilson. The date was December 14, 1892. Starr was wanted for several robberies when Floyd spotted him riding toward him on Lenapah's main street that dreary winter day. In fact, Wilson was carrying a warrant with Starr's name on it. The officer shouted for the outlaw to "hold up." Starr answered, "You hold up," and both men went for their Winchesters. Wilson got his shot off first, but he missed and his weapon immediately jammed. Starr charged, firing as he rode. Wilson went down, struggled for his pistol, but collapsed as one of the outlaw's bullets ripped into his heart. Witnesses claim that Starr's rifle muzzle was so close to Wilson's chest when he fired his last shot, the lawman's coat caught fire from the powder blast. As Starr fired the final shot, his horse bolted and he slipped off. The outlaw quickly mounted the dead officer's horse and raced out of town.

Henry Starr was eventually convicted of the Wilson killing and sentenced to prison, but while in jail at Fort Smith, Arkansas, awaiting an appeal, he disarmed a fellow prisoner who was attempting to escape, and was rewarded by a pardon.

## Marshall
### Logan County

Five miles southwest of Marshall, just off State Highway 51 where Skeleton Creek enters Logan County, a posse of sheriffs' deputies closed out the career of Oklahoma hard case Nathaniel "Zip" Wyatt. Wyatt, at the time riding under the alias "Dick Yeager" with sidekick Ike Black, had terrorized settlers in Major and Blaine counties during the summer of 1895. Black finally fell before lawmen's guns on August 1 near Canton.* Wyatt, although wounded in the encounter, escaped and headed northeast toward Garfield County. A posse picked up his trail near Skeleton Creek and on August 3 found him nearly unconscious in a cornfield on the Alvin G. Rosse farm outside Marshall. Weak from his wound, Wyatt tried to reach his guns as the deputies approached, but two bullets tore into the outlaw's body, one shattering his pelvis and the other ripping internal organs. As the lawmen disarmed him, Wyatt asked, "Who are you?"

"We are deputy sheriffs," was the answer.

"Thank God for that," said the outlaw, "the marshals [federal] would kill me."

Wyatt was taken to Enid where, "fetid with gangrenous smells," he lingered until September 6, finally succumbing to, as medical men in attendance put it, "septic chill or putrescent decomposition of the body."

## Muskogee
### Muskogee County

Christmas Eve 1894 was the night of the "Great Muskogee Scare." Earlier that day a gang of outlaws was discovered camped four miles west of town "in an advanced state of intoxication." Led by the mean and wild "Tulsa Jack" Blake, they had recently come from Ingalls in Payne County. There they had demolished a saloon because the owner, a man named Nicholas, had, according to Tulsa Jacka, betrayed the gang and probably caused the death of former member Bill Dalton at Ardmore, Oklahoma,* the previous June. Their next target, so it seemed, was Muskogee.

Drunk and defiant, the renegades sent a series of taunting messages to local peace officers, challenging them to come out and try to arrest them. Rumors ran wild through the community about an impending raid on the town, and the citizens scurried about gathering up firearms.

A posse of lawmen was finally organized and rode out to investigate. The gang had gone. The tension, however, was not relieved. It was now speculated that the threats were really a diversion, and that the outlaws, in a replay of the trick the Bill Doolin gang pulled on Coffeyville, Kansas, following the Dalton disaster (see *Coffeyville*), were in fact going to attack one of the night trains. Telegrams were rushed to neighboring towns along the railroad lines, and special officers were assigned to guard the passenger coaches and express cars. But it was all a hoax. Christmas Day 1894 dawned without incident.

## Ned's Fort Mountain
### Adair County

They called it Ned's Fort Mountain, a Cherokee outlaw's fortress cliff from which he held off posses for three years.

Ned Christie ran afoul of the law in 1885 when he

Ned Christie. *University of Oklahoma.*

Posse that killed Ned Christie. *Western History Collections, University of Oklahoma.*

was accused of killing Dan Maples, a lawman sent to arrest him for running whiskey. After the shooting, Ned retreated into the wilderness twelve miles southeast of Tahlequah, at the north edge of the Cookson Hills, and fought off pursuers for the next four years, wounding at least five deputy U.S. marshals in the process.

In 1889 Christie was shot in the face and his cabin was burned to the ground. When he recovered he built his "fort" on a forbidding cliff. From this two-story bastion, said to be braced with walls two logs thick and lined with oak two-by-fours, Ned commanded a 360 degree field of fire. On alert twenty-four hours a day, Christie and a handful of Cherokee companions stubbornly held off attackers until November 1892 when, after failing to blow a hole in the fortress with a three-pound cannon, a posse finally succeeded in setting the structure on fire with a blast from six sticks of dynamite. Christie made a dash for a nearby woods but was killed before he could reach safety.

To find the site of Ned's Fort, drive southeast out of Eldon on State Highway 51 and ask for directions.

## Norman
### Cleveland County

Southwest of Norman, between the Canadian River and Interstate 35, lie the remains of outlaw "Bitter Creek" Newcomb, one-time member of both the Dalton and Bill Doolin gangs. Following Newcomb's death on May 2, 1895, at the Dunn ranch outside Ingalls, Oklahoma,* the outlaw's body was claimed by his father, James Newcomb, and buried on the family farm at what was then called "Nine Mile Flats," on the north bank of the Canadian River.

## Oklahoma City
### Oklahoma County

Oklahoma City must hold some kind of record for frontier unruliness. The town was hardly an hour old when it suffered its first shootout. On April 22, 1889, a 21-year-old Texan, Clyde Mattox, already handy with a sixgun, got himself appointed marshal by the temporary city government. A rival political faction had also appointed a marshal, and the two new peace officers clashed. Mattox survived, but with a bullet in his lung. His opponent was dragged off to be buried. After Mattox recovered from his wound, he was acquitted of the shooting on a plea of self defense but was convicted of another killing shortly thereafter.

June 30, 1895, was long remembered in Oklahoma City as the day of the big jailbreak. The previous April, two Pottawatomie county outlaws, Will and Bob Christian, gunned down a deputy sheriff who was serving them with a warrant. Convicted of the murder, the brothers were housed in the Oklahoma County jail pending an appeal. On June 27 the boys' father and several friends smuggled in three revolvers. Three days later, a Sunday morning, the Christians and a fellow prisoner, James Casey, overpowered the jailer and fled into the street.

The jail was located at the junction of an alley running north from Grand Avenue and another alley connecting Broadway and Robinson avenues. The fugitives ran south down the first alley to where police chief Milt Jones had tied his horse. Will Christian leaped into the saddle and raced south on Broadway, then west into an alley between California and Reno. Meanwhile, Bob Christian and Casey ran out into Grand Avenue and turned east toward Broadway, where they tried to commandeer the buggy of a man named Gus White. At this moment they were spotted by Chief Jones, standing on Broadway a few feet north of the intersection. Jones ran toward the buggy with his gun drawn, but before he could fire, Christian shot him in the chest. Two police officers came running up, as did several citizens, all firing at the outlaws. Casey took a bullet in the head above the ear and another in the neck. Gus White was also hit, but his wounds were not serious.

Bob Christian raced down Grand Avenue in a hail of gunfire. One slug struck him in the fleshy part of the neck but did not slow him down. At the Santa Fe tracks he encountered a blacksmith in a road wagon and ordered him to climb down. Taking the wagon, he drove east, then south over the bridge that crossed the North Canadian River, and then east again to a wooded area. There he abandoned the wagon and fled on foot. Backtracking to the river, which was high and swollen from recent rains, he found a large log and escaped by floating downstream. His pursuers, seeing a trail of blood leading from the woods to the river, assumed that he was too weak to survive the current and gave up the chase.

# Orlando
## Logan County

The McGinn farm, three miles southeast of Orlando near the Logan-Payne County line, was used as a hideout by the Dalton gang in 1891. In May of that year, the gang spent a few days in a dense patch of woods there while eluding authorities who had tracked them following a train robbery at Wharton (see *Perry, Oklahoma*). The Dalton bunch was aided by Mrs. Hugh McGinn and her brother Oliver (Ol) Yantis. Yantis later joined the Bill Doolin gang, successors to the Daltons, and was in on the holdup of the Ford County Bank at Spearville, Kansas.* The Spearville holdup was Yantis's last, however. On November 15, 1892, Yantis was identified by Tom Hueston (also spelled Huston), city marshal at Stillwater, as a probable participant in the Spearville affair, and two weeks later Hueston, George Cox (a Stillwater town constable), and Sheriff Chalkley M. (Chalk) Beeson of Ford County, Kansas, cornered Yantis at his sister's place near Orlando.

It was early dawn and foggy. Yantis came out of the house to feed his horse, and Beeson called for him to surrender. Ol opened up with his pistol in the direction of the sheriff's voice but missed, and a volley of gunfire from the lawmen knocked him to the ground. One bullet severed his spine, and he died that afternoon in the office of an Orlando physician.

# Pawnee
## Pawnee County

Pawnee is west of Tulsa at the junction of State Highway 18 and US 64. The Farmers and Citizens Bank of Pawnee fell victim to the Bill Doolin gang during its winter rampage in 1893-94. At 3:30 P.M. on January 23, 1894, Doolin and sidekick William "Tulsa Jack" Blake entered the bank and put a sixshooter to the head of cashier C. L. Berry. When Berry could not open the safe, claiming it was equipped with a time lock, Doolin settled for $262 in currency and coins from the teller's cage. Taking Berry along as a shield, the two outlaws, joined by a third who had been left with the horses, rode off down the street, firing several shots into Bolton's Meat Market where a bank customer, Dolph Carrion, had fled to give the alarm.

A posse later trailed the outlaws to Black Creek where their tracks showed they had joined up with four more riders. This made seven. If all were in on splitting the proceeds of the robbery, each man got just under $40. If they had waited a half hour to raid the bank, one of the largest in the Cherokee Outlet, they would have ridden away with a fortune. The time lock was set to open at 4:00 P.M.

In November 1896 Pawnee citizens witnessed a shootout between Pawnee County deputy sheriff Frank Canton and Bill Dunn, enigmatic rancher, rustler, bounty hunter, stool pigeon, and part-time posseman. Dunn had worked both sides of the law for many years. At his ranch outside Ingalls, Oklahoma, he first hid outlaws from the law and later arranged for their capture or demise. It is believed that he played a major role in the killing of Charlie Pierce and "Bitter Creek" Newcomb in May, 1895, (see *Ingalls*) and was along when a posse ended the career of his one-time friend, Bill Doolin (see *Quay, Oklahoma*).

While Dunn was a favorite of some of the lawmen, Frank Canton despised him and continually hounded him about his shady operations which allegedly included part interest in a Pawnee butcher shop that sold stolen beef. On November 6, 1896, Dunn had had enough of Canton's harassment and challenged the lawman on Pawnee's main street. As Canton came abreast of Dunn, the latter stepped in front of him and said, "Frank Canton, God damn you, I've got it in for you!" Although Dunn already had his hand on his gun, Canton, who was lightning fast on the draw, got off the only shot, which struck Dunn in the forehead. Witnesses said Dunn dropped like a rock to the board sidewalk, "working the trigger-finger of his right hand" as if he still held his revolver.

It was said that the morning after Dunn was buried

in the Ingalls cemetery, a pile of fresh hog entrails was found on his grave, placed there by Payne County residents to show their disdain for a man who profited from betraying friends.

## Perry
### Noble County

On May 9, 1891, the lonely Santa Fe depot at Perry (then called Wharton) was the scene of what probably was the Dalton gang's first train robbery. (Bob and Grat Dalton were accused of robbing a Southern Pacific train in California the previous February [see *Earlimont, California*], but the evidence against them was weak.) The gang—then composed of Bob and Emmett Dalton, "Bitter Creek" Newcomb, and Charley Bryant—had heard that there was a large shipment of money being carried by the Santa Fe express. In what would become their classic style, the outlaws invaded the locomotive cab and ordered the engineer and fireman to climb down. But as they were marching their prisoners back to the express car, the express messenger saw them coming and began hiding the money and valuables. After a token resistance, he opened up his door and let the outlaws help themselves. At first it appeared to be a good haul, but twenty or so miles out on the prairie, when the bandits reined up to count their loot, they found they had been tricked. An enticing, bulging package, which looked large enough to hold thousands of dollars, turned out to be stuffed with cancelled waybills, old telegrams, and similar worthless paper. The gang's total take was said to be only about $500, which came to $125 per man.

Perry is at the junction of US 64 and US 77, just east of Interstate 35. On the west edge of town is the Cherokee Strip Historical Museum which has an excellent exhibit depicting pioneer life on the Cherokee Strip in the 1880s and 1890s.

## Pocasset
### Grady County

A midday robbery on the Rock Island line on October 1, 1897, at what is now Pocasset, was described by a local newspaper writer as the "boldest holdup in broad daylight ever attempted in history." It is arguable whether the affair was that bold, since the robbers picked one of the most remote spots on the line: a high prairie divide about eight miles south of Minco where one lookout could observe the countryside for miles around.

In 1897 the site was nothing more than a section house and a siding. Prior to the arrival of the train, six horsemen, led by lawyer-turned-outlaw Al Jennings, overpowered the section gang and ordered them to flag the southbound express. When the train came to a stop one of the men jumped up to the cab and covered the engineer and fireman with his Winchester. Two more took charge of the passenger coaches, and the final three entered the express car. Here, however, the robbers encountered trouble: two dynamite charges failed to blow open the American Express Company safe.

The Jennings gang seemed plagued with this problem. A month and a half earlier they encountered the same difficulty on the Sante Fe line at Edmond.* At Pocasset, however, they did not ride off empty-handed. Turning to the mail car, they rifled the registered packages, taking an undetermined sum. Next they ordered all passengers out of the coaches and lined them up along the track, a rare practice in the annals of Western train robberies. One by one the victims were forced to drop their money and valuables into a bag. During this procedure the leader of the gang, Al Jennings, let his mask slip, and the conductor, a man named Dacy, recognized him as the former lawyer from Woodward, Oklahoma.

On finishing with the passengers, the outlaws rode off toward Walnut Creek, then doubled back, rode west through the uninhabited area of the Wichita Reservation, and then turned north. Later, at a farmhouse outside El Reno, they rested, divided up their loot, and finally headed toward an old Dalton gang dugout on Cottonwood Creek southwest of Guthrie.

## Pond Creek
### Grant County

The attempted robbery of a Rock Island train on the night of April 9, 1894, at Pond Creek (located in northern Oklahoma at the junction of US 60 and US 81) is memorable mainly because it was an apparent attempt by amateurs to emulate the recent successes of the notorious Dalton and Doolin gangs.

Things seemed to go well at first, thanks perhaps to the only experienced robber in the bunch, Bill Rhodes, who allegedly had at one time ridden with the James brothers in Missouri. As the train pulled away from the water tank at Pond Creek station, two men slipped out of the shadows and climbed aboard. One positioned himself behind the tender and the other somewhere on the baggage car—probably on the roof. After about a mile, the engineer spotted a bonfire on the track ahead and slowed down. As he did, he and the fireman found themselves staring at sixguns. To show he meant business, one of the outlaws fired into the locomotive cab, the bullet ricocheting off the boiler into the roof.

After the train came to a stop, the engineer and fireman were marched back to the express car, where they were joined by more bandits who had been hiding in the brush near the fire. To keep the passengers in line, the outlaws fired a few rounds alongside the coaches. The express messenger, John Crosswight, was then ordered to open his car.

At this point the outlaws made their first mistake—not guarding the rear door of the express car. While they were shouting at the messenger to open the side door, an express company guard—former Wichita, Kansas, policeman Jake Harmon—slipped out the rear into the car behind and then down onto the track. About the same time, the brakeman also dropped to the ground and ran back toward Pond Creek to spread the alarm.

Messenger Crosswight refused to open up, and the would-be robbers thrust a stick of dynamite under the door plate. When it exploded, it knocked the messenger down but only stunned him momentarily. As his head cleared, he heard his attackers shout that they were going to throw two sticks in next time. With that, Crosswight agreed to open up. In the meantime, however, express guard Harmon, still unnoticed at the rear of the train, leveled his double-barreled shotgun at one of the outlaws beside the car. It was Rhodes, and the charge killed him intantly. As his stunned comrades stared at his shattered body, they heard riders coming from the rear—a posse from Pond Creek. They called it a night and raced for their horses.

# Purcell
## McClain County

Eight miles west of Purcell, at the edge of a deep ravine near the junction of State Highways 39 and 24, lies the decayed remains of an old cabin once used by outlaws Will and Bob Christian during the summer of 1895. The Christians had escaped jail on June 30 in a bloody shootout in Oklahoma City,* and quickly formed a gang that swept across a three-county area during July and August. On August 9 they barely survived an encounter with lawmen near Wilburton*. Circling back west, the two outlaw brothers headed for the hideout cabin near Purcell while a third gang member, John Reeves, sought refuge with friends near Paoli in Garvin County. While in Paoli, Reeves was captured and disclosed the Christians' hiding place.

A posse surrounded the isolated cabin on Friday morning, August 23. Reeves had told the lawmen of a prearranged signal he was to use on joining the two outlaws: he was to fire off one shot before approaching the cabin, and the Christians would come out and meet him. One of the possemen fired off the shot, and sure enough, the outlaws suddenly appeared. But instead of coming out of the cabin, they emerged from the nearby brush, less than thirty yards from two of their pursuers. Posseman W. E. Hocker took a bullet below the shoulder blade, but before he went down he was sure he hit Bob Christian with at least one shot. Hocker's horse was the closest to the outlaws, and they both jumped on and plunged back into the brush. The rest of the posse was on the opposite side of the ravine and could not get across in time to give chase. The outlaws headed west toward Dibble and escaped.

# Quay
## Pawnee County

In the 1890s Quay, which straddled the Pawnee-Payne County line about twenty miles northeast of Stillwater, was called Lawson. In August 1896 it was the scene of the killing of the famous Oklahoma outlaw Bill Doolin. Doolin, who once rode with the Daltons, formed his own gang after the Daltons' demise at Coffeyville, Kansas,* and terrorized Oklahoma for three years. The gang split up in the summer of 1895, and Doolin was captured the following January, only to escape from the new federal jail at Guthrie* in July.

Married and the father of a small child, Doolin, while on the loose, made periodic visits to Lawson where his wife was living with her parents, the J. W. Ellsworths. Tipped off about Doolin's presence by two Lawson blacksmiths Tom and Charlie Noble, deputy U.S. marshal Heck Thomas and a handpicked posse surrounded the house on August 24, 1896.

The Ellsworth home was in the rear of the town post office and general store, both operated by Ellsworth. The Noble brothers, who had been hired by federal officers to watch the place, spotted Doolin's wife packing belongings into a wagon as if she was planning a long trip. By the time the federal officers arrived, the wagon was loaded, presumably ready to take Doolin and his family out of the county.

The lawmen were certain the outlaw would eventually appear; he did, that night. Emerging from a nearby stable, he walked toward where the officers were hidden. Thomas shouted for the outlaw to halt. Instead, he raised his Winchester and fired. Thomas later wrote:

> He shot at me and the bullet passed between me and B. Dunn. I had let one of the boys have my Winchester and had an old No. 8 shotgun. It was too long in the breech and I couldn't handle it quick so he got another shot with his Winchester and as he dropped his Winchester from [a] glancing shot, he jerked his pistol and some of the boys thought he

shot once and the others twice—and about the time I got the shotgun to work and the fight was over.

Although eventually dispelled, a rumor arose that there had been no gunfight—that Doolin had died naturally and Thomas arranged for the outlaw's body to be riddled with bullets so he and his men could collect the reward. The rumor is believed to have orginated because there was very little blood on Doolin's body when he was turned over to the undertaker.

On her husband's death, Mrs. Doolin composed a poem about the outlaw, which she had printed on cards and sold with pictures for 25¢ each, the proceeds of which were to be used for his burial. The government buried the outlaw, however, in Guthrie's Summit View Cemetery, with a twisted, rusty buggy axle driven into the parched earth as the only marker.

Following the killing, the town declined. In the early 1900s it revived under the name Quay and thrived for a while as a modest farming and livestock trade center, nourished by the Eastern Oklahoma Railway Company. In 1914 oil was discovered nearby, and for the next ten years the town boomed. But as production declined, the population dwindled once more, and today only a few scattered homes remain.

## Red Fork
### Tulsa County

Southwest of Red Fork, now a Tulsa suburb, near the junction of Snake and Duck creeks, there was a popular outlaw hangout called the Spike S Ranch. In the late 1890s it was a favorite hideout of the Jennings brothers, Al and Frank, both of whom had given up the practice of law in Woodward, Oklahoma,* to ride the outlaw trail. The ranch was owned by John Harless, reportedly a "cattleman with a habit of rustling other people's livestock."

After a brief stint at train robbery, the Jennings brothers and their gang rose to near the top of the wanted list in Oklahoma. On November 28, 1897, they were spotted at Red Fork, and federal officers closed in the next night.

There was a blinding dust storm blowing as the lawmen surrounded the ranch house. To get an idea of what they were up against, the officer in charge, deputy U.S. marshal James F. (Bud) Ledbetter, sent in a neighbor of the Harlesses, a man named Kelly. Kelly was supposed to just "drop in," visit a moment, and then report back to the officers how many outlaws were present, their descriptions, and how they were armed. But once in, Kelly's nerve left him, and he stammered something to the effect that he "had got lost" in the storm and came to the house when he saw the Harless' light. After he left, Mrs. Harless mentioned that it was unlikely that someone who knew the area so well could "get lost," and the outlaws became suspicious. That night they put gang member Morris O'Malley outside to stand guard.

O'Malley took a position in a wagon between the house and the barn, but he had hardly got settled when he felt deputy Ledbetter's rifle sticking him in the ribs. O'Malley was quickly tied, gagged, and deposited in a corner of the barn.

Near dawn Mrs. Harless's brother, Clarence Enscoe, came out for a bucket of water. He, too, was captured and stashed in the barn. When he did not return to the house, Mrs. Harless came looking for him. Ledbetter took her aside, explained what was going on, and instructed her to go back into the house and tell the outlaws to come out with their hands up. She did as she was told, but the outlaws were in no mood to surrender.

Mrs. Harless and another woman, a hired girl, were allowed to leave, and then Jennings and crew gave Ledbetter their answer with a volley of gunfire. The officers responded in kind, and soon the outlaws found themselves pinned down in a hailstorm of bullets. A bullet tore into gang member Pat O'Mallay's right leg and blood spurted everywhere. Al Jennings took three quick hits: glancing wounds in both legs just above the knees and a solid hit in the upper left thigh. Frank Jennings was also wounded but apparently not seriously. Staying put meant sure death, and the three outlaws, limping and leaking blood, made a run for a thick orchard immediately behind the house. Luck was with them. Deputy marshal Lon Lewis's shotgun blast ripped into Frank's clothing but failed to strike flesh, and deputy Jack Elliott's rifle jammed on his first shot. All three outlaws reached the orchard safely and disappeared into the dense brush of Snake Creek. Later that day they commandeered a wagon belonging to two Indian lads and escaped south toward Okmulgee.

## Redrock
### Noble County

The Santa Fe Railroad almost put an end to the Dalton gang on a muggy June night in 1892. The gang had planned to rob the southbound express at Redrock, which today is just north of the Will Rogers Turnpike between Interstate 35 and US 177. But word leaked out, and the train was packed with railroad and Wells Fargo detectives. As the train pulled into the station, one of the gang apparently noticed that the passenger coach behind the express car was dark. It was only a little after 9:00 P.M., much too early for the passengers to be asleep. The outlaws let the train leave without molesting it, and they were about to ride away when they heard another whistle—a second train. This one looked normal, and the gang spurred their horses and surrounded the express car.

Although the outlaws guessed right about the train, they still did not have an easy time of it. The Wells Fargo messenger E. S. Whittlesay and guard John Riehl held them off with their rifles for nearly fifteen minutes before giving in.

When word went out over the wire that the train had been held up, it was first reported that the robbers had ridden away with $50,000, which would have been an all-time record for the Daltons. Later this was reduced to $1,600 on official company records. Years afterward Emmett Dalton claimed they actually picked up $11,000 in the raid, but many details in Emmett's memoirs are not to be trusted.

Nine years after the Dalton holdup, on March 10, 1901, Redrock erupted again when Ben Cravens, an Oklahoma outlaw wanted for killing a guard during an escape from the Kansas State Prison, tried to rob the Redrock post office with the help of a fellow fugitive, Bert Welty. The postmaster came in as the two were rifling the cash register and fired a shot at Cravens. He missed, and the outlaw whirled and killed him instantly. As the two outlaws dashed out of town in a stolen buggy, a sudden thunderstorm struck, and the buggy, apparently being driven by Welty, overturned on the slippery road. Cravens, evidently in a rage over his companion's carelessness, shot Welty, then righted the buggy, and rode off.

## Robber's Cave
### Latimer County

Robber's Cave, five miles north of Wilburton on State Highway 2, was supposed to have been a favorite hangout for Belle Starr and other outlaws in the area. Although serious researchers have found little evidence that Belle was the "Bandit Queen" early writers made her out to be, some outlaws may have used the cave, and the nearby "Robber's Trail," during the latter half of the 19th century.

The cave, an impressive recess high on a sandstone cliff in the wilds of the San Bois Mountains, would indeed have made an ideal bandit's lair. The Jameses and the Youngers are most often mentioned in connection with the site, since it was near the route they reportedly took between their homes in Missouri and their favorite spots in Texas. There is some evidence that Jesse James did visit Belle Starr's place thirty-five miles to the north (see *Youngers' Bend*), so he may have been in the area one time or another.

The site is now part of Robber's Cave State Park, an inviting 8,000-acre nature preserve which offers overnight camping facilities, lodging and interesting trails.

## Sacred Heart
### Pottawatamie County

It is difficult to find this tiny town on a map today. Nestled just northwest of Konawa near the Seminole-Pottawatamie County line, on what is now State Highway 39, this settlement was once the site of the Sacred Heart Catholic Mission. Today the town is barely a memory, all but forgotten except perhaps by a handful of Dalton-Doolin gang buffs who remember it as the place Bill Dalton and "Bitter Creek" Newcomb tangled with W. H. (Bill) Carr, an aging deputy U.S. marshal who came out of retirement for one last gun battle. Once Bill Carr had ridden with the best, but by 1894 he had all but hung up his guns, content to mind the general store at Sacred Heart and leave the pursuit of outlaws to younger hands.

The last week of March 1894 Carr received a wire from federal officers that Bill Dalton, last of the famous brothers to ride the outlaw trail, might be in his vicinity. The old deputy probably thought little more about it, until Sunday evening, April 1, when Dalton and sidekick Bitter Creek Newcomb entered his store to buy corn for their horses. Carr wasted no time. He promptly picked up his sixgun from the shelf near his cashbox, walked around the counter, and informed the two bandits that they should consider themselves under arrest. Newcomb's words were "I guess not," and he reached for his pistol. Both men fired. A bullet tore into Carr's right arm above the wrist, and his shot struck Newcomb in the left shoulder. The old deputy's gun fell from his hand, and as he stooped to retrieve it, Newcomb's second shot splintered the wood at his feet. A third bullet struck him in the belly just above the navel. The two outlaws, figuring they had finished the old man, rushed out the door. But Carr was not through. He picked up his pistol and with his left hand got off three more shots before he finally slumped to the floor. It was a close call for Dalton and Newcomb and a fitting swan song for an aging lawman.

Visitors to Sacred Heart today will find scattered foundations and outlines of the original mission around which the town was built. A two-story log structure, said to be part of the first building, still stands. Some restoration of a bakery and the home of the mission priest was attempted in the 1960s. The old cemetery is

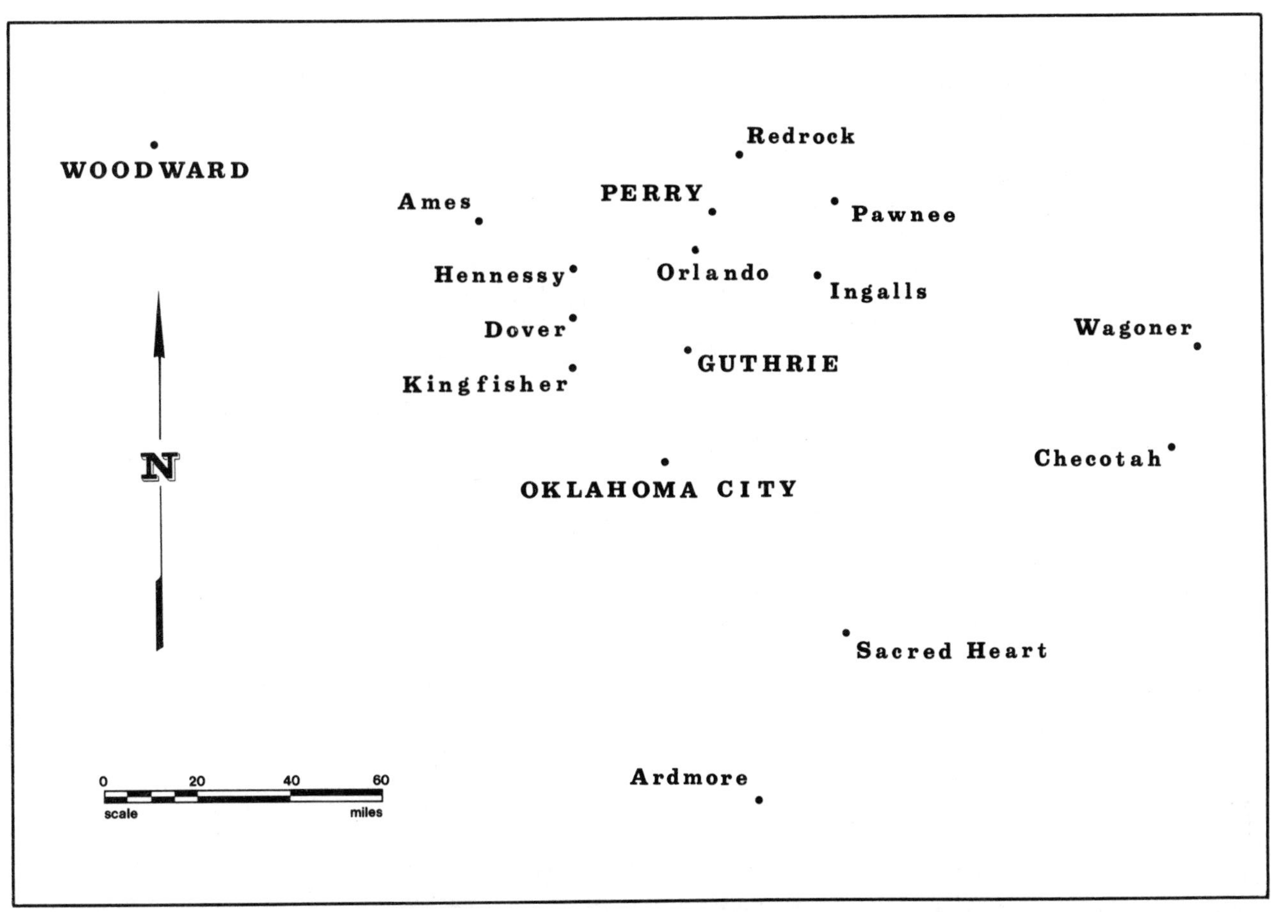


**The Dalton and Doolin gangs in Oklahoma. Ames:** Just southwest of Ames, the Doolin gang fought with a heated battle with lawmen on April 4, 1885, resulting in the death of outlaw Tulsa Jack Blake. **Ardmore**: The Houston Wallace farm on the outskirts of Ardmore was the end of the trail for Bill Dalton in June 1894. **Checotah**: In November 1897, Doolin gang stalwart Dynamite Dick Clifton was killed at a hideout cabin 10 miles west of Checotah. **Dover:** Scene of a Doolin gang robbery on the Rock Island line in April 1895. **Guthrie:** Bill Doolin's and Dick Clifton's escape from the sturdy Guthrie jail in July 1896 raised doubts about the competency of local officials. Doolin and gang member Charlie Pierce are buried in Guthrie's Summit View Cemetery. **Hennessy:** Scene of the capture of Dalton gang member Blackface Charlie Bryant in July 1891. **Ingalls:** Site of the famous "Ingalls Raid," an unsuccessful attempt to finish off Doolin and his comrades in September 1893. **Kingfisher:** The Dalton family home was located near Kingfisher Creek six miles north of town. **Orlando:** The McGinn farm, three miles southeast of Orlando, was a Dalton hideout; Ol Yantis, who rode with Bill Dalton after the end of the Daltons, was killed there by lawmen in November 1892. **Pawnee:** Bill Doolin and Tulsa Jack Blake robbed the Farmers and Citizens Bank of Pawnee in January 1894; also the scene of Frank Canton's killing of Doolin gang betrayer Bill Cunn in November 1896. **Perry**: Generally believed to be the site of the Dalton gang's first train robbery in May 1891; the town was then called Wharton. **Quay:** Bill Doolin was killed at Quay, then called Lawson, in a gunfight with lawmen in August 1896. **Redrock:** Site of a Dalton express car holdup in June 1892. **Sacred Heart:** Scene of Bill Dalton's and Bitter Creek Newcomb's shootout with aging lawman Bill Carr in April 1894. **Wagoner**: One of the quickest train robberies in history was pulled off by the Daltons four miles north of Wagoner in September 1891. **Woodward**: Bill Doolin and Bill Dalton robbed the Santa Fe Depot at Woodward in March 1894.

still there. Remains of some store buildings on the main street can be seen, and the Catholic church on Bald Hill survives.

## Stillwater
### Payne County

Many a hard case passed through Stillwater during the territory's lusty frontier years, but perhaps best remembered is a feverish week in May 1894 when the town nearly became an armed camp. The event was the trial of Arkansas Tom Jones, the only member of the notorious Bill Doolin gang captured the previous September during the famous "Ingalls Raid" (see *Ingalls, Oklahoma*). Jones was being tried for the murder of a federal officer during the attack. Before the trial began, Judge Frank Dale, who was to preside, received a handful of letters, allegedly from the Doolin bunch, threatening his life. A bodyguard was provided, but on the first day of the trial more threats arrived, and the judge ordered the federal marshal's office to provide a "strong posse of deputy marshals" for his protection and to guard against an attempt to rescue Jones. Once the trial began, no one was allowed to enter the courtroom without being searched, and officers were distributed throughout town to watch for strangers. An article in the Stillwater *Eagle-Gazette* proclaimed that a "veritable walking arsenal is stationed around the courthouse" so that "any attempt by the outlaws to rescue the prisoner will surely cost them their lives."

The trial itself proceeded undisturbed, and Jones was convicted of first degree manslaughter. Following sentencing, Judge Dale reportedly called the federal marshal in charge into his chambers and informed him of his displeasure with having to deal with such a tense situation. He made it clear that with the remaining members of the Doolin gang he preferred avoiding the normal legal process and informed the marshal, "I hope you will instruct your deputies in the future to bring them [the rest of the Doolin gang] in dead."

## Stroud
### Lincoln County

No serious student of outlaw history can hear the name Stroud, which is just off Interstate 44 midway between Oklahoma City and Tulsa, without thinking of the hapless bank robber Henry Starr. In March 1915 Starr and six companions tried to duplicate the Dalton gang's trick of robbing two banks at the same time—in Starr's case the Stroud National Bank on Main Street and the First National, two blocks away. It did not work for the Daltons (see *Coffeyville, Kansas*), and it did not work for Starr and his bunch. Their nemesis was a seventeen-year-old boy, Paul Curry, who shot Starr as he was escaping, knocking him off his horse and into the hands of the law. Curry also picked off another member of the gang, Louis Estes.

Following Starr's release from prison in 1919, he bought into a Tulsa film company, Pan American Motion Pictures, and set up on location in Stroud to film the story of his ill-fated raid. Starr played the lead in the picture, and as supporting players he used Stroud residents, including employees of the very banks his gang had robbed. Also to prove he held no hard feelings, he even engaged sharpshooter Paul Curry to play himself. The film, entitled *Debtor to the Law*, turned out to be a success, and under his profit-sharing agreement with Pan American Pictures, should have earned Starr $15,000, nearly a fortune by 1919 standards. But Starr later claimed he never saw his money—that his partners had cheated him out of his share. Several Hollywood producers were impressed with the picture, however, and offered Starr some attractive deals to make films, but because of an outstanding warrant against him for an 1893 robbery in Bentonville, Arkansas, Starr was afraid to leave Oklahoma, where he was safe from extradition.

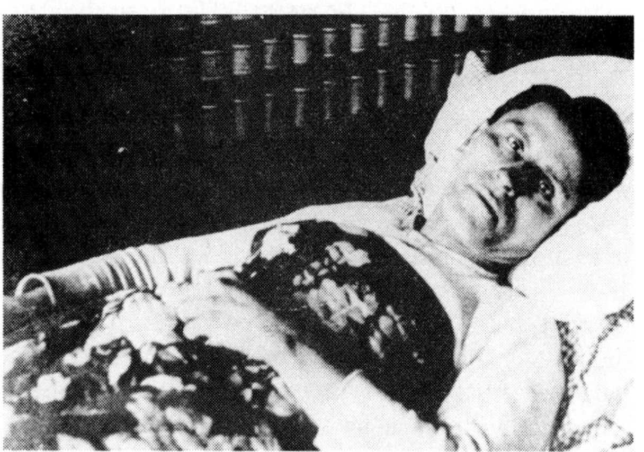
Henry Starr, following disastrous bank robbery at Stroud, Oklahoma. *Charles C. Goodhall Collection.*

There were some film companies still making pictures in Oklahoma, but Starr probably needed a stake to get back into the business there. Perhaps for this reason, he returned once more to bank robbery. On February 18, 1921, he was shot while holding up the People's National Bank at Harrison, Arkansas, and died four days later.

There is an interesting sidelight to Starr's robberies at Stroud. Another familiar name in Oklahoma's frontier history, federal lawman Bill Tilghman, had also entered the motion picture business, and when he heard about Starr's capture at Stroud, he rushed a camera crew down from Tulsa to film the robbers in captivity. Later, he worked the scenes into the picture he was producing at the time.

## Sugar Loaf Peak
### Cimarron County

Near Sugar Loaf Peak, just off the old Santa Fe Trail in the western end of Oklahoma's panhandle, may lie the richest buried outlaw treasure in the West. Most stories of buried loot are supported by scant documentation, except for the occasional and always questionable "treasure map." The Sugar Loaf cache, however, seems to be backed up with slightly better evidence.

According to a family history kept by the descendants of a Spanish metal worker, José Lopat, a gang of French prospectors, turned road agents, buried 500 gold ingots somewhere in the area in 1805. Lopat was around at the time (it was he who melted the gold into ingots), but since he was only in the employ of the Frenchmen and not part of their band, he was not allowed to see where the loot was hidden. Apparently the gold came from northern New Mexico where Spanish records show that gold was mined as early as 1798. It is believed that the Frenchmen acquired the treasure by raiding placer mines north and east of Santa Fe, during which attacks they may have killed as many as twenty miners.

Lopat died in 1856, apparently under the impression that the gang never returned to claim their loot. His story, recorded by his son in the back of the family Bible, received added credence in 1878 upon the discovery of what may be markers left by the bandits to guide them back to their treasure. That year three sets of carefully placed stones, almost a quarter of a mile long and each spelling out a Roman numeral, were found about six miles apart. Some time later a fourth set of stones was found. Together they form a thirty-six mile square. At the approximate center is Sugar Loaf Peak. Some treasure hunters believe the stones (some of which have become displaced) and the Roman numerals offer a key, in code, to the exact location of the cache.

Today most of the area enclosed by the square, including Sugar Loaf Peak, lies on private property—a cattle-spread locally called "Stone's Ranch."

## Tulsa
### Tulsa County

On the western edge of Tulsa, across the Arkansas River west of 31st Street, is a high hill called Lookout Mountain. For years rumors circulated the Tulsa area that on this hill, or somewhere nearby, a treasure lay buried, left there either by outlaws or the Spanish.

Landmarks like Lookout Mountain often stimulate such tales, and probably few people really believed the rumor. However, if one local man's story is true, there may very well have been something to this tale of buried treasure. In the early 1930s a young oil refinery worker named Roy Vance was approached by an Indian who had arrived in town by train. According to Vance, the Indian said he had come to find a certain cave on Lookout Mountain, and he was willing to pay Vance to help him. The cave, said the Indian, was supposed to hold a cache of gold stolen from a wagon train during his great grandfather's day. When Vance agreed to take the job, the Indian sketched out a map showing several landmarks that presumably would help them in their search. Vance and the Indian spent a week searching but found no cave. The Indian said he had to leave but would return. He never did.

Over the years Vance occasionally returned to the hill to hunt squirrels and rabbits, always, of course, keeping an eye out for the lost cave. In the mid-1970s he found what might have been a cave, but if so, the entrance had been closed up, possibly blasted shut with dynamite. Vance spent several weeks digging and blasting at the site, eventually reaching a depth of about six feet. He had not told anyone about what he was doing, and he had tried to conceal his work to look like he was building a stock pond. But it seems somebody had been watching. According to Vance, he finished up one night after dark, just after reaching another layer of hard rock which he figured would have to be blasted. But when he returned the next day, he found that the rock had been only a slab—and it had been removed during the night! In the soft earth below, he saw the impression of at least fifteen bars, presumably gold. There was nothing else in the hole.

For a while in 1911-12, the old outlaw Emmett Dalton served on the Tulsa police force. No doubt expecting to capitalize on the Dalton reputation, the city hired Emmett, the only outlaw survivor of the Coffeyville, Kansas, shootout of 1892,* as a special officer. Emmett had served his time in a Kansas prison, had later married, and was for all purposes reformed. But his name still meant something to the criminal element of the southwest, and he spent a brief, but apparently effective, period in Tulsa handling hard cases who drifted into town looking for easy pickings.

Tulsa was probably where Dalton formed the idea of making a motion picture based on his outlaw days. (He would later go to California to form his own production company [see *Los Angeles*].) About the time he was patrolling the streets, a local film producer, William Smith, was launching a motion picture company in Tulsa. Smith's films were a success, prompting others to follow. Memories of Oklahoma's outlaws were still fresh in the minds of movie fans, and Tulsa seemed an appropriate place to film their stories. False-fronted frontier buildings soon dotted Tulsa's Sand Springs Road, where a number of small studios cranked out Wild West thrillers. Old Oklahoma outlaws had a chance to ride again, if only on celluloid, and the pay was not too bad. One who joined the new industry was former bank robber Henry Starr who, perhaps using loot buried after one of his holdups, celebrated his parole from prison in 1919 by producing and starring in a film story of the bank robbery that sent him to prison (see *Stroud, Oklahoma*).

## Wagoner
### Wagoner County

Four miles north of Wagoner, at a little cattle-loading station and water stop on the old Missouri, Kansas & Texas Railway called Leliaetta, the Dalton gang robbed an express train on the night of September 15, 1891. This robbery has gone almost unnoticed on the list of Dalton holdups. The take was modest, about $2,500, which had to be split up among seven or eight gang members. (In his book, *When the Daltons Rode*, Emmett

Dalton claimed the gang picked up over $19,000 that night, but here and in many places, Emmett tended to exaggerate.)

If anything, this holdup probably stands out as one of the smoothest and quickest accomplished by Western train robbers. The affair took only a few minutes, and the passengers in the coaches did not even know the express car had been raided until the train was well on its way to Wagoner, the next stop.

# Wilburton
## Latimer County

Five miles south of Wilburton, which is on US 270 at the junction of State Highway 2, is the site of a battle between lawmen and a a band of outlaws from Pottawatomie County led by two brothers, Will and Bob Christian. The Christians' escapades began in the spring of 1895 when they broke out of jail at Oklahoma City* following conviction of the killing of a deputy sheriff. The brothers and several companions then ravaged Pottawatomie and Seminole Counties for a month before heading for the Wilburton area.

Deputies from Pottawatomie County picked up the trail of four of the outlaws and tracked them to their campsite below Wilburton near sundown on August 9. Charging into the camp, the lawmen waged a thirty-minute battle before night closed in. The officers suffered no casualties but did lose their horses. One of the outlaws, John Fessenden, was found dead at the scene. Another was wounded, but he and his two comrades escaped in the darkness.

# Woodward
## Woodward County

Woodward is in western Oklahoma, on US 183 at the junction of State Highway 15. On March 13, 1894, the Santa Fe depot at Woodward was the scene of an unique early morning robbery by Bill Doolin and Bill Dalton. Three days earlier, a dispatch from Fort Leavenworth, Kansas, appeared in the Kansas City *Times* describing the intended route of the army paymaster. How the newspaper obtained the information is not known, since the details of army pay shipments were always kept secret. This account, however, contained the amount of money destined for each post and the means by which it would be transported. According to the article, an estimated $10,000 was to be sent by rail to Woodward to pay the troops at nearby Fort Supply and others stationed in the general area. The article did not go unnoticed by Bill Doolin, whose gang was at the time staging a crime wave throughout Oklahoma and Indian Territory.

About 1:00 A.M. on the 13th, Doolin and Dalton surprised the sleepy Santa Fe station agent, George W. Rourke, in his room at the Woodward railroad hotel. Rourke was ordered to dress quietly and march over to the station. On the way the three men encountered a young boy, Sam Peters, and the outlaws forced him to join them. Once inside the station, Rourke reluctantly opened the Santa Fe safe from which the robbers helped themselves to $6,540 in currency. The station also had a small route safe, and the outlaws ordered the Peters youth to pick it up and follow them. They made Rourke and the boy accompany them about a quarter mile east of the station where they stopped and broke open the box. This one was empty. The three men and the boy then walked to the town stockyards where the outlaws had left their horses. After giving the boy $1.50 in silver for his help, Doolin and Dalton rode off in a southwesterly direction along Wolf Creek. Troopers at Fort Supply were immediately dispatched in pursuit, but they lost the robbers' trail in the winding gulches near Lipscomb, Texas.

On October 8, 1895, Woodward was in the news again as a result of the killing of Ed Jennings by Temple Houston, the incident which reportedly launched Ed's brothers Frank and Al on a career of outlawry. Houston had gotten into an argument in court with Ed Jennings and another lawyer brother, John Jennings. Ed had questioned the admissibilty of certain testimony, and Houston mumbled something about Ed being "ignorant of the law." Ed jumped up from the counsel table and rushed at Houston, calling him a "damned liar" and tried to slap his face. Both men drew their guns, but others stepped in and tempers cooled.

That night, Ed and John Jennings found Houston and Jack Love, a former sheriff, sitting in the back room of Jack Garvey's Cabinet Saloon. As the two lawyers walked in, Huston rose and said, "Ed, I want to see you a minute," apparently motioning toward the rear door.

Ed Jennings responded "See me here and now, you son-of-a-bitch," and reached for his gun. Houston, no stranger to a sixshooter, was already drawing his. As the guns erupted, the lights in the saloon went out. Witnesses claimed all four men fired their weapons, with Houston emptying his at Ed, who had stepped behind a large dice table. When the lights were put back on, Ed Jennings lay on the floor with a portion of his skull blown off. John Jennings had taken hits in the shoulder and elbow and had retreated to the street. Houston and Love were unhurt.

Houston and Love were tried and acquitted. Al Jen-

Lawyer-turned-train robber Al Jennings. *Curtis Publishing Co.*

nings and his brother, Frank, who had been in Denver at the time, left town soon after the acquittal, according to Al, because "we did not trust ourselves in Woodward, where Love and Houston would offer continual temptation." The two brothers rode south, then probably east, toward Tulsa, intending, Al said, to "establish among the outlaws some base from which . . . we could make a raid and kill those two men." Instead they became outlaws themselves, engaging in several train robberies with remnants of the Dalton and Doolin gangs.

It was not the last time Temple Houston would draw his gun in anger. In October 1896 Temple gave his son Sam a new pony, with instructions to ask a local farmer, J. B. Jenkins, to let him graze it on his land. Jenkins no doubt was a client of Houston's who probably owed him money, but Jenkins apparently did not like the idea. When young Sam approached him, Jenkins became testy and spat in the boy's face. A short time later Temple Houston found the farmer in the street in front of Woodward's Cattle King Hotel, and both men went for their guns. Once again Huston was quicker; his first shot ripped into Jenkin's chest and shoulder, and his second disabled his right arm. Once more Houston went to court as a defendant. This time he pleaded guilty to "unlawful shooting," a misdemeanor, and paid a fine.

## Wooster's Mound
### Osage County

You will not find Wooster's Mound on a road map. It is just that, a mound, near State Highway 99 about seven miles south of Pawhuska. On August 3, 1903, it was the site of the battle between federal law officers and the Martin gang, holdup artists responsible for the most spectacular highway robbery in Oklahoma history (see *Bartlesville*).

At Wooster's Mound the officers were led by deputy U.S. marshal Wiley G. Haines. Accompanying him were the chief of the Indian police Warren Bennett and constable Henry Majors. The officers dismounted about 100 yards from the mound and approached cautiously. The outlaws' campsite was nearly ideal from the standpoint of defense—a wooded knoll surrounded by deep ravines. The outlaws spotted the lawmen before they could get close enough for a good shot. There were three at the campsite: brothers Will and Sam Martin and Clarence Simmons. Sam Martin and Simmons immediately opened fire, while Will ran for the horses. Will was hit first; the initial bullet slowed him down and the second killed him. Sam Martin was next, taking hits in the right shoulder and the left wrist. Thinking Sam was finished, deputy Haines rushed him, only to take a bullet himself in the shoulder. In the confusion Simmons escape. The entire battle took less than a minute. By best count, twenty-seven shots were fired.

Haines began to bleed badly and was rushed to the nearest town where he remained in critical condition for several days. Sam Martin was given prompt medical attention but soon joined his brother in death.

Some say the battle at Wooster's Mound was the turning point for outlawry in Osage country. It is believed the publicity given the incident helped persuade other criminals that they could no longer operate safely in the area.

## Youngers' Bend
### Haskell County

South of Porum, near where the South Canadian River makes a sweeping curve between Briartown and Whitefield, lies history-rich Youngers' Bend, frontier home of Sam and Belle Starr. Although stories of Belle's escapades as a "Bandit Queen" were largely fiction, the Starr property, nestled in picturesque lowlands nearly inaccesible most of the year except through a narrow canyon leading to the uplands off the old Briartown-Eufaula Trail, was an outlaw's dream of a hiding place. The Starrs' rough cedar log cabin stood on a rocky knoll within fifty feet of a thick woods and commanded a full view of a wide meadow, where a visitor could be sized up easily coming in off the canyon trail. If intruders did approach, one could quickly slip from the cabin to the woods and head for the river, where along the south bank (reached by a boat provided by the Starrs) a network of crags and crevices offered concealment from the most persistant of pursuers.

Belle Starr's grave at Younger's Bend. *Charles C. Goodhall Collection.*

The Starrs settled on the place in the early 1880s, partly because of its isolation and, according to some old-timers in the area, partly because of a rumor that the Cherokee Indian who occupied the cabin previously had buried $10,000 on the premises. (Nobody knows whether the money, if there, was ever found.)

Tales abound about the Starrs' wild and criminal ways while at Youngers' Bend. Most of the stories are without basis. In 1882 Sam and Belle were convicted of stealing a horse in Indian Territory, and both served nine months in the federal house of correction at Detroit, Michigan. On their return, Sam did apparently engage in several burglaries, and in 1885 Belle was again charged with stealing a horse. However, she found plenty of witnesses to testify she was elsewhere at the time and was acquitted. It is believed that other outlaws did visit the Starrs on occasion, including Jesse James.

In December 1886 Sam Starr was killed at a dance at a neighbor's home on Emachaya Creek near Whitefield, the result of a shootout with an Indian Territory policeman named Frank West. He was buried in the Starr family cemetery southwest of Briartown. Following Sam's death, Belle was faced with losing her land because she was not Indian. She solved this problem by taking up with Bill July (alias Jim July Starr) who was part Cherokee. They lived together as man and wife, which satisfied both tribal and federal laws as they applied to property rights.

Belle lived peacefully on the river until February 1889 when she was mysteriously killed by a blast from a shotgun while visiting a neighbor. A tenant of Belle's, Edgar Watson, was charged with the crime but was released after a grand jury failed to find sufficient evidence against him. Belle was buried near her cabin. Vandals began to work on the site shortly thereafter, and on March 20, 1890, a newspaper account reported that the grave had been disturbed, apparently in an attempt to recover jewelry and an expensive pistol that were buried with the body. Soon after, Belle's daughter, Pearl, had her mother's resting place walled up with stone and concrete and hired a stonecutter to carve an elaborate marble tombstone.

## Yukon
### Canadian County

Today Yukon is a modern community of 17,000 on the western edge of Oklahoma City. In 1894 it was a sleepy, out-of-the-way hamlet that enjoyed, for the most part, a quiet existence. But not so on May 21 of that year—the day the Casey boys came to town. Twelve days earlier a Rock Island express had been held up at Pond Creek.* Rumor had it that several outlaws were now in the vicinity of Yukon and were plotting to rescue a suspect who had been arrested in connection with the robbery.

Around noon on the 21st the sheriff at nearby El Reno wired deputy Sam Farris at Yukon that the men were thought to be heading his way. The men, later identified as James and Vic Casey from near Arapaho, reached the town about 3:00 in the afternoon. Deputy Farris informed them that he had a telegram ordering him to arrest them. The men seemed peaceful enough and agreed to accompany the deputy to the jail, but after a few steps, Vic Casey whipped out his pistol and fired, hitting Farris in the groin. Although staggered, Farris drew his weapon and returned the fire, striking Casey in the foot. Both Caseys then ran. Farris, his eyes clouding with pain, emptied his gun at the fleeing outlaws but failed to hit them. The deputy's brother Joe Farris was standing nearby and tackled James Casey around the waist. Other townsmen came to help, and the outlaw was quickly subdued. Seeing his brother in trouble, Vic Casey returned and began firing, striking an old man named Snyder in the head. The townsmen, unarmed and unaccustomed to gunbattles, ran for cover, allowing Vic to hobble back to his horse and escape.

Sam Farris died, and Vic Casey was later captured and charged with his murder, but before he could be tried, the wound in his foot developed gangrene and he too died.

OREGON
1886
SCALE OF MILES
Population ........................ 174,768
Area, square Miles .............. 94,560
PACIFIC OCEAN

Oregon 1886

# OREGON

## Astoria
### Clatsop County

Probably the roughest town in frontier Oregon was Astoria, a fishing village in the northwestern corner of the state at the mouth of the Columbia River. In 1877 the town could boast of forty saloons and a generous assortment of gambling dens and bawdy houses. It was the fisherman's version of the rowdy mining camp, a good place to trade a week's wages for a night of entertainment then lose your life in a dark alley. Drifters in for a good time headed for the "swill" district, or "Swilltown" as it was called then.

The well-known renegades seldom ventured as far north as the Columbia, but local hard cases kept Astoria's reputable citizens off Swilltown's boardwalks after sundown. As was the case in so many western communities, the outlaw element got out of hand, and honest merchants and residents resorted to vigilante tactics. Most of the toughs were driven out in the 1880s, but the town had built a reputation for lawlessness which clung to it long after it had cleaned out its undesirables.

Astoria, Oregon. *Oregon Historical Society.*

# Kamela
## Union County

Kamela is a tiny town in northeastern Oregon just off Interstate 84 about thirty miles southeast of Pendleton. On June 14, 1914, a few miles west of the town, three Wyoming outlaws tried to pull off what they hoped was to be the "last great train robbery in the West." The robbers—Charley Manning, Al Meadors and Clarence Stoner—had information that the fast mail train out of La Grande carried a valuable shipment in its express car. Carrying a suitcase loaded with dynamite, the three boarded at Kamela as passengers. Once underway, they drew their guns and worked their way forward, marching the conductor, two porters, and a brakeman ahead of them. When they reached the spot they wanted, they pulled the emergency cord and stopped the train.

At this point things began to go wrong. The express messenger offered no resistance, and when they entered they discovered why: the car carried no treasure, only a small amount of cash. Because of a printer's error on the timetables, the locomotive carried the wrong train number. The bandits had stopped the wrong train. In the meantime, back in the second coach, a deputy sheriff, George McDuffie, was on his way home to Heppner, Oregon. When the train stopped he suspected trouble and came forward. One of the bandits spotted him and fired. The bullet struck the deputy just above the heart but was deflected by the contents of his breast pocket—a comb, deck of cards, and a metal pencil holder. McDuffie returned the fire and killed Charley Manning instantly with two bullets in the heart and one in the head. The remaining two outlaws fled into the brush.

A posse was formed immediately but lost the bandits' tracks. Ten days later, however, Meador and Stone were picked up seventeen miles west, walking along the tracks near Hilgard Station. Under questioning, Stoner, who was just a youth, broke down and confessed.

# Portland
## Multnomah County

Except for an occasional train robbery, northwestern Oregon was never "outlaw country" in the tradition of the Old West. The city of Portland had its criminal element, but mainly it was confined to the North End, where the police "walked in pairs as a precaution against the husky loggers and sailors out to celebrate after months in the wilds or at sea." The respectable citizens tried to pretend the district did not exist, but near the turn of the century the "slime overflowed" as one observor put it, and a local newspaper, the *West Shore*, launched a cleanup campaign. The Portland police force received the brunt of the attack for ignoring the problem and letting it get out of hand. Reform was attempted with few results, except that some cribs and sporting houses were closed which merely turned the "daughters of Aphrodite" out on the street to pursue the loggers and sailors who formerly came to them.

Bill Miner. *Charles Goodhall Collection.*

Among the occasional train holdups in the area, probably the best remembered is the one by "Old Bill" Miner and his bunch on September 23, 1903. Miner, who has become something of a folk hero following a 1983 Canadian movie about his life (*The Gray Fox*), stopped the Great Northern's Oregon and Washington Train No. 6 just east of Portland. In traditional fashion two of the gang had boarded earlier, near Troutdale, and about 9:30 P.M. crept over the tender and shoved guns into the backs of the engineer, Ollie L. Barrett, and the fireman, H. F. Stevenson. The train was halted at Mile Post 21, where two more gang members appeared carrying eighteen-foot willow poles with sticks of dynamite attached. But after blasting the express car door, the would-be robbers encountered three tough customers in the car—express messenger F. A. Korner and two mail clerks named Tipton and Kelley. No sooner than the door was blown, Korner leaped into the opening with his Winchester blazing. His first shot caught bandit Jim Connors in the chest, but the bullet went through his body and struck Barrett, the engineer, in the shoulder.

While Bill Miner was a veteran robber, he disliked gunplay and called his men off when he saw Korner barricade himself inside the darkened car with an obvious intent to make a stand. As the outlaws retreated, Korner once again rushed to the door and picked off another bandit, Charlie Hoehn. Hoehn went down but, with Miner's help, struggled to his feet and kept going. He eventually weakened, however, and his companions had to leave him behind. A posse found him the next day. Miner and the fourth bandit, believed to be a man named Harsham, split up, and Miner headed north into Washington.

Of the outlaws who did frequent Portland shortly after the turn of the century, the most famous was Harry Tracy, the scourge of the Northwest. Many variations of the Tracy story have been written, and he probably has been credited with many more crimes than he ever committed. However, it is generally agreed that he and a partner, Dave Merrill, invaded Portland in 1900 or 1901, donned gaudy Halloween masks, and engaged in a series of daring holdups of banks, stores, and post offices. Evidently Tracy was content to call Portland home and even took out a marriage license, settling down with Merrill's sister Rose in a small cottage on the banks of the Willamette River. But apparently Tracy's choice of a partner in crime was a bad one. It seems Merrill suffered from a loose tongue when drinking, and before long he left a string of clues to the identity of the "False Face Bandits." On being captured, Merrill reportedly made a deal with the authorities to lure Tracy into a trap in return for a light sentence. Both were convicted and sentenced to the Oregon State Penitentiary at Salem, where on June 2, 1902, they made a daring escape that is still talked about throughout the Northwest (see *Salem*).

# Prineville
## Crook County

Prineville is in the center of the state, on US 26 at the western edge of the Ochoco National Forest. About thirty miles northeast of the town, somewhere above the old Mill Creek Road where it winds past a towering 350-foot rock formation called Stein's Pillar, may lie buried a fortune in outlaw loot.

In the 1860s the area that is now Ochoco National Forest was a rich mining region and as such attracted the usual ornery element that eventually infests gold country. On a Saturday night in 1863, six of the area's hard cases rode into a rich placer field called Whiskey Gulch while the prospectors were cleaning their sluice boxes and robbed them of all the gold in sight. Flushed with success, the gang headed east toward Dayville, where they added to their loot by burglarizing the town bank. From Dayville they worked their way back west in the general direction of the rugged mountain area above Prineville. A posse from Dayville tracked them relentlessly, but got no closer than a cold campsite, and finally gave up.

In the weeks that followed the local authorities listened for word of somebody in the surrounding area spending unusually large amounts of money, but nothing turned up, and eventually the robberies were forgotten.

Almost fifty years went by before thoughts again returned to the six outlaws and their weekend spree. The year was 1911. A prospector riding through the virgin

Prineville, Oregon. *Oregon Historical Society.*

ponderosa pine above Prineville, near the summit of the Ochoco Mountains about ten miles north of Stein's Pillar, suddenly came upon a strange sight in a tiny glade: an ancient log lying on the ground with six evenly-spaced notches cut in it. Tied around the log at each notch was a halter chain. Below each notch lay the skeleton of a horse. Amid the skeletons were the rotting remains of expensive saddles, bridles, and halters. The six horses had been tied to the log with their saddles and tack still on. Left to die, the animals apparently had chewed the notches in the wood in a desperate attempt to satisfy their hunger and thirst.

Who would have abandoned six valuable horses, saddles, and tack in the wilderness? Finally, someone remembered the six outlaws. One theory offered was that the men had a change of horses waiting for them so they could not be identified by the animals they rode during the robberies. Another theory was that the outlaws tied up their horses fully intending to return, but the posse had come closer than expected, and the outlaws had to flee on foot, possibly to become lost. Also, they may have left the horses tied while they carried their loot deeper into the wilderness to bury it, then became lost, or perhaps argued and ended up killing one another.

The chance that gold might be buried nearby has, over the years, drawn many treasure-seekers to the site. If you visited there today you would see many holes dug around the log and beyond the glade into the woods, but as far as anyone knows, the gold, if it is there, has never been found.

## Salem
### Marion County

Salem is on Interstate 5 about fifty miles south of Portland. On June 2, 1902, at the Oregon State Penitentiary at Salem, outlaws Harry Tracy and Dave Merrill engaged in one of the most spectacular prison breaks in the history of the West.

The break occurred about 7:00 A.M. as the guards were checking off the prisoners shuffling from the chapel to the prison foundry to begin the workday. Tracy, a steely-nerved killer known also as an escape artist, suddenly leaped toward a packing crate marked with an "X" in chalk. He quickly withdrew two short-barreled rifles, apparently smuggled in by another convict who had recently been paroled, and tossed one to Merrill. Two guards were covering the prisoners. Tracy killed one with a single shot. The other dashed into an adjoining room. As Tracy started after him, a fellow inmate, Tom Ingraham, tried to stop him, and Tracy put a bullet into his belly.

The pair had also hidden a ladder behind a stack of lumber, and they grabbed it and dashed for the wall. A guard in the northwest tower, S. R. Jones, fired several shots at the fleeing convicts, but in doing so he leaned far out, exposing himself to their fire. Tracy's second shot knocked him out of the tower. The other guards could not get clear shots, and the two inmates threw the ladder against the wall and scrambled over the top. As they hit the ground on the outside, Tracy spotted another guard, B. F. Tiffany, on the wall just above them. One shot brought him down, on the outside, nearly at their feet. Using Tiffany as a shield, they dragged him a hundred yards into a heavy stand of fir trees. Seeing he was dying and too weak to be of further help to them, Tracy put a bullet into his brain.

Beyond the fir trees, Tracy and Merrill climbed into a culvert and stretched out in about a foot of water, which apparently kept the guards' bloodhounds from picking up their scent. After dark they sneaked into Salem, forced their way into a house, and changed clothes. Working their way in a zig-zag pattern, they headed north toward the state line, where eventually they would part company at Napavine, Washington.*

## Siskiyou Station
### Jackson County

Siskiyou Station consisted of a cluster of mountain railroad shacks at the Siskiyou summit, just north of where the Southern Pacific tracks crossed the California line. On October 11, 1923, three brothers, Roy, Ray, and Hugh D'Autremont slipped aboard the S.P.'s San Francisco-bound No. 13 during a momentary halt at the summit for a routine air break check. In minutes they had scrambled forward across the tender to the locomotive cab, where they pressed a gun against the head of the engineer, Sid Bates. The train was just entering a tunnel, and the bandits' orders were to pull to a halt when the locomotive reached the other end.

Roy D'Autremont stayed with the engineer and fireman while Ray and Hugh dropped to the ground and headed back to the mail car. When the mail clerk refused to open up, Ray placed dynamite against the car door and pushed the plunger. Overeager, he used too much explosive, and the entire front of the cab blew apart, killing the clerk instantly. The explosion brought the brakeman, Coyle Johnson, from the rear of the train, and one of the bandits ordered him to uncouple the mail car from the rest of the train. When he was finished, the bandit ordered him to go forward and tell the engineer to pull ahead. But when he did, he startled the other two bandits who were up front, and they shot him dead.

About this time the would-be robbers heard the whistle of the second section of the train coming from the rear. Realizing they did not have enough time to search the ruins of the mail car, they brutally shot the engineer and fireman to keep them from identifying them and disappeared in the wilderness.

Although the robbery itself was a failure, the D'Autremonts had planned their escape carefully, even to the point of sprinkling pepper along their trail to confound the sheriff's bloodhounds. Weeks before they had hollowed out a shallow hideout cave deep in the timber country and stashed away camping gear and provisions. For three weeks they hid in these damp quarters while posses scoured the area and search planes droned overhead. But the D'Autremonts had made a very serious blunder. The brothers had left a pair of overalls, several knapsacks, and other items, including a gun, at the scene of the crime. In one of the pockets of the overalls was a postal money order receipt. The receipt number was traced to Eugene, Oregon, where the records showed the money order had been purchased by one Ray D'Autremont. A quick investigation disclosed that Ray, along with his two brothers, had gone on a "hunting trip." When the knapsacks were identified by a Eugene merchant as having been purchased by Hugh D'Autremont, the authorities knew they had the right men.

But the manhunt would continue for over three years. Hugh D'Autremont was eventually discovered in the Phillipines, serving as a private in the United States Army. Several of his buddies had become suspicious when he seemed to know so much about the crime, much more than had been reported in the newspapers. Soon after, Ray and Roy were found living under assumed names in Steubenville, Ohio. All three pleaded guilty and were given life sentences at the Oregon State Penitentiary.

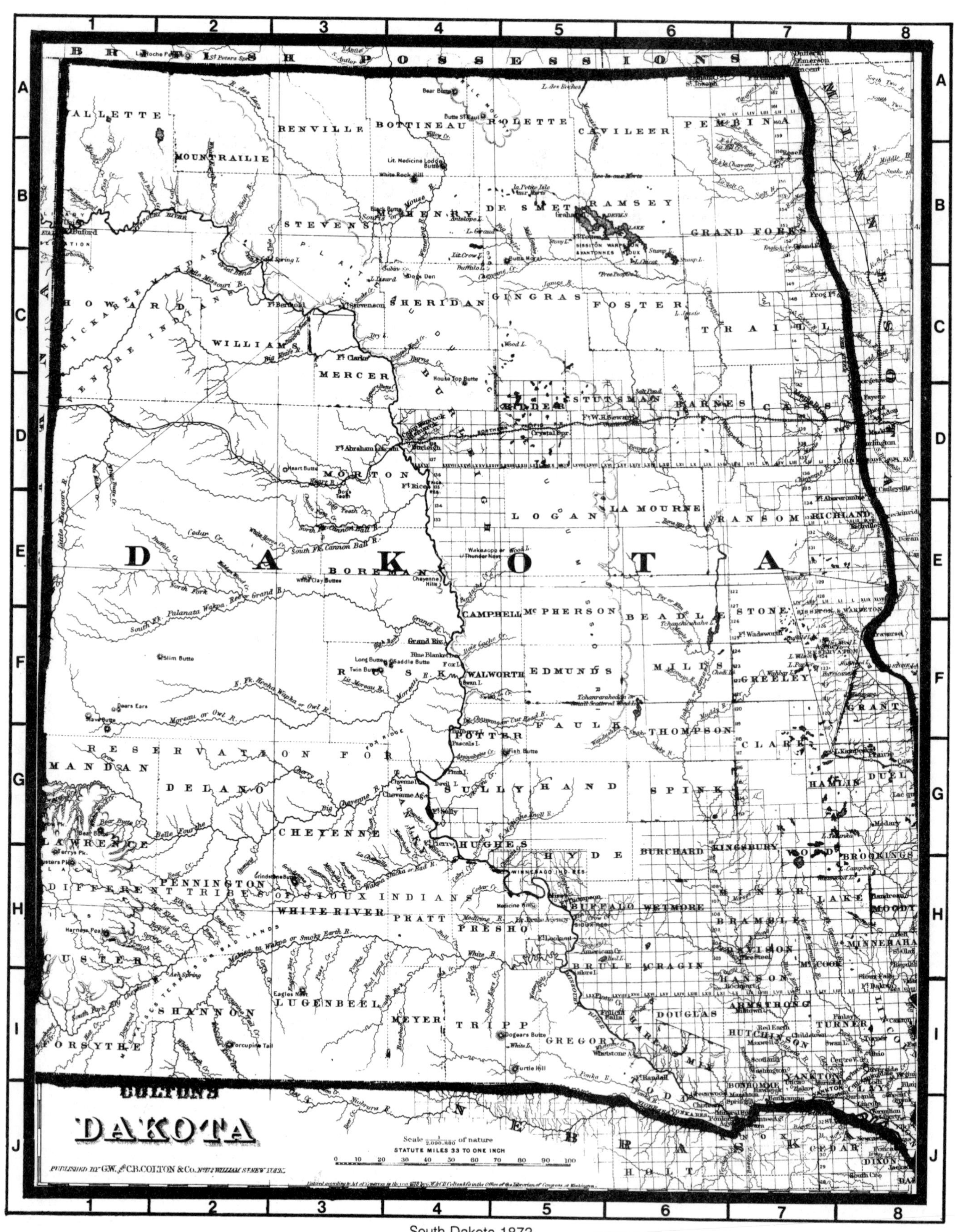

South Dakota 1873

# SOUTH DAKOTA

## The Badlands
### Pennington and Shannon Counties

Many areas of the West have been called "badlands." Most are regions that have been worn into steep buttes and deep gullies by wind, rain, and floods. The best known area is east of South Dakota's Black Hills, the 244,000-acre Badlands National Park, a labyrinth of ravines, ridges, buttes, domes, spires, pyramids, and knobs of a thousand colors. Many people mistakenly believe the region got its name from the danger it presented from outlaws bent on waylaying travelers. Actually, the area was avoided during Dakota's frontier days, mainly because it was unsuitable for farming or grazing, difficult to cross, and inhabited by less then friendly Indians. The region was not near a main route in and out of the gold-rich Black Hills, and it received little attention until western South Dakota became a tourist area. But if the Badlands did not play a role in outlaw history, it should have. Its picturesque buttes and spires are straight out of a Hollywood western of the 1960s.

If heading to the Black Hills from the east (Interstate 90), set aside at least an afternoon to wind through the park.

## Belle Fourche
### Butte County

"Belle Fourche" means "beautiful forks" in French. While the name has a gentle ring to it, the town of Belle Fourche was far from gentle in the early days. It is said that in September 1895 the entire community was nearly destroyed when feuding outlaws set it on fire. The town, which is much tamer today, is located at the western edge of the state, just north of the Black Hills at the junction of US 85 and US 212. In outlaw history it is best remembered for the famous Belle Fourche bank robbery of 1897.

The assault on the Butte County Bank on June 28 of that year showed that the major members of Wyoming's Wild Bunch had yet to perfect the fine art of bank robbery. Their first mistake was to send in gang member Tom O'Day to scout the town. Tom was known to take a nip now and then, and when he finally dragged himself back to camp, it was too late to stage the robbery, and it had to be rescheduled for the next day. The gang's second mistake occurred once they were in the bank. They ordered the customers to hold up their hands in plain view of the street, and Alanson Giles, who owned the hardware store across from the bank, saw something was wrong and spread the alarm. The robbers had to cut short their visit and thus missed $30,000 that was tucked away in the safe.

Western writers have never been sure just who among the Wild Bunch members were in on the raid. Ed Kirby, biographer of Harry Longabaugh (the Sundance Kid), seems fairly certain they were Longabaugh, Tom O'Day, Harvey Logan (Kid Curry), Lonie Logan, "Flat Nose" George Currie, and Walt Punteney. According to Kirby, Longabaugh, Harvey Logan, and Currie entered the bank while O'Day was assigned to hold the horses, and Lonie Logan and Punteney were stationed down the street with instructions to create a diversion if their comrades ran into trouble. This Logan and Punteney had to do when one of the robbers in the bank, believed to be Currie, fired a hurried shot through the window at Alanson Giles as he ran to give the alarm.

Five of the six outlaws made clean getaways. The unlucky one was Tom O'Day. Apparently again well-lubricated, Tom had trouble climbing into his saddle, and his horse finally bolted and ran. Tom then slipped into the crowd that had begun to gather on the street outside the bank. Hurrying west along the sidewalk, he crossed a vacant lot and ducked into a privy behind a saloon. Rusaw Bowman, a local butcher, saw him enter and waited outside with his gun drawn. When Tom finally emerged, he was arrested and tossed in jail.

The following September Harvey Logan, Walt Punteney, and another man were arrested near Lavina, Montana,* and charged with the robbery. They were returned to South Dakota and housed in the jail at Deadwood* but escaped on October 31.

## Black Hills

During the gold rush days in the Black Hills, the stages between Cheyenne and Deadwood carried millions of dollars in ore and other treasure. But the Cheyenne and Black Hills Stage Company had hardly begun operations when bandits began springing out of the shadows. When, in an early attack, two Wyoming mail carriers were found killed and scalped, Indians were blamed, but then it was discovered that only registered mail had been taken.

Deadwood residents received their warning of things to come on March 26, 1877, when stage driver Johnny Slaughter, son of city marshal J. N. Slaughter, was killed in an attempted holdup about two miles south of town—probably the work of the Sam Bass–Joel Collins gang. Four days later two robbers stripped another traveler, Edward Moran of Cheyenne, of $260 in gold dust, a watch, and some cash and left him tied to a tree about two miles south of the site of the Slaughter killing.

Foul weather during April and May 1877 temporarily discouraged further robberies. At times the trails became impassable, halting nearly all traffic in and out of the Hills, but when the weather improved, the outlaws returned. On June 1, a little over eight miles north of Hat Creek Station, a southbound stage was stopped by a horseman standing in the middle of the road. As the stage pulled to a halt, two more bandits leaped out of the underbrush, but this time the passengers were traveling well-armed. They began shooting and the attackers fled. Orders immediately went out to put two armed guards on every stage carrying a strongbox, but it did not seem to help. Two weeks later, on June 14, two outlaws with blackened faces easily took a strongbox from a stage in a narrow ravine about twenty-five miles north of Hat Creek Station.

On June 26 a southbound coach was stopped by five masked men about ten miles north of the Cheyenne River. There was a quick exchange of gunfire, and the driver, a man named Hawley, was shot in the side. The outlaws then emptied the pockets of the passengers (getting about $400 in cash and three gold watches) and took an undetermined amount from the strongbox. Several months later, Robert "Reddy" McKemma, a former Sam Bass gang member, confessed to the shooting. According to McKemma the other bandits were Bill Bevans (also called Blivans), Clark Pelton (alias Billy Webster),

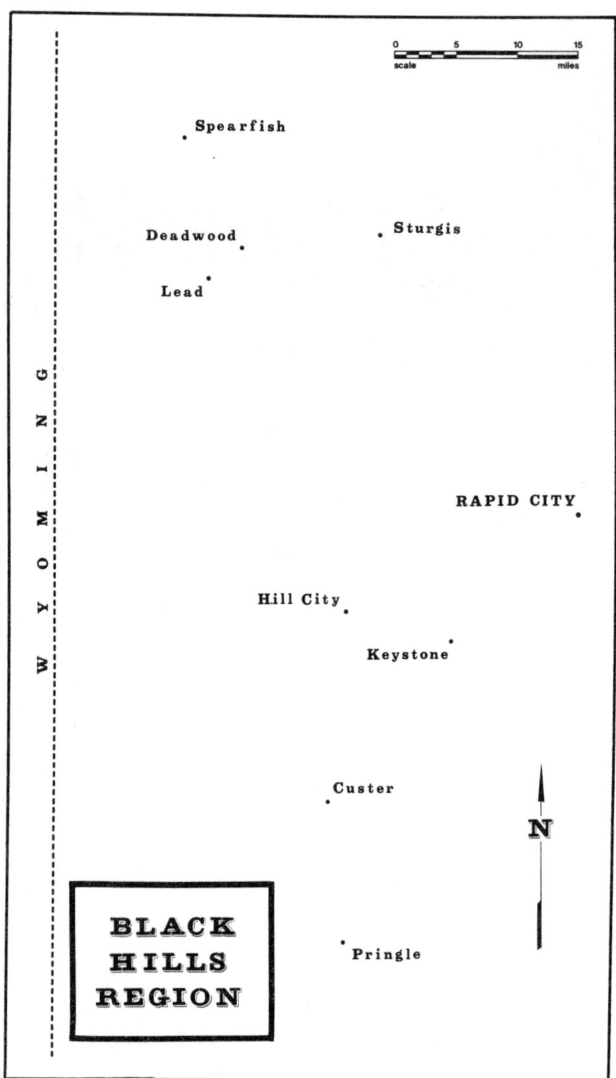


Dunc Blackburn, and James Wall. The same gang was also blamed for robberies on June 25 and 27.

Robberies were so numerous in July that many of the details have been lost to history, the stage line officials being reluctant to release any more information than necessary because it discouraged business. On the night of July 18 the same southbound coach was struck twice near the Cheyenne River. A few miles away the northbound was hit. Following these robberies, gold shipments were discontinued pending the installation of a new strongbox called the "Salamander." This new box, steel-lined and heavy, was equipped with a combination lock which the manufacturer claimed could not be opened by bandits in "less than six days." The box was put into use on August 24, 1877, accompanied on some runs by extra armed guards and an occasional cavalry escort. For a while the holdup rate was reduced considerably.

As the Black Hills area prospered, the owners of the Cheyenne and Black Hills Stage Company invested in

Hat Creek Station, Black Hills. *American Heritage Center, University of Wyoming.*

a "treasure coach," a special Concord lined with 5/16-inch steel plates capable of withstanding rifle bullets fired as close as fifty feet. Two port holes in the doors allowed guards to fire from the inside. Nicknamed the "Monitor," this battle wagon went into service in May 1878. A second model was put on the line the following September. While the Monitors could always be stopped by shooting the horses, armed guards with a generous supply of ammunition were expected to hold off would-be robbers for quite a while. But on September 26, one of the Monitors proved to be of questionable value at Canyon Springs Station. When the coach pulled in, robbers had already taken command of the station, and they quickly disposed of the outside guard on the stage with a rifle bullet through the chest. A shot from above then stunned an inside guard, Gene Smith. (The top of the coach was not armor-plated.) The other inside guard, Scott Davis, found he could not get a clear shot at the attackers through the port holes, and he abandoned the coach and ran for help. Meanwhile, the outlaws were able to smash open the Salamander strongbox in two hours and they escaped with $27,000.

The defeat of the Monitor so angered the commercial interests in the Black Hills area that vigilante groups began to spring up. These were soon joined unofficially by peace officers, and an all-out effort was made to round up every outlaw in sight. A half-dozen felt the rope, and many more were convicted and sent to prison, among them probably the culprits in the Canyon Springs affair. From then on, until the coming of the railroad, the Cheyenne and Black Hills stages rolled virtually unmolested.

# Custer
## Custer County

Custer, at the junction of US 16 and US 385 in the south central section of the Black Hills, was the first town settled after gold was discovered during General George A. Custer's expedition to the Hills in 1874. The town was laid out on the north bank of French Creek, just west of the site of the Custer party's discovery. The settlement began with a population of six, but in a month grew to over 1,000. According to one report, there were over 2,000 tents and 400 wooden buildings by the fourth month.

In the beginning Custer, then called Custer City, was the typical boom town—no law and order and mainly two thoughts on the minds of most of the inhabitants: find gold or find somebody who had gold and take it from him. But the boom soon ended; five months after the town was laid out, stories began to trickle in that richer deposits were being found fifty miles to the north, in Deadwood Gulch. The rush to Deadwood began in March of 1876, and by summer Custer was nearly a ghost town. Several merchants remained, however, as did a few prospectors, and the town did not die.

As the gold fever in the Black Hills leveled off, Custer slowly began to grow again. In 1878 interest in the French Creek region was renewed, and a second boom developed the following year.

Many of the badmen who eventually gave Deadwood its reputation passed through Custer at one time or another, especially before the opening of the stage line out of Sidney, Nebraska, via Rapid City. If many of these hard cases failed to break into the press dispatches while in Custer, it probably was because many of the law-abiding members of the community were just as tough as they were. The feeling in Custer was: "Stranger, maybe you shot some prospector up in Deadwood like they say, but we don't know for sure and we ain't asking—just don't do no shooting down here." And when a troublemaker did not take heed, justice was often swift.

Outlaw Jim Fowler, alias "Fly Specked Billy" (so-called because of a face full of freckles) discovered this fact in January 1881. Fowler started an argument in George Palmer's saloon on Main Street (now the site of the Custer Cafe), and before it was over, he killed another customer. Fowler, who had once ridden with outlaw "Lame Johnny" Donahue, had broken Custer's rule. Despite a valiant effort by Custer County sheriff John T. Code, the outlaw was dragged south of town toward French Creek, where there were several trees with limbs within an easy throw of a rope. The scene the next morning was later described in the Custer County *Chronicle*: "Judge Lynch had executed his inexorable sentence cleverly and secretly, and Fly Specked Billy, with his hands warm with the blood of his inoffending victim, had paid the tortures of an eternity of punishment."

Several nights a week during the summer months the shooting and lynching are reinacted for tourists by Custer thespians.

Deadwood in 1876. *University of South Dakota Museum.*

# Deadwood
## Lawrence County

In outlaw history Deadwood probably is best known as the town where Wild Bill Hickok died. The date was August 2, 1876. Hickok's law enforcement days were about over, possibly because of failing eyesight. He had come to Deadwood to look for gold and to gamble in the town's notorious saloons; also, there was a rumor that he was being considered for the job of town marshal.

The story that Hickok did not like to sit in a public place with his back to a door probably was true, and that afternoon in Carl Mann's Number Ten Saloon he was sitting with his back to the rear door. It is surprising that he would have done this; there is evidence that he knew he had enemies in town, and several persons who had talked to him the previous week recalled that he seemed depressed and may even have had a premonition of death.

Jack McCall entered the Number Ten Saloon by the front door. Hickok may have seen him, but he would have paid little attention; McCall was a nobody. He sauntered down the bar to the rear of the room, well behind Wild Bill. Minutes later a shot rang out. The bullet entered Hickok's head at the base of the brain, just to the right of center, and exited through the right cheek between the upper and lower jaw bones. The old gunman's head jerked forward, and for an instant he sat motionless. Then he toppled backward off his stool. (The saloon had no chairs.) The cards he had been holding lay at his side: two aces, two eights, and a jack (some say a queen).

As he fired, McCall had shouted "Take that!" Then he backed toward the rear door, taunting the crowd with, "Come on ye sons of bitches." Once outside, he grabbed the first horse he saw but slipped off as he tried to mount, apparently because the owner had slackened the cinch. He scrambled to his feet and ran into a nearby butcher shop, where he was found hiding a few minutes later. He gave up without a struggle. When asked why he had shot Hickok, McCall answered that Wild Bill had killed his brother. There has been no evidence found that he ever had a brother. He also talked about an argument with Hickok over cards, but this, too, was ruled out. The real reason was never determined. Although a conspiracy was mentioned, it is possible the assassination was the kind that will forever threaten famous persons—a nobody who kills to become somebody.

Those who lean toward the conspiracy theory point to later statements by a witness, Leander Richardson, who said Hickok had been warned that he was marked for death by a local faction who did not want him taking the marshal's job. Richardson claimed he overheard Hickok say, "Well, these fellows over across the creek have laid it out to kill me, and they are going to do it or they ain't. Anyway, I don't stir out of here, unless I'm carried out." Two days later he was dead.

Hickok was buried in a graveyard called Ingleside, but in two years the town grew to the point where the site became impractical as a burial ground, and in August 1879 his remains were moved to Mount Moriah Cemetery, now a leading tourist attraction. During the summer of 1879 rumors spread that Wild Bill's grave had been robbed. It was reported that he had been buried with his expensive ivory-handled pistols and a fancy knife. The rumors were false. Later evidence suggests that if Hickok was buried with a weapon it was probably an old cavalry carbine. Wild Bill's grave can be visited today at Mount Moriah, high on a hill overlooking downtown Deadwood. The original wooden marker is long gone. In fact, thanks to souvenir hunters, there have been five markers: two of wood and three of stone.

The Hickok killing aside, Deadwood was not the lawless place some writers have suggested. Blood did not flow in the streets from nightly shootings, although during the 1870s the town's violent death rate was well above the national average. Deadwood did have the traditional prostitution and gambling dens, mainly in a row of two-story brick buildings called the "Badlands" which, by the turn of the century, stretched along the west side of Main Street from Wall Street to the north end of the block. Generally, the town's unsavory element kept to itself. Deadwood characters were more colorful than criminal, and while many outlaws rode through the Gulch at one time or another, most of their crimes were committed on the lonely trails that wound through the Black Hills.*

Two outlaws who did spend some time in Deadwood were Sam Bass and Joel Collins. Near the end of 1876 they tried gambling for a while, were only moderately

A Deadwood hanging, 1897. *South Dakota State Historical Society.*

successful, and then in rapid succession invested in a bawdy house, a quartz mine, and a freighting operation. After all of these enterprises turned sour, they crossed paths with a California drifter who claimed to be the Jack Davis who helped commit the first train robbery west of the Rockies (see *Verdi, Nevada*). With Davis's help, they organized a gang and began holding up stages on the Cheyenne and Black Hills line. But by the fall of 1877, heads began turning their way, and they packed up and headed south, toward the Platte River Valley region of Nebraska (see *Big Springs*).

Several members of Wyoming's Wild Bunch spent some time in Deadwood in 1897, courtesy of Lawrence County. Housed in the local jail were Harvey (Kid Curry) Logan, Walt Punteney, Tom O'Day, and an unidentified fourth man, all suspects in the June 1897 robbery of the Butte County Bank at Belle Fourche, South Dakota.* Although Logan and Punteney were known desperadoes, the suspects were allowed out of their cells to roam around in the outer corridor of the jail. On October 31 they overpowered the jailer and his wife and conveniently found horses saddled and ready for them just outside town. Punteney and O'Day were later recaptured near Spearfish. In April 1898 they were tried for the Belle Fourche affair and both were acquitted.

Deadwood remains the most picturesque town in the Black Hills. The frontier flavor has been preserved, and Old West fans will enjoy a walk down Main Street. Museums include the Adams Memorial at Deadwood and Sherman streets and the Western Heritage in the Old Towne Hall on Lee Street. The *Trial of Jack McCall for the Murder of Wild Bill Hickok* is staged in Old Towne Hall six days a week during the summer months.

## Hill City
### Pennington County

Hill City, on US 385 near the center of the Black Hills, is seldom mentioned in the annals of outlaw history, but no fan of the Old West should visit the Black Hills without seeing the historic Hill City depot-museum and taking a ride on the restored 1880 train which runs between Hill City and Custer.

Prior to the arrival of the railroad in the Black Hills, the stage routes were continuously plagued by road agents (see *Black Hills*). The railroad largely replaced the stage lines for commerce, but train robberies never became a problem, and outlawry gradually disappeared from the Hills.

Territorial Capital Building, Yankton. Scene of the trial of Jack McCall, killer of Wild Bill Hickok. *South Dakota State Historical Society.*

The 1880 train has been used often in motion pictures and on television, including several segments of the once popular Gunsmoke series (the two-part episode entitled "The Snow Train.")

## Yankton
### Yankton County

Yankton, in southeastern South Dakota on US 81, was the scene of the trial and execution of Jack McCall, killer of Wild Bill Hickok at Deadwood in August 1876. After being found not guilty by an illegal "miners' court" assembled at Deadwood immediately after the shooting, McCall was officially indicted for the murder at Yankton, the territorial capital, on October 18, 1876. Prior to the trial, McCall suggested a vague defense based on an argument that he had feared for his life; that he believed that Hickok was going to kill him. He claimed that Hickok had killed his brother and, in addition, mentioned something about a dispute over cards. No evidence was uncovered to support any of these claims. Then, the third week in November, after an unsuccessful jailbreak attempt, McCall suddenly announced that he wanted to "turn state's evidence." On November 24 the Cheyenne *Daily Leader* carried a report that a posse had been sent in pursuit of a Deadwood resident named John Varnes who McCall apparently claimed paid him to kill Hickok. Varnes either was never found or cleared himself of the charge. On December 6, 1876, a Yankton jury convicted McCall after deliberating less then four hours. He was hanged on March 1, 1878, and buried in Yankton's Catholic cemetery with the rope still around his neck.

Wild Bill Hickok. *Kansas State Historical Society.*

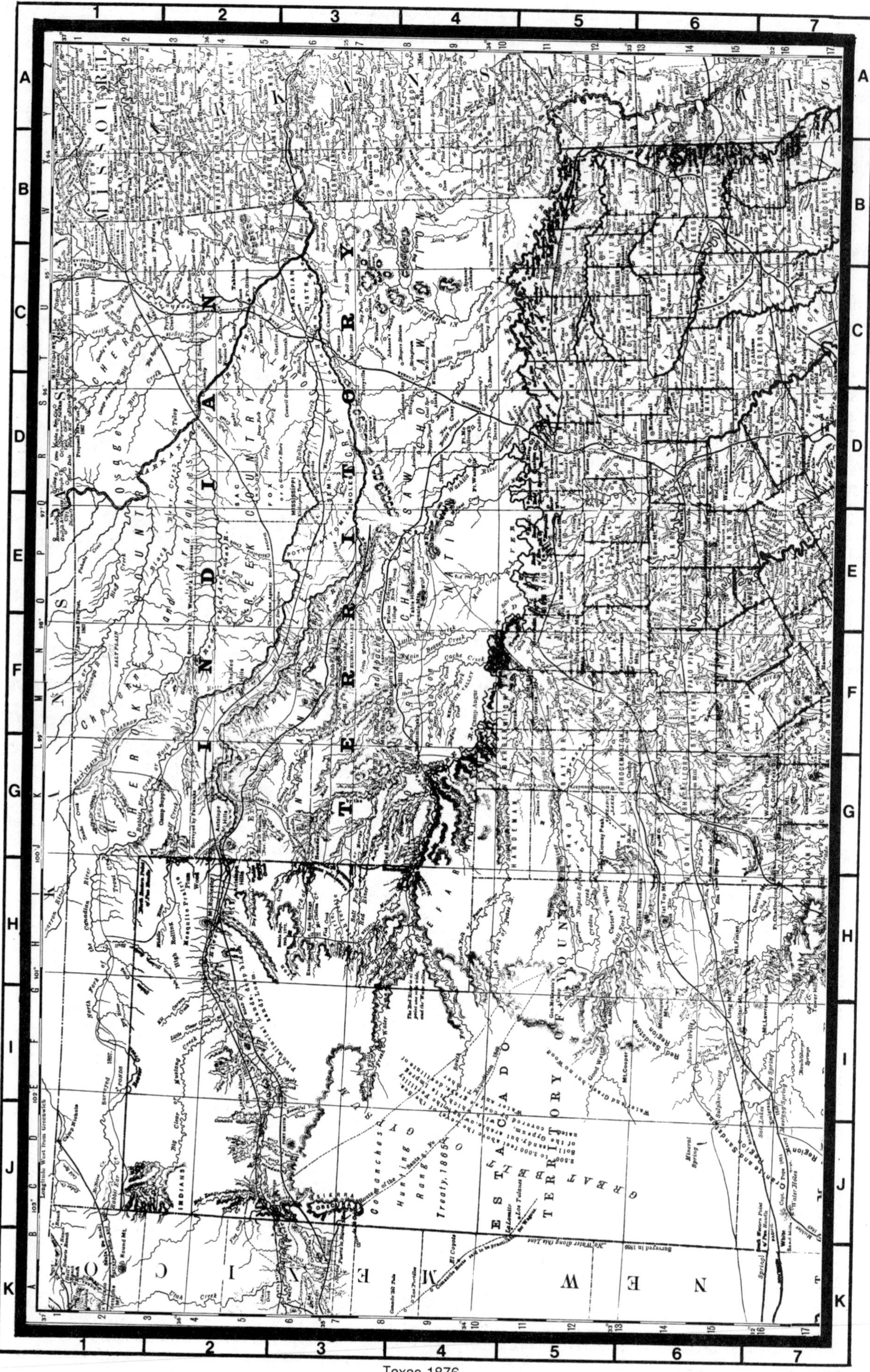

Texas 1876

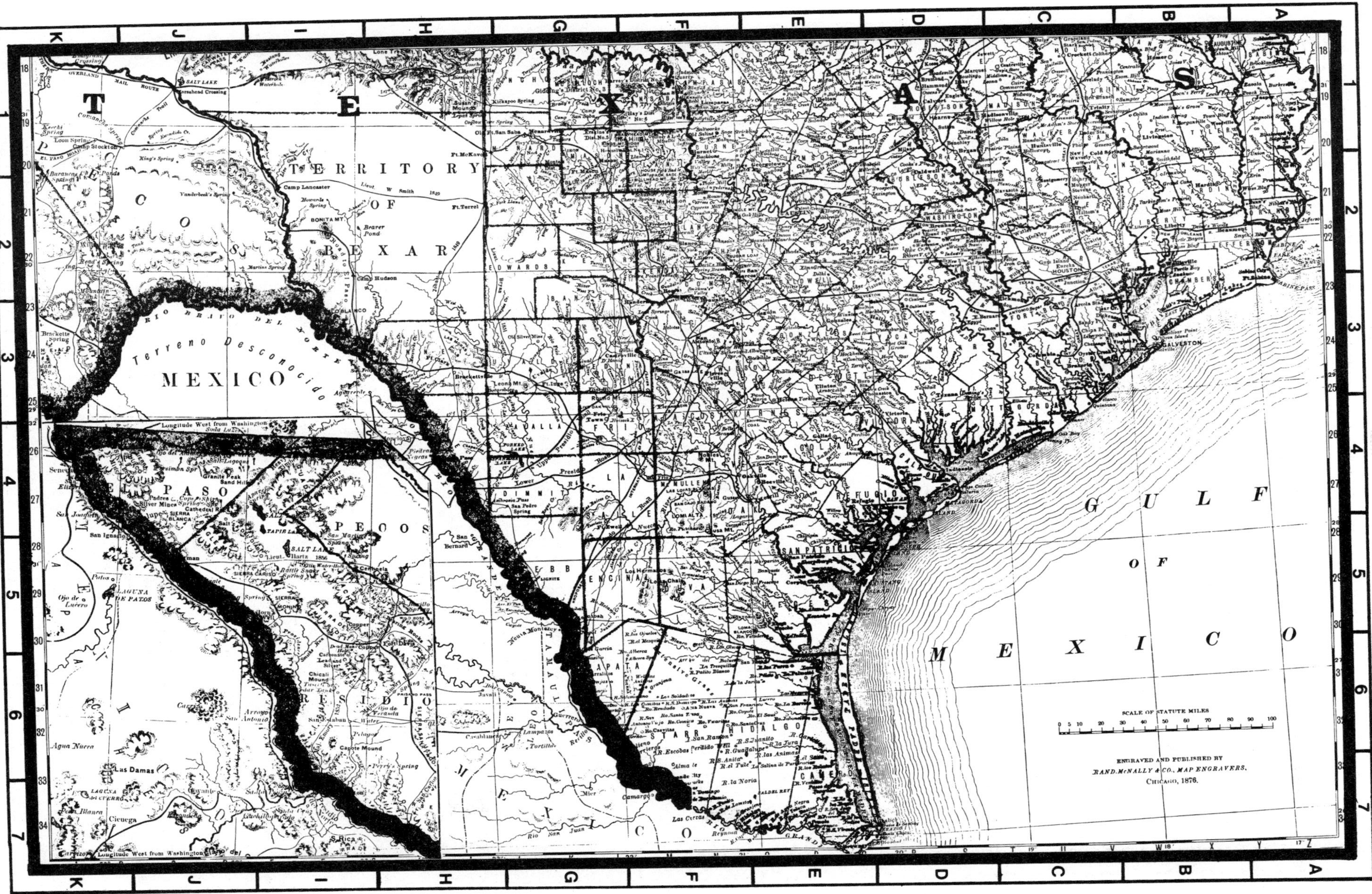
TEXAS
TERRITORY OF BEXAR
MEXICO
Terreno Desconocido
RIO BRAVO DEL NORTE
GULF OF MEXICO
EL PASO
PECOS
PRESIDIO
STARR
HIDALGO
CAMERON
GALVESTON
HOUSTON
SCALE OF STATUTE MILES
0 5 10 20 30 40 50 60 70 80 90 100
ENGRAVED AND PUBLISHED BY
RAND, McNALLY & CO., MAP ENGRAVERS,
CHICAGO, 1876.
Longitude West from Washington

# TEXAS

## Alexander
### Commanche County

Alexander, which is on US 377 about seventy miles southwest of Fort Worth, was the home of train robber William (Bill) Brock, member of the Rube Burrow gang in the 1880s. After a round of successful holdups in Texas, the Burrow gang robbed a Southern Express Company car at Genoa, Arkansas, on December 9, 1887. On making their escape, two of the gang members dropped their raincoats. The coats had handprinted price marks in them, and they were traced to a general store, Sherman & Thalwell's, in Alexander. Pinkerton detectives questioned a salesman, a man named Hearn, who remembered selling one of the coats to a cowboy named Bill Brock and another one to a stranger who was with him.

Brock lived with his in-laws just outside town. On December 31 he was arrested at their home, taken to Texarkana, and identified by the engineer of the Genoa train as one of the robbers. Under further questioning Brock revealed where he had hidden his share of the loot and named his confederates, Rube and Jim Burrow.

## Allen
### Collin County

Allen, which is just north of Dallas on US 75, was the scene of an express car robbery on February 22, 1878, by the notorious Sam Bass. The victim was the Houston and Texas Central Railroad. Bass had been hiding out in nearby Denton County following his holdup on the Union Pacific at Big Springs, Nebraska.* Bored with hideout life, Sam first robbed a couple of stages west of Fort Worth. Then, probably because of slim pickings, he turned to trains again.

Following the pattern set at Big Springs, Bass and four companions overpowered the station agent and another man just before the train was due in. The Texas Express Company messenger, however, a man named James Thomas, showed spunk, and stubbornly exchanged shots with the outlaws until he ran out of cartridges. Resisting the urge to go through the passenger coaches (probably because he had hastily put together an amateur bunch of robbers), Bass settled for the cash in the express safe—about $1,200. This was a measly sum for a bandit who up to that time held the record for the grandest haul ever taken from an express car—the $60,000 in gold coins he had garnered at Big Springs.

## Austin
### Travis County

Austin was gunslinger Ben Thompson's town, although he committed much of his mayhem elsewhere. Like many frontier hard cases, Thompson vacillated between enforcing the law and breaking it. While in Austin in 1868, he shot his brother-in-law and then threatened to kill a justice of the peace, all of which landed him in the state penitentiary for two years. Following his release he was in and out of trouble in several Kansas cowtowns before returning to Austin in the mid-1870s.

Thompson's most famous shootout in Austin occurred on Christmas Day 1876 at the Senate, one of the town's more popular entertainment dens. The fracas began over a game of monte. Ben was drinking heavily and losing, and he eventually picked a fight with the dealer. This brought over the owner, a man named Mark Wilson. Wilson knew of Thompson's reputation, but he was no coward, and he ordered Ben to leave. Thompson, probably realizing he was too drunk to shoot straight, fired one shot at the chandelier and stormed out, promising Wilson that he would be back to settle things.

The next day Ben's friends tried to talk him out of getting even, but he would not listen. "You tell Wilson that at four sharp, I'm entering the front door of the

Ben Thompson. *Texas State Library.*

Senate," was his reply. At four sharp he was there, and Wilson was waiting for him on the landing of the stairs to the second floor—with a shotgun. Wilson raised it and fired but missed. Thompson, however, seldom missed. His first shot struck Wilson in the throat, and three more bullets hit him before he toppled over the banister onto the floor below. Wilson's bartender, a man named Matthews, grabbed a Winchester from behind the bar and snapped off a quick shot, creasing Ben's hip. Thompson whirled, and Matthews ducked down behind the bar. Ben fired through the wood, just above the brass rail. The bullet struck Matthews in the mouth, and the fight was over. Ben handed a startled bystander his gun and told him to go find the marshal. A coroner's jury was convened and ruled that Thompson had shot in self defense. When he was later asked how he had come out alive after two men had the first shot at him, Ben replied that "they both shot too fast."

Despite his earlier brushes with the law, Thompson's reputation as a cool hand with a gun got him elected Austin city marshal in 1881, but he resigned the next year after another fatal shooting in San Antonio. Ben then took up serious drinking, and a final gunfight in San Antonio* in 1884 ended his life.

## Bellevue
### Clay County

This tiny tank town on the Fort Worth and Denver Railroad was the site of the first holdup by Rube Barrow, sometimes called the "king of the train robbers." Burrow and his brother Jim had drifted west from Alabama, developed an appetite for easy money, and decided to emulate the notorious Sam Bass who rode to fame out of nearby Denton County. Accompanied by two cowboys, Nep Thorton and Henderson Bromley, on December 1, 1886, the Burrow brothers held up an eastbound passenger train at the water tank 300 yards west of the depot at Bellevue, which is on US 287 about thirty miles southeast of Wichita Falls. Being rank amateurs, the new bandits bypassed the express car, and instead emptied the pockets of the passengers, which earned them a total of about $300. This meager take probably was due to the robbery being staged in broad daylight; the victims had plenty of warning and probably stashed much of their money and valuables away before the bandits entered the car.

This holdup almost was the Burrow gang's first and last. In a special car at the rear of the train, three soldiers were escorting several prisoners to Fort Worth. Without putting up a fight, the troopers allowed themselves to be relieved of their weapons, which later resulted in stiff disciplinary action and a sound reprimand all the way from Washington and the Secretary of War. This criticism was probably unjustified. It was reported later that the soldiers were ready to gun down the intruders when they were persuaded not to by several lady passengers.

# Benbrook
## Tarrant County

The June 4, 1887, robbery of a Texas and Pacific express near Benbrook, now a Fort Worth suburb on the southwest leg of Interstate 820, is significant in the history of train robberies in that the bandits, the Rube Burrow gang, came up with the ingenious idea of stopping the train so that the express car was just off a high trestle. All cars to the rear of the express were stretched out across the narrow bridge, which discouraged passengers and crewmen from dropping down to the track and coming forward to bother the robbers.

The robbery was handled in smooth fashion. The outlaws forced the engineer to pry off the express car door with a crowbar, and they helped themselves to approximately $2,500 from the safe. As they rode off, a hard rain began to fall, wiping out their tracks.

The operation came off so well the gang decided to repeat it a little over three months later. On September 20 they hit the same train at the same place. Even the same crew was in charge of the train. This time the robbers got $2,725. Other than the slightly bigger haul, the only variation from the earlier holdup occurred upon gaining entry into the express car. The second time the bandits riddled it with bullets to convince the messenger they meant business. Soon after the robbers' departure it even began to rain, just as before, leaving the authorities no trail to follow.

# Blanco
## Blanco County

While crime was hardly novel in central Texas in the 1870s, stagecoach robberies were rare. Therefore, when the S.T. Scott & Company line suffered a daring daylight robbery on April 7, 1874, about two miles east of Blanco (which is on US 281 about fifty miles west of Austin), worried merchants and law enforcement officials saw it as a warning that commerce between San Antonio and Austin might be seriously hampered. Although the bandits took only about $2,500 in cash and four gold watches from the passengers, a beleagured state legislature quickly authorized a $3,000 reward for the apprehension of the guilty parties. And although only one sack of mail was disturbed, postal officials kicked in another $3,000. To this was added $1,000 from the stage line, making a total reward of $7,000 which, as expected, induced a posse to hit the trail.

The chase was short-lived, however; the gang's tracks led east, along what is now Country Road 165, and a few miles out the mail sack was found, but the tracks themselves soon disappeared.

The leader of the gang was later identified as Jim Reed (who also rode under the aliases Bill Jones and Bob Miller), at the time married to Belle Starr. Reed was killed the following August near Paris, Texas.

# Bonham
## Fannin County

Bonham is in northeastern Texas on US 82, about thirty miles east of US 75. The town is the birthplace of the notorious Texas gunslinger John Wesley Hardin. Hardin, the son of a Methodist minister, was born there in 1853. He led a fairly normal life until 1868 when he allegedly killed a neighbor's hired hand who had been bullying him. Afterward, if Hardin's own account is to be believed, he added three soldiers to what would eventually be a long list of victims. (The area was then under the rule of Union troops, and the army apparently came looking for him.) These first three killings all occurred before Hardin turned sixteen years of age.

# Caddo
## Stephens County

In May 1878 on the dusty Palo Pinto Road just east of Caddo, the Sam Bass gang fought a gunbattle with a posse led by Stephens County sheriff Berry Meaders. The Bass outfit had abandoned its favorite hideouts in Denton County (see *Denton*) when the Texas Rangers and local authorities moved in. Fleeing west, they hid for a while in a secluded house on Big Caddo Creek about fifteen miles east of Breckenridge. They gave themselves away, however, when Bass carelessly spent some of the newly minted twenty dollar gold pieces he picked up at Big Springs, Nebraska.*

The shootout near Caddo, which is on US 180 about seventy-five miles west of Fort Worth, apparently resulted in no casualties. About forty shots were fired before the outlaws took refuge in the nearby hills. The posse, reinforced with rangers and volunteers from Palo Pinto County, trailed the gang throughout most of May, finally giving up on the 31st when it was rumored that the renegades had headed north for Indian Territory.

# Canadian
## Hemphill County

Canadian is in the Texas Panhandle on US 60 about twenty-five miles west of the Oklahoma line. On Saturday night, November 24, 1894, as the southbound Panhandle Express arrived at Canadian's Santa Fe depot, all hell broke loose. A gang of outlaws had quietly ridden in from the nearby Wichita Mountains and, in a fusillade of gunfire, lay seige to the express car, which was rumored to be carrying a package containing $25,000 in currency. When the battle erupted, Hemphill County sheriff Tom McGee was not far away, and he rushed to the scene, only to be nearly blown apart by the attackers' rifles. But more help came, and the Wells Fargo guards inside the car, encouraged by the sound of increasing support from the townsmen, kept up a steady stream of gunfire of their own. Eventually the attackers retreated to their horses and called it a day.

When the town was once again quiet, and sheriff McGee had been carried off to the undertaker, somebody suggested inspecting the package that supposedly caused all the excitement. To their astonishment, the Wells Fargo officials found that it contained only a few hundred dollars, neatly placed on top of a stack of blank paper. A local cattleman, George Isaacs, had shipped the package to himself from Kansas City. He was arrested and charged with a plot to defraud the express company. The plan called for the robbers to steal the package in return for a share of the insurance proceeds.

Four suspects were eventually arrested in connection with the robbery and murder. Two were identified as Jim Harbold and Jake McKinzie, believed to be members of the Bill Doolin gang. There was also some mention of Doolin gang member "Red Buck" Waightman being involved.

# Carrizo Springs
## Dimmit County

Carrizo Springs, about seventy-five miles north of Laredo on US 83, was an occasional stomping place for the notorious south Texas rustler-rancher King Fisher (see *Eagle Pass, Texas*).

Fisher had a ranch on Pendencia Creek southwest of Carrizo Springs near the Mexican border. He also had a favorite hideout to the east of town: a cave on the Neuces River "between the old 7D Ranch headquarters and Evans Lake, on the second bank of the river." A local resident, John Leakey, came across the cave in 1913, nearly thirty years after Fisher's death and found supplies stashed away in sealed buckets.

# Comanche
## Comanche County

Comanche, on US 377 about ninety miles southwest of Fort Worth, was the home of Texas gunfighter John Wesley Hardin's parents, James and Mary Elizabeth Hardin. Wes's brother, Joe Hardin, practiced law in Comanche for several years in the early 1870s. In 1874 Wes and two companions, Jim Taylor and Bill Dixon (who was Wes's cousin), got into a gunfight in Comanche with a deputy sheriff named Charles Webb from neighboring Brown County. According to the popular version of the incident, Webb, while attending a day of horse racing, began bragging that he would not leave Comanche without putting the famous gunslinger Wes Hardin in his grave. Before the day was out he had his opportunity. He even got the first shot, wounding Hardin in the side, but Hardin then put a bullet in Webb's head, and as the deputy was falling, Taylor and Dixon finished him off.

The town was filled with Brown County residents who were over for the races, and Wes and his companions barely escaped with their lives. The mob still raged, however, and eventually sought out Joe Hardin and two of Dixon's brothers, Joe and Bud, and lynched them all.

# Cottondale
## Wise County

Cottondale is in southern Wise County, just west of State Highway 51. In 1878 a gunbattle at nearby Salt Creek marked the beginning of the end of the notorious Sam Bass gang. Posses had been chasing the outlaws for nearly a week in and around Denton County (see *Denton*), when the gang suddenly headed west. On Thursday, June 13, a combined force of Texas Rangers and local volunteers surprised the bandits while they were camped in the brush on Salt Creek. Unable to reach their horses, the outlaws tried to escape on foot. One gang member, Arkansas Johnson, was killed. Another, Henry Underwood, eventually reached a horse and rode off. The four remaining bandits, including Bass, hid in a cave until night and slipped away in the darkness.

# Denison
## Grayson County

Denison is north of Dallas on US 75, about five miles below the Oklahoma line. The town was the early proving ground for Texas's famous lawman Lee Hall. As a deputy sheriff, Hall helped keep the lid on Denison as it threatened to run wild in the mid-1870s. Nourished by undesirables arriving almost daily on the newly laid KATY and Houston & Texas Central railroads, the town easily could have rivaled the worst in the the southwest, but thanks in part to Hall, law and order eventually prevailed. Legend has it that Hall was so much trouble for the hard cases of the county that he was the target of assassins' guns. When ambush proved unsuccessful, the local criminal element tried to frame Hall out of law enforcement, but this failed also, and the hard-nosed peace officer established an impressive record rounding up thieves and gunslingers, which eventually earned him an appointment as a lieutenant in the Texas Rangers.

In time, Hall became known as a compassionate peace officer, willing to try persuasion before force, a trait allegedly stemming from remorse over witnessing a terrified young thief commit suicide by downing a bottle of morphine rather then submit to arrest.

Some say Denison should be credited with originating the term "skid row." The town's down-and-outers frequented Skiddy Street, one block south of Main, which was named after Eastern socialite Francis Skiddy, at the time head of the KATY's Land Grant Railway and Trust Company. The nickname stuck, much to the dismay of Skiddy who would have preferred to be remembered in some other way.

# Denton
## Denton County

Denton was the home of outlaw Sam Bass from 1870 to 1876. Bass, an Indian boy who migrated to Texas via Missouri and Mississippi, generally behaved himself while in Denton, at least in the early days. (Denton is north of Dallas on Interstate 35.) At first he worked hard, and for a while enjoyed the reputation of being industrious and frugal. Later, however, he took to gambling, racing horses, and brawling. In 1876 he met up with a Dallas saloonkeeper named Joel Collins, and the two drove a cattle herd north to Nebraska. From there they drifted on to the Dakotas where they embarked on the outlaw trail.

Bass and Collins first tried robbing stages (see *Black Hills, South Dakota*), then pulled off one of the biggest train robberies in history (see *Big Springs, Nebraska*). Bass returned to the Denton area where he hid out in Cove Hollow, a cave-studded canyon wilderness southeast of Rosston in the northwestern tip of Denton County. Later, he roamed the wooded marshes of Hickory Creek, a few miles south of Denton. Although Sam's share of the Big Springs holdup was at least $10,000, he kept in tune that winter and spring of 1877-78 by robbing stages and trains in Denton and surrounding counties.

Bass and a newly-formed gang played hide and seek with posses for much of the spring and summer, engaging in several chases and gunbattles, one of which occurred near Pilot Knob, about six miles southwest of Denton. In that encounter, Denton marshal George W. Smith was seriously wounded. His fellow lawmen sent for help, but Bass intercepted the messenger, cut his bridle to bits, and turned his horse loose. Reinforcements finally arrived, and later in the day there was another running gunfight near Bullard's Mill, several miles to the east. The posse lost the trail that night but caught up with the outlaws the following day at Warner Jackson's farm, about a mile and a half from Bullard's Mill and eight miles south of Denton. The outlaws had made camp and were eating. Three of the gang were wounded in the fight, and one posseman was hit, but no one was

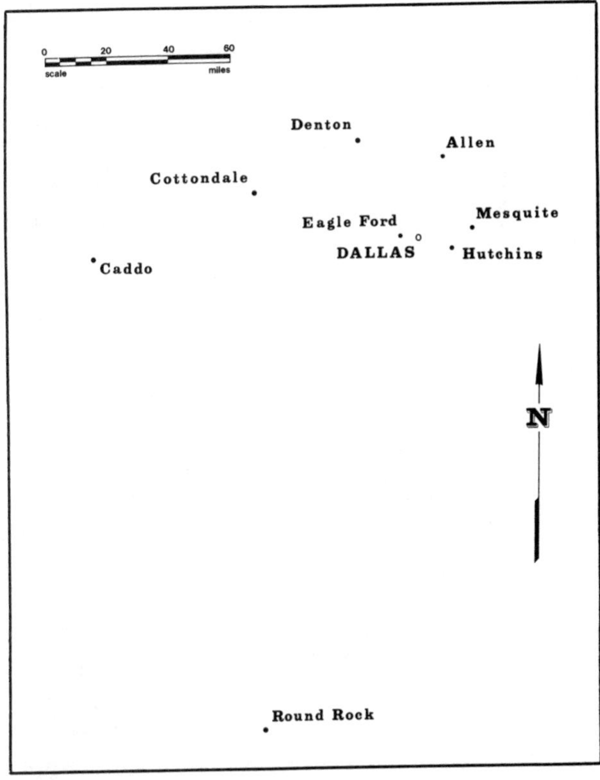


The Sam Bass gang in 1878. **Allen**: Express car robbery at Allen station on February 22. **Caddo**: Gun battle with posse on Palo Pinto Road just east of Caddo in May. **Cottondale**: Gunbattle with Texas Rangers on Salt Creek near Cottondale on June 13; gang member Arkansas Johnson killed. **Denton**: Bass's home town. The gang used the woody marshes and canyons around Denton to play hide and seek with the law throughout the spring and summer of 1878, engaging in several skirmishes with posses. **Eagle Ford**: Express car robbery at Eagle Ford on April 4. **Hutchins**: Express car robbery at Hutchins station on March 18. **Mesquite**: Express car robbery at Mesquite station on April 10. **Round Rock**: End of the trail; Bass and fellow outlaw Seaborn Barnes killed by Texas Rangers on July 19, following tip from gang member Jim Murphy that the gang was to rob Round Rock bank.

hurt seriously. The outlaws fled, outdistanced their pursuers, and finally lost them on the McKinney road, about six miles east of Denton. The gang headed north, and the following day, Monday, they picked up provisions at Bolivar. They were next sighted on Pond Creek in Cooke County, just north of the Denton County line. About thirty shots were fired, but the posse never got close enough to be effective. The bandits disappeared into the swamp on Clear Creek and eluded the lawmen for two more days. They were finally picked up again in neighboring Wise County where they lost one of their number in a shootout on Salt Creek near Cottondale.*

Denton was also the home of Jim Murphy, the "spy" in the Sam Bass gang who arranged for Sam's ambush at Round Rock, Texas,* in July 1878. Murphy had a ranch near Denton before joining the Bass crowd, but after the shootout at Round Rock he moved his family to a house on East McKinney Street in Denton where he felt they would be safer from possible reprisals stemming from the Bass ambush.

Charges against Murphy for robbery were dismissed after Bass' death, and he spent the next few weeks telling his story to a local judge, Thomas E. Hogg, who hastily put out a book on the gang's exploits. Murphy then tried to obtain an appointment as a law enforcement officer, claiming that he was secretly working toward the capture of other train robbers. He was unsuccessful and he became despondent. On June 7, 1879, he died from swallowing atropine in the office of a Denton physician, Ed McMath. The doctor, whose office was on the west side of the town square over Lipscomb's drugstore, had just given Murphy the drug to treat an eye ailment.

## Eagle Ford
### Dallas County

The robbery of a Texas & Pacific express at Eagle Ford on April 4, 1878, was the third in a series of holdups by the Sam Bass gang following his return to Texas the previous winter. The Eagle Ford holdup, about six miles west of downtown Dallas, was unspectacular and gained the outlaws little. Two earlier train robberies in the Dallas-Fort Worth area had put the Texas Express Company on guard, and when possible, it was sending many of its cash shipments by special messengers who rode inconspicuously in the passenger coaches. Bass apparently had not caught on to this trick and did not disturb the passengers.

Regardless of the deception practiced by the express company, it still expected its messengers and express car guards to put up a fight, and when they did not at Eagle Ford, they were both fired.

## Eagle Pass
### Maverick County

Eagle Pass, a border town on the western terminus of US 57, was King Fisher's hangout. Fisher, a rustler-gunman turned rancher, ruled Maverick County and much of the surrounding area in the 1870s and early 1880s. Locals tell of a sign nailed to a tree at a fork on the trail to Fisher's Pendencia Ranch which read: "This is King Fisher's road—take the other one."

Typical of men with power, Fisher dabbled in graciousness and developed a Robin Hood reputation. To this day he remains a hero of sorts to some Eagle Pass citizens. Although as early as 1878 Fisher was boasting that he had killed seven men "not counting Mexicans," he "always behaved like a perfect gentleman" at dances in Eagle Pass and would reimburse town officials for any damage caused by his raucous cronies. But King Fisher could be deadly. A witness told of Fisher's killing four Mexican wranglers he had hired to bring in stray cattle. Apparently the men were unhappy over their pay. King bashed one in the head with a branding iron, whirled and shot a second as he was reaching for his gun, and then picked the final two off a nearby fence before they could scramble to safety. The witness, another Fisher employee, helped his boss bury the dead. Other tales of Fisher's wickedness exist but are poorly documented.

In May 1876 a platoon of Texas Rangers led by Captain L. H. McNelly invaded the Fisher stronghold and captured King and nine of his men. But on arriving at Eagle Pass with his prisoners, McNelly discovered no outstanding warrants on Fisher and nobody willing to swear out a complaint. He turned his prisoners loose and wired his superiors to forget about trying to do anything about Fisher in his home territory. The Rangers persisted, however, and in May 1877 King was indicted for murdering a man named William Dunovan the previous year in the then unorganized county of Zavala. Other indictments followed, and by the end of 1877 there were fifteen in all, ranging from murder to horse stealing. But once again the state found Fisher difficult to put away. Prosecuting attorneys suddenly became unavailable, jurymen failed to show up, and court papers were mysteriously misplaced. After several acquittals, all charges were dismissed.

Ironically, however, Fisher's continuing battles with the law seemed to reform him. In 1882 he bought part interest in an Eagle Pass saloon and the Sunset Livery Stable. Already a strong family man, he "got religion" and presumably gave up his outlaws ways. In 1883 he moved to Uvalde County and became a deputy sheriff (see *Uvalde*).

# El Paso
## El Paso County

El Paso's unruly early years were flavored with colorful city marshals, the most ingenious of which may have been George Campbell, who served a little over a month in late 1880. Although Campbell—a transplanted Kentuckian with some brief experience as a lawman in Young County, Texas—was promised a salary, the city council was slow in providing it, and by the end of December, after thirty days on the job, Campbell concluded that the town fathers were content to let him live on what he could pocket from arrest fees. Thus, he concocted a plan. He got together with a dozen or so of the worst of El Paso's troublemakers, most of whom were his friends, and persuaded them to shoot up the town, to show the officials that he was needed and deserved a respectable salary. On the night of January 1, 1881, an alderman's door was nearly shot off its hinges, and the mayor's house was riddled with bullets. As hoped, the town was seized with fear. But word leaked out that Campbell was behind the riot, and the mayor sent for the Texas Rangers. The Rangers quieted things down, but the two men assigned to arrest the devious town marshal thought the whole affair was hilarious and failed to serve the warrant. The charges against Campbell were eventually dropped, and he was allowed to resign.

Campbell hung around town and continued to stir up trouble. On April 14, 1881, well-fortified with drink, he started an argument with town constable Gus Krempkau on El Paso Street in front of Keating's Saloon. A friend of Campbell's, John Hale, also under the influence, joined in and ended up putting a bullet in Krempkau. Dallas Stoudenmire, who had been appointed city marshal only four days earlier, came rushing out of the Globe Restaurant. Seeing Hale with a smoking revolver, he fired off a quick shot just in time to hit a Mexican who was desperately trying to leave the scene. Stoudenmire's next bullet, however, split Hale's skull. Campbell, suddenly sober, announced that he wanted no part of the fight, but he had drawn his weapon and was waving it about. Krempkau, dying from a bullet in the chest, squeezed off two rounds, striking Campbell in the hand and foot. Stoudenmire, still not sure what the fight was all about, put another bullet in Campbell for good measure.

Dallas Stoudenmire's quick action impressed El Paso citizens, particularly the lawless element who saw him as a threat. A plot was immediately hatched to do away with the new marshal. The man chosen to carry it out was Bill Johnson, an alcoholic former city deputy who had served as interim marshal until Stoudenmire arrived on the scene. Johnson had no love for the man who replaced him and eagerly took on the assignment. But Johnson's attraction to liquor made him a poor assassin. On the night of April 17, 1881, he tried ambushing Stoudenmire from high atop a pile of bricks being used to build the new State National Bank. His hand was shaky and he rushed his shot. Stoudenmire, accompanied by his brother-in-law Doc Cummings, ripped apart the blurry-eyed Johnson with eight bullets, the last one of which removed his testicles. As Johnson lay dying in the brick pile, guns opened up from across the street at Frank Manning's saloon, presumably from members of the element that had put poor Johnson up to the task he could not handle. Stoudenmire, enraged over the cowardly attempt on his life, charged the saloon with pistols blazing. His attackers, unnerved by his daring, broke and ran.

Street in front of El Paso State National Bank where Bill Johnson attempted to kill Dallas Stoudenmire. *El Paso Public Library.*

El Paso's new fighting marshal was not long on the job. He began drinking heavily and in May 1882 was forced to resign. Two months later he secured an appointment as a federal deputy, but his problem with alcohol continued to plague him. Plaguing him worse, however, was his long-standing feud with the four Manning brothers. Stoudenmire was convinced the Mannings were behind Bill Johnson's attempt on his life; furthermore, one of the brothers, Doc Manning, had killed Stoudenmire's brother-in-law Doc Cummings in a gunfight the previous February. Stoudenmire finally forced a showdown with Doc Manning in his brother Frank's saloon on El Paso Street on September 18, 1882. A bystander, J. W. Jones, jumped between the two enemies, hindering Stoudenmire's draw. Manning cleared his holster and, firing over Jones' shoulder, hit Stoudenmire in the arm and chest, knocking him backward. Manning then charged his victim and both tumbled out the door into the street. Stoudenmire finally got off one shot from a pocket pistol, striking Manning in the arm, but as the two wrestled, another Manning brother, Jim, rushed up and put a bullet into the back of Stoudenmire's head.

The streets of El Paso were dangerous enough, but in the early 1890s the town also became sandwiched between two strongholds of rough elements. To the south was the "Island," an international "no-man's land" of tangled river-bottom thicket inhabited by toughs who avoided both Texas and Mexico authorities by disclaiming citizenship of either place. And to the north of town lay a rugged area which served as home and hideout for dozens of rustlers who preyed on neighboring ranches. Their favorite trick was to pluck a small bunch of cows out of a herd and disappear through a gap in the mountains called "Smuggler's Pass," a name still used today. Lawmen usually stayed out of both areas, especially following the death of a federal deputy marshal, Charles H. Fusselman, who trailed a herd of stolen horses into an ambush in 1890. The spot where he fell is still known as Fusselman Canyon. His killer, a ruthless Mexican named Geronimo Parra, was tracked down ten years later by Texas Rangers and was hanged on January 6, 1900, in one of El Paso's more gory incidents. Somehow Parra's friends sneaked daggers into Parra and a companion, and on the day of their execution they whipped them out and carved up a squad of lawmen before they were finally subdued.

A small expedition was sent to the Island stronghold in 1893. Five Texas Rangers, led by Captain Frank Jones, plus El Paso County deputy sheriff Ed Bryant rode into the area on June 29. Like Fusselman, they were ambushed on the trail and Jones was killed. A monument was erected at the site, just west of Clint.

Tillie Howard's Sporting House in downtown El Paso was the scene of the killing of Bass Outlaw by John Selman on April 5, 1894. A former Texas Ranger and at the time a deputy U.S. marshal, Bass Outlaw (that was his real name) was a problem drinker with a short temper. When he was in El Paso, it was rumored that a policeman was assigned to him full-time, just to keep him out of trouble. On that day at Tillie's, Bass was simmering over losing some service of process fees to another deputy. While in the back room with one of Tillie's girls, he fired off his pistol, and Tillie called for help. Town constable John Selman, a former outlaw and gunslinger himself (see *Fort Davis* and *Fort Griffin*), was sitting in the front parlor, and he hurried to the back porch. Joe McKidrict, a Texas Ranger, was also nearby. They found Bass scuffling with Tillie. When McKidrict asked Outlaw why he had fired off his gun, the drunken Bass snarled, "You want some, too?" and he shot the ranger in the head. Selman drew his gun, at the same time leaping off the porch. Outlaw, within arm's reach, fired and missed, but the flash seared Selman's eyes, temporarily blinding him. As he staggered back he fired at the blurry figure he thought was Outlaw. Bass clutched his chest and squeezed off two more shots, striking Selman in the leg. Outlaw died four hours later. Selman would walk with a cane the rest of his life.

The notorious gunslinger John Wesley Hardin migrated to El Paso in the spring of 1895. While in prison he had studied law, and he attempted to build a practice in El Paso, but his clients were slow in coming. He maintained an office in his room on the second floor of the Herndon Lodging House on El Paso Street, but he spent many of his afternoons in the Acme Saloon, where his career mysteriously ended with a gunshot on April 19. On that day John Selman walked up and put a bullet in Hardin's head while he was shooting dice. Hardin was not wanted by the law, and Selman, then fifty-six years of age, had little to gain from the killing. Several reasons have been suggested. One was an argument over the arrest of Hardin's mistress, Helen Buelah Morose, by Selman's son, also a lawman. Another was a rumor that Hardin, Selman, and several others had conspired to kill outlaw Martin Morose (Helen's husband), and Hardin had failed to share money taken from Morose's body. At Selman's trial his defense was that Hardin was about to draw on him. He produced several witnesses who testified accordingly, and the jury was unable to reach a verdict.

John Selman's end came a year later, April 5, 1896, at the hands of a fellow law officer, deputy U.S. marshal George Scarborough. Selman and Scarborough met at the Wigwam Saloon on San Antonio Street. They exchanged a few words, then walked outside to the alley. A shout was heard—something on the order of, "Don't try to kill me like that!" Then there were four shots. Scarborough was found standing over Selman's body. The old constable had slugs in his neck, hip, back, and knee. He died the following day. Scarborough claimed self-defense and was acquitted. It was later rumored that Scarborough was involved in the Morose death and may have shared in some of the money Hardin had reportedly taken. Possibly Selman was attempting to blackmail him.

## Espantosa Lake
### Dimmit County

Espantosa Lake, north of Carrizo Springs and west of the Nueces River, was long associated with violence and death. Most tales are without strong foundation, but the area was an outlaw hangout in the 1870s and possibly earlier. (One explanation for the name "Espantosa," which means "frightful" or "horrible" in Spanish, is that road agents used the lake to dispose of victims after relieving them of their money and valuables.)

In August 1876 a platoon of Texas Rangers surprised a gang of thirty horse thieves hiding out at the lake and killed seven in a bloody hand-to-hand encounter.

# Evant
## Coryell County

It is possible that little Evant, a town of 450 inhabitants at the junction of US 281 and US 84, was the scene of the first murders committed by "Deacon" Jim Miller, the West's most famous professional killer. If the story is true, it was indeed a ghastly beginning to Miller's career as a steely-eyed murderer, because the victims were his own grandparents, and he was only eight years old at the time.

Miller's parents, who lived in Franklin, Texas, died in 1867 when Jim was only a baby, and he was sent to Evant to live with the grandparents. Seven years later, in 1874, the old couple were found murdered in their home. Young Jim was arrested, but because of his age he was never prosecuted. He was taken in by his sister and her husband, John Coop, on their farm at Plum Creek, eight miles northwest of Gatesville (twenty-five miles east of Evans). Jim returned his brother-in-law's kindness by killing him seven years later (see *Gatesville*).

# Fort Davis
## Jeff Davis County

Fort Davis, on State Highway 17 between Interstate 10 and US 90, was the center of operations for outlaw John Selman during 1879-80. Selman, after a bout with smallpox which changed his appearance, posed as a butcher in Fort Davis under the name John Tyson while spearheading an outlaw gang that ranged up and down the West Texas border country. The Texas Rangers were finally called in and uncovered Selman's role in the operation. He was arrested along with his lieutenants. The others were tried locally, but Selman was returned to Shackelford County (see *Fort Griffin*), where he had been indicted earlier for rustling.

# Fort Griffin
## Shackelford County

The remains of old Fort Griffin, established in 1867, and the nearby town of Griffin are now a part of Fort Griffin State Historical Park, located just off US 283 on the Clear Fork of the Brazos in northern Shackelford County. The town developed early as a trouble spot. As long as the military patrolled the area, things were fairly well controlled, but when Shackelford was organized in 1874, the civil authorities could not handle the unruly element that soon swept in. As one observor described it: "a wave of immigration brought in a mob of gamblers, gunmen, bad women, thieves, and crooks of every description. Griffin was headquarters for the long-haired buffalo hunters; the Dodge City cattle trail passed by it; and wild cowboys yipped and yelled in its dozen-odd saloons and honky-tonks every night."

Griffin was the stomping ground of Texas gunfighters John Larn and John Selman. Despite a shady past, which may have included killing a lawman in New Mexico in 1871, Larn was elected sheriff of Shackelford County in 1876. With sidekick Selman he began cleaning up the county, but he used questionable methods, which reportedly included collusion with vigilantes. On December 28, 1878, the Austin *Weekly Statesman* commented: "No wonder the highwaymen are seeking security east of the Colorado. Eleven men were hanged ten days ago at Fort Griffin and four more are enroute to that merciful village."

Larn's disregard for the finer points of the law probably led to his resignation in March 1877. No longer a peace officer, Larn was vulnerable. Local ranchers had suspected him of rustling for years, and in June 1878 his former deputy, Bill Cruger, now sheriff, arrested him at his ranch and took him to jail in nearby Albany. But Larn never saw a courtroom: that night a masked mob stormed his cell and riddled him with rifle bullets. He was buried at his home, the Camp Cooper Ranch, on the Clear Fork of the Brazos, north of town. The ranch is till there—a symmetrical six-room house which once sported a glassed-in cupola on the roof. (Some say the cupola was used as a watch tower to warn Larn of approaching enemies.)

John Selman was also supposed to be arrested that night, but a friendly prostitute from Fort Griffin rode out to warn him. He in turn hurried to Larn's ranch to warn him, but arrived just in time to see the posse taking Larn away. Selman fled Shackelford County for New Mexico, leaving behind his wife who died shortly thereafter carrying their fifth child.

# Gatesville
## Coryell County

The town of Gatesville is on US 84 about thirty-five miles west of Waco. A small farm at Plum Creek, eight miles northwest of Gatesville, was the scene of the second grisly chapter in the early life of hired gun "Deacon" Jim Miller. Young Miller was already labeled a killer, having been arrested for the murder of his grandparents nine years before at nearby Evant.* Too young to prosecute (he was eight at the time of the killings), Jim was released in the custody of his sister and her husband, John Coop, owners of the farm on Plum Creek.

As expected, young Jim and Coop did not get along. Although outwardly quiet, the boy possessed a terrible temper. The more Coop tried to discipline him, the more young Jim seethed. After a particularly bitter encounter on July 30, 1884, Jim waited until his brother-in-law went to sleep and killed him with a shotgun.

This time Jim was tried and convicted, but the Texas Court of Criminal Appeals reversed the conviction, finding that several technical errors had been committed during trial. By the time the second trial was scheduled, most of the witnesses against Jim had either left the state or had "mysteriously disappeared." Jim was turned loose, eventually to launch a career of killings that would never be equalled in the frontier West.

# Georgetown
## Williamson County

In 1933 a man named A. Modgling of Brownwood, Texas, claimed he had uncovered a cache of gold coins buried by the Sam Bass gang in the 1870s. (Bass and five companions robbed a Union Pacific express of $60,000 in twenty dollar gold pieces in 1877 [see *Big Springs, Nebraska*].) According to Modgling, who said he was eighty-five years of age, he had once been captured by the Bass gang and while held by them, witnessed the hiding of the cache at a place "eight miles west of Georgetown," which is about twenty miles north of Austin. He said he had decided to reveal the secret because he wanted to get the money, which was put "in a wagon bed, placed in a cave and covered over," and feared that "removal of the treasure might be a violation of the present act against gold hoarding." Because of this possibility, he said he filed an official request with the governor of Texas, Miriam A. Ferguson, for permission to remove the gold without penalty. He admitted, however, that he had already removed about $3,000 and put it in another place, "after bankers had refused to accept it for deposit."

The tale was probably a hoax, but those interested in more details can consult the December 21, 1933, issue of the Dallas *Dispatch*.

# Gonzales
## Gonzales County

Gunslinger John Wesley Hardin, following his release from prison in February 1894, moved in with an old friend, Fred Duderstadt, on his ranch outside Gonzales, which is east of San Antonio on US 183 at the junction of Alternate US 90. Then, on March 16, after being granted a full pardon, Hardin and his children were moved into a house in town. His wife, Jane, had died two years earlier while he was still in prison. While in Gonzales, Hardin attended church services regularly, made many friends, and led an exemplary life. Having studied law in prison, he applied for and passed an examination to practice and later in the year became involved in politics, especially the race for sheriff of Gonzales County. But one of the candidates for sheriff was W. S. Jones, a bitter enemy of Hardin's, and when Jones won Hardin left town. In December he opened a law office in Junction, Texas.*

# Gordon
## Palo Pinto County

Situated on the old Texas & Pacific line about sixty miles southwest of Fort Worth, the tiny town of Gordon (today, just off Interstate 80 near the Erath County line) was the site of the second train robbery by the Rube Burrow gang. The date was January 23, 1887. The previous month the gang displayed rank amateurism in a daylight holdup of passenger coaches on the Fort Worth & Denver Railroad at Belleville.* But in this second affair, the Burrow bunch showed they had learned from their mistakes (or from reading the newspaper accounts describing their mistakes). The Gordon robbery was staged at night, and the gang robbed the express and mail cars rather than the passenger coaches, collecting around $4,200 as compared to $300 at Belleville.

The Gordon holdup was conducted as if taken from a train robber's manual. Rube and a companion climbed aboard the tender as the train pulled slowly from the station. Five hundred yards down the track Jim Burrow and the others waited. Rube ordered the engineer to stop, and then marched him and the fireman back to the express car. A few shots were fired at the coaches to keep the passengers in line. The express messenger and mail clerk were persuaded to open their cars with threats that they would be burned alive. Everything went smoothly with one exception. A new recruit in the gang, Harrison Askew, panicked when he thought Rube was going to shoot the engineer, and he fled the scene without looking back.

The robbery went so well Rube decided to hit the same railroad at the same station in May. This almost was a fatal mistake. Although nearly four months had passed since the first robbery, railroad and express company detectives were still nosing around the area, and the gang likely would have ridden into their midst. But Rube and his bunch never made it to Gordon. Spring rains had swollen the rivers, and they could not cross the Brazos, which runs north of the town. After waiting several days for the water to subside, the gang turned around and rode back to their hideout.

## Hamilton
### Hamilton County

In the late 1940s an interesting story emerged from this small town on US 281 about seventy-five miles west of Waco. According to the tale, the notorious Billy the Kid had not been killed at Fort Sumner, New Mexico, in 1881, but was alive and well in Hamilton living under the name "Brushy Bill" Roberts. Roberts, who claimed to be ninety years old, *did* resemble the Kid: about five feet eight inches in height, around 165 pounds, with large ears and small hands; and, although he was nearly illiterate, Roberts could recite Lincoln County, New Mexico, history for hours—facts that would have taken an historian months to accumulate. He could also describe the layout of the Lincoln County jail and sheriff's office where Billy had escaped in April 1881, including details that had never been revealed. But there were also holes in his story, and at times under questioning Roberts suffered from lapses of memory. In the end, most historians discounted his claims.

## Hutchins
### Dallas County

Hutchins, now a southeastern Dallas suburb, was the scene of the Sam Bass gang's second train robbery in Texas. On March 18, 1878, Bass and two comrades held up the Houston & Central's No. 4 at the Hutchins station platform. As in their previous holdups, the Bass bunch overpowered the station agent and awaited the train's arrival. It pulled in around 10:00 P.M., and the robbers ordered the engineer and fireman to throw up their hands and climb down. But the railway mail clerk, a man named Terrell, and the Texas Express Company messenger, Heck Thomas (later to become a famous lawman), saw what was happening and managed to secret away most of the currency by stuffing it into the car's potbellied stove. Thomas briefly held out against the attackers, taking wounds in the neck and face, but had to give in when the outlaws made the fireman and engineer stand on the edge of the platform in his line of fire.

The robbers' haul was meager, less than $500 (one report says $89). Also, for the first time, the Bass gang encountered trouble from the passengers. Two trainmen, believed to be the conductor and a brakeman, ran through the coaches soliciting help, and a small contingent began firing at the outlaws from the rear of the the train.

The robbers rode off in an easterly direction toward the Trinity River, probably to mislead any followers. Soon they doubled back and headed northwest, to Denton County and their hideout on Hickory Creek. A posse was hastily formed but lost the tracks on hard turf.

## Junction
### Kimble County

Junction, Texas, is well named, being today at the intersection of Interstate 10, US 83, and US 377, about 140 miles west of Austin. In December 1894 the notorious gunfighter John Wesley Hardin opened a law office there. Hardin had studied law in prison and passed the state bar examination on his release earlier that year. He first tried practicing in Gonzales, Texas,* but left town when a political enemy was elected county sheriff.

Hardin had few clients in Junction, but he did win the heart of a young girl named Callie Lewis from nearby London. The two were married on January 8, 1895, but on the very same day Callie left him. Despondent, Hardin closed his office and moved to Kerr County. Little was heard from him until April when the hired gun "Deacon" Jim Miller, a cousin of Hardin's first wife, engaged him to help prosecute a man who had made an attempt on Miller's life. The case took Hardin to El Paso where he stayed on and reopened his office (see *El Paso*).

## Langtry
### Val Verde County

Langtry is in southwestern Texas, on US 90 about sixty miles northwest of Del Rio. Named after the English actress Lily Langtry (the "Jersey Lily") by her biggest fan, the colorful Judge Roy Bean, Langtry was actually three towns—the tent cities of Eagle's Nest, Soto City, and Vinegaroon—all created during the construction of the Southern Pacific Railroad in 1882 and all presided over by Judge Bean, who called himself "The Law West of the Pecos."

Contrary to popular belief, Bean really was a judge, or rather a justice of the peace. He received his appointment in August 1882 at the insistence of the Texas Rangers who were required to keep order in the area, and he officially held the office on and off for twenty years. He was required to run for re-election every two years. Occasionally he was defeated, but he continued to hold court in his saloon, the "Jersey Lily," collecting fines for minor offenses from unsuspecting strangers.

Judge Bean operated under his own ideas of jurisdic-

Judge Roy Bean's domain, Langtry, Texas. Bean is seated on keg at table. *Western History Collections, University of Oklahoma.*

tion and justice. His best remembered judicial opinion arose out of a criminal action against a railroad foreman accused of killing a Chinese laborer. As the story is told, the "courtroom" was filled with the defendants's fellow railroaders, a tough-looking bunch that undoubtedly made the judge uneasy. After the charge was read, Bean quickly flipped through his copy of the state's criminal code and promptly announced that "there ain't no law in the state of Texas against killing a Chinaman."

There were two Jersey Lilys during Bean's day. The first one burned to the ground in 1899. The second, much smaller, has been restored and is maintained today as a tourist attraction by the Texas State Highway Department. Among the features are six dioramas depicting various phases of Judge Bean's unconventional career.

## Longview
### Gregg County

Sometime in the spring of 1894, Bill Dalton, last of the outlaw clan to turn to banditry, broke with the Bill Doolin outfit and formed a gang of his own. Their first job was the First National Bank of Longview, which is in northeastern Texas, just off Interstate 20 about forty miles from the Arkansas line. On May 23, 1894, Dalton and three others—Jim Wallace, riding under the alias "George Bennett," Jim Knight, and his brother "Big Asa" Knight—rode into Longview and stopped in the alley behind the bank. Wallace and Jim Knight stayed with the horses, and Dalton and Big Asa Knight went inside. Dalton handed a note to the cashier, Tom Clemmons, which introduced the bearer as "Charles Speckelmeyer," a man "who wants some money and is going to have it."

The vaults were open, and the two bandits helped themselves to about $2,000 in currency and unsigned bank notes. Outside in the alley, however, things began to pop. The Longview city marshal, a man named Muckley, and his deputy Will Stevens spotted Wallace and Knight and guessed what was happening. A gunfight erupted, and soon bullets were flying in all directions. Muckley went down with a slug in his belly; then Stevens dropped Wallace who died almost instantly. Hearing the shots, Dalton and Big Asa forced the bank employees out the door ahead of them as a shield. By this time, a crowd was rushing to the scene, exposing themselves to the gunfire. J. W. McQueen, a saloonkeeper, was wounded but survived, as did Charles Leonard, who was hit as he was crossing the courthouse lawn. Another townsman, George Buckingham, was shot and killed.

Once on their horses, the outlaws raced north toward dense pine country. A posse was quickly formed but soon lost the trail.

## Memphis
### Hall County

Memphis, about seventy-five miles east of Amarillo on US 287, is the seat of what Hall County residents like to call the "Cotton Capital of the Texas Panhandle." Memphis is a friendly town today, but that was not always the case. At the turn of the century, deadly "Deacon" Jim Miller resided there as a saloonkeeper and self-appointed Texas Ranger. (Apparently Miller had the town convinced he was a ranger, but his name was never found on the organization's official rolls.) When Miller arrived in Memphis he already had a reputation as a killer, and before his life ended in a noose at Ada, Oklahoma,* in 1909, he became the most proficient hired gun in the West.

One of Miller's alleged victims in Memphis was a luckless attorney named Stanley. The year was 1899. Stanley, a capable lawyer, had made the mistake of vigorously prosecuting Miller on a charge of subornation of perjury. Miller was convicted, but the appeals court overturned the decision on a technicality. Stanley was no fool; he knew full well that Miller might seek revenge for the conviction, and when he had to make a scheduled business trip to Memphis that year he was probably well-armed and may even have been accompanied by a bodyguard. But neither did him any good. During his first evening in town he became sick shortly after supper. Thinking perhaps he had indulged too much in the rich and spicy dishes the Panhandle hotels seemed to favor, he retired to his room early. But near midnight he became feverish, and by late morning he was dead— a victim, according to a local doctor, of "peritonitis." Such maladies were common in West Texas in those days, and the incident was soon forgotten. Later, however, the doctor revealed to close associates that the real cause of death was arsenic poisoning. He also said that further investigation had revealed that the regular hotel cook had not been on duty that night, and Stanley's meal had been prepared by a new cook, a friend of Deacon Jim Miller's. Also, the day Stanley died, that cook left town. The doctor said he did not report his finding because he figured that he would be Miller's next victim.

## Mesquite
### Dallas County

Mesquite lies just east of Dallas. Today it is a community of nearly 70,000, a convenient mile off the eastern loop of busy Interstate 635. In 1878 the town consisted of a railroad station, general store, blacksmith shop, two saloons, and a few houses. On April 10 of that year the railroad station became the Sam Bass gang's fourth stop on what appeared to be an attempt to empty all the express cars in northeastern Texas.

By the night of the Mesquite robbery, the Bass gang had swollen to seven members, and at Mesquite they had to make use of all the firepower they could muster. In typical Bass fashion the gang disabled the station agent and awaited the arrival of the train. In the previous holdups that winter and spring, the gang had encountered some resistance from the express car messengers and trainmen but never enough to pose a problem. This night, however, conductor Julius Alvord, a crusty Civil War veteran, came from the rear of the train with his double-barreled derringer blazing. The tiny gun, however, was not designed for distance, and the furious Alvord raced back for his sixshooter. If this were not enough, across the track on a siding there was a special car loaded with convicts used for construction labor. Their guards, well-armed and with a good view of the affair, opened up on the robbers. The sound of all the shooting outside his car bolstered the courage of the express messenger, J. S. Kerley, and he let his attackers have five rounds through a crack in the door before he slammed it shut and locked it. And then from the baggage car, baggage clerk B. F. Caperton joined in with his shotgun. Even the train's candy vendor found a pistol and started to contribute, but a warning shot from the robbers gave him second thoughts, and he returned to the safety of the coach.

The outlaws must have felt they were in a war. Gang member Seaborn Barnes took bullets in both legs, and Sam Pipes was hit in the side, but just when the robbers were about to ride off, the firing slackened. Conductor Alvord took a hit in the shoulder and had to return to the nearest coach to bind his wound. Then the guards on the siding ceased firing, probably having decided they had better save some ammunition in case their convicts chose to try an escape. The outlaws took advantage of the lull by splashing the door of the express car with coal oil. Not wanting to go up in smoke with his car, the express messenger opened up.

However, for all their work, the Bass gang got little in return. On entering the express car they found but $150 in the safe and perhaps some small currency in three registered letters. They missed $1,500 which the messenger had stuffed under cold ashes in the stove.

## Millett
### LaSalle County

Millett, Texas, is on Interstate 35 about midway between Laredo and San Antonio. Just outside town, close to the roots of a large mesquite tree, there lies buried in a plain pine box a gunslinger once known as "California Jim." His real name was John Henry Hankins, and on June 17, 1882, he shot and killed a town marshal named Johnson at Laredo. It probably was not his first killing: his Colt 45 had a seven-inch barrel and seventeen notches on the handle the day he died. It is doubtful that every notch stood for a dead man but we will never know.

On the day he gunned down Johnson, Hankins was wanted in several territories, including New Mexico and Arizona. A newspaper account of the day described him as one of the coolest, nerviest desperados to ride the outlaw trail in southwest Texas. After the shooting at Laredo he headed northeast, along the newly laid tracks of the International Great Northern Railroad. Word was out that he was heading toward San Antonio. At Millett (then called Cibolo Station) Charley Smith, a Texas Ranger, and a young friend, seventeen-year-old Wesley DeSpain, spotted Hankins riding along a brushy ridge not far from the depot. When they were within thirty yards of him, Hankins drew and fired, striking DeSpain in the side and knocking him off his horse. Smith got off three quick shots with his Winchester before Hankins dropped from his saddle into the high sagebrush. He was fairly sure one had struck home.

Hankins was indeed hit. The bullet had entered at his hip joint and ripped into his bowels. He was bleeding badly, but was still conscious, and still had fight left in him. Smith discovered this when a bullet tore into his leg just below the knee. He was in a squatting position when hit, and the slug ripped through flesh and exited at an upward angle, re-entering his body at the breast. Both men were now in bad shape, as was young DeSpain.

Smith tried to stop the bleeding as much as he could and began a slow crawl back to the depot. On the way he met the section boss, R. T. Talbot, coming to help. Talbot wasted no time bringing the matter to an end. He rushed Hankins and ordered him to drop his weapon. Too weak to resist, Hankins let it fall. Taking no chances, Talbot picked up the outlaw's gun and smashed him in the head with it.

Hankins lingered until 3:00 A.M. the following morning, when he stiffened, took a deep breath, and gasped, "Well, Molly, it's all over now." And it was.

## Mobeetie
### Wheeler County

Old Mobeetie can be found in the Panhandle on State Highway 152 between US 60 and US 83. The town was born on land leased for Fort Elliott in an unauthorized camp of white squatters called Hidetown. When a shoe cobbler killed a young man in the camp in the late 1870s, the army kicked the squatters off government property, and they settled around the bend on Sweetwater Creek about a mile away. They called the new camp Sweetwater, and for a while it was the largest settlement in the Panhandle, drawing saloonkeepers, gamblers, dance hall girls, and the usual trade designed to entertain lonely soldiers and cowboys. In 1879, when Wheeler County was formally organized, the town's name was changed again, to Mobeetie (the Commanche name for "Sweetwater"), since Texas already had a town named Sweetwater down in Nolan County.

One of the most popular Mobeetie dance halls was the Lady Gay. In January 1876 it was the site of Bat Masterson's first shootout. One version of the story has the fight occurring over a dark-haired dancer named Molly Brennan, who was at the time being courted by an army sergeant from nearby Fort Elliott. The sergeant, Melvin King, caught Molly and Bat holding hands after closing hours. Molly jumped in front of Masterson as King fired. The bullet went through her body and struck Bat in the pelvis. But before he fell, Bat shot the sergeant dead.

A more legendary version of the tale is that Texas gunslinger Ben Thompson was on the scene. Reportedly he held off a group of King's soldier buddies until Bat could be taken away. This account has never been verified. Still another version denies any romance between Molly and Masterson or King, and has King gunning for Bat for some past wrong. Then in yet another version, there were two additional soldiers involved, both being wounded, presumably by Bat.

## Pecos
### Reeves County

The town of Pecos, which is in West Texas on Interstate 20 about forty miles northeast of where it joins Interstate 10, was the site of two wild gunfights between the notorious "Deacon" Jim Miller and Reeves County sheriff Bud Frazer. Miller and Frazer were once friends; in fact Miller had been Frazer's deputy, but a feud developed after Frazer discovered that Miller had killed a prisoner to cover up his own misdeeds. After losing his deputy's job, Miller ran against Frazer for sheriff (1892) but was easily defeated. Rather than leave town, as many would have done, Miller got himself appointed Pecos city marshal. The job paid little, but it gave Miller an opportunity to hassle Frazer.

In May 1893 while Frazer was out of town on business, Miller hatched a scheme to assassinate him. Two of Miller's friends were to stage a ruckus on the railroad station platform when the sheriff returned, and a third hiding in the shadows would see that Frazer was downed by a "stray" bullet. But details of the plan were leaked, and Frazer arrived in the company of two tough-looking Texas Rangers.

Things quieted down for a while, but word started going around that if Frazer could not handle Miller, he had no business being sheriff. This set the stage for the first shootout. On the morning of April 12, 1894, Frazer

Faro game in Pecos, Texas, saloon. "Deacon" Jim Miller is seated at left. *Western History Collection, University of Oklahoma.*

walked up to Miller on the street and started firing. The first bullet hit Miller in the chest but fell harmlessly to the ground. Frazer's second shot struck Deacon Jim in the right arm just as he began to draw. With his gun hand useless, he reached around with his left hand, drew, and fired. But Miller had never practiced shooting left-handed, and the bullet dug into the ground at Frazer's feet. Miller's second shot was even wilder, striking a bystander—storekeeper Joe Kraus. In the meantime, Frazer was pumping three more shots at Miller; they all hit him in the chest but none seemed to bother him. A final shot, however, struck Miller in the belly and he went down. Frazer jammed his empty gun back into its scabbard and returned to his office, thinking Miller was dead. He was wrong: a steel breast plate, which apparently Miller had worn since the first day he arrived in Pecos, had saved his life. Although seriously wounded, he would recover and meet Frazer again.

The second Miller-Frazer duel occurred on December 26, 1894. Frazer had been defeated for re-election the previous month and had left town. On this day he had returned to wind up some business affairs. His friends had warned him that Miller was still out to kill him, so when he saw Deacon Jim on the street he took no chances; as before, he whipped out his sixgun and commenced firing. The fight was nearly a duplicate of the earlier one. Frazer's first bullet struck Miller in the right arm. Again, Miller had to draw and shoot with his left hand, and again his shots went wild. A second slug tore into Miller's left leg. A third and fourth hit him in the chest, but as before, he was wearing his chest plate. Some say Frazer had not been told about the breast plate, and when so many shots found their mark and his enemy was still standing, he panicked. For whatever reason, Frazer did turn and run, ending the fight for that day. Once again, Miller survived, setting the stage for a third meeting, this time in the neighboring town of Toyah.*

Pecos was also a hangout for Barney Riggs, the Texas gunslinger who won a pardon from the Arizona territorial penitentiary for saving the warden's life during a riot (see *Yuma, Arizona*). Riggs was a hard case, and at the time was serving a term for murdering a rival in a love triangle. Following his release he joined up with the tough crowd that hung around Bud Frazer and was soon involved in the Miller-Frazer feud. In 1897 two of Miller's friends, John Denson and Bill Earhart, challenged Riggs in a Pecos saloon. The two Miller cronies got off the first shots but only grazed Barney. Riggs whipped out his gun and put a bullet between Earhart's eyes, but before he could do the same to Denson, his gun jammed, and the two men went at each other hand-to-hand. Denson, apparently getting the worst of the match, finally broke free and ran out the door into the street. Riggs found his gun, cleared the cylinder, and put a bullet in the back of Denson's head.

# Round Rock
## Williamson County

Round Rock is just north of Austin at the junction of Interstate 35 and US 79. A popular story is told that in 1871 the notorious gunfighter John Wesley Hardin spent some time in Round Rock seeking an education. Hardin was already wanted by the law as a hair-trigger killer, but for a few months that year he supposedly attended Professor Landrum's Academy at Round Rock, practically under the nose of the Texas Rangers. Even when he received word that the Rangers had learned of his whereabouts and were about to close in, he only temporarily interrupted his studies. After hiding in a woods outside of town, he later slipped back in to take his exams (which he passed). While this story has the earmarks of a tall Texas tale, Hardin was not your typical desperado. While serving a term in the penitentiary he studied law, and on his release he passed the Texas bar examination. Although he never had many clients, he was a practicing attorney at the time of his death in 1895 (see *El Paso*).

Round Rock was also the end of the line for outlaw Sam Bass and his gang. On July 19, 1878, Bass and three companions rode into town intending to rob the bank. Ordinarily such a holdup would have been easy for the Bass bunch, but there was a spy in the outfit, Jim Murphy, who had tipped off the Texas Rangers where the outlaws were heading.

On arriving in town, Bass and sidekicks Frank Jackson and Seaborn Barnes were supposed to head for Henry Koppel's general store which was near the bank. Murphy, in turn, was to check out another store in the old section of town. If all was clear, they were to meet at Koppel's and then head for the bank. But as they rode in, a deputy sheriff named Maurice Moore thought he noticed the bulge of a sixgun under Bass's coat. He told fellow deputy A. W. Grimes, and Grimes followed the three strangers into the store. Grimes, not realizing he was confronting the notorious Sam Bass, walked up and place his hand on the outlaw's coat where the gun seemed to be making the bulge, and asked him if he was carrying a pistol. Startled, Bass whirled, drew his gun and fired, as did Jackson and Barnes. Grimes stumbled backward and collapsed near the door. Moore, standing outside, put a bullet through Bass's right hand, nearly amputating his middle and ring fingers. The outlaws rushed out of the store, firing as they ran. Moore was hit in the chest, but continued shooting.

Sam Bass, *University of Texas.*

There were Texas Rangers all over town, and they converged on the scene. Bass was hit again as he neared his horse, which was tied in an alley beside the livery stable. The bullet, believed to have been fired by Ranger George Harrell, struck the outlaw about an inch to the left of the spinal column. Bass went down immediately. Seaborn Barnes, running at his side, took a slug in the head and died instantly. Frank Jackson, still unscathed, helped Bass to his feet and onto his horse, at the same time returning enough fire to keep the Rangers from moving in.

The outlaws rode north, toward Georgetown, then turned west into a dense oak woods. About three miles from town, Bass became too weak to go on and slipped to the ground. Jackson, after binding his companions's wounds, rode on. The following morning Bass crawled about a third of a mile to a newly constructed spur of the International and Great Northern Railroad, where section hands gave him water. A posse found him there a few hours later. He was weak but still alive. He died at Round Rock the next day, July 21, his twenty-seventh birthday. He lies today in the Round Rock cemetery, near his comrade Seaborn Barnes.

# San Antonio
## Bexar County

The colorful Judge Roy Bean called San Antonio home from around 1866 to sometime in the late 1870s. Bean married a young Mexican girl, Virginia Chavez, and in 1873 bought a stone house about two and one-half miles south of what was then the city limits. The house was on the west side of the San Antonio River just south of where it joined San Pedro Creek. Bean held numerous jobs during those years. He once operated a dairy which allegedly folded when he was discovered watering the milk from San Pedro Creek. He was also in the firewood business for a while, which likewise ran into trouble when he was accused of gathering wood from a neighbor's property. Bean spent some time in jail in 1875 when he was charged with resisting arrest while working for an attorney who was trying to evict some tenants for a landlord client. It was probably during this time that Bean became interested in the law, which may have led to his seeking the appointment of justice of the peace at what later became Langtry, Texas* where he became known as "The Law West of the Pecos."

A popular night spot in San Antonio was the Vaudeville Variety Theatre and Gambling Saloon. In 1880 Jack Harris, a part owner, made the mistake of incurring the wrath of gunslinger Ben Thompson. The feud simmered for two years, until July 1882 when Thompson left a message for Harris that he wanted a showdown. When he returned later in the evening, Thompson found Harris waiting for him just inside the front door with a shotgun. Harris raised his weapon but Thompson was quicker. The shot missed, but the bullet richocheted around the room and finally struck Harris in the chest, puncturing a lung. Struggling for breath, Harris made it as far as the second floor hallway before he collapsed. He died during the night. Thompson surrendered to local officials but eventually was acquitted.

On March 11, 1884, Thompson returned to the Vaudeville. He and a friend, former gunman King Fisher, had come to San Antonio for some fun and excitement. After hitting a few spots they settled in at the Vaudeville where they were joined by Billy Simms and Joe Foster, both former partners of Jack Harris. Present also was the house bouncer, Jacob Coy. According to an account later supplied by Simms and his friends, an argument started and Thompson, well-braced with whiskey, stuck his pistol into Foster's mouth and cocked the hammer. Coy grabbed at the gun, and Simms and Foster went for their weapons. Apparently everybody fired at once, except Fisher, who never got his gun out of his scabbard. Thompson and Fisher died instantly, Foster suffered a leg wound that would eventually prove fatal, and Coy was wounded slightly.

A popular San Antonio entertainment den, Fanny Porter's Sporting House at 505 South San Saba Street, was a favorite hangout of Butch Cassidy and the Wyoming Wild Bunch. The gang reportedly "frolicked with Fanny's girls, drank champagne, and cheered with the girls from a balcony while Butch rode a bicycle up and down the street," (which no doubt inspired the bicycle scenes in the successful 1969 movie, *Butch Cassidy and the Sundance Kid*).

## Sanderson
### Terrell County

Sanderson, in southwest Texas at the intersection of US 90 and US 285, straddles the Southern Pacific Railroad, the most frequently robbed railway in the Old West. The loot from one such robbery may still lie buried somewhere around Sanderson. Names and dates are sketchy, possibly because the records have been taken or destroyed, as occasionally happens in such cases. The holdup occurred sometime in the 1890s, and the amount may have exceeded $50,000. The robbers were caught several weeks after the robbery and still had the Wells Fargo sacks in which the money was being shipped, but they were being used to carry coffee and sugar. According to rumor, one or more of the Texas Rangers involved in the pursuit of the robbers resigned shortly thereafter to devote full time to locating the cache. There is no record of its ever being found.

The details of another holdup near Sanderson have been better preserved. On March 13, 1912, just east of town near an abandoned stop called Lozier, Ben Kilpatrick, the last active member of the famous Wyoming Wild Bunch, tried to rob one more train. Kilpatrick and a companion had climbed aboard behind the tender as the Southern Pacific's westbound Sunset Limited No. 1 pulled out of Dryden, about thirty miles east of Sanderson. Near Lozier they slipped over the coal pile and put guns into the backs of the engineer and fireman. After stopping the train, Kilpatrick's partner left Ben alone in the express car with Wells Fargo messenger Dave Trousdale while he marched the crew back to the locomotive. The safe was open, and all Ben had to do was to stuff the money into a sack, but as he bent over to pick up a package, Trousdale grabbed an ice mallet and hit the outlaw over the head. Picking up Ben's rifle, he then killed the second bandit when he stuck his head in the door to see what was detaining Kilpatrick.

## Scyene
### Dallas County

Scyene, Texas, now absorbed by the southeastern outskirts of sprawling Dallas, was the family home of "Bandit Queen" Belle Starr from the mid-1860s to the mid-1870s. Belle, whose real name was Myra Maybelle Shirley, was sixteen when her fmaily moved to Scyene from Carthage, Missouri, in 1864. Some writers have her frolicking with Missouri outlaw Cole Younger during these years, and some have written that she bore him a child. Records indicate, however, that in 1866 she was married to outlaw Jim Reed, and returned to Missouri to give birth to a daugher, Rosie Lee (nicknamed Pearl), in 1868.

Jim Reed was wanted by the law in several states, and Belle returned to Scyene off and on, depending on where he was hiding out at the time. He was finally killed in 1874, and shortly thereafter, Belle's father died, at which time her mother sold the family home at Scyene and moved into Dallas. Belle, however, remained in the Scyene area until sometime after the fall of 1876.

# Smiley
## Gonzales County

Smiley, Texas, the peaceful "little town beside the lake," is on US 87 about fifty miles east of San Antonio. In September 1871 Smiley's peacefulness was disturbed by Texas gunslinger John Wesley Hardin. The law had been on Hardin's trail for some time, and on that day two state officers, Green Parramore and John Lackey, were in town on a tip that Hardin was hiding out there. After questioning several residents, Parramore and Lackey stopped at the general store. Hardin, apparently in a devilish mood and eager for a fight, sauntered in and began taunting the two lawmen. According to the popular version of the incident, the outlaw asked the two strangers who they were looking for. When they told him, he asked: "Would you know Hardin if you saw him?" They said they had never seen him. "Well," said Wes, "you see him right now!"

Hardin's first shot struck Parramore in the head, killing him instantly. His second ripped through Lackey's mouth, knocking out several teeth. Stunned but still alive, Lackey dived behind a group of bystanders and scrambled out the door. Hardin, figuring the officer might be waiting for him outside, left by the back door. By the time he reached the street, Lackey was gone.

With blood rushing from his wound, Lackey raced to nearby Round Lake and plunged in. Hardin looked for him up and down the street but did not think to look in the lake. The cold water slowed down the bleeding, and the officer survived to tell a colorful story of the day he tangled with the famous John Wesley Hardin.

# Tascosa
## Oldham County

Like many Texas town, Tascosa flourished as an early watering hole for thirsty cowboys and then declined when the railraod passed it by. In 1881, on organization of Oldham County, things looked promising for the town. A stone courthouse was erected which still stands

Tascosa saloon. *Library of Congress.*

today. The community boomed, and by 1886 it was being called the "Cowboy Capital of the Great Plains," thanks to seven saloons and a night life that rivaled its Panhandle neighbor Mobeetie. Also, as a trade center, it was primed and ready for the anticipated arrival of the Fort Worth and Denver Railroad. But the rails never came; they passed to the east, beyond Mustang Creek, and Tascosa dwindled and died.

But the town's first six years were wild ones. Its Boot Hill Cemetery, which can still be visited, ranked with the best. Oldham County's first sheriff was shotgun-wielding Cape Williamson, and his chief deputy was the notorious Henry Newton Brown, who had once ridden with Billy the Kid and could never decide which side of the law he was on (until a lynch mob ended his indecision in 1884 at Medicine Lodge, Kansas*).

Quick-tempered lawyer-gunman Temple Houston also frequented Tascosa in the early 1880s but mainly as a district attorney, leaving the rough stuff to Sheriff Williamson. A tale has been handed down over the years involving Houston, Billy the Kid, and Bat Masterson. All were reportedly excellent shots with a six-gun, and one day a contest was arranged to see just who was the best. According to one version, the tin star trademark was removed from a currently popular brand of chewing tobacco and tacked up on a post. A second version has Masterson flinging the pack into the air. Both versions have Houston whipping out his weapon and, from twenty paces, plugging the star dead center. Billy, who was to shoot next, supposedly muttered, "Quien lo haja mejor?" (Who could do better?) and walked off. The tale has either been distorted drastically or is pure fiction, since when Houston first arrived at Tascosa, Billy the Kid was already dead, and Bat Masterson was a peace officer in Colorado. Billy the Kid did hang out in Tascosa but in the mid-1870s, before he migrated to New Mexico and the Lincoln County War (see *Lincoln, New*

*Mexico*). While in Tascosa, Billy apparently behaved himself. Townspeople remembered him as one who minded his own business, drank little, and enjoyed the company of young Mexican ladies at local dances.

What is left of old Tascosa can be seen just off US 385 north of the Canadian River. The courthouse is now part of Cal Farley's Boys Ranch which has taken over the townsite.

## Toyah
### Reeves County

Located on Interstate 20 nineteen miles southwest of Pecos, Toyah's saloons once quenched the thirst of many a dusty ranch hand. It was in one such saloon that "Deacon" Jim Miller ended the career of his arch enemy, former Reeves County sheriff Bud Frazer. On September 13, 1896, Miller and Frazer met for the third and final time. They had already fought two gunfights in Pecos,* which Miller survived only because he sported a steel breast plate under his coat. The third meeting was no contest. While Frazer was seated at a poker table, Miller carefully rested his shotgun on the top of one of the saloon's bat-wing doors and blew his foe apart.

After two trials Miller was acquitted, the jury probably finding that after their repeated encounters, Miller had done no worse to Frazer than Frazer would have to him.

## Uvalde
### Uvalde County

Uvalde, about seventy-five miles west of San Antonio at the junction of US 90 and US 83, was the last home of the enigmatic King Fisher. In his youth, Fisher developed quite a reputation as a rustler and gunman. Later, as a successful cattleman, he ruled Maverick and Dimmit counties with an iron hand (see *Eagle Pass*), but in 1883 he suddenly reformed. He bought a house in Uvalde (128 Mesquite Street) and secured an appointment as deputy sheriff of Uvalde County. He proved effective as a lawman and later in the year served for a while as acting sheriff.

In 1884 Fisher was scheduled to run for election as sheriff, but on March 11 of that year he was killed beside his friend, gunman Ben Thompson, in a shootout at the Vaudeville Variety Theatre in San Antonio.* His body was returned to Uvalde for a grand funeral, and he rests today in the Frontier Cemetery on the east side of town.

## Wharton
### Wharton County

Wharton, located on US 59 about fifty miles southwest of Houston, may never have been the West's wildest town, but the citizens of that city can still brag today about "the greatest shot" ever fired in a western shootout. The outlaw west had for the most part been tamed by 1917, but on September 15 of that year a troublesome bandit named Francisco Lopez drank too much tequila and began terrorizing the town. The city marshal was W. W. Pitman, a small, quiet man who had never shot to kill during his five years in office. That night Lopez and Pitman met in the street, which at the time was crowded with onlookers. Not wanting to risk gunplay and injury to an innocent bystander, Pitman calmly walked up to the bandit and informed him that he was under arrest. Lopez let out a laugh, replied that he was "not under anything," and drew his pistol. Two quick shots whizzed past the marshal. By the time Pitman fired, Lopez was getting off his third shot. The two shots sounded as one, and the bandit's gun flew out of his hand. According to witnesses, the bullet from Pitman's gun entered the barrel of Lopez's weapon, striking the bullet in that gun just after it left the cylinder. The stunned Lopez stared at his weapon as it lay on the ground. On the barrel, just in front of the cylinder, there was a bulge where the bullets had met.

The story was told and retold many times around Wharton County. In 1932 several of Pitman's friends entered the tale in a contest sponsored by Robert L. Ripley's "Believe It or Not" newspaper syndicate. It made the finals, and Pitman and his wife won a free trip to Cuba. Later, the gun was placed in Ripley's New York "Believe It or Not" museum.

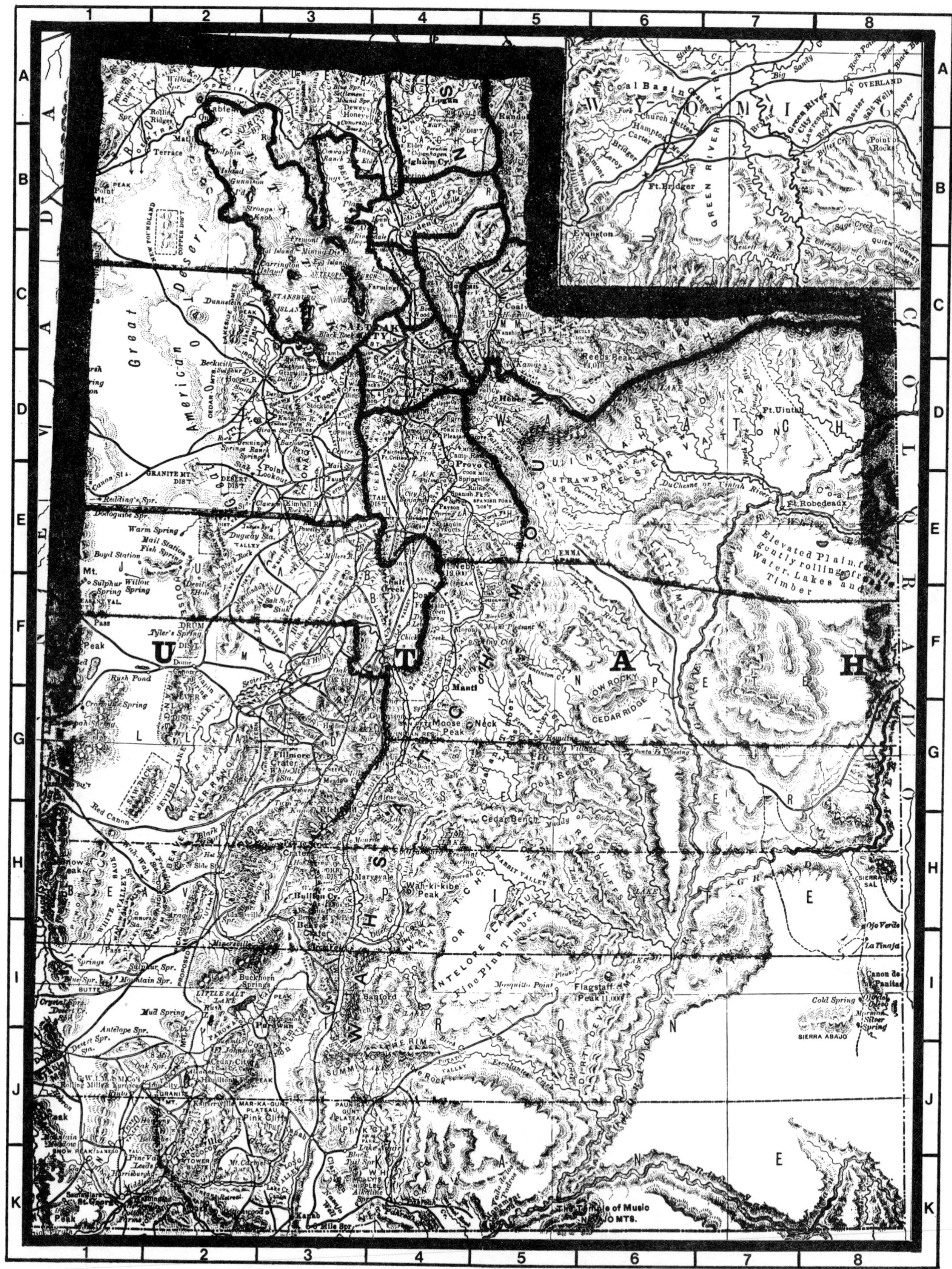

Utah 1876

# UTAH

## Castle Gate
### Carbon County

The remains of Castle Gate can be found in the heart of Utah's turn-of-the-century coal district, on a narrow stretch of US 6 north of Price. The town was the scene of perhaps the boldest robbery ever attributed to Butch Cassidy. On April 21, 1897, Cassidy and one other man, probably Elzy Lay, snatched the payroll intended for the employees of the Pleasant Valley Coal Company. The money was in three sacks and a satchel. Two of the sacks held silver (one $1,000 and the other $860), one sack held gold ($7,000), and the satchel contained coins and checks ($1,000).

The money arrived at Castle Gate on the noon Rio Grande Western passenger train from Salt Lake City. At the depot, Pleasant Valley Coal Company paymaster E. L. Carpenter, assisted by a company clerk, T. W. Lewis, signed for the shipment and headed across the tracks toward the company's store and offices—a two-story stone building about fifty yards away. As they reached the east side of the building, at the foot of the outside stairway leading up to the offices, a "rough-looking individual" (presumably Cassidy) stepped in front of Carpenter and ordered him to "drop the sacks and hold up his hands." Lewis, who was carrying one of the sacks of silver, broke into a run and escaped by dashing into the store. Cassidy did not try to stop him but deftly stooped and gathered up the remaining two sacks and satchel and handed them to his companion on horseback a few yards away. This second outlaw then spurred his horse, fired several shots in the air, and raced south down the street. Cassidy quickly saddled up and followed. Several of the office workers on the second floor saw what had happened and fired at the fleeing bandits, but by then they were out of range.

Pleasant Valley Coal Company, Castle Gate, Utah. *Charles C. Goodhall Collection.*

The outlaws rode to the south end of town where they tied up at a telegraph pole. One of them reached up and grasped the single wire leading out of town and, apparently using a pair of pliers, neatly clipped it. As he did, he dropped the sack containing silver and the satchel.

Once out of town, the outlaws headed toward the John U. Bryners ranch at the mouth of Spring Creek Canyon. On reaching the canyon, they rode into it about two miles, then turned south again, passed over a small ridge, and followed a trail which circled the towns of Helper, Spring Glen, and Price. On reaching the road between Price and the Emery County town of Cleveland, they once again cut the telegraph wire. At about 4:00 o'clock that afternoon they were seen by a mail carrier just outside Cleveland.

The coal company officials commandeered a locomotive and raced to Price where they spread the alarm. Several posses were quickly formed and were on the bandits' trail by mid-afternoon. Some sources say they got close enough at one point to exchange shots but were then soon outdistanced.

# Circleville
## Piute County

Circleville, in southern Utah on US 89 between Richfield and Panguitch, was the boyhood home of Robert Leroy Parker, alias Butch Cassidy. Butch's family moved into a small cabin on a 160-acre ranch outside of town in 1878 when Butch was twelve years old. Their previous home was in Beaver just across the Tushar Mountains. The Parkers were hard-working Mormons and during lean years Butch's father, Maximillian, cut ties and hauled timber for charcoal at nearby Frisco. Butch's mother, Ann, operated a dairy for a neighbor, Jim Marshall, and Butch occasionally worked for Marshall as a ranch hand.

Butch had his first brush with the law when he was around thirteen. On a trip to town to buy a pair of trousers he found the store closed. Rather than make another trip, he quietly let himself in, picked out the pair of pants he wanted, and left a note for the storekeeper that he would pay the next time he came to town. The storekeeper was not amused and complained to the sheriff. It has been suggested that the boy had no idea that he had done anything wrong, that since his "word was his bond," he felt the storekeeper should have known that he would have returned with the money.

Not long after, Butch got into more serious trouble. He began resisting his strict religious training and took up with a drifter named Mike Cassidy, who occasionally supplemented his ranch hand's pay by rustling steers. Mike Cassidy became Butch's hero and mentor, and soon the boy joined in on several raids. In the summer of 1884 a handful of steers carrying some of Butch's overbranding wandered back to their owners who sent the sheriff after the boy. Rather than bring shame to his family, the story goes that Butch packed up and hit the trail, adopting as he did, the name of his former saddlemate.

Butch Cassidy's childhood home near Circleville, Utah. *Utah State Historical Society.*

The Parker home is just west of US 89 about two miles south of Circleville and is open to the public.

# Corinne
## Box Elder County

Corinne is in the northern part of the state, just west of Interstate 84 about seven miles northwest of Brigham City. About four miles upstream from Corinne, along the banks of the Bear River, may lie buried the loot from the biggest train robbery ever committed in the state of Colorado. On an October night in 1881 a northbound Colorado & Southern express was robbed of $105,000 in cash and about $40,000 in jewelry. The holdup occurred just north of Colorado Springs.* The robbers, later determined to be George Tipton, Gene Wright, and Oscar Witherell, rode northwest across the Rockies to the Idaho line near Bear River, then south into Utah. At Corinne they began attracting attention and decided to hide their treasure, choosing, it is believed, a spot on the river bank where it "made a bend against a low timbered hill." The outlaws reportedly hid all but a few hundred dollars which they kept for a good time in Corinne, then a wide-open town catering to prospectors, stockmen, and soldiers.

But before long the outlaws encountered trouble. Out of money, Wright and Witherell tried to pawn one of the stolen watches and roused the suspicions of the local marshal. A gunfight erupted and Wright was wounded. In the confusion, Tipton, who had been standing on the sidelines, was hit in the leg by a stray bullet. Wright and Witherell were hustled off to jail. Tipton, however, was not arrested. His two pals probably expected Tipton to arrange their escape, but if he tried, he was unsuccessful. Wright and Witherell were eventually convicted of the Colorado robbery and sentenced to the penitentiary at Canon City.

Apparently in an attempt to work out a deal with the authorities, the outlaws revealed that the loot was buried along the Bear River. The deal was not made, however, and the exact location was not disclosed.

Tipton remained in Corinne, probably waiting until things cooled down so he could recover the stolen money. His wound did not heal properly, however, and infection set in. Eventually his leg had to be amputated. Probably suspecting the authorities were on to him, he left town one night, heading north toward the Idaho line. His wound was still infected, and he got only as far as a rancher's cabin just across the line. While laid up there he took sick with a fever, and several days later died of "gangrene poisoning." Before he died he told the rancher, a man named Lafe Roberts, something about the hidden loot. But Roberts, thinking the story was the product of a dying man's delirium, did not follow up on it. Only years later did Roberts visit the Bear River area to look for the treasure. When word of his search got around, he was paid a visit by Wells Fargo officials who apparently had never closed their file on his case. As time passed, interest lessened in the hidden cache, and it was nearly forgotten. In recent years, however, it has been listed in several treasure hunter's books.

## Fountain Green
### Sanpete County

For a while in 1945, Fountain Green, which is in central Utah about fourteen miles southeast of Nephi, may have been the home of the notorious outlaw Harry Longabaugh (the Sundance Kid). According to Longabaugh's biographer, Edward H. Kirby, the former Wild Bunch member and saddlemate of Butch Cassidy lived in Fountain Green under the name Hiram BeBee with his common-law wife, Glame Heasley, and two male friends, Frank W. O'Bannion and Paul A. Millet. Kirby says in September 1945 the clan moved on to Spring City, Utah.

## Manila
### Daggett County

A short distance east of Manila, just south of the Wyoming line and the Flaming Gorge National Recreation Area, there is a lonely grave marked only by two stones. The grave can be found on a hillside just off State Highway 44, before the road begins to curve south to skirt the Flaming Gorge Reservoir and eventually joins US 91. Few highway travelers know the grave is there. Local residents can tell you where to look; it is almost exactly on the old trail that crosses the dividing ridge between South Valley and Sheep Creek Canyon.

Why the interest in this particular grave? Outlaw researchers have identified it as perhaps the grave of a Pinkerton detective killed by the notorious Harvey Logan (Kid Curry) in 1895. Logan apparently used the area as a hideout in the days before he joined Butch Cassidy and the Wild Bunch. Old timers claim that during that fall Logan and a fellow outlaw, Tom McCarty, spent some time at nearby Linwood (no longer there), especially at a saloon owned by one Bob Swift. At times they were joined by a local lawman of sorts named Cleophas J. Dowd who it is said had more friends on the far side of the law than he should have. It was through the children of Cleophas Dowd that this story was pieced together, by researcher Kerry Ross Boren, who uncovered a letter said to be written by Logan himself which more or less confirms the tale.

While drinking at Swift's saloon, Logan, McCarty, and Dowd spotted a stranger asking questions. McCarty guessed he was a Pinkerton agent who had been on his trail for the robbery of the Farmers and Merchants Bank at Delta, Colorado* in September 1893. When the three men left Swift's, the man followed. At a spot on the ridge trail, near where the grave is located, Logan rode back and put a rifle bullet between the stranger's eyes. Dowd later claimed he tried to prevent the killing but was too late. The stranger was buried near where he fell, just far enough off the trail not to be noticed; however, a remorseful Dowd later returned and buried the victim deeper and erected the two stones as markers.

Further research here may be rewarding for Wild Bunch enthusiasts. If the victim was a Pinkerton agent, a search of the agency's records in New York City might turn up something.

## Mount Pleasant
### Sanpete County

If Wild Bunch researcher Edward M. Kirby is correct, the last member of that notorious gang shot and killed an off-duty town marshal in Mount Pleasant as late as October 15, 1945. According to Kirby, Harry Longabaugh (the Sundance Kid), who was then going by the name Hiram BeBee, got into an argument with the marshal, Alonzo (Lon) T. Larsen, in a Mount Pleasant tavern. Larsen grabbed the aging outlaw (Longabaugh would have then been 77 years old) by the collar and escorted him outside. Spotting BeBee's pick-up truck, Larsen stuffed the old man into the front seat. It was a mistake on Larsen's part—BeBee reached into the glove box, pulled out a 38-calibre Smith and Wesson pistol and shot Larsen in the chest. As the marshal tumbled into the gutter, BeBee fired again, putting a second bullet into his victim.

BeBee was tried for first degree murder at Manti, Utah, and on February 16, 1946, a jury found him guilty and recommended life in prison, The judge, however, sentenced him to death. On January 17, 1947, the conviction was set aside by the Utah Supreme Court. BeBee was tried again at Price, and again a jury found him guilty and recommended life. Once more the judge sentenced him to death, but this time the Utah Board of Pardons commuted the sentence to life. BeBee spent the next two years at the old Utah State Prison at Sugarhouse in Salt Lake City. In 1951 he was transferred to the new facility at Point of the Mountains south of Salt Lake City, and he died there on June 2, 1955.

# Price
## Carbon County

In Price's town cemetery lie the remains of outlaw Joe Walker, killed near Thompson, Utah, in May 1898 by a posse who found him asleep in his bedroll. Walker, probably a regular Wild Bunch member, was believed by some to have taken part in the April 1897 robbery of the Pleasant Valley Coal Company at Castle Gate,* although most outlaw researchers credit that robbery to Butch Cassidy and Elzy Lay.

Buried next to Walker is a young cowboy named Johnny Herring who died at his side that day. Young Herring carried no identification, and since he matched the description of Butch Cassidy, the authorities first believed they had killed Butch. Reports went out over the wires that the famous outlaw was dead, and Herring was buried with most in attendance convinced the body was Cassidy's. But the following day the body was dug up and viewed by a Wyoming sheriff who knew Cassidy and who stated postively that it was not Butch. Later, Herring was identified, and it was determined that he was just an innocent drifter who camped at the wrong time with a stranger he met on the trail.

Price is in east central Utah on US 6 about midway between Provo and Interstate 70.

# Robbers' Roost
## Emery County

Utah's Robbers' Roost country lies in the southeastern quarter of the state, roughly the high desert area around the heads of the side canyons of the Green and Colorado Rivers on the east and south and the Fremont River (also called Dirty Devil River) on the west. In relation to surrounding towns, the area lies directly within and slightly southwest of a triangle formed at the points by the towns of Green River, Moab, and Hanksville.

Butch Cassidy and the Wild Bunch of Wyoming are frequently mentioned in connection with Robbers' Roost. Actually, the area was known as hideout country for outlaws at least ten years before Butch passed through. Probably the first outlaw to use the Roost was a horse thief named Cap Brown, who may have built corrals in the area for his stolen mounts as early as 1874. Brown's major markets were probably the mining towns of Colorado. Between trips it is believed he lived in a shack in Bull Valley near Hanksville.

There is some evidence that Butch Cassidy, Harry Longabaugh (the Sundance Kid), and Elzy Lay spent the winter of 1896-97 at the Roost. According to researcher Edward Kirby, who obtained the information from Lay's daughter Marvel Murdock, the comely and mysterious Etta Place (later Longabaugh's consort) was at the time Cassidy's companion, and the two lovers shared a cabin with Lay and his new bride, Maude Davis.

Stories persist that because of the outlaw activity in the area, Robbers' Roost might still hold hidden caches of stolen loot. A local resident, Andy Moore, was pretty sure he encountered a Roost outlaw as late as 1930 shortly after he dug up a cache in a small cave southeast of the San Raphael Desert near North Springs. Moore, who met the stranger on the trail and camped with him one night, became suspicious when he acted nervous about what he was carrying in his pack outfit. After they parted, Moore backtracked the stranger's trail and found the cave with a freshly dug hole.

It is rumored that Wild Bunch member "Flat Nose" George Currie hid around $65,000 somewhere in the Roost and was killed before he could return for it. It is said that the day after Currie's death, two strangers, supposedly Currie's confederates, were seen in the area, perhaps intending to meet him and split the loot. If Currie was the only one who knew where the cache was buried, it could still be there.

# Rockville
## Washington County

Rockville is in the southwestern corner of the state, on State Highway 9 between Interstate 15 and US 89. According to Harry Longabaugh's (the Sundance Kid's) biographer, Edward M. Kirby, Longabaugh lived in Rockville in the early 1940s under the name Hiram BeBee. Little is known about the man. He was considered "grouchy" by his neighbors, some of whom say he was a whiskey bootlegger. There were reports that although BeBee was in his seventies, he could still draw and shoot a six-gun with the best of them. There were stories of how he could throw a can out into the street and "bounce" it along with repeated shots.

BeBee's house was just across the old bridge over the Virgin River. He and his common-law wife, Glame, rented it from a Rockville man named Arthur Terry. Disputes with neighbors eventually led to the sheriff being called, and soon after BeBee, Glame, and several other persons who lived at the same address (one of them possibly Glame's daughter) moved on.

According to Kirby, BeBee eventually ran afoul of the law in Mount Pleasant, Utah,* where he shot and killed the town marshal in 1945.

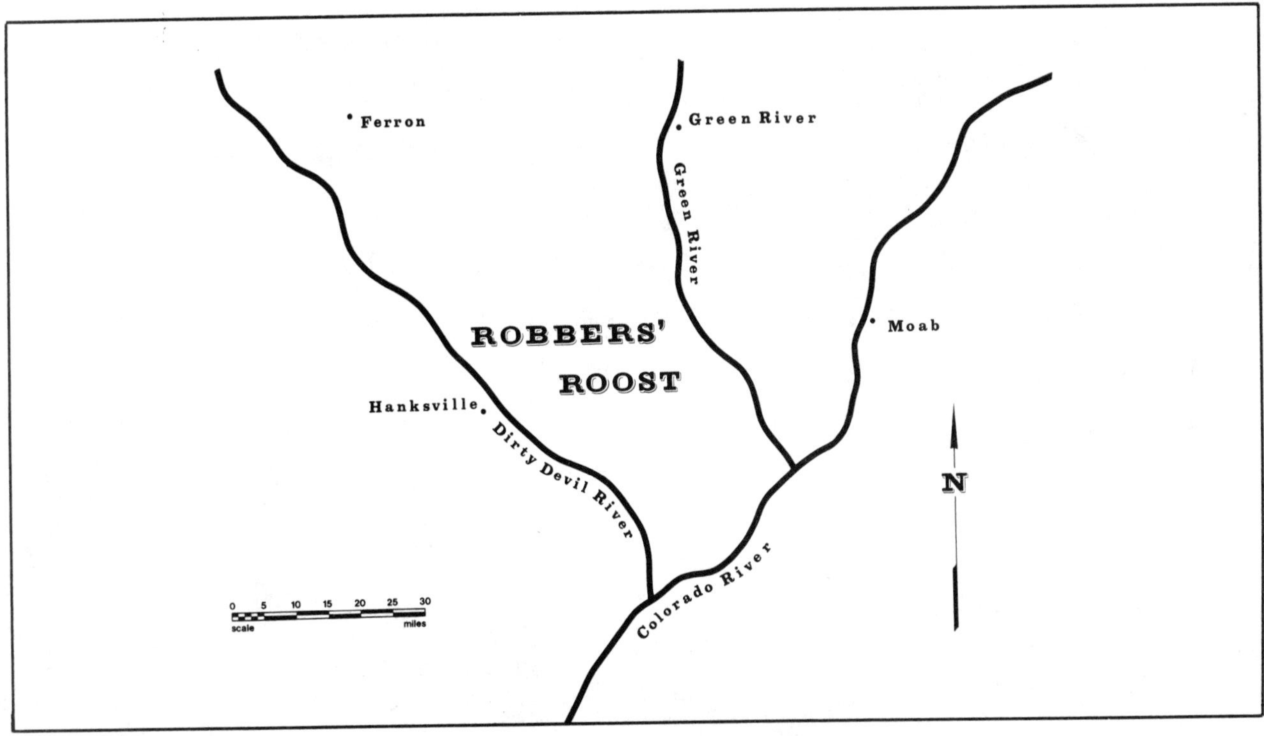


Robbers' Roost area of southeastern Utah.

## Salt Lake City

### Salt Lake County

In the old Salt Lake City cemetery can be found the grave of the notorious Captain Jack Slade, killer of Jules Reni (Beni) of Julesburg, Colorado,* and general troublemaker who was hanged by Montana vigilantes in 1864 (see *Virginia City, Montana*).

Around 1862 or 1863, Slade was put in charge of the Overland Stage station at Weber, Utah, just outside Ogden. Although basically a peaceful man, Captain Jack was a problem when drunk, and over the years he developed quite a reputation as a hard case. Mark Twain, in *Roughing It*, wrote of Slade that "it was hardly possible to realize that this pleasant person was the pitiless scourge of the outlaws, the rawhand-and-bloody-bones the nursing mothers of the mountains terrified their children with."

Slade liked to tear thing up when drunk, and after one such affair at Weber he was fired by the stage company. His wife, Virginia, went to live in Salt Lake City, and Slade headed for the gold camps of Montana. He got lucky, became fairly prosperous, and was soon joined by his wife and adopted son, Jimmy. But the bottle still plagued him, and after a particularly savage spree he irked the wrong faction in Virginia City. The vigilantes, still giddy over recent successes in doing away with troublemakers, put Jack to the rope. Virginia City had his body returned for burial at the Salt Lake City cemetery. Due to clerical errors, the location of his grave was lost for years. In the 1970s outlaw researcher Kerry Ross Boren dug into cemetery records and found the site (Block B, Lot 6, Grave 7).

There is an interesting but weakly documented story that sometime in 1900 Butch Cassidy slipped into Salt Lake City for a secret meeting with a local criminal attorney, C. W. Powers. Cassidy supposedly engaged the lawyer to approach Utah Governor Heber Wells and arrange a conference for the purpose of granting Cassidy amnesty, presumably in return for Butch's promise that he would forego the outlaw trail forever. According to the tale, Wells declined, but suggested an alternative: if Cassidy would ask for the Union Pacific Railroad to drop its charges against him in return for his promise to go straight, Wells would do what he could to persuade the railroad officials to accept the proposition. To make the deal even more attractive, Wells suggested that Cassidy offer to become a railway guard on the Union Pacific's express trains, thus allowing the railroad to keep an eye on him while at the same time, it was hoped, persuading other bandits to stay clear of the U.P. line. As preposterous as the plan was, the story goes on to say that Union Pacific officials did agree to meet with the outlaw to talk. A time and a place were set, and Butch showed up; however, the U.P. officials were delayed en route, and Butch, suspecting a double-cross, gave up and left.

Washington 1886

# WASHINGTON

## Creston
### Lincoln County

The state of Washington's most notorious outlaw was Harry Tracy (real name, Harry Severns) who together with a fellow fugitive, Dave Merrill, led authorities on a not-so-merry chase following their escape from the Oregon State Penitentiary in June 1902 (see *Salem, Oregon*). Following their escape, during which they killed three guards, Tracy and Merrill fled north into Washington, where Tracy may, or may not, have killed Merrill near the Lewis County town of Napavine.*

It was believed that the outlaws were heading for Canada, but after leaving the Napavine area, Tracy headed east. In late July or early August he crossed the Columbia River at Wenatchee and entered Lincoln County. Around August 3 he rode into a ranch owned by a man named Gene Eddy just south of the town of Creston, which is on US 2 about fifty miles west of Spokane. Somewhere along the way Tracy had picked up a young boy by the name of George Goldfinch. Some say the outlaw forced the youth to join him, but apparently the lad succeeded in convincing Tracy that he could be trusted: on August 5 he talked the outlaw into letting him ride into Creston alone, presumably to pick up supplies. The boy rode straight to the railroad depot and wired the Lincoln County sheriff at Davenport. A bystander overheard him sending the telegram and alerted four friends in Creston that the famous fugitive Harry Tracy was out at the Eddy ranch.

Hoping to get a sizable reward for capturing the outlaw, the eavesdropper and his friends rode out to the ranch. Tracy, probably suspicious over the Goldfinch boy's failure to return, was watching the road and spotted them coming. He grabbed his rifle and headed for a nearby field. Several shots were exchanged, and Tracy took cover behind a large rock in the middle of the field. A heavy gunfight erupted, and Tracy, only partially protected by the rock, took two hits in the leg.

Tracy managed to hold off his attackers through late afternoon, but around dusk, the sheriff's posse from Davenport arrived. Tracy tried to escape in the darkness, but shots sent him back to his rock. During the night, the posseman heard only one more shot from the outlaw. As dawn broke the next morning they closed in and found his body. He had ended his life with a bullet in the head.

The ranch where the outlaw made his last stand is still there. Local residents call it the "Harry Tracy Ranch." Today it is owned by a man named Everett Cole who lives nearby. According to Jim Dullenty, former Spokane newspaperman and now editor of *True West*, every year a half-dozen or so carloads of tourists drive out from Spokane to visit the site, especially the "Harry Tracy Rock." Most of the buildings have been restored and look pretty much the way they did when Tracy was there.

## Ellensburg
### Kittitas County

The Wild Bunch of Wyoming covered much ground near the turn of the century, but there is scant evidence they wandered as far west as Washington state, at least in their heyday. However, three outlaws who later were associated with that gang did spend some time in the state around 1891-92. They were Matt Warner (real name, Willard Erastus Christianson) and brothers Bill McCarty and Tom McCarty. Warner and Tom McCarty may have operated a cattle ranch in southeastern Washington, and it is likely all three were engaged in more than one robbery in the state during those years.

Matt Warner was reportedly jailed in Ellensburg (which is at the junction of Interstates 82 and 90) in 1892, shortly after he and the McCartys robbed the bank at Roslyn, Washington, which is about twenty-five miles north of Ellensburg. The holdup was a botched affair, and it is believed two townspersons were shot by Tom McCarty. Another man, George McCarty, possibly a brother of Tom and Bill, has also been mentioned in at least one account of the incident as having been jailed with Warner; however, it is more likely that it was either Tom or Bill. Somehow, probably through bribing a jail official, the two outlaws obtained tools and weapons and engineered an escape just days before their trial. Once outside they darkened their faces and wrapped themselves in blankets, hoping to pass unnoticed as Indians. It did not work, and they were picked up at the livery stable after a brief scuffle in which the man with Warner was injured.

Despite their attempted escape, Warner and his companion apparently left Ellensburg free men, possibly through more bribes. The following year Bill McCarty was killed during a bank robbery at Delta, Colorado.*

## Gray's Harbor County

He had a name, John Turnow, but to most he was just "the wild man." They said as a teenager he "was never quite right," and was a "brooding loner." As an adult he grew to an enormous six feet five inches and weighed at least 250 pounds. By age thirty he had become more animal than man, living most of the year alone in the wilds of the southern Olympic Peninsula, near the Wynooche River. He was a crack shot with a rifle and could track prey almost anywhere.

John Turnow in death. *Washington State Historical Society.*

Sometime in 1909 Turnow must have caused somebody trouble. That year he was taken from his beloved woods and sent to an insane asylum in Oregon. But they could not hold him in captivity. While in jail in Salem, awaiting transfer to another institution, he escaped and returned to the only place he felt safe, the misty wilderness of the peninsula.

The wild man was almost forgotten until a foggy day in 1910 when two bodies were found in the woods near his haunts. Loggers began to worry if they had to work in his area. "He could break a man in half," some said, and "shoot the eye out of a grouse at a hundred yards." A posse was organized, but they could find only his tracks, which would eventually disappear in the heavy underbrush. After a particularly cold winter, some argued that he had probably frozen, but others knew better. In March 1911 a trapper found his spring camp on the Satsop River near a clearing called Oxbow, thirty-five miles into the dense wilderness. Grays Harbor county sheriff Colin McKenzie and a deputy, A. V. Elmer, went in after him. Two weeks later a search party found their bodies near the site of the camp, each with a bullet in the head. A $5,000 reward was offered for the wild man, and manhunters searched the lower peninsula all summer with no luck. In the fall he broke into a logging company store house and stole a pair of boots for the coming winter.

Nothing was seen of the wild man throughout 1912, and many assumed he had either frozen to death or moved elsewhere. But the following April a deputy sheriff, Giles Quimby, and two loggers, Louis Blair and Charlie Lathrop, found a crude hut about a mile from where the bodies of McKenzie and Elmer had been found. All three men were armed, and they decided to work their way into the woods on the chance that Turnow was still around. He was. The three traveled only a few yards when a giant form leaped out from behind a hemlock tree. A rifle cracked, and Blair crumpled to the ground with a bullet hole in his forehead. Quimby got off a quick shot but missed. Seconds later, a bullet split Lathrop's skull.

Quimby hugged the ground, partially buried in the heavy brush. The wild man was still behind the hemlock. Now and then Quimby could see his furry beard as the giant glanced about, trying to locate the deputy. Slowly Quimby took aim, just at the point where the beard disappeared behind the trunk. When he thought the wild man was about to lean forward, he fired. The bark splintered and he fired again. More bark and another shot, then another and another, until the rifle was empty. Then Quimby ran.

Returning later that evening with help, Quimby found his dead companions. Cautiously the group approached the hemlock. Turnow was still there, on his back, clutching his rifle, his ragged gunnysack clothes soaked with blood: a grotesque, silent creature in death.

## Kennewick
### Benton County

Kennewick is in southeastern Washington on the Columbia River just southeast of Richland. Local history buffs still talk about a shootout that occurred near the town on October 31, 1906. The battle was fought at Poplar Grove, a hobo jungle then about four miles north of downtown Kennewick, near the Burlington Northern Railroad bridge over the river. The night before, somebody had burglarized two Kennewick stores—Tull & Goodwin's General Merchandise and the Kennewick Hardware Company—and Benton County sheriff Alex G. McNeill was called in from nearby Prosser to investigate. McNeill was scheduled to arrive by train the morning of the 31st. Joe Holzhey, his deputy, was already on the scene and had spotted two strangers out at Popular Grove acting suspiciously. It was later determined that one was a drifter, Robert A. "Kid" Barker, from Florence, Colorado, and the other was a sheepherder, Jake Lake, from Wallula, Washington.

Shortly before 3:00 P.M., Sheriff McNeill, Deputy Holzhey, Kennewick town marshal Mike D. Glover, and a local citizen, H. E. Roseman, rode out to the grove. As they neared the two strangers' campfire, they heard a voice call out from the trees, "Good evening, gentlemen. You are looking for trouble, and you'll get it!" With that, a rifle barked, and Holzhey slumped to the ground with a bullet in his belly. Glover was hit next and then McNeill. Only the sheriff was able to fire back; he emptied his revolver in the direction of the shots, then retreated to safety near the railroad tracks. Roseman, who was not armed, found him there and helped him to return to town for medical attention.

A large posse was organized and returned near dusk. They found Glover dead and Holzhey dying. Deeper into the poplars lay Jake Lake, apparently the victim of one of McNeill's shots. Barker was gone. Bloodhounds were summoned, and by dark over 200 armed men were gathered at the edge of the woods. Before the night was over there would be one more death. A posseman, Forrest Perry, stumbled across Barker in the dark and shouted for him to put up his hands. Several other possemen mistook him for the outlaw and opened fire. Perry died three hours later. Soon afterward Barker surrendered.

## Napavine
### Lewis County

Napavine is on Interstate 5 between Longview and Tacoma. A woods just north of the town may have been the end of the trail for outlaw Dave Merrill, companion of the notorious Harry Tracy. On June 9, 1902, Tracy and Merrill escaped from the Oregon State Penitentiary at Salem.* The two fugitives headed north into Washington. As they stopped along the way for money and supplies, they made no effort to hide their identities. Sometimes Tracy would engage in lengthy discourses on how he had suffered injustice at the hands of the authorities. These accounts made exciting reading, and afterwards newspaper reporters raced to interview his listeners. Reports of the chase spread across the country, and several eastern newspapers assigned special correspondents to follow the outlaws' trail.

Tracy and Merrill apparently were heading for Canada, but around Napavine their trail disappeared. Nothing was heard from them until mid-July, when a Napavine woman, Mary A. Waggoner, and her twelve-year-old son noticed a foul-smelling odor coming from a patch of bushes near where they were picking blackberries in a woods north of town. They investigated and

Harry Tracy. *Charles C. Goodhall Collection.*

Bloodhounds on the trail of Harry Tracy. *Washington State Historical Society.*

found a decomposed body with three bullet holes in it. Claiming the body was one of the escaped fugitives, Mrs. Waggoner requested a reward. A coroner's jury was convened and ruled that the body was indeed Dave Merrill's. They based their decision, however, soley on the testimony of several of Merrill's friends and relatives. Prison officials in Oregon refused to accept the verdict and refused to pay Mrs. Waggoner the reward.

Today most researchers believe the body was not Merrill's; that he, his family, and possibly Tracy staged the hoax. Years later a relative of Merrill's said members of the family received letters from the outlaw over the years from a town in eastern Washington. Tracy himself was eventually located near Creston, Washington,* where he was cornered by a sheriff's posse and died by his own hand.

## Spokane
### Spokane County

According to Butch Cassidy's biographer, Larry Pointer, Spokane was Cassidy's home from 1910 until his death in 1937. Evidence gathered by Pointer and also by *True West* editor Jim Dullenty, then a reporter for the Spokane *Daily Chronicle*, suggest that Cassidy lived in that city under the name William T. Phillips.

Soon after arriving in Spokane in December 1910 Phillips went to work for the Washington Water Power Company as a draftsman. Later he opened a small machine shop of his own. Operating as the Phillips Manufacturing Company, first at 1612 North Monroe and later at 1326 East Sprague, Phillips's shop produced "adding and listing machines" and also performed various machine work as a subcontractor for larger companies.

William Phillips and his wife, Gertrude, lived for a while above his shop on Sprague Street, then in 1925 moved to a comfortable home at 1001 West Providence. They adopted a son, William R. (Billy) Phillips, who later provided much information about his father to Pointer and Dullenty. Other sources of information on the connection between Phillips and Cassidy were two Spokane men, William C. Lundstrom and Charles F. "Fred" Harrison, both of whom lived in Wyoming at the turn of the century and knew Cassidy. Harrison owned the White Owl Saloon in Sheridan, Wyoming, and Lundstrom was his bartender.

It is believed that Phillips returned to Wyoming in 1925 for an extended tour of his old haunts and that later he went to Utah to visit his family home at Circleville.* He made another trip to Wyoming in the summer of 1930 after his business failed in Spokane, possibly to try to locate hidden Wild Bunch loot buried during the 1890s (see *Lander, Wyoming*). On returning to Spokane, apparently empty-handed, Phillips sold his home on Providence Street and bought a cheaper house on Kiernan Street. During the depression years he earned a living doing odd jobs. Following still another trip to Wyoming in 1934, Phillips returned to Spokane to write his "memoirs," a manuscript which he called *Bandit Invincible*. In it he did not admit that he was Butch Cassidy but wrote as a "bystander," implying that he was at least a member of Cassidy's outlaw gang. While containing much information presumably known only to a member of the Wild Bunch, the story was so poorly written that Phillips could not find a publisher.

Flat broke, desperate, and probably terminally ill, Phillips, if indeed Butch Cassidy, attempted to return to his criminal ways in 1935. Inspired by the wave of kidnappings for ransom that swept the nation in the early thirties, Phillips planned a kidnapping of his own. His intended victim was a local businessman, William Hutchison Cowles. The plan, which Phillips later revealed to his friend Lundstrom, was elaborate and included a carefully prepared hideout and a prearranged alibi. Apparently, however, Phillips could not convince anyone to assist him in whisking away the victim, and he had to abandon the idea.

Phillips made one last trip to Wyoming in 1936, presumably still looking for hidden loot. The following year his health deteriorated rapidly, and he was placed in a nursing home. He died on July 20, 1937, at Broadacres, the county poor farm at Spangle, Washington.

"Harry Tracy Rock," site of the death of the outlaw near Creston, Washington. *Jim Dullenty Collection.*

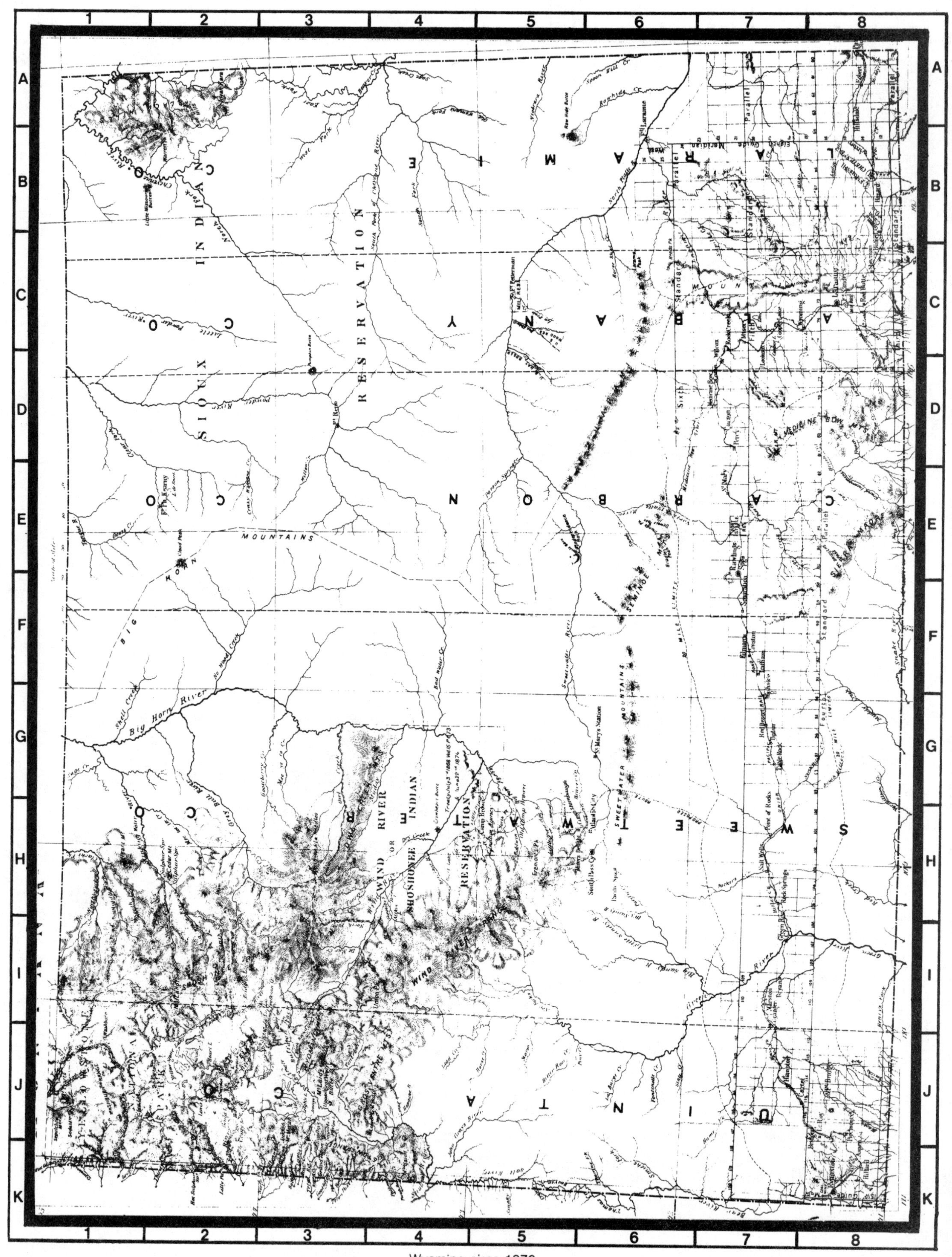


Wyoming circa 1876

# WYOMING

## Auburn
### Lincoln County

The only time the notorious Butch Cassidy was captured during his illustrious outlaw career was on April 8, 1892, at a ranch in Star Valley near Auburn, which is just off US 89 near the Idaho line. The man given credit for bringing Cassidy in was a Uinta County deputy sheriff named Bob Calverly, whose account of the arrest, if accurate, suggests that Butch's career nearly ended that day.

Cassidy, on being told that there was a warrant out for his arrest, answered, "Well, get to shooting," and he whipped out his revolver. Calverly said he drew his gun, too, and "put the barrel. . . almost to his [Cassidy's] stomach," but the weapon misfired. Butch apparently was prevented from shooting by a third man (possibly fellow-outlaw Al Hainer) who stepped between him and the deputy. When Calverly's revolver finally fired, the bullet grazed Butch's forehead, knocking him down. Calverly said from then on the outlaw offered no further resistance and was taken to Lander* where he eventually was convicted of having in his possession a stolen horse.

## Baggs
### Carbon County

Baggs, together with its sister community to the east, Dixon, are located in the south central part of the state, just above the Colorado line. Both towns, being within a couple days' ride from the outlaw country around Brown's Park (then Brown's Hole), Colorado, occasionally were forced to tolerate visits from renegade gangs, particularly the Wyoming Wild Bunch. An eyewitness tells of one such visit by the Wild Bunchers in the summer of 1897, shortly after the robbery of the Butte County Bank at Belle Fourche, South Dakota,* during which both Baggs and Dixon were literally "taken over" by the rowdy outlaws. The witness said the gang shot up the Bull Dog Saloon in Baggs but later paid the owner, Jack Ryan, one silver dollar for every bullet hole they made.

Baggs is also known for a colorful town marshal, Bob Meldrum, who served the community in that capacity in 1911 and 1912. Some say Meldrum, before he came to Baggs, was a hired killer on the order of Tom Horn. In fact, Meldrum may have ridden with Horn while Tom was a Pinkerton agent, before Horn hired on with the cattlemen to dispose of rustlers. From some of the stories about Meldrum, he may have been even more cold-blooded than Horn. It is said that in 1899, while working as a harness maker in Dixon, Meldrum discovered that a co-worker, a man named Wilkinson, was wanted by the law. As the two men left the post office (where Meldum saw Wilkinson's name on a reward poster), Meldrum dropped a few steps behind his friend and put a bullet in the back of his head. Another tale involving Meldrum, supposedly while riding with Horn, has him assisting in the assassination of two innocent cowboys whom he and Horn mistook for rustlers.

As Baggs's town marshal, Meldrum killed his last man on January 19, 1912. A cowboy named Chick Bowen and two companions got a little too noisy whooping it up in the Elkhorn Hotel. Meldrum followed them from the hotel to Calvert's General Store, where he grabbed Bowen and knocked his hat off. Bowen protested and Meldrum shot him in the stomach. Bystanders rushed the injured cowboy to the Red Cross pharmacy for treatment, but he died within the hour. In earlier times, a jury probably would have acquitted a lawman under such circumstances, but Bowen was well-liked in town, and Meldrum was not, and by 1912 the citizens of Baggs were in no mood to renew its reputation as a lawless frontier town. Meldrum drew a sentence of five to seven years in the Wyoming State Penitentiary for voluntary manslaughter. He served six years, and on release on 1918 apparently hung up his gun for good. It is believed he settled in Walcott, Wyoming, and returned to harness-making.

## Bear River City
### Uinta County

Bear River City was situated in the far southwestern corner of the state, east of Evanston where the Union Pacific tracks cross Sulpher Creek. Little evidence remains today that for a few months in 1868 the town boasted of 2,000 inhabitants. In late September of that year a rumor had spread that the site would be the new railroad's winter terminus, and within days the area was overrun by an assortment of fast-buck merchants, whiskey peddlers, land speculators, bunko artists, tin horn gamblers, powdery prostitutes, general roughnecks, and a few honest citizens. What only a few weeks before had been a tiny cluster of log and mud huts was now a twenty-four-hour town of tents and falsefronts, bulging with the means to satisfy nearly every popular form of greed, lust, and thirst.

As the unruly element that always followed new rails moved in to take over, a vigilance committee was hastily formed for midnight duty, and soon swift justice was ruthlessly applied. A local resident later wrote: "I got up one morning at my camp near Beartown (Bear River City) and noticed something hanging near the railroad track, and I walked down to see what it was. It was those three fellows whom I knew had been banished from Montana in 1864. A tag was pinned to their coats, 'warning to the road agents.' "

But the vigilantes' choice of victims was unfortunate. One of the lynched men had a brother working with the railroad construction gang camped at the edge of town. He stirred up a handful of the rougher members of the outfit, and they stormed into town seeking revenge. But their first stop was a saloon, and by the time they were ready to cause real trouble, they were unsteady on their feet. A group of vigilantes quickly disarmed them and marched them off to jail, but with three of their comrades lynched and another handful in jail, the crowd back at the construction gang camp began to ferment. Plied with whiskey and well-armed with rifles, pickaxes, and torches, they eventually fused into a mob and spilled into town. Their first stop was the jail, where they shot the marshal, turned the prisoners loose, and set fire to the building. Next they wrecked the tent occupied by the town printer and demolished his press. From there they turned toward Nuckoll's General Store where a group of townspeople had fled for safety. Fortified by Nuckull's supply of guns and ammunition, these man managed to fend off the attackers, preventing them from getting close enough to set the structure on fire.

The battle raged throughout the morning. Around noon the townsmen slipped a messenger out with instructions to ride to Fort Bridger for help. By late afternoon the mob began to tire of the seige and withdrew to the hills overlooking the town, vowing to return after dark and set all of Bear River City ablaze. The townsmen posted guards at the end of the street, but it was unnecessary. Filled with more whiskey, the mob finally slept off its rage. The troops arrived from Fort Bridger the following morning and declared martial law. The riot was over, and the citizens of Bear River City had their town back.

One of the leaders of the rioters was a tough 38-year-old ex-New Yorker named Tom Smith. Some say he had been a New York City cop and was accustomed to bashing heads. He had hired on with the Union Pacific in Nebraska in 1867 and was working his way west. At Bear River City he apparently was injured in the battle and was left behind to nurse his wounds when the rails moved on. Having picked up the nickname "Bear River Tom," he capitalized on his reputation as a hard case and hired on as marshal of several railroad towns during the next two years. In 1870 Smith drifted to Kansas, where he was in the process of taming Abilene when he was killed while serving a warrant (see *Abilene*).

## Carbon
### Carbon County

Carbon was the end of the trail for Dutch Charlie Burris, a member of the Big Nose George Parrott gang and presumed killer of Union Pacific detective Henry "Tip" Vincent in 1878.

That year some say Parrott and his gang joined up with Frank James, and possibly Jesse, to try their hands at train robbery. It was spring, two years after the James brothers' narrow escape at Northfield, Minnesota. Still on the run, it is said that Frank and Jesse may have drifted west, into the Powder River region of northern Wyoming. Prowling the area also was Big Nose George, who was then leading a makeshift band of former road agents out of Dakotas' Black Hills. How the Jameses and Parrott met is not known, but if they did, they may very well have joined forces.

There were few banks in Wyoming at the time, so the natural choice for a robbery would have been the Union Pacific Railroad. In early June the gang selected as their first victim the U.P.'s westbound No. 3 at a spot near Carbon, now a caved-in ghost town on the sun-blistered plains about ten miles west of Medicine Bow.

After breaking into a section house for picks and shovels, the outlaws pried loose a rail. But as they were wrapping a wire around it, in order to yank it aside as the train approached, they heard a handcar coming down the track. Scrambling for cover in the tall grass, they barely made it out of sight when John Brown, a Union Pacific section foreman came pumping by. Brown spotted the loose rail but kept on going; if he suspected it had been loosened by would-be robbers, he never let on. He sped toward the oncoming express and flagged it down. The Parrott gang's first try at train robbery was a flop.

When word spread of the robbery attempt, posses converged on the scene. They split into two groups: half rode north toward the Medicine Bow River and half headed west toward Hanna. However, two of the possemen, U.P. detective Tip Vincent and Bob Widdowfield, a coal mine boss from Carbon, had a hunch the outlaws might have fled south toward Elk Mountain. Before long Vincent and Widdowfield did pick up a trail leading toward Rattlesnake Pass. Unwisely, they followed the tracks right on in, apparently never suspecting the outlaws might be waiting in ambush. A bullet split Bob Widdowfield's skull. Vincent spurred his horse but got less than a hundred yards. The two bodies were found several days later.

Not long afterward, gang member Dutch Charley Burris was picked up in Montana and returned to Wyoming by train. On reaching Carbon, he was dragged out of the coach and into the depot by an angry mob. Surrounded by friends of the murdered Bob Widdowfield, Charley figured his only hope was to confess and plead for mercy. A railroad telegrapher was summoned to take down the outlaw's confession. But afterward, instead of being taken to jail as he had expected, Charley was marched outside and made to stand on a barrel. A rope was quickly placed around his neck, and the other end thrown over a telegraph pole. Someone asked the outlaw if he had anything to say before he met his maker. But before he could answer, Bob Widdowfield's widow stepped out from the crowd, "No, the son-of-a-bitch has nothing to say," and she kicked the barrel out from under him.

The following year Big Nose George Parrott met a similar end at Rawlins.*

## Cheyenne
### Laramie County

Cheyenne is in southeastern Wyoming at the junction of Interstates 80 and 25. The town suffered early at the hands of outlaws, but being a division point for the Union Pacific Railroad, it prospered and grew rapidly.

Tom Horn awaiting trial in Cheyenne. *American Heritage Center, University of Wyoming.*

Also, the town was blessed with an honest and courageous sheriff, Thomas Jefferson Carr.

Jeff Carr was elected in 1870 and wasted no time in cleaning up Laramie County. The worst troublemaker at the time was a hard case named Charlie Stanley who ran a bawdy house in Cheyenne's Golden Gate District on Ferguson Street, which also served as a "robbers' roost" for local muggers and thieves. Sheriff Carr and two deputies confronted Stanley in the street and marched him off toward jail on an assortment of charges. Stanley, however, always carried a Derringer in an inside pocket. He whipped it out and shot Carr in the ear. The sheriff, with blood spurting from his wound, wrenched the gun away and slammed his prisoner in the head with it. Now it was Charlie's turn to bleed. The blow cleared Stanley's thinking, and he allowed himself to be led to the lockup with no further trouble.

The following month sheriff Carr presided over the first legal execution in Wyoming Territory: the hanging of a "half-breed" named John Boyer who had been convicted of killing two men at a roadhouse outside of town. Carr let it be known that the hanging was his official announcement that Cheyenne was a town that outlaws had better avoid.

Cheyenne surged to life in the mid-1870s when gold was discovered in the Black Hills. Wild Bill Hickok arrived in 1875 and spent perhaps a year there. Hickok's name had become a legend and he no doubt was issued more than one challenge by barroom showoffs, but apparently his stay was relatively quiet. There is speculation that his eyesight had begun to fail him, either from glaucoma or a gonorrhea infection and that he did his best to avoid troublemakers.

The town was the scene of a classic gunfight on March 9, 1877. The participants were Charlie Harrison and Jim Levy. Harrison was a sporting man from the East who reportedly had put several former enemies in their graves. Levy came from Nevada, where he gained a reputation as a gunslinger in the early 1870s (see *Pioche, Nevada*). In Cheyenne the two apparently locked horns over a card game. Witnesses said remarks by Harrison about the Irish brought Levy to a boil, and the two agreed to meet later in the street. They did, in front of Frenchy's Saloon at the corner of 16th and Eddy, in what apparently approached a Hollywood-type Western showdown. Harrison fired first, possibly several times, and missed. Levy carefully took aim and drilled Charlie in the chest. Harrison went down, and Levy walked up and put a second bullet in him as he lay helpless on the ground. This second shot, deemed unsporting and unnecessary by bystanders, turned much of the town against Levy. However, any charges against Jim were evidently dropped.

Cheyenne was also Tom Horn's town. Between the day Horn, as a lad of fourteen, ran away from his father's farm in Missouri and the day he died at the end of a rope, his trail covered much of the West. But Tom Horn "the outlaw" belonged to Wyoming. To this day in some parts of the state, to lay in wait to kill a man is to "Tom Horn" him. Around Cheyenne, Horn was known as the "exterminator," a title he often used himself and one he became quite proud of.

National Guard troops patroling downtown Cheyenne prior to hanging of Tom Horn. Rumors circulated that Horn's friends might try to free him. *American Heritage Center, University of Wyoming.*

Joe LeFors, peace officer who engineered arrest of Tom Horn. *American Heritage Center, University of Wyoming.*

Horn's first trips through Wyoming were on the Union Pacific as a Pinkerton agent out of Denver. But Horn disliked the work and when he learned that several Wyoming cattle ranchers were looking for a "stock detective" to run down rustlers, he bade the Pinkertons farewell. Horn's first job with the cattlemen was with the Swan Land and Cattle Company north of Cheyenne on Chugwater Creek. Officially he was hired to break broncs; his real work, however, was to keep an eye out for rustlers, especially among his fellow wranglers. He did his work well, and during the late 1890s he moved on to similar jobs with other cattle outfits. However, sometime during those years Tom stepped over the line that the law draws on such conduct, and he became an exterminator. After tortuous weeks on the trail running down a range thief, Horn frequently would see him turned loose by a sympathetic jury. Tom pointed this out to his employers and suggested that justice might better be served if his prey never reached a courtroom. Eventually Tom proved his point. Quietly, among the cattlemen, he let it be known that he would lay a rustler out cold for a price. To prove that he had done the job he would leave a small rock under the victim's head.

How many paid killings Horn was involved in will never be known. The end came in July 1901 when a rock was found under the body of a fourteen-year-old boy, Willie Nickell, at the gate of his family's ranch near

Laramie. Horn was known to have been friendly with a family with whom the Nickells had been feuding, and he was suspected of committing the crime. But the only evidence was the rock, and this was not enough to gain a conviction. Five months went by, and it appeared that the matter would be dropped. Then, in December 1901, Horn received a letter from an old acquaintance, United States deputy marshal Joe LeFors of Cheyenne. LeFors invited Horn to Cheyenne to talk about a "stock detective" job in Montana that the lawman had heard about. Horn got liquored up before the meeting, and LeFors saw that he was kept well-supplied during the conversation. Talk turned to the Nickell boy's death, and Tom made several incriminating statements—statements that he later claimed were made only because he was drunk and eager to brag. But Tom's loose talk sealed his fate: LeFors had a deputy sheriff from Laramie County and a court stenographer hiding in the back room of his office. Every word of the conversation was taken down and used against Horn in court. In November 1903 the exterminator was himself exterminated on the gallows in Cheyenne.

## Dubois
### Fremont County

Butch Cassidy once owned a ranch where the town of Dubois now stands (in western Wyoming, on US 26 approximately sixty miles east of Grand Teton National Park). Cassidy and a partner, Al Hainer, bought the ranch in 1890 from two bachelors, Hugh Yeoman and Charles Peterson, possibly out of Butch's share of the proceeds of the robbery of the San Miguel Valley Bank at Telluride, Colorado.*

According to a local newspaper item, Cassidy and Hainer "made the appearance of going into the horse raising business," but were soon pegged by local citizens as "sports" who "spent their money freely" in the neighboring towns of Lander and Ft. Washakie. Cassidy and Hainer remained in the area for two years, during which time Butch apparently engaged in little, if any, outlaw activity.

## The Hole-in-the-Wall
### Johnson County

The Hole-in-the-Wall itself is unremarkable; in fact, you cannot even call it a "hole." It is more of a notch, roughly V-shaped, near the rim of the "Red Wall," a steep vermillion cliff in southwestern Johnson County, about sixteen miles southwest (as the crow flies) of Kaycee. Kaycee is a tiny town of 275 inhabitants on Interstate 25 about 50 miles south of Buffalo.

Tales about the Hole are endless and over the years have been widely embellished. One of the most popular, which has been told and retold until it has become fused into Hollywood westerns, is that behind the Hole once lay a classic outlaw town, replete with false-front stores, houses with picket fences, and raggedy children running about, all protected by towering cliffs through which there was but one narrow entrance, guarded day and night by sharpshooters. True, there is a valley behind the wall, and once there were even rough-hewn cabins here and there, but nothing resembling a town and nothing quite so defensible. In fact, few persons familiar with the area during the outlaw years could agree on just how valuable it was as a hideout. Butch Cassidy was supposed to have said that twelve men could stand off a hundred at the Hole's entrance, but the ability to defend the valley at the notch in the Red Wall meant little, because anyone familiar with the valley would not attack in that direction. To the north, west and south there were great rolling foothills, all of which contained passable trails used by Indians for years.

Although the valley behind the Hole was not impregnable, it was indeed secluded and thus offered a haven for outlaws. Thelma Gatchill Condit, a local historian

Harvey (Kid Curry) Logan, member of Wyoming's Wild Bunch. *Union Pacific Railroad Museum Collections.*

Hole-in-the-Wall area. *American History Center, University of Wyoming.*

who spent nearly a lifetime exploring the region, suggests why:

> It was one place, because of its wild bigness and rugged terrain, ideally safe and delightfully isolated, full of little grassy mountain pockets where tired, used horses, as well as pilfered broncs, could graze contentedly until moving-on time; full of little hidden canyons especially made for the leisurely changing of brands. It was not a hurry-up place at all; there was always plenty of safe time. Here train robbers could be swallowed up like magic, bringing sheriff's posses to a sudden halt, leaving them feeling furiously foolish to have been foiled so completely and unexpectedly when the moment of closing-in seemed so certain.

Condit also believed that the valley behind the Hole was popular with the outlaws because it was ideal training ground for their horses. Butch Cassidy in particular was obsessed with the idea that a bandit's fate rested with the quality of his mount. Before he became a familiar face on wanted posters, Cassidy owned a ranch in the valley on Blue Creek, about ten miles northwest of the Hole. It was said that Cassidy's corrals held some of the best horseflesh in the West. Cassidy's ranch is still there; the cabin still stands and is in fairly good condition. It is not, however, open to the public. Permission must be obtained from the owner, reportedly a descendant of the man who purchased the property from Butch in the 1890s.

The Hole-in-the-Wall valley probably was also a safe haven for outlaws because of the attitude of the permanent residents there. They were not inquisitive. Honest homesteaders and ranchers in the valley (and there were a handful) did not ask questions of those who might not be so honest.

The outlaw crowd usually behaved themselves behind the wall. For amusement, however, they occasionally plagued neighboring towns, especially Anderson (now Thermopolis) in nearby Hot Springs County. One day in the early nineties Butch Cassidy, in a rare fit of intoxication or anger, shot up the town cafe, and Harry Longabaugh (the Sundance Kid) did the same to the saloon. For general carousing, the boys from the Hole had two favorite haunts. One was the saloon at Kaycee, then just a crossroads, owned by two men named Tom O'Day and John Nolan, both of whom were said to be part-time rustlers themselves. The other hangout was Buffalo's Zindel Saloon, which in later years became the Rainbow Cafe, a popular stop for tourists.

No one knows for sure who first used the Hole to hide from the law. Some say it was a rustler named

Sanford "Sang" Thompson, who discovered in the mid-1880s that by shifting a few boulders about on the trail leading up to the notch at the wall's rim, one could make it appear there was no trail to the other side.

As a common hideout, the Hole finally fell into disuse following the Wild Bunch's last major holdup, the robbery of the Great Northern Coast Flyer at Exeter, Montana, in July 1901. The gang broke up after that, and without these renegades around, the region gradually became attractive to honest homesteaders who soon outnumbered their less savory predecessors.

But today a Hole-in-the-Wall gang still rides. Unlike the original bunch, the rules of today's gang forbid "gambling, guns, and women," while camping behind the wall. Each autumn the "gang," an incorporated Colorado group of ranchers and businessmen dedicated to "perpetuate the farfamed cow country traditions" while "engaging in robust pastimes of the Old West," rides through the Hole into the valley behind, to enjoy, undisturbed, a week-long session of "strong drink, windy stories, and horse-backing."

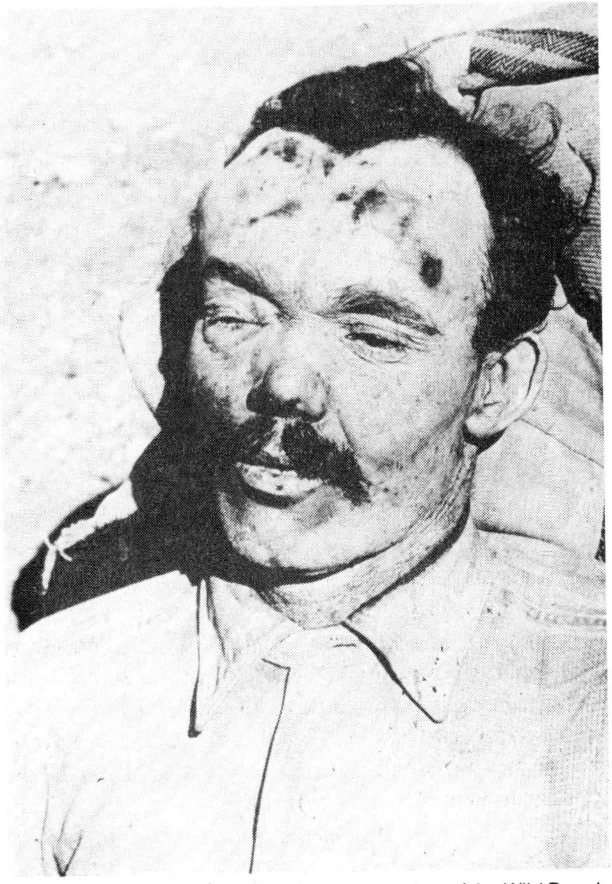

"Flat Nose" George Currie. This homely member of the Wild Bunch claimed he robbed trains "just for the fun of it." This photograph was taken in April 1900, shortly after Currie met his end at the hands of a Utah posse who mistook him for a rustler. *Pinkerton's Inc.*

Kaycee, Wyoming, nearest town to the Hole-in-the-Wall. *Wyoming State Archives, Museum and Historical Department.*

## Jackson Hole
### Teton County

Jackson Hole is the name given to the valley in western Wyoming that follows US 191 and the Snake River north from the town of Jackson to what is now Grand Teton National Park. Above the Hole, in Death Canyon not far from the site of the old J.Y. Dude Ranch on Phelps Lake, there is a tiny green meadow beside a deep, narrow mountain stream. It is said that if you get down on your hands and knees in that meadow and carefully part the fragile blue harebell and pale, elegant Columbine, you can still see the weathered remains of a 100-year-old drift fence, once said to house stolen ponies cautiously secreted away from prowling vigilantes who frequently combed the valley below.

The valley was at one time a popular hideaway for thieves and cutthroats who roamed the Teton range. Butch Cassidy possibly spent some time there and may have stashed part of the loot from one of his robberies somewhere along the willowy banks of Cache Creek. But despite the natural sanctuary offered by the valley, the area never became a true outlaw stronghold as did the Hole-in-the-Wall to the east, Colorado's Brown's Park, and Robbers' Roost in Utah. Generally, the Teton contingent of hell-raisers slipped in and out of the valley virtually unnoticed. Outlaws did venture into the town of Jackson from time to time for supplies and evening's entertainment, and occasionally they found the law waiting for them there. But if there were any spectacular shootouts between the good guys and bad guys (as presently portrayed on summer nights for the tourists), they have been lost to history.

Aside from Butch Cassidy, the most famous outlaw to roam the Jackson Hole region probably was a gunman and horse thief who rode under the name Teton Jackson (some say his real name was Harvey Gleason). Teton was downright mean and could be counted on to cause trouble of some kind wherever he went. Little is known of his early years, except that he ran a mule train for

Jackson, Wyoming. The wilderness in the distance was a popular outlaw hideout area. *American Heritage Center, University of Wyoming.*

the army during the Sioux War. Apparently he became dissatisfied with government pay and sold a few of the army's mules on his own. For this he ended up in the guard house, from which he promptly escaped by killing two troopers. He fled to the Tetons, took his new name, and joined up with a gang of renegades calling themselves the "Destroying Angels," whose specialty was raiding ranches and homesteads along the Utah and Idaho borders.

## Kemmerer
### Lincoln County

In the days following World War II, motorists traveling through southwestern Wyoming who happened to stop at a little cafe and gas station just outside of Kemmerer, where US 30 and US 189 intersect, probably paid little attention to the proprietor. He was ordinary looking, in his late fifties, with moderately rugged features. But this man was not ordinary: he could tell a story that would have kept a traveler spellbound for hours. The man was Bill Carlisle, last of Wyoming's notorious train robbers.

Carlisle's favorite target was the Union Pacific: the first time was in February 1916, just east of Green River. According to Bill, the idea came to him on the spur of the moment at a time when he was hungry, cold and jobless. He merely walked through the sleeper with a gun in the back of the porter, forcing him to collect money and valuables from the passengers. The affair went off so well Bill tried the same technique on the Overland Limited the following April, a few miles out of Cheyenne. His third robbery followed shortly thereafter—a passenger coach again, on the U.P.'s Limited No. 21 near Hanna, Wyoming, a small station between Rawlins and Medicine Bow. But this time Bill wrenched his ankle jumping off the train, and the next day a posse caught up with him in the willowed bottoms along the North Platte River. He was quickly tried and convicted, but in the fall of 1919 he escaped prison by hiding in a packing crate being shipped out of the workshop.

On November 21, 1919, Bill was back robbing trains, this time near Medicine Bow. But he picked a coach filled with doughboys returning from the war. A guard jumped him, and in the scuffle Bill shot himself in the hand. Weak from his wound, he was captured at a miner's cabin above Estabrook.

On his return to prison Bill became a changed man. He enrolled in a mail order business course and learned to use a typewriter. Later he became the prison librarian. By the time he was eligible for parole, he had so impressed the prison chaplain that he guaranteed Bill's return to an honest life, promising the parole board, "Should Bill Carlisle ever commit another crime, I will serve time either for him or with him." With the chaplain's help Bill borrowed money and opened a cigar store in Kemmerer. Later, he bought the gas station and cafe. Years afterward, when asked why he had returned to the very area where he was once known as a notorious train robber, Bill replied, "The best place to find a thing is where you lost it."

Kemmerer was also the home of Annie Byers Richey, possibly the only woman in Wyoming ever to be convicted of rustling. Annie and her husband, the Kemmerer school superintendent, owned the OXO ranch outside of town. On July 26, 1919, a neighboring rancher found two of his cows in Richey's herd with

Train robber Bill Carlisle following his capture. Bill later became a respected citizen of Kemmerer. *Wyoming State Archives, Museum and Historical Department.*

Green River Station, where Bill Carlisle launched his career as the last of Wyoming's famous train robbers. *Wyoming State Archives, Museum and Historical Department.*

his brand covered over by the OXO. A check of a boxcar load of cattle that Annie had recently shipped to market turned up several more suspicious brands.

Annie was arrested and charged with rustling. The case seemed routine until the day of her preliminary hearing. On her way to the courthouse she was shot and nearly killed by a "tall man on an iron-gray horse." Annie claimed she had no idea who the man was. When she recuperated, she was tried and convicted by a Lincoln County jury and sentenced to from one to six years in the state penitentiary. Her lawyer appealed, but the conviction was upheld. In the fall of 1921, while awaiting the court's order to report to prison, Annie was working on her ranch, repairing a fence. Neighbors saw her talking to a "tall man on an iron-gray horse." They thought they saw him ride off. After lunch, on returning to her fence work, Annie was heard to cry out, then fall to the ground. Shortly thereafter her hired man, Otto Palsenberger, also staggered and fell. Later it was discovered that both had been poisoned. Apparently while they were outside, somebody had sneaked into Annie's kitchen and laced a pot of stew she had simmering on the stove. The hired man survived, but Annie never regained consciousness. No trace of the mysterious stranger was ever found.

## Lander
### Fremont County

Lander is in west central Wyoming, at the junction of US 287 and State Highway 789. Butch Cassidy called Lander home for brief periods beginning, probably, around 1889. He had recently launched his lawless career with the robbery of the San Miguel Valley Bank at Telluride, Colorado.* One source says he worked for a while as a butcher in Lander and thus acquired his nickname. Other sources say he hung around with "hard cases" in town, but apparently he gave local peace officers no real trouble. One reason may have been a local girl, Mary Boyd, whom he might have married had he not chosen the outlaw trail.

In 1891 Butch did run afoul of the law. That year two Big Horn ranchers lost some of their finest saddle horses, and several were traced to Cassidy and a ranching partner, Al Hainer. Cassidy and Hainer had moved on by then, but were picked up near Auburn, Wyoming,* and returned to Lander. On June 23, 1893, they were found not guilty but were immediately arrested on a similar charge involving a second horse. Hainer got off again, but Cassidy was found guilty and sentenced to two years at hard labor at the Wyoming State Penitentiary.

After his release from prison, it is believed that Butch periodically returned to Lander to visit Mary Boyd. In May 1892 Mary gave birth to a baby girl, possibly Cassidy's. Mary later married a local cowboy named Rhodes but may have continued to see Butch on his return trips to Fremont County.

There is some evidence that Cassidy visited Lander as late as 1936, using the name William T. Phillips. It was said he was looking for loot the Wild Bunch had buried during their active years. At the time Phillips was living in Spokane, Washington.* Several Lander residents who knew Butch in the old days later swore that he and Phillips were one and the same.

North of Lander, on the old Emery Burnaugh Muddy Creek Road ranch south of Owl Creek Mountains, there is a lonely grave on a gravel point immediately above a partially hidden cave. It has been said the ranch was used by Cassidy and the Wild Bunch as a hideout in the late 1890s. The grave may be the last resting place of an outlaw named Harvey Ray who rode with the gang during the robbery of the Butte County Bank at Belle Fourche, South Dakota,* in 1897 and the holdup of the Union Pacific express car at Wilcox, Wyoming,* in 1899. Following the Wilcox holdup, the outlaws headed north and tangled with a posse outside of Casper, where a sheriff from Douglass, Joe Hazen, was killed in the fight. Descendents of Emery Burnaugh say the gang hid out at the Muddy Creek Road ranch shortly after the Hazen killing and that one of the outlaws, believed to be Ray, died from his wounds shortly after arriving.

The flavor of Butch Cassidy's Lander comes alive each summer, usually the first week of July, during the town's annual Pioneer Days and Parade.

Inner circle of Wyoming's Wild Bunch. Front row, left to right: Harry Longabaugh (the Sundance Kid), Ben Kilpatrick, and Robert Leroy (George) Parker (Butch Cassidy). Back row, left to right: Will Carver and Harvey (Kid Curry) Logan. *Denver Public Library.*

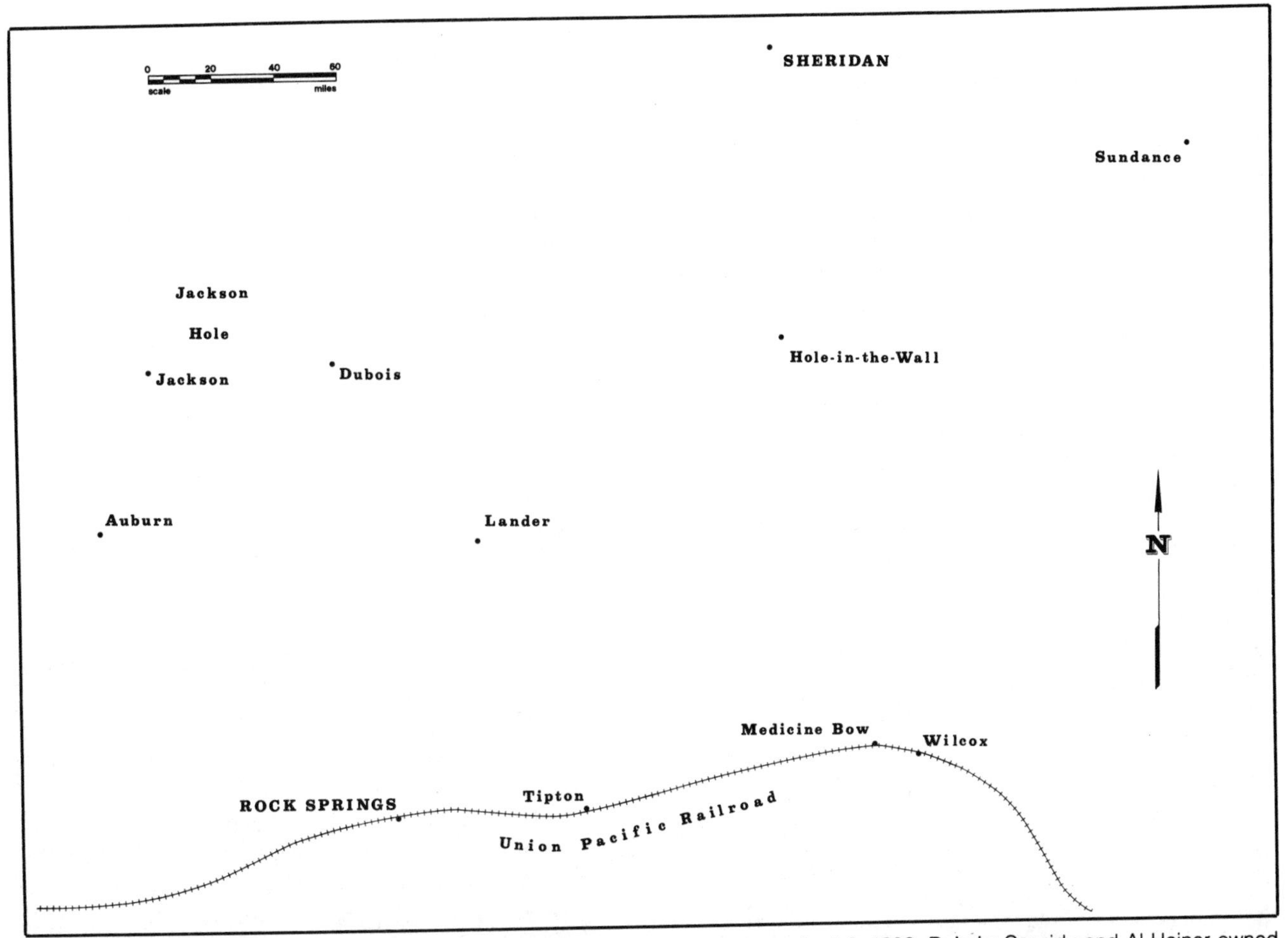


**The Wild Bunch in Wyoming. Auburn:** Butch Cassidy captured by Bob Calverly on April 8, 1892. **Dubois:** Cassidy and Al Hainer owned ranch where town of Dubois now stands. **Hole-in-the-Wall:** Famous hideout area for Wild Bunch and other outlaws in the 1890s. **Jackson Hole:** Hideout area; Cassidy may have buried loot there. **Lander:** Cassidy's home around 1890; he returned from time to time, possibly as late as 1936, looking for hidden loot. **Medicine Bow:** At times Wild Bunch used Weir Ranch, just east of town, for hideout. **Rock Springs:** Cassidy reportedly lived there in 1895; may have worked as butcher. **Sheridan:** In the summer of 1897, Cassidy worked on the Dan Hilman Ranch west of town; fellow Wild Buncher Elzy Lay may have tended bar in Sheridan saloon. **Sundance:** Harry Longabaugh's stretch in jail there in the late 1880s earned him the name of "The Sundance Kid"; the town also may have been a staging area for the Wild Bunch for their Belle Fourche, S.D., robbery in 1897. **Tipton:** Site of a Wild Bunch express car robbery on August 29, 1900. **Wilcox:** Site of a Wild Bunch express car robbery on June 2, 1899.

# Lusk
## Niobrara County

Lusk is in far eastern Wyoming, on US 20 about twenty miles from the Nebraska line. Sometime in 1886 a sullen cowboy calling himself Bill McCoy hired on with Luke Voorhees's LZ outfit near Luska. McCoy was not his real name, but ranch foremen seldom cared about such things. Apparently McCoy worked hard and caused no trouble—that is, until articles began appearing in the Lusk *Herald* suggesting that McCoy was actually a desperado named Dan Bogan who was wanted for murder in Texas.

McCoy should have moved on when the first article appeared, but he hung around and sulked. One night in early January 1887, after too many drinks at Lusk's Cleveland Brothers' Saloon, McCoy announced that the *Herald*'s editor, J. K. Calkins, had better find something else to write about. When the cowboy continued to grow more agitated, the bartender called the town constable, Charlie Gunn. Gunn, a well-liked and capable peace officer, quieted McCoy down and persuaded him to leave.

A few days later McCoy started up again in another saloon, Jim Waters' place. Gunn was called and this time the constable gave the cowboy a stiff warning, probably to the effect that if he was seen in town again he was going to jail. But McCoy did not take heed. The following morning, January 15, Gunn, sitting in Waters' place, spotted McCoy coming in the door. When Gunn got up to meet him, McCoy drew his gun and fired, hitting the lawman in the belly. As Gunn groped for his weapon, McCoy calmly placed his six-gun against the constable's head and, as a witness said, "splattered his brains over the floor and set fire to his hair." McCoy then raced outside and grabbed the nearest horse. But a deputy sheriff, Johnny Owens, had heard the shots and came running with his shotgun. A blast in the air failed to halt the fleeing McCoy, and Owens' second charge knocked the cowboy to the ground with a gaping shoulder wound.

The fight had gone out of McCoy but not the trouble he would cause. That night, despite his injury, he escaped jail. Weak from fever and in need of medical attention, he did not get far and finally turned himself back in. On September 8, 1887, he was convicted of murdering constable Gunn and was sentenced to hang. But shortly thereafter he escaped again and eventually fled to South America.

Johnny Owens, the deputy who blasted McCoy out of his saddle, later became a legend himself in eastern Wyoming. Like many lawmen of his day, Owens, a transplanted Texan, supplemented his meager deputy's pay by gambling. He usually won and eventually saved enough money to buy several saloons. He also dabbled in race horses. Despite these ventures, he continued to serve as a lawman and for twenty years served as sheriff of nearby Weston County where he rid the area of rustlers and kept law and order in the town of Newcastle* until 1912.

## Medicine Bow
### Carbon County

The town of Medicine Bow is on US 287 about fifty-five miles northwest of Laramie. Just east of town, the Weir Ranch once stood at the junction of Rock Creek and Medicine Bow Creek. The ranch was reportedly a popular hangout for outlaws in the 1890s, especially Butch Cassidy and the Wild Bunch during their travels between their hideouts at the Hole-in-the-Wall* in Johnson County and Brown's Park* in northwestern Colorado.

The ranch was started by a man named Wolf from Weir, Nebraska, in 1884. The ranch manager was named Billy McCabe. Along with many other outlaw hangouts in the West, the Weir ranch was occasionally called "Robbers' Roost" or "Robbers' Roost Ranch."

## Muddy Station
### Carbon County

Dan Parker was a young brother of Robert LeRoy Parker, alias Butch Cassidy. His name appears only once in the annals of Western outlawry—in connection with a stage robbery near Muddy Station, a midway stop on the line between Dixon and Rawlins. Muddy Station can no longer be found on the maps. Undisturbed for years, its faint remains lay near Muddy Creek, just off the route now roughly followed by State Highway 71.

On the chilly winter afternoon of December 29, 1889, stage driver Abraham Coon pulled his team to a halt four miles north of the station. Standing in the road before him were two horsemen, both waving revolvers. According to Coon's later testimony, each man wore a dark suit of clothes, a large heavy overcoat, and "had a little piece of buffalo rope put on to represent false whiskers and mustache . . . fastened on with a little small string around his ear on each side."

While one bandit covered the driver and his single passenger, a man named Allen, the other sorted through the registered mail. After taking what he wanted, he turned to Allen, but when the passenger informed him he had only four bits on him and offered to be searched, the bandit told him to "keep it." The robbers then fired their guns near the feet of the team and ordered the driver to "go north and not turn back."

The robbery probably would have gone unsolved but for one of the bandit's penchant for bragging. The following May, at a dance in Moab, Utah, a young man calling himself William Brown happened to mention that he had to leave the country "up north" because he had robbed a stage. The tale followed him and eventually he was arrested. His partner, who went by the name Tom Ricketts, was also picked up. On the way back to Laramie to stand trial, Ricketts broke down and confessed that his real name was Dan S. Parker, son of Maximillian and Ann Parker of Circleville, Utah. He also gave the names of his brothers and sisters, eight in all, but failed to mention his oldest brother, Robert LeRoy Parker.

Dan Parker served three years in prison for the robbery. On being pardoned in 1894, he returned to his family in Utah, and as far as anyone knows, was never in serious trouble with the law again.

## Newcastle
### Weston County

From 1890 to 1912 Newcastle, which is in northeastern Wyoming on US 16 near the Nebraska line, was the home of the "Gambling Sheriff," Johnny Owens. Johnny, originally a Texan, migrated to Newcastle from nearby Lusk in late 1889. At Lusk he was remembered as the hard-nosed deputy who captured the deadly Dan Bogan, alias "Bill McCoy," the night he killed town constable Charlie Gunn (see *Lusk*). On moving to Newcastle, at the time developing as a prosperous coal town for the fuel-hungry railroad, Owens first opened a saloon, the "House of Blazes" and later a music hall, the "Castle Theater," which featured traveling entertainers from the East.

Before taking the deputy's job at Lusk, Owens had been a professional gambler and could easily make a living off his own or anybody else's tables, but his reputation as an effective law officer had not gone unnoticed, and in 1892 Weston County needed a tough sheriff to rid the area of rustlers. Once elected, Owens wasted no time in cleaning up the county, and although some citizens complained about his penchant for the green cloth, he was reelected three times from 1892 to 1894.

Although Owens could be deadly with killers, he was compassionate with first offenders and often spent hours teaching the youth of Newcastle that "crime doesn't pay" by taking them down to the jail and showing them shackled prisoners. Sometimes his compassion was strangely applied, however, as in the case of outlaw Logan Blissard. In March 1906 Blissard escaped from Owens' custody while being escorted to the state penitentiary. On recapture, the outlaw informed Johnny that he would try to escape again because he would "rather be dead then in prison." And then he told Owens that when he did try, if luck was against him, "for God's sake shoot straight and don't cripple me!" A short time later Blissard made his try, and Johnny Owens put a single bullet in the middle of the outlaw's forehead.

Big Nose George Parrott. *Union Pacific Railroad Museum Collection.*

## Rawlins
### Carbon County

Rawlins is in south central Wyoming at the junction of Interstate 80 and US 287. In 1879 the town celebrated the demise of outlaw Big Nose George Parrott. Parrott was wanted for an attempted robbery of a Union Pacific train near Carbon the year before and for the killing of two possemen during the ensuing chase, (see *Carbon*). Parrott was eventually captured in Montana and returned to Carbon County for trial. While being housed in the Rawlins jail he was taken from his cell and hanged from a nearby telegraph pole.

Following the lynching, a local physician, John E. Osborne, made a death mask of Parrott's face, possibly the only death mask ever made of a Western outlaw. But Dr. Osborne did not stop there. Part of George's skull was removed, as well as skin from his chest and thighs. The skull went to Dr. Osborne's assistant, Lillian Heath, as a souvenir. The skin from his chest, so the story goes, was fashioned into a medicine bag for the good doctor, except for one piece which was given to an unknown party in Rawlins. This piece eventually

Big Nose George Parrott's bones found during excavation in Rawlins in May 1950. *Union Pacific Railroad Museum Collection.*

found its way to the Union Pacific Railroad Museum in Omaha, Nebraska, as did the piece of skull owned by Mrs. Heath. The skin from the outlaw's thighs, it is said, was used to make a pair of shoes. These ended up in the possession of the Rawlins National Bank.

On May 12, 1950, while workmen were digging a foundation for a new store in downtown Rawlins, they uncovered a tightly sealed whiskey barrel. Inside were a bottle of vegetable compound, a pair of shoes, and a human skeleton. Local officials later identified the skeleton as George's.

## Rock Springs
### Sweetwater County

The town of Rock Springs is in the southwestern part of the state, on US 191 where it crosses Interstate 80. According to Edward M. Kirby, one of outlaw Butch Cassidy's biographers, Butch spent some time in Rock Springs around 1895. While there, says Kirby, the outlaw (then using the name George Cassidy) worked at a local butcher shop, during which time he acquired his nickname, "Butch." Other sources suggest he may have worked as a butcher as early as 1890 or 1891, and probably picked up his sobriquet then (see *Lander, Wyoming*).

## Sheridan
### Sheridan County

Sheridan, the largest town in northern Wyoming, lies just off Interstate 90 about thirty miles from the Montana line. It is believed that Butch Cassidy and his sidekick, Elzy Lay, hid out in Sheridan County following their April 21, 1897 robbery of the Pleasant Valley Coal Company at Castle Gate, Utah.*

Lay may have spent the summer as a bartender in town while Cassidy worked as a hand on the Dan Hilman ranch, located west of Sheridan in Little Goose Canyon. The rancher's son Fred Hilman, during an interview in the early 1970's, said he was thirteen years old when Cassidy hired on at his father's ranch, and he remembered him well. He said his name was LeRoy Parker, and that he had been working for a rancher "up north" but had left when he did not get paid.

Apparently Cassidy was a hard worker and gave no indication that he was wanted by the law, except, recalled Hilman, that he had a tendency to "keep a saddle horse picketed near wherever he was working" and had a habit of always keeping an eye on the doors and windows when relaxing in the evenings. Also, there were occasional visits from a friend, presumably Lay, after which the two sometimes would ride off for several days. One such trip may have been to the Butte County Bank at Belle Fourche, South Dakota.*

At the end of the summer "Parker" failed to show up for breakfast one morning. On checking the bunkhouse, Fred Hilman found a note attached to the wall. "Sorry to be leaving you. The authorities are getting on to us. Best home I've ever had." It was signed "LeRoy Parker (Butch Cassidy)."

According to Hilman, Butch returned to the ranch for a visit in 1910.

## Sundance
### Crook County

Had it not been for Sundance, Wyoming, a peaceful town just off Interstate 90 in the northeastern corner of the state, the Sundance Kid probably would have ridden the outlaw trail under the unglamorous name of Harry Alonzo Longabaugh (his real name). In 1887, when Longabaugh was only nineteen, he made the mistake of stealing a horse, saddle, and gun from employees of the Three-Vee Ranch, which was located near the junction of the Belle Fourche River and Crow Creek in Crook County. The owner of the gun, Jim Widner, rode down to Sundance, the county seat, and complained to Crook County sheriff Jim Ryan. Longabaugh apparently had worked at the ranch for a brief period and was the prime suspect.

A short time later Sheriff Ryan learned that Harry was hanging around Miles City, Montana. The sheriff caught a stage north and soon had his suspect under arrest. But at the time, Ryan apparently had business to conduct in St. Paul, Minnesota, and rather than return to Wyoming, he shackled his prisoner and the two men boarded an eastbound Northern Pacific flyer. On the way, while the sheriff was using the toilet at the end of the coach, Longabaugh picked the locks on his chains and escaped. He was soon recaptured, however, and this time Ryan put him on a stagecoach and headed directly for Sundance.

In August 1887 Longabaugh pleaded guilty to stealing the horse and was sentenced to eighteen months at hard labor. He was supposed to be sent to the state penitentiary at Laramie, but it was full and instead he was kept at the Crook County jail at Sundance. Hence, the nickname.

On Longabaugh's release in 1889 he immediately got into trouble again. On May 17 he was involved in a shooting thirty-five miles north of Sundance at Salt Creek, during which law officers killed a small-time fugitive named Bob Miner. Longabaugh and another man, known only as "Kid Chicago," were with Minor when the lawmen closed in, and both were charged with threatening to kill the officers. (Some say "Kid Chicago" may have been Elzy Lay, who later rode with Longabaugh as a member of the Wyoming Wild Bunch.) The charges were apparently weak, however, and possibly were drawn up merely to chase Longabaugh and his companion out of Crook County. If so, it worked, and both men bid goodbye to the town of Sundance.

Longabaugh may have returned to the town for which he was nicknamed twelve years later. Some believe he and other members of the Wild Bunch may have used Sundance as a rendezvous point in June 1897 prior to their robbery of the Butte County Bank at Belle Fourche, South Dakota.*

## Tipton
### Sweetwater County

Tipton is a tiny tank town on the Union Pacific line about midway between Rawlins and Rock Springs. In outlaw history it is remembered as the site of an express car robbery on August 29, 1900. The holdup was nearly a repeat of one which occurred a year earlier at Wilcox, Wyoming.* Both have been credited to the Wild Bunch.

Wells Fargo express messenger Ernest C. Woodcock was the victim in both affairs. In the Tipton robbery, an armed bandit secretly slipped aboard behind the tender and halted the train at a prearranged spot marked by a raging bonfire. Shots were then fired alongside the coaches to keep the passengers in their seats. Woodcock was forced to open his car on the threat of being blown up with dynamite. (At Wilcox he had resisted, but here he was persuaded to come out by the conductor.) The dynamite was then used to blow open the express company safe.

Reports attributed to railroad officials immediately after the affair established the loss at only $54 cash, but other sources suggest a much higher amount. One report has the messenger admitting a loss in the vicinity of $55,000, and in an account written years later (some say by Butch Cassidy himself) the figure given was $45,000. According to this account the outlaws immediately buried the money "as it was too dangerous to try to dispose of it at that time." Following the robbery it is believed the gang rode west, eventually reaching Huntington, Nevada.

Some writers say it was the Tipton holdup that firmly established the Union Pacific's committment to their

Union Pacific express car destroyed by the Wild Bunch at Tipton, Wyoming, in 1900. *Union Pacific Railroad Museum Collection.*

Special posse used by the Union Pacific Railroad to chase train robbers. Horses and men were quickly transported to the scene of a robbery in the special "horse car" shown in the background. The device proved successful and was largely responsible for ridding the Union Pacific of the threat of robbery shortly after the turn of the century. *Union Pacific Railroad Museum Collection.*

special "horse car" trains which are generally credited with nearly eliminating robberies on that line. These special trains would rush an elite group of mounted manhunters to the scene of a robbery and within hours they would be nipping at the heels of the fleeing bandits.

Tipton can still be visited. There are still a few houses left, some inhabited, some not, most of which were built near the turn of the century to house railroad workers.

## Wilcox
### Albany County

Little remains of Wilcox today. The site, which is on the Union Pacific Railroad about fifteen miles southeast of Medicine Bow, is marked only by a trackside sign. In outlaw history the town is remembered for a train robbery by the Wild Bunch on June 2, 1899. Exactly which members of the gang were present has never been established. Butch Cassidy, Harvey (Kid Curry) Logan, and "Flat Nose" George Currie may have been there.

The assault took place in the early morning hours. The westbound express was halted by a red lantern, a device frequently used by train robbers in the 1890s. Several shots were fired into the mail car to encourage the clerk to open up. When he refused, the robbers set off a dynamite charge, blowing off a side door. While going through the car, the robbers heard a second train coming from the east and ordered the engineer to pull ahead across a small bridge. They placed dynamite under the bridge, set if off, then separated the express and mail cars from the rear of the train, and ordered the engineer to pull ahead again, this time about two miles. When the express company messenger, E. C. Woodcock, refused to open up, they blew out the side of the car, knocking the messenger unconscious. Next they turned to the safes, blew both open, and scooped out the contents. When they finished they headed north on foot, to a point behind a snow fence where they had hidden extra explosives and horses. From there their route was almost due north, past Medicine Bow, toward Casper.

# Yellowstone National Park

## Teton and Park Counties

In July 1914 Yellowstone National Park was the scene of the West's most ambitious stagecoach robbery in history. The culprits were Ed Trafton, a small-time outlaw from Jackson Hole, Wyoming, and a local man named Charles Erpenback.

Trafton and Erpenback were not the first outlaws to eye the Yellowstone excursion stages. Park regulations prohibited visitors from carrying firearms, which for years had made them attractive targets for bandits. The last holdup of a stagecoach, however, had occurred in 1908.

For their robbery, Trafton and Erpenback chose a site near Shoshone Point, between the Old Faithful Inn and Thumb Lunch Station. As the first stage of the morning slowed for the point, Trafton, his face hidden by a flowered bandana and his hat pulled low over his face, stepped from behind a giant boulder and pointed a Winchester at the driver. After warning the passengers that another robber stationed nearby also had them covered with a rifle, Trafton ordered them out and made them line up before him in single file. One by one, as they passed by, they dropped their money and valuables into the outlaw's sack. When they had finished, he ordered them back into the coach and shouted for the driver to pull on around the point and down the trail, reminding him again that he was under the constant observation of his fellow outlaw.

Minutes later a second stage arrived at the point. As before, Trafton ordered the driver to halt, and the scene was repeated. More stages arrived, and in each case the passengers were relieved of their valuables and the drivers were ordered to pull ahead around the point out of sight. Within an hour, fifteen stages had arrived and each fell victim to the highwaymen. When the sixteenth failed to show, Trafton figured they had pushed their luck far enough, and they rode off.

Park officials and local scouts combed the area for signs of the robbers' tracks. About a half mile south of Shoshone Point they picked up the trail of two horses leading due south and out of the park toward Jackson Hole. They also found other tracks of a lone man on foot, which lead southwesterly toward a cabin on Conant Creek. There they found Charles Erpenback. He was arrested and charged with taking part in the robbery, and he eventually confessed, naming Trafton as his accomplice. Trafton was arrested by federal officers at Rupert, Idaho, on May 22, 1915, and six months later he was convicted and sentenced to five years at Leavenworth penitentiary.

# NOTES

## ARIZONA

**Colossal Cave**: Kubista, 26-27, 62; Klien and Krell, 91. **Contention City**: Jahns, 166-172, 178-179; O'Neal, *Western Gunfighters*, 75-76, 180; Florin, 89-90. **Diablo Canyon Station**: Walker, D., 52-56. **Douglas**: O'Neal, *Western Gunfighters*, 271-272. **Fairbank**: Haley, 302-308; Florin, 100-107. **Flagstaff**: Kildare, "Dead Outlaws' Loot," 16-19, 52. **Globe**: Pointer, 216-218; Schreier, 52-54; Metz, *The Shooters*, 250. **Holbrook**: O'Neal, 249-250; Lesure, 149. **Kingman**: Kildare, "Vanished Stage," 22-24, 59-62. **Nogales**: O'Neal, *Western Gunfighters*, 57. **Pantano Station**: Kubista, "No Headlight in Sight," 30-33, 72-73. **Phoenix**: Kildare, "Fastest Gun," 16-19, 57-59; Lesure, 162. **Pine Springs**: Kildare, "Gold in Iron Boxes," 6-9, 55-59. **Prescott**: Dodge, "Hanging," 8; Walker, D., 52-56; Lesure, 168-169. **St. Johns**: Jensen, 30. **Smugglers' Trail**: Thomas, 28-29, 46. **Tombstone**: Bartholomew, E., 223-243; Jahns, 163-164; O'Neal, *Western Gunfighters*, 97; Trachtman, 27-33; Dullenty, "Tombstone's Love," 32-35; Dullenty, "Outlaw Hangouts," 28; Klien and Krell, 96. **Tucson**: Sonnichsen, *Tucson*, 124-126; Secrest, "Jim Levy," 57-58; McCarthy, 31; O'Neal, *Western Gunfighters*, 96-98. **Willcox**: O'Neal, *Western Gunfighters*, 100. **Yuma**: Neumann, 14-15, 38; Secrest, "Return of Chavez," 13, 32, 38; O'Neal, *Western Gunfighters*, 262.

## CALIFORNIA

**Badger**: Glasscock, 179-180. **Bakersfield**: Patterson, W., 5-7. **Bodie**: Nadeau, 203-210. **Campo**: Mills, 16-17, 32. **Camptonville**: Drago, 15-20. **Cedar Ridge**: Beebe and Clegg, 184-187. **Ceres**: Glasscock, 45-51. **Earlimont**: Glasscock, 37-44, Preece, 97-101. **Farmersville**: Patterson, W., 5. **Firebaugh**: Drago, 15-25; Secrest, "Chavez," 8. **Fresno**: Preece, 82-84; Glasscock, 232-240. **Goshen**: Glasscock, 34-36. **Kerman**: Glasscock, 65-75. **Los Angeles**: Secrest, "Fast Guns," 11; Drago, 42-43; Shinn, 79; Kennelley, 32-33, 53; Shirley, *Belle Starr*, 86-93; Pointer, 154-155; Kirby, *Butch Cassidy*, 13; King, 16-17, 36-37; Hitt, 18-19, 21, 58; Preece, 285-287, 305. **Murphy's**: Rosenhouse, 36-37; Nadeau, 93-94; Florin, 238. **Nevada City**: Dimsdale, vii., 256-259; Nadeau, 133-139. **Paso Robles**: Preece, 36, 65; Patterson, R., *Train Robbery*, 159; Shirley, *Belle Starr*, 90; Norin, 29-30. **Pixley**: Glasscock, 27-33. **Placerville**: Drago, 61; Nadeau, 52, 55. **Porterville**: Patterson, W., 5. **Raymond**: Secrest, "Holdup!" 24-26, 53. **Redding**: Drago, 26-34; Nadeau, 156-157. **San Andreas**: Drago, 46-57; Nadeau, 85-91. **San Francisco**: Gard, *Frontier Justice*, 152-158, 161-167. **Sequoia National Forest**: Glasscock, 127-143, 150-153, 193-210, 213. **Stockton**: Secrest, "Fast Guns," 11; Rosenhouse, 47. **Tehachapi**: Bartholomew, V., 28-29, 44, 46; Patterson, R., *Train Robbery*, 45. **Tres Pinos**: Horan, *Authentic Wild West: The Outlaws*, 188, 201-202; People v. Vasquez, 560-563. **Ventura**: Norris, 44. **Visalia**: Glasscock, 79, 88, 101-104, 164, 183, 190, 273-283; Patterson, W., 5.

## COLORADO

**Brown's Park**: Pointer, 52, 53, 142; O'Neal, *Western Gunfighters*, 327; Dullenty, "True Story of Harry Tracy," 42; Hill, 38-39. **Colorado Springs**: Kildare, "Bear River Loot," 14-15. **Creede**: DeArment, *Bat Masterson*, 331-335; O'Neal, *Western Gunfighters*, 111; Florin, 300. **Delta**: Baker, 205-211; O'Neal, *Western Gunfighters*, 204. **Denver**: McCarroll, 26-28, 58-59; Dodge, "The Lynchers," 23-24; Ferdom, 20; Smith, A.J., 16; DeArment, *Bat Masterson*, 226-231, 327-330, 344-347, 364-367. **Georgetown**: Rosa, 151; Florin, 314; Dorset, 199. **Glenwood Springs**: Jahns, 276-285; Palmquist, 26. **The Higgins Ranch**: Jones, R., 38, 61. **Julesburg**: Lee, 18-19; Rosa, 11. **Lake City**: Florin, 320-322; O'Neal, *Western Gunfighters*, 103, Wolley, 341-343. **Las Animas**: Berrier, 39; O'Neal, *Western Gunflighters*, 21-22. **Leadville**: Griswold and Griswold, 156; O'Neal, *Western Gunfighters*, 284-285; DeArment, *Bat Masterson*, 184-185; Jahns, 258-274; Dutschmann, McKinney Papers. **Meeker**: Rockwell, 20-21, 56. **Park County**: Crow, 16-18, 54-55. **Pueblo**: DeArment, *Bat Masterson*, 148-154; Patterson, R., "Battle for Royal George" (unpublished manuscript). **Rifle**: Patterson, R., *Train Robbery*, 187-189; Pinkerton, 74-76; O'Neal, *Western Gunfighters*, 186, Kirby, *Butch Cassidy*, 18. **Routt County**: O'Neal, *Western Gunfighters*, 149-150. **Silverton**: DeArment, *Bat Masterson*, 300. **The Spanish Peaks**: Drago, 140-145. **Steamboat Springs**: Pointer, 144. **Telluride**: Kirby, *Butch Cassidy*, 23; Pointer, 46, 50-52. **Trinidad**: DeArment, *Bat Masterson*, 219-222, 224, 235-237, 246-248; O'Neal, *Western Gunfighters*, 195; Metz, *Pat Garrett*, 126-127. **Virginia Dale**: Boren, "Jack Slade's Grave Located," 25. **Wray**: Kirby, *Sundance Kid*, 45; Patterson, R., *Train Robbery*, 190.

## IDAHO

**Boise**: Winther, *The Great Northwest*, 246; Winther, *The Old Oregon Country*, 287-288. **Florence**: Taylor, 1; **Fort Hall**: Winther, *The Old Oregon Country*, 287. **Idaho City**: Drago, 94-100; Taylor, 4; Sparling, 40. **Lewiston**: Winther, *The Old Oregon Country*, 287-288; O'Neal, *Western Gunfighters*, 256-257. **Montpelier**: Sweet, 9, 38; Behymer, 26-27, 54; Pointer, 108. **Salmon**: Martin, 23-24, 53-54; Taylor, 4. **Twin Falls**: Winther, *The Old Oregon Country*, 286.

## IOWA

**Adair**: Settle, 47-48. **Albert City**: Buchan, 13, 58-59, 62-64. **Bellevue**: Gard, *Frontier Justice*, 194-195. **Corydon**: Breihan, *Younger Brothers*, 86-87. **Tama**: Pointer, 101, 110.

## KANSAS

**Abilene**: Horan, *Authentic Wild West: The Gunfighters*, 160, 175-180; Rosa, 122-137, 139-142; Nordyke, 103-108. **Ashland**: O'Neal, *Western Gunfighters*, 224. **Bluff City**: Nordyke, 109-111; O'Neal, *Western Gunfighters*, 129. **Burden**: Shirley, *West of Hell's Fringe*, 324. **Caldwell**: McNeal, 189-193; O'Neal, "Caldwell: The Border Queen," 20-25. **Caney**: Shirley, *West of Hell's Fringe*, 117-121. **Cimarron**: DeArment, *Bat Masterson*, 312-314; Shirley, *West of Hell's Fringe*, 139-141. **Coffeyville**: Elliott, 42-50; Preece, 19, 30-31, 40-44, 204-207, 213-215. **Dodge City**: Faulk, 149, 161, 163, 167, 174, 175; DeArment, *Bat Masterson*, 1, 5, 76-77, 87, 104-107, 128, 204-214, 278-279; Jahns, 90-122; Vestal, 247-257; West, 29; O'Neal, *Western Gunfighters*, 195, Rosa, 102. **Douglass**: Gard, *Frontier Justice*, 195-196. **Ellsworth**: Rosa, 102; Bird, 31; DeArment, *Bat Masterson*, 58-61. **Fort Riley**: Rosa, 63-72. **Galena**: Settle, 103-104; Shirley, *Belle Starr*, 135-137. **Goodland**: Steel, 45-47. **Hays**: Rosa, 102-109. **Kinsley**: Vestal, 109-119. **Medicine Lodge**: McNeal, 153-159; O'Neal, "Medicine Lodge Bank Robbery," 53-56, 94; O'Neal, *Western Gunfighters*, 204-205. **Mill Creek**: Rosa, 7-8. **Muncie**: Settle, 75. **Newton**: McNeal, 37-39; Price, 12; Nordyke, 94-96. **Park**: Gard, *Sam Bass*, 85-89. **Sedgwick**: DeArment, *Bat Masterson*, 9-14, 22-23. **Spearville**: Shirley, *West of Hell's Fringe*, 122-123. **Wichita**: O'Neal, *Western Gunfighters*, 226.

## MISSOURI

**Blue Cut**: Settle, 111-113. **Carthage**: Shirley, *Belle Starr*, 31-62; O'Neal, *Western Gunfighters*, 260-261. **Forsyth**: Hartman, 61. **Gads Hill**: Settle, 49-50. **Gallatin**: Horan, *Authentic Wild West: The Outlaws*, 15-21; Settle, 38-39, 42. **Glendale Station**: Settle, 102-103, 114, 148; Patterson, R., *Train Robbery*, 40. **Hughesville**: *State v. West*, 1072. **Kansas City**: DeArment, *Bat Masterson*, 193; Thorp, 39; Breihan, *Younger Brothers*, 93-94; Garwood, 186-197; Settle, 165. **Kearney**: Settle, 6-9, 76-80, 166; Dullenty, "Bombing of Jesse James Home," 21. **Lexington**: Settle, 34, 70-71. **Liberty**: Settle, 33-34. **Mexico**: Gard, *Sam Bass*, 90-95. **Monegraw Springs**: Settle, 60-61; Breihan, *Younger Brothers*, 111, 116. **Norwood**: *State v. Kennedy*, 293; Garwood, 191. **Otterville**: Settle, 88-90. **Pineville**: Federal Writers Project, *Missouri*, 507. **Princeton**: Rosa, 159. **Richmond**: Settle, 35, 50. **Ste. Genevieve**: Settle, 47; Croy, 274. **Savannah**: Settle, 34. **St. Joseph**: Settle, 117-119, 166. **South West City**: Shirley, *West of Hell's Fringe*, 191-192. **Springfield**: Rosa, 54-58, 60-61. **Winston**: Settle, 107-109, 141-144.

## MONTANA

**Bannack**: Gard, *Frontier Justice*, 168-179. **Bearmouth**: Block, 168, 174-176. **Cook Stove Basin**: Pointer, 104-105. **Deer Lodge**: Breihan, *Younger Brothers*, 147-148; Simmons, F., 12. **Harlem**: Horan, *Authentic Wild West: The Gunfighters*, 195-203. **Helena**: Dimsdale, 228-238. **Landusky**: Horan, *Authentic Wild West, The Gunfighters*, 191-199. **Laurin**: Florin, 425. **Lavina**: Pointer, 130-131. **Malta**: Kirby, *Sundance Kid*, 39, 46-48. **Miles City**; Pointer, 48; Kirby, *Sundance Kid*, 30-35. **Missoula**: Pointer, 256. **Virginia City**: Gard, *Frontier Justice*, 180-185, Boren; "Jack Slade's Grave Located," 57. **Wagner**: Pointer, 181-183; Kirby, *Butch Cassidy*, 61-62; Dullenty, "Rare Old Photos Reveal Aftermath of Wagner Train Robbery," 40.

## NEBRASKA

**Big Springs**: Gard, *Sam Bass*, 74-81; Best, 30. **Chadron**: Gipson, 28-29, 72; Dullenty, "Outlaw Hangouts," 31; Patterson, R., *Train Robbery*, 191-192. **Long Pine**: O'Neal, *Western Gunfighters*, 222-224. **Ogallala**: Gard, *Sam Bass*, 75-84, 90, 96; DeArment, *Bat Masterson*, 185-192; O'Neal, *Western Gunfighters*, 260. **Rock Creek Station**: Rosa, x, xi, 14-33. **Sidney**: Rosa, 192-193; Rybolt, "Legend Becomes Reality," 32-36; Rybolt, "Doc Holliday Sold Gold Bricks Here," 41-43.

## NEVADA

**Aurora**: Drago, 76-84. **Carson City**: Drago, 68-71; Drury, 159-160. **Elko**: Kirby, *Sundance Kid*, 66. **Eureka**: Drury, 145. **Genoa**: McMillan, 22; Drago, 79. **Humboldt**: Kirby, *Sundance Kid*, 65-66; Wood, S., 152. **Huntington Valley**: Pointer 169-170. **Montello**: Patterson, R., *Train Robbery*, 45-49. **Pioche**: Secrest, "Jim Levy," 25-26. **Verdi**: Patterson, R., *Train Robbery*, 19-24, 214. **Virginia City**: Drury, 151-157, 161-163; **Winnemucca**: Pointer, 169-171; Kirby, *Butch Cassidy*, 37-39; Berk, 24-25, 53.

## NEW MEXICO

**Alma**: Pointer, 148, 161; Heslip, 44-45; Florin, 606. **Cimarron**: Pointer, 160-161, 268; Berrier, 38-39; O'Neal, *Western Gunfighters*, 19-21. **Clayton**: O'Neal, *Western Gunfighters*, 176; Romero, 27-28. **Columbus**: Judia and Ball, 12. **Corona**: Metz, *Pat Garrett*, 68-69. **Engle**: Shirley, *West of Hell's Fringe*, 322-323. **Folsom**: Florin, 620; O'Neal, *Western Gunfighters*, 176; Metz, *The Shooters*, 41-42. **Fort Sumner**: Metz, *Pat Garrett*, 98-119; Sanchez, 16. **Hillsboro**: Metz, *Pat Garrett*, 213-226; Florin, 625. **Las Cruces**: Metz, *Pat Garrett*, 275, 287-306. **Las Vegas**: DeArment, *Bat Masterson*, 95-96; Metz, *The Shooters*, 128-129; Jahns, 141-142; Metz, *Pat Garrett*, 84-86. **Lincoln**: Metz, *Pat Garrett*, 42-52, 92-94. **Messila**: Metz, *Pat Garrett*, 88. **Orogrande**: Metz, *Pat Garrett*, 205-210. **Outlaw Rock**: Weisner, 48-52. **Raton**: DeArment, *Bat Masterson*, 306-311. **San Patricio**: Sanchez, 15. **Silver City**: Simmons, M., 40; Cline, 15; Preece, 75-80. **Stinking Springs**: Metz, *Pat Garrett*, 76-80. **White Sands National Monument**: Metz, *Pat Garrett*, 88, 161-163, 170-172.

## OKLAHOMA

**Ada**: Shirley, *Shotgun for Hire*, 95-98, 101-115. **Adair**: Preece, 187-195. **Ames**: Shirley, *West of Hell's Fringe*, 274-277. **Arapaho**: Shirley, *West of Hell's Fringe*, 343-344, 349-351. **Ardmore**: Preece, 279-280. **Bartlesville**: Haines, 44-47, 50; Preece, 148-157. **Black Mesa**: Packer, 14-16, 50-52; Osteen, 17. **Bond**: *Shirley, West of Hell's Fringe*, 393, 411. **Caddo**: Walker, W.T., "The Doctor Who Rode with Sam Bass," 12-15. **Canton**: Shirley, *West of Hell's Fringe*, 311-314. **Checotah**: Shirley, *West of Hell's Fringe*, 406-407. **The Corner**: Shirley, *Shotgun For Hire*, 92-100. **Cromwell**: Morris, 59-60; O'Neal, *Western Gunfighters*, 325. **Curtis**: Shirley, *West of Hell's Fringe*, 341-343. **Cushing**: Shirley, *West of Hell's Fringe*, 398-399. **Dover**: Shirley, *West of Hell's Fringe*, 272-274. **Edmond**: Shirley, *West of Hell's Fringe*, 392-393. **Guthrie**: Shirley, *West of Hell's Fringe*, 281, 357-361, 371, 398, 413-415. **Hennessy**: Preece, 129-132. **Herd**: Shirley, *West of Hell's Fringe*, 318-320. **Ingalls**: Shirley, *West of Hell's Fringe*, 151-153, 156-162, 277-282; Morris, 101-102. **Inola**: Shirley, *Belle Starr*, 149. **Kingfisher**: Shirley, *West of Hell's Fringe*,

## OREGON



## SOUTH DAKOTA



## TEXAS



## UTAH



## WASHINGTON



## WYOMING

# BIBLIOGRAPHY


Allen, Stookie, "The Greatest Shot." *Frontier Times*, December, 1969.

Bailey, Tom. "Oklahoma's Buried Gold Mystery." *True Western Adventures*, August, 1959.

Baker, Pearl, *The Wild Bunch at Robbers Roost*. Los Angeles: Westernlore Press, 1965.

Barnett, Lana Payne, ed. *Presenting the Texas Panhandle*. Canyon, Texas: Lan-Bea Publications, 1979.

Bartholomew, Ed. *Wyatt Earp: The Man & the Myth*. Toyahvale, Texas: Frontier Book Company, 1964.

Bartholomew, Virginia. "The Mason-Henry Gang." *Frontier Times*, June-July, 1967.

Beebe, Lucius, and Charles, Clegg. *U.S. West: The Saga of Wells Fargo*. New York: E.P. Dutton & Company, 1949.

Behymer, Bruce. "You Don't Chase the Wild Bunch on a Bicycle." *Frontier Times*, August-September, 1970.

Berk, Lee. "New Evidence Suggests Butch Cassidy Didn't Do It." *Old West*, Fall, 1983.

Berrier, Deborah. "Clay Allison Never Killed a Man Willingly." *American History Illustrated*, Summer, 1982.

Best, J.C. "Where the Daltons Stopped." *True West*, April, 1983.

Bird, Roy. "Ira Lloyd: Gun-Toting Lawyer in a Lawless Town," *Real West*, Spring, 1982.

Block, Eugene B. *Great Train Robberies of the West*. New York. Coward-McCann, Inc., 1959.

Boren, Kerry Ross. "Jack Slade's Grave Located." *Frontier Times*, April-May, 1976.

———. "The Mysterious Pinkerton." *True West*, August, 1977

Bossennecker, John. "Bob Devine: 'We Raided Hole-in-the-Wall.' " *Real West*, January, 1980.

Boucher, Leonard Harold. "How Wild Bill Lost His Head." *True West*, May-June, 1959.

Braly, David. "Mysteries of the Ochoco Forest." *Old West*, Fall, 1984.

Breihan, Carl, "The Outlaw Who Became a Pair of Shoes." *True West*, January, 1983.

———. *Rube Burrow: King of the Train Robbers*. West Allis, Wisconsin: Leather Stocking Books, 1981.

———. *Younger Brothers*. San Antonio, Texas: The Naylor Company, 1972.

Brown, Dee. "Butch Cassidy and the Sundance Kid." *American History Illustrated*, Summer, 1982.

Buchan, Don. "Iowa's Terrible Gun Battle." *Old West*, Summer, 1975.

Castel, Albert. "Men Behind the Masks: The James Brothers." *American History Illustrated*, Summer, 1982.

Cline, Don. "Secret Life of Billy the Kid." *True West*, April, 1984.

Cole, Joe A., and Cole, Terry. "Charly Smith (1856-1882) Still Wears His Six Gun." *True West*, April, 1978.

Crow, Vernon L. "Trail of the Broken Dagger." *True West*, July-August, 1964.

Croy, Homer, *Jesse James Was My Neighbor*. New York: Duell, Sloan and Pearce, 1949.

DeArment, Robert K. *Bat Masterson: The Man and the Legend*. Norman: The University of Oklahoma Press, 1979.

———. "The Outlaw Trail of Dan Bogan." *True West*, January, 1984.

De Mattos, Jack. "Gunfighters of the Real West: John Kinney. *Real West*, February, 1964.

———. "Those Guns of Bat Masterson." *Frontier Times*, February-March, 1977.

Dimsdale, Thomas J. *The Vigilantes of Montana*. Norman: University of Oklahoma Press, 1953 (Reprint).

Dodge, Matt. "Hanging: The Media Event." *Real West Anual*, Spring, 1982.

———. "The Lynchers." *Real West*, August, 1983.

Dorset, Phyliss Flanders. *The New Eldorado: The Story of Colorado's Gold and Silver Rushes*. New York: The Macmillan Company, 1970.

Drago, Harry Sinclair. *Road Agents and Train Robberies: Half a Century of Western Banditry*. New York: Dodd, Mead & Company, 1973.

Drury, Wells. *An Editor on the Comstock Lode*. Palo Alto, California: Pacific Books, 1936.

Dullenty, Jim. "Bad Blood: The True Story of Harry Tracy." *Old West*, Summer, 1983.

———. "Bombing of the Jesse James Home." *True West*, January, 1983.

———. "He was a Stranger in Globe, Arizona." *True West*, September, 1983.

———. "Outlaw Hangouts You Can Visit." *True West*, March, 1983.

———. "Rare Old Photos Reveal Aftermath of the Wagner Train Robbery." *Old West*, Spring, 1983.

———. "Shootout at Poplar Grove." *True West*, January, 1984.

———. "Tombstone's Love." *True West*, March, 1983.

Dutschmann, R.P., Jim McKinney Papers. Jim McKinney Research Group, Terra Bella, California.

Elliott, David Stewart. *Last Raid of the Daltons*. Freeport, New York: Books for Libraries Press, 1971 (Reprint).

Faulk, Odie B. *Dodge City: The Most Western Town of All*. New York: Oxford University Press, 1977.

Federal Writers' Project: *Missouri: A Guide to the "Show Me" State*. New York: Hastings House, 1954.

Ferdom, John. "Street of a Thousand Sinners." *Real West*, September, 1962.

Fisher, O.C., and J.C. Dykes. *King Fisher: His Life and Times.* Norman: University of Oklahoma Press, 1960.

Florin, Lambert. *Ghost Towns of the West.* Seattle: Superior Publishing Company, 1970.

Gard, Wayne. *Frontier Justice.* Norman: University of Oklahoma Press, 1949.

———. *Sam Bass.* Lincoln: University of Nebraska Press, 1969 (Reprint).

Garwood, Darrell. *Crossroads of America: The Story of Kansas City.* New York: W.W. Norton & Company, 1948.

Gipson, Dade. "'Red Jacket' of Chadron." *True West,* January-February, 1967.

Glasscock, C.B. *Bandits and the Southern Pacific.* New York: Frederick A. Stokes Company, 1929.

Griswold, Don L., and Jean Harvey Griswold. *The Carbonate Camp Called Leadville.* Denver: The University of Denver Press, 1951.

Haddock, Neil. "The 'KATY' Called it Denison: Some Folks Called it Hell." *Real West,* July, 1981.

Haines, Joe D. "A Sensational Holdup." *True West,* January, 1984.

Haley, J. Evetts. *Jeff Milton: A Good Man With a Gun.* Norman: University of Oklahoma Press, 1948.

Hardin, John Wesley. *The Life of John Wesley Hardin.* Norman: University of Oklahoma Press, 1961 (Reprint).

Hartman, Viola R. "Alf Bolin's Reign of Terror." *Old West,* Summer, 1983.

Heslip, John R. "Graveyard of Violence." *True West,* August, 1981.

Hill, Wilford, "The Outlaws' Thanksgiving Dinner." *Real West,* February, 1984.

Hitt, James. "Real to Reel Outlaws: Badmen Who Made Movies." *True West,* June, 1983.

Horan, James D. *The Authentic Wild West: The Gunfighters.* New York: Crown Publishers, Inc., 1976.

———. *The Authentic Wild West: The Outlaws.* New York: Crown Publishers, Inc., 1977.

Hunt, Daniel D., and Joseph W. Snell. "Who Killed Oliver Yantis?" *True West,* January-February, 1966.

Hurst, Irven. "Robbingest Robber." *Frontier Times,* Spring, 1960.

Jahns, Pat. *The Frontier World of Doc Holliday.* New York: Hastings House, 1957.

Jameson, Henry B. "Lay Off Abilene!" *True West,* September, 1982.

Jensen, Jody. "Birth of the Arizona Rangers." *Old West,* Spring, 1983.

Jones, Bill. "Hole-in-the-Wall Gang Rides Again." *True West,* June, 1984.

Jones, Ralph. "Colorado Outlaw Cache." *Frontier Times,* December-January, 1980.

Judia, Bert, and Ball, Eva. "The Buried Money." *True West,* May-June, 1974.

Kennelley, Joseph. "Vengence Riders of the Monte." *True West,* January-February, 1966.

Kildare, Maurice. "Bear River Loot." *True West,* July-August, 1968.

———. "Dead Outlaws' Loot." *True West,* January-February, 1967.

———. "Fastest Gun in Phoenix." *Frontier Times,* December-January, 1968.

———. "Gold in Iron Boxes!" *Frontier Times,* February-March, 1968.

———. "Loot of the Vanished Stage." *Westerner,* March-April, 1974.

King, A.M. (as told to Lea McCarty) "Wyatt Earp's 'Million Dollar' Shotgun Ride." *True West,* July-August, 1958.

Kirby, Edward M. *The Rise and Fall of the Sundance Kid.* Iola, Wisconsin: Western Publications, 1983.

———. *The Saga of Butch Cassidy and the Wild Bunch.* Palmer Lake, Colorado: The Filter Press, 1977.

Klein, Rene, and Dorothy Krell. *Sunset Travel Guide to Arizona.* Menlo Park, California: Lane Publishing Co., 1978.

Kubista, Bob. "No Headlight in Sight." *Frontier Times,* August-September, 1968.

———. "This Robber Made It Back to His Cache." *Frontier Times,* December-January, 1968.

Lee, Wayne C. "Julesburg: The Wandering Town." *True West,* March, 1983.

Lesure, Thomas B. *All About Arizona.* Floral Park, New York: Harian Publications, 1978.

Lucia, Ellis. *Tough Men, Tough Country.* Englewood Cliffs, New Jersey: Prentice-Hall, Inc., 1963.

Martin, Don. "The End of Old Man Bender?" *True West,* March-April, 1959.

McCarroll, Ralph. "The Bane of Thieves." *True West,* March-April, 1967.

McCarthy, Donald. "Bill Brazelton, Stage Robber." *Frontier Times,* January, 1980.

McGinty, Brian. "John Wesley Hardin: Gentleman of Guns." *American History Illustrated,* Summer, 1982.

———. "Reining in the Iron Horse," *American History Illustrated,* Summer, 1982.

McMillan, Mark. "Lucky Bill Gets the Noose." *Badman,* 1971 Annual.

McNeal, T.A. *When Kansas Was Young.* New York: The Macmillan Company, 1922.

McPeak, Robert. "Robbers' Cache in Texas." (letter) *Frontier Times,* February-March, 1967.

Metz, Leon C. *Dallas Stoudenmire.* Norman: University of Oklahoma Press, 1979.

———. *John Selman, Gunfighter.* Norman: University of Oklahoma Press, 1980.

———. *Pat Garrett: The Story of a Western Lawman.* Norman: University of Oklahoma Press, 1973.

———. *The Shooters.* El Paso, Texas: Mangan Books, 1976.

Mills, James R. "End of the Murrietta Gang." *True West,* March-April, 1958.

Moffett, Cleveland. "The Pollack Diamond Robbery." *Western Frontier,* October, 1983 (reprinted from *McClures,* April, 1885).

Morris, John W. *Ghost Towns of Oklahoma.* Norman: University of Oklahoma Press, 1977.

Nadeau, Remi. *Ghost Towns and Mining Camps of California.* Los Angeles: The Ward Ritchie Press, 1965.

Neumann, Ross. "Devil's Island on the Desert." *Frontier Times,* Summer, 1962.

Nordyke, Lewis. *John Wesley Hardin: Texas Gunman.* New York: William Morrow & Company, 1957.

Norin, William. "The Daltons Were Our Neighbors in California." *True West,* September, 1983.

Norris, Rudell Murray. "Bank Robbery: California Style." *True West,* September-October, 1968.

O'Neal, Bill. "Caldwell: 'The Border Queen.'" *True West,* October, 1980.

———. *Encyclopedia of Western Gunfighters.* Norman: University of Oklahoma Press, 1979.

———. "Medicine Lodge Bank Robbery." *True West,* August, 1983.

Osteen, Ike. "Coe's Castle on the Carrizo—1867." *True West*, July-August, 1967.

Packer, C.L. "Coe's Castle on the Carrizo—1867." *True West*, July-August, 1967.

Palmquist, Robert R. "Good-bye, Old Friend." *Real West*, May, 1979.

Parker, Watson. *Deadwood: The Golden Years*. Lincoln: University of Nebraska Press, 1981.

Patterson, Myron. "Custer City Justice." *Real West*, July, 1975.

Patterson, Richard. "The Reno Gang." *American History Illustrated*, Summer, 1982.

———. *Train Robbery: The Birth, Flowering and Decline of a Notorious Western Enterprise*. Boulder, Colorado: Johnson Books, 1981.

———. *Wyoming's Outlaw Days*. Boulder, Colorado: Johnson Books, 1982.

Patterson, Will. "Wanted for Murder: Jim McKinney." *Heartland*, August, 1982.

Pence, Mary Lou. "Petticoat Rustler." *American History Illustrated*, Summer, 1982.

*People v. Vasquez*, Supreme Court of California, No. 10,154, January, 1875.

Pinkerton, William A. *Train Robberies, Train Robbers and the 'Holdup' Men*. New York: Arno Press, 1974 (Reprint). Privately published, 1907 (from address before the Annual Convention of the International Association of Chiefs of Police, Jamestown, Virginia, 1907).

Pointer, Larry. *In Search of Butch Cassidy*. Norman: University of Oklahoma Press, 1977.

Preece, Harold. *The Dalton Gang: End of an Outlaw Era*. New York: Hastings House, 1963.

Price, Carter. "Jim Riley's Strange Courage." *Real West*, September, 1962.

Raymond, Dora Neill. *Captain Lee Hall of Texas*. Norman: University of Oklahoma Press, 1940.

Richardson, Leander. "Last Days of a Plainsman." *True West*, November-December, 1965.

*Richey v. State*, 28 Wyo. 117, 201 Pac. 154 (1921).

Rickards, Colin. "Bill Miner: 50 Years a Hold-up Man." *English Westerner Brand Book*, January, 1966, April, 1966.

Rockwell, Nelson. "The Case of the Bungling Bank Robbers." *Frontier Times*, Fall, 1960.

Romero, Trancito (as told to R.C. Valdez). "I Saw Black Jack Hanged." *True West*, September-October, 1958.

Rosa, Joseph G. *They Called Him Wild Bill: The Life and Adventures of James Butler Hickok*. Norman: University of Oklahoma Press, 1964.

Rosenhouse, Leo. "The Missing Loot of California's Bandits: Where Is It?" *Golden West*, February, 1974.

Rybolt, Bob. "Doc Holliday Sold Gold Bricks Here." *True West*, August, 1983.

Rybolt, Robert T. "Legend Becomes Reality: Whispering Smith is Real!" *True West*, February, 1984.

Sanchez, Lynda A. "They Loved Billy the Kid." *True West*, January, 1984.

Schreier, Konrad F., Jr. "Pearl Hart: More Sad Case than Hard Case." *True West*, April, 1983.

Secrest, William B. "Fast Guns in Old California." *Real West*, June, 1980.

———. "Holdup!" *True West*, November-December, 1964.

———. "Jim Levy: Top-Notch Gunfighter." *True West*, August, 1978.

———. "The Return of Chavez." *True West*, February, 1978.

Settle, William A., Jr. *Jesse James Was His Name*. Columbia: University of Missouri Press, 1966.

Shields, Mike. "Terror in the Mist." *True West*, January-February, 1967.

Shinn, Charles Howard. *Graphic Descriptions of Pacific Coast Outlaws*. J.E. Reynolds, ed. Los Angeles: Westernlore Press, 1958.

Shirley, Glenn. *Belle Starr and Her Times*. Norman: University of Oklahoma Press, 1982.

———. *Shotgun for Hire: The Story of "Deacon" Jim Miller, Killer of Pat Garrett*. Norman: University of Oklahoma Press, 1970.

———. *Temple Houston: Lawyer with a Gun*. Norman: University of Oklahoma Press, 1980.

———. *West of Hell's Fringe*. Norman: University of Oklahoma Press, 1978.

Simmons, Frank. "Ghosts and Near Ghosts." *True West*, July-August, 1959.

Simmons, Marc. "Billy the Kid and the Lincoln County War." *American History Illustrated*, Summer, 1982.

Smith, Alson J. "Gay Days on Denver's Holladay Street." *Frontier Times*, February-March, 1966.

Smith, Lew. "Take Your Time—and Aim!" *True West*, September-October, 1958.

Sonnichsen, C.L. "Justice After Dark." *True West*, January-February, 1966.

———. *Pass of the North: Four Centuries on the Rio Grande*. El Paso: Texas Western Press, 1968.

———. *The Story of Roy Bean: Law West of the Pecos*. Greenwich: Fawcett Publications, Inc., 1972.

———. *Tucson: The Life and Times of an American City*. Norman: University of Oklahoma Press, 1982.

———. *Tularosa: Last of the Frontier West*. Albuquerque: University of New Mexico Press, 1980.

Sparling, Wayne. *Southern Idaho Ghost Towns*. Caldwell: The Caxton Printers, Ltd., 1974.

Spring, Agnes Wright. *The Cheyenne and Black Hills Stage and Express Routes*. Glendale, California: The Arthur H. Clark Company, 1949.

Stanchack, John. "Charles 'Black Bart' Boles." *American History Illustrated*, Summer, 1982.

*State v. Kennedy*, 55 S.W. 293 (1900).

*State v. West*, 57 S.W. 1072 (1900).

Steel, Rory. "The Jones Boys." *Old West*, Winter, 1982.

Stoner, Mary. "My Father Was a Train Robber." *True West*, August, 1983.

*Sunset Travel Guide to Idaho*. Menlo Park California: Lane Books, 1969.

Sweet, Richard D. "Gramps, Butch Cassidy, and the Black Cat Cafe." *Frontier Times*, August-September, 1979.

Taylor, Dorice. *Ghost Towns on the Yankee Fork*. Boise: Idaho Department of Commerce and Development, 1972.

Thomas, Robert L. "Smugglers' Trail." *Frontier Times*, August-September, 1967.

Thorp, Raymond W. "Gambling Kings." *Frontier Times*, February-March, 1965.

Thorpe, E.J. "The Gambling Sheriff." *True West*, July-August, 1967.

Townsend, Ben. "Hell Train Out of Yuma." *True West*, November, 1982.

Trachtman, Paul. ed. *The Gunfighters*. New York: Time-Life Books, 1974.

Vance, Tom. "The Treasure of Oklahoma's Lookout Mountain." *True West*, August, 1978.

Vestal, Stanley. *Queen of Cowtowns: Dodge City*. New York: Harper & Brothers, 1952.

Walker, Dale L. "Buckey O'Neill and the Holdup at Diablo Canyon." *Real West Annual*, 1980.

Walker, Wayne T. "The Doctor Who Rode with Sam Bass." *True West*, April, 1983.

———. "Ned Christie: Terror of the Cookson Hills." *Real West Annual*, Winter, 1980.

Warren, Sidney. *Farthest Frontier: The Pacific Northwest*. New York: The Macmillan Company, 1949.

Webb, Walter Prescott. *The Texas Rangers: A Century of Frontier Defense*. Boston: Houghton Mifflin Company, 1935.

Weisner, Herman B. "Outlaw Rock." *True West*, March, 1982.

West, Elliott. "Wicked Dodge City." *American History Illustrated*. Summer, 1982.

Winther, Oscar Osburn. *The Great Northwest: A History*. New York: Alfred A. Knopf, 1950.

———. *The Old Oregon Country*. Stanford: Stanford University Press, 1950.

Wolley, Muriel Sibell. *Stampede to Timberline: The Ghost Towns and Mining Camps of Colorado*. Denver: Sage Books, 1949.

Wood, Lamont. "Wanted: Roy Bean." *True West*, January, 1984.

Wood, Stanley. *Over the Range to the Golden Gate*. Chicago: R.R. Donnelly & Sons, Publishers, 1908.

# INDEX